The Jayhawker

Also by Norm Ledgin

Nonfiction

Diagnosing Jefferson

Asperger's and Self-Esteem

Naomi said, "I *know* you'll return, Malcolm. Your heart is in Kansas, and you're in *my* heart."

The Jayhawker

A Novel

Norm Ledgin

Illustrations by Jay Reinhardt

Tenderfoot Writer
Stanley, Kansas

This book gathers historical events, noteworthy persons,
and familiar locales into its story line, but it is a work of fiction,
and all such references to them are fictitious.
Other incidents, places, or characters and names are
products of the author's imagination, and any resemblance
to persons living or dead is purely coincidental.

Tenderfoot Writer
P.O. Box 23571
Stanley, Kansas 66283-0571

http://tenderfootwriter.com

Printed in the United States of America

ISBN-13: 978-0-9790589-0-5
ISBN-10: 0-9790589-0-2

Library of Congress Control Number: 2006909904

To those who look past others' outer features
and understand the longings in their hearts.

Prologue

In a perfect world—a perfect Kansas—a celebration would take place October 19, 2007, marking the sesquicentennial of "the rescue of Kansas from slavery."*

But it's doubtful we'll see such a public observance. The old excitement for marking historic events seems to have waned. Instead, history has been absorbed into our escape from reality and has become storytime material for books, TV, and movies.

So, we writers simply feed that appetite. We and our readers live and love vicariously through men and women bathed in glory. We show how those people, the real ones and the made-up ones, turned corners and made possible whatever benefits of progress we now enjoy.

One such turn was the outcome of the Kansas-Missouri Border War, which in a critical way led to the Civil War. *The Jayhawker* is less about the run-up to that deadly implosion of a young United States than it is about a mixed-race leader in it, Malcolm Erskine, about his triumphs and disappointments in a fight that was all about race.

The Jayhawker first appeared as an adventure serial in *The Blue Valley Gazette,* a country weekly newspaper that served Kansas's Stanley-Stilwell area in the early 1980s. The 114 illustrated episodes excited the historical interests and imaginations of many readers. Soon after the tale ran its course, the paper and much of the land in its circulation area yielded to metropolitan Kansas City sprawl, which began as "white flight" and continues insanely.

As violent as the portrayals and scenes in this book may be, chroniclers have shown that the actual Border War was worse. As an example of disturbing gore, when *The Jayhawker* first came into print a quarter century ago it anticipated lifesaving self-amputation. That became the basis for a news event about a mountaineer in 2003.

I've tried then and now to be faithful to local history and geography of the period. If there's confusion over place names like

Blue Valley, Pleasant Valley, and Camp Branch, that's because those names appear also in locations not far from the story's south Johnson County, Kansas, setting. To some, use of the designation Lykins County may be confusing, for the place didn't acquire its present name of Miami County until 1861.

My primary aim has been to show how people of varying temperaments and motivations carried Kansas past warring to a watershed moment, the political triumph of Free State forces late in 1857 over proslavery intruders.

The struggle I've described features both strengths and weaknesses by the principals: heroism, family devotion, romance—then there's incest, along with the vengeance, corruption, treachery, rape, butchery, and slaughter that "won" the West.

Norm Ledgin
October 27, 2006

*This description of pivotal 1857 events is attributable to the contemporarily witnessing newspaper editor, Dr. George W. Brown, of the *Herald of Freedom*, Lawrence, Kansas.

Part One

Fall of 1855 through
Spring of 1856

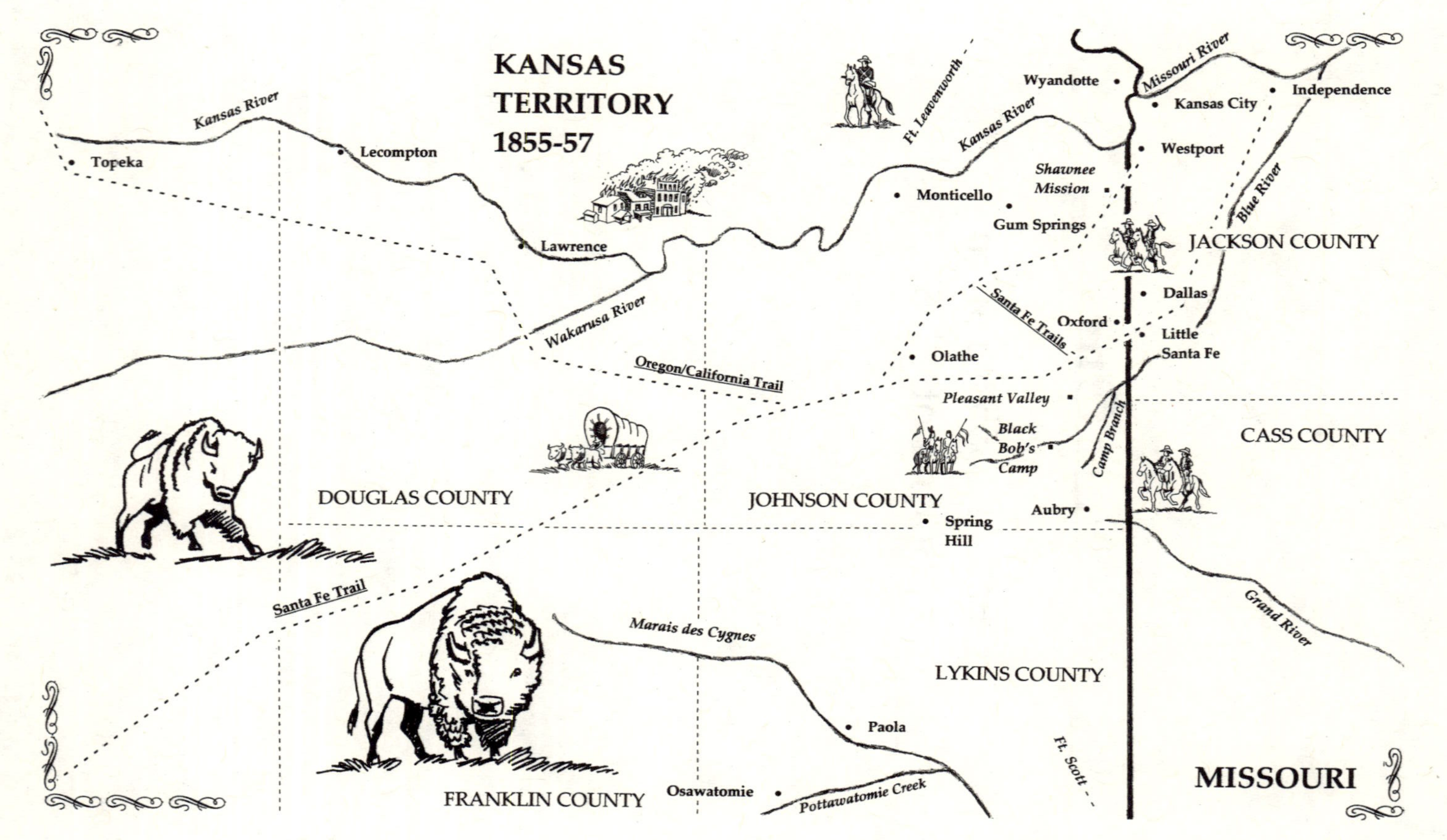
KANSAS
TERRITORY
1855-57
Kansas River
Topeka
Lecompton
Lawrence
Wakarusa River
Oregon/California Trail
Santa Fe Trail
DOUGLAS COUNTY
FRANKLIN COUNTY
Ft. Leavenworth
Kansas River
Wyandotte
Missouri River
Kansas City
Independence
Westport
Shawnee
Mission
Monticello
Gum Springs
Blue River
JACKSON COUNTY
Dallas
Oxford
Little
Santa Fe
Santa Fe Trails
Olathe
Pleasant Valley
Black
Bob's
Camp
Camp Branch
CASS COUNTY
JOHNSON COUNTY
Aubry
Spring
Hill
Grand River
Marais des Cygnes
LYKINS COUNTY
Paola
Ft. Scott
Osawatomie
Pottawatomie Creek
MISSOURI

1

Malcolm felt a sharp poke in his ribs.

"Wake up, son," the crusty old man barked in his ear.

Malcolm Erskine opened only one eye. The other stuck till he knuckled it. His first deep breath caught their odor of weeks on the trail without bathing. The October morning dewfall was turning it into a blanket of stink.

"Not yet light," Erskine mumbled to John Brown. "Tired. ... Cold."

"Snap awake, son. Come *on,"* Brown commanded.

Malcolm shut his eyes again and shifted his body several inches along the Missouri clay to move beyond Brown's reach. His lips and tongue touched the ground. He spat dirt.

The crouching Brown moved with Erskine and kept poking him.

"Let's be up, Malcolm. I want to walk into Kansas with the sun at our backs, in bright morning. Praise the Lord, I can see it already. We're within a spit and holler of the Territory."

Erskine lifted his face to peer through the murk.

Brown grabbed Erskine's head roughly and aimed it west. "Yonder. Lamps in cabins on the ridge. We're nigh the border."

"What place is that? Let go my head." He'd wanted also to ask John Brown—wanted to several days—why so much more night-travel lately. Brown had begun seeking trail ruts to let the horse pull the wagon along in them, like a train on rails.

But Erskine already figured the answer. Just wanted to hear it from Brown. It was on account of him, Malcolm, being so dark-complected. Traveling together as apparent equals in western Missouri was bound to raise too many suspicions. Maybe fire up a dangerous reaction, jeopardize their mission.

"What place is that?" Malcolm repeated. John Brown was standing fully and releasing the horse from its tether.

"The Lord's with us, son. Slow-flowing water in that draw below. Must've rained here a day or so back....That there's Little Santa Fe, they call it. Been there almost since this Santa Fe Trail opened. Settlement's smack on the Missouri border, overlooking Kansas Territory."

Brown nodded toward the cluster of buildings taking shape in the pre-dawn. Malcolm noticed a few cabins and barns were in the process of expansion.

"Yonder," Brown said, pointing, "along the draw and northwest, there's campground the wagon travelers use. And that way, about ten miles," he said, aiming a crooked index finger due north, "the newer Santa Fe Trail leading from Westport, a place of mixed allegiances but thick with proslavers. Beyond that, Missouri River landings. A new town anchoring, they call City of Kansas—or Kansas City."

From a lying position, Malcolm Erskine slid to his knees and was soon on all fours. He pushed himself erect and felt the morning urge to go into the bushes. Brown halted him with instructions.

"Secure that tarp on the wagon again, son. The boxes may be marked 'Bibles,' but anyone with half a brain would have his doubts."

"Where's your son-in-law to do that? Or—" Malcolm peered around in the half-light. "Or Oliver?"

"When you collapsed in snoring, I saw a good moon and sent Thompson and Oliver ahead. They'll meet my other boys at Lone Elm. I told Oliver, have them stir a ruckus—a diversion to draw Bushwhackers from here, from the border."

Erskine thought in slight panic, *Just Old Brown and me, walking a load of Sharps rifles into Kansas.*

As though hearing Malcolm's thoughts, John Brown added, "I told Oliver to send back a guard before we cross the line. Now secure that tarp, and I'll water the horse....Sun's starting to rise now."

Brown led the bay mare down the slope to the nearly dried-out draw. Malcolm moved to the wagon and found a tarp-end that had come loose. Broken rope. Forward, under the seat that went unused—for the weight of the cargo was all the horse could pull—he sought a coil. He pulled his Bowie knife and cut a length to repair the tarpaulin.

Erskine wished for a cup of steaming coffee. He knew Brown would have no delaying their triumphant entrance into Kansas Territory. No pausing to build a fire. He also wished for a cigarette, which he liked to roll every morning between sips of his first tin cup of strong coffee.

He glanced over his shoulder down the slope and saw John Brown on his knees, occupied in prayer, the horse seeming to root in the draw to find enough water.

Malcolm reached for a canteen and rubbed a splash into his eyes, over his face. He needed a shave, but Brown wouldn't have that kind of delay either. The old man was caught up in some holy significance about stepping into Kansas like it was the Promised Land.

Presently, John Brown returned with the mare. The two of them fell to hitching her, not speaking. Malcolm saw tears in Brown's eyes. His companion was evidently moved by reaching this place at last after walking and ferrying, but mostly walking. Henry Thompson and Oliver Brown rode, but John Brown walked, hundreds and hundreds of miles. And Malcolm walked, too, leading the mare.

With the backs of his rough hands, Brown wiped his sunken cheeks, sniffed loudly, then ducked to check the horse's lines. Straightening himself, he said, "Must ask you, Malcolm, before we enter Kansas. Are you prepared to die for the cause of freeing the Negro?"

The question caught Erskine off guard. "What?"

"Our cause, son. Our cause. Are you prepared to *die* for it?" Brown seemed now to be probing Malcolm's soul with his ice-blue eyes.

Die?

Erskine considered his own relative youth—he was twenty-eight. He fidgeted, putting on his hat. Embarrassed, shifting from one foot to the other as Brown stared hard, he tried to avoid the abolitionist's eyes. He also needed to relieve himself. Then he fiddled with his mustache and scratched the stubble on his chin. At last he dared to say, "Hell, *no,* John."

Brown was obviously taken aback by the response. Malcolm knew he must explain. The old man might have "smote" him in anger from misunderstanding, Erskine surmised, so he added quickly—

"Being at least a quarter Negro, I'm prepared only to *live* for this cause, not die. If I *must* die, so be it. But I doubt I'll *ever* be ready." In a softer tone, "Can you accept that, old friend?"

Gradually, Brown's demeanor softened. What seemed a smirk spread across a face that resembled a broken rock. "Haven't found God yet, have you, son?" The older man looked away resignedly.

"John, I've only just begun finding my pitiful *self,* much less a force I can't see," Malcolm said. "You know I haven't done much to be proud of."

Erskine was now eager to get on with their walk into Kansas. He wanted an end to this pointless conversation. He didn't like to seem irreverent. Just wanted to be honest.

Abolition was a common cause that had, by 1855, attracted all kinds. Religious zealots and intellectuals, financiers and poor ex-slaves, adventurers as well as idle dreamers. In Malcolm's case, "drifter," a name he'd earned on the waterfronts of New Bedford and Boston.

Maybe here in the West his drifting would end. Maybe he could find purpose in his life.

"Far better," John Brown said tensely, gazing at a thick line of bushes south of the settlement, "to put faith in an invisible force than— *DOWN!"*

Brown, in his middle fifties, threw himself to the ground nimbly, shoving Erskine down in the same motion. Rifle bullets whizzed overhead, and the delayed sounds of shots rang out.

Malcolm wet his pants.

2

Erskine shouted, "John! Stay down! What are you *doing?*"

John Brown got to his feet, evidently convinced the riflemen in the thicket meant no real harm.

"Warning shots, son," Brown said, "purposely high. I believe those proslaver devils only mean for us to be on our way, for us not to approach their community. They've stopped firing." Brown slapped his hat against his knee to get rid of dirt. He picked burrs from a sleeve.

Malcolm rose and checked that his Bowie knife hadn't slipped from its sheath. It was the only weapon he carried. "Why don't we," he suggested, hesitatingly, "pop off one of the box lids and—"

"They'd kill us before we got the first cartridge loaded in," Brown said. "Even if we were quick enough to get most of them, surely one would get away realizing what's in the wagon isn't Bibles. Later others'd be on us like angry hornets to take the guns and leave us for the buzzards. No," Brown said, replacing his hat on his shaggy grey head, "we'll move out, peaceably for now. Should be a guard party joining us soon. Lead the horse, son."

Malcolm calmed the mare, which was still skittish from the earlier rifle fire. He wrapped the lead rope once around his hand and tugged gently. When the horse balked, he tugged more firmly and she followed.

They moved faithfully in the wagon ruts of the old Santa Fe Trail. The border of Kansas Territory lay perhaps two hundred yards ahead, if Brown's crude map was true.

The younger man was uneasy knowing hostile riflemen were watching, uncomfortable also because of his unexpected incontinence. They would receive no hospitality from Little Santa Fe up the ridge, not by present appearances. Any observer could see his skin color in the morning light. Their mode of travel likely posed a puzzle whether Malcolm was a free man or a slave.

Old Brown, eager to join his sons, had been pushing himself too hard and needed rest. Their main cargo destination, Lawrence, was still three or four days west. For all Brown's wiry toughness and resoluteness, the man needed a good sleep, Erskine thought, and some hot food. And a bath.

Yet there was danger that if they lingered in Little Santa Fe, someone might discover the "Bibles" were modern Sharps rifles, plus ammunition for Free Staters settling new communities like Lawrence.

There was the additional danger that John Brown wouldn't hold his tongue. He would instead preach to proslavers the errors of their ways, invoking God's commandments in the fashion of Moses, with whom he was sometimes compared.

Malcolm conjured a plan, picturing himself stumbling, falling, urging John to pick up a stick and pretend to whale him to get him going again. If the Little Santa Fe people could see that and believe he, Malcolm, was a preacher-man's slave, and if Brown would play along—

"I know what you're thinking, Malcolm," Brown said, still facing west and walking slightly ahead of Erskine. "I know exactly what you're thinking."

Malcolm's blood froze at the realization of his companion's insight.

"I know," Brown continued, "because you once suggested degrading play-acting, and you're hanging back. Put it out of your mind."

"But you need rest, John," Erskine protested. "Let's do it to throw them off and get a meal out of it. Fresh water. Maybe a bath. A half-day's sleep in one of their barns. You sleep while I guard the wagon. Lawrence is farther off than we've come from Independence."

"No."

"John, please."

"No!"

Erskine heard something behind him and turned to look. Then he laughed, showing deep irony more than amusement. "Ah, well, old friend. The decision's being made for us. They've circled southeast and are now right behind us."

John Brown stopped and turned.

Three riders—two of them holding rifles at the ready, reins hanging loose—approached casually from where the line of bushes played out. Malcolm had no doubt they were the same men who'd fired over their heads. One was a young lad who appeared to have no weapon.

"M'awnin'," one of the armed men called, pulling up near them. "Ah 'pologize fer shootin', but me 'n' m'brother Bill took y'all fer gun-runners. Then we was thinkin', nobody'd be fool enough t'come through this-away cartin' guns. But we'd sure like t'take a closer look't what's in that there wagon."

"Malcolm," John Brown directed with a flourish, "untie that tarpaulin and show the gentlemen we mean no harm to anyone righteous and God-fearing."

"Yassuh, Reverend," Erskine said with a slight bow, dropping the lead rope and shuffling to the corner of the tarp he'd repaired earlier. He untied and lifted it. The word "Bibles" was plainly lettered near the corner of a box.

"Sa-ay, boy," the armed spokesman said slowly, a bit menacingly. "Bein' y'all are peaceable church folks, explain us why a Nigra totes a Bowie knife."

"Oh, yassuh," Malcolm said, removing his hat and pressing it to his chest, bowing slightly again, grinning. "I sure enough found this here rusty old worthless thing dropped on the trail, and it sure enough comes in handy for a work knife is all, suh. Sure enough!"

"Yew mighty light fer a Nigra," the man pressed, dismounting slowly and still gripping his rifle.

Malcolm turned away, putting on his hat again and pretending to check the wagon further, studying every angle of his and Brown's defense in case of an assault.

"Bet y'mammy was one fine-lookin' high-yaller gal," the man said, stepping closer.

Erskine, his heart pounding, slid his hand toward the knife handle, knowing he could turn and have it unsheathed and deep under the man's ribs before the other "gentleman" could aim his rifle. He knew he could also tear the Bowie from the man's innards, grip the blood-wet blade, and send it deep into the chest of the so-far silent "brother Bill"—before his first victim's knees buckled in a death fall.

He *knew* he could, because he'd learned well on the brawling New England waterfronts. And he knew John Brown knew he could. As for the lad with these men, Malcolm decided he would spare the unarmed youngster.

What Erskine hadn't calculated—what startled them all—was the appearance of a screaming woman riding a paint horse bareback down the ridge, full-tilt—the very image of what Malcolm's Scottish father in his storytelling had often described as a "banshee."

3

The dismounted rifleman nodded toward the woman. He turned to his brother. "Bill, yew goin' have t'do somethin' 'bout that crazy woman o' yern." He shook his head and sighed, lowering his gun.

Erskine let his hand fall to his side, away from the knife handle. He was fascinated by the approaching spectacle, the carelessly-clad woman racing the paint. She was young, strong-featured in face and body, dark-haired, dark-eyed. Her fully-exposed thighs showed curves and strengths that aroused him.

"Jimmy!" the woman shouted hoarsely. *"Get* along home—this *instant!"* She drew up the horse by pulling at its mane, glaring at the youngster who'd accompanied the two riflemen. "Go *on!"* she instructed him.

"Now, Sis," the boy of twelve or thirteen whined, his chin on his chest, his hands fiddling with the pommel of his saddle. "I was just ridin' along."

Malcolm figured the relationship was that she was married to the silent one called Bill, and the boy Jimmy, her brother, lived with them. The man who was still dismounted, however—her brother-in-law, name unknown to Malcolm—apparently was competing with her for bossing this little clan.

"Jane-Ellen," that one said, his tone scolding. "Leave the boy be. Bill 'n' me ain't leadin' him t'no mischief, if that's how come yew all het up."

A hatred Erskine had seldom seen in any woman's eyes clouded Jane-Ellen's. "Who's talkin' to *you,* you pile o' horse apples?" She accented her frown with a menacing display of teeth.

Suddenly her expression shifted. "Oh! A message for you, Hank. Catron left word, you and Bill catch up with his bunch on the trail to Lone Elm. Some goings-on over there." She slid forward

Jane-Ellen ambled over to John Brown. "Sir, you have an interesting face that begs to wear a beard."

on the paint's bare back, her skirt hiking perilously. "So why don't you just *git!*"

The rifleman—Hank—fairly jumped at hearing the name "Catron." He remounted, then pointed to Brown. "Old one's a preacher-man, boss o' this Nigra—'n' might hear yer confession....C'mawn, Bill." The two men rode off west. The boy, Jimmy, trotted his horse toward Little Santa Fe.

Malcolm observed that although Jane-Ellen was barefooted and rough in frontier ways, her accent showed little of the coarseness of Hank's. She was probably a Marylander, maybe a Virginian. From her manner he estimated she was in her mid-twenties, but on the other hand—

"Confession. *Shoot!*" Jane-Ellen watched Bill and Hank canter off. She laughed, as though at a private joke. "Confession," she murmured. Then, skirt riding up far past decency yet with no apparent embarrassment, she slid off her horse.

Blood rushed to Malcolm's head and other parts. His heart beat wildly over the treasure she'd exposed.

Jane-Ellen ambled over to Brown, one hand extended and the other pulling down the hem of her crude dress. "Name's Jane-Ellen Mulligan O'Brien. Please take this kindly from a straight-talking woman, sir, but you have an interesting face that begs to wear a beard."

Brown gave a rare chuckle. He took her hand and bent to kiss it. "I'll surely think on that, Mrs. O'Brien. I'm John Brown, lately of upstate New York, originally a New Englander like my companion here, Malcolm Erskine, of New Bedford, Massachusetts. Son of a fine Scottish sea captain, he is. Mother's Egyptian."

Malcolm heard her gasp in response to Brown's explaining his color.

"Egyptian," Jane-Ellen said, surveying Erskine. Now he heard a tremor in her voice and noticed her sudden blush. She rested a hand against her horse's flank, as though steadying herself. After inhaling deeply and seeming to force her smile, she said, "Malcolm Erskine. Not your darky."

"No, ma'am," Brown replied. "Free man. I own *no* man or woman. Against my principles to do that."

"But Bill and Hank *think* he's your slave," she pressed, still eyeing Malcolm with uncommon interest.

"I suppose so."

"Keep it that way," she suggested, turning to look into John Brown's eyes. "Especially if you value your lives....Look, head that wagon up the slope and around to my place just over the ridge. The two of you *stink* to high heaven and could use a bath, and maybe some hot food and rest."

John was hesitant, indicating Hank and Bill's dust swirling over the trail.

"Oh, don't worry about them. Might not be back for days. Likely Catron'll lead them on raids across the line, burning barns of Free Staters. It's what they like to do. Your stopping here on foot is what annoyed them. They expect wagons to drive on through. I'll have you on your way before they're back."

She walked beside Brown. Her horse trailed off to the side and followed without needing to be led or clucked to. Behind them a respectable distance, Malcolm pulled the bay mare into motion again. The wagon creaked forward. The outline of Jane-Ellen's buttocks under her short skirt mesmerized him.

She said, "The mean one's Henry—Hank, he goes by. In spite of what he said about confession, he's a hypocrite. Has the devil in him. I hate him, but he's kin. Except for my little half brother Jimmy and me tending some stock and gardening, we'd have nothing to keep body and soul together. This damned Kansas question's changed everything here, and Bill and that bastard Hank are always off—"

Jane-Ellen stopped and put her hand to her face. "Oh! Sorry, Reverend. I just cuss so much nowadays without thinking."

"Mrs. O'Brien, I'm not actually a preacher, though I'm a strong believer," Brown said. "I'm— Mr. Erskine and I are visiting Kansas for the very first time so that we may join my sons to—"

Malcolm was embarrassed for Brown because of the abolitionist's faltering effort to conceal their mission. Erskine's hopes—

that John Brown might successfully steer from the truth—were dashed, however, when Jane-Ellen said, "Well, it would have been believable, about your being a preacher, considering all the do-gooders wearing the cloth. You may think you've got Hank and Bill fooled, but not me, and maybe not even them."

Resuming the stroll, she added with an air of cockiness, "I'm not sure you should tell me what's truly in the wagon, for you can mark me down as a loyal proslaver. I'm not touchy as you about owning anyone. I'm just too strapped to buy a good slave, is all. We're not on the same side, but I say you both still need a bath and some tending to. Simple as that." She glanced back, staring at the wet spot on Malcolm's trousers.

Brown ventured, "And you don't seem readily persuadable to an opposing political view."

"That's right, Mr. Brown," she said, facing forward, "so don't bother to preach how un-Christian or undemocratic my attitude is and all. I'm a fairly educated woman in spite of appearance and the present style of my life, and I'll be glad to debate the slave issue with you some time. But for now it's only important you be cautious."

"Cautious," John repeated, his brow crinkling.

"I had suspicions about your cargo straight off and still do, as I suspect was true for the men. But now I wonder they might be weaker than I'd thought, those two."

"Weaker?" Brown asked.

"I was in a tub in the barn and heard shooting. Figured they were trying to drive someone off. They do that a lot. I don't like Jimmy mixing in that. I grabbed an old seaman's glass I brought from Maryland. In first light I calculated the situation and figured Hank might suspect guns in the wagon. Then I saw that big knife hanging from Mr. Erskine's belt. I'm certain Hank was scared of a Bowie in the hands of a half-breed, not knowing what experience your friend's had with it."

She turned again as she walked and glanced at Malcolm up and down. He simply touched his hat brim in acknowledgement, the corner of his mouth turning up in a slight smile that tipped his mustache crooked.

She faced forward, and Malcolm resumed observing her strolling rhythms from the rear. "It'd be a blessing if your Negro friend was ready to rid me of Hank O'Brien, but I surely didn't want also to be a widow-woman—and lose my brother in the bargain. It was then I threw on this old thing and rode down fast, screaming all the way. I must look a sight. Forgive me....Am I right, Mr. Erskine?" she called back to Malcolm, still facing forward.

"About not looking good? No, ma'am," he said, half hoping she'd find that to be impudent. "Quite the contrary, if you don't mind my saying so. About my being ready to kill the men, yes, except I'd have spared your brother. I had planned to spare him."

Jane-Ellen O'Brien stopped and turned around, causing the others to halt as well. She blinked rapidly, Erskine realizing she held back tears. "I thank you for that, Malcolm Erskine. I truly do." One tear escaped, and her lower lip quivered.

Seeing that, John Brown put an arm around her shoulder and led her forward again, toward her house and the hospitality she'd offered.

Impulsively, still strolling with Brown's gentle support, Jane-Ellen turned to look at Erskine one more time. To Malcolm, who'd lived an adventurous life and had known women of all colors, her latest glance spoke to him of something promising.

In that moment, as the shabbily clothed, naturally attractive woman seemed so at ease ambling shoeless beside John Brown in the chill of October—poor, but offering kindness to men set against the traditions she clung to—Erskine felt somehow bound to Jane-Ellen Mulligan O'Brien.

4

Jane-Ellen pointed to a ramshackle barn on the south slope of the ridge.

"Make your way there. You'll find a tub I was using. The water should still be fairly warm, and soapy. Sorry I can't offer you water clean and fresh, unless you want cold. The fire's already died in the cabin stove."

"That's fine, Mrs. O'Brien," John said. "We'll take turns in the tub just as it is. And we thank you. You're everything a Southern lady is reputed to be." Erskine observed that Jane-Ellen seemed flattered by Brown's comment..

"I'm going to a neighbor's over by the church," she announced, "for a fat chicken. I'll kill and dress it and cook it for you. Please tell Jimmy to get a fire going again."

Brown turned to Erskine and said, "Son, you lead the horse and wagon and do as she says, find the boy. I'll go with our hostess, for I'd like to meet some of these people hereabouts. I'd like to learn anything useful I can, to settle some of the differences among us."

Jane-Ellen snorted. "Don't get your hopes up for that, Mr. Brown. Likely all the men are gone following Catron for mischief, and the women-folks don't talk much about anything anymore. There's too much warring that's started here. The women don't like it, seeing farms and homesteads neglected because of it. But come along if you want."

Malcolm watched as they turned from the ridge toward a neighbor's house, past what looked like a church. Before leading the mare and the wagon, he watched Jane-Ellen once more from behind as she went off with Brown.

I don't know how, or when. But, Jane-Ellen, I'm going to have you, and I think you know it.

* * * * *

Erskine stopped and faced west into Kansas, marveling at the vastness of the land he could see from atop the ridge. It was gently-rolling and covered with the same prairie grass they'd first noticed after crossing the Blue River out of Independence. A meadowlark perched on a stump and serenaded him. He watched it fly off into Kansas, as though beckoning him to follow.

This was the land men had started fighting and dying over, the dispute being whether it would be taken into the Union as a slave state or free.

This was the land where he and others would either live side by side as free men, Negro or white, or put up with proslaver Missourians' blocking that vision. Blocking the soon-to-be next-door state from also becoming a refuge for freed slaves and runaways, as Malcolm saw it.

Erskine imagined the maternal grandmother he'd never seen, an African described to him as "a remarkable beauty, so dignified, and black as the ace of spades." He knew by the blood flowing in him, he must give every ounce of strength and every spark of intelligence to winning this fight for freedom.

He'd witnessed his father beating a fellow foreign-trade captain senseless in New Bedford for having run a slave ship from West Africa. He'd heard people call Morogh Erskine "nigger-lover" for taking the woman he loved, a mulatto cabaret dancer from Cairo, home to Massachusetts. There she bore him Malcolm. For as long as she could put up with humiliations, she settled for being a wife in common law. Countless pious preachers refused to join her to his father in God's eyes.

Thanks to a racism unbecoming of New England's Christian ministers, Malcolm was illegitimate, and that galled him. It led him away from interest in religion—not God necessarily, but religion. His faith in anything but himself was uncertain. He envied old Brown for drawing strength and determination from a deep attachment to God and the Scriptures. John Brown's religious drive gave the old man youth and energy.

Thoughts of Brown turned Malcolm's mind again to his father, who woke him early one morning when he was going on nine. In a mournful Scottish brogue he said Mama was gone—vanished—probably frustrated by her failure of acceptance in her new land.

The New England of promise and enlightenment had failed that beautiful race-mixed daughter of North Africa, had proved narrow and hostile, so she went away. They hadn't seen nor heard from her for over twenty years. They assumed she was dead.

Morogh had taken to drink at first, losing his commission to pilot ships to Glasgow and Liverpool. But for the kindness of settlement-house people out of Boston who recognized the Erskines' plight and gave them food, clothing, and shelter, Malcolm's father would today be in debtors' prison. Instead he reformed and went off the grog and back to sea.

As for Malcolm, he'd fallen into a rough life on the docks. He'd known too long a motherless existence. As boy and man he'd compensated through a succession of ruinous love affairs. He might have continued as just another wharf rat—odd-jobbing as a stevedore or as a hand on a whaling ship, often in trouble with the law, if not for do-gooders from Boston and Providence. They took an interest in this strong youth of rich *café au lait* color but poor prospects.

In his wild days he'd killed men—two—in self-defense and on separate occasions. The disputes were over women. He'd shot one and knifed the other, lucky to have done both killings before honest witnesses.

Settlement-house people had provided legal defense. The attorneys suggested he might be safer in another environment than to remain in Massachusetts. At their suggestion he joined the New England Emigrant Aid Society, later teaming with the Radical Political Abolitionists and John Brown in Syracuse, New York.

The Kansas-Nebraska Act of 1854 made the border situation with Missouri explosive. The bill let the issue of Kansas's becoming a future slave state or free state be decided in elections. Missourians found it easy to pour over the border *en masse* and stake phony land claims before voting, rigging results in favor of slavery. The Emigrant Aid Society and abolitionists sought in defense to build stronger bases in Kansas Territory, particularly in Lawrence. But proslavers' provocations turned the antislavers increasingly militant under the Free State banner.

*****

After a long drought in the enjoyment of female companionship, Malcolm could think of little else than the promise in the eyes of the brazenly immodest and married Catholic woman, Jane-Ellen.

Don't be a bloody fool, the angel of his better judgment whispered to him.

Malcolm tugged the horse and wagon to the barn. He found Jimmy pitchforking hay out the loft hatch and gave the lad the stove-fire message. He unburdened, fed, and watered the horse.

By the tub he undressed for a bath and lowered himself into the tepid bath water, his knife close by. His thoughts drifted between his mission in Kansas and the border woman who might inspire a brief delay.

Erskine sat and enjoyed the fact that *she* had not long before bathed in this tub—same water. He looked for a sign, perhaps a hair. He soon fell into a doze, still weary from his and Brown's nighttime trek and insufficient rest.

In what seemed like hours but were actually minutes, Malcolm woke to the pressing of a pistol barrel against his temple. He glanced to one side and noticed his knife was gone. He shifted his gaze the other way to the gunman. The man was huge—*boy* actually, for his captor couldn't have been over eighteen—dressed splendidly and with long, reddish-blond hair and a drooping mustache.

"Name's James Butler Hickok, sir," the young fellow said in a deep voice, "and you just get up very carefully, if you wouldn't mind."

Malcolm gripped the sides of the tub, feeling the pistol press harder but refusing to budge until the youth explained his hostile purpose. For that delay, despite Erskine's full size and slippery condition, Hickok reached a mighty arm around Malcolm and lifted him bodily from the water.

And while Malcolm wriggled and struggled above the tub in Hickok's grip, Jane-Ellen walked into the barn. She met this strange scene with unconcealed amusement, overly fixed on features of his nakedness.

What angered Erskine, however, was not the brazen sparkle in her dark-brown eyes over the sight, but his belief that she'd betrayed them, him and John Brown.

5

Jane-Ellen burst out laughing, watching Malcolm thrash about in Hickok's clutches. She fell back to sit on a hay bale, slapping her bare knees and obviously struggling to catch a breath.

"Hickok!" Malcolm managed to shout. "You've *shamed* me in front of a lady! Either *pull that trigger and finish me,* or I'll *kill you first chance I get!"*

Between gasps, giggle-tears running, Jane-Ellen pointed and directed, "Put him—*down!* He's— Oh, I'm weak. He's—one of *yours!"*

The powerful youth released Erskine, who rushed past the tub to retrieve his trousers and sought to cover himself. He burned at Jane-Ellen's continuing, brazen staring and laughter.

Malcolm felt he should say something to cover his embarrassment. When he started, "Ma'am, I—" Jane-Ellen stopped him with a surprising command. "Oh, stow it!" she snapped, causing Erskine to wonder at her nautical slang. And earlier she'd mentioned using a seaman's glass.

Jane-Ellen addressed Hickok wryly. "Notice, freed from your grip and choosing between modesty and satisfying his honor, Mr. Erskine chooses modesty. This is the man traveling with John Brown. The old man's comforted down, asleep in my cabin."

Malcolm, rebuckling his belt, saw Hickok nod and holster his huge pistol, one of two guns the youth carried. He wore an outfit that would have earned him the name "Dandy," though trail dust had settled on him. The lad extended his hand to Erskine.

"I'm sorry, sir," he said. "Please accept my hand and my apology. Soon as you do, I'll return the Bowie knife."

When Malcolm hesitated, Jane-Ellen rose and approached, saying, "You'll be in worse trouble if you don't accept. Mr. Hickok is bodyguard to Free State General Jim Lane out of Lawrence. He's the most feared man in these parts for his dead-aim with pistols."

"Asked by Brown's boys to ride guard into Lawrence," Hickok said.

Jane-Ellen said, "If it helps to know this, I was coming in here to scrub you, Mr. Erskine—Malcolm—now that I've got a chicken going. There's less so-called 'shame' over some matters on the frontier than in Massachusetts, but there are other standards of honor. So *shake his hand."*

Malcolm reached in obedience to Jane-Ellen's direction. After a handshake, Hickok reached under his brocade vest and gave Erskine the knife, handle first.

Malcolm said, "I—guess I've got a lot to learn." He replaced the knife in its sheath and took his shirt from where it hung, still damp as his trousers from slapdash washing.

"Mr. Hickok," Jane-Ellen said, turning to exit the barn and speaking as she went, "you go ahead and discuss whatever vile, murderous plans you've come to talk about. You're invited to share chicken for an early lunch. Then I suggest you *all* high-tail it out, or neighbors will accuse me of harboring the enemy."

She turned back to face the youth and furrowed her brow. *"Shoot,* Hickok. You must know there's a price on your head right here in Little Santa Fe, dead or alive. Or *New* Santa Fe, they're trying to get us to call it now. The men are gone, but I can name you a couple-three desperate neighbor women who'd love to collect the bounty."

"Thank you for the warning, Mrs. O'Brien," Hickok said, touching his hat and nodding, "and for the hospitality. I plan to bring you no harm but only to furnish Mr. Brown and his companion safe passage into Kansas. Until you happened in, I had no idea of this man's identity. I'd say you probably saved Mr. Erskine's life."

Jane-Ellen paused at the barn door. She jutted her chin in Malcolm's direction and asked, "Did you hear that, Mr. Erskine? Now you're very *deeply* in my debt. Remember that." She stepped away, then turned back to call, "Hot vittles in an hour, gentlemen. I'll awaken Mr. Brown beforehand to come in here for a good wash, with my practiced help at necessary scrubbing."

She relaxed and lingered in the doorway, shook her head, glanced at the dirt floor. She spoke idly, as though to no one in particular. "John Brown told me he'd fathered twenty children by two wives, not all surviving. Small wonder the old man's weary and beat-up looking. I suggested again he'd be handsomer with a beard." She looked up again, brightly. "And, oh, about that scrubbing, Malcolm? I'd have made you enjoy that." Then she sashayed out.

Erskine said while buttoning his shirt, "Hickok, before you say what you have to say, I want you to know I'm worried about her."

Hickok replied, "I doubt there's any danger from her. She's quite different from the rest of these proslavers and wants to see peace."

Erskine waved away Hickok's answer impatiently, then tucked in his shirt. "I don't mean danger *from* her, but *to* her—from having put us up like this."

Hickok strolled to a hay bale and sat, stretching his long legs and pushing his hat farther back on his golden hair by the brim. "Yes," he said quietly, "it's a valid worry." He reached in his vest and pulled out papers and tobacco to roll a cigarette, next offering them to Malcolm, who accepted. "Careful with all this hay when you light," Hickok cautioned. "We Jayhawkers haven't scheduled the O'Brien barn for burning yet."

"What's a 'Jayhawker'?" Malcolm asked. "I never heard that word."

"It's what these Missourians call some of us Free Staters, especially anyone who rides in to retaliate against their raids. You *do* have a mighty lot to learn, Mr. Erskine. *They're* the Bushwhackers—people like Christopher Columbus Catron—and *we're* the Jayhawkers. Funny-looking birds from the East, mostly, who strut around looking like we all own Kansas Territory."

Malcolm shook his head as he lighted up and sat on the barn floor, opposite Hickok. "I'm not used to women like Mrs. O'Brien getting involved in these things," he said. "I wish now old

Brown and I hadn't put her on the spot by coming to her place. We should have gone straight on."

"Mr. Erskine, women butt into men's matters whenever they choose. You've been around. You know that. What do you suppose raised her interest, or did you just happen by this place?"

"Before they were called away, her men fired over our heads to scare us off. I think she disapproved of that," Malcolm said, shrugging. "She likely felt she had to make it up to us. When *you* snared me, though, I thought she'd set me up for—what's the word?—Bushwhacking."

"Well," Hickok said, drawing on a cigarette while eying Erskine studiously, "maybe that's why she invited you, and maybe it's not. Doesn't matter. Anyway, General Lane's more interested in those Sharps rifles than in you or Brown or the O'Briens. The guns are my main focus—to see they get through safely."

"Safely? What danger past here? We'll be in free Kansas Territory."

"I said we *look* like we own the Territory, Mr. Erskine, but I didn't say it was yet ours or free. We have to police it constantly against Missouri proslavers, Bushwhackers. This is an undeclared war. A war respecting no boundaries." Hickok glanced from side to side. "I hope to *tell* you there's danger both sides of the line. Better have the stomach for it or turn back."

Erskine stared hard at young Hickok, finally saying softly, "I can handle myself."

"With a Bowie knife? I think you should outfit yourself better than that. Ought to carry pistols and get yourself a horse. Pack along a rifle and ammunition." Hickok, neither changing his expression nor flinching, snuffed out his cigarette in the palm of his hand, careful not to let lighted ash hit the straw.

Erskine gulped, realizing his grit was being tested. He did the same quickly, amazed he felt no more pain than a brief stinging. He looked up, asking calmly, "What will the O'Brien brothers do to her when they hear she took us in, fed us and all?"

Hickok got to his feet and looked over at the tarp-covered wagon near the barn door. The unhitched mare stood in shade in a small corral, drinking from a trough. Off-handedly but with candor, Hickok said while lifting his huge shoulders in a shug, "Don't know, Mr. Erskine, except maybe they'll only beat her. Then again, maybe they'll beat her real bad and leave her for the buzzards. Or maybe they'll be merciful in their outrage and simply kill her. There's no law or ethic or, uh, moral, uh—"

"Restraint?"

"Right. There's none of that in anything having to do with this border fight. There's only war and people dying. But dying for a reason, I suppose. I may seem fairly young to you for the responsibilities given me by General Lane, Mr. Erskine, but I'm sharp to seeing one thing today."

"What's that?" Malcolm asked.

"If Mrs. O'Brien pays with her life over this or in any other way, somehow I get the feeling, watching her— You mustn't take offense if I say this, but— I think *you're* the reason."

6

"Bow your heads," John Brown said. Jane-Ellen had placed him at the head of the table. Neither she nor her brother Jimmy sat with the three men but knelt on Brown's call to prayer and crossed themselves.

"Lord God," Brown intoned in a voice assaulting the cabin walls, "hear this plea of your servant, John Brown. We at this table are sworn to uphold your word that all men are brothers. For reasons of greed and slothfulness, others have brought our Negro brothers under enslavement."

Malcolm saw Jane-Ellen cast a sideways glance at Brown from where she knelt, roll her eyes in supplication, and shut them again.

Brown continued. "We do not expect, oh Lord, that this matter in violation of your holy word will be settled peaceably, yet we wish it were so. We hope earnestly—we trust—that we are proceeding with your grace and your blessing in everything that we do, even in the most troubled circumstances we may face. Guide us to take proper steps. Enlighten us. Show us the way. Help us bring peace with freedom in this land of Kansas.

"And bless this household of the O'Briens, dear Lord, for in it lives a charitable woman, your daughter, Mrs. Jane-Ellen O'Brien, and her fine young brother, Jimmy Mulligan. Let them not be apart from you in their minds and hearts, for others seek to lead them away from your ideals. Protect them, dear Lord, and give them wisdom and strength for the trials ahead.

"Bless young Mr. Hickok and Mr. Erskine, my strong companion. And please, Lord, watch over my sons, flesh of my flesh, and my son-in-law in the Kansas Territory, doing your good work. Watch over my dear ones still in North Elba. They sacrifice so that we may all serve you in a noble mission. Bless this food that it may nourish our bodies for continued service to you. In Jesus's name. Amen."

Malcolm saw Jane-Ellen cross herself again, the rhythm of her act beautifully deliberate and unhurried. In that instant he knew he could love her. He was so moved by that realization that tears leapt to his eyes.

She got to her feet, served a platter of boiled chicken and potatoes and carrots with quiet efficiency, directed Jimmy with gestures to fill the men's tumblers with chilled milk, then withdrew with her brother. The two went outside.

When the door was shut, Malcolm spoke. "John, I'll not be going as far as Lawrence with you. Hickok will guard you. I'll remain near this place."

Brown, already tearing at a chicken leg, nodded as though prepared for the news. "Understand completely," he mumbled between chews. Then, after indicating the woman outside wordlessly yet questioningly, Brown received confirmation by Erskine's nodding. Returning his attention to the meal, the old man added, "Don't like it, but where a man or woman's passion is involved, I certainly understand."

Hickok spoke up. "I think Erskine *should* stay, but for other reasons than—" He chose not to finish that thought, evidently attuned to Malcolm's embarrassment. "I mean for several reasons." The large youth punctuated his thoughts with cuts of his fork into a boiled potato, popping in a piece following each item.

"First, we need someone here—or near—to watch Catron. The man's a common Bushwhacker trying to get a political foothold in the Territory. He plans to build a proslaver settlement across the line and call it Oxford. So far he hasn't got far with it, but there's reason to believe he'll succeed."

Hickok devoured that piece of potato, swallowed, then—

"Second, General Lane wants to position me in this area, nearer the border than Lawrence. Wants me in what's just been organized as Johnson County. The place is a problem to Free Staters because of the easy way Missourians cross in and because of how Johnson County's leaders tolerate that. I may work as constable for villages organizing northwest of here, well-placed between here and

Lawrence. Meanwhile, Mr. Erskine's, uh, 'interest' will help us secure a strong watch we need right here at the border."

Another piece of potato.

"Third, about uncertainties. President Pierce tripped us when he fired Governor Reeder this summer, putting in Shannon, whose sympathies we don't trust. You may know Wilson Shannon, Mr. Brown, from Ohio? Isn't that where you lived much of your life?" Old Brown nodded, spearing a carrot with his fork. "In a few days," Hickok continued, "there'll be a convention in Topeka to set up our own government and press for easing out Shannon. Likely that will bring more trouble. I've got to be at that convention and otherwise stay close to General Lane."

Hickok paused to eat again.

"Fourth, trouble means we need those rifles right away. Proslavers will no doubt move against us heavily after the convention. We can't let them get past the Wakarusa River and threaten Lawrence. Only the force of arms can stop them. You can see how important these few hundred Sharps rifles are to us right now, and why I have to personally guard you through."

Hickok put down his fork, drained the milk from his tumbler, and wiped his lips with a napkin. He pulled the cigarette fixings from his vest and prepared to roll one, placing the papers and tobacco on the table to offer Erskine. Brown did not smoke.

Malcolm knew old Brown must have felt completely in Hickok's hands at this point, as he himself now felt. He anticipated that young Hickok had something more specific in mind for him to do here, as a "strong watch," a spy. And it came—

"Mr. Erskine—"

"Call me Malcolm."

"Malcolm, then," Hickok acknowledged. "What do you know about Indians?"

Malcolm stared blankly, not knowing how to answer.

Hickok pressed on. "You understand I'm acting under General Lane's authority."

Erskine nodded, hesitantly.

"You'll be living with a friendly tribe for a while, just four or five miles southwest of here. Shawnees. Chief's name is Black Bob. Sympathetic to Free Staters. Their brothers up at the Shawnee Mission, on the other hand, seem in line with Reverend Thomas Johnson, the slaveowner this county is named for. The Black Bobs have horses, pistols, rifles. Get in with them. They won't let you make a land claim, but they'll take you in and set you up with everything you need."

Malcolm was puzzled. "How do I arrange that? I'm frank to admit now—hearing your scheme—I know nothing about Indians."

Hickok snuffed the cigarette in a saucer and fell to eating again, causing Erskine to wonder whether his negative response was about to alter the young man's plan. But Hickok looked up chewing, staring at Malcolm with no indication there was a problem.

"What you do," Hickok said between chews, "is get yourself wedded to a Shawnee."

"WHAT!?" Malcolm nearly flew back from the table in reaction.

John Brown failed to react at all, continuing with his lunch.

"You just," Hickok said, sucking his teeth, savoring a chew of chicken, "get you an Indian lady and marry up."

7

Erskine rose from the table, looking first toward Brown, then back to Hickok. The plan was outrageous. "I— I see what's hap—happening here," he stammered in agitation.

John Brown went on completing his meal calmly, mopping his plate with a chunk of bread. Hickok seemed to have exhausted his appetite. He showed slight distress over Erskine's discomfort, frowning.

"This is the second—the *second* time today," Malcolm emphasized, "that you've compromised me where Mrs. O'Brien is concerned and—"

"Son!" John Brown boomed, dropping a piece of bread on his plate and rising, his chair scraping over the rough cabin floor. "You had better stop right there." Brown's intense grey-blue eyes burned into Malcolm's and held him transfixed. Slowly, emphatically, old Brown said, "I didn't walk with you hundreds of miles—and bend my back *and* my soul into getting that wagonload of rifles this far—to watch you jeopardize our mission because of a sudden and sinful infatuation. Malcolm, I remind you that you are a *soldier in a war!"*

Brown's face was showing color. Erskine feared the old man would get indigestion.

"You took an oath," Brown continued, "when you joined the Radical Political Abolitionists. The clothes on your back, the food you've eaten on the trail, were bought you by the New England Emigrant Aid Society. You have a duty. You consented to that duty. You will discharge that duty honorably."

Malcolm sputtered, "By marrying an *Indian?* Some poor creature I don't even know and haven't yet seen? Using her so I can spy? That's *honorable?"* He added a chuckle of irony.

Old Brown moved quickly and, with the back of his hand, struck a hard blow across the side of Malcolm's head. Erskine staggered backwards. Hickok looked away from the scene, obviously embarrassed.

Brown dropped his arm to his side and stood before Malcolm, looking straight into his eyes. "Young as he may be," he said, indicating Hickok, "Jim Lane has trusted him to come here and direct us further."

Brown's tone had calmed after his striking Erskine, as though by modulating his voice he might soften the effect of the blow. He continued, holding Malcolm's attention with his iron stare. "What Hickok has told us comes together logically. Simple fact is, we need an observer near this place, near this—this *Catron* and his Bushwhacker operations. You can do that. You're the logical one to do that. You *will* do that."

John Brown drew a hand across his chin and scratched. "Your ill-placed interest in Mrs. O'Brien is of no importance to me. Except I must remind you, tied to a murderous Bushwhacker though she may be, she is nevertheless a married woman, and a Catholic at that."

The old man, visibly shaken from the need to scold and discipline, returned to his seat and indicated Erskine should reseat himself. Malcolm did so, with impatient gestures of resentment.

"Curiosity, Mr. Hickok, compels me to ask," Brown said in a more reasoned voice. "Why the extreme, that of Malcolm's actually taking a wife among the Shawnees? Why can't he simply camp with them? Depend on them for some of his information? Report to your contacts near here or in Lawrence and otherwise move freely about on the Kansas side of the line?"

Hickok pulled a small jeweled box from the pocket of his vest. He removed what appeared to be a gold toothpick and proceeded to dislodge bits of chicken from his teeth and suck them in noisily.

"There are more shades of opinion among the Shawnees about how their tribes are to be run," Hickok said, "than you can shake a stick at. Plus they're trying to adjust to white settlers moving in close by, after they received false assurances in the Indian Removal program that sent them here. In short, it's keeping hold of fertile *land* they're worried about. And if it's trust and help Malcolm'll be needing from them, it's their land interest he's got to serve."

To punctuate his explanation, Hickok began aiming the toothpick at Brown and Erskine, a gesture so annoying that Malcolm wanted to grab it out of the burly youth's hand. "Game has gotten scarcer, so many Shawnees have turned to farming. Under the new treaty last year, a bunch took their head rights of two hundred acres apiece, and they're working the land. The group that's broken away and lives closest—the Black Bobs—they're handling things differently."

"In what way?" Brown asked, a creased brow reflecting his wish to cut through complicated tribal quarrels toward understanding.

"They hunt what they can, and they farm, but they hold their land in common. No claims of theirs are staked with form poles or other means, like it's all one piece. So to keep Free Staters from crowding them— What's the word? Encroaching? —they're making every alliance they can with neighboring settlers."

Young Hickok glanced down at his empty plate and began to giggle. "This," he said, "came close to being funny." He looked up again. "I was in Black Bob's camp last week and learned four or five young women have gotten to be of marriageable age, but they're short of eligible braves. An elder in the tribal council mentioned he wouldn't oppose any of our unmarried Free Staters furnishing insurance against future dealings with settlers. He asked *me* to take a squaw," Hickok said, the giggle rising to laughter. "But I begged off, that I'm committed in the service of General Lane."

"Say no more," John Brown instructed Hickok. "It's settled then. Malcolm," he said in firm declaration, "we are in grave need of the help of Black Bob and his people. They hold the key to your being able to move freely in this part of Johnson County, and they've got a vested interest in someone like you. No question but that we must meet them halfway if we're to establish a strategic position here."

"We? A legal marriage?" Erskine pressed. "For life?"

"*Mal*-colm," Brown said in a manner Erskine knew would lead to the old man's rhetorical philosophizing, "in terms of the dangers inherent in our cause to make Kansas a free state, how long is life?"

* * * * *

Soon they were ready to leave. Brown was resigned to the impracticality of walking across the border symbolically and was, instead, seated behind Hickok on the latter's huge white Arabian. Twin lead ropes stretched to the mare that was pulling the wagon.

Erskine received directions to walk the Santa Fe Trail a few miles to the next campground, then turn south to reach Black Bob's tribal settlement. He hung back, preferring that Brown and Hickok start so he could have a word or two with Jane-Ellen O'Brien, alone.

John Brown had given Mrs. O'Brien a warm and grateful farewell. She'd responded, "*Shoot,* Mr. Brown. I only did what any good Christian woman would do under similar circumstances."

"Hope you don't suffer for it," old Brown added.

She looked up at him where he sat astride the horse behind Hickok, shielding her eyes against the high sun. "I can take care of myself, Mr. Brown. You just mind *you* do the same. Stay clear of Little Santa Fe from here on, you and Hickok both, hear?"

"I hear, Mrs. O'Brien," Brown replied. With a touch of the hat brim and a short wave to Erskine, he and Hickok rode toward the ridge that would carry them over the line into Kansas.

Malcolm regretted that his separation from John Brown had been marked by disagreement, even bitterness. Brown's motives were not difficult to understand. The man was not only fanatical on the subject of Kansas's future as a free state, he was also disapproving of the adultery he figured Malcolm intended.

Ah, well, we'll make it right between us one day, you and I, John Brown.

Erskine turned to Jane-Ellen and reached a hand. She took it and squeezed it firmly, revealing nothing more in her touch than a good-natured farewell. "You take care," she suggested. Malcolm nodded. He looked deeply into her eyes, searching, but they told him nothing.

"Mrs. O'Brien," he began, shifting his weight from one foot to the other, "you ever need help, for any reason—"

"Don't," she said, stopping him, turning away. "Don't go on with that."

"All the same, I've got to say it. You need help, you hang a piece of string or a length of yarn or some such from the crook of that sapling." He pointed to a small tree near the ridge, just off the trail.

"All right, you've said it," Jane-Ellen acknowledged. "But don't look for it. I won't do it. Now please go before any of Catron's men happen to have turned back. Our luck could run out. I couldn't even tell you at this moment where my brother Jimmy's loyalties are. He's got his eye on us, peeking from behind the barn. Just go and don't complicate this border trouble more than it is. And you, too—especially you—stay clear of this place."

Malcolm frowned. He touched his hat brim. "Thank you for packing me something for the trail."

"You won't go far on it. I hope a New Englander can survive alone out there."

"Thank you, Mrs. O'Brien." He walked toward the trail and turned back once to see Jane-Ellen watching him. Again, he failed to read any meaning in her look and wondered whether he'd gain by forgetting her entirely.

About an hour later, three or four miles into Kansas, Erskine sat on a flat limestone boulder and untied the faded neckerchief in which Jane-Ellen had placed a few things for him to eat. No, he wasn't hungry, yet he longed to look at what she'd assembled for him. Something was wrapped in an old piece of newspaper and mixed among a few apples and carrots and an onion.

Malcolm opened it and felt as though his heart had jumped into his mouth. Then he felt pain—gut-wrenching pain.

The newspaper wrapping contained a small stone scarab, about the size of a thumbnail. A carved Egyptian scarab.

Its size and shape, its colors—black with orange flecks along the side—were unmistakable. The object had rested in a corner of his memory over twenty years.

The stone carving had belonged to his mother.

8

Timber made the Shawnees feel secure, Malcolm learned quickly. Chief Black Bob had explained it, had sketched a rough map in the dirt showing the creeks that fingered southern Johnson County, creeks that were lined with a modest wealth of timber.

The Shawnees now built cabins, having abandoned wigwams because they no longer needed portable homes to follow game. They were now "rooted," the Chief explained, and hoped to remain so. They used the wood also to produce tools for farming. Game had been thinned by early white trappers, so the Shawnees were now serious farmers.

The white man, Black Bob told Erskine, "is a fool to treat all that he comes by as his personal possession, to use badly." Furthermore, many whites "own a foolish pride over the color of their skin and allow such pride to govern their behavior." Malcolm learned in their first meeting that Black Bob had decided in his youth to belittle such pride by using his own dark color as part of his name.

They sat cross-legged before a campfire. It was evening. They ignored a raucous wrestling match among several youthful braves nearby. Chief Black Bob offered a cob of boiled corn to Malcolm, who reached into a small pot with his knife to coat the corn with butter prepared from the milk of the Shawnees' cows.

The Chief observed, "Not a matter of my knowing the white man well, my friend. I know him *too* well and therefore find him generally not to be trusted."

Erskine found it difficult to disagree. Yet he wished to offer balance in terms of his own understanding. He said, "The white man taught you to farm when game became too scarce to hunt."

Black Bob appeared surprised, but he let Malcolm go on.

"The white man taught you to build homes instead of your living in drafty wigwams. The white man will bring shops and wagons and railroads and schools and will teach you to trade and move your crops to markets and teach your children to do numbers and read and—"

Malcolm now stopped, hesitated about going on—then took a bite of corn, because Black Bob was shaking his head emphatically.

The Chief looked down and chuckled. "My friend," the Indian said, "you have been to school, yet you know so little." He looked up again, smiling softly. "Tell me, do you think corn to be an important crop in the future of the white man?"

His mouth full of soft, buttered kernels, Erskine could only nod.

"Then," the Chief said, "please learn that the white man knew nothing of corn until he found the Indian cultivating it. That was nearly four hundred years ago. And homes? We used wigwams because we were nomads. *All* the land was ours," Black Bob said with extravagant gestures, "to go where the game went—whenever we chose, wherever we chose. The white man forced us to stay in small places." He paused, then pointed to a nearby dwelling.

"Cabins?" Black Bob said. "They are nothing to build, and there are many ways to build them, provided the white man does not strip the land of its timber. As for trade, we bartered for centuries with other tribes, long before the Spanish arrived. I will not go into differences between what we teach our children and what your white man's culture teaches them, except to say our society seems more closely bound—individual to individual, tribe to tribe—than the white man's."

Black Bob closed his eyes, evidently pondering his next thought. When he opened them, squinting toward the firelight, he said, "The Shawnee—the Indian—lives in harmony with the land. Because my tribe keeps its land in common ownership, we are able to farm what is clear and let the timber stand until it may be cut for good use. And what does the white man do?"

Malcolm shrugged and shook his head, not sure where the Chief was going with this.

"The white man gives us the notion of individual land ownership—the right to personal property as separate from community property. So? A white man must do what he can with his small, individually-owned patch of ground. His crops suck all the nutrients from the earth, and his shelters require much of the timber, but does he ever replenish nature? Not very reliably."

Malcolm nodded agreement, wiping butter and bits of corn from his face with the backs of his hands.

"When he grows old and is ready to die," the Chief said, "he either wills his land to his oldest son or divides it among all his sons, thus carving his land-wealth into small, unprofitable units and caring little for the rights of his daughters. Did you know women of our tribe have equal rights of inheritance and ownership? And the right of service on the tribal council?"

Malcolm said, "No, I didn't know."

Without using his hands for leverage, Black Bob raised himself from a sitting position to his feet. He smiled down at Erskine. "My friend, it is the curse of my life that my people will be outnumbered, outfought, overrun, overcome by white fools."

Malcolm, getting up by bracing his hands on the ground, said, "Surely the white man has given the Indian something."

"Yes," Black Bob conceded. "The Spaniards brought horses across the ocean, and all the whites brought better tools and weapons. We use them as well as we can, as we will use you—as you apparently wish to be used, though you are only half white."

"Three-quarters," Malcolm corrected him.

"What difference? So long as you and your Free Staters may bargain in behalf of the Shawnees with— Who is Territorial governor now? I can never keep it straight, the whites change leaders so quickly, so arbitrarily, so often undemocratically."

Erskine had the presence of mind not to remind Black Bob that his own brother Shawnees in northern Johnson County were undergoing similarly frequent changes in chiefs, having adopted the principle of electing them. He answered simply, "Shannon."

"Ah, yes. Like the river that the Irish teamsters sing about on their path to Santa Fe."

They walked together casually, the Chief nodding to his braves and their women and bright-eyed children. Their smiles reflected the several cooking fires illuminating the camp. "So long as you deal for us with Shannon, we may use each other in friendship. By the way, my friend, do you know where the Shawnees came from?"

Malcolm admitted he did not.

"From where there is now South Carolina. That was our home, before we were driven by the white man to Tennessee. Then into Ohio, partly because the Cherokees were displacing us after being driven by whites also from the Carolinas. Then we settled in Missouri. Now we are in Kansas. Where next? The Cherokees are already in Indian Territory. Must we be forced there and be placed in contention with them again? And did you know some of the Cherokees keep Negro slaves?"

"No, I didn't know that either," Erskine said, frankly surprised.

Black Bob faced Malcolm in the firelight and said, "There is much we can do for each other. I have no liking for these Bushwhackers and slaveowners such as the teacher, Reverend Johnson. I will help you if you will champion our need to keep this land, if you will do that among your friends in Topeka and Lawrence. But you must always be honest with me."

"I deal honestly in all things," Malcolm responded, puzzled.

"I cannot approve a marriage with one of the virgins of the tribe when I know your heart is elsewhere. You have not said it, but I read it in your face," Black Bob said.

Malcolm was relieved—and as joyful as a fish that got away, "off the hook."

But Black Bob delivered a surprise. "A poor widow, Sylvia Parks, has come to join us from the Shawnee Mission. Her husband died there of some white man's illness. She is childless. She is educated and skilled and works very hard. If you promise me you will treat this kinswoman of mine with kindness—yes, she is a full-blooded Shawnee—I will arrange both a tribal and a Christian wedding. What do you say? Are we to help each other? Are we to help the white man recover some of his dignity, by teaching him to be human toward both the black man and the red man?"

Malcolm Erskine laughed at Black Bob's wit, and the Chief joined him in laughter and put a hand on Malcolm's shoulder.

Then, "Go to your cabin, my friend. It is agreed. We will work together and serve General Lane and John Brown and—"

"And," Malcolm finished it with, "Black Bob."

They said goodnight to each other cheerfully, and Malcolm proceeded to the home of the family that had taken him in, thinking as he strolled.

The mystery of Jane-Ellen O'Brien plagued him still. The link between her and his long-absent and probably dead mother nagged at his brain until his head ached. When he arrived at the cabin where he was staying, the host family was gone, an absence he found strange. But tired as he was, he thought about them little and readied himself for bed, his head still throbbing.

In some pain, he dropped off to sleep. During the night, however, he awoke and stirred, feeling someone next to him in the darkness. A woman with an intoxicating juniper scent, a woman whose skin felt like silk, whispered with a trace of nervousness, "I am Sylvia."

Within moments, the pain of Malcolm's earlier torment left him.

9

"Tell me about her," Sylvia said. She stooped to pick up kindling and tossed it onto an old blanket she would later carry, filled, to their cabin. Despite the chill in the air, Malcolm sweated freely while he chopped firewood.

"About who?" he asked, uncertain but half-knowing whom she meant.

Sylvia continued her search for dead branches on the brown-leafed floor of the grove, not looking up. "About the Jane-Ellen you talk of in your sleep, when you're restless," she said.

Erskine stopped and leaned on the axe handle. He wiped his forehead with his sleeve, the action pushing his hat farther back on his head.

"I won't dishonor you," Malcolm said, watching Sylvia. They had been wed quietly about two weeks before by a circuit-riding Methodist preacher as well as by Chief Black Bob.

Malcolm thought Sylvia very appealing, warm and wise, and comfortable to be with. At forty-two she was slender, full of energy, very attractive. Her high cheekbones accentuated hazel eyes that spoke possibly of a French fur trapper in her ancestry. Her black hair was thick, long, usually combed straight but at times pigtailed in back or in twin braids in front. In Massachusetts he'd known older women and determined they were more agreeable in some ways than those his age or younger. Sylvia with her passionate kisses, with her deep, melodious voice, was far ahead of them.

"No," Erskine said, resuming his attack on logs that required splitting, "I won't discuss Jane-Ellen with you." He brought down his axe with a *choonk* that echoed from limestone bluffs nearby, the split pieces falling to the sides of the chopping stump.

Malcolm wondered how much he owed Sylvia after all, whether he was being too tight-lipped generally with someone who had obviously and rather quickly come to care for him a great deal.

She'd been helpful in so many ways, teaching him nearly-forgotten methods of the Shawnees that could prove useful in following the movements of proslavers, in reporting their activities to the Free State command in Lawrence.

Because the Shawnees now depended so little on hunting as was true in the old days, they practiced their tracking skills only occasionally—skills that had enabled them to read signs of the woods, along creeks, on open prairies just as clearly as the white man knew printed words or pictures on paper.

Sylvia still knew all tracking signs and taught them to Malcolm. She showed him how to distinguish among tracks in order to count the numbers of animals and people who'd passed that way. She showed him how to estimate the size and weight of those he tracked from the distance in their stride, from the depth of footprints made in various weather conditions—even the age of the prints. She showed him how to recognize the significance of tiny breaks in tree branches, how they added to tracing a traveling party's route and whether the travelers were in a hurry.

Communication with friendly settlers and with Shawnees was crucial, Sylvia pointed out. One needed to know whether it was they who had passed through an examined area or whether it was hostile Bushwhackers they may have seen.

Gradually, Malcolm learned to distinguish an enemy from signs alone. Settlers and Indians generally went about their business in the open, often using wagons. Proslavers frequently sought the cover of woods. Most were far from home, in unfamiliar surroundings, so they watered their horses spontaneously, more randomly, uncertain where the best springs lay.

With marriage to Sylvia, Malcolm had acquired a horse once belonging to her late husband. The black animal was serviceable enough, actually a stallion in need of a strong rider and regular attention. After weeks and weeks of walking to Kansas, Erskine was grateful for the freedom of getting about much more easily. He saw to the animal's every need.

Sylvia rode a grey mule, causing Malcolm to tease her good-naturedly in front of others over preferring half-breeds, a joke she pretended embarrassment about but seemed to enjoy hearing him repeat.

Besides the Indian knowledge that she gave their marriage-of-convenience, she contributed political opinion and fervor. Educated at the Shawnee Mission, she'd also been quick to observe the border issues and as quick to take sides. She loathed her former teacher, the Rev. Thomas Johnson, for what she called his "superciliousness," causing Malcolm to search in her Noah Webster dictionary.

And it was she who brought Malcolm the first hard evidence of James Butler Hickok's prediction—that proslavers would react strongly to the recently concluded convention in Topeka. There in late October, Free State forces had adopted a constitution outlawing slavery.

Kansas now had two governments, two policies affecting its bid for statehood—the one led by proslavers whom fraudulent voting had empowered, and the government established by convention in Topeka.

The evidence Sylvia brought Malcolm showed Bushwhacker plans were on a larger scale than even Hickok might have imagined. No mere stepping up of raids against Free State settlers this time, nor would Missourians muster two hundred skirmishers here, three hundred there, to go against the defenders of Lawrence.

Sylvia had brought a report, more in the nature of tentative conjecture than fact, that the Missourians hoped to make war by the thousands. Such a report, Erskine concluded, begged for confirmation.

It pained Malcolm that she had taken such risks. She'd ridden her mule into Missouri, conspicuous as she was in Indian dress, and had acquired freshly-composed lists of Bushwhacker leaders and the network data relating to their forces.

Only at great peril to her safety could she have come by such lists, which she said had been stolen for her by a Bushwhacker leader's slave. Sylvia was truly a resourceful woman and wise in many ways, but Malcolm was irked by an occasional sign of foolhardiness she displayed in her devotion.

Loyalty was one thing, but abandonment of common sense and safety in his behalf was quite another. He changed his mind about what he had said earlier and stopped his work again, beckoning her to him. She sat on the chopping stump, looking up, waiting for him to speak.

"Understand," he said, "that I will never dishonor you. Everything considered, I married you more from will than from duty. I might have walked away from duty, as I can and have walked away from my past. But I stayed. I'll tell you all in due course. About Jane-Ellen O'Brien there's hardly anything to tell, except the sudden raising of a mystery. A connection between her and my own mother that somehow bridges twenty years of my life."

Malcolm reached a hand to cup against the side of Sylvia's face in a gesture of tenderness. She closed her eyes at his touch and leaned into it for a moment. Then she looked up at him and said, "I will go back to Missouri to learn more, for we need to know precisely when they plan to move and the route they will take."

Malcolm withdrew his hand as though burned, taking his breath in a hiss. Instinctively he wanted to strike Sylvia for giving him so much more than he asked—that she was so willing to risk her life serving him and his work.

She smiled up at him. "Yes, Malcolm. Now you know I'm nourished by seeing you worry over me. My husband—my late husband—never displayed any such concern. To have it now from you? That's something I could get drunk on."

This was yet another turn in Erskine's experience he hadn't expected. "You put an unnecessary burden on me," he protested. "I didn't bargain for this."

"Take life as it comes," Sylvia said. "Accept love as it comes. Let me feel the joy of giving as I believe it necessary to give. If it brings trouble—well—" The buckskin fringe of her bleached dress danced as she shrugged. "Trouble is part of life. We have time enough later for peace."

"Later—" he repeated, puzzled.

"When we're dead," Sylvia said.

10

Malcolm's snooping throughout Johnson County was a cautious undertaking. For some settlers unused to seeing a free Negro in these parts, he took getting used to. He kept careful lists and relied as much as possible on ties with transplanted New Englanders. They had in common an accent and memories of familiar places.

Information about the possible new strength of the proslaver force had proved useful to General Lane and abolitionists in Lawrence, critical to their planning. Word came back to Malcolm in dispatches through a settlement in northwestern Johnson County—a place named Monticello—that Lane and John Brown were gratified with the manner in which he was carrying out his assignment.

Occasionally a dispatch runner would hand him a sealed packet of cash for his own use or to buy information. As a participant in the New England Emigrant Aid Society and the Radical Political Abolitionist movement, he knew those organizations were the main source of funds nourishing the Free State cause.

Erskine began sorting out various political, military, and even social maneuverings the proslavers were undertaking. Quickly he came to know who was whom in groups they had formed. One of the units, Sons of the South, was a popular front with a following in Johnson County, broad appeal in Missouri, and leadership headquartered in Westport.

From his connection with the Shawnees, he obtained much information about Sons and their allies who convened with Reverend Johnson at the Shawnee Mission. Independent Shawnees led by Black Bob in southern Johnson County maintained regular communication with kinsmen at the Mission and saw that Malcolm was provided all useful information they could gather.

Erskine had himself ventured into the Mission once. He was so sickened by the condition of black slaves Johnson owned that he vowed never to return, unless that was absolutely necessary. He also resolved to discuss with Brown, when there might be time, the question of how Christian ministerial service could reconcile with slave ownership. The old abolitionist drew an exactly opposite view from the Scriptures.

Malcolm also learned of a secret society among proslavers and Bushwhackers—the Blue Lodge. He knew that several men from Little Santa Fe were among its members. They included Christopher Columbus Catron, who was hard at work trying to establish the community of Oxford just opposite on the Kansas side, and the O'Brien brothers, Hank and Bill.

Erskine reasoned that his best information about war plans lay potentially with his tracking Little Santa Fe members of the Blue Lodge. Weather was in his favor. A period of what some referred to as Indian summer had begun, warming the countryside and sharpening tracks and other signs Sylvia had taught him to follow.

One such set of tracks led him off the prairie to a relatively secluded and hilly place on Catron's land, a short distance southeast of where Tomahawk Creek flowed into Indian Creek. The spot was well-timbered, containing a spring pond trapped by a limestone formation. There he found evidence of campfires and of possible meetings involving at least a dozen men, judging from the variety of boot prints. He also found a place on a bluff above the camp where he could lie quietly, fully concealed, to await convening of what he hoped would be a meeting of Catron's Blue Lodge.

Malcolm equipped himself with bread, dried beef, and a canteen of water. He indulged himself the luxury of an entire day's surveillance. He was prepared to spend the night and wait another day if necessary, on the chance the Little Santa Fe group would meet to discuss its next moves.

Waiting, waiting, the unseasonably warm mid-November weather causing him to perspire freely and uncomfortably, Malcolm soon saw his vigil pay dividends. The O'Briens rode in toward evening and dismounted.

The brothers spent more time than was warranted discussing whether to build a fire in view of the high temperature. Bill finally convinced Hank they would need light to see by. As the brothers talked alone, Malcolm learned why they were so unlike the recent immigrant Irish—victims of the potato famine—with whom he'd become familiar.

The O'Briens reminisced on their youth in Louisiana, their roots there dating back more than a century. Their father had lost a modest sugar cane plantation in a New Orleans gambling den, prompting the boys to reconstruct their lives elsewhere. This circumstance led them to meander upriver to St. Louis and eventually westward.

It was in St. Louis where Bill had met the respectably Catholic Jane-Ellen Mulligan and her half brother Jimmy, orphaned and newly arrived from Baltimore to claim a deceased uncle's pathetic legacy of small acreage at Little Santa Fe. They played on her fears of the frontier and offered protection.

In the course of the brothers' conversation, Bill confessed—as he had probably done on previous occasions—that his interest in taking a wife at that time was subordinate to his enthusiasm over her being heiress to some land. But the ground was poorer in size and quality than he had hoped, which brought bitterness to his outlook.

Learning that, Malcolm resolved to free Jane-Ellen someday of the curse of being chained to two lazy, good-for-nothing louts. Two ignoramuses who'd fallen away from their immediate family in hard times and from ties to their church, eventually to become common border ruffians in defense of slavery.

At sundown others rode in. The first was greeted as Catron, well-dressed and a smaller man than Erskine had expected, though owning a commanding voice pitched high. Catron announced—to what finally became a group of eight other men sitting about—that he was freshly arrived from Leavenworth. In that city the previous day an event took place that he said would go down in history as most significant to their interests.

Territorial Governor Wilson Shannon had thrown in with proslavers by attending an organizational meeting of the Law and

Order Party. The new organization was sworn to regard as treasonable the acts of the Free State Party and its "illegal convention" in Topeka three weeks earlier.

Yes, Catron said, war would come—and soon—though that had not been discussed in Shannon's presence.

Lawrence would be "cleansed of unlawful, nigger-loving Easterners." The city would be claimed by Missourians and "right-thinking Kansans for a righteous cause" to which the Blue Lodge and the Sons of the South were committed. New alliances under the Law and Order banner, Catron said, would easily muster three thousand men from western Missouri.

Shouts of approval went up from the gathering near the pond, with Catron continuing his attempt to share details of Law and Order Party aims.

Malcolm found it difficult to hear Catron in the clamor and wriggled to the edge of the bluff. In doing so he dislodged a rock and lost part of the foundation on which he was lying in concealment, plunging headlong into the enemy's meeting place.

11

Malcolm lay where he'd fallen near the campfire, hands and chin skinned and bleeding. He gazed from face to face of the hated enemy, their leader's face last.

The well-dressed Catron appeared curiously thoughtful, as though not terribly disturbed by Erskine's sudden and awkward intrusion among them. Hank O'Brien, however, had been quick to get the drop on Malcolm with his rifle. He drawled, "Shoulda strung him up when we fuhst run inta him."

"You've seen him before? Where?" Catron demanded.

"Trav'lin' with a wagon 'n' a preacher-man. They was haulin' Bahbles."

"Bibles?" Catron shouted in his high-pitched voice, *"Beecher's* Bibles! Sharps rifles! They load and fire *ten shots to the minute!* Not like these damned muzzle-loading squirrel-shooters!"

"Well, now, C.C.," Hank protested at Catron's tone, "Ah kinda suspicioned, but y'all sent word fer me 'n' Bill t'come lickety-split."

Catron lectured further. "And that was no preacher he was with. It was *John Brown."* The Lodge leader approached for a closer look at Erskine, continuing to admonish Hank O'Brien. "You had the chance to dispose of John Brown and capture *hundreds* of Sharps rifles. And you let them slip away. *Damn!"*

By the light of the campfire, Malcolm stared back, deep into Catron's eyes. He saw what appeared to be a man of intelligence, but with passions opposite his own.

"Boy!" Catron shouted from within two feet of Malcolm's face. "That *was* Brown, wasn't he?"

Malcolm Erskine continued to stare, not responding. He expected he would be dead in a little while, so there was no sense giving up a particle of information.

Catron hovered even closer and in a slightly softer tone asked, "Son, tell me your name." Malcolm leaned back against the rocks, swirling up a mighty reservoir of saliva. He released the charge with full force into Catron's face.

The Bushwhacker chief pulled out a lace-edged handkerchief and wiped off the spittle. "Get that knife away from him," Catron instructed the others. "Tie his hands behind his back."

"When yew goin' hang 'im?" Bill O'Brien asked from nearby. Malcolm, while the men were binding his hands, studied more deeply the man whose wife had treated Brown and Hickok and him so kindly that October day.

Though he would die, Erskine hoped for confirmation Jane-Ellen hadn't been harmed for her gesture. He might never learn the mystery of how she'd come into possession of a scarab once belonging to his mother. He might never know why Jane-Ellen put the charm among his things before he left for the Black Bob camp. But he yearned to know she'd been safe these past weeks.

Catron responded to Bill. *"I'm* not going to hang him. The rest of you are. I have other plans for what I'll be doing this night." He studied Malcolm's knife, inquiring sarcastically, "What did you idiots do when you first saw him? Take him for a slave? This man's obviously a free man, though a mulatto, or more likely a quadroon."

"A whut?" Hank frowned at a term he seemed not to comprehend.

Catron turned to confront his rough companion. "You're from Louisiana and don't know what a quadroon is?" He shook his head. "Never mind. You others—get this boy's feet tied, too, and sit him against the bluff. We've all got talking and work to do."

The nine members of the Blue Lodge seemed satisfied Erskine couldn't escape. They reassembled to sit around the light of the fire. Malcolm decided, on the chance a miracle might get him out of this alive, he'd better do some hard listening.

Catron told his group he would deliver the Bowie knife to Sam Jones in Westport, together with a full description of their captive. By the time Jones received the news, "the darky should be dancing on the end of a rope."

They talked late into the unseasonably mild, Indian-summer night, working out plans Erskine listened to with care.

Jones was Postmaster of Westport, Missouri. By some quirk, he'd also been appointed Sheriff of Douglas County, Kansas, of which Lawrence was county seat. The appointment had come from the Territorial government formed by proslavers after an illegal election, Missourians participating by the thousands.

The election was under investigation by the United States Congress, but the illegal proslaver government of Kansas was, nevertheless, operating with the tolerance – perhaps the blessing – of Territorial Governor Shannon. Also important in the political power struggle, key proslavers such as Jones had law-enforcement credentials.

The proslavery regime thrived on tacit Federal recognition, despite its illegality. Its leaders pledged to destroy the competing government established by convention in Topeka. For Sheriff Jones there was no question how that would be done, Catron told his gang. Jones was the kind of leader "just itching" for some provocation to organize Sons of the South and Blue Lodge members, now under the banner of the Law and Order Party, into a warring force to ride against Free Staters at Lawrence.

Jones, whom Catron described as a stickler for justifying all he did, would now get relief from that itching. If the presence of this armed and "obviously dangerous spy" could be shown to have had hurtful consequences against a citizen of, say, Little Santa Fe, Jones would be able to move with a semblance of legal pretext against the spy's sponsors in Lawrence.

Catron said, "We're going to show that this Nigra – a Free State agent – tried to take advantage of Bill's wife. Bill, can you get Jane-Ellen to go along with that story?"

Malcolm watched Bill O'Brien mull over his leader's plan. He also noticed Hank O'Brien grin and turn to another man seated with him on the ground. Erskine heard Hank whisper, "Hell, Ah done more with the li'l wildcat m'self," causing the pair to giggle privately while the weaker-willed Bill weighed Catron's proposal.

"It's important, Bill," C.C. Catron pressed. "Sheriff Jones needs every bit of legitimate grounds he can find to move with force against those mongrelizing abolitionists. Assault of a white woman by their own buck spy is just about all Jones needs to get us moving. We can wipe out Lane and Brown and Hickok in one big fight over this. Can you do it?"

Hank continued whispering to the next man and giggling.

"Shut up!" Catron commanded Hank, half-rising from the tree stump he was sitting on. "I'm trying to talk to your brother about something damned important!"

Malcolm strained against the ropes. He wanted to strangle the sneering Hank O'Brien for his confessed violation of Jane-Ellen, not to mention the sin the man committed against his own brother. Malcolm didn't care whether he died on the spot, so long as he died with his hands squeezed around Hank's dirty throat.

"Ah s'pose," drawled Bill O'Brien. "But Jane-Ellen, she got a mind o' her own. Ah can beat her good t'go along, mebbe."

Malcolm observed Hank stifling giggles so as not to upset Catron again.

Catron rose. "I'm riding into Westport with this knife to turn it over to Jones before morning. Bill, you go get Jane-Ellen now—"

"She'd be asleep."

"Never mind! Bring her here so she can swear in front of these witnesses that this Nigra Free State agent tried to force himself on her. Let her point to him and swear it."

Bill grumbled and got up, finding his horse. Soon he rode out, still grumbling unintelligibly. "The rest of you guard him until Bill returns with Jane-Ellen. When it's all done, string him up." Catron strode to his horse, wrapped the blade in a neckerchief, then slipped the Bowie into a saddlebag. He mounted and rode out, heading north.

The men decided to take turns napping and guarding Malcolm while awaiting return of Bill with his wife, Jane-Ellen. Then they would all go through the charade of a witnessed accusation.

The wait wore on through the misty night, but Malcolm didn't sleep. The longer they waited, the more hopeful he became that Jane-Ellen had balked at taking part in such a ridiculous ruse. Surely this Jones, if he was a responsible person at all, would dismiss Catron's word as either fabrication or insufficient cause to go to war.

By dawn, only Hank O'Brien among his captors was awake, wandering nearby. Malcolm was certain O'Brien watched him periodically. Though Erskine strained against his bonds, he couldn't do anything about them, they were that tight.

At last, Hank cried out to the others as the sky lightened over Missouri to the east. "Ah found his horse!" The others woke up and got to their feet. "Git that black horse o' his 'n' set him on it. Ain't waitin' no more."

One of the men protested they had better follow Catron's instructions. Hank O'Brien dismissed that. Summoning another man, he cut the rope binding Malcolm's ankles and helped hoist him onto the black stallion given him by Sylvia. They led him to a tree, where Hank immediately rigged a noose and leaned far back to swing the business-end over a branch.

After tossing it, O'Brien seemed pleased at the length hanging down. Another man mounted his own horse and rode up alongside Malcolm, reaching to slip the noose over their captive's head and draw it tight around his neck. He muttered, "Say yer prayers, nigguh."

Erskine sat forward, seething with hatred but silent, unable to move without drawing the noose tighter. Though he felt satisfaction Jane-Ellen had apparently refused to go along with the plan, his thoughts turned also to Sylvia.

SYLVIA!

Distinctly, he heard his wife's voice mingling with that of other women of the Black Bob tribe. Now he could see them in a group, five of them, advancing through the muggy dawn toward Catron's Blue Lodge meeting place. They giggled and chatted casually, seeming oblivious to the hanging scene not far from them and pulling off their dresses.

Soon they made unmistakable sounds of jumping into the pond for an Indian-summer morning dip. All the Bushwhackers, including the rider who'd placed the noose and was now dismounting, scampered on foot to watch the Shawnee women bathe.

Sylvia appeared off to the side, unclothed and running toward her husband with a knife in hand. She leapt onto the rear of the horse, swiftly severed the rope above the noose and then the one binding Malcolm's hands. She kicked the horse's flanks to get the animal going.

"What about the other women?" Malcolm called back to her as they headed southwest at a gallop.

"They'll be safe. Several armed braves are concealed and on guard."

"Where did you get *my knife?*" He plunged it back into its sheath.

"From Catron. He made the mistake of riding out alone. We all waited for the right opportunities to make our moves." As apparent afterthought, she said, "When you're family, we take care of you."

Sylvia, unclothed, leapt onto the rear of the horse and swiftly severed the rope above the noose.

12

"I shouldn't leave at a time like this." Malcolm was frustrated by depending on Shawnee riders for passing information to Lawrence. He believed he should step up his activity because of new reports of the enemy's strength. "But maybe I ought to go to Lawrence myself, share what I know."

"You won't have to," Sylvia said. She was spooning cornbread and gravy to go with the pork on Malcolm's dinner plate in their cabin. "Hickok sent word last night he's in Monticello and wants to meet you in Kansas City tomorrow. You can tell him what you know there."

At the sight and scent of the meal, Erskine felt his saliva running. In twenty-four hours he'd eaten only dried beef and dry bread while waiting at C.C. Catron's Blue Lodge hideout. The experience of being captured, bound, falsely accused of assaulting Jane-Ellen, and readied for hanging—well, all that had left Malcolm famished.

"Why," mumbled Erskine, who'd fallen to the job of eating ravenously, "Kansas City?"

Sylvia watched him, seeming at peace to know he was safe again. Malcolm thought but never mentioned she mothered him too greatly. In fact he enjoyed it, her being wife as well as behaving maternally toward him. He hadn't seen his own mother since he was a child. Never considered marrying to have the comfort of a woman's care again, till Hickok suggested it as a means for establishing an effective spy base.

Again, thoughts of his mother brought him to Jane-Ellen. What *was* the connection? The mystery vexed him. Without breaking the rhythm of shoveling food into his mouth, he touched a shirt pocket containing the scarab Jane-Ellen had given him.

Impatient with himself for lingering on such thoughts, he looked to Sylvia with an appeal in his eyes for more cornbread, more pork and gravy. Reading his unspoken request, she got up to fetch it while he repeated his earlier question. "I asked, why Kansas City?"

Sylvia turned to her husband with a look reflecting surprise. "I just told you, but your mind seemed elsewhere. He's receiving rifles by riverboat."

Malcolm realized his daydreaming had blocked what she'd told him. He vaguely recalled hearing the sound of Sylvia's voice and not paying attention to what she'd been saying. Caught at being inattentive, however, he chose to attack. "Well, so *what* if you tell me again? I want to be clear on everyth—"

"Don't fib. You weren't listening. You were thinking of *her* again."

Malcolm stiffened. He was ashamed he'd provoked all this—to mask his own deficiency. Yet he felt now he couldn't back down. Turning and pointing a fork at Sylvia, he raised his voice to say, "I've never beaten you, though I have the right. Do you understand what I'm saying, *squaw?"*

"I hate how you say that word," she said, "as though I'm something dirty. I'm your *wife,* both in tribe and church. Jane-Ellen O'Brien is someone *else's* wife, if you'd just learn to accept that."

He was hurting her and didn't know how to undo the situation he'd let tumble beyond control. He felt he must continue to assert his role, however, and he added menacingly, "I'm *warning* you." Then he threw in, testing her to the limit, *"Squaw!"*

Sylvia served the additional food, raised her chin in a show of prideful dignity, and sat down opposite him. Her lower lip trembled slightly, reflecting hurt and self-enforced silence, self-discipline. She stared, which annoyed Malcolm further.

"Don't do that."

"Don't do what?" she asked.

"Don't stare. The truth is, I'm ashamed sometimes, the way I treat you. Especially on the very day you saved my life. I don't know what's the matter with me."

Malcolm threw down his fork, his appetite gone. He got up and walked to the window that looked out on the other cabins of the Black Bob Shawnees. Because they held land in common, they'd been able to cluster their dwellings and establish a village where Wolf and Coffee Creeks met the Blue River.

"You know," Sylvia said hesitatingly, "that I have quickly grown to love you. Truly. Partly because of the honesty you always come around to, without too great a delay."

"Yes, I know—though I'm not sure," Malcolm confessed, "what love is. I thought I felt it quickly for her—for Jane-Ellen—and was in some ways happy to get this assignment to be near her. I no longer control my thoughts when she enters them, but now, I think, it's all because of—" He reached into his pocket and held up the stone scarab. "—this."

Sylvia smiled grimly. "Ah, yes. You spoke of a connection the day we gathered wood together. I saw that stone charm when I washed your clothes, and I drew conclusions. Please give that to me—lend it to me—and I'll try to untangle the mystery for you."

"You think you can?" Malcolm now turned fully toward her, feeling a sense of true humility. "Understand, it has less to do with Jane-Ellen than it has to do with my mother."

"I understand," Sylvia said. "Please let me try." She reached her hand, palm up.

Malcolm hesitated. Then he pondered her faithfulness to their arrangement, her ways of gathering information even at peril to her safety, her initiative in the waylaying of Catron. He concluded this might be something she could carry out at little or no risk. It was unconnected with the Border War. He set the scarab in her palm.

Sylvia grasped it into a fist, as though glad to take possession of something that caused him so much pain while he possessed it. "Put it out of your mind," she said. "If any harm should ever come to me, you'll find it here." She bent and lifted the hem of her fringed dress, showing him a secret pocket.

"Why should—?"

"You never know," she said, shrugging. "Just a precaution."

Malcolm reached to indicate she should stand, which she did. They embraced warmly, and he whispered, "I'm sorry."

"And I," she said, "for using such a tone about her. You're mine—for the time being—and for that I thank the gods."

"God," he corrected her, holding up an index finger. "One God. You're a Christian. You should know about that."

"And do *you* know it, husband? Is any of us sure of anything?"

Malcolm felt he might choke on words he must utter. "Of one thing I'm sure," he said. "In all my life I've never been certain of anything, any*one.* But of your love I have no doubt and will never betray you. It means a lot— It means everything to me now, and for me it's pushing ahead of this cause we're fighting for."

Sylvia breathed a deep sigh and pulled him close, then whispered a suggestion. He laughed, and they left the kitchen for the bedroom.

*****

Next morning Malcolm rode out on the black stallion. The weather had turned chilly again, and he was dressed for it in buckskins Sylvia had tailored for him several days earlier. He also wore revolvers given him by Chief Black Bob.

He took the military road that led from Ft. Scott to Ft. Leavenworth, turning north toward the Shawnee Mission but planning to avoid that place. He felt good recalling his time with Sylvia following their quarrel. Then he remembered—and felt a chill in his bones over it—that she'd volunteered to clear up the mystery of the scarab. Could he have been wrong about a lack of danger in that? Now it was worrisome to him, along with her other risks in his behalf.

At last he shrugged to shake off his fears. He realized freshly that in this quest, given her skill at building networks for gathering information, Sylvia should face little jeopardy.

Perhaps he would use some of the money sent from Lawrence for his support to buy his beautiful wife a gift in Kansas City.

A family of Shawnees approached as he bypassed the Mission. He struck up a conversation, learning northern Johnson County tribe members had begun selling the head rights to their land to proslavery Missourians. This family had done so and was moving on to Indian Territory. Other families would follow.

Erskine, they suggested, had better advise people of the Black Bob tribe to do the same, an option they held under last year's treaty, even though the Black Bob people pooled their ground. The Kansas land market among Missourians was very good right now, they said.

Malcolm thanked them for the suggestion and wished them well in their journey. He made mental note that this development, too, was going against the strength of the Free State side. He would report it.

By mid-afternoon he was in the small but booming town called Kansas City, hard by the Missouri River. It was his first visit. Though Hickok's message had been unclear where in the town Malcolm might find him, it was apparent the place was so small he could walk it in a few minutes and find Hickok easily. He did, near the river depot.

Hickok greeted Erskine warmly. The two began strolling through town, evaluating much of what they had learned since the last messages they exchanged. They reminisced about the bathtub incident of their first meeting and the short time they were together for breakfast in Little Santa Fe.

It became obvious to Erskine, the sight they made strolling the plank sidewalks of Kansas City caused others to take full notice of the pair. A dark-skinned man who was possibly a Negro yet two-gunned and wearing a Bowie knife at his side. A burly and fair-haired Hickok, whom many must have recognized as a celebrity, linked to Jim Lane and a legend for his marksmanship.

Hickok suddenly darted his eyes about under the brim of his hat and said, "Malcolm, don't break stride. Keep your wits about you. I think we're headed for a gunfight with some of these people before this day is done."

Erskine rocked slightly off balance at the news, but he kept putting one boot in front of the other, moving with Hickok. He felt as though his heart had jumped into his gullet.

13

"Do you know," Hickok asked, "how to use those revolvers you're wearing?"

"What do you *mean,* do I know? Of *course* I know. You think I'd risk my life to wear them conspicuously if I wasn't prepared to use them?" As Erskine spoke, he looked about to see whatever Hickok had seen that might make his companion believe they were headed for trouble.

"I just thought," Hickok said, "you were strictly a Bowie knife man."

"Well," Malcolm said, "a lot's changed in my life, thanks to you telling me how to live it. I may not be as keen a shot as you yet, but I think I'm as fast."

"We'll see....There, up ahead. It's those two, moving away from that wagon. They've been eyeing me ever since I got to town," Hickok said. "I've seen one of them before. Friend of Frank Coleman, who's got some land near Lawrence and is in a dispute with a friend of *mine* over it, Charlie Dow."

Then Hickok snorted a quick laugh. "Land. 'Cept what I said about Shawnee value on it, this all has less to do with land than with *politics* lately. When land's as plentiful and cheap as it is in Kansas, you can bet any fight over it isn't who gets it. It's whether he can keep *slaves* on it to do his work for him."

Wondering momentarily how an eighteen-year-old like Hickok could have come by wisdom so soon, Erskine noticed suspicious movement up ahead and said, "They're stepping between those buildings. Look, some others on the street are taking cover."

"Good. You're learning. Always watch what others are doing if you want some idea what's about to happen. We may make a gunfighting Jayhawker out of you yet, Erskine. Now stop short of the corner of the next building. I'm going to move out into the street to draw their fire and bring them out."

"You'll be in the open. Are you *crazy?*"

"Oh, hell, Malcolm. They're more scared than we are and won't be able to hold their guns steady till they've discovered what they got themselves into. Trick is not to let them live long enough for that. Stop here and cover me."

Hickok stepped off the plank walk into the dusty Kansas City street and turned at an angle as though to cross it.

Their intended assailants, ready for ambush but apparently confused to see Hickok break away alone—no doubt wondering what had become of Erskine—started to exit the alley.

Coming out that way, their guns drawn, one of them faced Erskine at the corner of the building and took aim.

Malcolm pulled back and dropped to the planks as the first bullet left the proslaver's gun in an explosion that seemed to fill the street.

Gripping one of his weapons in both hands and with time to take aim, Erskine got off a shot to the man's heart from a range of about twelve feet.

The impact sent Malcolm's victim backwards and head-first against the far wall, blood spurting from his chest in a high arc. If he didn't die from his heart being torn open, he surely did from his neck being snapped by the wall.

The other man had lowered his gun in apparent surprise, causing Malcolm to wonder why he saw no shooting from Hickok's direction. He glanced over and noticed his young friend standing with hands to his sides, his guns still holstered.

The remaining assailant seemed puzzled about where to aim first. Malcolm was still on his belly and had a clear shot, which he decided he'd better take without waiting for Hickok to make his move.

Erskine's bullet winged the man's gun arm. The wounded man brought up his other hand to take aim at Malcolm, but another shot by Erskine went to the neck—possibly the jugular—and finished him. He fell into a quick-forming pool of his own blood.

Hickok strolled over and pulled cigarette fixings from his vest, calmly preparing a smoke, shaking his head and commenting, "What a bloody mess."

Malcolm scrambled to his feet, shouting angrily, "You never *did* draw! What the hell kind of fighter are *you,* leaving it all to me? Damn it, Hickok! I could have been *killed* for all the help you gave! And it was *you* they were after!"

Hickok nodded, rolling the tobacco in cigarette paper, then running his tongue along the edge to provide a seal. "Malcolm, have you got one of those new Swedish striking matches?"

Erskine reholstered the one revolver he'd used and threw up his hands in frustration, looking to heaven for some kind of guidance. He turned away, then back to ask, "Are you going to just stand there smoking while someone comes to arrest me for killing two men?"

Hickok raised his eyebrows. "I'm not smoking at all till you give me a match, if you've got one. As for the law coming after you, a dozen witnesses including me can say it was self-defense. You handled yourself very well, Malcolm."

Erskine sputtered. "What did you do? Put me to some kind of *test* just now?"

"What are you worried about?" countered Hickok. "You've killed before, from what I've heard. You'll kill again. I have no taste for it either, Malcolm. But it's our job." He dug into a vest pocket. "Ah, a match. My last till I pick up supplies. As for testing you, not really. I knew you had them both when you went belly-down. There wasn't any need for me to draw. Look, why don't we just forget this, stroll over to the constable's office, give a statement, and get on with our talk?"

They walked, Erskine still seething but beginning to calm himself. "Where can I buy some tobacco? And I want to get a present for Sylvia," he said.

Hickok laughed. "*Now* you're talking! That's the way it is these days, my friend. While other men's blood is still hot on the ground, life goes on." He threw a strong arm around Erskine's shoulders as they strolled. "Life goes on," Hickok repeated, beaming at his half-breed friend.

"Me," Malcolm said, lapsing into the dialect of his father without realizing it, "I could use a wee bit o' the grog."

*****

After a brief formality they discharged at the constable's office, the pair sought and found a saloon with tables. The place was filled with or surrounded by every objectionable human and alcohol-related odor imaginable, yet it seemed a proper enough setting for additional sharing of information.

Malcolm told Hickok real danger lay in Territorial Governor Shannon's coziness with proslavers. His insistence upon being housed and headquartered at the Shawnee Mission under the influence of the slave-owning Reverend Johnson. His naive participation in forming the Law and Order Party in Leavenworth earlier in the week, which lent the enemy legitimacy.

"Without his recognition of the rights of Free Staters—the legitimate claims of Free Staters—" Malcolm said, "every dirty, slavery-supporting, low-life, murderous Bushwhacker along the border from St. Joseph south to the Butler settlement is going to be in hog heaven."

Erskine paused for a sip of whiskey, then went on. "When anyone like Sheriff Jones has his legal excuse and is ready to move against Lane and the rest of you in Lawrence, Wilson Shannon's blessing on that is going to let you be totally overrun. There's big numbers in these scum-of-the-earth slavers, Hickok. You can tell Lane he'll soon be looking down the gun barrels of every one of them."

"How many?" Hickok asked.

Malcolm knew the number of men the Free Staters could summon in defense of Lawrence would likely be in the hundreds. The answer he felt obliged to give about Missourians' strength was far greater.

"Three thousand," Malcolm replied.

Hickok winced hearing that, thought a moment, then tossed off a shot of whiskey. "They won't all show up," he said, shaking his head.

"That depends how successfully Jones rallies them," Erskine said.

"Have you met Jones?"

"No," Malcolm confessed. "Never saw the man."

"Big man," Hickok said. "About my size, but a bully. An ordinary bully, and deep-down spineless to boot. That kind's the worst. I don't mind fighting anyone who'll face up to me, but I can't abide a blustering bully with no solid backbone. You never know what that breed of man will do next."

"But," Malcolm reminded Hickok, "he has a following."

Hickok nodded. Then he caught Erskine off guard with a comment about Governor Shannon. "What I just said about Jones in a fight? We're getting some feeling in Lawrence that Shannon behaves much the same way at his council tables."

"I don't understand what you're saying," Malcolm said, leaning forward to hear better above the noise at the bar. It was the weekend, and a number of Kansas Citians were pouring their pay down their throats.

"I'm saying we can get Shannon over to our side. At least get him to where the fight can be a standoff. While Jones is only deep-down yellow, where you can't see it straight off, Shannon is beginning to look like he's all-over yellow. Missourians are too drunk with the success of winning him over to see it. But *we* see it, and we'll use it."

"How?" Erskine could scarcely believe what he was hearing.

"We're going to scare Shannon so bad, Malcolm, he'll dirty his drawers."

14

Malcolm nearly choked on a swig of whiskey he'd timed incorrectly. Never, he told himself as he gagged, should he ask James Butler Hickok a question without being prepared for a surprise answer. Hickok leaned and thumped Erskine on the back to help clear the windpipe.

Feeling flushed, Malcolm attempted to repeat his young companion's statement as a question. "You're going—to settle this fight—by scaring the Territorial Governor—into—?"

"Messing his drawers, right. See, we want him to come to Lawrence. We want him to look at what we've done there. We want to show him the full range of our military readiness. We want to show him—"

Hickok interrupted himself to dig into a vest pocket and throw some coins on the table. "Come on," he said, getting up. "I'll show *you.*"

They left, Erskine wondering—even dreading—what the next surprise might be.

They paused at a shop where Malcolm bought Sylvia a generous length of yellow, imported silk goods, which he hoped she'd make into some kind of dress for herself. He also picked up a little grub for the roundabout ride he planned homeward, and some tobacco.

The pair reclaimed their horses and rode out of Kansas City heading south. They followed a path up the bluffs that work crews were still in the process of excavating. They aimed toward Westport but avoided the center of that bustling town. Near Westport they boarded a leaky ferry whose "seaworthiness" Malcolm had doubts about. They crossed the Kansas River.

Now in Kansas, Hickok led their way by a circuitous route to a relatively concealed building. Not built as a barn, the place seemed nevertheless large enough to serve as one. Malcolm realized as he dismounted that this was some sort of Free Staters' secluded warehouse. Two men armed with rifles recognized Hickok. They indicated that what he was looking for was out back.

They walked around to the other side, and Malcolm stopped in his tracks. Hickok continued and stood beside what appeared to be a vintage but serviceable cannon.

Erskine put a hand to his forehead, pushing back his hat, laughing at his friend's latest surprise. Hickok seemed to enjoy hosting a demonstration of the point he'd been making in the saloon.

"When Governor Shannon realizes we've got artillery," Hickok said, "and plenty of shot and powder to go with it, thanks to our backers in New York and New England, he'll turn tail and tell his slavery-supporting friends it's time to let us alone."

Malcolm was still trying to recover from laughing. "You really—believe that— antique'll work?"

"I *know* it will," Hickok said.

"When are you moving it to Lawrence?" Erskine asked.

"Tonight."

"And what's my next assignment?"

"To get word to us, by the fastest means available, about *when* they're riding against us. We want to know a full two days ahead of their arrival."

Erskine nodded, serious this time. "Consider it done."

* * * * *

Malcolm left to reconnoiter among the Shawnees of northern Johnson County. He hoped to get a better understanding of the gradual exodus under way. He carried a letter from Chief Black Bob asking Shawnees to shield him from proslavery whites—"his color being one reason I entreat you to grant quiet protection," the letter said.

The family of the Rev. Charles Bluejacket put him up for the night. Bluejacket worked often as an interpreter and conducted services at the Shawnee Indian Mission, when Reverend Johnson was away on Territorial business.

The Shawnee minister was a man of indefinite political views who dressed as white men did, very much a family man whom Malcolm judged to be about forty. He judged also that, in spite of what he regarded as Bluejacket's unaccountable naiveté in current events, he liked him.

They discussed the present chief in the north area, Captain Parks, brother of Sylvia's late husband. The name was not a military designation but yet another tribally adopted first name. Parks was the first chief to be elected under a system that this branch of Shawnees had recently instituted, a system Bluejacket endorsed. He said he intended one day to be a candidate. His grandfather had been a chief when the tribe's leadership followed a bloodline.

"Why didn't you stay with hereditary chiefs, as Black Bob's people do?" Malcolm asked.

Bluejacket seemed surprised at the question. "We follow carefully," he replied, his small beard bobbing with every syllable, "the lessons of democracy."

Erskine decided to spare the minister the bitter response he considered over the white man's capacity for establishing political puppetry. He believed whites promoted democracy symbolically and vaguely among the unprepared, then hovered with one hand on the reins and soon turned to patronizing and domineering their pupils.

Malcolm asked himself, *Should I let this trusting and innocent man discover how little democracy there'll be for the Indian when treaty pledges must be honored?*

Talking late into the night, Erskine learned from Bluejacket that although the Shawnees near the Mission had begun offering their lands for sale, the number of takers had begun to slacken. The report he had heard from departing Shawnees on his way to Kansas City was true, but there was more to the story.

The market was good when land buyers could afford to speculate. But serious settlers from the East were people of limited means and, for safety's sake, were now avoiding border counties. Interested Missourians, similarly cash-poor, still worked the ground they owned in their home state. They hoped a defeat of Free Staters would result in an eventual sell-off of Kansas land at low prices.

Bluejacket said he had faith that existing treaties would keep Shawnee land at fair value, whatever the outcome. "Desirable land of well-defined bounds doesn't depreciate, so what can the Shawnees lose by holding out?"

Erskine asked, "You're confident of the integrity of your treaties? And those charged with keeping and enforcing them?"

"Reverend Johnson," Bluejacket said, "has given me assurances on that score. I feel confident and secure, and I have told my followers they have nothing to fear."

Malcolm looked down and shook his head in dismay, but Charles Bluejacket either failed to notice or attached no importance to that.

Deliberately Malcolm yawned as he raised his head, which his host apparently recognized as a sign Erskine wished to retire for the night.

There was little to learn about border maneuvers from these Mission Shawnees, Malcolm decided, secluded as they were from the firestorm raging around them. Reverend Johnson had strongly influenced their views and rendered them blind to the conflict and politically impotent.

* * * * *

Next day Malcolm continued westward, hoping to learn how near to Lawrence— and how concentrated—was the proslaver penetration of Johnson County settlement. That might also tell him the precise route or routes the Missourians would take when ready to strike, where they might convene on the way, at whose home, with whose blessing.

Erskine stopped in a new settlement taking shape, Gum Springs. There he found fresh tension among Free Staters he had met in previous excursions to this part of Johnson County. They feared they might be "done for," they said, because of the casualness with which Governor Shannon tolerated the enemy cause, especially since formation of the Law and Order Party. They spat at the mention of Shannon's name.

Malcolm found little proslavery sentiment either in or west of Gum Springs. Occasionally a fellow New Englander recognized Malcolm's accent. Such a settler might descend a ladder or set aside an axe with which he'd been splitting firewood or quit digging a post hole. He would invite Erskine to share a jug or some tobacco, then confide he'd heard from someone who'd heard that so-and-so living nearby "had been seen" at a Blue Lodge meeting in Westport or some other place.

Malcolm nodded at these third- and fourth-hand confidences, made notes, and placed question marks beside all reports he considered little more than hearsay.

Erskine rode into the developing hamlet of Monticello. Sam Garrett, a young English stonecutter who also had a Shawnee wife, greeted him warmly. A few of the original settlers there had intermarried upon their arrival several years earlier, among them Isaac Parish and John Owens.

The community drew its name from Thomas Jefferson's home. Common perception was that this place would be, in part, a refuge against further indignities to Shawnees by whites.

Garrett insisted that as the day was wearing on, Malcolm must stay the night. That evening he would invite Parish and Owens to join them for conversation. And what had Erskine heard lately of young Hickok?

"I just left him yesterday near Kansas City. Hasn't he been through here with a shipment?"

"No," Garrett said, scratching his chin. "Possibly he took another route....You know," he added, brightening, "Hickok's agreed to be our constable when we can afford one and when things quiet down at Lawrence. Actually, when he's here he serves that role voluntarily."

Erskine decided not to tell Garrett that Hickok had failed even to draw a revolver the day before, leaving the disposal of attackers to Malcolm. "It'll be a while, Sam, before things quiet down.

The Sons of the South and the rest are preparing to move against us heavily."

"Through *here?"* Garrett appeared genuinely agitated to learn the news.

"I don't know. I hope not, for your sake and your family's."

Sam's wife, Betsey, served a fine supper, though she seemed to Malcolm to be distracted. Afterwards, when her husband stepped outside to help Isaac Parish unsaddle and water his horse, Betsey sat opposite Erskine and a frown came over her otherwise bright, round face.

"I don't know how to say this," she said, "because it isn't my business to pry in your personal affairs. But a message was posted for you today."

"A message? What message?" Malcolm asked. "What do you mean, 'posted'?"

"The woman at Little Santa Fe. Didn't you instruct Black Bob's people to watch daily for a length of yarn on a certain tree? A sign of danger or urgency?"

The questions jolted Malcolm. Though loyal now to Sylvia, he had volunteered an obligation before he met her. Still, he would keep his word, let no threat to Jane-Ellen go unchallenged. More to the point, if it was possible he would go to Jane-Ellen's aid quickly.

"Yes, I did so instruct them," Erskine admitted. This alarm was coming at the worst possible time of border troubles.

"The yarn has been there," Betsey Garrett said, "since early this afternoon." She burst into tears.

"What is it?" Malcolm insisted.

"Sylvia!" Betsey wailed. "She's kin to me. She's *missing!"*

15

"How can Sylvia be missing?" Malcolm asked. "I just left her yesterday morning! Before I went to meet Hickok in Kansas City!"

Betsey regained her composure with some effort. It was obvious she was trying to remember every detail of the report from Black Bob's camp. "She left the cabin shortly after you rode out. It's not her habit to fail to return by nightfall, regardless where she goes. Though Black Bob accepted her in the tribe when she became widowed—with the idea of watching over her—he never denied her freedom to come and go as she pleased. By evening, though, he'd become worried and sent out a party. She'd left on her mule."

Betsey paused to reach for a handkerchief, blot tears, and blow her nose. "They came back late, reporting the prairie ground had finally hardened and it had become so dark they found the search impossible to continue. This morning they took up where they'd left off. They think they found tracks on the prairie north of the camp that were hers and— Oh, Malcolm!" Tears ran again.

"There were other traces," Betsey said, "possibly Bushwhackers. They couldn't be sure. They all led to the water's edge. They followed the creek into Missouri."

"You don't mean the creek. You mean the Blue River, the south part close by their camp."

"No, the creek. Indian Creek."

"Indian Creek!" Malcolm got up quickly. He struck his right fist into the palm of his left hand. *"Damn!* What led her *that* far north!? Are you *sure?"*

Sam Garrett and Isaac Parish entered, realizing quickly from Malcolm's agitation and Betsey's state that something was wrong. They looked from one to the other.

"Sylvia," Erskine explained, bitterly, "has been taken by Bushwhackers."

"Where exactly?" Isaac asked. "Do you know?"

"I figure to Dallas. The Watts Mill area, right on the border," Malcolm said.

Garrett moved forward to put a hand on Erskine's arm. His next words were ominous. "Watts Mill," he said, "is like a military camp right now. A Bushwhacker gathering place."

Malcolm prepared to leave and considered further the dangers of the place where Sylvia was thought to be. The flow of Indian Creek was boosted by Tomahawk Creek just inside Kansas Territory. The combined waters flowed across the border and powered the mill. Anthony Watts and his sons had lately acquired the facility. Mrs. Watts—Sally—was related to Col. Albert G. Boone of Westport, grandson of Daniel Boone and now political mentor of Sam Jones. Boone was an architect of the Law and Order Party.

This time of year milling was at peak. Proslavery farmers were in and out of Dallas frequently, from all directions as it lay on the north-south road between Westport and Little Santa Fe. The legendary scout, Jim Bridger, had just bought land near the mill and was likely aiding Missourians. The place had also become a center for rallies that doubtless inspired raids against Free Staters.

Garrett said, "Isaac, you'll have to saddle up again. Gather as many as are strong-hearted enough to ride through the night into Missouri. We've got to find Sylvia."

Isaac Parish approached Malcolm. He, too, gestured by touching Erskine on the arm. "Try to take comfort," he said, "in knowing how resourceful are the Shawnee women. I know. I'm married to one as well." Parish returned outdoors.

Betsey Garrett looked up past tears into Malcolm's eyes. "Thank you, Malcolm, for not pressing me about the other one—about the O'Brien woman."

"I haven't forgotten about her," Erskine said, slightly annoyed over Betsey's implications and realizing her suspicions slowed her sharing the report of the signal.

"She may in fact be safe," Betsey said about Jane-Ellen, "though I know that doesn't reconcile with the alarm she gave. She was seen after the yarn was discovered on the tree, and she appeared not to have been harmed."

Malcolm straightened, wanting to shout in frustration, knowing *now* the meaning of the yarn hung by Jane-Ellen—not placed there to tell of *her* jeopardy but of *Sylvia's.*

Erskine's vanity and curiosity had led Sylvia to risk her life—for *what?* For his wanting to know the secret of Jane-Ellen's connection with his mother. He'd acted like a child. Now he hated himself for it.

Sam Garrett asked, "What is it, Malcolm?"

"Nothing, except that I loathe myself," Malcolm said in his darkest tone, his face clouded, "that I allowed such extreme danger to come to my Sylvia."

Garrett, before leaving to saddle his own and Erskine's horse, muttered something Malcolm did not hear fully, something to Betsey about her failure to share promptly the report of the signal.

Erskine stood facing the door, trying to regain control of his emotions, trying to rid his brain of the enormous self-hatred, the overpowering guilt that caused a throbbing pain there.

Behind him, from where Betsey sat at the table, Erskine heard, "Malcolm, you used the words 'my Sylvia.' I hope—" Betsey could barely speak for all the emotion he detected welling inside her. "I *hope* you told her you loved her—before she—"

Erskine didn't want to hear any more and reached for the cabin door, opening it quickly, stepping outside, closing it with a noise behind him. He looked to the darkened sky to assess what illumination might be available. The moon was at barely more than first quarter. Some light, but not much. Better than nothing. He was *thinking* again, no longer letting himself simply be drained by emotion.

Garrett hurried their saddled horses from the barn. Then Parish rode in, leading three other men. Malcolm recognized one of them as John Owens. That made at least four of the six in the party who'd married into the Shawnee tribes.

Malcolm would lead. "We'll take the most direct path," he said, "letting every Blue Lodger know we're coming. Make all the noise you like. That way they won't mistake us for Jayhawker raiders. If any confronts us, we'll say we're on a peaceful mission, looking for my wife." He peered into the eyes of the others to make sure they understood. "If any resist our being armed, I'll cut them down."

"We're with you all the way," Owens said, patting the stock of the carbine sheathed to his saddle.

The six rode eastward on a trail bordered by bleached grass that reflected the faint moonlight. When they felt surer of their horses' footing, they increased their speed. By the time they neared the main part of Gum Springs, they were at full gallop, causing settlers to run out in nightshirts to call after them. Because none blocked their way, they continued without letup and ignored inquiring calls behind them.

Past Gum Springs they turned southeast, avoiding the draws that fed Mill Creek. Soon they dipped with the ground toward Turkey Creek and plunged across, keeping their bearings southeasterly. Malcolm decided to follow Indian Creek and keep following it till it crossed the Kansas-Missouri line directly into Dallas.

As the night wore on, there was less and less chance they would be stopped. It must already have been well past midnight. Only once did Sam Garrett call out to caution that they should rest and water the horses.

Malcolm pointed to a place they could barely see in the dark, indicating Indian Creek. There they pulled up. Two of the men dismounted to rub their buttocks vigorously and be rid of the hard ride's pain they were unused to.

The horses drank, their breath steaming in huge clouds along the water's edge.

After perhaps ten minutes and hardly a word among them, Erskine directed that they should start again. This time they would stay with the creek bank, which provided less-certain footing.

Progress grew slower. Within an hour, however, they were at the border. Malcolm signalled them to stop.

"If they've harmed Sylvia," he said, "and I fear they have, they want me to find her. They want me and anyone I bring with me to react immediately. Then they'll punish me and will have broken the link I represent between the border area and Lawrence. So," he said, turning and looking into the eyes of each man as clearly as the night's dim light would allow, "we are *not* to react unless blocked or confronted directly while we try to carry on our—our mission, which is only to find Sylvia and bring her back."

"Whether—" Garrett had started to say something but rejected the notion of going on.

"That's right, Sam," Malcolm said with understanding and some gentleness. "Whether alive or dead."

They crossed into Missouri and found Watts Mill and Dallas eerily quiet. Erskine took that as a sign the people there knew what was happening. Otherwise they'd have come out of their homes at the sound of horses.

Yes, he thought, *they want me to find her. And they'd like to be watching when I do.*

Slowly they paced their horses through what remained of the night. They went back and forth over the area for what seemed like another couple of hours. They looked for any clue that might help them. Not one Missourian had approached them, though from time to time they saw a whale-oil lamp or candle flicker in a window, then shortly afterward be extinguished.

At first light, Malcolm indicated they should halt again. For an instant he faltered, looking as though he might collapse. "We're near Sylvia, and she's dead," he said. "There's no mistaking the odor of a dead human left in the open more than a day."

"There!" Owens shouted, pointing toward a stout tree. "Look!"

Erskine dismounted before turning, certain of what he would see.

When he wheeled to gaze upon the naked form of Sylvia hanging from the tree, her torn and bloodied dress on the ground,

Erskine raised his head, allowing a deep, growling, otherworldly scream to rise from inside.

it was as though he had already visualized—*this* was how he would find her.

Garrett, also now on foot, came over to Malcolm. "Let go, my friend. Don't stay hard at this moment. *Let go.*"

Malcolm Erskine knew he must rid himself of the pain—pain he'd begun carrying hours before, half-knowing what he would find. He must do this regardless who was present or who else might be observing. He must let it out, as any man worth calling himself a man would do for his woman. He raised his head, allowing a deep, growling, otherworldly scream to rise.

The long scream filled the dawn of the Missouri countryside near Dallas. It sent a covey of quail flapping and a startled doe and her fawn dashing.

John Owens shuddered visibly at the sound. One or two of the other men were moved to sobs at the sight of Sylvia, especially at the sounds of Malcolm's honest grief.

16

Malcolm turned away momentarily as Garrett and Owens reached from astride their horses to cut the rope. They draped Sylvia's body over the black stallion's saddle. Parish dismounted to gather her torn buckskin dress and stuff it into Malcolm's saddle pocket. He fetched a blanket from his pack and started to cover Sylvia.

Malcolm stopped him. "No, Isaac. Let everyone we pass see what they've done. Then the guilty ones may understand, their days are numbered."

"When do you plan to strike back?" Garrett asked. "Do you have a plan?"

"In due time," Erskine said. "In due time. Not today, not tomorrow, nor the next day. Do I have a plan? I'll learn the identity of all who took part, whether they did it or simply stood close and allowed it to happen. And I'll kill every last one of them."

With that declaration, he mounted his horse behind the cold, death-odored body of his beautiful wife. He led the group out of Dallas southward, toward the Santa Fe Trail.

The sun was visible, but a mist hung in the air to prevent its having any warming effect. When the slow-moving procession came within sight of Little Santa Fe, Malcolm recognized Jane-Ellen O'Brien. She was waiting on her paint horse.

They hadn't seen each other since the day he arrived at the border nearly two months earlier. She wore a man's jacket loosely over her dress, which was hiked up for riding like a man, and high boots. A mourning shawl covered her head and shoulders.

Garrett ventured, "Is that—?"

Malcolm nodded, observing that Jane-Ellen took care not to approach. She started her horse and rode parallel at a distance, as though part of the slow procession.

Erskine touched the brim of his hat in acknowledgement. Seeing that, she halted her paint, hesitated, crossed herself in the Catholic fashion, then wheeled her horse to return home at a canter.

"Why did she ride along like that?" Sam asked. "She was the only person to come out."

"I don't know for certain," Malcolm said. "It may have been her way of asking me not to make her a widow."

"It was her *husband* did this?"

Erskine nodded. "I'm reasonably sure he was in it, though it's more the style of her brother-in-law to have led it. Punishment—for Sylvia's rescuing me last week when the O'Briens started to hang me, when they caught me spying on their Blue Lodge meeting. I'll learn everything I need to know, in due time."

Erskine sighed. He looked down at Sylvia's body that was turning ash blue. "Our time together was short. The circumstances of our joining were not the best. But I loved her for what she was and what she taught me. She transformed me, from a stupid, fickle, moonstruck Yankee fool into a man with solid purpose. She had more courage and love in her than anyone I've ever known. For Sylvia, love and courage were bound together. It was impossible to show one without the other."

When they approached Black Bob's camp, the riders discovered the Chief had already prepared a place on a nearby ridge, as well as a casket for the Christian burial he evidently knew Sylvia would have wanted. Word of Sylvia's fate had gone ahead out of Dallas, in the mysterious manner of Shawnee communications at which Erskine continued to marvel.

Malcolm had considered cremation in traditional Indian fashion, but on the ride he'd concluded—and knew Black Bob would, too—that Sylvia deserved enshrinement. Erskine dismounted and embraced Chief Black Bob, whispering hoarsely, gratefully, "She was an inspiration."

Women of the tribe had found a suitable garment to dress Sylvia. The strange combination of their Methodist training at the Mission and their remembered Shawnee rites led them to embellish burial preparations—ears of corn and several apples placed around

Sylvia's body as food for a journey, a silver cross placed on her bosom as guidance for her eternal soul, mournful Indian dirges sung softly by weeping tribeswomen as John Owens read from the Scriptures.

Before the lid was placed, Malcolm got to his knees and bent to kiss Sylvia lingeringly on her cold, blue lips. He placed a cluster of late-blooming purple chrysanthemums beside her. He rose and joined Shawnee braves in nailing the lid, lowering the coffin into the ground, shoveling earth to cover it, and setting a temporary wooden cross above it. He gazed in all directions from the ridge and nodded acknowledgement that the Chief had selected a splendid place.

"If anything happens to me," Malcolm said, pointing to the ground alongside Sylvia's grave, "please put me here."

The Chief nodded. The burial party mounted up and followed Black Bob to the Shawnee camp.

Erskine noticed Sylvia's mule had somehow made its way home and grazed near their cabin. Silently, he shook hands with each of the men from Monticello, who were to be fed before riding out.

He accepted the offer of a Shawnee youth to attend to the stallion. He recovered Sylvia's bloodied dress from the saddle pocket and felt for the stone scarab. He retreated to his cabin.

* * * * *

Erskine busied himself for several days by riding out to observe signs along paths and gather evidence. To dispatch helpful Shawnees and direct what they should watch for and of whom they should ask questions. To instruct them how best to collect and record useful data. Each evening he returned to the camp and consulted with them.

By oil-lamp and candlelight he prepared charts in his cabin. He composed outlines, drew diagrams and rough maps, studied the recorded routines of several Missourians in order to chart schedules. He rounded out lists that Sylvia had helped him start weeks before—lists of Blue Lodge and Sons of the South members. Lists of

Bushwhackers. How they spent their days and nights. Names and other data relating to their family members.

Malcolm corrected and then redrafted the lists and charts with new information brought to him daily. He tacked these on the cabin walls and restudied them when he woke each morning.

Women of the Black Bob tribe delivered food to Malcolm, for he took no time to cook for himself. When they picked up the baskets in the morning and saw he hadn't eaten, they shook their heads and mumbled complaints that Erskine chose to ignore.

Each day Black Bob entered the cabin to watch Malcolm at work, to review his charts, his lists, to suggest corrections where he knew information to be in error. He joined Erskine for rolling cigarettes, smoking, and small talk.

Malcolm overheard tribe members outside when the Chief left the cabin. They inquired about his health and his state of mind. He heard Black Bob assure them, "He's fine—at work for the Free Staters *and* to preserve the honor of Shawnees."

Though Malcolm grew thinner, he felt stronger, more determined in his work than ever, firmer in his convictions. He knew what steps he must take that would serve combined causes of a free Kansas and frontier justice over Sylvia's murder. There was no question what he must do—no question but one that Black Bob put to him one evening: "How many?"

"Twenty-three," Erskine replied. "All to be disposed of in due time, so as not to trigger Jones's moving against Lawrence. Twenty-three."

"That many," Black Bob responded, shaking his head. "Come, eat something. I have freshly roasted pig in my cabin."

"Yes," Malcolm agreed. "I'm famished."

*****

Erskine was interrupted while bathing to learn he had a visitor—a boy. Drying, dressing, curious, Malcolm approached a group clustered at the north entrance to Black Bob's camp.

Several Shawnees stood about the lad, whom Malcolm recognized as Jimmy Mulligan.

Jimmy removed his hat respectfully and grinned.

Erskine asked, "Why are you here?"

"Jane-Ellen sent me, sir."

"Why? She's not in any danger, or you wouldn't be grinning like that."

"To— To—" Jimmy seemed confused momentarily. "I think she sent me to help you. I have, uh, information."

17

Malcolm approached the lad and put a hand on his head. "Come to my cabin and we'll talk. Do you drink coffee?"

"Yes, sir. Sometimes Jane-Ellen lets me, if I put milk in it."

"I have a pitcher of milk. You can help yourself. What sort of information do you have? Why did Jane-Ellen send you?"

Jimmy Mulligan glanced back to where his horse remained tethered. He evidently was anxious that the Indians should not disturb it.

"Don't worry," Malcolm assured him. "They don't need it and will watch it well for you."

Jimmy sighed and let Malcolm lead him. He grinned again and looked up at Erskine. "Yes, sir, I was worried. I'm not used to Injuns. I'd just as leave have that coffee before I give Jane-Ellen's message. It was sort of a dry ride. Also I want to say it just right, the way she told me."

"I understand," Malcolm said, smiling. "How old are you?"

"Thirteen come January."

"How old is Jane-Ellen? About twenty-three? Twenty-four?"

"Nineteen."

Erskine stopped, and the boy did, too. "Nine*teen?* Are you *sure?* She looks older."

"Yes, sir. Well," Jimmy said, shrugging, "it's a long story. She's been through misery, I guess you could say."

"Misery," Malcolm repeated.

"I'm not supposed to talk about it," the boy said. "I'd just as leave you didn't press it, sir."

Erskine pictured again what kind of life she must be leading, wedded to a no-account such as Bill O'Brien, and his brother Hank taking liberties with her.

Malcolm asked, "How do *you* get along with the O'Briens?"

"Sir," Jimmy said, his eyes pleading as he looked up into Malcolm's, "I'd just as leave you didn't press any of that either."

They entered Erskine's cabin. Malcolm stirred embers in the small fireplace and added short lengths of branches to set it blazing again. He took a pitcher from a cupboard, actually a cubby that stuck out from the side of the cabin to receive increasingly cold outdoor temperatures. He set the milk on the table with a clean mug for Jimmy.

They stood as Malcolm poured the coffee. The boy stopped him when the mug was half filled, added milk himself, and lifted the mug for a generous swig.

"Sit down, Jimmy," Malcolm suggested. "Pull the chair to the fire, if you like. Why didn't you wear your coat today?"

"I don't own a coat. Jane-Ellen sometimes borrows one of Bill's, and sometimes I use it, but—" He shrugged again.

Erskine went to Sylvia's wardrobe and found a faded buckskin jacket. "Here," Malcolm said, tossing it onto the table. "It's yours. It may hang a little loose, but you'll grow into it. Just don't tell Bill or Hank how you came by it. Say you helped a wagoner on the trail who gave it to you as pay."

"I don't like to lie, sir."

Malcolm turned to face the lad, to study him. "Considering possible reasons against admitting you came to see *me,* God will forgive you."

"Well," Jimmy said, nodding, crossing himself quickly, "I'll do it then. And thank you for the coat."

"You're welcome." Erskine sat opposite Jimmy, trying to find the lad's gaze and hold it. "Now, tell me."

The boy drained the mug and set it on the low hearth, then moved his lips silently. He seemed to be rehearsing by rote what his sister had sent him to say. "Jane-Ellen's afraid you plan to kill Bill."

"Aye." Malcolm nodded. "No question about that. I will kill him, and I will kill Hank. The only question is when. Continue."

"She'd just as leave you didn't."

"Oh? Won't she be better off rid of them? I'd have figured she might thank me."

"She'd be—*we'd* be worse off."

"Explain."

"As little as the O'Briens help around the place, they do bring us money from time to time. Not much, but enough to keep us going."

"Money? I doubt they do any honest work."

"Honest or not," Jimmy said, "some consider what they do as work."

"Mercenary Bushwhackers? *Paid* to be border ruffians? Jane-Ellen's content with blood money?" Malcolm shook his head and looked into the fire.

"Begging your pardon, sir. But word is you're in the same line of work."

Erskine turned and stared harshly, raising an index finger to caution Jimmy Mulligan. "Not to raid or kill for pay, my lad. It's not the same thing."

"But you *do* kill, and that's part of why I'm here to talk with you."

"How so?" Malcolm sat up straight, not understanding. "And what killing?"

"The men you gunned down in Kansas City, after you got loose of Hank and Bill."

"Oh, them." Malcolm gestured with a hand-wave. "I'd forgotten. Anyway the constable ruled it self-defense."

"Just the same, sir, they were friends of Frank Coleman."

"I'd heard that," Erskine said, acknowledging with a nod. "And now that snake Coleman has killed Charlie Dow. Did him in the other day in Douglas County. I've also heard Coleman's hiding at one of the Law and Order bases, the Shawnee Mission, under Sam Jones's protection."

"Sir," Jimmy ventured. "That's part of what Sheriff Sam Jones has been waiting for. Now that Coleman's at the Mission, he's been talking about the, uh—the, uh, Nigra who shot his pals in

Kansas City. That would be you, sir. Jane-Ellen says word's reached Little Santa Fe that you're a wanted criminal."

"Criminal?" Malcolm repeated, eyebrows raised, the palms of his hands on his chest. "Me?"

"Not just a spy, Mr. Erskine, but under a murder warrant. I don't understand all the words I'm using, such as 'warrant,' but that's what Jane-Ellen told me to say."

"Warrant is a paper," Malcolm said, taking cigarette fixings from a nearby shelf. "Worth this," he added, holding up a cigarette paper and then blowing it out of his hand, "when signed by bogus officials like Jones." He watched the paper float to the floor.

"Well," Jimmy said, "let me keep going or I'll forget. A man named Jack Branson went and burned down Coleman's house and was arrested by Jones day before yesterday. That night a bunch of Free Staters led by Colonel Sam Wood stopped Jones and his men and rescued Branson—"

"Good for them," Malcolm said.

"And now Jones claims Colonel Wood gave grounds for Law and Order Party action. Jane-Ellen said what it really means is *war.* The men from Lawrence were carrying Sharps rifles. Jane-Ellen said word's around *you* brought them in—you and that old man, John Brown."

"What if I did?" Erskine asked.

"Jones is making what Jane-Ellen calls a 'case' out of it against you, along with your shooting those men in Kansas City. Never mind what the constable said, you're just plain *wanted,* Mr. Erskine."

"Tell me, Jimmy. As Jane-Ellen understands it and has passed it to you, what does 'wanted' mean when Jones says it?"

Jimmy Mulligan frowned and sat forward. "Jones has asked Governor Shannon to call for three thousand men to go against Lawrence. He claims that because of the way he was forced to sur—surrender Branson and because of how the Lawrence men were armed, Law and Order must take action in all stra—strategic places."

"Places? Where besides Lawrence?"

"Here."

"Here?"

"In Black Bob's camp. If you want to protect the Shawnees, you have to get out, sir. That's what Jane-Ellen says you should do."

Malcolm stood up, threw his cigarette into the fire, and ran a hand over his face. He pulled himself straight, looking about the cabin he was reluctant to leave but knew now he must abandon. Jane-Ellen was right.

"I thank you, Jimmy. You can spread news I'll be gone from Black Bob's village within the hour—by the time you return to Little Santa Fe. I refuse to bring trouble down on the Shawnees. Now I'll see you off. Thank you."

"There's more," the boy said, standing, reaching for the jacket. "Just one thing more."

"What's that?"

"Jane-Ellen said the reason your wife died was, she—the Indian lady—helped you escape Hank. She was recognized when she talked with my sister about the—the, uh—"

"Scarab. This." Malcolm pulled the stone from a pocket to show Jimmy.

"Yes, sir. They caught your wife on the trail, after she left Jane-Ellen. Anyway, Jane-Ellen says she'll be glad to tell you the whole story of that stone if you both meet somewhere, except you mustn't do anything to Bill."

"Go now," Erskine instructed Jimmy Mulligan. "Get on your horse and ride out. Put on the jacket—here's your hat. Go."

"Don't get angry."

"I won't do you any harm. Just go. I've heard enough."

"What should I tell her?"

With no meanness nor roughness, Malcolm took Jimmy by the arm. He walked him up the path to his horse. He helped hoist the boy into the saddle.

Jimmy looked down, child's eyes appealing to Erskine's for response. "What should I tell her?" He looked as though he might weep, as though it might be the end of their rope—his and Jane-

Ellen's—if they were left destitute by Malcolm's planned vengeance against the O'Briens.

"Go tell her I said, 'No'." Malcolm slapped the horse's flanks to get it going, shouting after Jimmy. "Tell Jane-Ellen I'll never make such a deal. Bill and Hank O'Brien will *die!*"

Chief Black Bob came up and stood beside Erskine. "It is no use. He cannot hear you anymore. Calm down, friend."

Erskine drew several short breaths to regain his composure. "She thinks she can play on a link to my mother to interfere with my honor? Never."

"What will you do?"

"I can't stay here. Bushwhackers will raid your camp if I stay."

"You are welcome to stay," Black Bob said, "as long as you like. We can defend ourselves."

"I don't want it on my conscience if they carry through on their threat. They're calling men to arms against Lawrence right this minute," Malcolm said. "I must send a message there. And you must let the Law and Order people know I've left this camp for good—else they'll come make a bloodbath."

"Where will you go? We have discussed safe hiding places, but you would be alone," Black Bob said. "How can you do your work alone?"

"I'll manage. I'll stay in contact. For now I'll pack and be gone in fifteen minutes. I can't bring further grief on the people, the family, I've grown to love."

Malcolm reentered the cabin of his short happiness with Sylvia. He returned to her wardrobe and inhaled deeply, closing his eyes to savor her juniper scent.

18

Malcolm surveyed his new quarters—a limestone cave adjoining an unnamed creek. He checked cracks in the cave ceiling, to be certain they were dispersing smoke from fires he would need for warmth and light. He wanted no telltale column, but fine channels of exhaust to help him escape attention.

He reached for a leather bucket to water his horse, pouring from his canteen. He held it for the animal, which was able to stand upright in the cave. He spoke in soft tones to maintain the horse's calm, guard against a whinny that might reveal their hideout.

Erskine had dared move closer to Little Santa Fe. He was northeast by about three miles from Black Bob's place. Only the Chief, a few in the Shawnee council, and now Malcolm knew of this cave.

Black Bob had presented Erskine with a sturdy bow and a quiver of arrows, a weapon no longer used commonly by Shawnees but not forgotten for its value.

In the cave, alone after two days' absence from the tribe, Malcolm felt the bow's smooth curves. He placed his hand around the grip and was newly impressed how comfortably it fit. He set the bow aside and sought his papers and charts. A calendar among them reminded him, the final month of 1855 would start the following day.

Erskine kneeled before the fire. He spread one sheet after another to one side until he found the particular list he had by now memorized. With the stub of a pencil he made a small check against the name, "Zeke Larson, Leavenworth, printer."

Of the twenty-three names on the list—the murderers and accessories to murder of Sylvia Parks Erskine—Larson's alone had puzzled Malcolm, until now.

All the Bushwhackers involved in Sylvia's slaying were from Missouri except Larson. All were either from Westport, Dallas, Little Santa Fe, or from small Missouri places between.

This morning Malcolm had unexpectedly spotted Larson from a description of the man's horse, a roan with large light spots on its rump. More accurately he had first seen the horse, then later the man. The animal was tied outside the shack of a white woman, Penelope Taylor. She lived not over a mile from Erskine's cave.

The woman was a prostitute. The Shawnees had long tolerated her presence on their land. Ever since the start of the Mexican War, she'd been servicing teamsters using the Santa Fe Trail. Lately, according to observers, her business had fallen off. Malcolm had seen her a few times and understood why. She seemed comfortable with filth. The smell wafting from her place was so strong that even sweating, trail-riding passersby couldn't ignore it.

Erskine had been amused to see Penelope stand in her filthy dress, lift her skirt high, and wave at wagoners on the trail ridge. They, in turn, coughed or made a face and prodded their oxen to step more lively. For all Malcolm's time in Kansas she'd been unwilling to talk with him, unwilling to provide information. She referred to him as a "darky" and made a show of trying to ignore his comings and goings near her place.

This morning Malcolm had waited until Larson woke and left the Taylor shack, at nearly noon. But his quarry's sudden, fast ride eastward had caused Erskine to wonder whether Penelope had spotted him through a window. Whether she'd cautioned Larson about his presence and suggested her customer seek help from Little Santa Fe.

Erskine had then retreated to his cave to begin formulating a plan. When he was sure he could carry it out, he would go on foot to a clearing past which any reconnoitering team of locally based Bushwhackers was certain to ride.

He checked a pocket watch left him by Sylvia. It was now 4:12 p.m. He estimated by the distance that thirty minutes remained for him to position himself, be ready for what he suspected would be only a small force returning with Larson.

Malcolm reckoned the force would be small because Law and Order bands, Sons of the South, and Blue Lodge members were, at that moment, arriving in the campground by Little Santa Fe for both ceremonious and serious business. From there and other points on the border they would launch a mass invasion. Erskine reasoned Larson couldn't successfully recruit many for a hunt near Penelope's place on the small chance of chasing him down.

When would the strutting invaders move into Kansas? Erskine was unsure.

He checked both revolvers, picked up a Sharps rifle, checked the horse's tether to be certain it was secure, and left the cave. The day had been bright and cloudless but was beginning to grey in the east from approaching sundown. He trotted toward the military road by which Larson must originally have traveled from Leavenworth.

A quarter mile south of the Santa Fe Trail, he entered woods bordering a clearing next to the military path. The place was a common stop because of a small, natural spring that trickled from a limestone outcropping. Opposite him, across the clearing and nearer the road, the wooded ground rose unevenly and would tempt his trackers to take cover there.

Likely they were approaching along byways now, planning to continue till dusk or darkness as they sought Erskine, the wanted slayer of Frank Coleman's cronies.

At 4:44 Erskine heard hoofbeats from the north, men turning off the trail. He chose a stout tree to stand behind, pocketed the watch, and placed his index finger on the rifle trigger. When the horsemen rode into view—four of them—he fired a shot with casual aim, to make it raise dust on the east side of the clearing.

All four reined up and dismounted quickly, scrambling for cover at the precise spot Malcolm had anticipated they would. Within seconds, rifle fire from them rang around him. Erskine was able to ignore it under protection of the sturdy but autumn-stripped tree.

The clearing was narrow enough, Malcolm had estimated, that he could dash across in about four seconds, too short a time for anyone firing old-style rifles to reload and take good aim. Now he glanced over his shoulder and saw the brightly setting sun directly behind him. That would blind anyone looking straight through the stand of young, bare trees.

With revolvers drawn, Erskine darted from his cover and broke into a run directly toward Larson and his three companions, firing as he sprinted. With each of the first two shots he felled startled and confused Bushwhackers. The two who remained, one of them Larson, rose to reposition rifles for short-range firing. Their movements were not quick enough. In his next two shots, still on the run but with steady hands, Malcolm caught one man in the chest and Larson in the forehead.

He continued up the slight rise until he was among them. Three were dead. His first shot had only caught the neck of one of the men, seriously but not fatally. He pressed a revolver to the back of the injured Bushwhacker's head. He fired and then fought sickness from seeing the man's skull split apart like a melon.

Despite the gore around him, Erskine began searching their pockets. He gathered billfolds and papers. He stuffed them into his shirt and ran back to recover his rifle.

Malcolm returned to his cave at the creek by a steady trot. He dumped his pickings on the floor near the fire. He took the pencil and, still breathing hard, crossed Larson's name from his list.

He sifted through the other men's papers, keepsakes, personal belongings, and he beamed in the knowledge he could now cross through three more names. Two were teamsters out of the milling depot of Dallas and one a cowhand from near Little Santa Fe.

Malcolm was about to throw the small pile into the fire when he realized Larson's papers were more substantial than ordinarily carried by such a man. He unfolded one that was a Law and Order Party handbill, reproduced from the proslaver newspaper, the *Leavenworth Herald,* where Larson had worked.

Another paper was an order to Larson. It explained the man's presence in the vicinity of late. A native of Cass County, Missouri, he was to aid C.C. Catron in organizing entry into Kansas Territory by the south area's proslavery forces. The torchlight entry from Little Santa Fe was to be simultaneous with others along the border, as far north as St. Joseph. It was to start at 5:30 p.m. on Friday, November 30, 1855.

Malcolm pulled out his watch. It was 5:34. While he had been busy with his own mission of revenge, the armed invasion of Kansas had begun.

19

Erskine left the cave and looked northward into the increasing darkness—and listened.

The gathering Law and Order force at Little Santa Fe was most likely to use the old Santa Fe Trail part way to Lawrence before turning northwest on the Oregon-California Trail. For the present, all was quiet along the Santa Fe.

Malcolm weighed his next moves, fearful of giving Lawrence false or premature alarm. Were the orders he found on Larson accurate? He had to assume the invaders would move on that schedule.

First he should wait till he could see torchlights on the ridge. Then he faced a choice, riding roughly forty miles to Lawrence, slower by night than by day, or turning to other options.

He could short-cut across the invaders' path and reach Monticello in less than an hour, tap a rider there with the information, and so on by relay to Lawrence. That should give Free Staters good preparation time. But depending how hard and fast the Missourians were riding, they could, even with cumbersome supply wagons, arrive at the city by mid-morning.

There was a key, Malcolm reasoned—the overall speed of the entire force, especially factoring its burden of loaded wagons. He should calculate how they were paced for joining other similarly equipped Law and Order units.

A warning too *late* would prevent Hickok's positioning of his precious cannon and General Lane's deploying the Lawrence defenders effectively.

Too *early* a warning would sap the defenders' strength, placing them on garrison standby for too long. And worse, the appearance of the cannon could be signalled back to proslavers by their own scouts or spies.

Every advantage of surprising readiness to meet the attack must be given the inferior-numbers force at Lawrence.

Only one course of action was logical, Malcolm realized. To *join* the invading group. To join long enough to learn when and where they planned to rendezvous with units out of Westport and other border launch points.

As for signaling Lawrence, he would fall back on a clever contingency Black Bob had readied. The Chief had shown impatience with communications methods used by white Kansans, who lacked the telegraph employed in the East. So, as some said of showmen, Black Bob had a "trick up his sleeve."

Malcolm reentered the cave, kneeled in the light of the fire to observe his reflection in a backwater pool of the creek, and unsheathed his Bowie knife. He proceeded to shave his mustache. Without scissors and lather the process smarted. But thanks to a finely honed blade, the job was soon finished with only three bloody nicks.

Next he unrolled a blanket containing articles of old clothes for possible masquerading in his work. He took off his buckskins and shirt and began to pull on what amounted to rags, making certain all holes were overlapped against the chilly night and against a telltale peek at the dun shade of his body.

A tin of boot polish added deep color to his face, neck, hands, and forearms. He worked the polish in to make certain it wouldn't rub off lightly. Afterwards, he pulled an old hat down to his ears, hiding most of his straight hair, seeking his reflection again in the pool to be satisfied.

He strapped the bow and quiver to his horse and covered the animal with the blanket to conceal them. He saddled the steed, making certain the bow rode the animal's side in a way not to discomfort it.

Finally, Erskine threw all papers into the fire. Over time he'd memorized their contents. What was in progress now—the invasion—would likely change everything. It would certainly alter the significance of information he'd gathered for nearly two months, whether for the Free State Party or, lately, his own campaign of revenge.

The Bowie remained strapped to his calf, hidden by a loose trouser leg. Into his customary clothing he tucked his revolvers, rifle, and watch and placed the bundle in a corner of the cave. With them went a leather pouch containing items saved from Sylvia's belongings. The scarab he dropped into one of his boots.

Malcolm slipped a box of Swedish matches into a pocket, looked around, then kicked dirt to extinguish the fire and glowing ashes. In the darkness he found the horse's lead and walked him outside.

There! Some distance to the northeast a glow seeped into the blackening sky. The march had begun. When it passed the trail intersection with the military road, he would join it.

Malcolm walked his horse northward. He would wait near the crossroads. When he arrived there, he sat on a rock to listen, to watch. The faint sound of men singing reached him first, then the *clank-clank* of wagon apparatus. Several wagons. They'd used the time at Little Santa Fe to stock up, to prepare for a possibly prolonged presence in the Territory.

The sound of a woman's laughter punctuated noises of the invading party. Had the sanctimonious Law and Order force dared invite women for pleasurable company? He had heard the illegal voting intrusions into Kansas described as "picnics." Would they try making *war* in the same manner? If so, then all he'd heard about those who followed Sam Jones and other proslavery leaders was true. Lowest of the low, dumbest of the dumb, undisciplined, the scum of Missouri.

Malcolm was freshly reminded of men he'd encountered on the docks of New Bedford. Loafers, ignorant brawlers satisfied with short-term work and long-term pleasures wherever they could find them. Men whose mature strengths were sapped by involvement with diseased prostitutes, by liquor, by rough saloon-environment sport.

Erskine spat in disgust. To face such an enemy would diminish the honor of Free State fighters.

Now he could see the lighted procession. Christopher Columbus Catron led, trotting a white horse. Other Blue Lodgers including the murderous O'Brien brothers were at Catron's sides or closely trailing. Most carried torches that wisped smoke skyward.

A rider from the rear suddenly dashed past the line to pace Catron and speak to him above the din of the lusty singing. Catron shook his head in negative response, but the rider pressed him. The Blue Lodge leader appeared to relent. He raised his hand to halt wagons, riders, and a walking "infantry."

The stopping point was near Penelope Taylor's shack. In fact, the whore was standing outside waving, raising her skirt and gyrating her hips, shouting invitations.

The force must have numbered four hundred by Erskine's reckoning of torchlights and the glinting rifle barrels breaking the darkness. With units coming out of more populous Westport and St. Joseph, as well as those from Weston and Dallas, the total force could easily reach the predicted three thousand.

Several men dismounted with shouts of *"Whoop-Whoop!"* and left the party to run down the ridge slope to Penelope. A buckboard came up the line, its driver yahooing loudly and two men standing high in its bed, pouring water into a huge washtub. A laughing, heavily-painted woman pranced forward on foot to meet the wagon. She carried a rough brush and what appeared to be a cake of soap.

From the way the men pulled at Penelope's rag dress, it was clear she was to be bathed in the open, in the cold of the December's-eve night, in plain view of hundreds of raucous spectators.

The cry of approval was deafening. Catron retreated to the side to allow his troops their sport and lit a cigar. Malcolm sympathized with Penelope over the indignity her wailing protests failed to dissuade.

They dumped her unceremoniously into the tub. Two women fell to the task of scrubbing her, to the accompaniment of cat-calls, shouts, the raising of whiskey jugs, torches stabbing the night in a rhythm to the burgeoning chant of "Yay! YAY! *YAY!"*

After a few moments they blanketed a cleaned Penelope. She seemed none the worse for it. They carried her to a covered wagon. Soon they reorganized into a riding, marching—more accurately strolling—force headed for war. When the still-boisterous procession had continued another quarter mile westward, Malcolm stood in the restored darkness and sighed heavily.

To his horse he mumbled, "Theirs is a dirty business—un-Christian, indecent, murderous—all in the name of piety to keep Negroes at a level lower than theirs, if such a level exists."

The black-faced Malcolm mounted, clucked his tongue to urge the horse toward the trail, then at full gallop rode west-by-southwest in pursuit of the invaders. Overtaking the tail of the procession he began shouting, *"Massa!* Ah gots ta find my *massa!"*

"What's your master's name, boy?" someone called out, but Erskine ignored that and continued his slave-like cries.

"Massa! His lady gwine birth a *ba*-by. Massa gots ta go *back!* Oh, Lawdy," Malcolm whined as he rode toward the head of the procession.

"What the *hell* is going on?" he heard Catron shout. "Whose Nigra is that? Boy, who're you looking for?" The leader stopped the singing and shouting procession once more and yelled to Malcolm above the noise, "What's your master's *name?"*

Erskine reined up and blubbered, "Massa *Robert."*

"Robert *what?* We've got maybe *fifty* Roberts here!" Catron replied impatiently.

"Ah don' rightly *know,"* Malcolm said with a stereotypical bleat, scratching through his battered disguise-hat. "All Ah knows is Massa Robert, is all. He gots ta come *quick!* His *lady—"*

"Someone *help* this dumb nigger," Catron commanded. "Find whoever he's talking about and do it quickly, else we'll *never* rendezvous at the Wakarusa by evening Sunday."

Hearing that, Malcolm turned and rode back at full gallop past the noisy procession and its camp followers. He passed the wagon in which they'd deposited Penelope. He saw her stand shamelessly in the costume of her trade, despite the night's chill, and point at him.

"That's— That's the darky *spy!*" she screamed. "You say Zeke Larson ain't come back? Ask *him!*"

Before anyone could sort out her cries, Erskine was riding hard on the trail into the darkness, bending forward over his horse's neck and whispering every prayer in his sparse repertoire that the horse would not lose footing.

At some distance he dismounted and removed the bow and quiver from under the blanket, found an arrow he'd wrapped earlier, and dug the matchbox from his pocket. By sound he could tell at least one horseman was in pursuit of him. Yet cautiously Malcolm struck a match, ignited the wrapped arrow, drew the bow tight, and fired the flaming arrow high and westward into the night.

Erskine removed another arrow from the quiver. He continued to watch the sky and observed how a responding flaming arrow soared from perhaps two miles distant, arcing in the same direction. And farther and more faintly, yet another. The alarm message was on its way to Lawrence and would be there within minutes.

The torch-bearing horseman who rode up with a shout of "*Die,* nigguh!" had no means for taking good revolver aim. He caught Malcolm's next arrow in the gut.

After he fell, Erskine set down his Shawnee bow and seized the dropped torch. Malcolm crouched, kneeled, held the light to his pursuer's face. His heart pounded with joy. Hank O'Brien grasped the arrow shaft, whimpering for mercy.

Malcolm drew his Bowie knife and growled, *"For what you did to my Sylvia! For what you've done to Jane-Ellen!"*

Then in quick, sure swipes he ripped open the front of Hank's trousers and performed a bloody surgery. O'Brien's long, shrill screams filled the night, hurting Malcolm's ears.

Erskine saw several torchlights leave the trail in response. He slung the bow and quiver over his shoulder, remounted, and sent a hoarse cry of glee into the darkness. Then he bent into a fast ride southward.

20

Malcolm rode aimlessly. He was unable to think clearly, so wild in the brain was he over the atrocity he'd just committed against Hank O'Brien.

To kill in retribution is one thing, he told himself, *but to do what I've done was savage, senseless. Still, given the chance to do it again, I would.*

Erskine wandered through the night astride the black stallion, cantering, then trotting, walking, then breaking into full and pointless gallop. He felt the side of the animal and realized it was frothy. They must both rest.

He must ease his mind and heart that he'd chosen the right course, that he was a man whose honor needed satisfaction in whatever way his instinct for justice dictated.

Not everything that seems morally fitting is Christian. But then, neither is everything moral that's being done in the name of Christianity. He decided he knew less on the subject than he should.

In the darkness he reached his cave by the small creek. He dismounted and entered, leading the horse. He set aside the saddle, tack, blanket, and the bow and quiver. He built a small fire and tore the rags of his disguise from him, using a bunched garment to brush down the animal.

"I'll name you Ebony," he muttered to the steed impulsively. "You're a good friend."

Malcolm saw to the horse's watering and comfort. He lay beside the fire in hopes he would sleep. Tension ruled that out. His thoughts were with the men in Lawrence. They would be organizing themselves through the night, probably building redoubts to fortify their position, dispatching women and children to safety beyond the city.

They could not possibly muster more than two hundred fifty men among them, though the farmers and ranchers of surrounding areas might swell that number.

Even if only half the force of Missourians held to the poorly-disciplined advance on the Santa Fe and Oregon Trails, they would arrive with fifteen hundred.

No, he couldn't sleep. The orders for his mission—what he was to do after the invasion had begun—didn't summon him to Lawrence. They didn't prohibit his going there either.

So, he decided, he would go.

First he would rest, the best he could in the torment of mulling military realities, and knowing God might never forgive the behavior that hard circumstances had turned him toward. Was it forgiveness he sought? Or understanding—an opportunity to explain—and if so, to whom?

Yes, of course.

Erskine thought out a plan, one that would allow his circling the invading force in time to arrive at Lawrence before Jones, Catron, and the others. The names of Lawrence men he had only heard—Lane, Robinson, Wakefield who would command use of the cannon, Judge Smith—would come alive for him when he reported for duty. He would rejoin Hickok, and old John Brown.

But first—yes. In charting his next moves, a mood of peace came to Malcolm. He fell asleep.

*****

Next morning at dawn Erskine gathered his things in preparation for quitting the cave. He would not shave—nor wash. No, the washing, he mused, would come later, elsewhere.

In a leisurely manner and fully packed, Malcolm rode toward the Santa Fe Trail. He turned eastward, to Missouri. The dawning of December's first day was crisp, dry. The sun broke in the southeast and soon began warming him in his resolution and his plan. He rode the few miles to Little Santa Fe, knowing every man-jack was gone. Was it cowardly to visit at this time? Or cunning? He preferred to think the latter.

At the O'Brien house, he leaned from Ebony to rap boldly at the door. Jimmy Mulligan answered, sleepy-eyed, then wide-eyed in realization who his visitor was. He summoned Jane-Ellen. She came wearing a frayed robe and blinked at the morning light. "*Shoot.* It's you—with grease or something on you. And with your upper lip smooth as a baby's ass."

"Get the pot going," Malcolm directed, "and have the boy fill the tub in the barn. I need a warm bath. You can come scrub me." Though he knew the niceties of good manners, he took the luxury of forgoing them.

Jane-Ellen turned to Jimmy and nodded, then came outside. "Aren't you afraid I'll think you yellow? I mean, for you to come here knowing the men are gone to war?" She walked alongside Ebony as Malcolm aimed the horse unhurriedly toward the barn.

"You're confessing, Jane-Ellen, that you know I'd care what you think. As for yellow—" By breaking off, Erskine indicated the subject warranted no further talk.

Jane-Ellen said, "You're right on both counts." She opened the barn door for him. He walked the horse in and dismounted. "*Phew!*" she said, recoiling exaggeratedly. "Yes. Wash up. We've got talking to do. I'll scrape together something to eat, then send Jimmy off and come back to scrub." She turned to leave.

"Why send the boy away?" Malcolm asked, hoping he knew the answer but wanting to fish for it anyway.

Jane-Ellen turned and smiled. "There's something we both want, Mr. Erskine—Malcolm. And we're both smart enough to know the right opportunity. First you get started. Jimmy'll come fetch your clothes. I'll see whether I can un-stink them."

* * * * *

In the warmth of Jane-Ellen's humble but clean cabin, and disregarding this was the place of his enemies, Malcolm felt relaxed contentment.

Jimmy had agreed to spend the better part of the day at the schoolhouse play yard with friends. "Mr. Erskine and I must—talk," Jane-Ellen had explained to her brother.

She'd set aside her work dress and dug out a green and white calico frock. "I feel silly wearing this," she said to Malcolm, "but it's the only decent thing I've got."

After they'd all breakfasted and Jimmy had gone off, Malcolm smoked and asked, "Are you romancing me, Mrs. O'Brien?"

"You know what I want from you," she said, sitting opposite. "I'll do what I must to get it. The life *I've* led—"

"It's not like that," Malcolm said, flushing, annoyed. "I won't have it for us like that—to be *bought* with your favors. Pretended affection to spare the life of your murdering husband? No."

"He's all I've got standing between me and the poor-farm. Won't you let him go, please?" Her tense demeanor softened. She began to weep.

"Don't beg, woman. I—"

"I know what you did to Hank. I don't know whether to thank you or despise you for it." She wiped the tears and sniffed, firming her face against further crying.

Malcolm sat back in the chair, stunned. "How could you know?"

"You think Catron's so stupid as to go to war without a surgeon? They found Hank where you left him and sewed his arrow wound on the trail. Then they took him to a hospital in Westport. He was delirious, but he told them you mentioned both Sylvia and me as the reason. They're not sure he'll live, but they're working to save him."

"I don't know what came over me," Malcolm confessed. "I should have just finished him. For all the bleeding, I thought maybe I *had.*"

"Yes, it was awful what you did. Uncivilized. Though I'm not sure killing is more civilized or merciful. It's a hard time for being certain about such things. But castrating him for Sylvia's and my honor? In that way I owe you thanks."

Erskine studied Jane-Ellen. The dress offset her dark hair nicely. But the freshness of her frock couldn't hide signs of weariness aging her young face, nor the poverty in which she lived.

What contact could she have had with his lost mother? How could Jane-Ellen know of her? What circumstance would have given her the scarab? Explaining it was part of the deal Jimmy had said she wished to make.

Just as he was about to speak of it, to ask, she said abruptly, "Malcolm, let's stop fencing. I'm a woman, first and foremost, and my affection's *not* pretended. In a lonely and confused moment in St. Louis, I let myself be talked into marriage. He was a down-and-out adventurer from New Orleans—a foolish man who promised to take care of me on the frontier, in return for sharing my inheritance. Maybe Hank put him up to it. I was fearful about what lay ahead, with a tag-along brother to watch over."

She glanced from side to side and bit her lip before continuing. "In a sense Bill kept his part. I know you think the little he earns is 'blood money,' but it's money nonetheless. I couldn't keep my part, because the legacy turned out poorer than lawyers had led me to believe."

Jane-Ellen sought eye-contact with Malcolm. "I *don't* love him, Malcolm. If I did, you wouldn't be sitting here. At least I had sense enough not to be married in the church. Yes, I'm troubled by sins, but I've become increasingly helpless. Hank is—a brutal pig. You must know how he cuckolded Bill."

"You *let* him?"

"He—took me by force. At first it was habit for him every chance Bill was away. After a while it became a choice for me—between yielding or suffering painful bruises from struggling. I'd run out of lies to Bill how I'd gotten black and blue. Nor could I be truthful. If the two had faced off, Hank would have killed him."

"Leave this dung heap. Come away with me," Malcolm said, regretting he hadn't gone for Hank's heart with his Bowie knife.

"I can't. I don't believe in your cause. And there's Jimmy to take care of. You're not a landowner—"

"I expect to come into two hundred acres of Sylvia's, as soon as the legal problems—"

"Malcolm, you have nothing, except maybe unstoppable passion. I'm well aware how the Black Bobs pool their land. You're far from having a clear claim. And you're too involved in this Border War to settle down."

"You call the man you depend on 'settled down'? Bill O'Brien's a damned mercenary. Where's your security in that?"

"I'm afraid to make a change. Not only would I be a fool to tie myself to an outlaw, but your side will lose. They're going to wipe out Lawrence." Jane-Ellen looked down at the table, speaking sadly. "And I'm sorry to say, your days are numbered, Malcolm. Just when—"

Erskine stood and drew Jane-Ellen to her feet. He said, finishing the thought for her, "Just when, everything else being equal, you'd have grown to love me."

She looked away, then nodded. "Very likely. God forgive me, but it's much more complicated than that. More than I can talk about now."

Malcolm grasped her to him, but not roughly. They kissed—she with a passion that surprised him. When he lifted her into his arms, carrying her toward the loosely-curtained sleeping area of the cabin, she asked softly, "Did you love Sylvia?"

"Yes, he replied. "More than *I* can talk about—now."

21

"We haven't yet talked enough," Malcolm said, reaching to the nightstand for the pocket watch, "and Jimmy will be coming home, expecting supper."

Jane-Ellen sat up, grabbing a blanket to cover her nakedness against the chill. "What time is it?"

"Past four. The Law and Order group will probably pull up and spend the night on lands of Chief Fish at the Douglas County line."

"I don't suppose anything I say will keep you from going," she said. She lay back again and turned, idly running a finger across the place where he'd shaved his mustache.

"That's right. Lucky for me—lucky for us—they've got so many on foot and overloaded wagons, they've had to go at a snail's pace. On Ebony I could make it to Lawrence without a stop in five-six hours, even at night."

"You must get some rest. I can arrange something for Jimmy if you'd like to stay the night. And you're right. We haven't talked enough." She reached both arms to embrace him, to pull him close under the cover. "Nor will we ever have enough of this."

Malcolm took Jane-Ellen's face in his hands and studied her in the dimming light. He kissed her impulsively, as he'd done often through their passionate day.

"No," he said. "We'll have to find another time. I want to hear what you know of my mother, and I'd like to have talked of it today, but we were—"

"—busy," she said, laughing. "Oh, Malcolm, my feelings are so confused. I'm not sure now I *can* tell you everything. I'm too much involved with you, and I fear—" She broke off.

"Fear what?"

"Telling you all of it, and what you'll think afterward. I just—can't go into it right now. But about Bill. Will you promise to let him alone?"

"No, Jane-Ellen. I won't promise. I have two reasons now to kill the bastard. He and the others violated and hanged Sylvia. Reason enough. The other is to do away with him so we can be together. Even if you think my days are numbered—which I doubt—I'd like to spend more of what's left like this, like today."

"Shoot." She drew back and sulked. Then she slid over and got to her feet, rubbing her arms to warm herself, reaching for her robe.

Malcolm drank in the sight of her body. Just as he was becoming newly aroused, she said, "Get on with your bloody business, Malcolm. Go to Lawrence. I hate you."

Malcolm laughed. "You mean you love me."

"*Yes,* you savage. I love you. And I hate you for what you're going to do, because it'll send me into starvation."

Erskine got up, searched for his things while still laughing. "Do you honestly think after today I'm going to let such a thing happen to you—or to Jimmy?"

"How are you going to prevent it? Will you explain that to me, Mr. Drifter with no money in his pocket?"

"I don't know how, woman. But on my honor—"

"Your honor? Malcolm, your so-called honor has nothing to do with reality in times like these. This— This damned slavery and border dispute controls us."

"No—"

"The people who live here on either side of the border don't know one day to the next whether riders will come, make false accusation about sympathies for or against slavery, burn the house— And you off and working for those holier-than-thou hypocrite Yankees from Boston, think *you'll* have the—the means to take care of me? With me stuck on the border?"

Jane-Ellen's frown troubled Malcolm, who quit laughing, no longer taking her worries lightly. "I'll find a way."

"Malarkey!"

"Don't be shrewish at a time like this, Jane-Ellen. I thought you loved me."

She seemed ready to melt where she stood in her loose robe, turning, fidgeting, apparently confused. "Oh, Malcolm, I do, I do. But all I ask is that you *think*—and try to understand what you may be doing to me before you do it."

Momentarily, Erskine considered pressing once more the principle from which he would never back down—that he would kill Bill O'Brien. But the occasion called less for argument than for a sweet parting. He nodded. "I'll—think about it."

Later, as he was readying to leave, Malcolm searched his brain for ways to make a believable commitment about when they would be together again. Though the wish burned inside him, nothing of any sense occurred to him to say to Jane-Ellen. That made him wonder whether she was right—that in this time of border trouble, events controlled people and not the other way around.

"Take care. I'll be back," was all Malcolm could say.

"I'll take care," she said, "and you. And let your mustache grow back."

"About Sylvia—"

Jane-Ellen put her finger to his lips to quiet him. "She was very special, I know. And you loved her."

"Yes, I did."

"And now you love me."

"From the time I first met you," he confessed.

"I know you don't understand my situation completely. You're a dreamer and a romantic at heart. You're not a very practical man about some things."

"You still hate me as well as love me?" he asked, almost childishly.

"Sometimes," she said, nodding, "and I probably will hate you again. I feel—" She looked out a window into the advancing darkness. "I feel as though our lives are in each other's hands. I'm not sure how to explain that. I feel it, and that makes me uncomfortable. Then there's the other thing—the complicated story of our—

of your mother. In many ways that's still a mystery to me. If I say more, I could lose you."

Malcolm took her in his arms once more, whispering, reaching under her robe to touch her in delightful places. "I don't see how anything could make you lose me." He kissed her once more, his passion renewing hers. When they broke away, he said, "Till our next time."

"Yes. God go with you and protect you—and guide you to do the right thing," she said.

He left the cabin for the barn, where he saddled and mounted Ebony. He rode off toward the trail, the words of her prayerful wish echoing in his mind.

*****

Erskine soon turned northwest to cross Tomahawk Creek. While trail riders followed the ridge so as not to let their wagons become mired in mud, he was at an advantage on horseback and intended to use it. He would make Lawrence easily by morning, even with a stop in Monticello.

It had been some time, two or three days, since he'd slept more than a couple of hours at a stretch. Yet he felt refreshed, crediting his marathon lovemaking with Jane-Ellen. Rather than sap his strength, it had energized and emboldened him.

In his mind he replayed the remaining list of eighteen—no, nineteen, for Hank O'Brien still lived. The nineteen he'd targeted to kill. With each name he pictured a description of face and stature, a favorite manner of dress, or a detail relating to a horse. He would know them anywhere, every one.

Doubtless all but Hank were in the procession to Lawrence. Jane-Ellen was probably right about the result of this war, he believed. Lawrence faced destruction against such odds. If he didn't die as a wanted outlaw, he might die in battle just the same. More reason to be in Lawrence. *His* choice—not Lane's nor Brown's nor Hickok's calling him to join.

Honor again was what pressed him. Honor that Jane-Ellen refused to understand in a man, unless— It could be that *her* honor was now in conflict with his. What dignity was there in the poverty she was certain to face if he killed her husband?

For the first time he regretted his vow of total vengeance. He was beginning to understand her position. Still, understanding it, would that deter him? He thought of Sylvia. No, the O'Briens and the other murderers of Sylvia must die. As for Jane-Ellen, he would work things out for her.

After dark Malcolm reined up at Monticello, at the home of his stonecutter friend, Sam Garrett. He called to the family. Sam came out carrying a rifle and lamp. "You look different," he said.

"Shaved for a disguise," Erskine explained, dismounting. "Put me up for a few hours? I'll gladly take a place in the barn."

"Nonsense," Garrett said. "I'll spread something comfortable by the fire inside." Betsey came out and greeted Malcolm. Sam said, "I was about to tell Malcolm we're off to bed early and—"

Erskine interrupted. "Will you join me in the morning to ride to Lawrence?"

Betsey Garrett recoiled. "No!" She turned to her husband and clutched at his shirt. "No, Sam! Tell him you *can't!*"

"I—" Garrett was obviously embarrassed. Malcolm wanted to put him at ease. He considered saying that someone had to cut the stones to mark the Free Staters' graves, but that would have been a cruel joke. Sam found words. "Understand, Malcolm, it's—not from fear."

"Even if it were," Erskine said, "I would understand. If Sylvia was still alive, I'd have second thoughts myself. No, my friend. I shouldn't have raised the point."

"Come in. You look more worn out than your horse."

"I will," Malcolm said, "if you and Betsey forgive my foolish suggestion."

"There's nothing to forgive," Garrett said, "only a great deal to try to understand. Malcolm, it's all going out of control."

"I know, I know," Erskine said, head down while entering the house.

Despite his anguish over the plight of Lawrence, confusion over conflicting loyalties he was witnessing, annoyance over trying to sort *right* behavior from foolhardiness, he lay down where he was directed.

Soon he slept.

* * * * *

Before dawn Malcolm was up, letting himself out quietly. Today was a day he must, once again, start to think like the warrior he'd proven himself capable of being. The cold morning sharpened his instincts. He would soon near one or another of the lines of enemies marching to Lawrence.

Recent construction of crude bridges across creeks of the region had given Missourians a more direct route. Signs of their having passed through were everywhere. He must be cautious not to venture *too* near them. He paused to consider a turn southwest, putting Ebony across the creeks on a route paralleling that of the invaders.

In that pause, Malcolm detected hoofbeats coming from the south. He dismounted, pressed his ear to the cold ground, and decided a single horseman was approaching at a canter.

At this hour it could mean a messenger on assignment circulating among various advancing Law and Order units. Erskine looked about sharply and decided on a logical north-south route the rider would probably use—not a well-worn trail but ground traveled enough to constitute a path, actually an ancient, flattened creek bed.

Malcolm concealed Ebony at some distance. He removed a coiled rope and tied one end to a tree branch. He then trailed the rope loosely and kicked dead leaves and torn grass over its path along the ground. He worked quickly to camouflage it, as well as he could in the short time he figured he had. He ducked behind a thicket on a banked area to wait.

The rider appeared, moving not so quickly as Erskine had earlier estimated, yet heading northward at a fair pace. When horse and rider were about ten feet before the rope, Malcolm snapped it quickly to rider level.

The horseman saw the rope and started to pull rein, but not quickly enough. The rope caught him in the neck and toppled him. He thrashed on the ground. Any faster ride and he'd surely have been broken-necked—and dead.

Erskine drew a revolver and ran to the fallen man, who seemed little harmed though badly shaken. Malcolm failed to recognize him. His captive, however, looked up wide-eyed, clutching his injured neck with one hand and pointing to Malcolm with the other.

"You—" He gasped to find his voice, still choked from colliding with the rope. "You're the Nigra savage what cut Hank O'Brien!"

Erskine holstered his revolver, grinned, stretched his hand in an offer to help the man to his feet.

"Sir, you're mostly correct. I'm proud to confess I did justice to O'Brien. Malcolm Erskine at your service, sir."

The man refused help and continued to lie on the ground, squirming, still rubbing his neck. Erskine planted a boot on the man's chest and pressed weight on his victim. "Sir, let me instruct you in manners. I declare you at *my* service. In other words, you're now my slave."

"Your *what?"*

"My slave, by law of the Kansas Territory," Malcolm added.

"Go on. Ain't no law but what them with the most guns *says* it is."

Jerking his thumb, Malcolm indicated the distance to the man's horse and rifle. And the messenger bore no sidearms. "Exactly what I thought you'd say. So, because I have the most guns, I order you to your feet, *slave."*

22

"Tell me your name," Erskine instructed his captive.

The man mumbled something inaudible, brooding where he sat on the cold ground. Malcolm crouched and eyed his prisoner squarely.

"Let me explain the situation," he told the unhappy Law and Order messenger. "You already know my reputation. I would kill you without hesitation if it suited me."

As confident as Malcolm was about his new-found power, he took little joy from it, but he went on. "My former misspent life has left my brain free for exercise of which I never knew it capable. Now I'm going to tell you something that may startle you. I'll do it to reinforce the necessary relationship between us for the next hour or so."

"You mean," the puzzled captive asked, "you'll let me go?"

Malcolm nodded. "Exactly, Ben. I give my word, provided you do as I say."

The courier recoiled in surprise. "How'd you know my *name?"*

"A close look at you and the insignia you wear tells me you're a member of the Blue Lodge in Independence," Erskine said. "I know that Catron has maintained contact between his Little Santa Fe group and Independence through a liaison named Ben Morton. That's who you are."

"Oh, well." The man sighed. "That was easy to figure."

"Your wife's name," Malcolm continued, "is Greta, maiden name Hostetler. She's from Indiana, where she was shunned by her people for carrying your baby without benefit of wedlock. The baby is now your son Peter, age sixteen. You also have a fourteen-year-old daughter, Mary, who is a celebrated beauty and flirt, a bit light in the brain and in her choice of clothing, causing you and Greta considerable worry."

Morton got to his feet, his face gone white as a ghost's. Erskine rose also and pressed on.

"Ben, I know your age, origin, trade—you're a carpenter—and even the size of your bank account and the nature of your current debts. I know where you live and would not hesitate to visit."

"You're the damned *devil!*"

"No, Ben, it's simply my habit to store more information than I thought I'd need. I can recite this sort of personal data about many of your comrades because—"

"Don't touch me!"

"Morton, stop carrying on so. I'd expected a better-reasoned response from a 'brave' Bushwhacker."

Ben Morton dropped to his knees. "Anything! I'll do *anything* you say, but don't bring no harm to my family."

Erskine bent closely for signs that the messenger would listen carefully to everything he was about to be told. "You are to continue to Jones's camp—that's where you were headed, right?"

"Yes, *yes!*" Morton said, nodding animatedly, obviously scared half out of his wits, still kneeling, shaking.

"I'm not even interested to know the message you were carrying," Erskine said. "I knew by your leisurely cantering it couldn't have been very important, but here's what you're to do when you end your assignment delivering it...."

Malcolm gave Ben Morton the names of three of Sylvia's assailants he knew to be in the Westport group on its way to the Wakarusa. "You're to gather them and tell them you saw Hickok and me—just the two of us—camped on the south face of the old, dried bed of Captain Creek, where it's at its widest. They'll know the place. Do you know it?"

"I *know* it!" Ben said, still nodding, teeth chattering. "I— I *know* it!"

"If they get there several minutes before ten o'clock this morning, they'll likely see movement, which means Hickok and I are breaking camp on the south side. Tell them you were hidden and overheard one of us call to the other, ten o'clock sharp's the time we'd move out. If they want their chance at me, at Hickok, they should take cover on the other side, the north side, and start shooting like crazy. Now, call your horse. Get going. Report back to me here in twenty minutes. Don't jeopardize your home and family by failing me."

Ben Morton mounted up and pressed his horse northward as though chased by demons. Malcolm watched him go, checked his pocket watch, and sat on a fallen tree trunk to roll a cigarette.

At the exact time he was due, Morton returned. Though out of breath, perched nervously in his saddle, he told Erskine, "I—done like you said—*exactly!* Them three plan to *be* there!"

"Good." Malcolm next instructed the courier to return southward to Catron's group, to gather another three on Erskine's list. This time the trio must include Bill O'Brien. He made only one change in the instructions. Morton was to tell the second group that he and Hickok were camped on the opposite side, on the *north* face of the wide, abandoned creek bed. That the second group should occupy the south side.

"After *that,* what do I do?"

Erskine shrugged. "After that, Ben Morton, I have no further use for you. I'll rescind my claim on you as my slave, under the rule of Kansas Territorial law you acknowledged when we met, and declare you a free man again. But—" Malcolm held up a finger in warning. "—you must carry out this part of the assignment to the letter as well, or face consequences."

"I *won't* fail! My *word* on it!"

"I know you won't, Ben, for you're a man who truly loves his home life and will do anything to keep his loved ones secure. I'm mystified why you'd ever have made a habit of visiting the Oxford whore, Penelope Taylor, as would Greta be mystified. A shame, betraying a lovely wife who can still make an exciting bed for a truly attentive man, husband or otherwise."

Malcolm raised his eyebrows in quest of acknowledgement from Ben, who nodded vigorously.

Erskine continued. "Your son Peter is at an age for weapons. Yet he could be hurt or killed from lacking experience in a confrontation. And there's that sweet, ripening, daughter Mary, the sight of whom sets grown men like me, white or black, on *fire*—"

"I'm *going!* I'll do *just* like you say! Short of ten o'clock and you'll be on the *north* bank!" Morton clucked his horse and bent into his ride, heading speedily for Catron's armed force.

Malcolm sighed. He called Ebony and rode the short distance to the appointed place. He pastured the horse to the east and found a position behind low-lying brush, where he could conceal himself to observe.

At five minutes before ten o'clock, according to his watch, he saw three crouched riflemen scurrying from tree to bush to tree, down the north bank of the area. Almost simultaneously he heard rifle fire from the south face of the small valley. He spotted what must have been O'Brien and two companions selecting cover on that side.

Because of Hickok's reputation for gunmanship—which made it seem to his enemies he was every place he wasn't expected to be—Malcolm knew that the disparity in the origin of the shots, the number of guns going off, would make each side believe it truly had Hickok and Erskine in its sights. The valley was wide enough for faces or outfits not to be recognized, unless anyone rose fully from concealment. Yet it was narrow enough for marksmen to find their targets.

Erskine spread himself low, rifle alongside, and watched as the shooting increased in intensity. Before long he could tell one man had caught lead on the north side—soon another on the south. From time to time he would see the remaining Law and Order gunmen crawl to select new cover, then resume firing. Another man on the south was silenced suddenly, but the remaining lone rifleman there kept up fire and picked off the two on the north.

When all was silent, the survivor stood. It was Bill O'Brien. Malcolm slid his rifle into position and took aim. Just as he pressed the trigger, however, O'Brien darted forward down the bank, as though to investigate results on the other side.

Yet, hearing the charge from Erskine's rifle, O'Brien stopped, turned, then beat a retreat on foot westward, along the old creek bed. All the Bushwhackers' horses had evidently scattered at the sound of rifle fire.

"Damn!" Malcolm muttered, for missing his best chance at a shot.

With Bill O'Brien fleeing and the skirmish over, Erskine knew it was necessary to verify the other five were dead. Leaving his rifle and drawing both revolvers, he headed first for the north bank.

Two of the men there were beyond quick recognition. Their faces were torn and bloodied generously by rifle bullets from zealous comrades across the way. Malcolm searched pockets for identification and was satisfied they were among those he'd summoned. The third man stirred and called out, "Help me!"

Erskine grabbed him by the ankles, crossing them to flip the man onto his back. It was Philip Bilbo, an aide to "Sheriff" Sam Jones, one ear gone where a bullet had torn the side of his head, but not fatally.

Bilbo apparently recognized Malcolm. His face became clouded, for he knew he was about to die.

"You expect me to kill you," Erskine said, "don't you?" Bilbo, his lower lip quivering as he lay helpless, muttered a feeble assent. "Then no sense disappointing you."

As Erskine bent to place a revolver into Bilbo's drooping mouth, the injured man brushed it away and babbled, "I *took* 'er fore we strung 'er up! How ya like *that,* nig—" Malcolm jammed the barrel past the man's teeth and pulled the trigger. The effect caused him to turn away in disgust.

He next crossed to the south face of the valley and found both men dead. A shot had entered the shoulder of one and evidently found its way to his heart. The neck of the other appeared to be broken by a bullet clean through where his Adam's apple had been.

Malcolm holstered his revolvers, made his search, and mentally crossed five names from his list. Only fourteen of the original twenty-three remained. But it disturbed him that the targets at large included both O'Brien brothers.

Bilbo was about to die. "I *took* 'er," he said, "'fore we strung 'er up. How ya like *that*?"

He sought his rifle and horse and, realizing Bill O'Brien may yet be hiding somewhere rather than returning to his camp, Malcolm proceeded cautiously along a circuitous path toward Lawrence.

When he felt secure enough to do so, he began to sing a Scottish sea chanty he'd learned from his father—one to take his mind from the fact he was riding to war.

23

Except for occasional cries of cattle ranging nearby, Erskine found the southern approach to Lawrence deathly quiet. He had crossed the Wakarusa River and was hours ahead of the planned Law and Order assembly there. He guided Ebony toward the city—if it could yet be called a city.

Malcolm was at first surprised that ahead lay only low buildings, log cabins and sod homes mostly. He could now make out the sturdy barricade across what he knew to be the main street, named for the origin of most settlers, Massachusetts. The settlement was but a year and a half old, product of New England Emigrant Aid Society efforts to establish a western base of freedom.

Though Erskine felt little patience for religious leaders' dominating meetings back in Massachusetts and New York—meetings that led to the settlement effort—he approved of their aim. He wished now that more of them were present to shoulder rifles against the approaching enemy, men like John Brown and his sons, religious yet unafraid to enforce their principles with guns.

"HALT!"—he heard when he came within a hundred feet of the barricade. He glanced from side to side to survey the city—more a village—and could see redoubts for defense on every side. He was impressed that Lane, Robinson, and others had evidently secured the place well.

A man picked his way over the barricade and approached on foot slowly, handguns at the ready. No doubt Malcolm was covered also by a dozen rifles he couldn't see. "Identify yourself!" his greeter commanded.

"Malcolm Erskine of New Bedford, Massachusetts, employed in the service of the Free State Party. Take me to my friends and companions, John Brown and James B. Hickok."

The man broke into a grin and holstered his revolvers. An older man, probably a rancher judging from his appearance, he extended his hand and moved to where Erskine remained astride Ebony.

"*Wel*-come!" he said with what seemed genuine warmth, grasping Malcolm's hand and shaking it vigorously. "Not a man here hasn't heard of your good work. I'm Abe Milford. Come." He turned toward the barricade and shouted, "Let him through! It's *Erskine!*"

Half a dozen or more men scrambled over the barricade, shouting happily, greeting Malcolm, grinning their approval at his arrival. Because of the unexpected excitement he caused, Erskine felt a tear pop at the corner of each eye. He dismounted and one of the men embraced him. That broke restraint, and he touched the backs of his wrists to his dampening cheeks.

Milford shook hands with him again and said, "I don't know whether you realize it, Erskine, but you're a hero in Lawrence. The same as those who rescued Jake Branson from Jones."

"I'm no—hero," Malcolm protested in genuinely-felt modesty.

"Well, no matter what you say," Milford continued, "much of what you've done has appeared in both our newspapers—"

"Both? I thought Lawrence had three," Erskine said.

"The Tribune moved on to Topeka last month, but we still have the Free State and the Herald of Freedom. They've just carried stories how you and the Shawnees arranged to give us that flaming-arrow warning, everything about your defending Hickok in a Kansas City gunfight, how you were rescued from being hanged as a spy, and—"

Malcolm waited during Abe Milford's self-interruption, trying to read the man's suddenly clouded face.

"—and we're all sorry about your wife."

"Thank you," Erskine said. "And thank you for your friendship. Now, please take me to Brown, and I'd also like to see Hickok."

*****

The attack they expected the following morning did not come.

All the men now in Lawrence—between three hundred fifty and four hundred, more arriving from Topeka every hour—were deployed with Sharps rifles and other arms in a well-fortified circle around the community.

They had the advantage in defense of being on higher ground than the invaders, whose torchlights they'd seen all night several miles distant along the Wakarusa. They were prepared to retreat to even higher ground on Mount Oread at the west side of Lawrence, if necessary.

Malcolm's hopes rose with each observation of Lane's and Robinson's efficiency, the discipline they exercised over their troops, the amount of ammunition on hand, the placement of the single cannon and the extra manpower assigned for possible rapid fire.

He couldn't help but draw contrasts between their sobriety and spirit on the one hand and the character of the enemy on the other.

While he knew invading Missourians to be behaving as drunken and whoring rabble in their camp, the men of Lawrence were keen-eyed and extremely well-organized.

John Brown introduced him to the Lawrence leaders, the top-ranking men of the Committee of Safety for the current crisis. Men of little patience with nonsense. Men as serious as the occasion warranted. Lawrence leaders had before encountered invasions on a smaller scale for purposes of Missourians' illegal voting, a circumstance now under Congressional investigation. This time they neither underestimated the enemy nor seemed awed by the Law and Order force's superior numbers, known to be about fifteen hundred
.

The day wore on without action—Monday, December 3—and the vigil continued. The Missourians did not cross the Wakarusa, except for a couple of scouting parties.

"The longer they wait," Hickok pointed out to Erskine, "the stronger we get." He nodded toward the north, where at least fifty men were riding in to join the defenders.

"How many are we now?"

"Hard to keep up with it, but we may be coming on to six hundred. Brown's boys have been out scouting the countryside and have rallied more than anyone thought would come. They'll be going out again."

Only once was discipline broken sharply, but for joyous reason. John Brown and Malcolm were seated at dinner in Brown's cabin that evening when an excited shout went up from everywhere outdoors.

Judge G.W. Smith rushed in, grinning from ear to ear. To Brown, who remained seated and was coolly continuing his meal, Smith said, "John, we've just heard from our northeastern scouts. Governor Shannon and Jones asked Colonel Sumner at Fort Leavenworth to send the First Cavalry against us, and Sumner *refused!*—lacking orders from Washington."

Brown nodded approval, eyes twinkling at the news. He wiped his lips with a napkin, saying to the judge-turned-soldier, "I will offer a prayer of genuine thanks. I do believe, and have always believed, that God is on our side."

Smith left, and Malcolm observed to Brown wryly, "No disrespect, but things done in the name of God—" He shook his head, unable to finish that. "I suppose down at the river the other side's making the same claim. Anyway, something odd must be taking place there. I can almost feel it in the air."

"Only thing odd, my boy," Brown said, "only thing of significance, is that Sam Jones has undertaken to lead that entire operation without first finding his courage. Why would he need Army assistance when he already has us outnumbered?"

* * * * *

Two more days of siege passed, the only relief from tension being provided by men in the ranks composing raw jokes about the invading leaders—Eastin of the city of Leavenworth, Jones of Westport, Catron of the southern force, and Territorial Governor Wilson Shannon.

At one point Erskine saw the Free State leader, James Lane, interrupt the telling of tales among several men at a fortified position on the east. "Keep in mind," Lane said, "they are no more nor less scared than we are. The difference lies in what we're doing, the cause we serve. We know we're right, and they—when their liquor wears off—are obviously having doubts about their mission."

Erskine later rode off from the group with Lane and learned from the Lawrence officer that Governor Shannon was due to visit that day, to see whether he might resolve the impasse. "I'd like to be present for that," Malcolm requested.

"I don't see why you shouldn't be," Lane said, shrugging. "Meet us at the south barricade in an hour."

Wilson Shannon arrived by wagon, accompanied by a driver and two armed guards on horseback, each of the latter carrying a white flag.

There to greet the Governor were Brown, Lane, Hickok—who still considered himself Lane's bodyguard—as well as Charles Robinson, with whom Lane shared command, and at least thirty Lawrence defenders.

Robinson took it upon himself to introduce each man to the Territorial Governor by name for a perfunctory handshake. Governor Shannon seemed only mildly annoyed by the courteous exercise, until introductions got around to Malcolm Erskine.

Shannon withdrew his hand quickly and stepped back. He pointed to Erskine. "I *refuse* to make the acquaintance of this—this *bloody murderer.* In less than two weeks he has been solely responsible for the cold-blooded killing of *eleven* men—nine in the past *week.* And the—the atrocious humiliation and maiming of another."

Hickok chewed on a matchstick and muttered, so only Malcolm would hear, "I know about the two in Kansas City, but what the hell else is Shannon talking about?"

"Sir," Malcolm said, addressing the Governor. He ignored Lane's hand-waving to be silent and stepped toward Shannon. "I'd be happy to explain—"

A symbolic gesture by Shannon interrupted Erskine. The Governor turned fully around, his back to Malcolm, and called to his wagon driver. “Return me to the Wakarusa. There’ll be no peace talks today with this man present.”

24

Jim Lane took a place beside Charles Robinson and addressed Shannon. "Governor— Sir, I'm duty-bound to remind you, the side you represent consists largely of citizens of Missouri. On the other hand, *we* are the true constituents President Pierce has appointed you to govern and serve."

Shannon frowned, apparently for being lectured about his status in the situation.

Just as the Governor seemed about to respond, young Hickok pulled a surprise. The young man turned to face Malcolm and said in a voice for all to hear, "I arrest you, Malcolm Erskine, in the name of the Committee of Safety of the City of Lawrence and the County of Douglas. The charge is murder."

Malcolm's mouth flew open in surprise at the action of his young friend.

"I order you," Hickok continued, "to surrender your weapons immediately and accompany me to the city jail, where you will be held for consideration of the charge by the justice system of Douglas County."

Erskine looked past Hickok into the faces of John Brown, Jim Lane, Charles Robinson, and finally Governor Shannon. He saw the Governor relax his earlier fury, so he resigned himself to arrest and looked into the eyes of Hickok—who winked.

In order not to betray his seemingly duty-conscious friend, Erskine brought his hand up to his mouth in a false wipe. He turned a spontaneous grin into what he hoped would look like a grimace. Then he dropped his hands to his sides and gingerly unholstered his revolvers, handing them to Hickok.

"Your knife, too," Hickok commanded. To Malcolm it appeared Hickok was fighting hard within himself to suppress a giggle. He unsheathed his Bowie knife and extended it, handle first.

Head down, Erskine turned and allowed himself to be led away. When they'd proceeded far enough to be out of the others' hearing, Hickok said, "Lord, I hope I can make it the next few hundred feet without falling on the ground, laughing fit to bust."

Erskine continued to look downcast and muttered, "You conniving son of a— *How* am I going to be any help around here sitting in jail? Have you lost your *mind?*"

"We have to show Shannon we're civilized, Malcolm. Everything he's heard about us up to now has him convinced we're a bunch of outlaws. Lucian Eastin and that Law and Order crowd have him completely buffaloed with lies. Remember in Kansas City we talked about Shannon being yellow? Lane is counting on that. He's going to trot the Governor around on a tour of the city—let him see our defenses—let him see the cannon."

"You think it'll work? You think those proslaver drunks camped by the river will stay put?" Malcolm asked.

"It's sure worth a try, now that Shannon has shown up and has a chance to see we mean business. But it also requires a little play-acting—which reminds me, who else *have* you plugged since I last saw you? I mean, it came as a shock to everyone here when we heard about Sylvia, but nobody's heard the rest."

"Go back for Brown later, and you both sit with me in the cell. I'll tell you everything."

*****

Brown and Hickok listened for about an hour to Erskine's recounting of his plan and his partial carrying out of vengeance. There was a long silence in the crude cell.

Finally, Brown heaved a sad sigh. "In your position," he said, "I'd have done the same, though perhaps not so efficiently." He got up and looked out the tiny cell window at besieged Lawrence. "The Scriptures treat such matters in a way that leaves a man some choice, depending whether he leans to the Old Testament or the New."

Erskine looked up. "You mean, 'eye for an eye' versus 'turn the other cheek'?"

"Exactly. It's surprising how we keep turning back to Biblical sources as guidance even for violence. And it's surprising that no matter what words we light on, no matter what phrase or passage we depend on to justify actions, in the end we're left with one truth." The old man paused and looked into Malcolm's eyes. "In the end, God will judge you."

Erskine, sitting on a low stool, put his elbows on his knees and his face in his hands. Through them he mumbled, "Does God even know me, or care about me? He seems to get farther from me instead of nearer."

"Farther?" Brown asked. "He's with us now, not only listening but looking into your heart. And it's on the basis of what's there that the Lord will make his judgment."

Despite recurring misgivings, Malcolm now wanted to believe that. Still looking down, he said darkly, as though in question, "You're sure."

"Surer than anything else I've seen or learned in life," John Brown said. "Yes, I'm sure."

Hickok observed in silence from where he'd been sitting on the cell cot. Possibly he recognized Erskine's emotions could go either way—joy at learning that motives more than actions would be in evidence before God, or surrender to confusion and remorse. "Here, Malcolm. You want me to roll you a cigarette?"

That was the right thing to put to him, Malcolm knew, nodding in gratitude. It broke tension.

As he accepted a light, he grew more confident about the turn of discussion and decided to raise a question he'd carried for some time. "John, let's talk about you and your motives on the one hand, and someone I can't figure out for his motives."

"Who?"

"Thomas Johnson of the Shawnee Mission. *Reverend* Thomas Johnson, owner of slaves and an advocate of slavery. Where do you calculate *he* stands with God? Being he's a man of the cloth, I figure that's a valid question."

"I've never met the man," Brown responded, returning to the window. "No opportunity to size up his character."

"I haven't been able to figure out," Malcolm continued, "where Johnson finds moral justification for his position. I know where you find yours, but yours is opposite. *He's* the ordained man of God."

Brown kept looking out the window. "I have only a theory with respect to men like Johnson. It makes his being a clergyman incidental rather than basic." The grizzled abolitionist turned and found a place on the cot next to Hickok. "Without knowing the man," Brown continued, "I'd say early in his life he was troubled by an inadequacy, something missing in himself or something missing in one of his closest personal relationships."

Malcolm leaned forward, intensely interested. He drew a long puff on the cigarette and waited for more.

"Unable to reconcile the troubling inadequacy, whatever it was, with his own sense of perfection as a creature in God's image," Brown continued, "Thomas Johnson accepted the only alternative—a view of superiority. A relative view."

"Superiority over the black man," Malcolm said.

"And the red man," Brown responded, "for his work as he sees it is to convert them from savage status to civilized and Christian status."

"But Johnson has become more than a teacher and slave-owner. He's *partisan* for slavery."

Brown shrugged. "The more justification and consent he seeks among others for his position, for his own prejudice," he said, "the deeper must lie his self-doubts."

Malcolm stamped out his cigarette butt on the cell floor. "And that's it? That's all of it? There's nothing really Biblical supporting him?"

"Nearly as I can interpret," Brown said, "that's all of it. The Bible is too devoted to human dignity to be a basis for slavery, though there are contradictory references in there. I wouldn't call them justification. The man—Johnson—is simply ill emotionally, in my view. Not clearly a hypocrite."

The three were interrupted by arrival of General Lane in the jailhouse. Hickok sprang to his feet, asking his chief, "How goes it? Has the Governor seen the cannon?"

Lane, looking through the bars, smiled and nodded. "I think your quick arrest of Erskine helped. But the cannon—and the buckets of nails we said we could load into the exploding shells—Well, they may have clinched matters. Shannon is closeted with Robinson now, working on a treaty."

Suddenly Lane broke off, laughing. "And you recall Shannon's failing to bring the First Cavalry against us?" He shook his head, seemingly in the grip of some irony. "*Now* he's talking about summoning them against the mob on the Wakarusa."

Brown stood, closed his eyes, raised his hands to the ceiling of the cell, and called out, "Praise the Lord."

They congratulated one another. Victory seemed assured through quick conversion of the Territorial Governor. With Hickok and Brown stepping out to talk further, Malcolm was left alone in the cell. But the conversation continued so that he could hear. The topic soon came around to him.

"No, no," he heard Jim Lane say. "Erskine stays in there and will stand trial."

"You *can't* be serious," Brown protested. "You *must* let the lad out when Shannon leaves."

Hickok also spoke up. "General Lane, we've heard Erskine's story. I think you should hear it."

"Plenty of time for that when we convene a jury," Lane said. "I won't have the Free State cause jeopardized by *anyone's* lawlessness, for whatever reason."

Immediately, even as his incarceration was being enforced by Lane's authority and attitude, Malcolm began plans for escape. He would sooner become a true outlaw—a deserter and renegade—sooner abandon service to the Free State Party than give up settling the score for Sylvia's murder.

Before the visitors left the jail building, Hickok came close to the bars. In a low voice, he tried to give Erskine some assurance. "I'll do what I can." He turned and left.

For Malcolm, thoughts of escape were too compelling to waste time on self-pity.

Abe Milford, his new rancher-soldier friend, visited and was admitted to Malcolm's cell. "Well, my comrade, this is both a sad and happy day," he said, the latter reference evidently to imminent peace.

"Don't be sad for me, Abe. I'm getting out of here as soon as I calculate how."

"No need to plot that. Leave that to me. And it's not you I'm sad for. It's myself."

"How do you mean?"

"While I was here in Lawrence, soldiering—" He seemed not to know how to go on, and his voice was breaking. "Eager for some action while they idled by the river, the Bushwhackers— I just learned— They ranged and happened on my ranch and burned my home, barn, outbuildings, killed my stock, and—"

Milford's knees buckled, and Malcolm grabbed the man to help him sit on the cot. "Not your family. Oh, no, Abe. Not your *family!*"

Milford collapsed in grief, nodding, sobbing. "All of them," he said.

25

"Word of this should go to Shannon immediately," Erskine said.

But Abe seemed no longer to care about peace or war between Free Staters and Missourians, or those attempting to manage it.

Malcolm watched the man try to pull himself together. Obviously Abe was here because he realized Erskine had some understanding of the pain in his heart.

"Malcolm," Abe said, "I'll get you out of here. We'll ride together from now on— I have nothing else to live for. I have friends who'll join us. They helped bury my loved ones today. Good men. All I need do is give them the word."

"Abe, I—" Erskine groaned. "I don't think that sort of thing is for you. Your work is ranching. You know nothing of hiding and running and plotting and striking quickly—and running again."

"I'll learn. You'll teach us. You'll lead us."

"I'll *what?*"

"They call us Jayhawkers when we strike back. So be it. Malcolm, we have to band together and become as strong as they are. After they ride into Kansas to terrorize a farmer, a rancher, *we'll* ride into Missouri and do the same."

"No, that's—"

Milford interrupted Erskine, as though driven, spinning out his plan. "Trouble is we've depended on brave souls like you to do our dirty work. The rest of us who've been victimized must join and give those murderers measure for measure, regardless whether Lane or Robinson approves. And you'll teach us."

Malcolm protested. "You're ready to commit your life to terror? Just help me out of here and let me go my way alone, finish what I set out to do."

Abe said, "You're not seeing how the deep passions of victims like us can shape the politics of this region. We already have leaders who are good for thinking and talking, but that's all. Your blood and now *mine* runs for *action.*"

Erskine sat on the small stool in the center of his cell, studying Abe Milford. He calculated that his new friend was in his forties. He was a chunky man, all muscle and heart. His square face could break as quickly into a smile as a frown.

Milford continued. "We're up against crazy zealots who won't let go of living off the labors of Negroes. They see us over here, trying to prove that men of all colors and origins and religions can work together in absolute freedom. If we succeed, their slaves'll be escaping over here at every opportunity."

"I realize that," Malcolm said.

"Those Blue Lodgers, Bushwhackers, are so committed to slavery, they'll fight to the death to keep it. There'll be no peace, Malcolm. Understand? This entire exercise by Shannon and Lane is a sham. A delay, until each side calculates more clearly what to do about destroying the other."

Malcolm noticed that in spite of the chill in the cell, Milford was working up a sweat.

"John Brown knows what to do," Abe said. "He's smarter than the rest, for he'd just as soon blow Missourians' heads off than stand there waiting for the bloody Bushwhackers to see the light—see the error of their ways. But John's too old to lead an effective force. Hell, *I'm* too old. You, Malcolm, still have your youth, and you've been trained by the Indians—"

"Correction," Malcolm said, "by one Indian. My late wife."

"You know the countryside at the border. You're crafty, precise, smart—and we *trust* you. You came into this an idealist, and you still show signs of that, but your wife's murder brought you down to earth, to reality, as happened to *me* today."

Abe reached to touch Erskine on the upper arm, seeking eye contact. "Malcolm, you're getting *your* revenge. I want mine. That's what'll give me strength and keep me from going crazy. But you must show me how to be effective. Lead the way. Face it—we'll be outlaws. I'm willing. We're both victims, with nothing to lose. And we'll find more men like ourselves."

Erskine nodded.

Milford was right.

The course of action he suggested would in no way distract Malcolm from his planned revenge. It might even help him reach his goal—and serve as an object lesson to Bushwhackers.

"All right," Malcolm said. "All right."

He stood and then paced. "Here's the situation. We've had mild weather for the approach of winter up to now, but that's soon to change. Both sides will be numbed quickly by the cold, as both sides are numbed by this uneasy peace. I think most Missourians will straggle home, except for some who'll take cowardly opportunities to vent frustrations over the aborted war. They'll use winter to lay plans for another invasion. They'll carry it out by spring."

Erskine paused to consider the near future. It seemed bleaker than Brown had painted it during their walk to Kansas.

"You make a good point, Abe. They have no intention of letting matters rest after this. They just weren't ready to destroy Lawrence, but they'll try again. And Kansas will need us, doing in our own way what we've committed ourselves to do—whether Free State leaders like us for it or not." Malcolm chuckled in irony.

"Meanwhile, we'll pick a camp and look for alternative refuges. We'll build shelters. Gather food against the winter. Prepare for the time winter starts to break. Set up our network of information and our striking force. We'll sharpen our skills and be certain about every move we make."

"*Now* you're talking," Milford said.

"We have arms—that's easy. And you say you can gather men. But we need money," Erskine said. "We can't disturb the Black Bob Shawnees for support. We can't expect subsidy from the Emigrant Aid Society or the Free State Party. Not when we'll no longer be taking Lane's orders."

"Money will be no problem," Milford said.

Malcolm turned, surprised by Abe's comment. "How do you figure that?"

Milford stood, removed his hat to smooth down his thinning hair, replaced it, and drew a hand across his face. "Can you trust me with that part of it?"

"You're going to *steal* it?"

Milford didn't respond but turned to leave, calling the jailer to let him out. Then he faced Erskine to say, "Be ready in thirty minutes, Malcolm. Your horse will be saddled. The realities of what we've been through are justification enough for me, my friend, to face uncertain prospects. We'll talk and plan once we're camped away from here. We must go when there's still a generous piece of daylight. Just be ready in thirty minutes," Abe repeated. Then he left.

*****

When the time approached, Erskine looked out his cell window and saw Milford walking toward the jail carrying a middle-sized wooden box. He heard Abe enter and talk with the jailer about a meal prepared by someone named "Della," evidently a woman who'd chosen not to leave the city with the other women. He also heard Abe invite the jailer to look inside the box if he didn't trust that Milford was telling the truth. The jail-keeper demurred, obviously not wanting to appear distrusting of so good a local citizen as Milford.

Abe entered the cell and was locked in again with Erskine. He invited Malcolm to lift the lid, recover his revolvers and knife, and follow his lead. Abe borrowed one of Erskine's guns and turned again to the trusting jailer outside, ordering the cell unlocked again.

The hoodwinked jailer threw down his cigarette and shouted at Milford, "You can't get away with this!"

"I *can't?* I'll blast off your foot if you don't unlock this, so don't tell me about 'can't'. I bloody *can* and *will!* Open up!"

Free and outside, Malcolm saw six horses approach, two of them led by men mounted on the others. One steed they led was Ebony. The other horse was Abe's. "Easiest thing I've ever done,"

Milford cracked as he and Erskine mounted up. "Your weapons were in Brown's possession."

"John Brown *helped* you?" Malcolm was astonished.

"And wished you God-speed. Let's ride!"

At the first corner they turned, James Butler Hickok was strolling along the walk and stopped, evidently realizing what was happening. Malcolm gave his young friend a quick salute.

"I'll *find* you!" Hickok shouted after him.

"No, you *won't!*" Erskine threw back, digging his heels into Ebony and taking the lead for the group's escape.

They rode westward, Malcolm planning to circle widely to avoid the Law and Order force still camped to the southeast. And they rode hard.

Occasionally Erskine turned to see whether his Lawrence allies—his former allies in the city—were in pursuit. He knew he was cutting himself off completely, and he felt a strong sense of guilt. He was now a renegade and outlaw, leading a band of outlaws.

A band of Jayhawkers.

26

Erskine led his new companions south toward Franklin County. He would skirt all known trails and later take an eastward course that would carry them almost to the Missouri border.

Malcolm had in mind a position at the edge of the Black Bob Shawnee lands, south of the Blue River and farther south of the Santa Fe Trail. It was important to establish a secure camp in a relatively uncharted place before the weather turned harsh. He wanted to be near important trafficways of Bushwhackers so his new group could intercept and strike them. By positioning his band at approximately an equal distance from the Santa Fe Trail and the north-south military road, Erskine would have ready access to both. He would also be within a mile or two of the border, ready to ride into Missouri when the occasion warranted.

Southeast Johnson County provided a number of hiding places heavily wooded. That meant ample means for building shelter and finding small game. Malcolm would ask no help from Chief Black Bob for fear of jeopardizing the Chief's already shaky position between the two warring sides. His Shawnee friend had sacrificed and helped enough in Erskine's behalf.

The hard ride was beginning to tire the horses. The band stopped to dismount and rest. Abe Milford suggested to Malcolm that he learn the names of the men, tell them at least tentatively what lay ahead, listen in time to what drove them to choose an outlaw existence in his service.

Erskine addressed the men with gratitude for aiding his escape. He disclosed his plan for establishing a hideout and where—along a creek called Camp Branch—and why that location. All nodded in agreement it was a good plan, but worry arose again about financial support.

One young man, Peter Iverson, said he had given up his trade as a teamster not only because work was slow this time of year but because Milford had promised adventure.

Hearing that, Malcolm laughed. Then he fell into a short lecture about the seriousness of their mission. Yes, adventure it was, but only incidentally so.

As aides to a gunfighter responsible for the deaths of several men on both sides of the border, they would be branded outlaws. The first two rules for outlaws, Malcolm said, were escape and survival.

Under the circumstances of winter and the Border War, survival wouldn't be easy. They would live to see 1856 but could very possibly perish before the next winter, events would likely become that violent.

A man about Erskine's age, Jeremiah Adams, brought up the subject of money. He'd served once as a trapper in Missouri and could show them how to live off the land. But soon ammunition would run short. Certain staples would have to be bought.

Milford spoke up, turning first to the two remaining men, Philip Baxter and Ezra Renfro, and receiving their nods. "I may as well tell you now. Renfro here once worked in the bank at Westport and has a plan that will help us. Baxter and he and I will take care of that just as soon as you've got us settled in, Malcolm."

"I don't like that," Erskine said. "I don't like taking depositors' money, largely humble people just like us—or just as we were. No, it's dangerous and wrong."

Renfro spoke in an Ohio River Valley drawl. "What would you say, Erskine, to some thirty thousand dollars in gold and currency Colonel Boone's got stashed in the bank office? He's been using it to buy the loyalty of some border ruffians who have no way of supporting themselves."

"The mercenary Bushwhackers?"

Renfro nodded.

"Boone's own personal funds?" Malcolm pressed.

"And a little of Jones's mixed in. Don't ask me where they got it. But I know where it is, what it's used for, and how to take it without anyone getting hurt. I could use the help of one other man."

"What would I say?" Malcolm asked, his mood changing. "I'd say you've got my blessing. You can do it a day or so after we locate camp and settle in. Any other questions or suggestions? We'll talk more at Camp Branch. Now, mount up and let's ride."

*****

By evening, the December chill blowing into their faces and promising snow, they rode north from Lykins County into Johnson, very near the border. Malcolm pointed ahead, shouting above the wind, "Along that creek, then east to the next branch! Near the border!"

Abe pulled his horse alongside Erskine's. "Malcolm, are you sure there's time to get there before snow or freezing rain hits? It looks mighty threatening. We've been riding hard."

"Trust me. We're nearly there. It's not totally dark yet. We can slow down and still make it easily in a very short time."

Milford dropped back and Erskine heard him tell the others to draw collars up and head into the wind, that Erskine knew this terrain and was certain their chances were better continuing while there was light left. Despite scrunching themselves and pulling rein ends up into their sleeves—only Milford had gloves—they cursed the cutting cold loudly.

"Three more miles!" Erskine called back to the others, tracing the route ahead carefully with eyes narrowed against fast advancing darkness.

Malcolm considered that the general course of action he'd chosen might possibly be a fatal one. But what other choice did he have? How actively they might be sought by Kansas Territorial lawmen was unpredictable. When word spread of their flight from Lawrence, the enemy—Missourians—would most certainly put a price on their heads, if they hadn't on Malcolm's already.

Again he ran through the list of his enemies mentally, a list topped by the names of Hank and Bill O'Brien. Because of the savage manner in which he'd carved Hank, never expecting the man would survive, he'd now stimulate far more vengeful attention by Bushwhackers. At every chance they'd be after him with a passion, as though performing a holy service by exterminating him and his kind.

Now only the finishing of Hank O'Brien would come close to making it right in Erskine's mind, though not in anyone else's.

He tortured himself with imagination about Sylvia's final hour—for perhaps the hundredth time—fighting against crying out over the worst he pictured.

He remembered the last defiant words of Philip Bilbo before he blew Bilbo's head apart— "I took 'er 'fore we strung 'er up!" Exactly how many of those dirty killers had violated Sylvia's nobility? He could never be sure, but what did it matter now? They would all die.

And Hank's ravishing of Jane-Ellen? To where she submitted for fear of a showdown between him and his brother? That galled as well and was as much in his mind when he wielded the knife as was Hank's role in Sylvia's death. For that dual motive, Malcolm piled on more guilt.

Death would be a welcome finish to this existence, Malcolm thought in renewed anguish. Head down, bent into the gathering darkness and biting wind, he continued to lead Ebony toward Camp Branch.

What was left to live for? Jane-Ellen? She was so troubled over his plan to finish Bill O'Brien that she'd surely turn against him. The Free State cause? He needed more evidence it wasn't a hopeless venture, even as strongly as he believed in its principles. The safety of the men who followed him? Now *there* was something to consider. A responsibility.

And there was one thing more, and Jane-Ellen held the key. A joint relationship with his lost mother. That mystery nagged at him, giving him a faint resolution to go on.

Looking up, Erskine realized they were close to their destination. "Over there!" he shouted to the others, none of whom would dare straggle in this wilderness. "Into those woods!"

The trees, though bare, broke the force of wind well, giving the six frozen horsemen some respite. They peered into the darkened area that was to be their home.

As he led them into the woods, Malcolm allowed himself the luxury of reaching into his back pocket for a handkerchief to blow his nose.

Raising his head on completing that, he sniffed the cold atmosphere of the woods. The sign he picked up by scent froze his blood as no north wind could. He reined Ebony and lifted a hand to halt the others, hoping his fingers weren't so cold he couldn't squeeze a trigger.

Seeing Malcolm draw, the others did as well—just as shots rang from up ahead. Philip Baxter was hit in the face by a rifle shot and died instantly, falling back over his horse's rear.

Malcolm threw himself to the ground and came to his knees firing. His men did the same. His second shot caught a Bushwhacker in the act of finding better cover. Milford picked off another peering past a limestone outcropping.

The firing continued, however, Erskine calculating two of the enemy were still alive.

Milford caught lead in the thigh and fell sprawling sideways. *"Play dead!"* Malcolm instructed the others hoarsely. With shots peppering trees and ground around them, horses scrambling away, they fell one by one into mock stillness.

Within seconds, two Bushwhackers whooped a victory cry and leapt from behind cover.

From under his hat brim, Erskine peered through the deep dusk and recognized Bill O'Brien. Malcolm turned a revolver barrel along the ground and groped for the trigger, continuing to play possum, mystified over how O'Brien knew to lay for him in *this* secret place.

O'Brien rested his rifle at port position, laughing as he strolled toward where Erskine played dead—where Erskine concluded quickly, *It must be done now!*

27

Malcolm waited for O'Brien to approach and stand directly over him. He calculated the choices carefully.

If he didn't wait long enough, Bill O'Brien and the other Bushwhacker could counter a sudden move and reposition their rifles. But if Malcolm waited too long, Bill would most certainly draw a pistol, press it to Erskine's head, and deliver a *coup de grace.* Then there was danger Malcolm could get off a revolver blast to finish O'Brien but be beaten to his next shot by the other man.

The surviving four of his Jayhawkers—one of them wounded—lay in the grove similarly poised, awaiting Erskine's move.

Would his companions be quick enough?

When the scuffed toes of Bill O'Brien's boots were within inches of where Erskine took shallow breaths, watching from under his hat, he noticed the second man's boots lined up almost directly and closely behind Bill's.

Think like a cat, Malcolm told himself, straining to be perfectly still. He concentrated on every part of his body that pressed the frozen ground and readied himself to spring.

With a speed surprising even himself, Erskine leapt up and forward, butting his head into O'Brien's groin, knowing his enemy would fall back against the other man.

All three went down in a shouting, growling heap, Malcolm on top and bringing his revolver barrel to Bill's chest. He squeezed the trigger to a deafening explosion and felt a rush of O'Brien's body heat from the bloody hole he'd opened.

The second man struggled to wriggle from under O'Brien's weight that had suddenly gone slack. But young Peter Iverson was already on him, firing repeatedly into the Bushwhacker's head and making a mess that Malcolm would just as soon not have witnessed.

"Enough!" Erskine shouted to Iverson.

The dying O'Brien still drew breath and, with each inhaling, forced a stream of blood from his chest that Erskine moved aside to escape.

All the others were up, even Milford despite the bullet hole in his thigh.

"Adams! Renfro!" Malcolm shouted. "Into the woods and scout for others! Iverson, check Baxter."

"He's dead."

"I said *check,* damn it!" Iverson shuffled back to where their comrade had gotten one of the first blasts in the face.

"Abe, can you walk?"

"I can limp, Malcolm," Milford said. "I'm all right. I'll expect you to dig this lead out of me."

"You may be in luck, Abe. One of the first things I smelled riding in—what made me draw—was liquor. These Bushwhackers must have been here a while. The alcohol will purify your wound. Let's find it. Look around if you can. See if those other two Bushwhackers are finished. Go through their things and get me their names. Take their money."

"They's—dead," Bill O'Brien offered, obviously sinking fast.

"I don't need *your* help, you scum!" Erskine said, sneering at the dying O'Brien.

"Whut yew—done t'brother *Hank*—'n' *yew* call *me*—" A fit of coughing interrupted him.

Malcolm figured the man had only a few minutes to live, and there were questions he wanted to ask O'Brien.

He heard Iverson return from checking Baxter, reporting him "definitely dead." Then Abe limped back from looking at the two other Missourians, shaking his head in a sign they were dead, too.

Bill O'Brien appeared to be staring past Erskine, in Iverson's direction. He seemed to want to say something but couldn't get it out.

Malcolm asked O'Brien, "How did you know we were coming here? I thought you were all still at the Wakarusa."

O'Brien coughed and said, "We quit camp there—yest'dy. Got tahred—waitin' fer—action."

"But how could you know we were coming here? Nobody knew but us."

O'Brien tried to shake his head. "Jes' a—good—place t'hole up....Nigguh, he'p me. Ah don'—wanna die."

"Neither did my Sylvia want to die. Nor Abe's family. You're going to die, Bill, and soon. There's nothing I can do for you."

"Then—leastwise finish me," O'Brien begged.

"No. I won't waste another bullet on you."

Malcolm considered telling O'Brien what his brother Hank had been doing to Bill's wife, Jane-Ellen. And about her resigned submissions. But he couldn't bring himself to that sort of meanness—nor dishonor Jane-Ellen.

O'Brien said, "Sorry—'bout yer—squaw. Jes' went—'long with whut—Hank done. But didn't—tetch her. Not me....*Please*—finish me."

Hearing that, Erskine drew a revolver and placed the barrel against Bill O'Brien's forehead. "You weren't one of those who—molested my wife?"

"Ah—*swear*....Pocket," O'Brien mumbled. "Pocket."

Malcolm reached his other hand into Bill's shirt pocket and found rosary beads. Surprised, but impressed, he placed them in the dying man's hand.

Then he squeezed off a ringing shot directly into Bill O'Brien's brain. After that, he went through the other pockets.

He got up, seeing Renfro and Adams return from the woods to indicate there were no signs of others.

Erskine collected papers Abe Milford had found on the dead Bushwhackers, including the man Iverson had finished off. He stuffed them inside his shirt. He would check their identifications later to see whether any were on his list. Probably they were.

"Gather all their weapons and ammunition. Store them temporarily there," Malcolm said, pointing to a hole beneath a ledge. "Find their horses and bring any saddle blankets here. We've got to stay in this grove, at least tonight. Even in this cold, the corpses will start stinking up the place, and the ground's too hard for burial. Get ropes, bind their ankles, and have the horses drag them half a mile up the draw. Leave the bodies there."

"Baxter, too?" Iverson asked.

Erskine nodded. "Baxter, too."

The men set to work.

Malcolm said, "Abe, let me have a look at that wound."

Milford reached into his jacket and pulled out a half-filled bottle of cheap whiskey. "Found this over there." He handed it to Malcolm, who pulled the cork, put the bottle to his lips, and tasted the stuff.

"Bad for drinking," was Erskine's verdict. "Good for cleaning wounds. Plenty of alcohol in it. Let's see that leg." He pulled his Bowie knife and—with the square-faced, lips-pursed Milford sitting on a fallen tree—ripped open the man's trouser leg. "It's deep."

"But you'll get it."

Malcolm looked into the older man's anxious eyes. He smiled and nodded. "Yes, I'll get it. You just sit there—keep it covered. Keep drinking this. I'm going to build a fire first."

There was a hatchet in one of the men's packs. They began collecting limbs to build a lean-to.

Malcolm had directed them to build a couple of temporary shelters—over Iverson's objections that it was too dark to work. *"Do it!"* Erskine had commanded in a tone leaving no doubt he was ready to enforce his leadership.

Milford, sitting by the fire Erskine was tending, asked, "Will we be staying here more than one night, Malcolm? Evidently the Missourians know about this hideout, too."

"I'm not sure they do. Nor am I certain it was the coincidence O'Brien made it out to be."

Abe went pale, hearing that. "Malcolm, I assure you, every one of these men is to be trusted to the limit. Besides, there was no way any could have passed information while we were riding here."

"Abe, why don't you just keep pulling on that bottle and let me worry about that?"

Milford did as Erskine directed, making certain to leave enough of the liquor for the wound.

"Hold on to something, friend. I'm going in with my Bowie."

Malcolm sterilized the knife point in the fire. He began his probe for the pellet.

"Oh!" Abe yelped. Then he clamped his mouth shut, held a branch, and tried to hang on.

"Don't squirm. Be still and I'll get it quicker."

Milford looked as though he didn't dare relax, tensing increasingly for the unanesthetized surgery.

"Take another swig," Erskine said.

"No! *Ssss!* No, *get* it!"

Malcolm probed deeper, finding the bullet lodged against Milford's thigh bone. "I'm going to have to sew you when I'm done." Despite the bitter cold, sweat ran from under Erskine's hat. Abe, too, was beaded with sweat and showing signs of shock.

With one more cutting thrust, Malcolm brought the knife blade under the rifle slug and worked it out. Immediately he took the bottle from Abe and poured the contents into the wound until it was empty.

"AAAAGH!" Milford shouted, fainting and falling from the log. Erskine directed Adams to fish inside a saddlebag on Ebony for a sewing kit.

"Let's do this while he's passed out," Malcolm said.

When it was done, Adams, Iverson, and Renfro secured all horses on the lee side of an outcropping and retreated to a lean-to. Erskine moved Milford under the other shelter. He told the trio to huddle close in order to fight the cold—and to try to catch some sleep.

He arranged the unconscious Abe for the man's best possible protection, covering him under and over with saddle blankets. Then, the luxury of a free moment available, he removed the papers from his shirt one by one, studying them before the fire.

Within minutes he was smiling, happy to confirm they'd finished off not one but four whom he'd sought. His revenge was progressing successfully—but there was a hitch represented in one of the scraps of paper, a note.

Malcolm burned all but that paper and warmed his hands by the fire. He pondered what he should do about the sorry fact he'd just learned.

His thoughts drifted to Jane-Ellen. At last he'd made her a free woman, which she would doubtless resent unless he could find a way to support her. With only about twenty dollars collected from the dead, there wasn't enough of a purse to start her widowhood properly.

Perhaps they could share with her some of what Renfro planned to steal from the bank at Westport. Would he be able to justify that to the men? No. Not a chance.

Erskine sat near the protection of the lean-to and the fire, drawing up his knees, crossing his arms, stuffing his hands inside his jacket. He let himself doze. And he dreamed.

He dreamed of visiting Jane-Ellen, but it was a fitful and complicated dream. It threw him awake, and he wondered momentarily where he was.

The night's chill—and sleet starting to fall and freeze on and around him—caused him to draw tighter into himself to shut out the cold. He inched closer to the fire and protection of the lean-to.

While replaying the brief nightmare, he wondered how prophetic it might be. In the bad dream Jane-Ellen had opened her cabin door and promptly blasted him in the face with a shotgun.

28

Malcolm fought sleep in order to avoid a repeat of his nightmare. He worried about Milford. He fueled the fire to keep them both warm through the night. He considered his next moves.

Ten men remained of the twenty-three who'd either brutalized and hanged Sylvia or stood by without protest. Most of them, he expected, were still at the Wakarusa River near Lawrence or by now returning from the siege.

Very likely they were bitter that their march to war had been thwarted, first by Sam Jones's cowardly reluctance to attack Lawrence, then by Territorial Governor Shannon's interceding to effect a truce to the Free Staters' advantage. The Missourians would be bitter that their effort had gained them nothing.

Soon all remaining targets of Malcolm's vengeance would be back in their homes along or near the border, securing themselves against the hard winter, postponing Bushwhacker activities.

Soon they—most of them family men—would be warm in their beds, cozy with their wives, preparing a Christmas for their children. They would be attending to the winter chores of their farms or working at other trades.

Without doubt they would be aware that he, Malcolm, was free and in hiding, now fortified with helpers committed to gunfighting. They would consider that four more of the group that had hanged Sylvia near Watts Mill were missing and probably dead.

They, too, would count down the list and realize Philip Bilbo of Westport was gone, Bill O'Brien of Little Santa Fe was gone, Zeke Larson of Leavenworth was gone, that several other cronies were gone—and that Hank O'Brien lay in a Westport hospital, less of a man at Erskine's hands.

They would mull what Ben Morton of Independence must by now have shared with them about Erskine's diabolical methods, his bloody determination.

Occasionally, Malcolm mused, they would meet one another and talk about how to finish Malcolm before he had the chance to finish them. They would study maps, seek information about who had joined Erskine, estimate the strength of arms of this new Jayhawker threat.

They would live their winter nervously, Malcolm knew. He smiled to himself that he had so quickly assumed power unmatched by any other border fighter.

But the smile faded quickly as Erskine assessed also the liabilities of his own position.

His chief aide, Abe Milford, himself a widower as well as a grieving father at the hands of Bushwhackers, lay unconscious at his side. Would he succumb to cold, to shock, to infection? Morning would yield some of the answer.

The group had little money. Not enough worth spit. True, Ezra Renfro had a plan for that, but Malcolm had his doubts. Only Jeremiah Adams, wilderness-wise and practical, seemed of meaningful help for now.

Young and hot-blooded Peter Iverson was likely a traitor, by Erskine's reckoning.

Should he jeopardize Renfro and the Westport bank mission by sending Iverson to help? Should he risk his own survival, an injured companion on his hands, by sending the steady and mature Adams?

Assuming Iverson had betrayed them, *when* might he have had the opportunity to do so?

Of course! When they'd stopped to rest in their flight from Lawrence. Malcolm had himself identified their hideout foolishly, naming Camp Branch.

Back in Lawrence, earlier, Iverson could have sent word to Bill O'Brien that Malcolm was to be set loose. O'Brien would watch and either follow or plan his interception.

During the rest period, Iverson could have scribbled the note Erskine now had in his pocket—the one picked from a dead Bushwhacker—containing the penciled words, *Camp Branch.* Maybe

Iverson left it under a prearranged small stone weight, where O'Brien and his men would see it and then outride them here.

O'Brien's failure to destroy the note, his seeming recognition of Iverson as he lay dying, sealed the young man's fate—perhaps. Malcolm must be sure it was Peter. For why not Renfro—or Adams?

Which one had a pencil in his kit? Which had note paper such as the piece of evidence? Which could even read and write, or not do so? He knew little about his companions and trusted implicitly only Milford, who lay helpless.

No food, insufficient funds, no durable shelter, and they were low on ammunition.

If Sylvia's surviving murderers knew such facts and his whereabouts, they'd be on him in an hour, two at most. They'd shoot him, skewer him, hang him, or cut him into little pieces just to make certain he hadn't the nine lives of a cat—for he'd once survived hanging. Thanks to Sylvia.

There was nothing Malcolm could do about hiding their vulnerability if there was a traitor here. And there most certainly was. Yet he would move against no one until he knew who was guilty.

What must be constant, Erskine thought, staring into the fire, occasionally dropping in a frozen branch and hearing its reassuring crackle, was his own cunning. Most of the shrewdness in which he took new pride had flowered and grown under Sylvia's guidance, then matured under pressures of conflict and violence.

Use your head, Malcolm, he demanded of himself in the night. *It's nearly all you've got that's truly your own.*

In the morning, Milford awakened sore and hungry, the latter a good sign. The sky was clearing and the sun would come up.

Adams went out to check a trap he'd left and returned with a large, male possum as well as a pot from his kit. He promised the tastiest breakfast they'd ever had. Melted snow would provide the water he needed for cooking. He had spices in his saddlebag and a tin of lard.

Erskine told them that after breakfast they'd revisit Baxter's body, say a prayer over it, but not try to bury it in the frozen ground. "Abe," he whispered before leaving for the rites, "is that little prayer book still in your saddlebag?"

"No, Malcolm. I carry it in my coat—right here." He handed it to Erskine.

Later, Adams, Renfro, and Iverson stood with him. Milford was unable yet to move such a distance, even by horse, so he stayed in the grove. Erskine held the book upside down and pretended to be reading from it as he prayed aloud. He passed it first to Adams, who confessed illiteracy believably. Then it went to Renfro, who begged off as a non-believer, and finally to Iverson.

The young man hesitated, but he righted the prayer book and read a sentence or two haltingly. That narrowed Erskine's suspicions. He decided to set Adams and Iverson to work felling trees the best they could with the hatchet, to start building a cabin. He directed Renfro to carry out his mission in the bank at Westport, right away.

Renfro wasn't unwilling, though he was apprehensive about doing it alone. "I—*think* I can pull it off," was his reply.

"Do your best," Erskine said. "And be careful. If you're caught and they realize we're cohorts, they'll torture you to find me."

Those remaining—Erskine, Milford directing construction from experience but unable to help physically, Iverson, and Adams—started the cabin, more a lodge. No carpenter's tools. No nails. Just hatchet-grooving of logs, tree-branch bracing for wall strength, lattice-improvising for small, paneless windows. And clay-mud—lots of mud for insulation.

Malcolm insisted it should be large enough for a dozen or so men and well hidden among the trees, sturdy as a small fort.

They worked all that day and into the evening. They spent the night in the shelter of partly completed walls and built fires on what would be the dirt floor, after the layer of snow melted.

Next morning they began again after the breakfast of a coyote pup from Adams's trap. Malcolm began to feel anxiety over delay in Renfro's return. Ezra should have been back by the previous evening.

Presently Erskine saw a lone horseman through the woods in the distance, the horse almost strolling. It was Renfro. From far off he looked disheveled. He dismounted and limped into camp, appearing to have been roughed up badly.

Renfro said he'd been waylaid at Little Santa Fe, and the money—all of it—had been taken from him. Malcolm's hopes for their survival collapsed. Much in his plans had been riding on the ability to use the $30,000 Boone held for mercenary Bushwhackers.

"Were you able to identify who did it?" Erskine pressed.

"Catron—and Hank O'Brien and their men, mentioning your jail escape."

"Hank is out of the *hospital?* And *riding?"*

"With blood in his eye for you like no man I've ever seen. I lied to them about wanting to start my own bank in the Paola settlement. They knew I once worked for Boone, so they believed that story. Only reason they let me go was I made them rich giving up the stolen money."

"Were you followed? What did you do about tracks in the snow?"

"They were too busy fighting over the money to see me slip away, but I came roundabout to mix my tracks with others on the trails. My horse's shoes are like anybody's. I'd have got here last night but for sidetracking."

"Did you see—?" Stopping, Erskine decided not to finish that.

"Bill O'Brien's wife?" Renfro asked. "Yeah. She's madder than a hornet that Bill didn't come home two nights back, and she fears you got him. Not crying about him though. Told Hank he had to share what they took from me. If she winds up widowed at the poor farm—she and her little brother—she plans to kill you herself, is what she said."

"Did Hank indicate that he'd take care of her and the youngster?"

"Oh, he took care of them, all right. Threw her and the kid out in the cold! Told her never to come back. Didn't have a use for her anymore, whatever that meant. No, Malcolm, I heard her again—before I slipped away—swear to kill you if it was the last thing she ever did."

29

Within a week Erskine's group finished building the lodge, topped with a serviceable roof Adams and Milford designed from tightly-woven saplings.

Next they fashioned cots over which they could drape saddle blankets. Lacking grass or hay, they tried thawing and drying ground moss and found it to be a good mattress under blankets.

Stacked limestone furnished a crude but efficient chimney. Adams saw that the fireplace was made roomy enough for cooking.

Possum became a favorite, but they were running out of salt, spices, and cooking fat. Occasionally they enjoyed wild fowl and once a raccoon. Though they tried rabbit, none enjoyed it.

Several times Adams begged permission to leave camp to find a lake containing fish, knowing the ice was not too thick to penetrate. Erskine said that would have to await his return from the Paola settlement, where he intended to try to obtain staples and ammunition on credit.

"Why must the fishing wait?" the frontiersman pressed.

Malcolm said, "Because I hope also to bring back recruits to make our numbers more secure. I can't spare you from here right now, Jeremiah. I can't afford to lose you."

Adams walked off, grumbling that Erskine had too little faith in his capacity for survival in the wilderness. Abe Milford approached, still hobbling slightly from his healing wound.

"Does he know?" Abe asked.

"Know what? That either Renfro or Iverson's a traitor? No."

"You really believe, Malcolm, that you can persuade men in Paola to join us?"

"I'm confident enough about it that I think you should direct the making of at least four or five more cots. I'll leave for Paola Sunday."

Two days before Christmas, placing the sufficiently recovered Milford in charge, Erskine rode south into Lykins County. The day was sunny, the snow melting. He marveled at the vastness of the undeveloped land, the apparent richness of its soil, and its ready resources of timber along creeks and of stone not difficult to quarry.

Except for the border troubles, Malcolm considered, he might have staked a claim by now and begun either farming or ranching.

On impulse, Malcolm reined up Ebony, pausing at the top of a knoll where he could view the Lykins County prairie in all directions. He dismounted.

Dropping to his knees in the snow, removing his hat, bowing his head, he spoke—

"Lord, you and I haven't gotten to know each other well. I've never been sure you're there, not in the form others ascribe to you—all-knowing and all-powerful. Still, I'll try.

"I've either killed or been responsible for the deaths of seventeen men, not counting Phil Baxter who died serving me. Two in Massachusetts, two in Missouri, thirteen in Kansas. I aim to kill ten more, and there'll probably be more after that.

"I've committed adultery and mayhem to add to my sins. To believe preachers, I'm probably beyond redemption. Still, Lord, I—Well—

"All that I am was made by my father and mother—he of principle and sensitiveness, a Scot, a captain riding the seas somewhere in the world, a man with strengths and weaknesses who loved a woman society didn't want him to love.

"My mother? A dark beauty, a dancer, a literate and wise Egyptian whose African civilized heritage dates earlier than any white person's. Yet she was denied a place in a supposedly free society, for loving a man they didn't want her to love.

"My life has tumbled ever since from one circumstance to the next. Now I'm told there's a price on my head in Missouri, and some of my comrades have turned on me here in Kansas Territory.

"I'm the most feared killer on the border and not proud of that. If the truth were known, I don't want to hurt even the lowliest creature much less a fellow human.

"I've known several kinds of love—a father's, distant and stern as he felt it must be, yet constant; a mother's, wonderfully warm but short-lived and tragic in the abruptness of her departure; an Indian woman's, loyal and constructive, though fatalistic and brief as the winking of an eye, and Jane-Ellen's, hot-blooded, clinging—but now she swears to be my enemy.

"Lord, I— I don't know *why* I'm talking to you and getting my knees wet and my body chilled through. But I figure you may make something good happen for me.

"Duty requires me to finish my mission. An 'eye for an eye' you once told the Hebrews, to whom I'm also probably related through Mama. Yet your Jesus was more charitable—sought to reach his enemies by love. His birthday's coming up, now that I think of it.

"Well, truth is, there's little room for love, Lord, when a man or woman whose skin is darker or nose is flatter isn't even regarded as a fellow human, with feelings like anyone else's.

"To cleanse others' souls of hatred I must continue my present course, make examples of those who murdered Sylvia. And make examples of those who would reduce me to slavery.

"I don't know what to ask of you, Lord. My needs are simple. I want the Catholic woman, Jane-Ellen, for I know deep-down she wants me. I want to keep her safe, provided she doesn't take a pot-shot and finish me.

"Let's see, what else? I want salt, sugar, spices, lard, guns, bullets, knives, money—more men to help me. And I want my enemies dead.

"From *you,* Lord, I ask understanding. I'll take care of the rest of my wants. It's somehow important to me at this dark moment of my life that I have your understanding....

"And I think that's all I want to say."

Erskine stood, starting to replace his hat, then added, "Oh, yes. Amen."

He reached Paola in mid-afternoon, going straight to the Lykinses, a family divided on the slavery issue. Brothers James and Joseph, however, had gone to Lawrence in support against the siege.

The Lykinses had worked with Indians, Malcolm knew, though mainly in missions. Still, they understood his position about Shawnee honor and personal honor and offered help.

They now introduced him to several young men, sons of farmers idled by winter, seemingly eager for adventure.

One of the young men, kin to the brothers and named Ralph, approached Malcolm after learning pieces of his story. "Sir, I've seen her. The O'Brien woman."

Erskine pulled him aside. "What news? Where?"

"She's gone to the poor farm outside Independence. Her little brother—Jimmy Maloney I think is his name—is ill with some kind of fever."

Malcolm bit his lip hearing that. "Mulligan. Jimmy Mulligan. Go on. Tell me whatever you know."

"I delivered a wagon of supplies contributed to the Mormon Mission that runs the poor farm. I was asked to look in on the boy because I've got some skills as a healer, though mostly with livestock. I couldn't help the boy, nor could any doctor who's been there."

"What kind of fever? Do you have any idea what it is?"

"All I know, Mr. Erskine, is I think he's going to die. I doubt he'll see the New Year.

30

James and Joseph Lykins and their kinsman, Ralph, woke Erskine the morning of the day before Christmas. The comfort of a real bed had refreshed him, allowing him to sleep longer and more deeply than was ordinary for him.

"Come meet your recruits," James said, poking his guest awake, "and we'll all have breakfast. Five good young men including Ralph have been mustered into your service—and one woman."

Malcolm sat up quickly. "Woman? Are you *mad?* A woman among ten of us *marked as outlaws?"*

James interrupted. "A Shawnee woman who can track, fight, cook, sew—and is herself an outcast. She's a good Christian woman now, very devout and repentant."

"Repentant for what?"

"For killing a tribesman of the Black Bobs who, uh, tried taking liberties. It was only because she sought to defend her honor that the Chief spared her life, but she was banished. That was a few years ago. She drifted to Paola and has done mostly housecleaning and some tending of stock."

While James Lykins talked, Erskine threw cold water on his face to come further awake, to face this newest challenge to his perceived order of things. All the while he shook his head and grumbled, "Impossible."

The more they tried to convince him of Rose Deerfoot's fitness for joining the recruits, the louder he said, "Impossible." Then he stalked from the bedroom into a roomful of young men—and Rose.

When Erskine saw her, he was absolutely certain of her complete lack of qualification for such a mission. *"Impossible!"* he shouted to all. She appeared scrawny, unkempt, and the sight of her caused him to wonder why a Shawnee brave might be so foolish as to make advances to her.

"Malcolm Erskine!" his name was called. It was she, Rose, yet the voice was almost detached, as though a ghost's. It was the *same voice as Sylvia's.*

"I am your sister-in-law," Rose said. "Sylvia was my half-sister."

Erskine stood transfixed. "Syl—" he mumbled, unable to say the name of his dead beloved.

"Acknowledge me as your kinswoman, related by marriage," she pressed, "and I can then—I must then serve you under tribal custom."

"Ah *ha!* I won't acknowledge you, if it's as simple as all *that."* Malcolm began laughing nervously, looking around at the others in some pride that he'd solved the problem so simply. "I *don't* acknow—"

Rose moved swiftly, caught Erskine by the ear, pulled him with unbelievable strength to the floor, and whispered very closely, distinctly, "Camp Branch." Then she released him.

"How did you know?" the subdued Erskine asked, looking up at Rose Deerfoot as she stood.

"Sylvia told you where to hide if you ever needed to. It's *my land.* You're trespassing on *my land.* Take me along, and I'll let you and your men be my guests. Refuse and I'll have you all kicked off."

Rose turned, her loose buckskin dress swirling in a flash. She threw a coat over her shoulders and left the Lykinses' cabin.

James Lykins started to laugh, a low laugh of irony at first. Soon the others joined, and before long Malcolm—still on the cabin floor—laughed as well at the joke on himself. When he could bring himself under control, he said, shaking his head, "I'll be damned."

James explained that through her banishment, Rose had received her property formerly held in common with the Black Bobs. Further, though she was a Christian, she chose to draw Old Testament justification for certain of her tribal customs, thus her commitment to acts of kinship. Most importantly, she saw an opportunity to repossess her holdings with Erskine's help and protection.

Rose pulled him with unbelievable strength to the floor, and whispered, "Camp Branch."

"She knows everything Sylvia ever knew," James said, "about your enemies, about—everything. Malcolm, she may be an asset to your cause."

"But she's such an ugly little thing—dirty, smelly. Nothing at all like Sylvia, except for her voice. Help me up. I've laughed myself weak."

Three of his new soldiers scurried to be the first to help Erskine to his feet. "I must write a letter to be delivered to Abe Milford," he said. "And *Ro-ose,"* he added derisively, implying by his tone that her condition was unsuited to her floral name, "will lead you all to the hideout. Heaven help us—she smells as though she might be the local hog tender."

"She is," James confirmed.

"Let me have paper and a pencil, please," Erskine requested. "When I conclude this, I'm going to Westport, alone."

"Eat first, Malcolm."

"Will you pull my ear if I refuse?" A new round of laughter shook them. They sat at the table together as James and Joseph introduced the other recruits and the Lykins wives served.

*****

Erskine started out ahead of them, hurrying due east to the military road and then northward. He pressed Ebony as hard as he dared, reaching the old Santa Fe Trail by early afternoon and boldly turning straight toward the hostile border.

There he went ignored or unrecognized, perhaps none believing a man so widely sought as Malcolm Erskine would ride alone into enemy territory. He turned north on the border road leading to Dallas.

Because it was Christmas Eve and not a common time for milling or transporting, Dallas was virtually abandoned. He led Ebony directly to Watts Mill and sought a teamsters' and millers' call board he'd seen there weeks before. One never knew what news might be posted that could prove helpful.

Among the notices he found a fresh one offering a $50 reward for information leading to the capture of Peter Iverson, teamster and embezzler. "Hmph!" Malcolm snorted, tearing the notice from the board and stuffing it into his shirt.

Erskine was elated to conclude the young man was innocent of treachery. The notice was authentic, signed by the sheriff of Jackson County—no doubt about that—so, by any stretch of reason, Peter couldn't be allied with these people.

By late afternoon he approached the outskirts of Westport. Many of his enemies lived there, yet that didn't deter him. He turned east onto the new Santa Fe Trail—the north trail serving as Westport's main street. Erskine proceeded directly to the Harris House, tethered Ebony, and entered the saloon.

"You a nigger?" the barman asked matter-of-factly. "We don't serve niggers."

Malcolm leaned across the bar and whispered so that only the bartender could hear. "Yes, I'm a nigger, name of Malcolm Erskine. And, for a glass of whiskey, I'll pay its price and let you keep your manhood."

The barman looked at the Bowie knife Erskine indicated. Apparently he was trying to decide whether this was indeed the Free State spy—and now renegade—whose reputation for swift vengeance was legendary. He reached for a glass and bottle and put them before Malcolm without another word about it.

"And speaking of Hank O'Brien," Erskine said, eyeing the barman to make certain he understood the reference, "I want to know his doctor, the surgeon who treated him."

Now the bartender looked about, seeking help, but the place had nearly emptied. Most customers had returned to their families to be in time for Christmas Eve dinners. Only a few derelicts and a gambler lingered at far tables, and they would be of little help.

Stuttering, the barman gave Malcolm directions to Dr. Horatio Green's home, not far from the Harris House.

"One more thing," Malcolm said, tossing down a whiskey. "Do you know Ezra Renfro?"

The bartender nodded, hesitatingly. Then he volunteered, "He's a k-killer."

"Oh? Tell me about it." Erskine poured another drink and threw it down his gullet.

Malcolm learned what Ezra was evidently loath to talk about. Apparently he was let go from Boone's bank for living in the quarter of Westport set aside for freed slaves by the town's founders, the McCoy family. A gang of ruffians entered Renfro's cabin one night and kidnapped his Negro mistress, apparently to sell her back into slavery and further punish Ezra. They held Renfro as others made off with the woman. He gave the Bushwhackers such a struggle that one of them dropped a revolver unnoticed. When the man returned later to look for it, Renfro garroted him quietly in the darkened cabin, then fled to Lawrence.

"Hmph!" Malcolm snorted a second time in his investigation, again pleased to have suspicions of possible treachery dispelled.

He paid and left the saloon at nightfall and went directly to the home of Dr. Green, knocking at the front door. A young lad answered.

"Merry Christmas!" Erskine said cheerfully to the boy, smiling. "Please let me in to see Dr. Green."

"Are you ill?" the boy asked. "You don't look ill."

"I'm feeling very well, as a matter of fact," Erskine said. "Call your father like a good lad."

"What is it?" a well-dressed man said, coming down the stairs into the living room.

"You will please come with me, Dr. Green. We're going to the poor farm near Independence."

"But this is Christmas Eve. If it's no emeregency, I plan to stay with my family. Besides, there are doctors a-plenty in Independence who—"

"If you can put Henry O'Brien back together as you have," Malcolm said, "then I believe you're the best damned doctor in Missouri."

"*You!* You're *Erskine!* How did you get here with half the Law and Order people looking for you?"

Malcolm stretched his arms and shrugged. "Spirit of Christmas kept me safe, I suppose. Either that or they're incompetent, which I suspect is more the case." More seriously he added, "Get your bag. It's a young boy with a fever of some kind, and it could be fatal."

Dr. Green did as instructed, telling his son to have one of their slaves saddle a mare. At the door, Erskine turned and suggested to Green, "Doctor, perhaps you'd better say goodbye to your family. If the boy fails to improve, or if he dies, you'll never return."

"It's to be like *that,* is it?" Green said.

"Yes, sir. I want to put as much incentive into the success of this mission as possible."

"Incentive! Yet I have no choice."

"No, Doctor. You have no choice."

31

A light snow fell on Erskine and Dr. Green through their night's ride eastward.

Malcolm was unfamiliar with this area. He couldn't count on a memory of his walk with John Brown, because they'd taken a southern trail out of Independence. This trail from Westport took them to a crude plank-and-pontoon bridge spanning the Blue River, at a narrow place below the Blue Ridge.

The low mountain itself proved something of a struggle. Malcolm's horse, Ebony, was beginning to show signs of weariness from the long day. "We'll camp," Erskine announced.

"Camp?" Dr. Green replied in an unbelieving tone. He pushed away the protective scarf across his mouth. "That's not possible! We'll *perish* in this cold if we stay out of doors."

Erskine dismounted. Without delay he demonstrated how a reasonably comfortable few hours' shelter and fire could be crafted on the lee of an open mountainside. He managed to come up with a small pot and soon served the surprised Horatio Green a tin cup of hot cocoa.

Before long the doctor seemed ready to relax, talk, draw Erskine out for conversation, but Malcolm suggested they nap. Green, acknowledging the superior experience of his captor, now seemed willing to follow every lead.

Later, refreshed by nearly two hours' rest, Malcolm checked their mounts and was satisfied their rest had been helpful. They broke camp and continued on.

"Back there," Dr. Green said, riding alongside Malcolm, "I could have slipped your knife from its sheath, or one of your revolvers from its holster, and killed you. I'd have been proclaimed a hero from here to St. Louis for it, in spite of breaking my oath as a physician."

"I know that you could have tried," Erskine acknowledged.

"Why did you trust me?" Green pressed.

"It's my natural inclination to trust until I have reason not to," Malcolm said. "Perhaps that will prove my undoing someday. In the meantime, I know no other way to behave."

"That's a dangerous attitude for a man in your position."

"Not entirely, Dr. Green. Had my trust proved unwarranted, I'd have felt your attempt and been at your throat before you could decide where to plunge the knife or how to pull the trigger."

"Yet you slept soundly."

"When I sleep, I sleep soundly. When I awake, I awake fully. I've only recently trained myself to do the latter."

Green appeared to think on that, then— "Why have you killed all those men—or caused them to die?"

"They murdered Sylvia, my wife. They violated her honor, her tribe's honor, and mine."

"Why did you castrate O'Brien?" Horatio Green asked with apparent academic curiosity.

"I thought it would kill him. I hadn't reckoned on your skills for keeping him alive."

"But why that—that savage choice?"

Malcolm turned to the doctor, barely able to read his face in the dark of night, their only light being from reflected snow. "I admit, I was plagued by guilt after that because I, too, thought it savage to remove a man's very manhood, whether or not as a means of intended killing. Now, however," Erskine said, facing forward, checking the trail, "I find it all very—poetic."

"Poetic!" Green fairly sputtered at Malcolm's surprising answer.

"Yes," Malcolm affirmed, "because Hank O'Brien is now a rich man, thanks to his continuing knavery and thievery. But what pleasure will he derive from his wealth?"

Dr. Green was silent the rest of the ride, perhaps pondering Erskine's observation. Soon Malcolm pointed to their destination at the faint light of dawn—Christmas Day.

After rousing a custodian and announcing that a physician accompanied him, Erskine was directed to a crude but large cabin—a sort of infirmary—in which they found Jimmy Mulligan alone. Green immediately began his examination, leaving to Erskine the securing of their horses.

When Malcolm reentered the building, he asked, "What's your finding?"

"I have no name for what ails the boy. But I think I can save him. I may even have the proper medicines in my kit."

Jane-Ellen burst in. Seeing Malcolm and a stranger near Jimmy, she flew into a rage, turning abruptly to Malcolm in an attempt to wrest a revolver from him.

With a swift movement, Erskine had Jane-Ellen locked in his grip, her mouth covered with his rough hand. "He's a doctor. The best. He'll cure Jimmy." As an afterthought, "Merry Christmas, my love."

The added greeting only infuriated Jane-Ellen further. Though she intensified her struggle, Malcolm removed her to an adjoining room and swung the door shut without releasing her.

"Listen to me, Jane-Ellen. In a few moments I'm going to let you go, and as I do you will be calm and totally comfortable in my presence. You'll end this talk of killing me for putting you on the poor farm, for endangering Jimmy's health and very life, for reducing you to further humiliation. I'm well aware the ill I've done you."

She continued to writhe in Malcolm's hold, the two of them working themselves into a sweat from the struggle. Yet Malcolm was determined she would be calm before he would release her. Slowly through the struggle he swung her around.

Removing his hand from her mouth, he replaced it with his own mouth for what proved a rough, biting kiss.

Though he felt blood drip to his chin he continued to press the back of her head toward him to hold her in that fashion, daring to search in the lingering and violent kiss for some response.

It took longer than he'd hoped, but it came. And with it a spontaneous passion for him that he knew to be among Jane-Ellen's strongest capabilities.

"Here and now," he whispered.

"No," she protested. "Not on the floor. Not here. Oh, Lord, Lord, Lord, what *am* I?"

"Here and now," he repeated.

*****

Later, looking up into his dark eyes, Jane-Ellen at last smiled. "And Merry Christmas to you, Brother Malcolm."

He laughed. "Why do you call me 'brother'?"

"Oh—pay no attention. This— This is a very religious place. It's 'brother' this and 'sister' that, all the time."

"No, no," he protested in mild amusement. "There was more in your tone."

"Please," she said, tracing his mustache with a finger, "pay no attention."

"When Jimmy is well enough to travel," Malcolm said, "I'll come for you both. You needn't stay here. I have some means to provide for you. They're primitive means at best, but for you to stay here much longer is unthinkable."

"I don't know," Jane-Ellen said, indicating she wished to get up. "I don't know whether to attach my life actively to yours when you're sworn to go on killing. I'm sick of all this killing. I'd like to be able to go back east."

"To Maryland?"

"*Shoot,* anywhere but this accursed border environment. Besides, I don't believe in your cause. I'm— I'm not sure *what* principles to stand on any longer, after everything I've seen—and a few things I've done. But those principles certainly don't include following a man living as an outlaw."

"Jane-Ellen, must I remind you—about principles, that is—you've just responded passionately to the lovemaking of a man who recently blew your husband's brains out?"

She straightened her rough, frayed dress and glanced at him while he rose. "As I confessed, Malcolm, I'm not sure of myself. And I know what I've done. You're right. For some time—until an hour ago—I was so angry I wanted to kill you, truly. I would have, too. Never doubt that."

"Your changing moods involve more than my shooting Bill, or causing you to be brought to the poor farm, don't they? Something's offsetting all that anger."

Jane-Ellen turned and sought his eyes in the flickering candlelight of the small infirmary room. "What are you seeing of us in your mind's eye?"

"A link that I— I can't explain. There's more in the things you *haven't* told me than in what you have, isn't there? What do you think I do with all the time I spend out there in the wilderness? You think my brain ceases to function?"

She held up a hand. "Don't go on with it, please."

"It's Dahlia—my mother. It's something to do with her. For God's sake, Jane-Ellen, tell me the story, will you? What do you know of her?"

Jane-Ellen covered her face tightly and shook her head, her uncombed hair flying behind her. "Don't go *on,*" she begged.

As though struck by a powerful blow, Malcolm stepped quickly back against a wall. He flattened himself to the boards. He felt as though he would choke.

"No," he said, almost in an inaudible gurgle. Then louder, "No, it can't be."

Still covering her face, Jane-Ellen began to nod. "I think it's possible, yet I love you," was all she could say, weeping.

"It *can't* be!" Malcolm shouted.

"I only know," Jane-Ellen continued, hiding her face, "that our love—God help us—will probably destroy us."

At that moment Dr. Green knocked and entered uninvited. "I must have quiet!" he commanded in a harsh whisper. "The boy is resting now. What on earth is going on in here?"

Malcolm rushed past him and found the outer door. Jane-Ellen followed him outside.

"Malcolm!" she screamed after him. *"Come back!"*

Erskine ran toward his horse and leapt into the saddle. He reached to untether Ebony and turned to face Jane-Ellen where she stood in the doorway.

The rising Christmas-morning sun revealed every secret in her tear-streaked face, causing him to shout in a blood-curdling cry. *"It can't be!"*

Ebony reared at the sound of his master's anguish.

Then Malcolm turned the steed west and rode away.

32

The Jayhawker band of Camp Branch found no joy in the approach of a new year. All agreed it was likely to be a bloodier time than the year just ended.

Political discussions took place daily, nightly. They depended on news from outside through their safest connection, the Paola settlement. From there they were also supplied by a relatively sympathetic community.

On credit they had stocked coffee, tobacco, sugar, salt, flour, lard, spices, soap, candles, and whale oil.

The resourceful recruits from Paola had obtained Bowie knives, two small barrels of gunpowder, several boxes of lead scraps, and molds enabling them to cast their own bullets and build their ammunition supply. The hard winter's days and nights would not pass in idleness.

Abe Milford had recovered fully from his wound and taken a position of effective leadership, Erskine having sunk into a mood of alternating silence and testiness.

It was Milford who distributed specific duties among the other eight men and those for Rose Deerfoot. He'd been instructed earlier to find a place for the Shawnee woman during Malcolm's Christmas visit to the poor farm.

Rose, meanwhile, appeared to view her presence among them as a right of ownership. It was her land they occupied and, therefore, by a quirk of what passed for law in Kansas Territory, her lodge they'd built.

She seemed to know better than to press such points in Erskine's presence. Just to look at him in this period of winter waiting gave indication any encounter could end violently.

While the others worked, Malcolm went his own way, riding out on Ebony for several days' absence at a time, or sitting before a lamp writing, sketching—ever silent. Not even Milford dared yet engage Erskine in conversation.

All knew that when their leader was ready to instruct them, he would do so. For the time being he was evidently satisfied with Abe's administration of the band, else he'd have issued swift and sharp instruction to the contrary.

Rose Deerfoot took charge of keeping the lodge tidy, aided from time to time by young Ralph Lykins. She also shared cooking duties with Jeremiah Adams. Milford had placed Ezra Renfro in charge of keeping track of supplies.

To Peter Iverson went the principal responsibility of attending the needs of the horses, seeing they were corralled properly, fed, watered, kept free of illness or predators. Iverson undertook construction of two crude pole barns to shelter the animals, with the help of the new men from Paola.

Abe had tried to make known to Malcolm shortly after Christmas his worry that Iverson might still warrant suspicion as the spy among them. But Erskine settled that in one brief incident, much to Milford's apparent relief—

It happened that one of the new young men from the Paola settlement—Daniel Goodman—called attention to rotting corpses lying half a mile from their camp. He reported that breaks in the weather had caused them to stink, which justified their burial. "At least a decent grave for the man you said was one of you."

Though Goodman was addressing Milford at the time, Erskine overheard and said, simply, "Let Baxter rot." From that, Abe concluded Malcolm had deduced, finally, who it was that had betrayed them to the late Bill O'Brien.

Goodman had a talent for carpentry. With a few tools he'd brought, and in spite of their lacking easy access to a sawmill, he crafted a sturdy cabinet, comfortable chairs, and other household furnishings.

They continued sleeping on the crude bunks they'd built before the Paola group joined. Rose showed them how to make better mattresses, miraculously producing bolts of cotton, spools of thread, and needles with which they learned to fashion bedclothes and mattress covers.

Rose fed the fire with the moss they'd originally gathered as bed stuffing. She set herself and others to collecting and storing the down and feathers of game fowl that Adams bagged. These she boiled and dried, gradually producing a more satisfactory stuffing for each bed. She offered the first such mattress to Erskine. He rejected it glumly and spread a blanket on the dirt floor near the fire, continuing to use that as his sleeping place whenever he was in camp.

All knew that Malcolm and Rose had accepted silently an ambiguous kinship as in-laws, even reopening contact with the Black Bob Shawnees despite Rose's banishment from the tribe. Though a few of the men expressed fears the Indians might betray their whereabouts, a simple command from Erskne ended talk of that. "Stow it!" he'd barked one morning to cut off such a conversation. And that was that.

The political talk ran to what the reconvening Congress in Washington might do as a result of its investigation of border troubles. And there was speculation whether President Pierce, in his final year in office, might alter the bloody course on which he and Congress had set people of the frontier by means of the troublesome Kansas-Nebraska Act.

They knew the truce Governor Shannon arranged during the siege of Lawrence couldn't last once the weather broke. Missourians had been shamed by the incident. They would seek satisfaction.

Upon his return from reconnoitering one evening, a weary Erskine summoned Ralph Lykins and three of Lykins's comrades from Paola—Alfred Willoughby, Eb Tolle, and Calvin Durham.

"Can you make dynamite?" Malcolm asked.

Ralph scratched his head and turned to Tolle, who nodded and replied, "How many sticks and what kind of fuses?"

"Eight sticks," Erskine said. "Bind every two with a weight that'll break a glass pane when thrown. Fuse no longer than it takes five seconds to burn."

"By when?"

"Tomorrow sundown."

Lykins and his group went to work, knowing the assignment would require precision and considerable caution.

Erskine sat at the table and looked toward Rose, who quietly held up a pot as a sign of offering coffee. He nodded, and she served him. She lingered and stood near him, evidently wishing Malcolm to become aware she'd taken to grooming and bathing. When he made it apparent her close presence wasn't worth his attention, she moved away grumbling in her Shawnee language.

Abe Milford saw an opportunity to break several weeks' near-total silence and sat. "It's time we talked," he said.

"No, it isn't," Malcolm said. "The dynamite is for me to use. The rest of you stay here."

"I wasn't even thinking about that," Abe said. "I trust that whatever it's for, you can handle it. What I'm worried about is you."

"I'm all right."

"Malcolm, you're like a walking dead man. The men—and Rose—don't know what to do to bring you back to the world of the living, to make you feel like our leader that we honor and trust."

Erskine turned to his friend. "They're doing all right. You run a fine camp, Abe. Just keep it going. There's much work ahead." He sipped coffee and indicated Rose. "As for her, let her choose someone in the band, and you read the book over it. Make it holy if not entirely legal. I won't have any whoring here."

"It's you she wants, believing it's her right. I think she truly craves you."

"Let it go, Abe. Besides, that skinny, savage hog-lady is more Christian than I'll ever be, despite her one murderous sin. She may even turn out worthwhile, now that I look at her. But not me."

Abe reached across to put a hand on Malcolm's shoulder. "Whatever it is, Malcolm, tell me. It's eating on you something fierce."

"I'm the worst sinner ever to walk the face of the earth," Erskine said. "There's not an evil in God's storehouse of judgment I haven't committed by now, except maybe treachery."

"What happened at the poor farm?" Milford pressed. "Time we talked about it."

"I'd rather not. It's revolting."

"Malcolm, you've got to let it out. You've got to break this mood. We need you. We need to know what comes next for the group we've put together."

"In due time."

"Tell me what you've done that I don't already know. You owe me that. I don't like reminding you, I saved you from a trial that would have led to your hanging."

Erskine turned and studied his friend. "I'll never forget my obligation to you, Abe. But it's hard for me to speak of my sin. It's truly awful and will put me in hell for certain."

"Say it. Say it low, so the others don't hear."

Malcolm sat back and looked down at the table, staring at a ring left by the coffee mug he'd moved aside.

Sighing, then slowly, so quietly that Abe Milford had to lean forward to hear, Erskine said, "I've been humping my own sister. I didn't know it at the time, but I think she knew all along."

33

Later in the evening Malcolm saw Rose pull Milford aside to talk. Before he made his confession he might not have noticed such things. But the relief from having shared his darkest secret with Abe seemed suddenly to reawaken interest in those around him.

He presumed Rose was again pressing her kinship claim which, if carried to a conclusion acknowledging ancient tradition, would have placed the hog-lady at his side, as his wife.

Erskine shuddered at the thought. There was no doubt she was his sister-in-law, as half-sister to Sylvia. Sudden realizations of sibling relationships were a new kind of nightmare.

There was little doubt Rose was a resourceful woman for one so unappealing to him in appearance. In some ways she reminded Malcolm of Sylvia, but not in looks nor build nor—odor. She was high-spirited and strong for one so small and thin. Extremely powerful, and quick. Proportioned like a boy, but *not* a boy, and possessing obvious designs on him. Better that she should select any of the other men.

Whomever she might choose would become well-propertied for life. There was much a man could do with two hundred acres. There was much *he* could do, if he weren't busy stalking enemies and organizing a retaliatory striking force against Bushwhackers.

Erskine looked around the lodge and rose from where he'd remained seated at the table.

"Men!" he called out. "Men, quiet down! Let me have your attention."

They gathered in a semi-circle before him, some seated on their cots, some folding their legs under them and sitting on the dirt floor near the fireplace.

"I apologize for being so out of sorts for so long. I commend every one of you for your patience, your loyalty, your industry, your good spirits. My sincere thanks go to Abe for providing leadership during my prolonged withdrawal. I want none to fear I've weakened in any way. I've had personal problems to work out. One of them is about to be solved completely, or nearly so."

From the corner of his eye, Erskine noticed Abe moving to a better listening position to catch the meaning of that, probably anticipating that it had something to do with the dynamite order.

"As you know I've been taking revenge for the murder of my dear wife, a truly remarkable woman, underrated in life even by me."

Now Rose appeared, moving alongside Milford to listen.

"Tomorrow night there'll be a meeting among the surviving assassins. Their purpose is to plan a strategy for my capture. They're weary of being stalked and seeing their numbers killed off. I know exactly where the meeting will be—an isolated place east of Dallas. I know what time it's to start, the layout of the small, ramshackle cabin where it's to be held, and who'll be present. My only fear is that one, Hank O'Brien, will be missing from the group."

Abe spoke up. "That still leaves nine. Malcolm, you *can't* tell us you're going up against nine men by yourself."

Ezra Renfro called out, "We'll go *with* you." Others echoed Renfro's pledge of help.

Malcolm held up a hand to restore silence. "Never mind. I appreciate what you're trying to do. But I've involved you in my own vengeance too long. That's not the true purpose of our being together. It's not right that I should expect you to solve my problem. And this is solely my problem.

"Here's how it will be— Tomorrow sundown, precisely, I'll leave Camp Branch for Missouri, taking the dynamite being prepared by Ralph and Eb and Calvin and Alfred. There's not the slightest question in my mind I'll succeed.

"On the slim chance I don't, on the chance I fail to return by midnight tomorrow, then I leave it to you all to decide whether to continue under Milford's leadership, or whether to disband and return to your homes."

"*I* can't lead these men in battle," Abe confessed. "None of us is seasoned enough in that."

Erskine nodded. "That's why I suggest you have the option of disbanding. But it won't come to that, for here's my pledge to all of you. I *will* succeed tomorrow night. I *will* return. And the very next day, as there seems to be approaching a mild break in the winter, we'll undertake a rigid program of training.

"Every trick used by Bushwhackers I'll teach all of you. Every element of scouting, attacking, use of a variety of weapons, occasions for retreat and reassembly—every method of counterattack, spying, masquerading— Every detail of survival I'll teach you so thoroughly that this outfit will be feared from St. Joseph to the Indian Territory.

"The proslavers will know when they inflict evil on innocent farmers and ranchers in Kansas, when they interfere with free elections, when they use terror to force their will on free men and women, they'll pay a deadly price at our hands. That's what we're here for. And that's, by God, the way it'll be."

The Jayhawkers voiced their lifted spirits. Cheers rang through the lodge. The young lads of Paola slapped one another on the backs in enthusiasm. Abe beamed over the clear sign of leadership renewed in Malcolm.

Rose managed a smile, the first Malcolm remembered seeing from her. He shook off the brief distraction of it and resumed speaking.

"Tomorrow, Iverson, check the horses carefully, for we must use them the day after in our training. Ezra, consign for the training period enough ammunition for three days' practice. Adams, consider what food must be carried for field operations to include at least one overnight encampment. Goodman, help Abe draw a schedule for rifle practice, revolver practice, whether on foot and running or mounted and riding. Rose, you know this land, so advise Goodman where to set targets in both wooded areas and open ground."

As an afterthought, Malcolm asked, "How many knives have we?" Four hands went up. He unbuckled his belt and pulled at the sheath containing his Bowie, sliding it off. "Which of you served as a blacksmith apprentice—Eb Tolle?"

"Yes," Eb called out.

"When you're done with the dynamite, make drawings of this. Goodman can help with the design. We'll have to build a small forge and find good steel. Over the next two weeks I want enough of these made to equip each man."

A movement by Rose caught his attention. He corrected himself. "I mean, to equip each member of our band. Return mine before I leave tomorrow."

Erskine rebuckled his belt and picked up his hat to leave the lodge.

"Where would you be going now?" Abe asked, obviously cheered by Malcolm's reclaiming leadership.

"To one of the horse sheds. I've much thinking still to do, Abe, for tomorrow night's mission isn't quite so easy as I've made it sound. I've nine or ten men to kill and must be relaxed in my mind to be clear in every move I make."

Abe nodded.

After Malcolm had been at the horse shed awhile smoking, he heard someone approach from the lodge. It was Rose. She'd fixed her coal-black hair and evidently bathed again. More and more, that was becoming a habit in her small room sectioned away. She'd changed into a beaded yellow buckskin dress and gave forth a pleasing artificial scent, a hint of lilacs.

Rose was silent and hoisted herself to sit on a rail beside Malcolm, placing her hand in his. He felt intermittently a pressure in her touch—nonverbal questioning through their handclasp. His longing to erase the stain of sin he'd committed with Jane-Ellen overtook him. He found himself responding to Rose Deerfoot, gladly.

*****

At sundown the following day, Erskine gathered the dynamite packets, placed them in a burlap bag, and suspended the bag from the pommel of his saddle. He mounted Ebony and rode north. He would follow unused routes to the vicinity of Dallas, approximately ten miles north and a mile or so east, smack on the border.

Malcolm avoided all settlements, sometimes strolling or trotting Ebony over now familiar ground of the vast area called Santa Fe Township. After two hours, by nightfall, he reached his destination east of Dallas without having encountered a living soul.

In the moonlight, outside the old cabin where his enemies gathered, he recognized from descriptions several of the horses in a nearby corral. Hank O'Brien's was not among them. He peeked through a window from two angles and counted nine men, all on his list. He circled the place and again—for he'd scouted here days earlier—estimated distances between windows and the approach he would use. There were four windows, two each on opposite sides, none on the ends of the cabin.

He felt for his matches. He lifted the burlap sack from the pommel and withdrew a weighted twin dynamite charge.

Erskine lighted the first charge, crashed it through a window, and moved on to the next. As the second broke through the pane, the first exploded amid shouts by those inside. Before a second explosion, he'd already lighted and released the third set of dynamite sticks on the other side. Then the fourth. He ran from the cabin to avoid fall-away effects of the explosions.

None inside escaped.

The cabin burned quickly.

Malcolm leaned on a rail of the corral and rolled a cigarette. He would wait for the fire to calm down some and then poke around.

34

Malcolm sought to reconfirm identities of the dead. Personal papers that hadn't burned he took from their pockets and read by firelight. He became doubly certain the nine charred bodies belonged to Sylvia's slayers.

Erskine called Ebony. He felt little remorse over what he'd just done. He mounted and began to head back to Camp Branch. If anyone lived within the sound of the explosions, none came to the scene nor blocked his leaving. Malcolm knew he had caused innocents to become widows and orphans, and he regretted that. He tried to move beyond guilt for wrecking families.

Costs of war, he told himself. *Bloody shame.*

Erskine arrived at Camp Branch about twenty minutes before midnight, approximately the time he predicted he would return. He found the entire company awake and now evidently breathing easier at the sight of him.

"Go to bed," he instructed them gently. "We have hard days ahead of us."

They did as he said—all but Rose Deerfoot, who boiled Malcolm a rich cup of cocoa and sat with him as he drank quietly. "You're tired," she observed. He nodded. "Where will you sleep?" He indicated his usual place on the floor by the fire.

"No," Rose said. "They all know and approve. There is your place now." She lifted her chin to indicate her room.

Pausing in his sipping, Malcolm glanced toward the sectioned area where Rose maintained some privacy. Then he looked back at her.

"Only because I can't dishonor you by refusing. Not because I wish very actively that it be so."

She smiled with obvious irony and shook her head on hearing his reasoning. "I'll work on making your wish more, uh, 'active'."

"You know I feel no deep passion toward you, Rose."

Her smile faded. "Let's face it, Malcolm. At this point in your life, you feel nothing." She got up abruptly and went to her room.

Erskine sat thinking about her latest words. Soon he put down the mug and walked to the entrance of the room. Rose was already lying in bed, a candle burning on a nightstand.

"You're right," he said softly, so as not to awaken the others. "But I don't *want* you to be right in that. You can help me."

In a swift movement, Rose slid naked from under the covers and stepped to him, throwing her strong arms about him and embracing him with a strength of which he'd never thought a woman capable.

She sought his mouth for a kiss and held him in that. Then, drawing back, her dark eyes probing his, she said, "At times you are ice. But I am fire. I must and *will* melt you, being careful you don't extinguish me."

"I have no intention of marrying you, you understand."

"I know that," she said, taking his hand and leading him. She sat on the bed. "I know that, Malcolm. You owe me nothing, for you've already given me more than I'd ever hoped to find in this wilderness."

He stared at her body in the candlelight, slender as that of a young girl but well-formed and starting to excite him.

Rose said, "After my wandering and becoming a brooding outcast, you helped me realize I'm more than a 'hog-lady,' a Shawnee without a tribe. I'm more than the tough boy some would mistake me for, if I didn't wear dresses. Those realizations are part of what you've already given me." She squeezed his hand and looked deep into his eyes, "And best? The knowledge that I'm a true woman, capable of loving a man."

Malcolm began to unbutton his shirt, and Rose unfastened his belt and undid his trousers and sought him all over with her love-hungry mouth.

He closed his eyes and whispered, "That you are, Rose. A true woman."

* * * * *

The Jayhawker band used the next several days of cooperating weather vigorously. The horses' steps seemed livelier. The men showed a keenness and willingness to learn. The occasions for camaraderie arose more frequently, in spite of the military atmosphere of the training program.

Malcolm shared all techniques of traditional Shawnee tracking, as well as use of all senses for recognizing meaningful signs of an enemy. He taught riding both saddled and bareback for warfare. He taught shooting accurately while running on foot and at full gallop astride horses.

After demonstrating the weighted effect of knives and hatchets, he showed the men—and Rose—skills of close fighting as well as accurate throwing. He encouraged wrestling as a way of learning physical balance and their own muscle structure. He taught how to deflect and use others' physical attack force to bring them quickly to disadvantage. He said this last method of fighting was taught him by an Asian sailor on a dock at New Bedford, that its skills required concentration, keen self-awareness, hair-trigger timing.

In wrestling, Rose proved the most adept pupil, pitting her mere hundred pounds against men nearly twice that weight. By effective and unerring use of all the leverage her strong, bony body provided, she upset the best of them.

Their appetites grew from the exercises. Jeremiah Adams gladdened them by dragging a deer from the woods by rope tied to his saddle. The deer carcass provided a few evenings' feasting. At night they fell into their cots wearily, happy in the knowledge they were better prepared to face their enemies.

At times the conversation turned to cravings for female companionship, but Malcolm wouldn't let anyone wander to Penelope Taylor's, as some suggested. He feared their being caught off guard by Bushwhackers, or returning to the lodge diseased.

Instead he asked Ralph Lykins to plan an outing, whenever cold weather might renew its numbing force and rule out training till another break. In Paola the men could develop acquaintanceships with decent and clean young women. In subsequent visits there they could pursue more responsible relationships.

Abe Milford seemed restless and dispirited when talk turned to such subjects as courting and raising families. Only recently bereaved by murderous proslavers near Lawrence, he tended to grieve silently for long periods over his loss.

Malcolm, seeing that, knowing a close companionship had developed between Abe and Rose, encouraged her to continue providing Milford sympathy and platonic warmth. Her attentions seemed to bring Abe around again.

"He's a good man," she told Malcolm one night in their room.

"Yes," Erskine said, smoking, thinking back. "He saved my life."

"I'm afraid you may both be expecting me," Rose said carefully, thoughtfully, "to hold his heart in my hands."

Malcolm at first brushed that off in denial. But on considering her deeper meaning, he turned and asked, "Could you?"

She nodded unhesitatingly. "If not for you, I could. He's a very good man."

Erskine looked at her profile as she evidently continued thinking on the subject. He asked, "Do you both talk about me, the way you and I discuss him?"

"Of course," she admitted freely, turning to Malcolm. "We are all family now. Why not? Would it surprise you to know that the need to sustain *your* happiness is probably Abe's chief concern?"

"No," Malcolm said, shaking his head, turning away again. "It wouldn't surprise me. He's been like a father, having lost his own children."

A few evenings later, Erskine accidentally overheard them. Rose and Abe had been talking when he started around a corner inside the lodge. He paused to listen—

"Egyptian," Malcolm heard Abe say, "gone since he was a child. I wonder—"

"What?" Rose asked.

"Oh, it's crazy."

"Tell me."

"It's too wild to consider."

"Abe, I'll throw you across the room if you don't spit out what's on your mind."

"Well," he said, haltingly, "the woman would have to be someone my age or older, possibly lighter than most Negresses, being from North Africa—"

"Go on."

"You say she'd been an entertainer—a dancer. Therefore, possibly well-figured, maybe even attractive in middle age."

"If you don't get on with—"

"Wait, Rose, wait. You know, a number of escaped slaves made their way to Lawrence and settled nearby. I've seen and talked with them, and— Rose, I think I *know* such a woman."

35

Ralph Lykins said, "I ran into Hickok. He was just leaving Paola. He shared information that'll interest you."

Malcolm, wielding a broom, was clearing snow from an overhang above the cabin door. News of Hickok caught him off guard. "What kind of information?"

"It sounded very tentative, but I think he's trying to get you back in the good graces of the Free State Party. And he wants a pardon for you from Governor Shannon. For himself, he's dickering with folks at Monticello about what they'll pay him to be constable."

"A pardon for me?" Erskine turned and spat. "I don't need a pardon."

"Yes, you do, Malcolm. Unlike the rest of us, you're a man without a country, an outlaw on both sides of the border. That's not good."

"Did you talk with Hickok privately? Just the two of you?"

"Yes," Lykins said. "I was surprised to find him so young—younger than I am."

"Did he mention John Brown?"

"He did. John Brown's settled in Osawatomie. He's formed a band similar to ours, except it's centered around his family, mostly his sons. Also he's helping escaped slaves."

"Well, then," Erskine said by way of settling a fact, "that leaves me no friends stationed in Lawrence. What makes Hickok think Lane and any other Free State leaders give a damn about me?"

"Hickok says they're all uneasy about the truce Shannon brokered with the Missourians. He thinks the Law and Order bunch will return to Lawrence, and next time they won't wait at the river but will sweep in and destroy the place."

Erskine considered that a moment. Then he said, "Lawrence's people can ward off an attack. Or they'll muster help."

"Hickok says they're not sure they can. They don't think the invaders will show their hand so clearly next time. They'll probably take the city by surprise."

Erskine rubbed his forehead vigorously, a habit he'd taken up under stress and frustration. "Thanks, Ralph. I'd hoped to hear that Lane acknowledged I've been right in all I've done, despite bloody consequences. But I see now he needs me to help stall or cripple or at least give another timely warning of the next invasion."

"That's the long and short of it," Lykins said, nodding.

"Arrange to get word to Hickok at Monticello," Malcolm said. "He and I should talk."

*****

On a clear, dry day in mid-February, Jeremiah Adams rushed into the lodge. He said Bushwhackers from Watts Mill had terrorized settlers in the northern part of Santa Fe Township—farmers. Homes and barns had been set afire, two or three men wounded, stock slaughtered—"and worse," Adams added.

"How, 'worse'?"

"Two of their women have been carried off."

"How long ago?"

"Less than an hour. One of the Black Bob Shawnees rode up to tell me, seeing me hunting. They know what we're all about and where we are, the Indians do."

"It was just a matter of time for the Shawnees," Erskine said. "Tell everyone, hand weapons and mount up."

Malcolm watched the men prepare and assemble, buckling gun belts, checking the positions of their knives. Rose approached. "Let me ride with you."

"No. You may be with child."

"I'm going. Later it will be risky for me to ride out."

"I said *no!*"

"We're wasting time. I'm going." Rose Deerfoot strapped revolvers and her knife around her slim, trousered hips and rushed out to join the others.

Standing alone in the lodge doorway, Erskine raised his eyes heavenward. "Lord, ain't leadership a bloody burden?"

Iverson led Ebony forward. Malcolm swung up and pointed the way.

The Jayhawker band pounded earth at full gallop toward the Santa Fe Trail, six miles north. Fording the Blue River easily, they continued up the rocky slope of the valley and rode hell-bent over the plains.

The well-worn Santa Fe highway on the ridge carried them in a few minutes over the remaining couple of miles east to the border. There they turned north to Dallas and Watts Mill.

Keen-eyed Jeremiah pointed to dust rising east of the milling community, Bushwhackers riding away hard. He pointed to where Indian Creek could be jumped by the horses so as not to lose time.

Two of the animals faltered, those of Eb Tolle and Ralph Lykins. "Try again!" Erskine shouted from the north bank as the others continued to pursue the Missourians. Eb backed his horse off and bent into a dash toward the creek, sailing across easily and inspiring Lykins to try the same.

"Come on!" Malcolm commanded. Seconds counted. Lykins looked as though he'd just as soon not be in this, but he set his lips firmly and imitated Tolle's example. He jumped Indian Creek and from that instant kept the pace.

That left Erskine behind the others. He bent low to where he could speak encouragement into Ebony's ear. "Show them what you can do." They soon overtook all in the company.

Malcolm drew a revolver and held it aloft, showing others they should also draw. He continued toward the dust cloud, their distance from it closing. About a dozen Bushwhackers were up ahead. Two in the lead rode with women caught between them and the reins—and that's what seemed to have slowed them.

Erskine figured they also must have dawdled on their return from the farm raid, to show off their captives to loafers at Watts Mill. When the Bushwhackers saw dust in the sky from Malcolm's approaching group, they must then have decided to high-tail it east.

Malcolm squeezed off a shot at the hindmost rider, catching him in the shoulder but not dislodging him from his horse. Another shot hit the Bushwhacker in the neck, and that brought him down.

Abe Milford held a rider in his sights and brought him down with the first bullet.

One of the Bushwhackers turned half around to see two empty horses at the rear. He seemed uncertain whether to surrender or continue on. That second's hesitation cost the man his life, for Peter Iverson got him in the heart.

From the corner of his eye, Malcolm was aware of something he'd never expected. Riding a pinto without holding reins, Rose goaded her small horse into passing the mighty Ebony, a revolver in each hand. She approached to within two or three horse lengths of the fleeing Bushwhackers.

First with her right hand and then with her left, she began a barrage of shots that took down three men. It was all she could do to keep her pinto on its path, from bodies spinning out of saddles onto the ground and the victims' confused horses veering away.

Malcolm saw the leader of the Missouri group raise his hand to halt for surrender, half his force gone. They drew up near a stone fence that they might have had difficulty jumping anyway. It was over for them.

"You've got us outfought and outnumbered," the leader said to Erskine, panting. "I suppose you're going to try to hang us on Missouri soil, which'll be your death if you do."

"Wrong!" Malcolm said. "We didn't outfight you, because you didn't fight at all. You're all yellow cowards who know only to terrorize innocent farmers. As for hanging you, I'll come back and pull the rope personally if one of the Kansans you hurt happens to die....Take their papers," Malcolm instructed members of his band. "Anything they've got for identification. I want to know all about these men and those back there on the ground. No telling what I'll learn. Help those women down. We're taking them back to their homes. That's all we really rode here to accomplish."

The "women" turned out to be girls, sisters of fifteen and seventeen. A few in Malcolm's band fell over themselves trying to show the girls every courtesy and consideration.

The younger sister was crying from fright. Rose aimed her pinto in a stroll to where the girl was standing and leaned from the saddle to extend a reassuring hand, smiling. "You're safe now," she said. Through tears and dust, the girl managed to smile back and nod happily.

Malcolm said, "I ever catch you in Kansas again—Walter Dunscomb is it?" He glanced at a paper, then at the leader. "You cross the border again, Dunscomb, I won't bother with hanging. I'll ride up and drop you wherever you stand."

"I ever go to Kansas again, Erskinigger, I'll do what they done your wife and take whatever slut is *now* your woman."

Daniel Goodman piped up with, "Uh-oh!"

Goodman and Erskine had seen Rose Deerfoot stiffen, hearing the Bushwhacker's words. All watched her ease her small horse slowly toward Duscomb, then dismount. She removed her gun belt and knife and set them on the ground.

Evidently recognizing the challenge and thinking he was confronting a long-haired Indian boy, Dunscomb willingly dismounted and dropped his gun belt as well.

Malcolm wondered whether there was really time for what he suspected was next. But he overcame his cautious side, curious and wanting to let Rose do whatever she was about to do.

36

Walter Dunscomb crouched in readiness for a free-ranging match—fists, wrestling, kicking, biting, anything but weapons. Such was the custom of hand-to-hand fighting.

Rose seemed just as ready as Dunscomb, though he had a considerable advantage of weight. His edge gave him cause to smirk, looking into Rose's angry eyes. Apparently he never doubted his opponent was a brash Indian brave trying to show courage in front of adult white friends.

Rose attacked first, simultaneously buckling one of Dunscomb's knees and locking his neck with her other arm. But the move proved a mistake, for the Bushwhacker was able to shake her off by regaining his footing. Rose went flying onto her rump, the other Bushwhackers laughing at the sight.

Instead of waiting for her to rise, Dunscomb turned to leap on his fallen opponent.

Rose evidently saw she could gain more by defensive maneuvers than by offensive ones. She might have moved away but didn't. Instead she brought her feet up to meet the Bushwhacker's face just at the right instant, jerking his head back with such force that his whole body followed.

The blow enraged Dunscomb, who scurried forward on hands and knees with a murderous growl. He doubled his fists and went for her groin, missing as Rose used her one advantage—speed—to escape.

Before she could rise to her feet, however, Dunscomb had Rose by the neck with a powerful left hand, pulling her toward him in a stranglehold she seemed unable to escape. Soon he had his right hand around her neck as well.

Abe Milford edged his horse forward and drew a revolver, but Malcolm waved him off. "No, Abe. It'll be a fair fight."

Abe sputtered in protest, obviously wanting to reveal to the fighting Missourian that Rose was a woman, but Erskine paid little attention.

In apparent realization there would be no intervention, no matter what, Dunscomb dared relax his grip to adjust to a better hold. But the relaxing was exactly what Rose needed to catch her breath and her presence of mind.

Imitating the doubled-fist action her opponent had earlier tried, she brought a blow to his groin that disabled him, causing him to release her neck completely and fall in a heap.

Even as he tried to regain his footing and thrash at Rose again, her light-footedness proved decisive. She found, upon Dunscomb's efforts to rise, that his face was lined perfectly with her most potent kicks. After getting in five or six such blows, Rose seemed to accept that it was all over.

She approached the bloodied and badly-beaten Bushwhacker and pulled at both sides of his shirt collar, saying into his dirtied face—loudly enough for his companions to hear and clearly in a woman's voice, "*I* am now Erskine's so-called slut, and sister to his dead wife. You still think you can do me *as was done her?* I should think," she said, directing her remarks now more to Dunscomb's aides than to him, "you're *shamed* for being beaten by a woman."

Malcolm, seeing she'd made her point, waved his revolver barrel toward the other Missourians to indicate they should leave. They did, one or two looking back in wonder that their leader had been unable to overcome a skinny squaw, shaking their heads and riding off.

Rose recovered her gun belt and knife and remounted, receiving cheers and pats on the back from her Jayhawker companions. Malcolm felt good about her glory, noticing and dismissing Abe's disapproval that he'd let it go on this way.

But just as he turned to lead his Jayhawkers and the two young women back to Kansas, Erskine caught a look from Dunscomb—one he'd not soon forget. The look was of such fierce hatred, it made Malcolm think again on a subject he'd confronted before—

Which was worse to his foes, steeped in Southern traditions—to kill them or shame them?

Clearly Malcolm had now been responsible for a violation of his enemies' sense of honor. Until a few moments ago, Walter Dunscomb was a defeated Bushwhacker, perhaps intimidated to the point of staying out of Kansas. Now, however, he was shamed beyond all reason and would be a new and insidious enemy, as was Hank O'Brien. That was an uncomfortable danger to have invited, Erskine realized.

* * * * *

By March Hickok had received and accepted an invitation to the Jayhawkers' lodge at Camp Branch. The understanding was that any lawman credentials he carried didn't extend that far, that he was out of his jurisdiction. Besides, he'd solicited the invitation and would have broken frontier propriety by making an arrest.

Daniel Goodman and Eb Tolle met Hickok riding in at an entrance to the encampment. They waved off the Shawnee who'd led Hickok there. They seemed about to ask the young constable to turn over his weapons when Malcolm rode up hurriedly. Erskine used a slight turn of his head as a sign to Goodman and Tolle to back off.

Hickok smiled, extended his hand to Malcolm, and chuckled. "No, they wouldn't have gotten my guns. But I wouldn't have shot them either, if that's what you were worried about."

"That's exactly what I was worried about. I'd forgotten to tell them never to ask for your weapons if you happened to show up here," Malcolm confessed. "How long can you stay?"

"I must be in Monticello before sundown. A rider there's waiting for me to give him word of your intentions, so he can carry news to Lane in Lawrence by tonight."

"Why am I so important to Lane now?"

Hickok turned fully to face Erskine, seeming amused. "'Why,' Malcolm? Don't be so modest. Don't you know you've built the finest little defensive force along the entire border? That if we had ten or twelve more like yours, we'd be secure till Congress can finally get around to statehood for Kansas?"

"Somehow I felt I'd one day be appreciated," Malcolm said, smiling, "but it had reached the point where I truly didn't give a damn."

"I don't believe that," Hickok shot back in quick disagreement. "You want a pardon. I *know* you do. I know you better than you give me credit for."

Malcolm stopped Ebony, and Hickok halted his horse alongside. "Tell me on what grounds I require a pardon. Every one of the men I've done in has been an enemy, fighting in the Missouri cause."

"A technicality. Malcolm, you got crossed up on a technicality. Think back," Hickok pressed. "Were they *all* Missourians?"

Erskine creased his brow, then the light of realization broke on his face. "Ah, yes. I keep forgetting about Zeke Larson."

"That's the one," Hickok said. "Citizen of Leavenworth, although on the Law and Order side. Lots of folks in Leavenworth are pressing to hang you for that alone. To hell with the other twenty or so you've plugged."

"But if I stood trial, with a jury of my peers— If I explained, I'd be ac—"

"Not acquitted, Malcolm. Convicted. See, you weren't always careful *where* you carried on your escapades. If you'd done it all here—even in Oxford—you'd maybe have been clean. If Larson hadn't been in the picture, you'd maybe have been all right. But some of it was in Douglas County, where law's firmly established. Technicalities of the law, my friend. You're not clean."

"What do I do?" He clucked Ebony forward again, Hickok riding along toward the lodge.

"Three things," Hickok said. "Accept a pardon. Swear allegiance to the Free State Party in behalf of your entire band and be ready to take orders. Help us train similar bands up and down the border."

Erskine thought. "And in return do I receive protection against Missourians hunting my head?"

"No. For that you're on your own. You'll have to take care of yourself."

"Thanks a lot," Malcolm said sarcastically.

"You're not worried you *can't* protect yourself, are you?"

"Not really," Erskine acknowledged. "Look, stay for coffee. Meet my group. Then send word back to Lane that I agree to all his terms."

Hickok reached a hand to Malcolm. They shook on it.

* * * * *

Within a few days, Erskine enjoyed the effects of being back in the good graces of Free Staters.

He received a brief letter from Governor Shannon pardoning him and those aiding his jail escape. He also received information about Bushwhacker operations that enlarged his own carefully collected data.

After months of official fugitive status, Malcolm would enjoy increased freedom west of the border. The purposes for which he'd organized his Jayhawkers would be helped by resources in Kansas, including financial support. He and his group could look forward to paying debts on supplies obtained in Paola and placing new orders.

Erskine was still reluctant to let too many Free Staters and allies know precisely where he and his band were holed up. Yet he realized it would be only a matter of time before Missourians would catch wind of their location and gather for a challenge.

Malcolm instituted more efficient systems of watch over the place, also insisting that Rose—now more clearly with child—never be left alone in the lodge while the others were chasing Bushwhackers.

To secure that, he'd successfully persuaded Black Bob Shawnee couriers to prevail upon the Chief for Rose's protection when warranted, despite her earlier banishment from the tribe. Accepting news of her condition, they and Chief Black Bob relented, principally because Malcolm's taking her as his woman honored a kinship custom. They accommodated Erskine's wishes.

During a foray into Missouri, in response to one by Bushwhackers into Kansas, an incident gave Malcolm a greater sense of belonging and of overall purpose.

Several of the Bushwhackers sought to occupy an isolated cabin for defense while Erskine's band was pursuing them. Malcolm, sitting astride Ebony, was horrified to see a Missouri woman, resident of the cabin, shoved out the front door to the ground. She held a baby in her arms and nearly lost her grip on the child.

Immediately Erskine dismounted and strode to the cabin, unchallenged by Bushwhacker guns. Others in the enemies' gang were evidently as shocked as Malcolm to witness their leader's lack of decency toward the mother and child.

Malcolm commanded the leader to step outside. Despite the Bushwhacker's drawing a revolver nervously, Erskine laced into the man with a speed and fury unmatched in his previous close encounters.

The Missourian let his gun slip to the ground and tried to defend himself with his hands and arms against Malcolm's hard-driving fists, but it was clear he'd soon be broken-faced and substantially lacking teeth.

"I've never seen him like that," Ralph Lykins observed to Abe Milford, loud enough for Malcolm to hear.

"I can understand it," Abe replied. "You're watching a man robbed of his sense of family. And he wants it back."

37

Milford approached Erskine outside the lodge one morning. "Let's talk, boss."

"Go ahead, talk," Erskine said while stretching a cleaned raccoon skin between two saplings.

"Not here," Abe said. "Let's ride out a bit. Everything's under control in camp."

They strolled to their horses, saddled up, and headed south on a leisurely and meandering course. "What's on your mind, Abe?"

"John Brown has made contact through Black Bob. He wants to meet with you."

"What in heaven's name is happening now? I select a place for its tight security," Malcolm said with gestures emphasizing his distress, "and soon comes evidence God and the whole world know where we are."

"Malcolm," Abe said in a mildly scolding tone, "how long did you really believe our whereabouts would stay secret?"

"Indefinitely. I don't like the fact so many are finding ready access to us. Next thing you know, it'll be Sam Jones or Hank O'Brien dropping by for tea."

"If you really believed Camp Branch was that secure," Milford responded, shaking his head, "then you're more naive than I took you for."

"Not naive. Just careful as possible," Erskine snapped.

"Correction," Milford said, holding up a hand. "Careful as reasonable. Too much to expect our comings and goings would forever stay secret among the Shawnees, or any on the Missouri side who saw us ride in by the same few trails. Be realistic."

Erskine sighed and shook his head. "You're right, Abe. It's my new responsibilities making me nervous."

"I know what you feel, but you should be less worried day by day. You've taught us enough to meet all dangers that lie ahead."

"What are you trying to say, Abe? Soon you won't need me as your leader?"

"I'm not saying anything of the kind. You *are* nervous. And I think it would be premature to arrange a new hideout. But while our position grows less ambiguous to others, the political situation affecting us grows moreso."

"How do you mean?" Erskine stared hard for an answer.

"A minute ago I called you naive. The message we get from John Brown," Milford said, "is that naiveté is what's placing the Free State Party in an extremely vulnerable spot. He knows a thing or two he wants to share with you and eventually others—with the younger men coming into leadership up and down the border."

"When?"

"He wants to come here tomorrow."

"Impossible," Erskine said. "Tomorrow I'm due in Gum Springs to start a training program for a new Jayhawker band. It's all arranged."

"Malcolm, form a committee among the others and send them. Learn to delegate some of your work, especially to those you've trained. Otherwise what was the good of the training?"

Erskine thought about the situation in Gum Springs, where settlers were talking of renaming the place Shawnee. The community was developing, strengthening, and so were its settlers' capacities for bold action. He stopped his horse. Ebony snorted, indicating he would rather move, perhaps canter. Malcolm leaned to pat the firm neck of his steed lovingly.

"Abe," Erskine said, "pick three who've shown the most progress in horsemanship, weaponry, and bivouacking. Send them."

"That would be Adams, of course, for the last. In weapons I'm impressed with Willoughby. And horsemanship seems to have taken hold of Iverson. The boy has come a long way since Lawrence."

"So be it. I'm ready for you to summon John Brown here."

* * * * *

Next day, the grizzled old man as legendary as Malcolm Erskine—in some ways more famous—rode into camp with two of his sons, Watson and Oliver, and his son-in-law, Henry Thompson. "The Lord bless and keep you," John Brown said in greeting Erskine.

"And God be with you as well, old friend," Malcolm replied. "Let this also be my first chance to thank you for helping Milford arrange my escape from jail."

"All in the interest of *living*"—Brown's emphasis was a rare jest, harking back to conversation at the border nearly six months earlier—"for the cause of freedom."

"In which cause," Erskine picked up with, "I'm at last prepared, if necessary, to die."

Brown, apparently delighted to hear such a commitment, embraced Malcolm warmly. "I pray the Lord reward you in the kingdom of heaven for your sacrifices of the past and those yet to be made."

"I don't know about that part of it," Malcolm said, "but thanks." He felt a warmth of spirit and purpose emanating from his charismatic mentor.

Introductions followed, Milford and Rose Deerfoot proudly showing the lodge to Brown's young men as the two independent-minded fighters in the Free State cause walked off together.

"There's no question in my mind," Brown told Erskine, "that General Lane provides sound leadership. But the situation is deteriorating for lack of coordination and dynamic resoluteness."

"I've heard some of that. What do you know that I should know?"

"Remember the young martyr of the Wakarusa, Thomas Barber?" Brown was referring to an incident during the early-December siege. Impatient Bushwhackers, camped in readiness for the Lawrence invasion that never occurred, killed a young Free State settler in cold blood about eight miles southwest of the city.

"Barber," Malcolm replied, "wasn't the only martyr. There were Milford's family and others."

"I know, I know," Brown said solemnly. "But for the moment let's speak of Barber. No doubt you've heard that one of the men responsible is George W. Clarke."

"I've heard that, yes."

"What's vexing is that Clarke enjoys the full protection of Governor Shannon and is one of the Governor's most intimate associates."

Erskine stopped in his path, digesting the full import of the news Brown had just revealed.

Brown continued. "Shannon has been called on the carpet in Washington for making an accommodation with Free Staters during the Wakarusa siege. Evidently President Pierce would rather that the Law and Order Party had overrun Lawrence. Clarke, as it happens, has extremely influential friends in Washington with whom Shannon has asked that bloody murderer to intervene, to save his political hide."

"So, Governor Shannon," Malcolm said, wanting to understand fully and spitting words bitterly, "is not only continuing to play both ends against the middle but consorting with proslaver murderers to do so."

"Exactly," Brown said. "And he lets General Lane believe his role as Governor is to balance the sides, bring Free Staters a measure of official protection."

"You want me to assassinate Shannon?" Erskine asked. "I'm the nearest fighter who can do it. He continues to use Johnson's Shawnee Mission as a base. I can go into disguise and make it look like the work of a Bushwhacker. Say it and it's done."

"No," Brown said, continuing their walk, shaking his shaggy head. He gazed at the ground. "I have a better plan—actually a principle to promote—one prompted by my thoughts of the Barber incident."

"Which is?"

"To persuade Lane and other Free State leaders toward an aggressive policy of 'eye for an eye.' Not a single known Law and Order murderer must be allowed to walk the Lord's ground unpunished, for a start. Nothing will so impress Missourians and Washington as the absolute policy of retributive justice."

"I'm with you totally in that," Erskine agreed. "I've long been impatient with the political maneuverings, the competing legislative conventions as means of effecting statehood for Kansas. Our side, the only legitimate side, should have a uniform policy to press under martial conditions."

"You're quick to see it, Malcolm," Brown said. "The Lanes and others of Lawrence must show Shannon they no longer accept his compromising and weak rule. They ought to deepen, declare more fully, their independence of him and institute martial law for as long as necessary. Arrange a retaliatory execution each time it's warranted."

"And I suppose," Erskine said, "I'm the one who's supposed to persuade Lane in that direction."

"*I* can't get involved in Lawrence right now," Brown replied, "so it must be you. I'm too occupied with receiving escaped slaves, caring for them, feeding them, finding them places inside the Territory where they'll be safe and free."

"But such work as that drains our strength and resources," Malcolm protested mildly, "at a time you and the Osawatomie group are needed for fighting."

Brown smiled. "Helping the Negro, I might remind you, Malcolm, *is* our strength. I must do both."

Erskine nodded. "Of course. I'll go see Jim Lane. Should I take Hickok with me?"

"That's unnecessary. Let him stay in Monticello. Lane respects you more than ever, believing the pardon has somehow cleansed you."

"Milford says you believe Lane to be naive. I see more clearly what you mean. Yes, I'll talk to him."

"Martial law committed aggressively to a policy of 'eye for an eye,' Malcolm," Brown repeated. "Nothing less. Lane must convince Robinson of that. These Jayhawker chases into Missouri aren't enough. The full authority of the Free State Party must support our ridding the countryside of at least one proslaver for every free man who has died. Full policy commitment. Let's deal with proslavers in the only language they understand—*violence.*"

When Brown spoke that last word, Malcolm saw the fire of strong commitment leap into the old man's eyes. He nodded and said, "For my part, not knowing how Lane will respond, consider it done, my friend. A proslaver, guilty or innocent of other transgressions, for every victim on our side."

*****

When Erskine told Abe Milford of his plan for seeing General Lane in Lawrence, Abe bit his lip. "What distresses you?" Malcolm asked.

"Nothing. Well, it's not the plan that bothers me. I can understand such a principle. Maybe you can persuade Lane to it, though I'd be surrendering some of my Christian ethic to fully support an Old Testament notion. No, it's something else I haven't wanted to tell you, not knowing how."

"I think I know what it is. I overheard you and Rose conspiring."

"There's a woman in Lawrence. Mind you, Malcolm, I don't know about this for certain."

"I recall you once spoke of a 'Della.' My mother's name was Dahlia. You think perhaps—"

"Yes, Malcolm. I think there's a chance, from what you've told me, that she's your mother."

Erskine's heart beat wildly. "I haven't fully believed it was possible, even after hearing Rose and you speak of that. Not after all these years. But now that I'm going to Lawrence—"

"Pay her a visit," Milford urged. "I— I could be wrong. But find out. You'll never be at peace with yourself until you do."

38

Rose was taking what Malcolm thought an unusually long time to come to bed. "When will you quit washing and fussing with yourself? I have a long ride, a lot to do tomorrow."

"One moment," Rose said. She'd combed her black hair and was pampering it into waves that had appeared in washing and drying. Her nightdress was fresh. She'd scented herself in a way evoking memories of Sylvia, a sweet muskiness through which he recognized only the faintest of her customary lilac.

"You're beautiful," Erskine said when she turned around in the lamplight.

"I love you for saying that," Rose replied, "but I'll never believe it's true."

"Something's been added by your impending motherhood."

Rose looked down at her belly. "It shows that much?"

"Not unflatteringly," Malcolm said. "There's a new light in your eyes, a new self-confidence in your face—your demeanor."

"However much I've become a woman," Rose said, "is due entirely to you. When you're finally gone from me, I—"

"What do you mean, 'finally gone' from you, as though permanently?"

Rose sat on the bed and brought a hand gently to Malcolm's face, framing it on one side, stroking his cheek. "Dearest, I've long known our love will never find the depth and substance it requires for permanence. You've known it, too. No—don't respond just yet. I'm grateful you did the right thing bringing me here to my land. I'm grateful you helped me meet my tribal responsibility, letting me become your mate in common law. Had we wished more, we'd have sought the circuit Methodist minister."

Malcolm turned to kiss the palm of her hand repeatedly, half-regretting and a little ashamed he'd held back in their relationship.

"It's all right," Rose said. "You owe me nothing more, except as I ask this one last night together. You've given me so much—*so much.*"

Erskine, for all his manly self-control, began dripping tears into her hand. "I know," Rose said soothingly. "I know your torture. The woman you're convinced is your half-sister is still the only woman you've ever *truly* given your greatest passion. It's hard for you as a loving man and as a person of principle."

Malcolm sought to speak but couldn't. He tried to halt tears but couldn't.

"Dearest Malcolm," Rose said. "Sylvia became your substitute mother, little more. She was both comfort and teacher to you. She knew it and wanted nothing but to serve you that way. She told me that." Rose sought the best eye contact the candlelight would allow. "Through your need, *her* life found meaning. Through your more recent need, *my* life has found meaning. Now we must all work on *your* happiness."

Malcolm reached for a cloth to dry his face, to blow his nose. He sat up slowly, looking around for his cigarette papers and tobacco.

"No," Rose said, "you don't need to smoke." She raised herself fully onto the bed and put her strong arms around him. "After tonight," she whispered into his ear, "our lives must go separately. We both know it. But through tonight we still belong to each other."

* * * * *

The following day Erskine took leave of his Jayhawkers, glancing back to see Abe place his arm around Rose. In Shawnee sign language she gestured to Malcolm, some sadness in her smile, "All our hearts are with you."

Abe waved, as though trying to communicate that Malcolm need not worry. Those remaining at Camp Branch would meet whatever was to come.

Erskine rode slowly at first then bent into his ride and spoke encouraging sounds to Ebony. The black stallion seemed livelier whenever he did that, and the ride became an easy prance over familiar ground.

They aimed for Monticello, where Malcolm wanted to see how his friends there were getting on. As he approached the place, he sensed a new peacefulness, apparently established by Hickok's settling there.

Among the first to notice Erskine's approach was Sam Garrett. He greeted Malcolm enthusiastically, instructing his son to summon Isaac Parish and John Owens to his cabin. Betsey Garrett embraced Malcolm and insisted he stay for lunch. "Where is Hickok today?" he asked the others.

"East of here at Gum Springs," Isaac said. "Actually, Shawnee. He's trying to persuade the townspeople there to become part of a constabulary that will include our own. He feels that will strengthen the peace of this northwestern area of the county."

"It will," Erskine agreed. "I wish all Free State settlements accepted rules of law and arranged for strong men to enforce them."

John Owens nodded and said, "That's the only way Kansas will rise from the hellishness of war, fulfill the peaceful purpose the white man's creating it for."

Betsey interrupted to say animatedly, "Creating it with the help of Indians and Negroes."

Owens smiled. "You're right. I'm too long in my upbringing with the false notion that whites are saviors to the world."

Malcolm thought on that brief exchange. The others continued debating the successes of resettling runaway slaves in separate communities north and west. They speculated aloud the future of unintegrated Indian tribes—the Wea and Piankeshaw, the Miami, Chippewa, Pottawatomie, Ottawa, and more than a dozen others.

Erskine finished eating while the others talked, picked up a napkin and ran it over his mouth. He heard the trailing end of a question put to him and asked, "What? What was the question?"

"Assuming we win the antislavery fight," Parish repeated, "what kind of state do you think we'll have, Malcolm? I mean its makeup. Its people."

"You want an honest answer?" Erskine asked. "Regardless how the races now mix easily on the frontier," he said with bitterness, "Kansas will be as Owens has frankly regarded it, a white man's land. Maybe better than most, freer than most, maybe not. But a white man's country nonetheless. And that," he said, flicking the napkin down beside his plate with a little more emphasis than necessary, then rising, "will stick in my craw."

"Oh, Malcolm," Betsey chided.

"I don't like seeing Indians moving out," Erskine said, preparing to take his leave. "I don't like seeing Negroes given separate corners of the Territory to settle in. I'll never understand why we can't all just be—" He sputtered, trying to find the right word. "*—people!*"

"You've been pardoned for the vengeance killings," Sam said, "because many of us believed it was wrong to treat you as a man without a country. Now you sound as though that's what you'll always be, regardless."

"I hope," Malcolm said, shaking hands all around in preparation to continue his way to Lawrence, "your half-Shawnee children need never learn what it's like. But yes. For as long as most whites categorize me as the black man I am—consign me to inferior status in some matters—I'll be 'without a country,' as you say."

"Then what do you want? What do you hope for? Why do you go on?" Garrett pressed, even as Erskine paused at the door before exiting.

"I still hope that a half-breed such as myself, such as any of your half-Indian children, will someday stand as a true equal to any of you three men—politically, socially—"

"As a matter of practicality, Malcolm—and I hate to be saying this—you wish for too much. You may as well wish for *women* to be so regarded equally."

"That, too. I wish only for what's right."

Without further bitterness, with only the warmest gratitude for such friends, Erskine left knowing he'd given the Monticello settlers something fresh to think about.

*****

Malcolm approached Lawrence speculating about the woman "Della" whom Abe had described. He talked aloud to Ebony. "It's been more than twenty years, good friend. Could it be true?" He was unable to calm his heart for its wild pounding.

It wasn't over Rose alone he'd wept the night before, as he remembered, but for all the significant women who'd entered and left his life. For lovely Sylvia. For the unerasable Jane-Ellen, despite his bitterness. And for Dahlia Bahari, his Egyptian mother, who'd quit New Bedford when white people shunned her.

On the main street—Massachusetts—he noticed several changes since he'd fled jail nearly four months earlier. Sturdier structures were in process of construction or had been completed. Earlier, nearly all the buildings had seemed temporary, too quickly thrown together. The new three-story Free State Hotel was imposing, a symbol of stability and prevailing notions of "progress" on the frontier.

That's where he was told to meet Lane, who evidently had been alerted to Erskine's arrival, for he came out into the street with his hand outstretched.

With Ebony hitched to a rail, Malcolm and Lane shook hands warmly. "Welcome, Citizen Erskine," the General said in acknowledgement of Malcolm's pardon.

"Nice to see you, sir. We have much to talk about."

"Perhaps you'd like to freshen up after your journey," Lane suggested.

"As a matter of fact, I would. I'll just go into the hotel and come back down, say, in a half hour."

"Oh! Well," Lane said in some embarrassment, "other arrangements have been made for you. You'll be more comfortable with people who've opened their home to you."

Malcolm glanced toward the hotel and the grinning Free Staters standing before it. They were watching the scene in the street with interest, some waving greetings to Erskine but making it clear by their casually armed presence that he was, in some respects, an outsider.

A pain shot to his head upon realization the Free State Party had not yet worked out the status of Negroes and half-breeds for such accommodations.

"Don't—" Lane said softly, noticing how the revelation affected Malcolm. "Don't make an issue of it, Erskine. We're still learning to live with the full consequences of what we've wrought."

Malcolm nodded. "If you don't mind my saying so, and I won't speak of it again, you're all a stinking bunch of damned, bloody hypocrites—*sir.*"

Surprisingly, Lane agreed. "You're absolutely right. But we're learning. Be patient."

"I should be patient? *Curse* you for saying that—to *me!*"

"I don't blame you. I'm working on it," Lane tried firmly to assure Erskine. "Some of us are hard at work on it."

"Where then do I stay?"

"With the café keeper, Della. She's expecting you. It's just down the street, on the left. You and I can meet in my office later. Take your time. Get yourself settled."

Without responding, Malcolm turned to Ebony. He released the tether and mounted. He stared solemnly and at length toward the group by the hotel, then spat into the dusty street and trotted off.

39

The homes of ex-slaves in Lawrence were more modest than those of whites but kept well. A few black men and women were tilling their yards for gardens. Seeing Malcolm among them, they paused to nod and smile, or wave and watch him pass.

A simple sign, "Della's," identified the inn and restaurant in the largest house of the city's Negro section. New doubts pulled at Malcolm, whether this was where he would find his mother. She was a literate woman who would never have allowed public bastardization of her real name, Dahlia. Erskine sighed over his certainty this would be a fruitless search. He dismounted and tethered Ebony and went in.

The place was gloomy, evidently not yet open for business. The shutters over all windows were closed. Malcolm bumped into one of a half dozen café tables before his eyes adjusted to the dimness.

No one was about. He heard no sound of anyone on the ground floor. Malcolm sought the kitchen, where he found the stove cold. There was no sign of recent activity, except for a sack of unwashed potatoes left on a counter and opened, as though soon to be used.

A door at the far end of the kitchen led to a yard and outbuildings. He saw a smokehouse and two privies. And there, stooped in the act of hauling up a bucket from a well, Malcolm saw the figure of a slender, barefoot woman. He watched.

From a distance he observed no clue to make him believe she might be his mother. She seemed drawn and tired, for someone who would be only a few years older than Sylvia was at death.

Erskine knew his mother had been a very young woman—a girl—when his father brought her to New England from Egypt. Adding her roughly nine years in New Bedford before she'd fled and twenty-one since he'd seen her, Malcolm calculated Dahlia Bahari would now be forty-seven.

The woman at the well grasped the handle of the filled bucket and turned. She faced Malcolm where he stood on the small landing by the back door. She surveyed him thoroughly, blinking against the sun. Then she reached to support the bucket with both hands.

Sensing it was heavier than she ought to be carrying, Erskine hurried down the steps and crossed the yard to take the bucket from her. As he did, he looked up and found her staring, smiling. He noticed she still had all her front teeth.

But even this close, he couldn't swear she was his mother. She looked somewhat like he remembered her—maybe. Still, was this the once loving woman who'd held him close, nursed him, read to him, bathed him, dressed him, comforted him, fed him, and taught him to do things for himself?

In a slow drawl not unlike that of most ex-slaves she lived among—her voice stronger than he expected—she said, still smiling, blinking, "Malcolm?"

This was not the reunion he'd yearned and dreamed about nearly his entire life. He nodded and sputtered, reflexively, "Yes'm."

"Don't you—recognize me?"

Erskine hesitated, then shook his head slowly. "Not entirely. Are you—" He choked on what he wanted to ask, but finally he got it out. "Are you—my mama?"

"Della" seemed amused. She placed a hand on her hip and twisted slightly away as though to get a better look at him. She said, "If you're Malcolm Erskine of New Bedford, Massachusetts, then I'm sure enough your mama."

Malcolm immediately let go of the bucket, causing it to spill. He sank to his knees. His hat, too, fell as he was gripped by unfamiliar emotions. He grasped at her hand to hold it close, to kiss it. He threw his arms around her knees and felt great sobs welling in his chest as he sought to cry out, "Mama! Mama!"—but speaking was difficult.

Erskine hesitated. "Are you – my Mama?"

A rush of strange feelings clouded everything, especially his vision. He bent to touch her bare feet and immediately fell to kissing them lovingly. At last he muttered audibly, "Mama....Mama...." As though doing so ritually, he kissed her feet again.

"Get up, son," he heard her command softly.

"Yes'm." He stood before her, a little amazed how much taller he was than she, remembering now that last time they'd faced each other he was a child.

"Hold me close," she said.

Effortlessly, Malcolm lifted her from the ground, half-afraid he'd break her, yet wanting to tighten his hug and keep her there. Then he heard her say, "You're blubberin' all over my neck, son."

Erskine put her down.

She hiked a thumb toward the well. "How about gettin' another bucketful? You spilled the first." While he reached to do as she instructed, Dahlia Bahari straightened herself from the roughness of their reunion and commented, "Now, *that's* what I call a greetin', sure enough."

Malcolm laughed, wondering how it was possible he was laughing while tears ran off his face into the well.

"When'd you see Papa last?" she asked.

"About— About a year ago," Erskine said with a slight stutter, nervous about this encounter, even about such a simple task as filling a bucket of water.

"I heard he hit the bottle bad after I left. Even lost his captaincy."

Malcolm nodded, finally getting the filled bucket in his grip, recovering his muddied hat. "Yes'm, it's true. But the settlement-house people straightened him around, and he was soon sailing again. And they took care of me, some."

"Couldn't have taken care of you very well," she said, snorting. "I heard you're a sure enough killer. Even killed men back in New Bedford."

He nodded again, looking at the ground. He didn't know why he felt ashamed. He'd never felt this way over anything he'd done. Regret, yes, but not this same brand of shame.

Then Malcolm realized he was playing out a relationship that had ended more than twenty years earlier. He was a child again, caught having done something wrong. And there was no one he would rather displease *less* than his mother.

"We've all done things, and had things happen to us," she said, "that none of us liked. Come on, son, let's go inside. I'll make you some potato pancakes."

Dahlia declined his offer of help in the kitchen and directed him to sit at a table. She washed and peeled the potatoes at the counter. She talked almost idly, moving by fits and starts into a recounting of her time away from Malcolm. She found an onion, peeled it, and then began grating all into a bowl. Malcolm moved his chair so he could watch her face as she spoke—

"I told your papa I wouldn't stay in a place where people were such hypocrites, talkin' about how evil it was that black folks were treated like dirt, then treatin' them like dirt themselves. We never did get married, you know. You're sure enough illegitimate, Malcolm, and I regret that, but—" She broke off, shrugged, shook her head, then went on.

"Other sea captains' wives were spiffyin' up every Sunday and traipsin' off to church on their husbands' arms. Me? I sat indoors a lot, mindin' you. I could hardly go anywhere for fear someone would say unkind things again—things to make me cry."

Dahlia paused and looked out a window over the counter. "Cry? Ha! You know, I'd give anything to be able to cry again. All the 'cry's' been taken out of me by what's happened over the years. I've seen everything there is to see about life and cruelty. Everything."

She reached into a cupboard and found eggs, flour, salt. "I told Morogh, much as it would break my heart, I might just go runnin' off by myself. I couldn't take any more humiliation, I said." She turned to face Malcolm. "Sorriest day of my life when I had to sneak off and leave you both, especially you, son. But I did it." She shook her head sadly. "Worst thing I ever did to myself." She turned to resume her work.

"If I thought myself humiliated *then* by bein' a half-black Egyptian livin' in white New Bedford, it was nothin' alongside the humiliations after that." She shook her head again.

Though Malcolm felt pain along with her, he wanted to find a way to ask about Jane-Ellen Mulligan—how it came to be that his mother had another child, one who could so easily pass for white. But he didn't dare interrupt her story. He felt ashamed even to think of Jane-Ellen at a time like this. No doubt his mother would come to that in time.

Dahlia struck a match and lighted kindling in the stove. She grabbed a frying pan from a hook and spooned lard into it. "Sorriest day of my life," she said with emphasis, "to leave bad for worse. I don't think I ever pined about leavin' Cairo, but I sure enough regretted walkin' out on you and Papa."

The lard soon crackled in the fry pan as Dahlia ladled in the potato mixture. Three scoops she kept separated from each other and watched closely. Malcolm got up and stood by her. The undersides of the pancakes flattened and sizzled in the grease. Dahlia held a spatula in readiness to turn them.

"I went to Providence," she said. "I thought I might find work there. I had the notion I might dance again, but none of the café owners was interested in a high-yaller who could wiggle around that way. They said it was indecent, the style of dancin' we did in the part of world I'd come from. Can you imagine?" she asked, turning. "Indecent. Why, it's an *art.*"

She shrugged and turned back to the stove, flipping the golden pancakes to fry their other sides.

"Wasn't long before I was down to my last twenty-five cents and walkin' along the street. A couple of drifters saw a chance to make some money off me. By the alley, one of them brought a sack down over my head. They carried me off and I heard them sell me for fifty dollars to a slaver. You know, durin' the bargainin', I almost hoped my captors would get the seventy-five dollars they'd asked, just so I'd feel worth the most I could feel, even knowin' *hell* lay ahead.

"I was put in a sort of big jail cell with maybe ninety-a-hundred other darkies. They gave us hardly a scrap to eat for days, and it stank like you wouldn't believe. Everybody was *scared,* those people, only they—we—were bein' treated like anything *but* people. Before long we were chained together and led aboard a ship," Dahlia said, "bound south for Baltimore. Some were fugitive slaves, some were fresh-brought from Africa, and some, like me, were free people abducted illegally and thrown in with the others."

His mother signalled Malcolm to hand her a plate. "I can tell you, son— Oh, yes," she said, her mouth tight. "I can tell you, there ain't nothin' worse in life than bein' a *slave.* And when I heard here in Lawrence that my son—my own son!—was number- one killer of proslavers on the border," Dahlia said, her eyes narrowing, "I realized— Worryin' about Christian ethics against killin' is a luxury right now. I hate violence, sure enough, but if there's one thing I hate worse," she said, looking hard at Malcolm, "it's heartless and cruel *slavers.*"

40

Malcolm couldn't figure how his mother expected him to eat potato pancakes when his emotions were running so high—first over their reunion, now over her story. Not to offend her, he dug in. *Oh, these are good!*

After she served Malcolm, Dahlia put a single pancake on her plate and sat opposite. He observed her picking at her food more than eating it. In time, she set her fork down and resumed the tale.

"Took a week for that tub we were chained in, Providence to Baltimore," Dahlia said. "On the way they put into New York to fix a rudder. You'd think when we laid over they'd have let us get up and stretch, but no—

"They just kept us lyin' on boards a couple days in that stinkin' hole, lyin' in our own urine and shit and vomit, most of us too weary to scream and cry. Some, even strong ones, already dead and their bodies bein' chewed on by rats. Finally, they took us out, hosed us quick, and put us right back down.

"Those were *Yankee* slavers and seamen haulin' us, the kind of scum Papa told me of, and I wouldn't believe could exist. But I believe it *now*. To them we weren't people. We were dollar signs in their eyes, like they'd cargo cattle or pigs or buildin' materials.

"I started that trip healthy and weighin' a hundred or so pounds but must have come off the ship in Baltimore down to less than eighty. Could hardly stand. Other slaves held me up, tellin' me, if I looked near death, the bosses would take their loss, kick me off the pier, and let me drown. Now, wasn't that Christian-like of our captors?

"I saw them do that to a boy while they hosed us on deck. Couldn't have been over fifteen years old. He'd weakened from rat bites and sickness to where they just unchained him and dropped him in the water. He bobbed up once, and I'll never forget the look in his eyes, and then he went down. I remember thinkin', maybe he was one of the lucky ones."

Malcolm put down his fork. He was unable to eat another bite while hearing such things.

"They put us in a shed on the waterfront, everything dark, everything cold, everything wet, everything stinkin'. We heard them arguin' outside whether to feed us before the sale, whether to fatten us up, to look good as we could for the sale. Evidently they were inexperienced slavers, or they'd have taken better care of us.

"Finally they gave us warm oatmeal. It was like sand, but we were so hungry it was like the best thing we'd ever eaten. I couldn't hold it down, though. How we made it through the night in that shed I'll never know, but next mornin' they tossed buckets of water on us and we were made ready for the sale. Malcolm, you ever been to a slave sale?"

He shook his head and muttered, "No'm."

"Like any livestock auction. You go on naked—else they strip you down—and they start pinchin' here and there and stickin' their fingers in you. They don't leave you a shred of dignity. They make you want to die. Before long you figure bein' paid for and given work and food and a shack to live in, well, it must be heaven compared to the boat ride and sale that got you there.

"Me? I only brought them fifty-five dollars in the bids, I was that emaciated. Just five dollars over their investment.

"Sean Mulligan must've seen a spark left in me to *want* me. He fancied me after the white hands on his tobacco plantation had their way. The more weight I gained back, the more he came around to my cabin to cluck over me like a damned rooster.

"Eventually I became more his wife than his own wife. One day he up and moved me into the big house and put me in charge of the other slaves there. He told me, never let on I could read and write. He urged me to talk like a nigger, else I'd be whipped and resold sure enough."

Though Malcolm wanted to let Dahlia tell it her own way, he saw an opening and urged, "Tell me all about the Mulligans. I want to know more about them."

Dahlia sat back and eyed her son carefully. "Oh, Lord," she said. Her face revealed a new interest. "That's right—Jane-Ellen. I'd heard you killed her husband, but I hadn't dreamed you'd go past maybe runnin' across her on the border. You *did,* didn't you?"

When Malcolm failed to answer, Dahlia pushed back her chair and got up, fidgeting at the counter.

"Tell me, Mama," he said. "I need to know it all."

Dahlia shook her head, her back turned to Malcolm. "I'm sorry, son. I never dreamed the two of you would *ever* get together like that. You've bedded her."

"Yes'm."

"Tch!" Dahlia resumed shaking her head. "That's a pity."

"Is she my half-sister?"

Dahlia suddenly spread her hands on the counter and looked down, slumping wearily. "Hadn't you best be gettin' along to see General Lane? That's the real reason you came to Lawrence, isn't it?"

"General Lane be *damned* for a hypocrite," Erskine said.

"No, no, son. He's trying to make it all work. Don't be hard on Mister Jim. On *Jim,* I mean. The habit's so strong the way I refer to white folks, I haven't broken it yet. No, Jim doesn't like anymore'n you do that escaped or free Negroes are set apart."

"About Jane-Ellen," Malcolm prompted her again. "About her family. What's so damned *hard* about giving me a straight answer whether Jane-Ellen is my *sister?"*

Dahlia whipped around and took a step to the table. She slapped Malcolm hard across his face. She breathed heavily immediately after that, her eyes dilated. She was obviously in distress that he'd provoked her—so soon after their long separation.

"Don't you raise your voice to me with 'damns' and demands, young man, you hear? I may be just another woman you think you can badger, but you'd better remember I'm your *mother!"*

Ignoring the blow—ignoring the lecture—Malcolm pressed her in a softer tone with, "Why can't you just say she is or she isn't?"

"Because I don't know!" Dahlia shouted.

Malcolm sat up straight, confused. "How is it possible? How can a woman *not* know whether she had a baby nineteen, twenty years ago? Will you tell me that?"

"I had a baby, *yes.* But so did Sadie Mulligan. We both had baby girls within a day or two of each other, and two more look-alikes you'd never believe." Dahlia pulled a handkerchief from her apron and blew her nose.

"Both milk-white skin but dark, dark hair. Both soft hair, not a trace of kink, like some's still in mine. Both dark-eyed. Yet, officially, one white by blood and all Irish and one as blood-black as you."

"You're telling me they got switched around in the house? Couldn't you tell which was your *own?*"

"I didn't stay long enough to know. Sadie took it into her head to put up a *row,* threatenin' to go to the priest. Sean was what amounted to a bigamist in common law, two wives with babies in the house. I got put back in a cabin. My baby was taken from me and wet-nursed. I didn't get to see either of the girls again till they were two-three years old. I went back to field-handin', and that was that.

"Sean—it became 'Mister Sean' after that—never came to my cabin again, afraid of being excommunicated. I took a black man in and we stayed together eight years till he got sold away. I made him be careful I didn't have more children, though the Mulligans' white overseers still came around every chance to do me. I didn't want any more children."

Malcolm looked down at his half-filled plate. He pushed it from him. Suddenly a new thought raced through his mind. He reached into a pocket, pulling out the scarab.

"If you didn't know, why did you give this to Jane-Ellen? Why not the other girl?"

Dahlia let a smirk play over her face. She turned and stepped to the counter, then turned around to face her son again, crossing her arms.

"Because the other girl died of pneumonia when she was five. And Sadie passed on soon after. I always wanted to believe my baby was still alive. I gave that stone to Jane-Ellen just before I escaped. I never said a word to her about what I suspected—or hoped. I figured when she got older she'd overhear enough kitchen talk about it.

"She was about ten, and Sean had remarried and a new boy baby was shaping along—James. I started to tell Jane-Ellen to keep the scarab always. Then a little devil got in me and I said, 'Missy Jane-Ellen, you keeps it, an' it gwine gib you good luck, lessn' you bye-'n'-bye runs across a man by name Malcolm Erskine, my son, which ain't likely. Then you gibs it him, y'hear?' And the little darlin' said that's what she'd do."

Malcolm nodded. "And that's what she did." He looked at the black stone in his hand, the carving and the orange flecks. He held it toward her. "You want it back?"

Dahlia snorted and turned away, saying, "Didn't bring *me* no luck. Though I carried it all my life till I gave it to her."

"What am I going to do, Mama?"

"About Jane-Ellen? While there's doubt, you stay *away* is what you're goin' to do. What else *can* you do?"

"What about birthmarks that would have distinguished the two girls from each other, when they were newborn?"

"Birthmarks?" Dahlia paused in the act of putting away some things, then she continued and removed boxes and small sacks from cupboards. She stopped again and put her hand to her mouth. "Birthmarks. I—" She shook her head. "I—don't—know. I'll have to think on that one. That's goin' back a long time, and I'd put all thoughts from my mind the first couple years of bein' separated from my baby. *That* was a pain I wanted to forget—like the pain of leavin' you."

"Will you work on remembering? For me?"

Dahlia turned again and studied her son's face. She nodded. "I'll sure enough try. Malcolm?"

"Yes'm?"

"I'm sorry I slapped you."

"I'm not. It felt good being reminded I had a mother again."

She smiled and swept over to where he sat, taking his head and hugging it to her bosom. Then, stepping back, still smiling down at him, she asked, "When do you see Lane?"

"The time's long past. I'll catch him tomorrow." Though it was only just coming on evening, he said, "I want to lie down. I could use about a month's sleep. I guess Lane won't like my snubbing him, but—" Malcolm shrugged.

"I'll explain to him. He's one of my regular supper customers. Got to open the place in less than an hour. Help'll be comin' by any minute."

Dahlia showed Malcolm to a guest room of the inn. He undressed and got into bed and considered asking Dahlia to tuck him in. Evidently anticipating that—or reading his mind somehow—she fussed with the cover awkwardly, smirking in embarrassment over the long-interrupted ritual. She bent to kiss him. She stroked his brow for what seemed a long time, smiling with lips set firm. Then she left.

* * * * *

Late at night, Erskine awoke to noises downstairs. Soon Dahlia in her nightdress opened the door and admitted someone that the dim light from the hallway revealed to be Abe Milford.

"Malcolm, we're *wiped out!* Dunscomb got together with Hank O'Brien and they brought at least forty men against us! Burned the lodge to the ground!"

"And *Rose?*"

"Wounded but alive at Black Bob's. She, uh, miscarried."

"The *others!?*"

"One or two besides us may have got away. I don't know which. Couldn't tell for all the smoke and shooting. The rest—dead."

41

Erskine scrambled out of bed and reached for his clothes. "Let's get going," he said.

"Where? There's nothing we can do now!" Abe said.

"We can try to round up survivors," Malcolm said. "We can gather more men and go after O'Brien and Dunscomb."

"That's foolish!" Milford protested. "We wouldn't know where to begin because—I'm telling you, I don't even know *who* got out except Rose and myself. For all the confusion and the fire and everything, I couldn't tell what was going on except that our men were being gunned down."

"Did they put up a fight? Did our side get any of *them?*"

"I doubt it. O'Brien timed it about an hour after we all went to bed. We were all dopey with sleep and the whole lodge was going up. They obviously brought in kegs of lamp oil and poured the stuff everywhere. Then they picked off those who ran out the door, or they shot through the windows at anything moving."

"How'd you and Rose escape?"

"Through the small window in her room. I ran in to see to her safety at the first sign of trouble. Just outside that window it drops into the ravine. While we were scrambling in the creek, Rose caught a shot in the shoulder. We kept running like hell, all the way to the Shawnee camp. To get here I used one of Black Bob's horses."

Erskine stood holding his clothes, not knowing what to do next. "All right," he said, "let's go see Rose."

"Let her rest. Besides, she's my responsibility now."

Erskine snapped a hard look at Milford.

"We're married, Malcolm. She insisted that Black Bob say some gibberish over us, so I'd get the land in case anything ever happened to her. I've grown to love her, and I think she cares for me. I know she was carrying your baby, but she lost it. I need this. I need to start another family."

Standing in the doorway with a wry grin and her arms crossed, Dahlia observed her son fussing with his clothes. "Wish *he'd* finally settle and do the same, sure enough. Anybody can see he's got the wherewithal."

Erskine covered himself in embarrassment. Then, relaxing, he realized he had nothing to be ashamed of in front of his own mother.

"Mama, we'd appreciate some strong coffee. We'll be down presently."

Dahlia left, shaking her head and muttering how her best chance for having family again—especially grandchildren—was probably never going to pan out.

Malcolm started dressing, asking Abe, "Who was on watch?"

"Doesn't matter who was on watch. They had their throats cut. We saw one at the north end of the lodge grounds, dumped into the creek."

"Who was it?"

"Jeremiah Adams."

Malcolm sighed heavily. "Who was on watch on the other end?"

"Ralph Lykins."

Malcolm shook his head. He sat on the bed and sighed once more. "Tell me who else you know for sure caught lead."

"Iverson. He was first out the door. There must have been two dozen guns trained on him, all going off at once."

"Who else?"

"Before he could duck back inside, where it was already a fiery hell, they gunned Eb Tolle in the doorway."

Malcolm sank his face into his hands trying to picture the massacre of his men, so many of them young men, hardly more than boys. And he'd recruited them.

After a long time that way, he looked up, found Abe sitting beside him. "That leaves Ezra Renfro, Dan Goodman, Cal Durham, and Alfred Willoughby."

"I think Durham and Willoughby were burned up in the fire or shot in the cabin, or both," Milford said. "Last I saw Renfro and Goodman they were trying to break through the roof where fire hadn't yet caught, but I don't know whether they made it."

"Let's hope they did," Erskine said.

"Amen," Milford muttered. "Now what? Have you talked with Lane?"

Malcolm made a sound and got up from the bed, pulling on his shirt. "Lane. I've come to realize he's a hypocrite. How can I deal with a hypocrite?"

"You'll deal with all kinds," Abe said, "because you have to get the job done."

Erskine buttoned his shirt. "I suppose you're right, Abe. I'm starting to lose my enthusiasm for this whole business, seeing how colored people are kept apart from whites here in Lawrence. And *this* is supposed to be the capital of freedom more than any other place on this bloody continent."

Abe squirmed. "I don't know what to say about that, Malcolm. I don't think of you as a colored man. Anyway I just married an Indian woman, I suppose against most racial tradition."

"Sometimes," Erskine said, as though talking to no one in particular, "I don't know *what* I am—black, white, in between. It's when I *don't* know, I like myself best. Then I can think of myself only as a man." Dressed at last, Malcolm said, "Let's get some coffee. Too much death. It'll be dawn in less than two hours, and we'll wake Lane and tell him what happened."

* * * * *

Erskine and Milford walked into the Free State Hotel lobby. Malcolm insisted the night clerk summon Lane and have him down soon while they sat smoking. "And bring us coffee, please."

"I can't do that, Mr. Erskine."

Abe stepped to the hotel desk and leaned across, his nose within three inches of the clerk's. "Yes, you can," he said evenly.

The clerk nodded, then said, "You realize he's a nig—"

"Waiting for coffee's what he is," Abe said. "And a hero of the Free State."

"Yes, Mr. Milford. Just as you say."

Abe turned and winked at Malcolm, who was shaking his head in disgust. "*Now* I know what we're fighting for," Erskine said, sinking into an overstuffed chair. "The right of high-and-mighty hypocrites to have clerks deal out their crap." He drew tobacco and papers from a pocket and rolled a cigarette.

Lane joined them in about fifteen minutes. "I expected you last evening. Della made apologies for you."

"I was busy—and tired," Malcolm said.

"Busy sulking?" Jim Lane had the nerve to ask.

Malcolm looked up, eyed his commander, then slowly nodded, a grim smile at the corner of his mouth. "Busy sulking—partly," he acknowledged.

"It'll change, Malcolm," Lane tried to assure the Jayhawker leader. "Rome wasn't built in a day. Neither will Kansas be."

"Nice to look forward to having another fight ahead," Erskine said, "if the one we're in is ever finished."

"We, uh," Abe Milford began, catching Lane's attention, "lost our entire group last night, except for a few who escaped. Hank O'Brien and Walter Dunscomb led three dozen or so men and burned our lodge. There are at least six dead, maybe more."

"Was C.C. Catron in it?" the General asked.

"I don't know," Abe said.

"What about Sam Jones? Was he involved?"

"Likely, but I don't know. I don't think he was *there,* but I couldn't say for sure."

Lane turned to Malcolm. "I'm sorry. Truly sorry. I know how comrades in arms can become friends. Whatever it was you came to Lawrence to speak to me about, is now a good time to go into it?"

"The best time," Erskine said. "We want a strong martial law and an eye-for-an-eye policy we can post everywhere."

Lane's mouth flew open. When the full impact of what Malcolm had suggested sank in, he shook his head and declared, "Impossible."

"Who says 'impossible'?"

"I say!" Lane responded. *"I'm* in charge now. Robinsons's up to his ears in the political side of this thing, so it's up to me."

"It's up to *all* free men of Kansas," Erskine countered. "Let's have a Free State Party meeting and put it to those here in Lawrence."

"In military and defense matters," Lane said, "I'm in charge." He reached calmly for the lobby's pot and a cup and poured himself some coffee. "None of John Brown's crackbrained Old Testament schemes will go around here. You'll see. I'll post word and give you your meeting, and then you'll see. Tonight. Right out there in front of the hotel. Lay out your proposition. See how they take to it."

"Agreed," Erskine said, getting up. Milford, evidently surprised that Malcolm wished to end the conference with Lane so quickly, rose and stood by his chief.

"Eight o'clock," Lane called after them as they walked out.

* * * * *

Erskine spent the rest of the day buttonholing shopkeepers to whom Abe introduced him—as well as teamsters, farmers, ranchers—laying out his and Brown's plea for a harder line against Bushwhackers.

"Don't you see?" Malcolm repeated often. "We've got to let the Missourians know—when one of *our* people dies, one of theirs will die regardless whether he was involved in attacking."

Most shook their heads. Several argued how un-Christian was such a policy.

By the time the sun went down that day, Erskine admitted to Milford, "We're going to lose this argument. Brown and I will be left on our own. We'll have to make our own policy."

"I'm with you all the way," Abe said. "You know that."

Malcolm looked at Milford a long time. "I haven't wished you happiness with Rose. I do, though. She's less than half your age, you know."

"You're not saying I'm not man enough, are you?"

Erskine hesitated. "No, just the opposite, Abe. I'm saying you may be too much man for that little filly."

Milford chuckled. "You're a liar, Malcolm. Let's go get a whiskey before these damned do-gooders make a law against *that.*"

* * * * *

By eight o'clock a platform had been placed in front of the Free State Hotel. General Jim Lane stood on it, waiting. Stationary torches lighted the scene. Two men were tying red-white-and-blue bunting at the platform's base. Nearly fifty men had gathered around, with more hurrying down Massachusetts to get there before any speechmaking.

Erskine stepped onto the platform and joined Lane. Immediately—with no introductions—Malcolm began addressing the crowd. Lane frowned from his first words.

Malcolm appealed in the names of abolition and of John Brown, in the name of all fighters for the Free State, for Kansas, that a policy be declared for harshest punishment against the intruders from Missouri, against any proslavers from within or outside Kansas.

To Lane's obvious dismay, Malcolm began to receive a few cheers from the crowd.

42

Erskine was strongly aware he was a legend "come alive." The Lawrence newspapers, *Herald of Freedom* and *Free State,* had exaggerated his border adventures and spread them to other papers. He was a folk hero. Add the broad "a" of his Massachusetts accent and his words rang like a voice from home to New Englanders in the street.

"We can't let them keep cutting our numbers," Erskine appealed to the crowd, "when they already outnumber us so heavily. Just as John Brown suggests, we should do everything in our power to cut them down as well—to let them know they risk losing a man for every one of *ours* they kill."

Shouts of approval went up from the enlarging group on Massachusetts Avenue, mostly men but some women, and more couples approaching.

Confident of his position and the support for it, Malcolm turned around during the cheers and applause to catch the eye of General Lane—and to grin defiantly.

Lane returned an icy stare, seeming to grow angrier with each stream of words Erskine delivered to the assembly. "Finish it, Erskine," Lane said through the din. The put-on smile left Malcolm's face. He nodded and turned to his audience again.

"General Lane doesn't like what I'm saying, folks. He's got different ideas about how to wage war, like moving a cannon around to scare Sam Jones. But I'm not talking about what *you* all do here in Lawrence to protect your position.

"I'm talking about the war on the *border,* where I've lived the past six months. It's *hell* there! Nightriders come across and push settlers around as though *they*—and not Kansans—*own* the place. They throw women and babies out of their homes and burn the cabins to the ground.

"They slaughter stock and smash water tanks and burn barns and wagons and fields. They say they've got a right because they're looking for their own escaped slaves, their 'property.' I say they have *no* right to bring the hell they're bringing.

"They have *no* right to shoot a man down for protecting his home. *No* right to carry off his women. *No* right to try to turn Kansas into another slave state by the force of terror.

"No right!" Erskine emphasized, smashing his right fist into his left palm.

This time the roar was deafening. The citizens of Lawrence were in Malcolm's power at that moment.

If they could forget completely they were being addressed by a half-breed, Erskine mused during the cheering, some of them might even invite him to sit down and have dinner in their homes, perhaps introduce him to their daughters.

"As you know, I organized a Jayhawker group to go after those raiders. I did it without money. I was only able to get help when Lane convinced you that my band and I were needed—*and* when Governor Shannon pardoned me.

"Well, we *were* needed. That was proved when other bands like ours sprang up in places along the border. And it was ours they called on to train them.

"We were ten men and a woman, every one trained with revolvers, rifles, knives—every one a crack horseman. We did our jobs.

"Now, thanks to Bushwhacker treachery, six of my Jayhawkers are dead, the remainder of us scattered." Malcolm hesitated as he surveyed the members of the crowd in the light of the torches. "I intend for Bushwhackers to *pay with their lives for that!"*

It appeared for a while the shouting, cheering people of Lawrence would scoop Malcolm from the platform and carry him on their shoulders in a spontaneous parade up and down Massachusetts Avenue.

They had enjoyed ceremonial parades ever since they founded the city two years before, and this seemed to be another occasion for such celebration. They moved about animatedly in the dirt street, a few dancing jigs in the excitement that Erskine's battle cries and warrior tongue had sparked.

Some held torches that danced up and down, like rising and falling punctuation marks in the spring night.

Malcolm stood with a pleased grin. Gently he resisted the overenthusiastic handling by which townspeople sought to show sudden affection. He backed politely from reaching arms, invitations for him to lead a march.

Unnoticed—unseen by all but Malcolm—a lone, slender figure approached from the direction of the Negro quarter.

Slowly she made her way toward the celebrating, singing, dancing crowd. When she reached the outer edge, she tapped a man on the shoulder and he stepped aside to let her pass.

Dahlia Bahari—"Della"—tapped the next man, and he stepped away and became quiet at the sudden appearance of the ex-slave café proprietress. And so it went until Erskine's mother reached the edge of the platform, her arrival by then having quieted most of the celebrants.

She looked up into Malcolm's eyes and commanded, "Lift me up there, son. I've got a few things to say to these folks."

Malcolm reached to hold her wrists and easily lifted her a few feet onto the platform. Dahlia turned to the now-silent gathering.

"I *wondered* where all my late-evenin' customers were," she said, getting a hearty, tension-breaking laugh from the group.

"I've got six apple pies and three cherry pies, fresh-baked, goin' to waste if I don't get more business before this day's over."

That brought more good-natured laughter and a voice from the crowd shouting, "Della's pies! Now *that*'ll beat a political meeting every time!"

Several in the audience called out agreement.

Dahlia held up a hand. "And that's another thing. You've been callin' me 'Della.' Don't know how that started except maybe someone couldn't pronounce Dahlia, like the flower, and the other name stuck. That's all right. I've got no objection to that.

"But it's time for truth and for you knowin' a few things you don't know—about me, about your speaker here, and about what he's sayin'."

She looked around at all in the street, then said with obvious pride, taking Malcolm's arm. "This here's my son. My own blood son I hadn't seen in over twenty years till yesterday."

A gasp went through the crowd, at least one woman so quickly caught by emotion that she said "Oh!" and began to cry.

"Last time he was in Lawrence most women and children were away, packed off to farms west of here for safekeepin', while you men had your non-shootin' war with the coward Jones.

"And, too, last time Malcolm was in Lawrence he got thrown in jail, and Abe Milford here let him out." She looked down at Abe, who was standing close to the platform. "Thank you, Abe, a thousand times over, for Malcolm would've been tried and found guilty—and hanged, sure enough."

Looking up, Dahlia said, "I have to tell you straight off I don't agree with much my son just told you. I *have* to tell you that. Maybe I have no right, bein' an ex-slave and a woman and colored and all that, but I reckon you'll listen to me anyway.

"Malcolm here thinks he's seen a lot of life, a lot of sufferin' and killin'. Well, I've been a slave," she said, pounding her chest with her fist, "and I'm here to tell you, he ain't seen *nothin'* compared to things I've seen. I could tell you stories— Well, another time—maybe.

"Before I was kidnapped and forced into slavery—in New England, mind you—I heard about Nat Turner down in Virginia and what *he* tried, almost the same as what Malcolm and John Brown are suggestin'.

"Turner was a slave who organized a revolt and tried gettin' even with whites. What did it get *him?"*

Someone shouted, "A hangman's noose!"

"You're *damned right!"* Dahlia answered, screwing up her face as she found her point being made for her.

"Lord knows, I don't cotton to slavers, especially the mean ones. I hate their guts. I hate the very breath they draw. I'd kill one if I saw him so much as *thinkin'* about movin' in my direction, and I mean that.

"They did every rotten thing they could do to a woman—" (More gasps from the ladies in the crowd.) "—and I'd like to pay back the guilty among 'em with the bullets they deserve.

"I'm not just a woman and born Egyptian and colored. I'm a person. A *person!* And I'm entitled to life without others runnin' it and interferin' with it, just like any other person.

"And Malcolm, son—" She turned to him. "—that's my reason for standin' up here and makin' a fool of myself along with you, by tryin' to address a political meetin'. You mustn't kill anybody who's innocent in his actions, even if he's guilty in his heart. That won't even things out.

"It's not human to do such a thing. It's not right in the eyes of God or man—or woman."

Turning back to the hushed audience in the street, Dahlia added in a lowered voice, barely loud enough for all to hear, "And you know it in your hearts, don't you?"

Malcolm was afraid Mama would add something like those last words. He knew such rhetoric could turn everything around.

A woman's voice was heard to say, "She's right!" Pretty soon a preacher with a turned-around collar shouted, "Amen!"

A lot of grumbling followed, men arguing with their wives or with one another. Malcolm's speech may have gotten them fired up, but Dahlia's had taken them to moralizing and intellectualizing among themselves.

Finally one man shouted to Lane, "Put it to a vote! We got nearly all the menfolks here!"

Lane stepped forward, quieting the large group that by now numbered over two hundred.

"All right, all right," he said, raising both palms for silence. "I declare this a meeting of the Free State Party, Douglas County branch, and it'll be officially recorded that a voice vote was taken on the question."

"Put the question to us," someone demanded, "simple-like!"

Lane looked at Malcolm, and Malcolm turned toward Dahlia and pushed back his hat, amused as she looked up at him to say, "Sorry to go against you, son. Sure enough sorry."

"It's all right, Mama. In a lot of ways, you just made me sort of—proud."

"The question," Lane struggled to shout, the crowd getting noisier in last-minute countless arguments in the street, "is whether to adopt John Brown's recommended policy of vengeance, one proslaver—innocent or not—to be killed for every Kansan who falls to Bushwhacker terror, said policy to be posted legally as warning. Call out 'yea' for adoption and 'nay' for rejection. You all grew up with town meetings and party meetings in New England, so you know the procedure. All in favor?"

A loud shout of *"Yea!"* went up from the street, torchlights dancing again. It took a while for the enthusiasts for vengeance to quiet down.

"All *against?"*

A much louder shout of *"NAY!"* filled the night. Women joined in, even though they had no privilege of voting in Free State Party matters.

"The nays have it!" Lane declared.

Dahlia Bahari stepped to her son and put her slender arms around him to hug him close. She looked up into Malcolm's face and said, "Whatever happens, son, know that I'm proud how you stand and fight for what you believe. And I've always loved you and always will, more than my own life."

43

The morning after the street rally Erskine awoke to a rich smell of coffee and sausages and buckwheat pancakes. He proceeded downstairs shirtless and found his mother busying herself in the kitchen.

She greeted him with, "You ready to forgive me for crossin' you, son?"

"There's nothing to forgive, Mama," Malcolm protested. "You said what you had to. It's your right, and I admire you for speaking out."

"You're holdin' back, sure enough. I hear it in what you're *not* sayin'." She served him a stack of pancakes and indicated he should help himself to butter, syrup, sausages, coffee, milk.

"I just don't see how we can win against superior odds unless we're ready to give them measure for measure," Erskine said, digging into his breakfast. "Eye for an eye," he added.

Dahlia turned and waved a spatula in his direction. "Now see here, son. You can win if you believe in what you're doin'. For if it's right, the principle will outlast the fight and all involved in it. No need to try to win by sinkin' to the level of the enemy."

"I'd like," Malcolm said between chews, "to live to see victory. Not watch our efforts drag out—*fail* because they have numbers to outlast us."

Dahlia waved that aside with a scowl. "Victory," she muttered with disdain. "There's never goin' to be anything like 'victory' in this. Fightin' over something isn't what settles who's right or who's wrong. It only settles who's stronger or cleverer or dirtier at fightin'. Sure, you've got to defend yourself. But killin' innocents? No."

"Then what *does* settle who's right?" Erskine asked his mother.

"Believin'. Knowin'. And bein' so informed and sure and *stubborn* about what you believe and know is right, others will pay attention and become persuaded. You need more coffee?"

"Yes'm, please. I guess I missed a lot when I no longer had you to grow up with. You sure wrote the book on 'stubborn,' didn't you? Meaning no disrespect, of course."

Dahlia finished pouring coffee and strolled back to the stove, evidently deep in thought. "I know what you're sayin', son. Papa had his weaknesses. He gave in too easily to the people around him, instead of givin' those church elders and preachers the tongue-lashin' they deserved. Funny, his bein' a tiger at sea and a pussycat ashore.

"You know, he could've made everything right for us in New Bedford, but they had him out-talked about the sins of interracial marriage. He believed in me and loved me, but he wasn't stubborn enough about it—about us—when it was important to be. I left because my stubborn streak was stronger, but it—" She shrugged and, fussing with the skillet, appeared to choke on her words. "—turned out—bad for me after all."

"Yet you're not sorry he brought you to America from Cairo? That he started out intending to marry you?"

She turned. A sad grin played on her face. "Seein' you, Malcolm, and the man you grew to be? No, I'll never be sorry. For all my sufferin', both in New Bedford and later as a slave, *you're* what made it all worthwhile. I know that now, son, more than ever—sure enough."

Malcolm looked up and smiled, then went back to eating. "I'm leaving in a few days, you know. Don't know when I'll be back."

"I expected that. You've got more killin' to do. That's your occupation, isn't it?"

"It's what I seem to do best," he said matter-of-factly, even knowing Dahlia had intended sarcasm.

"What then? What comes after that?"

"I'd like to ranch, if I live long enough. I'd like to raise beef cattle."

"That's what your papa's family was in. In Scotland, I mean, before he went to sea. That's what he told me. Maybe you can get him to come west and give you some pointers."

Malcolm nodded. "Maybe I can, though here Papa'd miss the ocean. I'll write him." He finished his breakfast quickly, then got up. "Meanwhile, I'll be joining John Brown in Osawatomie."

Dahlia snorted, then carried some things to the deep sink to be washed. "John Brown. He's a good man, but crazier'n a coot. I hope you know that," she said.

"I know that."

"He's either goin' to stop a bullet or be hanged. I'd hate for the same to happen to you."

"Crazy or not," Malcolm said, "as you say, he's a good man. A great man. With him you know where you stand. Not so with these politicians playing at war and freedom in Lawrence. And seeming half-hearted about both."

"Is Abe Milford goin' with you?"

"Not to join Brown, but to live with the Shawnees for a spell. With his—bride. We'll leave Lawrence together."

"And what are you goin' to do about Jane-Ellen, son? Where does she fit in all this?"

"I'll find her and settle things between us."

"You haven't thought things out yet. I told you, don't go bein' intimate again, because there's a chance she may be your sister. Didn't I tell you that?"

"Yes'm. You did. I *have* thought things out. I came to a conclusion. Now, listen to me, Mama. Don't fight me on this."

"I'm listenin'."

"I think you know it was *your* baby died in the Mulligan home. Having already given up one family before they took you into slavery," Malcolm said evenly, trying to hold Dahlia's gaze, "you only *hoped* Jane-Ellen was yours, and you acted from that hope. Am I right?"

Dahlia turned away.

"No, no, Mama. Look at me." He held her by her thin shoulders and stared deep into her dark eyes, seeing them glisten.

She said, "You're very bright to be reasonin' things out that way, son." Her voice broke slightly.

"Jane-Ellen's not my sister, is she?"

Slowly, then more definitely, Dahlia shook her head, looking straight into her son's eyes. "I have doubts, but honestly, I'll never know for sure. There were enough differences between the girls that I'd— I'd *prefer* now to tell you it's unlikely. I'd been hopin' to hold onto the fantasy the rest of my days that she was mine, but I see where it's hurtful. Go make it right with her and explain, the best you can. The poor girl must be in torment—or maybe not. The confusion is my fault. You tell her, this may be one of those times when people say, give it the benefit of doubt."

He embraced his mother and held her that way a long time. At last she moved back and said, "And go put on a shirt, ticklin' my nose with all that chest hair. Shame on you for comin' to breakfast that way." Then she allowed herself a lapse. "Is *that* how yo' pappy done brung you up?"

They laughed, Malcolm picking up Dahlia and swinging her around the kitchen.

"Put me down, you *hear?*" But her protests were subdued by the new joy they found in Malcolm's remaining days in Lawrence.

*****

Abe Milford turned in his saddle to gaze back at Mount Oread, which overlooked the city that was now a focal point for the nation. Then he said to Malcolm, "It's going to get worse before it gets better, isn't it?"

"I'm afraid so, Abe," Erskine said, nodding. "Afraid so."

They rode for Monticello. There Erskine visited Hickok and other friends, testing their mood for helping him form a new Jayhawker unit.

"It's not in us," Sam Garrett said. "We're settled down to our trades and to building our community. We've got too much at stake here, Malcolm, and we're not going to leave."

"Hickok, what about you?" Malcolm urged.

The young man shook his head. "You know I'm something of a loner. I only plan to stay here long enough to help these people establish the peacekeeping, build their town, then I'll move on."

"Doing what?"

Hickok shrugged his huge shoulders. "Don't know. I'd like to see more of what's west of here. I may even take a turn at driving wagons or stages just to be staked for travel. I don't know."

After a brief lunch that Betsey Garrett fixed for them, Milford and Erskine were on their way again, aiming south through Johnson County. Malcolm planned to scout for men in Paola and Osawatomie.

"Here's my turn-off, Malcolm."

Erskine looked around to get his bearings. He recognized a trail that led to the Black Bob Shawnee camp. He knew his companion was ready to break away from war if he could, and settle down.

"Give Rose my best," Malcolm said, taking Abe's hand in his, covering both with his other hand.

"I will."

"And tell Chief Black Bob I still try to carry all the wisdom he and Sylvia put in me. Tell him we'll all reunite one day—in the happy hunting grounds."

Abe Milford looked a long time into Malcolm's eyes, as though trying to read the future there. At last he turned and rode for the wooded trail.

Erskine sighed and headed Ebony southward.

*****

The Paola settlement was bustling with new arrivals and with construction. Sturdy store buildings were going up around a square. Few people paid attention to the lone, dark figure of Malcolm as he dismounted and hitched his black horse to a rail.

Suddenly a strong hand from behind grasped Erskine's wrist and caught him in a spin that sent him backwards, rump-first into a horse trough filled with water. Standing and laughing before him as he went down was Daniel Goodman.

"Why, *you*—" Malcolm stopped short of completing the thought, because they'd already begun to attract amused onlookers. He'd just as soon the new settlers caught no drift of who he was. No telling which ones had kinfolks in Missouri who could inform his enemies.

"Bet you thought I was a goner," Goodman said, beaming.

"Help me out of this," Erskine said, reaching a hand. "Didn't bargain for getting wet with my clothes on, you dumb squirt." Goodman helped Malcolm extricate himself from the trough. "I hope *your* weapon's dry in case trouble comes, Daniel lad. *My* guns are soaked."

"You won't find trouble here in Paola, Mal—"

Erskine stopped him. "Go easy on identifying me to strangers," he mumbled low.

Goodman looked as though he realized what Malcolm's apprehensions were, and he nodded. "New people moving in here every week now, and we've got a real town taking shape. Let's walk."

They strolled, while Goodman told of his escape through the lodge roof the night of the fatal raid on their camp. He was happy to hear Abe and Rose survived the attack, but he reported sadly that Ezra Renfro had fallen back into the burning building and perished there.

"That makes seven dead," Erskine said.

"Seven dead," Goodman repeated, nodding. "It was *hell.* I was bleeding and dizzy and headed the wrong way out, but I made it, as you can see. The raid was all over in a few minutes."

"What do you know of who did it?" Malcolm asked.

"Hank O'Brien. And Dunscomb. And a bunch of drifters from around Watts Mill."

"Catron? Jones?"

Goodman shook his head. "No sign of them. O'Brien was leading. If either of the others was there, one of them would have led."

"That's probably so," Erskine agreed.

"I landed over in Cass County—got there running. A woman that people took me to—she stitched me up and bandaged me. By morning she sent me on my way with a horse and saddle. Turned out she was O'Brien's sister-in-law. A widow-woman. She asked about you. Said she knew you from when she lived at Little Santa Fe."

Malcolm stopped and turned to face Goodman. "A poor woman? Dressed shabbily?"

"Oh, no. She seemed well-fixed enough. Nice home. Has a little brother, otherwise alone. Name's Jane-Ellen O'Brien, she told me straight off. She's got herself what looks to be a rich spread and cattle. She was elegant enough for *my* eyes. Matter of fact, Malcolm, I've, uh, been back to see her since. I'm—you might say—sort of sweet on her. And I truly think she fancies me."

44

Daniel's description of Jane-Ellen's current circumstances stunned Malcolm. The young man had spilled the information in ignorance of Erskine's past relationship with her. Of the Camp Branch group, only Abe Milford and Rose Deerfoot had shared that confidence.

Malcolm tried to mask both his feelings and his curiosity over the double-edged news. He must have succeeded, for Goodman seemed not the least suspicious of the extent of Erskine's interest.

"Come to my house for dinner," Daniel declared. "Stay with us while you're in Paola. Dinner will be a very special occasion."

"How can my arrival," Malcolm screwed up his face to ask, "make dinner a special occasion? You didn't know I was coming."

Goodman's mouth popped open in evident surprise. "Your arrival? No, no," he said, starting to laugh. He slapped Malcolm on the back. The slap reminded Erskine he had just spoken like a vain fool.

"No," Daniel continued. "It's Passover. This evening my family is having a *seder*—the feast of Passover."

"I can't intrude on a solemn religious ceremony," Erskine protested. "Thank you, Daniel, but no. Surely there's an inn here in Paola by now, judging from the growth I see around the square."

"Malcolm," Daniel said in a commanding tone, "you won't go to an inn. You'll stay with us. As for intruding, there's always an extra place set at the table by custom—an empty chair. For thousands of years, Jewish families have carried on the tradition of setting an extra place at the *seder*. That's in case the prophet Elijah should drop in. And it's a joyous occasion, not solemn."

"Elijah," Malcolm repeated.

"You'll be our Elijah." Goodman said happily. "My parents—my whole family—will be thrilled. You must come."

Erskine stared at Daniel and saw only earnestness in his eyes. Small wonder to Malcolm that Jane-Ellen might be attracted to this intelligent, exuberant young man. Goodman had proved himself capable as a warrior. Now Erskine would observe him in a peaceful setting.

"I'll come to dinner," Malcolm agreed, "but let me arrange lodging and wash up and—"

"Nonsense. You'll stay in my home. My family wouldn't have it any other way."

Erskine looked at the ground and then away, in frustration. He disliked anyone's taking charge of him, but Daniel Goodman's genuineness was too compelling to put aside. At last he nodded.

They retrieved Ebony. Daniel led the short distance to the Goodman home, not far from the square.

*****

Morris Goodman was a small man with a round face. A few strands of light-brown hair were combed straight across his bald head, which was topped by a *yarmulke,* the traditional skullcap of religious Jewish men. He wore a dark, fashionable suit, and a cravat.

His wife, Sarah, was slightly taller, her dark red hair turning generously silver. Aproned and a bit disheveled, she seemed to have taken charge of arrangements, instructing the Goodman children in preparation for the *seder.*

"How many are you?" Malcolm muttered to Daniel.

"I have three brothers and five sisters. I'm the oldest. Here, let me show you to your room and where you can wash up."

"Moishe!" Erskine heard Sarah commanding her husband soon after introductions. Her next words flowed in a combination of English, German, and what must have been Yiddish. As Malcolm pieced it together, she was cautioning her husband to stop persuading their smaller children that Elijah had truly come to the Goodman household.

Erskine was obviously no prophet. He was the soldier of the Kansas frontier about whom Daniel admitted he'd told them a great deal, and he was armed to the teeth.

Erskine knew religious occasions generally prompted renewal of old customs, making such events meaningful to young children. And there were enough of *those* around, giggling and bounding in and out of the kitchen.

"It would be better, more fitting," Malcolm whispered to Daniel, "if I put away my weapons."

Goodman nodded in agreement. "You have nothing to fear here. We're all safe."

"Safe," Erskine repeated. "That's a good condition for people to feel."

Morris Goodman began describing to Malcolm how he had brought his family to Paola in a covered wagon for the purpose of opening Goodman's Dry Goods on the square. The store started to prosper almost immediately.

Erskine unbuckled his gun belt and handed it to Daniel's small brother Aaron, who stared open-mouthed at the twin revolvers and their gleaming handles protruding from the holsters.

"My kid brother Samuel is seeing to your horse," Daniel said. "He loves animals. I wouldn't be surprised if he has Ebony unsaddled by now, and wiped down, brushed, watered, and eating a bucket of oats."

"The saddle and gear are very complicated—" Malcolm started to say.

"Samuel can handle it. He saw the Indian bow and quiver slung and wrapped. Why do you still carry it?"

"A gift from Black Bob. Sentimental value, and it may come in handy."

"May I see your knife?" Morris asked as Malcolm was detaching the Bowie sheath from his trousers belt. Erskine handed it to Mr. Goodman and watched as his blade and the weight of the weapon caught the dry-goods merchant's admiration.

"It is truly," Morris said slowly, turning the knife over and over in his hands, puckering his lower lip outward and nodding, "a magnificent weapon. You actually *use* it?"

Erskine gave a short laugh in slight embarrassment. "Yes, sir. And I regret to say I expect to again."

"I've never seen anything like it," Morris said, slipping the Bowie back into its scabbard and handing it to Aaron to set aside. "I have heard of such knives. Why do they call them 'Bowie'?"

"After the inventor," Erskine said, "a southerner, lived mostly in Louisiana, Jim Bowie. He died at the Alamo in San Antonio twenty years ago."

"Ah," Morris said, brightening. "Another hero of the frontier such as yourself."

"I'm no—" Malcolm began, but Daniel interrupted.

"Whether you believe it or not, Malcolm," he said, "to many people you represent what Kansas has needed for these times. We all wish there were a dozen—a *hundred* more like you."

Malcolm put a hand on his young comrade's shoulder. "Thank you, Daniel. You do me more honor than I deserve. And in front of your family I testify to your bravery and good contributions as well."

"Come," the now beaming Daniel directed. "I'll show you where you'll put up." He led the way, turning to say over his shoulder, "And you can stay as long as you like."

"No, I—"

Erskine stopped in his tracks, Daniel continuing ahead. At the end of a hallway Malcolm saw the most attractive woman he'd ever seen, tall and stately, with auburn hair worn flatteringly in waves to her shoulders and beyond. Her features were perfect. He drew closer, her green-hazel eyes and dimpled smile entrancing him.

"My sister. Naomi," Daniel backed up to say, realizing what had halted Erskine. "She'll get you whatever you need."

"Welcome, Mr. Erskine," Naomi said with a slight curtsy, then advancing with her hand outstretched. Malcolm took it. It was either a strong hand or she was applying pressure to the handshake that he didn't expect. He gave a perfunctory bow of the head.

For the present, Malcolm was speechless, feeling his heart beating so strongly it pulsed clear to his throat. "You appear flushed," she said in a low-register, melodic voice. "Are you not well, Mr. Erskine?"

"I am—"

"In *love!*" Daniel shouted teasingly. "Happens all the time, Malcolm. Naomi has broken more hearts than any woman west of the Mississippi."

"I—can understand that," Malcolm acknowledged.

"Please," Naomi said, turning her face away and blushing.

Yes, Erskine admitted to himself, this stunning young woman, slender and yet well formed, tall, dignified, was a creature of beauty beyond belief.

"You take over," Daniel instructed Naomi. "I've got to help Mama." Then he left them.

"This way," Naomi said, leading Malcolm to a small but comfortable room. "This is Daniel's room. You'll stay here. I've filled the pitcher and there's a wash basin and soap, cloths and towels. You're very dirty from the trail."

"I— I think you're very beautiful, Miss Goodman."

"Thank you, Mr. Erskine, but you know nothing of my character, and that's much more important. Still, I thank you for thinking me well turned out. If you'll please sit down, I'll help you with your boots."

"I need no—" Malcolm realized protests were futile. The Goodmans had taken charge. She worked swiftly to slide his boots off, a Derringer pistol dropping from each.

Erskine observed she didn't appear surprised. She simply set the weapons on a nightstand, then started stripping his high socks away, finding a small dagger concealed in the leg of one of them and again remaining inscrutable over that.

Sitting in wonder at her swift, efficient movements and her overpowering reserve, Malcolm failed to realize she was about to set to the task of washing his feet. "No! Stop!"

"Be quiet, Mr. Erskine. I won't have a smelly man sitting at my parents' *seder* table. I'll do this and *you* will take care of the rest. There's no time for a tub bath before dinner."

She applied a warm, wet cloth and bathed his feet, careful to go between his toes. Malcolm felt simultaneously embarrassed and humble, as she was humbling herself in what he figured was some sort of Jewish ritual.

"Why, Miss Goodman—Naomi? Why do you do this? Are you this accommodating with all your guests?"

"We haven't many guests, Mr.—"

"Malcolm," he corrected her.

"We're a Jewish family in a Christian frontier community. We're somewhat isolated," she said, looking up and straight into his eyes. Her lips were full and parted, almost pouting. He wanted to kiss her, and more, but he fought the urge.

"No, Malcolm," she said. Her voice broke over the sudden familiarity he'd encouraged silently—making him believe for an instant that she read his thoughts. Then, with evident courage, "I simply decided when I saw you, I would do this." She looked down again, engaged in her swift labors. "I don't think I can explain why," she said, shaking her head. Her lovely hair bounced. He wanted to touch it but held back.

"Can you smile again for me?" he asked. She lifted her gaze, breaking into a slow, warm smile. The effect was more startling than Malcolm had surmised it might be. "Someday," Erskine said evenly, looking into her eyes as she was ending her task with a brisk towel-rub, "I'll return the favor, Naomi, and wash *your* feet."

Naomi nodded. "Perhaps," she said with surprising acceptance. "Now," getting up, pointing here and there, "Samuel has brought some of your belongings and they're in the top dresser drawer. You'll change—clean socks, clean underthings. Use the washstand. The privy is out back, of course. I think I'll leave you now."

She started to exit, then turned at the door, her reserved look having returned. "You're a legend, Mr. Ers— I mean, Malcolm. That's part of it."

"And the rest?" Malcolm was quick to blurt.

She smiled again, softly this time. "I think you know the rest. You're not ignorant or blind and neither am I. But we'll speak of it no more just now." In an instant she was gone.

Later, Samuel and Aaron helped explain the *seder* to Malcolm. The ceremony moved along with symbolic questions by the youngest children and answers by Morris. There were pauses for apparently ritualized tasting of appetizers.

Morris Goodman told how his people annually celebrated their Moses-led exodus from Egypt thousands of years earlier. "We were slaves," he added, almost proudly.

"My mother is Egyptian," Malcolm said, "and was a slave in this country."

"And *our* people were slaves in *hers,*" Morris said matter-of-factly, shrugging. "Human history is very peculiar," the merchant said, "very remarkable for its twists and turns."

* * * * *

The next several days, Erskine circulated in Paola. He revisited the Lykinses, who were bereaved by the loss of young Ralph in the attack at Camp Branch. He also paid respects to the Durhams, the Tolles, and the Willoughby family for the loss of their sons. He felt only slightly resented for having attracted the young men to war, but by and large respected that he'd gone personally to the families to offer condolence.

"I've reminded them all," Daniel Goodman said, "we volunteered. Some feel their boys might not have done so but for your reputation. That's all there is to the resentment you've sensed."

"I carry that as a heavy burden, Daniel. I hope you know that."

Turning to happier thoughts, Malcolm inquired, "Why do I see so little of Naomi?"

"She's my father's principal help in the store. For a clue to her personality, I suggest you simply let it be," Goodman said. "Whatever comes, if anything, must be natural."

"You're right," Malcolm said, nodding. "I'll give the matter of Naomi no sense of anxiety."

"Good," Daniel said. "That's the correct way."

Malcolm rode out often to learn more about the Lykins County countryside, crossing once into Cass County, Missouri, in hopes of observing Jane-Ellen O'Brien's new place, perhaps to visit her with Dahlia's message.

Caution prohibited him from asking precise directions of Daniel, whose own interest must be respected, Malcolm believed. Moreover, he couldn't reveal himself to Cass Countians, so he avoided contact with them and never learned Jane-Ellen's whereabouts.

In fact, the only eventful discovery across the border was a "wanted" poster about himself on a tree, which noted he was worth $15,000, dead or alive, "preferably dead."

Returning to the Goodman home, Malcolm was surprised by Daniel with a package. "It's from Jane-Ellen. I told her only that you're here, on your way to see John Brown, and she sent this. There's also a letter."

Opening the package quickly, Malcolm discovered money, a fast count revealing a cash sum of—*five thousand dollars.*

45

"Dear Malcolm," the letter from Jane-Ellen began. Erskine decided to read it aloud in Daniel's presence after scanning it in vain for affectionate references.

"I will explain my new financial circumstances in due course, not now. Meanwhile, take this money and give it to the abolitionists in Osawatomie to aid them in their work with runaway slaves.

"As you can see, I have changed my formerly reasoned and now admittedly provincial view on the subject, the change partly owing to my recent experience at the Jackson County Poor Farm.

"While I can never know the feeling and indignity of genuine slavery first-hand, I am reformed to the principle that poverty and condition of race should never be cause for a human being to be thus fated for such servitude.

"I came as close as any white person could come, believing anyway as I do that I am partly Negro, to knowing what harsh dependency and slavery must be like. I now detest it totally and, though I can afford them now, keep no slaves.

"Turning to more urgent matters, please avoid entering Missouri as there is a reward for you dead. The place crawls with bounty hunters and mercenary Bushwhackers. Hank O'Brien is now well-situated financially, but he is sworn to use all his resources to find and kill you. Beware, everywhere you go.

"Daniel tells me you seem smitten with his sister, Naomi, and that is good, I think, except that you should not subject her to an alliance so fraught with danger of tragic consequences as that arising from your adventurism.

"I wish for an end to this accursed border conflict and fear for your safety and Daniel's, yet he is not known so widely, nor is he so committed to a cause and to vengeance and killing as you.

"Help John Brown, with my warmest regards and confession of past error, and take care.

"Your sister in freedom's lingering fight,

"Jane-Ellen"

Daniel Goodman appeared agitated over portions of what he heard from the letter, which he obviously had the good character not to read earlier while serving as courier.

"Is she your sister or not?" he asked Malcolm point-blank.

"Evidence seems to be that she's not. Regard what she's written as a figure of speech."

"Yet she believes she's part-Negro. She said that before to me, and it never disturbed me one whit," Goodman said. "But I never made the connection with your own background. Now I'm confused about the kinship between you two."

"As far as I can tell, there is *none,"* Malcolm declared a bit too sharply. "Jane-Ellen was in close contact with my mother while growing up in Maryland. I've since seen and talked with my mother, in Lawrence as a matter of fact. She's eager that confusion—a confusion over baby girls born almost simultaneously to her and the plantation mistress—be cleared up once and for all. The mistress raised Jane-Ellen as her daughter, and in all likelihood that was rightly so. The other child died."

Daniel paced the Goodman parlor in a state of increasing anxiety.

"This places me in an awkward position," the young man said. "I now believe there's more between Jane-Ellen and you than I'd had the faintest suspicion of." Daniel turned suddenly. "Oh, my God. You've taken her to your *bed,* haven't you?"

"No!" Malcolm shouted, grateful in his heart it was only a half-lie on a technicality. Actually, Jane-Ellen had taken him to hers.

"But you *would* if you had the chance," Goodman persisted.

"Yes, of course," Erskine confessed. Then he demurred, adding, "I *would have,* though not if I suspected we were siblings. Now, with you in the picture, Daniel, I'd respect our friendsh—"

"The *hell* you would. No, *I* won't try to clear up whether or not she's your sister. Let her believe it as long as she likes—or not. My position isn't yet that secure with her. She might still come running for you."

Malcolm decided not to disclose that the possibility of incest mattered far less to Jane-Ellen than it did to him. Didn't matter to her at all, as a matter of fact.

Goodman paced more, then turned and added, "I didn't know these things. I'm glad I know them now. Regardless of the difference in our religions, I plan to make a life with Jane-Ellen."

"*Marry* her?" Malcolm asked, his face twisted in such irony that Daniel must have gotten the message. Erskine found the notion ridiculous.

"Very likely, yes. I've got enough trouble with my parents over it without running into trouble with *you,* so I'm telling Jane-Ellen nothing except your thanks for the money."

Erskine sighed in weariness of the discussion, saying, "As you like." He folded the letter and put it away in his shirt with the cash funds.

"I *do* know what I must do, however," Goodman added.

"Nothing foolish, I hope." Malcolm tried to omit from his tone any sign of warning. He felt he knew Daniel Goodman well enough that the young man meant no physical nor armed challenge—in which Daniel would be the inevitable loser.

"No, nothing foolish. I must find and talk to Naomi." Goodman turned and hurried from the room.

That night, the last that Malcolm planned to spend with the Goodmans before riding for Osawatomie, he was awakened by hearing the door of his room opening. He reached for a box of matches at his bedside and lit a candle.

Naomi stood before him in a translucent nightdress only partially covered by a robe. She was shivering. Her auburn hair appeared recently washed and dried, and it glistened in the candlelight. "I'm doing this for my brother, you know."

Malcolm nodded.

"I've never been with a man. Even while away at medical school, I never let a man touch me."

"You studied to be a doctor?" Malcolm asked. "That's a surprise."

"I haven't completed it. I'm not here to talk about that. You know why I'm here."

"Yes. Are you cold? Come quickly, in here with me," he said, drawing the cover aside.

"I'm not cold. I'm shivering from nervousness, not from the chill. It's all new."

"It's all easy and natural," he said, "provided we both play it out slowly—touch, explore."

"I said I've never been with a man. I didn't say I don't know what to do."

"And this is for your brother, of course," Malcolm said wryly.

"Of course," Naomi replied, removing her robe and gown and lying down, the hint of a smile on her full lips.

Erskine pressed a finger on the candle flame to snuff it.

*****

When Malcolm awoke Naomi was gone—not only from his room but evidently from the house.

Mrs. Goodman saw to his breakfast, and Daniel helped with his readying for departure. The younger boys and girls had left for school and Mr. Goodman for work. Daniel saddled Ebony for Erskine and brought the horse around front.

"Thank you," Malcolm said from the saddle, probing Daniel's eyes, "for everything." He wanted to ask Naomi's whereabouts after their long night of glorious fulfillment and little sleep, but he decided against further discussion.

Had Naomi given up her virginity because Daniel prevailed on her to distract him from Jane-Ellen? Erskine preferred to believe the attraction that was evident before the *seder* might have driven her to his bed anyway. "Thank you," he muttered to Daniel again.

Goodman sighed in a way indicating relief. "You are my brother now," he observed.

"Perhaps," Erskine said.

"Stay in touch," Daniel urged.

Starting Ebony southward, Malcolm failed deliberately to respond to Daniel's suggestion of continuing an association. He was still unsure how the prospect of a union between Daniel and Jane-Ellen suited him. His feelings for her were now a jumble, a mixture of passionate longing and moral revulsion.

And now there was the unexpected breath of fresh air—the extraordinarily bright, candid, stimulating, gorgeously proportioned Naomi. Thanks to her ease of familiarity upon their first meeting—and last night her ardor in lovemaking—the auburn-haired woman's arrival in his life was, at the very least, compelling. Perhaps *eclipsing.* His hands still carried the scent of their hours-long experience, and he sniffed them repeatedly.

Just as his wool-gathering about the women in his life was at its deepest in the short ride between Paola and Osawatomie, Malcolm heard a shot. Simultaneously a piece of bark splintered wildly, high on a tree trunk—not over five feet from his head.

Quickly he dismounted and chased Ebony to a gully beyond the tree for safety, managing to slip a Sharps rifle from its sling as the stallion obeyed and fled.

For balance, however, and in his haste to find a retaliatory position, Malcolm put his left hand down hard to the ground before looking.

His first thought when a bear trap snapped around his left forearm was that Sylvia's teachings of personal defenses had, in that awful instant, slipped from his mind. He'd *lost control!*

He looked down. He'd also lost the ability to use the rifle, and—with the advance of intense pain—he concluded he may also have been about to lose half his arm.

Whipping out a revolver, Erskine fired in the direction of the shot that had originally sent him scurrying. More shots were returned. Rifle shots they were, indicating a pair of attackers, no more.

"We done got yew now, nigguh!" he heard Hank O'Brien call from the distant brush. "Ah *know* we got yew in a trap if y'ain't usin' yer rifle!"

Malcolm glanced about and saw, here and there along the ground, a dozen or so similar traps along the route—the only well-used trail between Paola and Osawatomie. He'd been methodically bushwhacked by O'Brien, who'd caught wind of both his whereabouts and his plan to join Brown.

Doubtless the traps were spread during the night by O'Brien and Dunscomb, any innocent travelers being diverted by the pair on a pretext. The shot that had missed him was intended to force him from Ebony into taking defense on foot.

He must free himself or lose his life, Erskine decided. There was only one way to do it, for the trap was chained around the tree as others nearby appeared similarly secured. There was little hope of prying it open, no hope if it were to be done quickly.

He drew his Bowie knife and, glad he'd honed the blade to a razor's edge, began cutting away his own forearm.

At the sound of movement in the brush, he dropped the knife and resumed firing with his revolver. He would soon need his other revolver, for reloading would be difficult if not impossible.

Whether to spend more time warding off shots still flying overhead or continue cutting himself away became a sudden choice he resolved quickly. Get *free*—so that he might alter his position at will, not stay a sitting duck.

Clenching his teeth against the pain, Malcolm picked up the Bowie again. He dug and twisted at gristle and tendons to separate his arm at the elbow.

Ignoring the pain, the shock, the sweat, the rush of blood, he reached a point where he could no longer distinguish between pain from the trap's grip and that from his own cutting.

All that possessed him was the notion of cutting himself *free,* as foxes and other animals are known to do, chewing off their own legs to escape with their lives.

With one final cut and a shriek of pain, Malcolm broke loose and resheathed his bloody blade. He also vomited at the sight of his severed forearm in the trap and his dripping stump hanging from his torn jacket.

But he was *moving* again. And instead of moving toward Ebony to flee, he scurried swiftly toward his enemies, crawling one-handed between the other traps along the ground.

46

Erskine calculated his strategy.

He tossed one revolver aside and reached for his other. Eight shots left, counting a full revolver and a one-shot Derringer in each boot. No bullets in his belt, assuming he could even manage reloading one-handed.

Hank and Dunscomb were likely to have come well prepared, judging from the continuing but aimless rifle fire. But why not with more men? Was this thing a matter of pride for them? Or greed over the posted reward for Erskine, to be dragged to Missouri "preferably dead"? O'Brien's $30,000, taken months ago from the late Ezra Renfro's looting in Westport, couldn't have played out this soon. Could it?

The firing stopped. Malcolm listened. Dunscomb's voice came from possibly twenty-five yards distant. "He ain't there no more, Hank. He's out of the trap somehow."

Erskine heard O'Brien answer in a hoarse whisper, "Shut yer mouth, fool! Stay low. He ain't run off or we'd o' heard."

Malcolm next heard what sounded like rifles being tossed to the ground and then, unmistakably, revolvers being cocked. That meant they knew he was approaching in the brush.

Suddenly a long series of rapid shots peppered the shrubs around him—in front, behind, on either side. O'Brien and Dunscomb unloaded revolvers randomly in hopes of finding their target. One bullet grazed Erskine's boot.

If they'd separate, Malcolm thought, *I've got a chance.*

Without stirring a leaf or a branch, bypassing other planted bear traps, Erskine inched forward. He tried to forget the pain and avoid the sight of his stump—a bloody rag of sleeve still dangling there.

He concentrated on setting up the kill.

"Yew," he heard Hank call in a forced whisper. Evidently they were both reloading and assessing the new circumstances. "Git *that*-a-way." O'Brien was obviously directing Dunscomb to a spot he thought would be on Malcolm's flank.

Quickly, Erskine calculated where he could jump immediately after firing and not be caught in another bear trap. It would also have to be a spot providing cover.

A young tree was all he saw close, barely wide enough to shield him. But its base was clear of traps and surrounded by heavy weeds and brush. And it was only six or eight feet away.

He heard Dunscomb take off clumsily toward his left. Malcolm raised up slightly, threw two revolver shots in quick succession toward where he figured O'Brien was, then raised up higher to aim carefully.

In the split second of O'Brien's ducking, Erskine turned and squeezed off a bullet into Dunscomb's temple and leapt for the tree. Instantly he made himself as narrow a target as he could, while O'Brien plugged away with two revolvers.

Now that they were sure of each other's positions, and with Dunscomb likely dead, Malcolm felt free to talk while planning his next move.

"You're a dead man, too, Hank!" he called.

"Yew wrong! *Yew* good as dead, but after yew larn how it is bein' *cut up!* Ah'm goin' bring yew down hurt, then *do like yew done me!"*

"You can't do any of that by yourself against me," Malcolm said. "Where's all your help?"

O'Brien didn't respond, but Erskine heard his enemy mumble to himself while working, apparently, to push more shells into his revolvers.

During Hank's unintelligible rantings, a realization came to Malcolm. O'Brien had run into a simple, practical problem. He hadn't been able to muster help for this adventure because other men were busy planting.

O'Brien's and Dunscomb's tracking, the setting of traps and preparing for ambush, must have taken time too precious to others in this season. Only drifters and mercenaries such as O'Brien could afford the luxury of gambling time in Kansas, stalking quarry for a posted reward.

Malcolm brought his dizzying brain back to the immediacy of his problem and how he would solve it.

He needed an edge. He had three shots in his revolver. The one-shot "toys" he also carried would require closer range.

O'Brien was concealed behind a stout tree with ample ammunition.

The edge came from O'Brien himself, who asked, "How'd yew git loose o' the trap?"

"How's that?" Malcolm had heard perfectly well, but it was time to stall. Following a brainstorm through the fogginess overcoming him, he started ripping at his dangling sleeve.

"Ah *axed* yew, how'd yew git yer black butt *loose o' the trap?"*

"Oh, *that.* I cut off my arm."

Silence. Then– *"Yew – done – WHUT?"*

"I, uh, cut off my arm." Careful not to let any part of himself stick out past the tree, Malcolm set down the revolver and drew the dagger from inside his sock. He used it to pin a length of bloody sleeve to the first limb. "Take a look."

Recovering his gun and figuring which side O'Brien might use to peer from his cover, Malcolm sank low. He began a new crawl through the brush in that direction, careful not to stir stones or twigs.

By the time Hank showed his face in irresistible curiosity, Erskine was in a totally new angle robbing O'Brien of protection. Through the heavy thicket, Malcolm took aim and fired.

But his shot wasn't true, merely blasting off the end of O'Brien's nose. Still, Hank dropped one gun and clapped a hand to his face in pain, firing wildly with the other. Malcolm fired again, but that bullet was deflected by a stout shrub in front of Hank.

O'Brien had Malcolm's range and, despite blood gushing over his face and into his eyes, blasted away. He hit Malcolm's revolver, spinning it from his hand and out of reach. Erskine was still

"Yew – done – *WHUT?*"
"I, uh, cut off my arm."

too far from his enemy to get a true shot with a Derringer. That left his Bowie knife.

He drew it, hefted it by the razor-sharp and now bloody blade. He estimated the distance at ten yards, farther than he had ever been able to get the precise accuracy he needed. Nevertheless, he pressed his feet hard to the ground and pushed to stand for leverage.

His standing and the sight of his bloody stump appeared momentarily startling to the wounded O'Brien. In that split second's hesitation by his enemy, Malcolm *threw*—sending the blade clean into Hank's heart.

O'Brien toppled back, kicking and writhing. Erskine closed the distance with a sprint and pulled the knife. He plunged the Bowie into Hank's neck, the angry force of the thrust half severing the man's head.

Crazed by his own deliriousness and rage, Malcolm struck again, then once more, decapitating O'Brien. Panting hard from the effort of battling while maimed, he watched the head roll away.

"Now I know," he said, still trying to catch a full breath, fading from loss of blood, "you won't come back to life again."

With that he passed out, falling across the headless corpse of his enemy.

*****

Erskine's next conscious moment was cloudy but marked by surprise. Abe Milford was leaning over him, covering him, trying to make him comfortable and cautioning him to lie still.

Even more remarkable was the hazy presence of Jane-Ellen, of Rose, and Naomi Goodman. For a moment Malcolm let himself believe he was dead, gone to where his dearest friends somehow gave comfort through magical images.

Yet Abe's touch was real.

"Don't try to speak, Malcolm, assuming you can. The truth is, my friend, you were nearly a goner. We've got work to do on you. Try to sleep. If you don't, I'm ready to fill you with whiskey."

Erskine stuck the end of his tongue between his lips to indicate he would welcome the bottle. Milford uncorked it and slanted it toward him, pouring generous swigs into Malcolm's mouth.

Half aware of what was about to happen, Erskine strove to cooperate. He swallowed the whiskey freely. He blinked in hopes of prompting Abe to tell what had brought them all out. How did they find him?

"The shooting out here," Milford explained, "attracted attention in Paola. Daniel figured it was you in danger. He and his sister found you. She stopped the bleeding and cleaned the stump. Goodman held a compress while she arranged to send for Rose and me. I sent for Jane-Ellen. You were unconscious the hours it took us all to arrive. Wasn't safe to move you—couldn't get you to a doc because there's none hereabouts. Daniel's now gone to try for one in Osawatomie."

Abe said Rose was sterilizing the Bowie to use for cauterizing Malcolm's stump. Naomi would stitch it. As for Jane-Ellen, she was clutching rosary beads and absorbed in prayer.

Malcolm blinked again, between gulping great drafts of whiskey. The drink dizzied him in a way he half welcomed.

"What is it?" Abe asked. Erskine continued blinking, feeling as though he might pass out again at any moment. Abe turned and called, "Jane-Ellen!"

She came quickly and fell upon Malcolm with kisses and tears. "You're awake—alive! Oh, Malcolm, *live* dearest. Live! Daniel said you learned from Dahlia we're not—you know—as we'd thought." She rubbed her tearful face over his, breathing kisses and sweet breath into his mouth as though that might help.

"Everything's changed, dearest. At the Poor Farm a priest came. I convinced him to talk with Hank about the money. At first we thought Hank was going to return it to Colonel Boone, but the priest worked on him. That was some fast-talking *priest,*" she said, laughing. *"Shoot,* he wound up with five thousand for the church—and fifteen thousand for me, leaving Hank with ten, which I inherit now as his nearest known kin.

"Oh, Malcolm, we're rich. When you're well, you can still deliver what I gave you for John Brown. But with my place in Cass County, we can be comfortable. You can change your name, grow a beard, raise cattle.

"They'll let us alone, I'm sure. And now we can belong to each other and—"

As she rambled on, Malcolm could think only of Daniel Goodman, who'd displayed strength of character by confessing to Jane-Ellen what he'd learned—little substance to the belief that Malcolm and Jane-Ellen were brother and sister.

Erskine's dimming eyes took on a look of sudden anger that she evidently couldn't read. When she backed away slightly to look at him, she smiled past her tears and blurted, "Now we can get married."

With all the strength he could muster, and even to Abe Milford's apparent surprise, Malcolm began to rock his head in a negative sign.

"Yes, Malcolm, we can," she said, unable—unwilling, perhaps—to understand what he was trying to say by gesture.

Thoroughly weakened by the effort, made drunk by the whiskey, Erskine sank again into a near state of unconsciousness.

Abe leaned to assist a shocked Jane-Ellen to her feet, cautioning her. "Be strong, woman. He said 'no.' Let it go at that. Now we've got to work on him while he's passing out." Abe called, "Rose! Quickly!"

"He couldn't!" Jane-Ellen protested.

Milford repeated, "He answered 'no.' A moot point anyway if he dies."

47

Malcolm's next fully conscious moment was marked by the droning of men's voices at a distance. Yet, when he opened his eyes, except for voices it appeared he was alone.

An early morning mist clung to the woods around him. The dampness was slightly chilling. A blanket covered him and another was under him. His mouth felt like he'd swallowed cotton.

Sticking his tongue between his lips, Erskine wished for water. Surely—as he remembered now—Rose or Abe would still be here, would hold a canteen to his lips.

A voice up close—a woman's—startled him. "You're awake!" A face came into view, that of Naomi Goodman, her fine features clouded by worry. Still, her eyes spoke happiness over his coming awake. Her appearance was of a woman who'd spent one or two nights outdoors and was unused to that.

She put a hand on his cheek. He heard water drops. Evidently with the other hand she was squeezing a cloth into a bucket. With the soaked cloth she wiped gently at his lips, allowing drops to seep into his mouth.

"No," she said, reading the command in his eyes. "I can't let you drink fully yet, or you'll retch. Your system gave back the whiskey while you were under, while we worked on your arm."

Another face came into his range of vision—John Brown's. They had summoned the old man.

Yes, Daniel Goodman had gone to Osawatomie, as Abe had told him. Remembering now the events just prior to his lapse into unconsciousness, he wished also to see Daniel and Jane-Ellen. He tried to speak. "Jane—"

"She's with Rose at the creek, bathing," Naomi said. "She'll be along presently."

Milford stepped up beside Brown, a half-smile lighting his broad face. "I do believe," Abe said, "the warrior's going to make it."

From under the blanket, Malcolm raised his right hand with some effort, moving it across to feel the stump of his left arm. The recollection of his necessary self-mutilation was a sickening one.

"Learn to accept it," Naomi said softly, trickling more water into his mouth, then washing his face.

On impulse, Erskine tried to form a response. "Can y—"

"Can *I* accept it? We'll talk of that another time. The important thing is to make you well. Mr. Brown will take you to Osawatomie for rest and recovery. I'll," she said, getting up, "visit you there."

Naomi Goodman turned to Brown and Milford. "No food or drink until he's been conscious a good while longer, then only a bit of soup. He's lost a lot of blood. Without our coming and Rose's help, he'd have perished out here, probably of infection."

Malcolm remembered that Rose, just before his going to sleep or losing consciousness again, had been readying his Bowie for cauterizing his arm. He reached and found the knife replaced in its sheath.

"Don't fidget around so much," Abe instructed him. "Lie still."

Naomi turned back to Malcolm and knelt again, putting both hands behind her neck to undo the clasp of a gold charm. She showed it to him up close. It was shaped like a table—a table with one leaf raised.

"This," she said, "is a *chai.*" Her pronunciation was strange to Malcolm, who concluded the word was from Hebrew. "It means 'life.' You'll wear it always." She put it around his neck, hooked it, and drew the charm forward to rest on his chest.

"You will," she instructed him further in seriousness, "dedicate yourself to life and living. I know that it won't be easy nor always possible for you, but you must try. I want you to turn away from killing and death."

Then Naomi leaned forward and whispered closely. "Will you promise to try? Will you become a man of peace?"

Malcolm whispered, with difficulty, "While—slavery—lives, no—peace."

"But you'll find other ways to fight that evil, Malcolm," Naomi said. "If you do, I'll help you—if you want me."

Unashamedly in front of others, she kissed him fully on his cracked lips. Her kiss, he thought, was the best medicine he could ever have wished.

"I—promise," Malcolm fairly grunted. Instantly he regretted making a commitment so difficult to keep.

Naomi got up again and walked away. Erskine wanted to know when he might see her again but had no strength to call after her. He heard her say to Daniel, "I'm going home now. He's in good hands. God and Mr. Brown will watch over him."

The sound of footsteps along the path indicated Daniel was accompanying his sister to her horse.

John Brown summoned his sons. Malcolm figured they'd brought a wagon for him. Dimly in the distance, the morning mist now lifting, he could see one in readiness.

Abe used the opportunity of their being alone. He knelt beside Malcolm. "Do you want to talk more with Jane-Ellen? Maybe you owe it to her, but are you up for it?"

The best he could, Erskine nodded.

Then Malcolm said, "Kicka— Kicka—"

"Kickapoo Rangers. You heard me talking to Brown?"

Erskine nodded again.

Abe frowned. "Time enough to worry about that later, when you're well." Malcolm reached and used all the strength he could to grasp Abe's arm, squeezing. "All right, all right," Milford said. "But first settle things with Jane-Ellen. I'll ask Brown to tell you the rest on the way to Osawatomie."

Jane-Ellen came forward and hesitated, then crouched beside Erskine. Abe got up and stepped away. "Why do you reject me now, Malcolm, after all we've meant to each other?" she asked.

"It's—no—good," Malcolm said. Speaking was still difficult. "You—let—us—" He found it hard also to speak the bold truth of what was in his heart. "—become—lovers—while—"

"While I still believed you were my brother. *Shoot.* I figured that was it." She glanced away and shook her head. "Deep down you're a pious man, Malcolm. An unusual man. Not always good on the surface when you're riled, but I guess you've got your rules."

"I—just—can't—" was all he could add, feeling as though he might pass out again if he spent any more effort speaking.

"Can't what? Forget? Or can't forgive? Never mind, I know what you mean. I made confession about it weeks ago with that priest, so I've acknowledged the corruption in my heart for some time."

Erskine managed to form the name, "Dan—"

"Yes, Daniel," Jane-Ellen said, sighing. She looked around, distractedly, sadly. "It's not the same. I love him, but not in the same way I've loved you, Malcolm. He's strong and warm and comforting," she said, "but he hasn't your fire. Do you know what I mean?"

Malcolm could no longer speak. Instead he moved his hand about in a way evidently strange to Jane-Ellen.

Rose had walked up behind her. "Indian signing," she said, "is difficult for a one-armed man. He's trying to tell you something about his growing up."

Erskine was grateful. He continued moving his hand. "As nearly as I can make out," Rose said, "he's saying the fire you speak of belongs to youth. It can't blaze forever. He has no ill feelings. He'll think of you always as his— Oh, I can't say this."

"*Say* it," Jane-Ellen demanded.

"As his *sister* in spirit," Rose said, finishing. Malcolm dropped his hand to the ground, exhausted.

Jane-Ellen got up, looking somewhat vexed.

Rose approached and took her by the wrists. "He's right," Rose said. "I've been through it myself with him, when our band shared the lodge. Of all the men here today, he's the only one who hasn't found himself. He hasn't yet matured emotionally. You should work on something steady and solid in your life now."

Jane-Ellen bit her lip and studied Rose's face, then looked down again at Malcolm. Next, after embracing Rose impetuously, Jane-Ellen left the two of them. She called in another direction, "Daniel? Daniel, wait for me!"

Rose then turned to Malcolm and leaned to pull the blanket away. She lifted a bandage on his stump to observe the work she'd done to stop infection. Satisfied, she covered him.

"We all love you, Malcolm, despite your childish moods and brutal savagery. Your fickleness and unpredictability. Don't ask me why, half-breed, but we all love you. People like Abe and Daniel will give Kansas its future, but people like you somehow give it glory and passion. Yet, it's peace in your heart you need now."

With that, his Shawnee sister-in-law covered his eyes with her hand, saying, "Sleep for a while."

* * * * *

Malcolm later woke to the sensation of being lifted. He concluded several men were placing him in the wagon he'd seen. He saw John Brown directing the move. "Careful," Brown said. "Gently. He's like my son, too, so he's your brother."

Milford came alongside, holding Ebony's reins and saying to Brown as he tied them near the tailgate, "I know he should rest. But he desperately craves news from Lawrence. He overheard us talking about the Rangers. I think you should tell him everything. Still, I wouldn't let him entertain the notion of doing anything about it."

"You say he found his mother there. He'll be anxious about her," Brown said.

"The Committee of Safety in Lawrence generally moves the women and children out when there's danger. Not all the women comply. Yes, he'll worry," Abe said. "But you can't deny Malcolm the truth."

Erskine heard that exchange and saw them shake hands. Milford then reached into the wagon bed and took Malcolm's hand, squeezing it warmly. "Goodbye for now," he said. When they unclasped hands, Malcolm waved a farewell.

Brown directed his sons to help him into the wagon, where he would ride beside Erskine. The wagon got under way.

Brown said to Malcolm, "Shortly after you left Lawrence, Sam Jones entered the city, in part seeking you, in part on other business. It's difficult to comprehend, but you must remember, though Jones is little more than a coward and Law and Order lackey, he still carries credentials as Sheriff of Douglas County, bogus or not.

"Unfortunately for Lawrence, Jones was fired on while there and wounded. That and other events have now stimulated an impression among United States officials of lawlessness by Free Staters. Federal Marshal Israel Donelson has been assigned to keep the peace.

"In the meantime, a force of three hundred Southern mercenaries, known as Kickapoo Rangers, have arrived in the region to assist the Law and Order Party and put down Free Staters."

Brown spat over the side of the wagon as it rolled bumpily along. "Law and Order Party," he said with a snort. "Gives concepts of law and order a bad name." Another snort. "At the moment, Lawrence is totally without leadership. For reasons unclear, General Lane has not only left the city but is no longer in the Territory. Charles Robinson is also absent—to try to appeal to Northern forces for aid. On his way to St. Louis he was taken under arrest. So much for political solutions."

Brown spat again.

"Even former Governor Reeder, that saint of a man so dedicated to our cause, has been forced to hide and is wholly without influence in the present circumstances. And Governor Shannon? He's done another about-face, supporting Marshal Donelson and Jones, abandoning our side altogether. He's given endorsement to the occupation of Lawrence. You know what that means."

Malcolm nodded.

"Lawrence will be destroyed," John Brown said.

After a long pause, he said, "Only one abolitionist group remains in all Kansas showing any guts for the fight, albeit a meager force by comparison with the huge army the proslavers are mustering."

Erskine looked at the old man quizzically.

"What force?" Brown said in response to Malcolm's raised eyebrows. "All hope for a free Kansas," Brown bent his head sadly to say, "strange as it may sound, is vested in the few who're riding in this wagon."

48

Despite John Brown's analysis of a weakening Free State position, Malcolm resisted yielding to a defeatist mood. He knew the old man would never give up the fight, regardless of the odds.

Brown filled the remaining time of the wagon ride describing operations of the Underground Railroad. He personalized tales of runaways, sharing anecdotes and accounts of their lives in slavery. He spoke of close calls, the pursuing Missourians threatening to close in and recapture their "property."

"In every case," Brown said, "we were successful in eluding those devils."

At the moment, he said, he doubted there was a single fugitive slave in Lykins County. All had been transferred successfully north out of Kansas or to Canada. But more would arrive within days, and many more after that.

"We run the most efficient 'railroad' that has ever operated," the old man said, emitting a rare chuckle to add, "with or without tracks. And Mrs. O'Brien's generous gift will smooth the journey for many."

More than any other new town in Kansas, and partly because of Brown's work, Osawatomie had become a second city to Lawrence in tactical importance to Free Staters. The sounds Malcolm heard, the scenes he glimpsed indicated a busier and possibly larger population than Lawrence's.

Brown called for the wagon to halt in the middle of town. He got out.

By turning his head slightly, Erskine saw they were in front of a drugstore called "Darr's." Brown entered the place and was gone for a very short time. When he came out and was helped again into the wagon bed, he explained that "Doc" Darr was the closest professional the city had to a physician. Darr would visit Brown's camp to look at Malcolm as soon as he could.

They drove off again and within a half hour arrived at Brown's place.

John Brown directed that Erskine use his room in the rambling cabin for convalescence. It had a view of the Marais des Cygnes River. The spring air floated through opposing windows to give the place a freshness it needed, for no women were about to see to cleanliness. The bedding odor was foul.

Remembering his most recent comfort in a bed, Malcolm let his thoughts drift to Naomi Goodman. Then he recalled his promise—to *try* to forgo violence. While wondering whether he could or would keep such a pledge, he fell into a deep sleep.

*****

In a matter of a week, buoyed by the companionship of the Browns and by "Doc" Darr's frequent ministrations, Malcolm was up and about. He tried earnestly to transfer his attentions to helping fugitive slaves. He asked Brown for the privilege of serving as a "conductor" on the Underground Railroad.

The abolitionist said he feared Malcolm would become strenuously active too soon. He allowed the Jayhawker to witness movements of slaves in the immediate area, to talk with the wretched souls, to learn what these escape opportunities meant to them and to the white people making them possible.

After another few days, Malcolm mounted Ebony and joined a party at one of the nearby "stations" to greet thirteen Negroes under cover of darkness. And, despite Brown's raising a fuss because he feared slowing Erskine's recovery, Malcolm also volunteered as a day guard to patrol the area with a Sharps rifle and revolver.

Malcolm believed at first that using weapons would be a problem with half his left arm gone. Yet he was soon able to raise his stump to rest the rifle barrel for aim. Shortly after that he found—through practice and practical necessity—he was virtually as successful operating and aiming the rifle unsupported, one-handed. He used his knees to grip the stock while breech-reloading, his mouth for storing bullets.

Brown's family and a few followers held occasional matches to test and sharpen their skills. Erskine volunteered to compete. He then outpointed half the other shooters with his disciplined and steady one-armed method. He vowed afterwards—aloud—to become champion in another week.

Malcolm missed most in his recovery the companionship of women and the warming effect of an occasional swig of whiskey. Brown had made no hard and fast rules about women and whiskey, but the example of celibacy and temperance he set was eloquent enough for all to follow.

Erskine thrived in this Spartan environment. He estimated his health progressed faster toward full recovery than if he'd been too closely nursed and indulged.

Often he went swimming in the Marais des Cygnes or in Pottawatomie Creek, testing and strengthening his left upper arm, building his upper-body strength and right arm for extra demands on them.

During one such swim, while at midstream in the Pottawatomie, he was surprised to see the white hair of an old Negro pop up in the brush on shore. The man emerged fully and proceeded to the creek, followed by a young woman evidently his daughter.

Malcolm waved them back, indicating they should return to hiding in their nearby "station." He wondered why their safety hadn't been better guarded by others supposed to be standing watch. He swam as quickly as he could for shore, the young woman turning away as he reached for his trousers. All the while Malcolm scolded them for coming out of hiding.

The old Negro explained that he, too, longed to swim, having spotted the creek from the ramshackle cabin where half a dozen fugitive slaves were resting. His daughter had tried to dissuade him, but when he insisted stubbornly she came along as a lookout.

Malcolm groped in his shirt that was hanging on a bush to find his cigarette fixings. Rolling a cigarette one-handed was an art he'd recently perfected with the help of his stump and his teeth. He felt the need for a smoke now, to consider what to do in this minor crisis.

"Go ahead. Have your swim," he said. The old slave stripped the rags from his body and stepped into the creek, revealing whip marks that caused Erskine to wince.

The man dipped himself into the cooling water and then, in a burst of energy, struck out for the creek-bend downstream, using graceful, long strokes. There he turned and retraced his smooth path through the water.

"Onliest wish Papa has," the young woman explained, "is he be back in Africa, free like this again."

"How much more family do you have?" Erskine asked, blowing a stream of smoke as he talked and watched the man, his weapons close for defense and Ebony grazing nearby.

"We's all. Mama, she was sickly and died last yeah."

"Do you have a husband?"

"A *hus*band? They don' 'low us no *hus*band on the plantation we worked." The woman explained she'd had a man and a baby in Tennessee, near Memphis. The man had been sold and the baby had died of a rattler bite in their slave shack. "How's come *you* free?" she asked.

"What do you mean?"

"You a nigguh, ain't you?"

Malcolm thought, turning to survey the woman whose youth had been robbed by slavery. She appeared barely more than seventeen and was strong and supple. During his silence, she smiled and added, "You gwine let me swim, too, Mistuh White Nigguh?"

"I don't think so," Malcolm said quickly, angry with himself for feeling tempted to exploit the situation. He threw his cigarette to the ground and stamped it out with his bare foot. Then he summoned the old man back to shore.

"The two of you," he directed, while the refreshed old man dressed in the rags of his escape, "get back into hiding."

When they turned to leave, the young woman stopped and looked at Malcolm. "I wish it all be different. Don' you?"

Erskine saw a look in her eyes—of longing for simple and serene happiness. He nodded to her and said, "Yes, I do."

With that, she smiled once more. Then the two trudged through the brush to return to the cabin hideout.

The following day, with no slaves in the region and little to do, Malcolm strolled with his horse from Brown's camp to the nearby Marais des Cygnes and again swam, exercised, smoked, thought, tried to plan his future.

A sound in the brush behind him and a slight whinny by Ebony alerted him to someone's approach on foot.

Abe Milford! His valued friend embraced Malcolm, remarking on the recovery with lavish approval. After exchanging personal news, Abe waited for Erskine to sit and relax. Then his face became clouded.

"I have terrible news, Malcolm. Your mother has been killed. Yesterday Jones and his drunken company—with the U.S. Marshal's men and Kickapoo Rangers—sacked Lawrence. They swept in so quickly there was no time to organize a defense.

"They burned the Free State Hotel to the ground—rode around raising general hell. They destroyed the newspapers and burned other buildings, then ranged through town like Crusaders searching for infidels.

"In a way it was good they met little resistance, for the loss of life turned out to be relatively small. But when they got to your mother's place to torch it, story goes she came out carrying a revolver, blazing away, cursing slavers loudly, vowing to kill any who touched her or her building.

"One rode up and shot her in the head, and that was that. I've tried but failed to get his identity."

Malcolm received the news in an anguish arising partly from having gotten to know Dahlia Bahari—truly know her—after their long separation. More than his mother, she'd become a friend.

Yet one burning truth leapt from the news. As Malcolm turned everything over in his mind, he fingered the *chai* Naomi had given him. That truth was that he was the blood of Dahlia's blood—and her death must be avenged.

49

After Malcolm calmed himself, he accompanied Abe the short distance to Brown's cabin.

They found the place in a state of turmoil.

John Brown, looking fiercely agitated, was shouting orders. His sons Fred, Owen, Watson, Salmon, Oliver—and his son-in-law, Henry Thompson—were calling back in apparent confusion about what the seemingly crazed patriarch meant them to do.

Erskine noticed the absence of John Brown, Jr.

Neighbor Jim Townsley made a dusty arrival by wagon and called out to Brown that John, Jr., had successfully mobilized a company called the Pottawatomie Rifles and struck out for Lawrence to assist.

"To do *what?*" old Brown responded. "There's not a bit of use for that *now.* Assist!" Brown spat into the dust at his feet.

Erskine sought Brown's attention while Milford went to greet Ted Weiner and his company, now riding into camp.

"John, what can I do to help?" Malcolm asked. "Who do you want me to lead—or follow?"

"You," Brown said, pointing to Erskine, "will go nowhere. You're not well enough to fight."

Malcolm protested that his *mother* was among the victims, that he was as strong and ready as any.

Brown picked up a rifle, turned, and walked off, brushing aside with a gesture further remarks and offers by Erskine.

"Leave off," Henry Thompson suggested to Malcolm. "He's not rational. He'll listen to nobody." Thompson then hurried off to help load Townsley's wagon with rifles and ammunition.

Abe raced back to Erskine and said, darkly, "There's to be a blood bath. Vengeance through the slaughter of nearby innocents. Just because their sympathies are with the other side."

"You're not serious," Malcolm responded. "Where did you hear of any such plan as that?"

"Ted Weiner told me. That's what this is all about. And why are you surprised, Malcolm? Isn't that like the policy you urged on General Lane? What *we* urged on people in Lawrence? Eye for an eye, regardless? As long as the targets are known proslavers?"

"Well, *yes.*"

"You never thought you'd see it carried out," Milford said. "You thought an announced policy might just intimidate Bushwhackers against riding in."

"Yes. Post it as a deterrent, but—" Erskine tried to look sharply into the eyes of all the men about him. He hungered to know what was in John Brown's heart.

Abe said, "I'm leaving. I suggest you do the same. Stay out of this one." Abe went to his horse, mounted, paused to wave goodbye to Erskine. Then he rode northeast, seeming headed for Paola.

Brown appeared in no condition to listen to anyone. He walked about barking orders as though singlehandedly mustering a regiment. He'd surely cut down anyone now—maybe one of his own sons—if any was so foolish as to stand in his way.

Malcolm found the situation ironic. As slayer of more men than all here combined had killed in the Border War, he wandered through camp ignored.

Of course he wanted to do something over what happend in Lawrence. *Yes,* he wanted to hunt down those who'd killed his mother. But seek out fellow Kansans whose sympathies lay with slavery, who'd never lifted weapons in violence? No.

Before long Brown, still on foot, had his force assembled in readiness for a bloody ride. Erskine stood far to the side, a lonely witness.

John first instructed Owen Brown to stand ready to lead most of the men along Pottawatomie Creek, then to break off an advance party that would call back John, Jr., and his force.

He, old Brown, with Townsley and the others, would proceed to the homes of known proslavers, the Doyles and others he named. At that point in Brown's delivery of preliminary instructions, Townsley appeared to balk. Sitting in the driver's seat of the wagon, he fidgeted and fussed and made opposing remarks.

"Shut up!" Brown commanded. "You're trying to discourage my boys!"

Brown drew a revolver but did not aim it. The gesture was clear to all, a reminder Brown was in charge and would tolerate no breach of discipline. When quiet was restored, he reholstered the handgun.

"Hear me!" John shouted, lifting a rifle above his head, clenching his other hand into a fist.

"Hear me! The words of Free State politicians have failed to protect Lawrence. Now the time is past for negotiations and political solutions. I call on the power of Almighty God to help us rid Kansas of her enemies," Brown said, next raising his eyes to the heavens.

"Lord, your humble soldier, John Brown, has come to this place in obedience to your command, that the evil of slavery must never be allowed to flourish here."

In that instant, in a brief second's pause by Brown, Erskine knew he must separate himself totally from this man. The fanaticism of anyone's claiming to have had two-way conversation with God was more than Malcolm could accept.

"There's been talk of so-called 'innocents'," Brown said. "Talk that we seek to destroy men who've not taken up arms against us." Brown paused, shifting his gaze from the sky momentarily to spit into the dust below. "Who is innocent, Lord, if guilty in his *heart?* Who is innocent if he judges a man inferior by the shade of that man's skin? And," Brown said, lowering his gaze and flashing his eyes at those about him, all of whom listened awestruck, "who is innocent if he doesn't soldier to rid the land of *all* believers in slavery?"

Pausing, energized to hoist himself onto the wagon without help, he then shouted, *"An eye for an eye!"*

With that, a cry of *"Forward!"* by Owen Brown, who brandished a cutlass, started the force from camp. Townsley's wagon and several on horses raised a huge, dusty cloud that was caught eerily by the setting sun.

*****

That long night Malcolm lay in John Brown's bed, unable to sleep. Just before dawn, dazed by the torment in his mind and lack of rest, Erskine stirred to the sound of a few horses riding into camp. He reached for a revolver and rushed to the window.

A man and two women entered the clearing—Daniel and Naomi Goodman and Jane-Ellen O'Brien, covered head to foot by the dirt of their ride. "We've come to pay our respects," Daniel said, dismounting quickly and rushing to take Malcolm's hand.

"Oh, Malcolm," Jane-Ellen said tearfully, her face streaked. "I'm so sorry about Dahlia—*our* Dahlia." She sobbed freely and was helped from her horse by Daniel.

"Where is everyone?" Goodman asked.

"Gone for revenge," Malcolm said.

"East to Missouri?"

"No. South, then along the Pottawatomie in a campaign of madness. Invoking God's name as they go."

Hearing that, Jane-Ellen stepped back and crossed herself.

"I'm finished here," Erskine said.

"You're leaving Brown's place," Goodman observed.

"And leaving Kansas."

50

The foursome spent the sultry day in and around John Brown's place, with only the sounds of chickens and an occasional owl relieving the multiple tensions.

They considered going to Lawrence, then argued themselves away from that course. Naomi tried to persuade them all toward Paola, but Malcolm refused. Making do with what was in Brown's cupboards, they ate mostly in silence. They walked in the woods, sat by a stream with their bare feet in the water, idly identified birds that darted among the trees, and returned to the cabin.

They sat, each with separate thoughts.

"I appreciate your spending today with me," Erskine said. "I know it's from respect for my mother."

Naomi sought to lighten the mood. She picked up a cloth napkin and reached to tickle Erskine's face with the corners of it, saying, "It's also from simply wanting to be with you, Malcolm. There's a great deal of feeling for you among us."

Daniel said, "I think we should follow Brown's group, see what he's been up to."

Jane-Ellen said, "I'm afraid of what we'll find."

"It's a good suggestion," Malcolm said, "if for no other reason than to learn Brown may have backed off. May have had second thoughts and *not* struck innocent men. That could bear on my staying or leaving the Territory."

Naomi straightened in her chair and raised her eyebrows.

Malcolm continued. "Even if we chose to track Brown, it's getting late in the day. We'll lose light before we can turn back."

Naomi rose and said, brightly, "Jane-Ellen, you and I will find fresh linens, make up clean cots or beds as best we can. We're staying the night. Daniel, you slaughter and pluck a fat chicken for dinner. Malcolm, get a fire going in the stove and fill a large pot with water. Find some vegetables in the larder."

*****

That night Malcolm's anxieties insured sleeplessness again.

Brown's room was stocked with books, and he'd found among them Harriet Beecher Stowe's latest attack on slavery, *Dred: A Tale of the Great Dismal Swamp.*

Long before coming to Kansas, he'd read and been moved by *Uncle Tom's Cabin.* While he now found the reading freshly inspirational, he doubted the Beechers and Stowes, whom he'd met back East, were aware of extremes to which co-abolitionists such as John Brown had gone.

Erskine set the book aside and reached for his tobacco and cigarette papers next to the candle. He thought about Morogh Erskine, his father. He wanted to see Papa, tell him face to face what he'd learned of Dahlia's whereabouts the past two decades and her final, brutal fate.

The door opened. It was Naomi. "May I come in and talk to you?"

Malcolm surveyed the beautiful woman in candlelight, wondering at her motive for coming. He still believed her last visit in this manner was a planned seduction, to free Daniel from competition over Jane-Ellen. "Yes, Naomi, come in."

She sat on the edge of the bed, again projecting her calm beauty eye-to-eye. "If you leave Kansas, Malcolm, I'm going with you."

"That's impossible. There's a heavy price on my head in Missouri, which I'll be crossing the full breadth of. I'll go alone."

"I'll follow you. Or we can go north to Nebraska and then through Iowa."

"Forget 'we' for a trip of a thousand and a half miles, nearly all of it overland. You'll remain in Paola with your family." Malcolm then crushed his cigarette into a crude stonewear dish, probing Naomi's gaze for the secret behind her suggestion. "Are you pregnant?"

She nodded. "It's been only weeks, but there are ways a woman can tell."

"That won't hold me, you know. I consider myself a man of honor, but—"

"Oh, cut the horseshit, Malcolm," Naomi said in the first flash of verbal emotion he'd ever witnessed from her. "If I'm to have your child, I'm proud—regardless of shame it might bring my family. Don't think I seek to *hold* you by it. By my own code of honor, I hadn't planned to tell you. Because you asked, neither can I keep it from you."

Malcolm thought long on that last statement, and he softened. "I'm grateful for what you've just said, your candor. I respect your courage and your independence."

Naomi again looked Malcolm in the eyes by the candlelight. "My only reason for coming to you tonight was to prepare you for my decision to join you."

"I overrule that. It's final. Now, go back to your room."

"First, hug me. Let me know you're not made of stone."

"A one-armed man finds embracing difficult."

"I don't care about that. It's your soul I look at, not your missing forearm."

He reached instead for her hand, drew it to his lips, and kissed the palm. "I need time away—alone," he said. "All I can offer is to remind you, this child was created in a moment of love's passion."

"*Love's* passion? Do you really know the meaning of love? I mean, I hope you do, but—"

"I'm—in the process of finding that out, among other things. Now go, Naomi, please."

As she rose to leave, they were startled by the door's opening again. It was Jane-Ellen, who said, "Oh! Excuse me."

Quickly, gently, Naomi took Jane-Ellen by the arm. "Is it Daniel you're looking for? He's asleep farther down the hallway. Come, I'll show you."

Obviously taken aback and outmaneuvered, Jane-Ellen threw a melancholy look at Malcolm while yielding to Naomi's guidance.

For Erskine's part, he felt like a pawn in a game between two strong-willed women. He decided to put all thoughts of them away—if he could.

*****

By five in the morning all were up. Daniel seemed particularly cheerful, the two women strangely quiet.

Malcolm packed his small kit. He and Daniel readied the horses while the women fried bacon and eggs. They ate quietly, Naomi's serenity seeming to prevail against Daniel's boyishness, Jane-Ellen's divided heart, and Erskine's brooding.

Suddenly, when they were finished and straightening the kitchen, Malcolm announced, "The women must return to Paola. Neither is to engage in this search of the Pottawatomie." Daniel appeared surprised.

"That's ridiculous," Naomi said, putting dishes away. "What do you fear from our possible exposure to the sight of death?"

"Don't you know?" Erskine asked in a way seeming to puzzle Daniel and Jane-Ellen.

Naomi hesitated, then nodded, "I think I do."

"What *is* it?" Daniel pressed.

"I'm pregnant," Naomi said, causing Jane-Ellen to gasp. "He fears a bad effect. I don't accept such old wives' tales."

Erskine now found every excuse to put off their leaving. It was mid-morning before he broke the stillness of their wait, broke the boring buzz of flies inside the cabin to say, "All right, take some extra food and some blankets. Let's ride out."

Though Malcolm could have found it relatively simple to use Shawnee tracking methods to follow Brown, even on dry ground, he led them deliberately astray.

"But the wagon went that way!" Daniel protested, pointing along the creek.

"We'll look north," Erskine said. "There's a clearing near the Marais des Cygnes that Brown uses for a rendezvous when his band becomes separated. We'll start from there, then work our way west and south again."

Malcolm knew Daniel suspected he was delaying the search purposely on account of Naomi. "I'll talk to them," Daniel offered in a low voice. "See if I can't send them back to Paola."

"Thank you," Erskine replied.

Daniel dropped back to ride alongside the women.

The unseasonable heat made the sight of the Marais a welcome one. Jane-Ellen bravely insisted on a swim. "You're as dusty as I," she called to Naomi. "Will you join me?"

"Farther along," Naomi said. "I'm still influenced by modesty. Let the men stay here."

When he and Malcolm were alone, Daniel said, "It's no use. They're stubborn in this. We have no hold on them, to be giving orders. They're not soldiers, you know."

"I'll confess," Erskine said, sitting on the bank and rolling a cigarette, "part of it is protectiveness I feel from Naomi's news, part is knowing what we'll find, and—part is wanting to savor the companionship of the three of you before I leave Kansas."

Goodman was clearly moved. He placed a hand on Malcolm's shoulder and squeezed. "When will you return?"

"I have no plan to return," Erskine said, "else I might not have caused this delay."

"This is a beautiful place," Daniel observed. "Why don't we camp? You need the rest. You've hardly slept for two nights."

"It's already past mid-day. I'll nap," Malcolm agreed. "You guard the women and the horses."

* * * * *

When Malcolm awoke, wood had been gathered for a campfire to be lighted later. The horses had been unsaddled and brushed and were grazing together, loosely tethered. Naomi and Jane-Ellen were laughing companionably.

Erskine went to the stream for a quick, refreshing wash.

After supper, Daniel told stories of the Goodmans' emigration from New York and of their starting the family business in Paola, sprinkling his tale with amusing anecdotes that eased Malcolm's mood.

With darkness, there was little doubt how they would arrange themselves. In the soft firelight, covered with a blanket, Naomi pressed close to Malcolm and whispered, "Can you ever put Jane-Ellen from your thoughts?"

"I'm not certain, in all honesty, though she seems happy with Daniel."

"'Seems' is the correct word, I'm afraid," Naomi said. "I'm glad you had a long rest this afternoon. Will you please resign yourself to our accompanying you along the Pottawatomie?"

Malcolm buried his face in the rose-scented area of her neck and shoulder and said, "Tonight, Naomi—at this moment—I'm resigned to anything you demand."

*****

By first light of morning they were off and riding, returning south.

In an hour they reached a sorry scene—several settlers gathered around a corpse evidently pulled from the Pottawatomie. Malcolm inquired after the identity of the man and was told he was William Sherman, slaughtered by several sword thrusts—chops, slices—mutilated.

"Navy cutlasses," Malcolm said, realizing immediately Brown's mad campaign was more insidious than he'd expected. The younger Brown boys had been brandishing the swords. And such execution is done only when an assassin fears alarming others by sound of firearms.

Furthermore, the killing was freshly done. That indicated a full *two days' hesitation* by Brown in contemplation of how he would administer his "eye for an eye" policy.

Dismounting, approaching a farmer who was apparently a neighbor to this place, Erskine asked, "What manner of man was Sherman? Where did his sympathies lie, do you know?"

"I know only that Sherman is kin to Dutch Henry and happened to be here when Dutch was not. Dutch, as you may know, is a proslavery man. I heard and then saw Brown and his sons and a few others ride off in the night, obviously after doing this."

"You're positive it was Brown, and just a few with him."

"I saw them all by their torchlights. Yes."

Malcolm remounted, observing bitter reaction by the two women and Daniel. *"Shoot!* Is this," Jane-Ellen protested, "what I sent Brown money to do?"

"I assure you," Erskine said, "it's not. Brown has helped many slaves escape and has used your contribution well. What he fails to use well is his good sense when his passions are fired."

Daniel asked, "How many do you think were involved, Malcolm?"

"Not many, from the tracks leading away. Eight or ten. I think some abandoned the project, and old Brown waited for his other forces. When he realized after two days they'd defied his orders, continued to Lawrence or returned to their homes, he struck—out of frustration as well as madness. Let's continue upstream."

After another quarter-hour or so they came upon a dog in the road that appeared to be summoning them. The wretched animal wagged its long tail sadly at the sight of them, then kept bounding to the roadside as though to show something there.

Both Daniel and Malcolm dismounted to investiage. They found a body, similarly cut and brutalized by swords. "It's Allen Wilkinson," Erskine said. "I recognize him. Dead not over six hours."

"A proslaver?"

"Yes, of course. In Franklin County, widely known to be."

"One sword thrust would have done it. Why so many?"

"I don't know," Erskine replied. "I don't know. Brown's boys tend to go a little crazy. I blame myself for delaying this search, for idling. I hadn't realized Brown would hesitate. But knowing it now, I think I might have been able to dissuade him, had we caught up sooner."

Daniel appeared vexed over Malcolm's self-criticism, a condition he'd witnessed in his leader at Camp Branch. "No one could have stopped Brown, from the way you described his mood. Where to now?"

"To James Doyle's place. I have no doubt Brown intended to go there."

When they arrived soon at the Doyle farm, others had gathered and were placing the bodies of young Drury and William Doyle in a wagon bed. Malcolm could see at a glance that the pattern of cutlass chops and apparent mutilation of the young Doyles was similar to the deadly work done others. Jim Doyle was the only one shot—and stabbed as well. He'd taken a bullet in the forehead, no doubt fired by John Brown himself. A neighbor woman wailed at the horror as the four saddened companions led by Malcolm walked their horses through the scene.

"Let's leave," Erskine said. "I've seen enough butchery. And I've committed enough as well. But never like this, against unarmed, innocent men and boys."

They mounted and rode east. Soon Malcolm pulled up and dismounted. They were near Osawatomie. Paola lay north a short distance. "We'll say our goodbyes here," he announced.

Daniel, Naomi, and Jane-Ellen also dismounted. Naomi said, for all to hear, "Will you now, Malcolm, give up killing once and for all? Dedicate yourself and your work only to life?"

Malcolm reached impulsively to touch the *chai* she'd given him, recalling his rash promise. "I've known and felt madness similar to what we've seen today. But never against innocents. Give up killing? Tell me, Naomi, what do you expect me to do in defense if attacked? Offer no resistance? And what of my honor when those dear to me are taken?"

Naomi said, looking away, "It's significant to me you haven't directly answered my questions. Maybe there are no answers."

Malcolm took each in a farewell embrace, Daniel first, then Jane-Ellen, who began to cry, then Naomi. She whispered to him, "I *know* you'll return. Your place is here. Your heart is in Kansas, and you're in *my* heart."

Erskine stepped back to look at her. Rather than speak, he nodded—ambiguously. He released Naomi and turned to mount Ebony.

In the saddle, he paused to say, "I don't know how, but Kansas will someday be free and secure. Meanwhile, I want to break the torment in my soul over things I've done and seen. When I do, *I'll* be free and secure."

He started Ebony forward and cantered toward the morning sun.

Naomi said, "I *know* you'll return, Malcolm. Your heart is in Kansas, and you're in *my* heart."

Part Two

Fall of 1856
through 1857

51

A faint tinkling of piano music relieved Malcolm's depression, but only slightly.

The after-midnight atmosphere in New Orleans was thick with a stifling dampness. He labored to draw a lung-filling breath. Even a yawn felt incomplete.

Erskine's coming to New Orleans had proved a serious error. The Vieux Carré was populated with whores and thieves, gamblers and drunks. Some son of a bitch had stolen Ebony.

Behind him lay the city made for night-living yet possessing an irresistible beauty in daytime. Ahead of him, where he sat on the wharf, lay the inky Mississippi.

Unconsciously he raised the point of the hook on his left arm, scratching his nose. Consciously—*I've no money, no horse, no future prospects.*

Malcolm regretted the impulse that had steered him to serve a hitch as a sailor. He'd traded passage for himself and Ebony on a fourmaster out of Boston by double-shift menial chores. Couldn't hire on as a sailrigger with only one good arm. He handled some cargo, but mostly he took jobs fit for cabin boys—waiting tables, cleaning decks, and dumping slop, human as well as animal. Stops at Baltimore, Charleston, Tampa, and now New Orleans.

And it was here he'd lost Ebony.

Erskine's visit to Massachusetts had been disappointing. When he brought his father news of finding Dahlia in Lawrence and then of her martyrdom, Morogh Erskine became confused. Two decades of the man's grief over her leaving had frayed into ragged memories of her.

Malcolm learned that Morogh's mind had lately begun playing tricks on him, damaging his effectiveness at captaining large sea vessels in foreign trade. He'd also begun slipping in and out of recognizing his own son. A doctor told Malcolm his father was entering a state of dementia, that recovery was unlikely. A maritime board of inquiry was weighing whether to recommend Morogh's entering a seamen's rest home.

Before leaving Massachusetts this time, Malcolm signed all necessary papers to see to his father's best interests and care.

Malcolm's visit to Baltimore was also frustrating. He'd equipped himself in New England with forged papers showing him to be "James Jefferson," a freed slave "with all accompanying privileges." But moving among the gentry—seeking information about the Mulligans and Jane-Ellen's uncertain origin—proved impossible. No whites in Baltimore wished to share that kind of information with a darky. Blacks were suspicious of the stranger who wore a hook.

Malcolm was a man between, neither enjoying true freedom in the white-dominated world nor accepted as part of "slave society." Freer in New Orleans than in cities north to Baltimore, at least he was among mulattoes and quadroons like himself. But still a man between.

After Baltimore, service at sea was more drift and idle curiosity than purpose. This last stop, when he observed the relative freedom of half-castes in the Vieux Carré, some even entrepreneurs, he vowed never to work a ship again. He thought he might stay here for a time and maybe, eventually, ride Ebony to California.

But at a bawdy house one afternoon on Rampart Street, believing Ebony was safely hitched at a rear railing reserved for customers, he came out and found an empty place where the stallion had stood. Malcolm set out searching the Vieux Carré for Ebony, carrying his knapsack with his weapons stuffed inside. He searched the surrounding city of New Orleans. He learned, at last, that a stallion fitting Ebony's markings had been seen herded onto a ship aimed for Memphis, day before yesterday.

A small Mississippi River sternwheeler was due to dock below the spot where Malcolm sat. Visible in the glow of the city's streetlamps, clanking like a broken machine, the ship was now approaching the wharf. Grey belches puffed and poured from two chimneys. Dark water sloshed over low gunwales.

Two white stevedores stirred themselves from where they'd been dozing on cotton bales, grumbling at the work ahead. Apparently they were to unload more bales as well as sugar cane, with little prospect of additional help.

In the faint light one of them turned, as though considering whether to invite Malcolm to cut in with them. Seeing his color and his handicap, however, the man spat and made a gesture to forget that course of action.

Later, as the small ship edged away in a din of clanks and wheezes, the dock workers headed for the nearest saloon. Malcolm removed his shirt, stuffed it into his knapsack, and slipped into the river while holding the knapsack aloft with his hook.

Soon he climbed aboard. A river sailor later described his sudden appearance at the rail. "I seen first this knapsack throwed over the rail, then a goddam hook! Then this jigguhboo come aboard!"

Several sailors seized Malcolm immediately and searched him and his knapsack. When they discovered weapons, they stripped him and threw him into what passed for a brig—actually a filthy cage he couldn't stand up in, used to transport fighting boars.

Malcolm was locked there overnight.

In the morning the ship's captain peered at him through the bars of the overhead hatch. "Whut *is* you, anyways?" the river pilot asked, giggling.

Malcolm shook the effects of a fitful sleep and recognized his chance for freedom. He reached his hook through the bars between the captain's knees and pressed upward.

The captain went ghostly white, realizing the hazardous position in which this dark-skinned captive held him.

"Whut you wawnt? Anythin' you wawnt, you *got!* Only don't move that hook 'ceptin' *away!*"

"I want my weapons, my clothes, my freedom, and passage to Memphis."

"I ain't stoppin' in Memphis! Goin' straight to Saint Looie!"

Malcolm pressed the hook higher in the man's crotch, asking him, "Ever hear in Missouri about Malcolm Erskine, the border fighter? The Jayhawker?"

"Why shore, *evuh*body— Oh my *Lawd!*" The river pilot reached into his jacket and fumbled for the padlock key. "P-Puts me in mind, whut you was sayin' 'bout M-Memphis, I recollect I *do* has business theah-bouts."

"No you don't. I won't ride with a fool cracker who makes me want to puke. See that I get a ticket on a bigger ship out of Baton Rouge. Else I'll find you again and tear off your balls. Make it first class."

"*Done!* Corn-sider it *done!* Yes-suh, Mr. Er—"

"Jefferson."

"Yes-suh," the captain said, reaching gingerly to unlock the cage, then yelling for a ship's hand to toss down the prisoner's things.

"Mr. *Jefferson's* your name o'course," he prattled, not daring to move an inch. "An' I'll quick as lightnin' make you out a ticket from Baton Rouge, soon's you're dressed and care to step up to the b-bridge. Please be careful with that there hook 'tween my legs! *Please!*"

52

Ticketed and ordered let alone, Malcolm took in sights during the rest of the trip upriver to Baton Rouge, cypresses hung with Spanish moss, an occasional alligator napping on shore. He was still depressed over not knowing whether Ebony was safe or was being mistreated.

The sun began to draw off vapor, and Erskine took deep breaths. From the knapsack-arsenal he'd taken to wearing over his shoulder, he drew a volume of Whitman's work, *Leaves of Grass,* turning to favorite lines:

"This is what you shall do: Love the earth and sun and the animals, despise riches, give alms to every one that asks, stand up for the stupid and crazy, devote your income and labor to others, hate tyrants, argue not concerning God, have patience and indulgence toward the people, take off your hat to nothing known or unknown or to any man or number of men, go freely with powerful uneducated persons and with the young and with the mothers of families, read these leaves in the open air every season of every year of your life, re-examine all you have been told at school or church or in any book, dismiss whatever insults your own soul, and your very flesh shall be a great poem and have the richest fluency not only in its words but in the silent lines of its lips and face and between the lashes of your eyes and in every motion and joint of your body...."

Walt Whitman the poet was at one with Erskine the freedom-fighter, he concluded. What the Eastern poet-traveler wrote was true and believable, as much for a black in slavery as for any man in freedom, just so long as the man stood straight as he could—and bravely.

For a man between, such as himself—well, it was even truer.

Where Malcolm stood near the bow, with water splitting into waves that broke in opposite directions, he was confident a scent of the plains was reaching him. It came as a surprise. He was sure, or possibly imagining, the scent had traces of blowing dust and cattle, dung and farmer's sweat, woman's milkiness—all blended. Wisps of wind must also have crossed over sweet prairie flowers, picking up as well the pungency of dark earth under a plow.

And there were sounds in the breezes, and mind-pictures—

The low voice of Sylvia in a Shawnee cabin, her buckskin dress at the foot of their bed. The giggling of the brash Jane-Ellen while she brushed her paint pony. The whispers by Rose, who could either kill or love passionately. The frank counsel of Naomi, a giving woman of rosy pinkness and countless delights.

Tears leapt to Erskine's eyes. He returned the book to his knapsack, feeling inside also for the security of his weapons and for the security of keepsakes—the stone scarab, the gold *chai.*

He knew he couldn't linger in Memphis after he recovered Ebony, which he was confident he could use his tracking skills to do. Together they must somehow cross Arkansas, past the Buffalo River and the Ozarks to Kansas Territory.

California could wait.

Sounds and scents of the plains were beckoning.

* * * * *

The dock at Baton Rouge bustled with activity. The river captain directed Malcolm to a huge sidewheeler he would board for Memphis. "That one, Mr.—ah—Jefferson."

The captain winked. Erskine ignored that, as well as the man's extended hand. He headed directly for the larger ship, the *Delta Queen.*

At the foot of the gangplank he displayed his ticket. The ship's crewmen surveyed him curiously for his questionable color. The purser observed, "This ticket is made out for a *white* man. Beggin' your pardon, Mr. Jefferson, but you are surely the darkest-complected white man—"

"Stamp it," Malcolm commanded him quietly.

The purser hesitated, then did so, holding it up uncertainly.

Erskine whipped his left arm forward and speared the ticket on the hook point, proceeding up the gangplank with a defiant hoist to his knapsack.

Inquiring of a startled steward, he sought his first-class cabin. The accommodations were more than satisfactory—except for an argument in progress opposite his door. He peered into the cabin across the way and observed another steward attempting to reason—in both English and French—with an obviously infuriated Creole.

As nearly as Malcolm could determine, a woman accompanying the Creole was not the man's wife but his sister. She wasn't present. Ship's rules wouldn't allow an adult brother and sister to share a cabin, and no other was available.

The angry passenger said he would neither pay for two cabins nor be moved from the ship to await another passenger vessel. Brother and sister must be in Memphis in two days. The next ship would get them there too late.

"Excuse me," Malcolm said, standing in the doorway and addressing the steward. "I'm James Jefferson. I would be happy to offer the hospitality of my cabin, which is directly across, if this gentleman wishes to share it for the trip. In that way, his sister may have this one to herself."

The steward appeared mightily relieved, in spite of Malcolm's being a man of color.

The Creole protested, however, on grounds it was too generous of "Monsieur Jefferson" to allow himself such inconvenience. No, he insisted. The ship's rules must bend to allow for family custom. He and his sister have shared accommodations all their lives.

"Mon Dieux, un frere et une souer?" He gestured to show that evil in such a relationship was unthinkable—and that even to *think* it was an insult.

Malcolm, not inexperienced with matters of such delicacy, approached the agitated passenger and rested his hook gently on the man's shoulder. He couldn't let further disturbance draw attention to that part of the ship and wished an end to this argument.

With a slight shift of his head and a quick, dark look at the steward, Erskine commanded the officer to leave. The man obeyed with apparent knowledge this "Jefferson" fellow would work out the arrangements as he'd suggested.

"What's your name?"

"Eugene Fontenot," the Creole said. "My sister is called Audrey."

"Where is, ah, Mademoiselle Audrey?"

"I asked her to her wait on deck until the matter was settled."

Malcolm said, "The matter, *mon ami,* is settled."

Fontenot shrugged. "As you wish, Monsieur."

"What's your business in Memphis?"

Before Fontenot could answer, a curly-haired brunette with mischievously flashing blue eyes appeared at the doorway. She was dressed elegantly in emerald. She carried a closed, matching parasol in one hand and a folded newspaper in the other.

The woman announced, "I saw the steward come out. The discussion is finished?" She couldn't have been over twenty, Malcolm calculated.

Fontenot explained the arrangements Erskine offered, introducing him by the false name he was using.

"Ah, yes. Then it was *true,* what our parents said of our third President and the slavewoman he loved."

Malcolm bowed and said, "Mademoiselle Audrey," kissing her extended hand. He was awed by her remarkable figure that was stylishly revealed in high fashion, possibly Parisian. But the smirk she maintained following their introduction puzzled him.

Later they took a quiet dinner together, the three of them. Audrey Fontenot continued to clutch the folded newspaper closely to her or rest it beside her on the chair. She seemed to be pressing a pose of knowing something no one else knew. She was quite clever in conversation, Malcolm observed, and evidently well schooled.

When the time came to retire and before they closed their opposing doors, Malcolm received a generous wink from Audrey, unmistakable in its meaning.

With Eugene snoring at last, Erskine tiptoed out and tapped a knuckle at Audrey's door.

When he was admitted to the still-lighted cabin, he found her wearing only a diaphanous yellow negligee and an intoxicating scent. Magnolia? The newspaper was open on a table. The bed-cover was folded down, and a thick bath towel lay spread on it.

The paper was a week-old copy of *The New York Tribune.* On its front page a drawing of Erskine appeared, hook and all. The picture's pose and accompanying headlines were exaggerated representations of his Jayhawker adventures.

"It is coincidence," Audrey said, "that I have been reading about you, Monsieur Malcolm Erskine." Her voice had a purring quality, matching her feline air of combined possession and submissiveness.

Malcolm felt as though his heart had leapt into his throat. Would he be taken captive again through some seductive treachery planned by Audrey Fontenot?

"You have me at a disadvantage," he said, considering escape.

"Oui, je connais, vraiment," she said, advancing toward him. "On the chance I have the only copy on board, I will keep your secret safe—if you will do likewise with mine."

"Your secret?" Malcolm asked—at first confused but then delighted and surprised over the tempo at which their new acquaintanceship was suddenly progressing. He soon came to know the reason for the towel, yet another surprise.

* * * * *

After an hour or more, when he returned to his cabin, Malcolm found Eugene stirring awake. "I thought I heard you," Fontenot said. "Where have you been?"

"Uh— Down the hall, to the, uh—"

"Aboard ship they call it a 'head'," Eugene observed, laughing. He sought his pillow again, then as an afterthought— "Ah, I was beginning to tell you earlier—"

"It is coincidence," Audrey said, "that I have been reading about you, Monsieur Malcolm Erskine."

"Tell me what?" Malcolm asked.

"The business that takes us to Memphis. It is for an arranged marriage involving a very rich, older gentleman. Our family is to receive a handsome sum for my delivering Audrey as a bride of beauty, wit, good breeding, and education. And most importantly, she is untouched."

53

Between eighty and one hundred slaves boarded the side-wheeler at Vicksburg. Malcolm lost count as they were herded below by men with sidearms and bullwhips.

Audrey Fontenot, leaning with Erskine against an upper deck railing, turned and studied him quietly, then said, "That is not at all to your liking, *mon cher, n'est-ce-pas?"*

Malcolm stood straight, pulled a tobacco pouch from a pocket to fill and roll a cigarette with one hand and his hook. He said nothing as he lit up but continued to stare at the cargo deck below, watching the ship's hands replace planks and rails for the vessel's departure.

Audrey said, "My fiancé owns many slaves. He is in cotton and needs them, of course. Do you like me any less, knowing I will soon become mistress of slaves? Owner of slaves?"

Malcolm exhaled a stream of smoke that was caught by a river breeze quickly. Whatever his answer, it would be important to this cultured young woman. He turned to her, his dark eyes from under the brim of his hat holding her in a steady gaze. "Will you like *yourself* less?" he asked.

The effect was clear. Audrey gasped and clutched the railing tightly, her knuckles showing white. She hung her head and breathed hard. *"Mon pere –* My father is a gambler. He is heavily in debt. This marriage will save our family from ruin."

Malcolm looked at the retreating city of Vicksburg as the steamship moved out. "Why," he asked, "don't Eugene and your father simply go to work?"

"You don't understand," Audrey said in an apparent appeal to reason on her terms. "They are trained for nothing useful in Louisiana. We are not like the Cajuns who have been here for a century, and they farm or trap or fish." She punctuated her speech with animated gestures.

"We are Creoles. Our parents were well-to-do Parisians, dealers in art. They held grand illusions about this 'New World.' They did not know life here would be so harsh. My mother died here, bringing me into the world. Eugene was little more than a baby himself. My father has since given everything to educate us, and now it is our turn to repay him, to take care of him."

Erskine indicated he wished to walk on the deck, then he asked, "Pay him back by being miserable for the rest of your life? Would a father expect or want *that?*"

"If that is what it will come to," Audrey said, "so be it, but I doubt it. After all, I shall be a very wealthy woman. Monsieur Catron—"

"Who!?" Malcolm stopped, threw down the cigarette, stamped on it.

"The gentleman I am to marry. Ferdinand Magellan Catron. Quite an odd name, I confess." She laughed. "True, I have not actually *seen* him, but I understand he is very kind, very courteous, very—"

Malcolm stopped her. "No more," he said. "I don't need to hear any more."

"But I would *like* to tell you about him, so that your mind will be at rest that I am doing the right thing," Audrey pleaded, babbling on. "He is a mature gentleman, almost sixty in age, I believe, a survivor of the famous Texas battle for the Alamo, and—"

"On which side?"

She was peeved. "Malcolm, you are unfair."

"Not really," he replied, half-amused, half-disgusted. Educated as she was, she should know, he thought, the only survivors of the Alamo besides Mexican troops were a couple of women and a slave who were spared. And one or two men who went over the wall early, before Colonel Travis made his fatal stand.

Erskine gazed at the deck below, noticing a high-class clientele had also come aboard at Vicksburg. They greeted other wealthy plantation owners from Natchez who were taking a balmy autumn's river cruise. They would all spend evenings in the ship's small theater or in the saloon, watching a comic play, waltzing or dancing a quadrille, smoking and playing cards. They would pause in Memphis and later disembark in St. Louis, where wives would ask indulgence to view the latest fashions. They would dine elegantly in the hotels, flirt with and surreptitiously fondle or arrange liaisons with one another's spouses, and they would return relaxed and in a jovial mood by yet another luxury river craft.

Malcolm considered the Fontenots' current position, particularly the sweetness of this bright young woman who had given herself to him quickly, solely on the strength of his reputation as a man. Surrendered her precious virginity—as testified by blood on the towel—in unspoken desperation because she faced an uncertain marriage. He considered also the companionability of Eugene.

"Audrey, I want to know two things— How much is your father's debt? And how good are you and Eugene with horses?"

"Mais—pourquoi?"

"Never mind why. Just tell me."

"Papa owes nineteen thousand. And as for horses, we had excellent instructors. Eugene rides like the wind. I have managed well *side*saddle, but that was before last night's— Well, shall we call it 'liberation'?"

Definitely there was another way out for her. Erskine knew she was unable to assess realistically the man she was engaged to marry. He must persuade brother and sister to follow a different course, perhaps join him in his return to Kansas.

The Catrons, he thought bitterly. *Slavers from Texas. One now a Missouri Bushwhacker leader, the other a Tennessee cotton baron with a yellow stripe down his back.*

* * * * *

That evening Erskine wore a suit he'd borrowed from Eugene. As it turned out, a good fit. He left behind his menacing hook and joined the gentlemen and ladies in the ship's saloon.

Despite his color, Malcolm managed by strength of personality to ingratiate himself with some of the cream of Southern Bourbonism.

Sugar-tongued ladies clucked sympathetically over the loss of his arm, which Erskine lied was his sacrifice in Missouri, defending Southern traditions. Though obviously the product of suspiciously mixed ancestry, he claimed he owed his loyalty to the side that upheld *la bonne vie,* the good life.

Thanks to vivid descriptions of events in which he reversed the sides, he was toasted as a hero of the Border War, defender of Southern honor.

"James Jefferson" received a generous advance of chips at a game table. By midnight the poker turned into concentrated labor for Erskine, casual diversion for four planters wearing diamond studs in their cravats and diamond rings on pudgy pinkies. No apparent professionals at cards were present, to Malcolm's relief.

Over and over, Erskine asked himself what he was doing in such a predicament, for he knew little of these ways. Barely understood the game, as a matter of fact. He was certain of two things, however. That he must try for Audrey's and Eugene's sake, and that in the company of these rich men, flattery and bluff seemed all he required as tools for winning.

"Jefferson" played the role well, matching the planters in betting, losing or winning thousands in chips, smoking cigars, lathering his speech with accented suggestions that, yes, he was indeed a freed descendant of the long and poorly hushed liaison between Thomas Jefferson and the beautiful Sally Hemings. By evoking the name of the Sage of Monticello, he found, he could practically draw tears from his hosts' eyes.

An accident of sorts occurred. With all players remaining in this round of draw poker, it came the turn of each to show his five cards. Around Malcolm were a hand with a pair of queens, another with jacks over fours, another with three sevens, and another with three tens—the last being the apparent winner. Malcolm spread two kings and two sixes. But all except "James Jefferson," who remained in pretended innocence about cardplaying, noticed immediately that he had only four cards.

"Wheah's th' othuh *cawd,* Mistuh Jeffuhson?" a kindly old slaver inquired in a friendly tone.

Malcolm had, from all appearances, dropped a card unaware and in one-armed awkwardness. His gabbing in continued conviviality had shifted his concentration from the game, he explained. He looked on the floor around his chair and, discovering a card, exclaimed "Ah!" in a pose of surprise.

Reaching, he brought it up and tossed it onto the table face down, chuckling in feigned embarrassment.

"Turn it *ovuh,*" the older man urged.

Malcolm did. It was another six. "Mistuh Jeffuhson, suh. You've *won.* Yes, you've won a considubble 'mount of money, suh."

They were all happy for him. Erskine suspected these wealthy planters had *wanted* him to do well, for the game was declared ended.

Converting the chips to cash and subtracting what had been advanced, Malcolm came away with $23,500. It was the least he could do, he realized, to offer to buy them all a late-night round of drinks before retiring. Most begged off, weary and ready for bed.

Only one man, the old gentleman who'd insisted that Erskine locate his fifth and winning card, shared drinks with him. The pair chatted about horses and racing.

Malcolm glanced toward the table they'd left. He noticed a ship's Negro porter bending to retrieve three more dropped cards. As though wise to Malcolm's trick, the man smiled softly in his direction.

Yes, Erskine had earlier placed randomly selected cards under his boots against the chance he might require one for rounding out a winning hand. He risked being caught as a cheat if anyone counted the deck, but—

Now the familiar sound and feel of the ship's scraping a sandbar caused them to take special notice, for this time the sound was louder than they were accustomed to hearing. The ship ground to a stop.

"It 'peahs th' Cap'n is a lucky man this trip," the plantation owner observed.

"What makes you say that?" Malcolm asked, puzzled.

"Got a hold full o' dahkeys. He'll have 'em tooken ashoah, with rope to pull this ship off'n th' sandbah."

Erskine thought about that and made a grand decision. He took leave with thanks for the man's guidance in the game and for conversation.

Time to point the way for nearly a hundred slaves to find their freedom.

54

It was past midnight. Malcolm found the captain on the bridge, roused from sleep because of the accident. He greeted with obvious annoyance an intrusion by Erskine.

Because Malcolm continued to wear Eugene's fancy clothes, he decided to continue the role that had been so successful in the ship's saloon.

"James Jefferson, heah, ready to assist in any way I can, suh," Malcolm said in greeting, adding a slight bow.

"Captain Emanuel Chadwick. I have sufficient crew to cope with the situation, Mr. Jefferson. I thank you kindly."

"It was my thought, Captain Chadwick, suh," Malcolm pressed, "that if you were to wait until approximately dawn, the rivuh will rise one or two feet because of storms to the noath of heah."

In the dim light, it was apparent Chadwick sought to assess his visitor for any special talents that might equip "Jefferson" with such knowledge.

Evidently finding none from all that Malcolm's face revealed, Chadwick tried to dismiss his one armed visitor by giving instructions. He told an aide, "Make ready the slaves for shore and secure the lines." The blacks would be put to work tugging the craft free of the sandbar.

"No need of that, Captain, with all due respect," Erskine insisted.

Chadwick sighed heavily. "Mr. Jefferson, if you wish to help get this ship moving again, there are one or two things you can do. First, forget your theory about the river rising. Also, you might help by standing guard ashore over the darkies, so they don't go running off. My cargo, you know, and I'm duty-bound to deliver them in—"

"Gladly," Malcolm said, with a more pronounced bow than he gave earlier. "And I will enlist my friend, Eugene Fontenot, to accompany me for guard duty."

"You do that. Thank you. We shove off rowboats in twenty minutes. By the way, how do you know there've been storms north of here?"

"I, uh—" Erskine looked among the crewmen, expecting none to believe him, even though he'd be telling the truth. Yet the more incredible it sounded, the more likely Chadwick would proceed with his plan involving the Negroes. That was what Malcolm preferred Chadwick to do.

Erskine said, "I, uh, smelled it. The rain, I mean."

"You *what?*" Chadwick barked, the other men sniggering.

"I *smelled* it—yestuhday, just befoah the othuh vessel docked at Baton Rouge."

By now the crewmen were in full laughter. Chadwick himself was trying to maintain composure. Erskine left, feigning both minor embarrassment and eagerness to help. He made straight for his cabin to see Eugene.

"Wake up," he said, shoving his roommate roughly. "Wake up! We have less than twenty minutes."

"Quest-ce que c'est—?"

"I have the money for your father. When Audrey arrives in Memphis, she must pay his debt and return home on the first ship. She will *not* marry Catron. Understand?"

"I *hear,"* Fontenot said, fully awake now, "but I do not *understand."*

"I've won enough money playing cards to cover the debt. I won't have Audrey selling herself to that planter. That's final. Now, you and I have new business to discuss. Get into the roughest clothes you've brought and pocket your valuables. You're not returning to this cabin. Take your straight razor, because it can be a weapon. A knife, too, if you have one. And here's one of my pistols. Conceal it at your waist."

"I never carry a firearm. But *why?* Where am I *going?"*

"To Kansas. Get ready. And listen carefully while I tell you my true identity and purpose."

* * * * *

A few volunteers met the crewmen at the ship's two lifeboats. Each boat could carry approximately eighteen people. Each was scheduled to make three trips to shore to move slaves and their temporary overseers.

Malcolm inquired, "Are theah any Nigra children?"

A crewman nodded. "A baby and two or three other young 'uns."

"Fetch them."

"Why? They ain't big enough to help pull the lines."

"We'll be theah for hours. The baby will need its mama for feeding," Erskine said. "We'll need anothuh child to mind the baby while its mothuh works. That would leave one or two little ones alone in the hold for a long period, and that's inhuman. You agree, suh?"

The crewman thought about that a few seconds, then nodded. "You're right. I'll get 'em."

Malcolm had learned, happily, the tugging would be tried from the Arkansas side of the Mississippi. He'd brought writing paper, pencils, and matches from the cabin. He and Eugene would ride with the last slaves to be launched to shore.

Meanwhile, Malcolm used every minute of their time on deck to instruct Fontenot about what must be done over the next few weeks.

"We have a main station outside Pine Bluff—sympathetic non-slaveowning white families, with resources for this many people. When we get ashore I'll diagram the stations between. I'll write other information you'll need. I'm estimating we're near the mouth of the Arkansas River, maybe ten miles south of it. When you reach it, follow the south bank, traveling only by night."

Fontenot nodded, evidently absorbed completely by this adventure.

"Avoid farmhouses by at least half a mile. Stay downwind where there may be dogs. Deal only with slaves for information. They won't sell you out. We'll determine on shore who the natural leaders are in this group. Make good use of them to keep everyone in check, to keep everyone moving and the children quiet. *Tu comprend?"*

Fontenot nodded.

"Eugene, *mon ami,* we're three hundred miles from safety, and that's as the crow flies. Before you're finished, you'll have traveled overland to Lawrence close to double that, leading about ninety or so fugitive slaves. Can you do it?"

Fontenot appeared humbled. He ventured, "For you, Malcolm—for taking me into your confidence, trusting me, and for what you've done for Audrey and my papa—*anything."*

"Better keep calling me 'James Jefferson' while these crewmen are still about....Ah! The first boats are returning from shore and they'll load up again. As promised, there are the baby and the other children. It's *very* important, Eugene, that this entire group be kept together. They've been subjected too much to splitting up couples and families. We don't want any of that to happen by accident. Understand?"

"Oui. I intend to do exactly as you say, at risk to my life if necessary, on my honor."

Erskine studied carefully the face of Eugene Fontenot, in the misty light of the ship's whale-oil lamps.

Was Eugene in any way like him? All evidence pointed the other way, to Fontenot's being the spoiled son of a Baton Rouge dandy—yet he spoke believably of honor. It was as though Fontenot had been seeking a level of manliness, personhood, and had finally realized neither his nor his father's could be purchased at the price of Audrey's happiness.

At last, after the passing of nearly another half hour, all the slaves were launched. Eugene and Malcolm were separated temporarily, each to ride with a group.

By all appearances, Captain Chadwick had been in conversation with awakened passengers and had learned favorably of

"James Jefferson's" adventures, his general trustworthiness as a Southern hero and leader. So Chadwick was willing to have the one-armed adventurer take full charge of this work crew of consigned and valuable property.

Ashore, the slaves sought dry footing to tug the ropes. Malcolm persuaded three white volunteers that the situation was well in hand, that they may as well return to the ship for a good night's sleep. They glanced at one another, saw how well "Jefferson" and the Creole were controlling the effort, and agreed.

When all slaves were in place for the huge task, a few small campfires lighting the work area, the sailors rowed the other volunteers back. They also let out into the water the slack of the long, strong ropes they would shortly secure to the *Delta Queen.*

Malcolm summoned one of the children, a boy about ten years old. "Your name?"

"William."

"William, watch for a flare—a bright light that will suddenly flash in the sky above the ship. That will be our signal to start tugging on the ropes. Do you understand?"

The boy nodded and hurried to the river's edge to take up watch.

"The rest of you," he called, "gather around and listen while we have time. This gentleman accompanying me is Eugene Fontenot. My name is Malcolm Erskine."

Hearing Malcolm say his true name, a man and three women dropped to their knees in prayerful thanks. Another woman fainted and had to be caught from falling. Several slaves wept openly and clasped hands to look heavenward and cry, "Hallelujah! Lawd-a-mighty, Hallelujah!"

All soon realized, because of Malcolm's presence, they'd boarded the Underground Railroad, on their way to freedom.

The effect appeared to leave Eugene Fontenot awestruck.

"Malcolm! You are their *Messiah!"*

Erskine didn't respond, except to acknowledge with warmth and returned affection all slaves who sought to embrace him, to touch him.

"It's you, Eugene," he said, "who'll lead them to the promised land—to the freedom they deserve. There's no greater mission in life, *mon ami.*"

The boy, William, rushed to them from his watch, panting. He pointed toward the ship. "The light done went awn! See?"

Malcolm instructed the group leaders. They would make a few attempts to dislodge the ship from the sandbar—nothing that would cause any of them injury—and then they would all be on their way heading north and west.

An older man struck up a song—

"Every time I

"Feel the spirit"

—a lively spiritual the others chorused, taking positions on the ropes.

"Movin' in my heart

"I will pray...

"Yes, every time I

"Feel the spirit

"Movin' in my heart

"I will pray..."

The older man soloed in deep baritone—

"Jordan River

"Runs right cold

"Chills the body

"Not the soul."

The music must have sounded strangely crisp for such an hour in the Mississippi River valley, Malcolm thought. Surely people awake on board wondered at the primitiveness of Negroes who would sing energetically while pulling a stuck ship free.

Again, a solo—

"Ain't but one train

"On this track,

"Runs to heaven

"And right back."

Malcolm gasped to fight tears of joy, hearing the music shift into a counterpointed round from the hearts of *all* the slaves with him on shore.

"Yes, every time I
"Feel the spirit
"Movin' in my heart
"I will pray....
"Lawd, every time I
"Feel the spirit
"Movin' in my heart
"I will pray."

Eugene approached Malcolm during the slaves' tugging effort. "And what of you, Malcolm? Where will you be while I carry out this mission?"

"Soon as these ends of the lines are secured to trees, you'll strike me unconscious, back of the head, but on slightly higher ground than here. The river will rise shortly. You'll take the papers I've charted and lead them northwest as diagrammed, to freedom. Remember, Eugene, you'll be a *wanted man* from this moment on. Still willing to go through with it?"

"Malcolm, I don't know what to say. I am so thoroughly moved. The way I have seen these people respond to you—to the promise of freedom— Just *listen* to them. Malcolm, my new friend, it is the most glorious thing I have ever seen or heard in my life. I thank you for letting me have a part in it."

55

Malcolm felt a hand pushing against his shoulder. He opened his eyes. It was close to sunrise. He'd been asleep on the ground for a time. *Unconscious?*

Now he remembered. Eugene and his charges must have made a good start.

Captain Chadwick leaned over him, his face distorted by a scowl.

"Jefferson, let's be up and off. You've suffered a bad blow on the head, that's clear. That renegade, Fontenot, ran off with my cargo, every man jack. And you were right," Chadwick added, straightening and gazing across the wide Mississippi. "The river rose as you said it would. I don't know how you knew, but the ship is free. We're ready to move."

The river pilot walked around, examining the ground. "We know by these prints just where they headed, but I can't spare anyone to run off looking for them. I'll just have to inform the authorities—and the consignee. Yes," Chadwick said, tossing a pebble hard toward the beach in a show of frustration, "he'll be madder'n hell, Catron will, to learn I let his property be stolen so easily."

Malcolm sat up, eyeing the captain carefully. The man could lose his riverboat pilot's commission over such a huge loss in cargo. Except for that and the knowledge it might expose his own game, Erskine could have surrendered to laughter—learning it was Audrey's fiancé who'd been the loser.

Audrey....He wondered whether she was still asleep or up. Her life had changed in several ways overnight, and she didn't even know it.

Malcolm stood. With his one hand he brushed sand from his clothes, Eugene's clothes. Until they got to Memphis he'd be obliged to continue to play the dandy, "James Jefferson."

"I'm truly sorry, Captain Chadwick, suh," Malcolm said in his false pose, though the ache in his head was real enough. "I let my guard down neglectfully, causing you and Mistuh Catron a heavy loss and inconvenience. Indeed I am sorry, and if theah were some way I could make it up to you both, I—"

"There's no way," Chadwick said. "Let's just be off." They stepped into the waiting lifeboat to be rowed to the ship.

* * * * *

Erskine ordered hot water delivered to his shipboard room. He sought more comfortable togs of Fontenot's to change into. He pocketed the scarab and hung the *chai* around his neck, concealing it under a shirt of Eugene's. He decided, too, he must wear his hook, whether acceptable to the genteel Southerners aboard or not.

Because of the accident involving the sandbar, their arrival in Memphis would be delayed several hours. They would dock there toward evening.

A long day lay ahead. He must isolate himself and stay close to his cabin, or continue the tiresome role-playing—and risk error that might reveal him as one of the most wanted men in the West.

With luck none of his fellow cardplayers of the previous evening would seek him out. Malcolm hoped they would learn, or perceive, while he may have brought credit to the South by his border fabrications, he brought shame to himself by letting Fontenot overpower him and steal the slaves.

After the steward brought the water, Malcolm cleaned up, expecting that Audrey would arrive any moment to hear good news about the money.

The morning wore on with no sign of her, however, and he was tired from the night's business on shore. He stretched out on his bunk to catch some sleep.

When he woke, he left his cabin and knocked at her door across the way. No response. Surely she couldn't be sleeping through all the noises of passenger activity. His knocking should be rousing her. He considered asking a steward to unlock her door, but he had no valid excuse. And there was no need to call even more attention to himself for odd reasons. He would continue to wait.

He returned to his room and looked for the money where he'd concealed it the night before—under *Leaves of Grass* on a shelf, his winnings of $23,500.

It was gone.

In its place he found a letter.

"Mon cher:

"When you inquired about such skills of mine as horsemanship, it never occurred to you to ask about my swimming. In that, I am without peer.

"I sought you during the night—even at the risk of waking Eugene, to whom I planned to confess my adoration for you. I planned to renounce the marriage arrangement in Memphis and perhaps find some other way to help Papa and save our family honor. All for the love of you.

"When I found this cabin empty in the early morning hours, however, I sought clues to your and Eugene's whereabouts. Seeing your hook here and more of Eugene's clothes gone than he alone could wear, I made small inquiries and large guesses.

"I have found the money and will take it with me when I leave the ship at dawn. I will take riding clothes and go to friends in Mississippi who will lend me—or sell me—a horse, so that I may return to Papa in Baton Rouge.

"Thank you, cher, for all you have done—except that I am peeved by the suspicion you decided to manage my life without consulting me. For that I have left you without a penny.

"Still, I will not betray your identity, for I plan to burn the New York paper with your picture before I leave.

"Tell Eugene I am sorry to have missed saying goodbye. I am afraid it is he who will be obliged to explain to Monsieur Catron in Memphis that I could not go through with the wedding.

"Incidentally, I forgot to tell you that the slaves you and Eugene accompanied to shore—and with whom you will soon be returning to the

ship as I write this – were to be mine, that is until I decided to forgo all of that because of you. Monsieur Catron bought them to staff an elegant new home he is building us.

"We will meet again, cher, I am certain. I would like to know what there is to Kansas that fires your passions so.

"Au revoir.

"Je t'aime.

"Audrey Fontenot"

At that moment, except for his determination to find Ebony, Malcolm might have left the ship as well to pursue Audrey. He disliked himself for such thoughts, for they made him wonder whether he'd become more serious about her than was warranted. They'd known each other such a short time.

Yes, he'd miss her puckish charm and elegance, the chance to observe her internal struggle between dependency and independence. If she wanted to learn more of Kansas, however, she must go there on her own.

Furthermore, he was tied – more or less – to Naomi Goodman of Paola. She was to have his child.

There came a knock at his cabin door.

He'd been partly undressed while trying to decide his next step, so he put on Eugene's robe and opened the door.

Captain Chadwick stood facing him, his uniform cap still atop his square head, lines seeming deeper in his face this afternoon than this morning.

"Mister, uh, Jefferson."

"Yes?"

"James Jefferson?"

"Why surely, Captain Chadwick, my name hasn't changed since we parted this morning, suh."

"I'm afraid it has," Chadwick said, hands behind his back and stepping into the cabin to look around. Two burly sailors, both armed, followed him.

"I'm putting you under arrest."

"Whatevuh for?"

"Oh, that's easy, Mr. Malcolm Erskine!" Chadwick snapped, whipping around to face his prisoner now being restrained by the sailors. The river pilot brought one arm forward from behind his back to display a page of charred newspaper.

Apparently Audrey's intended act of destroying it was incomplete. Enough remained to make clear that he and the illustrator's representation of him bore exceptional similarities.

"Yes, Mr. Erskine, that's *so* easy. Fraud at the cardtable last evening. Grand larceny of ninety-one able-bodied slaves, valued in the neighborhood of fifty-five thousand dollars. And violation of the Fugitive Slave Law."

Chadwick stepped close to Malcolm and looked him hard in the face. "That's a Federal offense, Erskine. Regardless of anything else you're wanted for, you'll likely *hang* for that. And I'll be there to watch."

He instructed his sailors, "Hold him in the brig till we dock in Memphis. Then the U.S. Marshal can have him."

56

Conditions in the Memphis jail were worse than Erskine might have anticipated.

The odor was overpowering. Not a breath could be drawn that wasn't fouled by the stench of other prisoners and himself, of sweat and waste. Hardly a place in his cell was dry enough for Malcolm to sit, to lean, to rest. The ceiling, walls—everything—dripped.

Erskine saw no opportunity yet for escape. He was alone in a cell but could see others—black men and white men—who shared cells nearby. Often he would glance up and catch them staring at him, possibly in wonder over legends of his border exploits.

Either by some oversight or by some incomprehensible judgment, he'd been allowed to wear his hook. Possibly the jailers reasoned he would need it to handle his food tray—but he hadn't touched a morsel since entering his cell. Occasionally he took a sip of water. That was all. Everything else was too foul to consider putting in his mouth. Erskine decided he'd be more comfortable—readier for escape should the chance arise—if he refused solid food for a time.

It had been four days since his arrest aboard the *Delta Queen*. Though Captain Chadwick had indicated Malcolm would receive a speedy trial and be hanged, there were evidently complications.

For one, Erskine learned there was a dispute between civil and military officials about whose prisoner he should be. The chief United States Marshal for Western Tennessee was inclined to turn the famous Jayhawker over to military authorities. In that event, Malcolm would be prosecuted under the Fugitive Slave Act. But the Army and Federal justices were so divided on the slavery issue that Erskine's life might be spared when sentencing was pronounced. That was an outcome prosecutors wished to avoid.

The Sheriff of Shelby County and Memphis city officials, on the other hand, wanted Malcolm released to Missouri authorities on charges of murder. If he were simply shipped upriver to St. Louis, he'd be tried and hanged—probably within the same day—and the law establishment would be done with him.

Another complication arose by intervention of Ferdinand Magellan Catron. As soon as it was known throughout Memphis that Captain Chadwick had captured Malcolm Erskine—as soon as Catron heard about the circumstances—the cotton planter visited to take a look at the prisoner. For one brief moment Erskine and Catron studied each other, Malcolm seeing resemblance to the Missouri border leader, C.C. Catron. Then Catron the planter slapped a riding crop against his thigh, turned, and left.

Malcolm, soon after, learned of a convoluted involvement by Catron that surprised him. According to a conversation he overheard between a visiting newspaper reporter and a jail guard, Catron was negotiating to *buy* Erskine as a *slave.*

The planter would indemnify the State of Tennessee for expenses of arrest and incarceration. If he could successfully claim Erskine as his property, he would also contribute a recreational center to the military along with a freight-load of cotton to be processed into uniforms. If those offers failed, the reports went, he was ready to fall back on the more reliable custom of paying bribes.

As nearly as Malcolm could determine from the reports, Catron believed he might use ownership of Erskine to recover Audrey Fontenot, which would let marriage plans proceed as previously announced. The planter would simply hold Erskine's life as ransom.

Malcolm also heard that if Audrey complied, the plantation owner would insure against further trouble by turning his slave-stealing, bride-stealing antagonist into a eunuch, surgically.

*****

It was the sixth day. Malcolm stood leaning against the wall of his putrid cell trying desperately to imagine the clean air of Kansas, dozing despite all present discomfort. He suddenly snapped into full wakefulness at the *clank* of his cell door opening.

A scowling jailkeeper snarled at him, "Visitor. This way."

Malcolm noticed two additional jail guards waiting with revolvers drawn as he stepped into the aisle that gave access to the cells. He followed the man who'd spoken. The other two walked behind.

No, he wouldn't try for escape. Not until he knew more about the position of doors, windows, the building in relation to other parts of the city. Perhaps in this unexpected outing he might learn enough to raise hope. He studied everything he passed.

They led him to a small room containing only a table, two chairs, a suspended whale-oil lamp, no windows, and a gentleman who wore a hat and cape and sat with a notepad and pencil in front of him.

By an attitude of some authority, the seated gentleman waved the guards out. They closed the door to leave Erskine and this man alone.

"Sit down," the man instructed in a thin, piping voice.

Malcolm sat, finding it difficult to make out the features of the man's round face. His visitor appeared to be an older man, also a person of means, yet the notepad and pencil on the table indicated this might be a representative of the press.

"Are you a reporter?" Malcolm inquired. "Did you ask to see me, to interview me? Is that why they're allowing this?"

The visitor removed his hat and placed it on the table.

Erskine was certain, seeing the man more clearly now, that he'd encountered him somewhere before—or at least someone similar in appearance. He peered curiously at the gentleman's features. He leaned across the table to study the visitor closely.

"Are you an attorney? Did you come to defend me, to advise me? Who *are* you?"

The visitor, while darting his eyes toward the door, held up a finger and placed it on his lips. "I am here," the man said in a squeaky, barely audible voice, "to help you."

"In what way?" Malcolm whispered hoarsely.

"God help me," the man said, rocking his head from side to side and glancing toward the ceiling, then looking into Erskine's eyes. "I am here to help you escape."

Malcolm stood suddenly, believing this might be a trap.

The authorities in Tennessee as well as those in Missouri would be rid of him if he tried to escape, if he were shot and killed in the process.

No, this man's announcement was too good to be true. So it must be false.

"Sit *down,*" the man insisted. "Listen to me and don't behave like some ignoramus. Look into my face very closely. Tell me what you see."

Malcolm squinted and examined the man carefully. "I see someone who resembles a gentleman in Kansas." The man nodded, encouraging Malcolm to say more. "A gentleman—a merchant—in the Paola settlement."

"And that man's name," the visitor said. "Would it be Morris Goodman?"

"Yes."

"You're saying I look like Morris?"

"Yes."

"Do you have any idea *why?*"

"No."

"I am Noah, his brother. I am the great-uncle of your child, yet to be born to my niece, Naomi. I am, Mr. Erskine, *mishpocheh.* Do you understand? I am family."

57

"How does it happen that 'family'," Malcolm asked Goodman, "knows I'm here at all?"

"Son," Noah said, "news of your arrest reached Paola within two days. Putting together the new telegraph and fast-riding adventurers, there is little that escapes us. Besides, in the Territory you are widely celebrated. Particularly in Paola."

"How is she? Naomi, I mean."

For answer, Noah gestured, then said, "Approximately out to here. Estimates are the baby will come in January."

"I mean," Erskine pressed, "how is *she?*"

Goodman eyed him curiously, then asked, "You truly care? You would return to her? Perhaps marry her and give the child your name?"

Malcolm fidgeted, glancing from side to side. "Must I answer that to get a—a simple piece of information about—"

"About my *niece,* young man, it is necessary that you do the right thing. *Schwarz oder weiss,* we Goodmans are past caring, so long as you devote yourself, apply yourself."

Malcolm was pleased race was no issue with this family, but— "If you mean marry her, I can't honestly make that promise."

"Then I am probably wasting my time here," Goodman said, starting to rise.

"No, *wait.* You said you were here to—" Lowering his voice, "to help me escape."

"And I *am,*" Goodman said, also modulating, "but to escape to freedom as a *mensh*—a person—not as a *shlemiel.* You know what is a *shlemiel?*" Noah asked with some emotion.

Malcolm nodded. It meant fool, simpleton, worse than the worst of idiots, which he admitted to himself he'd been many times over.

He thought. Obviously he couldn't give his word about Naomi now, but he must feel Goodman out to see what was in the older man's plan. "How did you get here?"

"Ach!" Noah said, waving his hand in disgust, sitting back. "The worst wagon ride ever. You wouldn't *believe* how bad, because it was too fast over mountain trails, the shortest route."

"Through Arkansas?"

"Yes. I was en route here, then overtaken by, uh, others—so that I could receive news about you."

"Did you pick up any news about—?"

Goodman brought a finger to his lips to indicate silence. He said, "You mean a large shipment by 'railroad'?"

Malcolm nodded.

"Everything is proceeding well," Noah said. "The 'cargo' is intact."

"You're a veritable fountain of information," Erskine observed, "aren't you? What line are you in?"

"I am a simple *schneider."*

"A what?"

"A tailor. You know, I sew together goods and you put on the result and call it a coat or trousers."

"A *tailor."*

"That is what I said."

In a hoarse whisper across the table, his frown conveying total frustration, Malcolm snarled, "A *tailor* is sent to help me get out of this hell-hole? What are you, *crazy?"*

"You want, Mr. Malcolm Erskine, a gunman to maybe help you *shoot* your way out?" Goodman asked. "You think that will get you anywhere besides dead? Or you want, Mr. Malcolm Erskine, an explosives person to help you *blast* your way out? You have time to figure out how to do that effectively?"

Erskine shook his head, deflated in hope, totally in despair that Goodman was a man of good intentions but of no apparent talent useful to him now.

"Or do you want, Mr. Malcolm Erskine, a person of some *intelligence?"* There was a pause.

Malcolm looked up. "What do you mean?"

"The tailor who sits before you is managing and acting upon a plan cooked up by his niece, the brilliant young woman who is more patient with you than you deserve, and by his brother, Morris. From them, father and daughter—*family*—has come a perfect plan of escape."

Noah Goodman then rose and pulled from a pocket of his vest a tape measure made of cloth, indicating Erskine should rise as well. Before Malcolm could appreciate what was taking place, Goodman was measuring him—across the shoulders, around the chest, around the hips, from head to toe, and so on. Noah paused a few times to write figures. At last, seeming satisfied, he reseated himself. Malcolm did the same.

"I am no ordinary tailor, young man. I do a considerable business in leather goods—buckskin, suede. Memphis is one of my better outlets—though," with a shrug, "I may have to give it up. Anyway, I have brought with me a few hides and will soon have others."

Erskine appealed with his eyes and a small gesture of the hand, urging Goodman to continue, to explain, before a guard might cut short the visit and interrupt his learning what lay ahead.

In apparent realization of Malcolm's concern, Noah waved it off. "The guards are being well taken care of, or I would not have been able to see you at all. Their families will have enough venison to last for weeks."

Goodman placed his forearms on the table and brought his round face closer to Erskine's. "In two days you are to be taken to court. Naturally, you cannot go in your present state, filthy as you are. I, being family, have offered and will be allowed to return with a change of clothing for you, following your reasonably suitable bathing. The fact is, I have already made you clothing not exactly in your size. The measuring was for something else."

Erskine frowned, puzzled.

"Another gentleman will accompany me to assist. He will appear to resemble you in, well, a *few* respects. The fitting and dressing are to be completed in my enclosed wagon, just outside a door downstairs. We will be guarded, but not every moment. However—"

Malcolm was beside himself trying to figure how such a crazy plan stood a chance of being successful. He wished Goodman would move on to the essence of the escape method.

"—you will be sewn carefully but quickly into a very large buck's hide. A glass tube will be provided for breathing. I am afraid you will find the conditions for some time after that to be, let us say, quite uncomfortable."

Erskine nodded. "Downright stinking, I would guess," he said. Nevertheless, he liked the plan so far for its novelty.

"Exactly. You will appear to be a carcass not yet skinned. To be totally convincing I will have several such skins placed in my wagon, with heads, hooves, and tails intact. *That* is not routine, but the guards do not know that. Later we will most certainly be stopped and searched when your disappearance is discovered."

Malcolm wondered aloud, "What about the other man? The suit is for him?"

"He will step out in garments I have already shown the guards, a hook dangling from his left sleeve. As the downcast prisoner they expect you to be on the way to arraignment," Noah said, "he will play the role obediently—go off with the guards to court, a hat and other accoutrements concealing his false identity.

"Outside the court building, in what will most certainly be a crowded condition owing to your reputation, he will toss the hook into a bush easily, remove and conveniently lose false mustache, hat, and accessories including peel-away sleeves of a different material and color, and stand straight.

"From that instant, he will insist—*if* confronted—on a separate identity he can document with papers—"

Malcolm interrupted. "I want to meet the man someday who can pull off that maneuver, even though in a crowd."

"You already have," Noah countered. "He is Daniel, my nephew and former member of your Jayhawker band. He can do it, knowing your walk, your manner generally. He is the one who rode from Paola to overtake my wagon, a few days after I had left from there to come here. He is the one who explained the plan to me."

"And he is now *here?* In *Memphis?"*

Noah Goodman nodded.

"All this has already been arranged to *succeed?"*

Again Goodman nodded, adding. "And rehearsed to some extent, though we are still in contact with hunters for fresh deer in woods across the river. A kosher butcher here in Memphis is also assisting."

"What if the jailers shackle me for the trip to the courthouse? How will Daniel escape that?"

"I have already been assured, you are not to be so treated. With as many hides as I must deal in, you can imagine how much venison is at my disposal."

"Daniel in appearance is nothing at all like me."

"Touches of lampblack and boot wax and the false mustache will have changed that," Goodman said.

"You say Naomi and her father put together this scheme just a few days ago, and it's already being *rehearsed?"*

"Exactly."

"You are to spirit me away somewhere inside a deerskin, deer's head and all?"

"Exactly."

"Where?"

"Hanh?"

"I said where? Where are we going?"

"To *Kansas.* The wagon will proceed immediately to Kansas, first by a charter ferry, then eventually by trails through the Ozark Mountains."

Malcolm bit his lip considering that. He was silent a while, then he said, "We can't do it."

Noah did not appear to be thrown off by the remark. "Why not?"

"I came to Memphis looking for my horse, Ebony. I won't leave this place without him."

"You will not have to leave this place without him. Ebony will be one of the four steeds pulling the wagon."

Erskine sat stunned. How was it possible such miracles should come his way? Who was the moving force behind all this? "Explain that, *please.*"

"Daniel is at this moment," Noah said, checking a pocket watch, "purchasing your horse from thieves who stole him in New Orleans. They are regular dealers—rustlers up and down the river. They were easy to find. The ransom is not unreasonable."

Erskine shook his head. "This has got to be one of the most baffling conversations I have ever had in my life. And one of the most exhausting. Please tell me, Uncle— May I call you Uncle?"

"It is my sincere wish that you do."

"How did it become known my purpose in Memphis was to find and recover—"

Noah held up a hand to stop Malcolm. "Son, listen to me. You underestimate the resourcefulness of my niece. Once hearing of your arrest, she went to great lengths to learn everything quickly, from every source, including indirectly—" Goodman brought his voice to a whisper. "—Monsieur Fontenot. To calculate, plot, plan, arrange, persuade. And, as you can see, I am here as her kinsman to carry it out."

Erskine nodded, thinking about Naomi. "She is a very resourceful woman. More than I dreamed. But," he peered anxiously into Uncle Noah's eyes, "what if we fail?"

"If we fail, we die. But— You see, I have my own 'but,' Mr. Erskine. Do, please, unfasten your shirt button and touch what I believe hangs at your throat, given you by Naomi."

Malcolm felt the *chai*—the symbol of life.

"You see, my son," Goodman said, "it is expected we shall *not* fail. The welfare of your child depends on that."

58

Before Noah ended his visit, he pressed a letter into Erskine's hand. Malcolm was uncertain whether such a paper might be taken from him by jailers, so he slipped it inside his shirt.

When he returned to his cell, and although the light was dim almost to the point of darkness, Malcolm read—

"Paola settlement
"Lykins County, K.T.
"Sunday, the 19th of
"October, 1856

"Dearest,

"By now you will have heard all that is planned to aid you. (My language will be couched on the chance this falls into the wrong hands.)

"You must forgive me for interfering with all free choices you may have made for yourself in relation to the future. But I have an obvious stake, and left to your own devices only disaster lay ahead for you.

"Understand, please, that I make no demands, that I press no advantage because of obvious ties between us. My family feels differently, of course, but they don't know you as I do.

"I would happily surrender all that is comfortable and respectable to be at your disposal, even if one more night together were all I could look forward to.

"What I write reflects a foolish kind of love, and I am not a foolish woman, as you must know by now. But you have ignited my passions so, I cannot hide them from you.

"You are not the kind of man a woman can love wisely.

"From the manner in which I carry, the mothers of the settlement predict I am to have a son.

"If it can be managed, I invite you to join me and our son here, where you will be loved and cared for as no other man could ever be, where

there is work to be done and a place to be built and a dream of freedom to be made real.

"I love you, Malcolm Erskine. If anything is to come of that, however, it will be up to you.

"Yours in dedication to life,
"Naomi"

To protect the letter, Malcolm folded it small and slipped it between the stump of his left arm and the leather casing for his hook. During the next couple of days, while awaiting arraignment and the opportunity for escape, he would read it again and again.

Though night and the following day dragged mercilessly, Erskine was aware of something new coming into his life—*hope.*

Not since he took part in the border struggle had he felt anything but despair about the violence in which he was involved, anything but loss over the death and destruction around him.

Now he must form thoughts and words for his son—*their* son—to share at the appropriate time. To explain why it had all been necessary, what the future peace ought to be like—the "dream of freedom" Naomi said begged for reality.

* * * * *

When the guards came to take Malcolm for arraignment, events began to move so quickly that he was less conscious of the overall escape plan than of new circumstances carrying him along, minute to minute.

Dutifully, gratefully, he washed in a room below. He then followed a guard who was evidently complicit in the scheme. They stepped outdoors to a wagon. He glanced toward the horses and saw Ebony. He entered the wagon and found Noah and Daniel.

Malcolm greeted Daniel cautiously, not to arouse suspicion by other guards just outside. Noah gave instructions with gestures more than words. Obediently Erskine lay beside a buck's carcass and wiggled himself in. Noah began to sew him into it with rapid skill.

Erskine lay beside a buck's carcass and wiggled himself in. Noah began to sew him into it.

Daniel used a small mirror to apply makeup, disguising himself as Malcolm. He put on the trick suit Noah had made.

Soon Malcolm was enclosed entirely in the hide. Noah slipped a glass tube into Malcolm's mouth, instructing him by a whisper to breathe not through the nose but through the mouth only, using the tube.

With that, the tailor drew the last stitches tight.

Erskine could hear the action involving Daniel, though with difficulty. Because no commotion greeted Daniel's exit from the wagon, he could assume the guards had accepted the young man as himself and were proceeding on that basis. He felt the weight of the van shift from Noah's exiting, then the older man's climbing into the driver's seat. All was going on schedule.

The wagon moved slowly at first, then shifted direction several times. Malcolm heard Noah command the horses into a more lively trot, and the van picked up speed.

After approximately half an hour, the vehicle stopped. Malcolm heard what must have been police or sheriff's deputies shouting commands to Noah, to admit them into the van for a search. They completed the search quickly, apparently without suspicion that the buck's carcass contained an escaped prisoner.

From loud mutterings Erskine was able to hear among them, he deduced Daniel was already "at large" somewhere in the city, an occurrence that had evidently led to the van's inspection.

It soon became clear they found no reason to detain Noah.

The wagon moved again. Everything was going well enough, apparently, with Daniel soon to be making his way to catch up to them.

At last, Malcolm could hear the steps of horses' hooves on the wood-plank floor of a ferryboat. The short sailing was without incident. On the Arkansas side they rolled again. Noah presumably wanted to wait until they were well away from the city before releasing Malcolm from the carcass.

Meanwhile, conditions were becoming increasingly cramped and uncomfortable. Breathing through the tube was not so easy as Erskine had thought it might be.

For a reason Malcolm found difficult to deduce, the wagon stopped. Before long he heard a voice commanding loudly, "Git down from thar, dayumn Jew-drummer!"

Erskine heard Noah Goodman protest, evidently believing he could avoid robbery by indicating there was little in the van of value.

Then Malcolm heard a shot, followed by several more in quick succession. The first shot sounded like that of a small pistol.

Noah had apparently panicked, drawn on the others and been gunned down. A body fall, then a lifting of weight from the wagon springs, led Erskine to conclude—

Uncle Noah had toppled from the wagon, dead.

* * * * *

Malcolm was helpless inside the deer carcass, with no way of extricating himself.

Daniel, now the only person who could cut Malcolm out, was on his way to join them but would undoubtedly be waylaid by these robbers. Malcolm calculated there were three of them.

One opened the door of the van, evidently peered inside, then shut it.

Malcolm felt the wagon horses being led, by someone either on foot or on horseback taking the reins. The bouncing about made it apparent to Malcolm, the robbers were leaving the road for a clearing somewhere.

They had seen something in the wagon they wanted, regardless that all it contained were a couple of carcasses and several skins.

After about ten minutes they stopped. Malcolm knew wagon tracks would lead Daniel to them, and the young man would most certainly be gunned down.

Probably they had dragged Noah's body off the trail to hide it in the brush.

"Whah'n't yew build us a fahr," he heard one of the men command, "an we'll carve up that big buck in thar 'n' have us a feast."

They meant to plunge their knives into the skin Malcolm wore, to butcher it, in the belief it was venison for a meal.

59

Erskine's arms were immobile. One was stuck partway into the skin of the deer's front right leg. His left stump and hook were similarly trapped.

There wasn't a part of his body he could move except his face and head.

His situation allowed no opportunity for panic. He needed to concentrate on the difficult job of breathing through the glass tube.

"You gawt thet fahr builded yet?" he heard one of the men ask. "Ah'm a-gittin' hongry."

Malcolm realized he must use his head, literally, to get out of this. He couldn't let himself be slain at the whim of ignorant thieves on a lonely country trail in Arkansas. He had too much to do, a new life to look forward to.

Malcolm breathed more deeply as he felt his heartbeat accelerate. In breathing deeply, he felt his lungs fill. He must be careful that if the men opened the door of the van again, they would not detect breathing and think the deer was still alive.

At present they were otherwise occupied, but Malcolm had little time. He would fill his lungs so that he could hold his breath as long as possible.

For what he must do, he could only hope he wouldn't choke on his own blood.

Malcolm positioned the tube in his mouth so one end was between his molars. He held his breath and bit down hard. He worked the tube around so that the pointed and slivered end was at the opening.

In turning the tube he'd cut both his tongue and the inside of his mouth badly. He felt the blood running.

He continued holding his breath as he used the tube to *saw* the thread that closed the carcass.

It was a tough thread. But if severed, it ought to give easily. That would let him move his head to force the opening to expand.

There.

The thread snapped apart—but the skin *failed to give.*

Malcolm must attack another stitch with the broken glass, all the while fighting the inclination to vomit his blood before he could breathe air freely.

Quickly he worked at the tough thread once more. *There. Again.*

The thread parted, and an opening was visible even in the dimness of the wagon van's interior.

Malcolm pressed his lips against the opening and spat—glass tube and splinters, blood, saliva—then he gasped for air, wheezing mightily as he drew breath.

"Whut in hayell's *thet?*" he heard one of the robbers exclaim. They'd obviously heard his laboring for air.

Now he must work even faster.

With his teeth he attacked the seam to widen the opening. If he could loosen the carcass sufficiently, he'd be able to work one arm free and escape from the skin.

He was swallowing blood—a lot of it. He felt his tongue against his teeth to see how much of it remained. It seemed intact though it bled freely. From time to time, while working the small opening, he spat blood through the hole.

"Probably one o' them horses, is all," he heard another robber respond.

At last Erskine was able to move his head forward so that his entire face was protruding from the opening. Now, before they came to butcher the carcass for venison, he must work his arms loose.

Again and again he bent and turned his head so he could chew his way out of the opening, enlarging it as swiftly as he was able.

"Git us a chonk o' venison," he heard the leader command.

They were coming.

Malcolm felt room enough to turn a shoulder. He was able to get his entire head through the hole now, clear to the neck.

He wriggled, hoping somehow his twisting would work an arm free—either arm. But he mustn't set the van to shaking, or the men outside would hurry their moves to investigate.

He heard them outside the van door as he drew his left arm from inside the deer. He used his hook to attack remaining threads and was soon able to free his right arm.

"Whut's makin' this wagon *move* lahk thet?" he heard. "Whut in *hayell's* goin' awn?"

The van door opened as Malcolm was pulling himself free of the deerskin. The two men silhouetted against the light of the open door were transfixed, clearly unable to believe what they were seeing.

Malcolm got to his feet quickly, blood swirling in his mouth. With an expertness he didn't think he possessed, he spat a large stream of blood directly into the eyes of one of the robbers. He swung his hook point-end into the neck of the other, severing the man's jugular vein.

The temporarily blinded robber set up a wail that attracted the third man from outside—evidently the leader.

Erskine grabbed the revolver of the man who'd gone down with his neck sliced, firing it into the gut of the one whose face he'd bloodied.

The leader came to the door and recoiled at the sight of Malcolm—a gun in Erskine's hand, a hook serving as the other hand, deer blood mixed with his own from head to foot.

Malcolm allowed no exchange of amenities but simply fired directly between the robber's eyes at close range, taking off part of the man's head.

He listened carefully and heard no footsteps approaching. His calculations had been correct. Only three men.

The man he had attacked with his hook was still breathing, giving up blood freely on the floor of Goodman's wagon.

Malcolm pressed the revolver above the man's ear, muttering through blood that flowed from his mouth, "You picked the wrong man to mess with."

He pulled the trigger and watched the robber's corpse slide on blood halfway across the floor.

Erskine needed water. He had to find a canteen or a stream somewhere to fill his mouth and try to stop the blood flow, else he faced the prospect of bleeding to death.

He found no canteen among the robbers' gear. Possibly they were locals, not professional thieves or highwaymen. There might soon be a search party of relatives concerned over their absence.

Despite Daniel's being due, Malcolm thought only of putting distance between himself and this place. Of driving northwest toward the Ozarks and crossing first into the Indian Territory, then north into Kansas.

He would first do what he could to heal his mouth. Then bathe, if that could be managed, and bury Noah before driving off.

But for the ever-present need of horses, he'd simply have unhitched and taken Ebony. Now, however, he decided he should take the robbers' horses as well, tie them to trail the wagon. And take their weapons and anything else of value.

Malcolm approached Ebony, whose curiosity had already caused the magnificent steed to turn its head.

Apparently smelling his master's blood, Ebony began instinctively to lick—as though believing himself able to heal Malcolm's wound.

Regardless of aching mouth injuries, Erskine managed a chuckle and friendly sounds—to let Ebony know of his love. Then, staggering from loss of blood, he scampered to where he might find a stream.

A line of trees indicated a draw. Through sharp grass he made for it—but seeing movement there he threw himself to the ground, expecting a shot.

As he lay spread-eagled, hearing no response to his incautious scrambling, Malcolm figured he must simply have startled an animal. He rose again and trotted weakly to where he hoped he'd find enough water to start healing his mouth.

When he arrived, Erskine found it difficult to comprehend what met his gaze.

The earlier movement apparently had been thrashing snakes, for there were dozens of them near a small stream, at least half the serpents attacking a corpse.

The foul-smelling body was that of a Negro child.

Malcolm reasoned the child, a boy, had lost his way and wandered in the woods.

It was now being eaten and bitten by a succession of attacking cottonmouth water moccasins.

The horror of the scene and his own huge loss of blood combined in their effect.

Malcolm collapsed on the spot.

60

The next several days were confusing and feverish for Malcolm. His mouth injuries had made him unable to speak.

He was aware of many Negro faces—faces he'd never seen before. He was aware of someone's crying. Yes, something to do with the boy torn by snakes.

In a half-conscious state he made vague connections between what he'd seen before passing out and what was going on around him now.

In the care of these strangers, he tossed every night. He groaned, dreaming he was fleeing danger. By day his sleep was no less fitful. Those caring for him in wakeful periods forced water between his lips.

The passing of days and nights fed his agitations, his awareness of separation from the aims Naomi's letter had sparked. He worried about Ebony and about reaching Kansas. He worried about Daniel.

Yet he could do nothing but lie there, wherever he was, weakened and helpless and dependent upon slaves who tried to help him recover.

He remembered an argument between two of them. One said correctly, with a definiteness that prevailed, "He done *escape,* look lahk. We *cain't* take him to no doctuh."

So, he was being nursed by amateurs, who apparently hoped they would both cure him and protect him from further jeopardy.

The woman who had cried came into focus gradually, the same slavewoman who watched over him now constantly by day. Evidently she believed that Malcolm, as discoverer of the child's body, was somehow linked to the boy.

When Erskine felt the strength to do so, he indicated by signs that he wanted something to write with—a pencil and a piece of paper.

There were none.

"Iffen they was," the grieving woman whispered, "t'wouldn't do no good. We cain't read."

That cut Malcolm off from inquiring after anything these people might know to give him peace of mind.

One day the woman—Erskine learned her name was Marian—stepped away for several moments but not out of his view. He saw her pause, apparently thinking, then evidently realizing his need, for she turned and held up a finger. "*Ah* fahnds out things yew wawnts t'know." She hurried off.

Malcolm breathed easier, recognizing that she'd intuited his hunger for news. More than nourishment, more than rest, it was news he craved now.

He slept better that night, but in spurts. In the morning, hoping to see Marian, he saw instead a younger woman and became uneasy about that. Though she tried to help him, to make him take water and softened oats, he refused.

All day he lay in a mood the others found testy. "Ah cain't do a thang wid 'im," the younger woman declared.

Presently the face of a palsied old man appeared above him. The man looked to be maybe ninety years old, Erskine thought. The little hair he had was like snow against his black, deeply lined face.

Because the old man shook, he had difficulty getting words out. At last he gave Malcolm the only piece of news that would make him feel better for now, make him more cooperative in his own recovery.

"Marian," the old man said slowly in a piping voice that Malcolm could barely hear, "she be heah come a few days."

With that, he left, and the younger woman returned. This time Malcolm ate and drank, and rested easier.

Days later, his patience growing shorter and his strength returning gradually, Malcolm indicated he wanted to walk outside, to move around freely. He was refused, others explaining that he was too light in color not to be detected.

"Nod yo haid," the younger woman instructed him. "Yew coluhed?" Erskine indicated *yes.* "But yew also whahte?" Again he indicated *yes.*

"Dunno iffen *Ah* would confess t'bein' coluhed, iffen Ah could mebbe pass fo whahte," she muttered.

Malcolm understood. He could see much more clearly now, and he observed the conditions under which these slaves lived. Their shacks were awful, with hardly enough sturdiness to protect them against the approaching winter. The bugs came and went freely through the rotting walls as did the increasingly chilly night winds. There seemed little or no lumber available for repairs, certainly no paint.

Soap and candles appeared hard to come by. One would think with hog-raising being so popular in Arkansas, these slaves might make wider use of the fats for such necessities. But Erskine noticed they seemed poorly organized.

The crop here was cotton, Malcolm learned, and the harvest was in. But when slaves weren't working the fields they were set to clearing timber for roads, or the women worked as spinners and weavers—all to serve needs of "whahte folkses."

Unable to determine how much time had passed since he was found near the draw, Erskine measured time by the improved condition of his mouth. Improvement, however, meant only less swelling, less bleeding. He'd apparently lost a lot of blood.

He still could not speak. His tongue seemed unable to move in ways he could control. So he grunted to get attention, then varied his grunts and the movements of his hand or hook to give signs that might lead him toward two-way communication.

The others caught on, and he was seated and in the midst of such an awkward conversation when a woman appeared in the doorway. *Marian.*

She rushed to her patient and knelt, her face beaming. Though recently bereaved, she glowed as though in the presence of a wonder.

After touching Erskine's hand, she turned to the others and said, "This heah *Malcolm Erskine.*"

Malcolm heard a pair of hands clap together, and he turned to see an old woman raise her eyes heavenward and fall to her knees on the rough floor.

A slave standing near the doorway removed his hat as though that was the proper thing to do and held it awkwardly to his chest, lowering his eyes reverently, mumbling a prayer.

Marian bent to kiss Malcolm's hand. She raised the back of his hand to her cheek and rubbed her face against it, as though absorbing something holy or life-giving.

"This heah," she repeated, to no one in particular, visibly moved, "Malcolm Erskine."

She would not let go his hand.

A spiritual began in the customary style, as before on the Mississippi shore, one voice setting off a chorus of others after a few lines. It was a song of hope for deliverance. Erskine had heard ex-slaves sing it at abolitionist meetings.

"Go down, Moses,
"Way down in Egypt's land,
"Tell old Pharaoh,
"Let my people go."

Malcolm knew singing was one act of defiance white people never bothered slaves about, because they believed it was a sign of "happiness." Believed that slaves in general were so ignorant, they sang to show joy over being slaves, never mind the message.

"When Israel was in Egypt's land –
"Let my people go.
"Oppressed so hard they could not stand –
"Let my people go.
"Go down, Moses,
"Way down in Egypt's land,
"Tell old Pharaoh,
"Let my people go."

Marian explained what she learned by inquiry among slaves of neighboring properties – that a man identifying himself as

Daniel Goodman had arrived at the scene, assessed the situation with fair accuracy, buried Noah and her son side by side.

After searching in vain for Erskine, according to her informants, Goodman had taken the wagon and all the horses including Ebony to Kansas, but not before leaving word that he would send for Malcolm as soon as anyone might locate him and relay that discovery. That process was probably now in motion, thanks to Marian's describing her patient to others who had tried to help Daniel.

Marian's news included a report that the fugitives led by "the Frenchie"—Eugene Fontenot—had arrived in Kansas Territory and were now free. Some had elected to find homes in Kansas, others had moved on to Canada.

* * * * *

The day following Marian's delivering her reports, two braves of the Miami tribe arrived. They had a saddled appaloosa in tow. Daniel had sent them to guide Malcolm "home."

Able now to walk without help, Erskine made ready for departure. He gave unspoken but hand-signed acknowledgement of his gratitude for their care.

Marian had one last thing to tell Malcolm. Though it pained her she seemed compelled to announce it. "Mah son, the boy yew done fahnd? He's be name Stevie—Steven."

Erskine nodded in acceptance, as though of a gift. He leaned and kissed Marian on her forehead.

Within a few days—because of uninterrupted swiftness they were able to achieve in travel—Malcolm recognized the gently rolling prairies of northeastern Kansas. Soon Lykins County. Ahead lay the expanding community of Paola.

They rode into the square. Erskine sat straight in his saddle for the greeting he knew would come. The Miamis waved off and let Malcolm continue alone.

There, on the porch of the home of Morris Goodman, stood the woman whose cleverness had freed him from jail, whose strong will had brought him home.

Naomi, heavy with child, dressed warmly against the November chill, descended the steps and approached. She beamed. She stretched her hands to Malcolm. She said, "Tomorrow is a day we will observe with extra meaning, my love."

Dismounting, his heart racing, he looked at her questioningly.

"Thanksgiving," Naomi Goodman said as they embraced.

61

Morris was not among the Goodman family members gathering to greet the returning Jayhawker. Malcolm wondered whether he should take that as a sign of disapproval.

Naomi's mother, Sarah, was extremely gracious, open to Malcolm about having fixed her silvering auburn hair. He studied the older woman more carefully than before, realizing Naomi was truly her younger image, though taller. If this was how Naomi would age, he would be fortunate to keep her at his side.

Malcolm remembered there were nine children in all, Daniel being the eldest and Naomi next. Daniel was also absent, and the longer it took his comrade-in-arms to appear, the more uneasy Erskine became. He decided, however, not to call attention to that in any way.

Malcolm was reintroduced to Samuel, Benjamin—and little Aaron, who stared at the Jayhawker's hook and must have wondered at their guest's inability to speak. He reached his little hand and shook Erskine's.

The younger girls—Ruth, Miriam, Judith, and Esther—curtsied, blushed, giggled, squirmed, and were finally released at a sign from Naomi to run off squealing in embarrassed delight.

"Forgive them," she said.

Shaping his mouth around the words and trying to project a whisper, Malcolm replied slowly, "I—love—them." Then he wondered why he'd chosen to say *that* so unhesitatingly. Perhaps it was extreme, although Naomi was obviously pleased.

Sarah inquired, "How is your father? Is he well?" To that he simply nodded, deferring news of dementia's onset in Morogh Erskine, trying to show gratitude that she'd asked. It was clear from the way Naomi's mother had formed her words that she was also trying to be rid of her accent.

In Malcolm's studying Sarah, their eyes met and held a long time. He realized to his surprise that such communication can be clearer at times than spoken words. He was sure he read there—

Please, let's end any uncertainty about the future of this family. Let's live in peace and enjoy this baby you and my precious daughter have created. Just don't be running off again, all right?

Almost imperceptibly, Malcolm nodded again to Sarah, as though in answer to her unspoken appeal, her powerful stare.

"Forgive her," Naomi said.

Malcolm placed a finger to her lips, indicating she must stop apologizing for her family. With difficulty occasioned by the size of her belly and the awkwardness of his hook, he embraced her, prompting more giggles from the Goodman girls nearby—and an embarrassed grin from little Aaron.

Locked in a hug, Naomi murmured, "I love you, Malcolm. I hope soon you'll give me a sign that you love me."

Malcolm continued to embrace her, wanting desperately to make a commitment but knowing he'd be taking up responsibilities again in the Border War. He backed away and signed to Naomi that he wanted to know where her father and brother were. She understood quickly, saying, "I know why you ask after Daniel. It's unclear whether he's to establish anything permanent with Jane-Ellen."

Now Malcolm lowered his eyes, caught in his thoughts by a woman who was able to read his mind.

"Father and Daniel are in the barn, sitting *shivah."*

Erskine's inquiring look upon hearing such a word caused Naomi to explain quickly.

"It's a method of mourning, and this is the final day. They sit uncomfortably on boxes. They neither shave nor wash. It will all end at sundown today—seven days. Late starting because Daniel waited to deliver the news in person after his trip to Memphis. Tonight they will groom, come to dinner, and we will all eulogize Uncle Noah, and life will go on....Do you like hard-boiled eggs?"

Malcolm shook his head, then indicated they gave him gas.

"Well, tonight in addition to fish there will be hard-boiled eggs as a symbol of the continuity of life. Tomorrow, for Thanksgiving—which I wish someone would make an official holiday, though it's a short version of our Sukkos feast—we'll have besides turkey some foods that symbolize—" She stopped, catching herself at prattling, then laughing at herself.

Erskine showed by his demeanor that the endless symbolism pouring from Naomi and her family was a wonder. She asked as they left the porch and walked, "You find that in any way objectionable? That I'm tied to my culture and enthusiastic about it? Those ties aren't so overpowering, Malcolm, that I haven't room in my life for you."

Malcolm stopped and turned to her. She went on. "Yes, I'm frankly proposing—again, I suppose. Proposing marriage. I have money set aside to claim good land north of here. We'll raise cattle, you and I, with our son."

Erskine could not have asked for a better opportunity to make a commitment, but events were still out of control. He tried to form a word—one word that would explain all to Naomi.

First resting his hand on her belly to indicate he would refer to the baby, that his plans had much to do with their expected son, he worked his sore lips into a pucker and tried to find his voice.

Though it hurt to speak, his tongue only now beginning to follow the wishes of his brain, he uttered that one word—his first above a mumble since being sewn into the deer carcass for escape.

"Free."

Again, he placed his hand on her belly, then held up an index finger to emphasize that it was the infant forming inside her of whom he spoke. His eyes grew wide as he forced the word again from his throat, from his mouth and lips.

"FREE."

Naomi embraced him again, sobbing. "I know, my darling, I know. You must help make Kansas a free place for our little boy. But," and she stood back to face him again, "I fear for your life."

To that, Malcolm replied by unbuttoning the top of his shirt. He drew out the *chai* and fingered it.

Trying again to speak, Malcolm formed the words, pushing the air past his lips to say, "I—will—sur-*vive.*" He added, "For—you—*both,*" bringing his hand to rest again on her belly.

She replied, "I'll hold you to that promise."

*****

In the evening, after they'd cleaned up and come to the table, Morris and Daniel wore *yarmulkes* and spoke prayers for Noah.

Moved by the sacrifice Uncle Noah had made to save him, Malcolm bowed his head reverently. He found that their shared thoughts were filled with such strong emotion, he was unashamed to weep quietly before the entire family.

Seeing that, Naomi leaned to kiss him on the cheek. The prayers ended, and the Goodman men set the *yarmulkes* aside.

Naomi asked for everyone's attention and stood.

"I have something to announce. I love this man, this good and caring man, this half-breed warrior, Malcolm Erskine. And I believe in my heart he loves me, whether or not he can say it.

"But I'll have no more talk or speculation about our future. He has trouble enough. He can't make a commitment now. We have time, both of us. There's much that he must yet do, and I support him in all of it."

She sat. Then reaching a hand to grasp Malcolm's right hand, Naomi added, "The child is to be called—" Their eyes met, and Erskine nodded, encouraging her to go on. "Noah Steven Erskine. Steven for the dead slave boy whose mother nursed Malcolm back to health."

Daniel threw his napkin to the table, standing to the noise of his chair scraping backwards across the floor.

"That's outrageous! There's not a valid reason in the world he can't give *you* his name properly. I'm damned near sorry I had a part in saving his life."

Naomi stood to start after her brother, with a look so ferocious the smaller children cringed.

But before she could take a step, Morris Goodman rose. A short man, he nevertheless reached and slapped Daniel soundly across the face.

The noise was like a rifle shot in their full dining room.

Daniel's face reddened, his pride badly stung. He rested his hands on the table and leaned toward them all.

"Let me tell you all something. You may be glad to hear this, but Jane-Ellen will never wed me while he lives. He is her sickness. And *she* is why he won't do the right thing by Naomi. Go on, sister. Ask him whether or not that's true."

"I know all you speak of," she said, flushed over the highly emotional turn of events. "He owes me no explanation. He owes me nothing. He has given me more than you will ever understand. Yes, I want him, but I can never *own* him. And the problem isn't Jane-Ellen," she added.

Malcolm was surprised at that last observation. He stared at her as she reseated herself. "The problem holding Malcolm back is far more serious," Naomi said. "It's a problem of hatred and loathing, not anything involving a woman."

"Don't be a fool," Daniel said scornfully. "He's not that big a patriot against slavery, else why did he spend the last six months away from here?"

"Not hatred of slavery," Naomi said, looking down, biting her lip. "Hatred of—himself."

The room was deathly quiet.

Suddenly, Malcolm pulled a slip of paper from his pocket and a pencil. He wrote several words, then handed the note to Naomi's brother, Samuel.

Samuel read, folded the paper, and nodded. "Papa, may I be excused?" he asked Morris.

The father looked at the lad and, eager as anyone else to see what was to happen next, replied, "Of course. But—where are you going?"

"By Malcolm's request," Samuel said, "to fetch the Justice of the Peace."

62

"But why?" Naomi leaned to Erskine to ask, just after Samuel had left the house. "Why now? Because of what I said?"

Malcolm nodded.

"Even though I risked your contempt for revealing that much of you, you would instead want to *marry* me? For that?"

Malcolm nodded again, then reached for the pencil and a piece of paper to write once more. When he finished, Naomi read, silently—

"Because you know me that well. Because only you have discovered that it is self-loathing that drives me – that I have hated my life, hated myself, and wish to make a good mark, a meaningful achievement, before I die."

Sarah Goodman spoke up, directing her remarks to her husband. "Moishe—Morris, it may seem unimportant at a time like this, but the fish is getting cold. May we all go ahead while we wait for Samuel?"

Daniel reseated himself, subdued both by the slap from his father and by the spontaneity of Erskine's resolve to wed Naomi that very evening.

Morris nodded and began to eat.

Now, quiet, each with his or her separate thoughts, some happy over the unexpected shift of events, some perhaps harboring anxieties, they all ate—the near-dozen members of the Goodman household with their guest, minus Samuel on a joyful errand.

There seemed less interest in the fish, the hard-boiled eggs, the symbolism of the end of *shivah,* than in the forthcoming impromptu wedding.

The younger girls of the family were all a-twitter, but glances from Naomi and their parents prevented their bursting into noisy chatter.

Little Aaron looked as though he didn't know what to make of it. Between small bites, he scanned all with his big, brown eyes, then went back to picking away bits of eggshell and nibbling.

Suddenly the parlor, adjacent to the dining room, seemed to explode. The sound of shattering glass interrupted their quiet happiness.

Young Esther Goodman screamed. Malcolm and Daniel—within a second—had revolvers at the ready and rushed toward the darkened parlor to investigate.

A rock with a note tied around it lay on a small Oriental rug.

Daniel peered out the shattered window into the darkness, a night broken only by lamps and candlelight shining in distant homes of the Paola settlement. He set aside his gun and reached for the note. "Light that lamp!" he commanded to one of the children.

Malcolm placed his hand on Daniel's arm, shaking his head. He beckoned him with motions of his revolver barrel that they should all leave the parlor, not stand in a lighted room without knowing clearly what was happening outside.

They pushed plates aside to spread the note on the dining room table. Expecting a crude scrawl, Malcolm was surprised the composition was crafted so precisely.

"26th of November, 1856

"To Malcolm Erskine—

"Welcome back to Kansas Territory, nigger.

"I'm holding your intended brother-in-law, Samuel Goodman, until you put yourself in my custody. Then the Jew-boy will be released and returned safely to his family.

"I have resources letting me wait a reasonable length of time while you assess the situation and, finally, surrender to me.

"However, I won't wait forever. If in 24 hours you appear not to have been persuaded of the seriousness of my intentions, I'll deliver Samuel Goodman to the porch of his home, dead.

"When you appear on the porch with your hands—oh, excuse me, HAND up, a scout I have stationed here will know you wish to surrender. He'll instruct you further, and I'll come personally to collect you.

"With that accomplished, consider yourself under arrest for violation of the Fugitive Slave Act.

"E.A. Jones"

Malcolm looked up after reading the message, as did other family members. He saw Sarah cover her mouth to stifle a sob, Naomi as well. He shook his head vigorously, indicating—the best he could with limited power of speech—that he would never allow Samuel to become a victim. "He—will—be—safe," Malcolm said hoarsely.

Daniel instructed Benjamin to light a lamp in his bedroom. "You and I," he told Erskine, "have a great deal of talking and planning to do. There's no one to rely on close by for help—no one else to handle this except you and me."

Erskine stared at the more ominous phrases of the note. With his revolver barrel he traced the signature inquiringly.

Daniel responded with a name—"One-Eyed Emmett Anderson Jones, newly arrived in Kansas from Springfield, Missouri. Literate, as you can see. A killer. Distant kin to Sam Jones of Westport, but not a yellow-belly like him. Basically he's a bounty hunter and sometimes mercenary Bushwhacker, often working alone. He makes the late Hank O'Brien look like a sissy."

Naomi spoke with great anxiety. "He's the meanest proslaver ever to set foot in Kansas, is what I've heard. He incited Bushwhacker raids the past couple of weeks, Malcolm, and on his own has killed several people. He has, sort of—well, *taken over.*"

There was much Malcolm hadn't yet caught up on. Did Sam Jones still consider himself a Territorial lawman even though he lived in Missouri? It was he who'd led the sacking of Lawrence and was indirectly responsible for the death of Malcolm's mother.

Kansas was still without effective government. Congress over the summer had refused to seat either set of delegates from the Territory, the proslavers or the Free Staters. Complicating all was the recent election of James Buchanan as President, the Pennsylvanian sympathetic to the South. He'd beaten John C. Frémont, the Republican soldier-adventurer who'd visited Chief Black Bob years earlier on the old Shawnee Reserve.

Malcolm joined Daniel in the younger boys' quarters. Benjamin had not only lighted the room but had brought there all weapons in the household, all the ammunition, so that Daniel and Malcolm could measure their resources. The arsenal was modest, but Erskine calculated it should more than suffice.

"When will we move and how?" Daniel asked after Benjamin had left the room.

Malcolm scribbled on a sheet of paper. *"At first light we'll aim"*—and sketching a rough map of Lykins County—*"in this direction."* He drew a line toward the border, at the northeast corner of the county where it intersected with Johnson County.

Daniel appeared unconvinced. "How do you know he's headed there? I mean, what makes you *think* he's going there?"

Malcolm wrote, *"I know he will. Our leaving here could excite the scout to reveal himself, so we may have to deal with him. What I don't know is whether Emmett is taking Samuel alone or with help. We'll learn more when we ride out and examine tracks."*

Daniel argued, "Why can't we start now?"

Malcolm pointed to the lamp, then skyward, shaking his head. Daniel Goodman evidently didn't understand, so Erskine repeated the moves.

Then Daniel appeared to realize—no moonlight, no illumination available, one of several facts with which Malcolm routinely equipped himself before any action. Daniel pressed Erskine, however, on the latter's "knowing" Jones's planned direction.

Malcolm reached for a blank sheet and wrote—

"We're dealing with an outlaw, whether deputized or not. Lawmen don't throw rocks through windows or hold people hostage and threaten to kill them. This one will head toward his Missouri base mainly by creek beds to throw off tracking. Marais des Cygnes is too wide and winding for that, but Grand River is perfect. That's evidently how he came in, perhaps even camped there, and that's how he'll go out."

After Daniel's reading of Erskine's analysis, a loud knocking came at the front door, further alarming all in the Goodman household.

63

Benjamin Goodman, breathless, poked his head in at the doorway where Malcolm and Daniel were making plans.

"It's the Lykinses. They want to talk to you, Malcolm."

Erskine nodded that he'd be out shortly. He turned to Daniel inquiringly.

Goodman shrugged. "Everyone in Paola knows you're here. I doubt very many know Jones has been in town. Let's hear what they have to say."

The visitors said two of their family members were now posted on the porch as lookouts, so it was reasonably safe for all to gather in the Goodman parlor. Someone had already lighted a lamp and picked up the broken glass.

Zeb Lykins was spokesman. "We know how many are in Jones's group and which way they rode. One of the girls was at the well when she saw Jones's men grab Samuel. She came and told us, but by the time we could get outside with our guns, they'd already gone."

Erskine nodded, beckoning more information. "It wasn't quite as dark then," Zeb said, "so she could see a great deal. She thinks she saw six riders—actually was paying more mind to the fact they'd taken Samuel than anything else."

Erskine acknowledged that with another nod. He gestured to Daniel and Naomi so as to save his voice in communication. Naomi understood more quickly and asked, "Have you spotted the man Jones said he left on watch?"

Zeb held up two fingers. "He left two men behind. We've seen them—still mounted, guns in both hands and drawn—over about—there." He pointed northwest, where all knew a large grove of locust trees stood just beyond the Goodman home. "The others," he said, pointing northeast, "rode that way."

Malcolm considered all he'd just heard. He would much rather ride now if he could, knowing he need no longer examine tracks to determine numbers Jones had brought to Paola. Naomi said, "You men have probably saved us valuable hours with this news. Now we know things Malcolm would have had to use tracking in order to learn."

Malcolm nodded agreement. Once again he gestured to Naomi, whose brain seemed an extension of his own. "Is there anything else you know?" she asked Zeb Lykins. "Anything else you can tell us?"

Zeb hesitated, obviously embarrassed. "We'd go with you, but—" Zeb looked at the floor, finding it difficult to continue.

Naomi went to him, at no instruction from Malcolm, and said, "Nobody's asking you to make more of a sacrifice than your family already has, Zeb. That's what's bothering you, isn't it?"

Lykins nodded, truly humbled and grateful over Naomi Goodman's spoken observation.

Malcolm hadn't even given a thought to asking any of the Lykins men to go along, and he was glad his fiancée had made that clear now. He strode toward Zeb and extended his hand.

"No matter what you may have heard," Zeb said, a bit awkwardly, "we don't resent you for leading the others from Paola who died up in Johnson County. I mean that. We're glad you're back, Malcolm, and glad you're doing what's best for Kansas, what's best for all of us who're trying to make a life here."

Erskine was moved. He increased his pressure on Zeb's hand and felt the young man return the grip.

The Lykinses left. Erskine indicated the younger children should be sent to bed and that the rest should talk in the dining room.

Naomi and Sarah saw to preparing others for what they knew would be a long night of anxiety for Samuel's safety.

Morris Goodman sat in his place at the head of the dining room table. He looked grim over the abduction of his second son, over the risks in a rescue attempt.

When they were finally gathered—Morris and Sarah, Malcolm and Naomi, Daniel, Benjamin—Erskine began to scribble and pass his notes around—

"I have the advantage. There are only six – actually four including Emmett at their hideout – and not likely to be more than that."

"How do you figure advan—?" Daniel protested. "Wait. What do you mean, 'I'? This is my fight, too!"

Malcolm grabbed the sheet and added with pencil—

"The Lykinses' report changes the plan. No more unnecessary risks to this family. The safety of all of you is now as much my responsibility as anyone's, and the fight at their camp is my fight alone because everything will work better that way."

Daniel indicated agitatedly that Malcolm owed him an explanation.

Before writing again, Malcolm thought. He pondered how to communicate what he had to say to the Goodmans without alarming them, on the other hand without insulting Daniel. At last, he began to write again, this time at considerable length—

"Armed to the extent they are, from the way those placed on watch by Jones are described, they originally intended a raid on this settlement.

"Then, coming across Samuel and worming out of him the details of his errand, all Jones's plans changed.

"Because their force at Grand River will be small – likely only those four – and because I can do this best in darkness and am trained in Indian ways, I prefer now to go alone.

"You're not without assignment, Daniel, for I leave to you the elimination of the two on watch, an action NOT to be carried out until you're certain I've succeeded in rescuing Samuel. Otherwise word could be carried northeast by an escaping one of the two here – to kill the boy."

Reading that, Sarah gasped and placed her hand over her mouth.

"How will I be certain?" Daniel asked when he'd read the last part.

Malcolm rose from the exhausting scribbling, sighed, looked toward Naomi, and pointed to a clock on the mantel. He gestured as Naomi spoke.

"Malcolm," she said, "will be in this room, with Samuel safely returned, by noon tomorrow."

She watched as Erskine gestured further, then said, "He will then step onto the porch as instructed by Jones. As soon as their guard is lowered, you—Daniel—and others you should recruit for this, must move in and take the two out there in daylight. How that is to be planned exactly, Malcolm leaves to you."

Erskine pointed to Sarah. He leaned to touch Naomi on the left hand, shrugged slightly, then urged her to proceed with her seemingly expert interpreting.

"Furthermore, all plans for a Thanksgiving feast are to proceed—barring anything unforeseen—immediately following our wedding at—"

Malcolm held up four fingers.

"Four o'clock in the afternoon, tomorrow."

Daniel looked astounded. "I've known you for some time, Malcolm, but I never knew you to be this sure of yourself."

Erskine smiled and took Naomi's hand, squeezing it, prompting her to say to her brother, "He draws new confidence from our love." Malcolm nodded, confirming those were his sentiments.

At last he indicated he would make ready and that he wished to leave without knowledge by Emmett Jones's two men on watch, that he needed also to select the right weaponry.

Benjamin was dispatched to saddle Ebony in total darkness—and quietly.

Malcolm scanned the arsenal in the Goodman boys' room and selected one Colt, the latest in revolvers made in the East.

"Only one?" Daniel asked.

Malcolm held up his one hand, indicating he had little use for two-gun fighting as in earlier days, though he could carry a spare. He gestured that he needed but one and preferred to travel as lightly as he could. Much of the time he would be on foot.

Morris Goodman—either anticipating a wish or by other motivation—suddenly ducked out and in a moment returned, carrying a sheathed Bowie.

"After you showed me your knife," Morris said, "I admired it so much, I obtained one, but cannot yet determine what I will use it for. It is yours, my son."

Malcolm examined the knife, smiled, and accepted it with sincere gratitude. Truly, it was the most appropriate item he could have wished for in what lay ahead.

64

Everyone in the Goodman family had retired. None expected a good night's rest while Samuel was in the clutches of One-Eyed Emmett. Still, they took some comfort in the knowledge Malcolm was positive about recovering the boy safely.

Before heading out, Malcolm accepted a small sack from Naomi. "It's a hard, fruit-flavored candy," she said. "Mama says it will ease the pain in your mouth. You pop one in and let it dissolve slowly. I have a lemon-flavored one in my mouth right now."

Malcolm tucked the sack in his shirt and drew Naomi to him, hugging her and seeking her mouth for a kiss. After a time, knowing her playfulness matched his, he felt the lemon ball being transferred. Still kissing, they both began to laugh.

Breaking away, Naomi said, "I don't know how, in the midst of danger to Samuel, I can manage to find anything funny."

Malcolm formed the word soundlessly, *"Life,"* and touched the *chai* charm she'd given him. He indicated life produced its own unsought amusements, just as it did its unwelcome hazards.

He then tested the sharpness and weight of the Bowie knife Morris gave him and found it perfect. He was tempted to leave the Colt behind and rely solely on the knife. As though anticipating that, Naomi stopped his hand from unworking his gun belt.

"No," she commanded. "You must take a gun. You may need it."

Malcolm acquiesced. He spotted a twinge of pain reflecting on her face. He touched her shoulder, frowning, wanting explanation.

"The baby. He moved."

A surge of emotion raced through Malcolm. He knelt and placed his ear to her belly. He held her close that way for a time, shutting his eyes. At last he rose, sought his hat, whispered to her, "I love you," and left.

Mounting Ebony, he glanced back to see Naomi at the window throwing him a sad kiss and smiling bravely.

*****

In darkness relieved only by stars, Malcolm determined he'd reached the county line. He dismounted and tethered Ebony. The cautious ride through the northeast section of Lykins County had taken nearly two hours.

Half a mile farther lay the source of the Grand River, the timbered area where he concluded Jones would camp. As though confirmed in that, he was certain he saw the flicker of a campfire.

Yes, definitely a campfire.

If One-Eyed Emmett placed two on watch at this camp instead of one, Malcolm's approach would be extremely difficult. He decided to proceed by crawling.

Erskine knew he could kill a man in blackness of night within two seconds of fixing his whereabouts from a short distance. But he could never know whether that man would make a sound going down, alerting someone whose gun was cocked. Someone near in the blackness. He might be forced to take his first adversary by making complete body contact.

Because it was fall, Erskine cautioned himself against snapping a dry twig. He knew he must *slide* hand, hook, and knees forward.

Now he was at a place just south of the narrow river where he could observe the entire camp on the other side.

Two tents were pitched, Samuel evidently in one of them.

No man was visible, indicating to Erskine that while at least two slept, the Bushwhacker on watch had stepped far from the site and *might even be on his neck now.*

Instinctively, Malcolm rolled to one side in the dirt and grabbed for the Bowie, thrusting the blade upward on the chance—

The sharp knife found flesh, gristle, and bone. Malcolm could feel the heat of his intended attacker's blood spilling over him. It was over within a heartbeat's time.

And done quietly.

Had Erskine *heard* the Missourian above him? Or had he guessed?

No time to consider that now. There was another on watch coming into the firelight, a carbine at the ready and wearing at least one pistol.

Malcolm popped a hard candy into his mouth, then scurried along the ground, through the stream and probably making his Colt useless for a time because of the water. He came up on the north bank and continued silently. He didn't let his snaking movements produce the *swish* sound that any crawling animal might have made.

At a tree he rose, remembering every lesson the Shawnees of Black Bob and even the brawling longshoremen in New Bedford had taught him about the balance and trajectory of knives.

From a distance of perhaps twenty feet, he threw the Bowie and caught the other man on watch clean in the throat. At the falling of the carbine, Malcolm raced to catch it before it touched the ground, then turned toward the tent.

All was still, including the dying Bushwhacker in the lighted camp area. Erskine retrieved his knife, glancing at his eyes-open enemy in the last seconds of the man's life. Soon the watchman's face turned to one side and he was finished.

So far not enough sound had been raised to alert One-Eyed Emmett or the other man in one of the tents, Malcolm believed. Only the hoot-owls and an occasional crackling in the small campfire broke the still of the night.

Not even the breeze could raise a stir in the trees, for the leaves were nearly gone.

Samuel would either be with Jones or with the other man in one of the small tents—but which one? If he knew, he could easily slay the occupant of the other.

Distinctly, Malcolm heard a gun being cocked. Then a voice.

"Ver-ry *good,* Mr. Erskine."

One-Eyed Emmett walked into the lighted camp area, a pistol leveled at Malcolm.

"You're slipperier'n I thought. Yes, you're really *good.* I saw Mr. Applebee go down. I thought you did that rather neatly. And I can see from all the blood, you've also dispatched Mr. Bergen."

Realizing Jones's talking would wake the fourth man, Malcolm let himself glance toward the tents.

"Get back!" Jones commanded his man, but too late. Erskine let a blast from the carbine catch the revolvers-drawn Missourian in the head before he could straighten from the crouch of leaving the tent.

Instantly, Malcolm recocked and turned to Jones.

"Now, what'd you go and do that for?" Jones wailed. "You've left me all alone here in the wilderness, with no one for company 'cept a Jew-boy and a nigger. What's a real American like me to do on Thanksgiving with companionship like that?"

Malcolm found that sucking candy eased his mouth and vocal muscles. He would make a try—

"Samuel!" he called. "If you're not tied, go straight south! Find Ebony! Wait there!"

He heard the lad scurry from the other side of the tent and could tell in a few seconds that Samuel was already lickety-split across the stream.

"Now I ain't even got the *Jew* for company, Erskine."

Jones's playing was a stall, Malcolm knew. The Bushwhacker was figuring how to get the advantage, for the two had the drop on each other.

Malcolm studied the man in the firelight. He was everything he'd been described as being—mean-looking as hell, relatively well-spoken to the point where he might impress someone as being educated, and he was far from reckless in his movements.

Emmett Anderson Jones decided to sit on the ground. He lowered himself Indian-fashion, still holding a gun on Malcolm, who held the carbine on Jones.

"What say we powwow, now that you've found your voice again. I heard a hell of a lot about you, before coming up from Springfield. You've caused excitement around this part of the country. Where've you *been* the last six or so months?"

Malcolm heard a gun being cocked. Then a voice behind him. "You're slipperier'n I thought."

Malcolm had decided not to engage in conversation with this man, not give One-Eyed Emmett even the tiniest clue to his personality, his reasoning capacities, his patience or impatience during palavering. He would just let Jones go on.

"Sit down, Malcolm," Jones invited with a tone of amusement. "You're not *my* nigger. You don't have to stand out of respect for your superiors. You're quite a legend. I'd like to know what makes you tick."

Erskine studied Jones, watched how he moved—body, hands, feet—how he held his head, how he looked at things from his one eye.

Malcolm made a decision. "It's a stand-off, Jones," he said hoarsely. "Take one horse and leave. Head east, out of Kansas."

"I could get you while you're helping yourself to the other horses and weapons," Jones said. "Why don't *you* be the one backing away?"

Erskine wanted an end to this. He couldn't talk much longer without popping another candy, and he couldn't take a chance of reaching for that.

Jones apparently realized Malcolm wasn't to be messed with. He'd already killed three of his men. "As I say, I *could* get you, but you know I'm not damned fool enough to try. Not this way."

Erskine watched him uncock carefully and holster his revolver. Jones strolled to where a white horse was tethered beyond the tents.

Mounting, Jones walked the mare several steps back into the firelight to add, "See, no gun in hand, Erskine. And that, besides skin color, is the difference between us. You're a man of honor and won't shoot. I'm not. You can be trusted. I can't."

Jones rode off slowly, entering the river and heading east in its bed.

Almost simultaneously, Malcolm heard Samuel call his name from far off.

The boy sounded troubled.

65

No need for crouching, sliding from tree to tree, Erskine believed. Samuel's tone conveyed no physical threat but rather confusion, weariness.

Now it was quiet ahead—too quiet—making it more difficult for Malcolm to find his way in the darkness. Should he call out?—provided he could make enough sound with his hurting mouth.

Malcolm heard a man's voice exclaim, *"What?"*—as though reacting to something incredible. He realized young Samuel Goodman was having a conversation. But with whom—here, halfway between midnight and dawn?

Malcolm also heard a horse nicker and realized that animal wasn't Ebony. He moved faster. A man and another horse were there.

Just as he was about to call out to Samuel, he heard, *"Malcolm."* It was Eugene Fontenot.

Accustoming to the darkness, Malcolm tried to greet his friend warmly. But he noticed a pulling back by the Creole.

Samuel, however, heaved an audible sigh of relief at Malcolm's arrival. The boy was seated astride Ebony, as though he wouldn't leave Erskine's horse for anything. Malcolm thought back to when he was Samuel's age, about thirteen, and recalled things he clung to for security, particularly in a state of motherlessness.

Erskine asked Fontenot, "Something wrong?" He was certain a distant attitude had taken hold of his friend.

"Nothing, nothing." Eugene said. "I am happy to see you recovering from your experience in Arkansas."

Malcolm was dubious. "What were you two talking about?" he managed to say. He pulled juices from the last of his hard candies to moisten his mouth.

"I understand from this young man, you are planning to be married today," Fontenot responded. "That is—wonderful news."

"Thank you," Malcolm said. Maybe Fontenot would clear the air later.

They would all ride back to Paola, where Eugene had learned of Samuel's abduction and Malcolm's likely whereabouts. Fontenot admitted brushing aside Daniel Goodman's advice against going to the Grand River.

Malcolm mounted Ebony behind Samuel. Fontenot mounted his horse, a bay mare as nearly as Malcolm could tell in the dark. The Creole began to describe his adventures with the slaves from the *Delta Queen.*

All instructions Erskine had given the Louisiana man proved true for charting the escape through Arkansas. Not everything went without a hitch. There were three occasions when teams of bounty hunters rode straight up to the Underground Railroad stations while the escapees were in or near them.

In one place there was barely enough room for the huge company of fugitives under the barn, which had a false floor. The hole had been shored cleverly to prevent anyone's discovering, by hollow sound, that it wasn't solid.

But one spot gave trouble. It thumped differently when a horse's hoof stepped on it. As luck would have it, one of the Arkansas proslavers heard it.

Fontenot confessed to having nearly dirtied his trousers in fright. But he heard the farmer explain, an old cistern had been covered during the building of the barn. "They's holla spots here 'n' there," the farmer said. The bounty hunter accepted the farmer's tale rather than tear up the floor for proof.

On other occasions elaborate tunnel and cave systems protected the fugitives.

There were nights they feared someone had been lost while they were moving from station to station, that a child had wandered off.

Fontenot taught the slaves to keep track. He divided them into small groups. Members of each group were responsible for one another and for reporting their safety to the next group ahead.

Fontenot described John Brown, whom he'd seen in Osawatomie the day before. He reported the old man's resolve to begin insurrections by Negroes in key places throughout the South.

Malcolm shook his head in dismay and said to Eugene, "A pipe dream."

In the haze before dawn on the way to Paola, their faces grew visible. Erskine reached and stopped Fontenot. Their horses halted.

They were still about five miles from the settlement, and the sun would rise in less than an hour. Malcolm wanted to smoke. He dismounted. He sat on a fallen log and rolled a cigarette. The boy remained astride Ebony.

Fontenot dismounted as well and strolled over to sit alongside.

"Audrey is with me," Eugene said with voice lowered. Samuel had begun to doze in the saddle. "She is at this moment in the home of the Goodmans."

Malcolm had almost guessed, almost figured from the way Eugene was behaving that Audrey was somehow involved.

"Over Daniel Goodman's protests, I left immediately to find you. I didn't know about wedding plans till I stumbled upon Samuel. In the course of chatting, from nervousness I suppose, the boy spilled the news that you are to marry— I'm sorry, what is her name?"

"Naomi. Whom I love," Malcolm thought to add, turning to face his friend.

"Yes, yes, of course. Naomi. I notice she is with child. Yours, I suppose."

Malcolm nodded.

Fontenot sighed. After a time, he said, "That is too bad."

Malcolm again found enough voice to say, "I'm thrilled over it. Why bad?"

"Because Audrey— Well, see, she would have stayed in Baton Rouge once matters were settled over our father's debts, but— Well—she visited a physician and learned— I don't quite know how to put this, *mon ami,* but—"

Malcolm puffed on his cigarette, knowing full well what was coming—or believing he did.

"She is also to have your child."

"That is," Malcolm said, "truly unfortunate."

"She did not think so. She came to Kansas—first to Osawatomie to locate me, then accompanying me to Paola to find you—because she wishes to wed you."

Erskine began to laugh.

Fontenot took offense. "I see no reason to be amused over my sister's sense of honor, which can best be satisfied by your carrying out her wish."

"Eugene, my friend," Erskine tried to say, now with hoarseness, "this is Kansas, not Louisiana."

Fontenot appeared baffled.

"This is where a man is free," Erskine said. "He's neither bound—" He began to cough, starting to lose again his power of speech until he could be soothed by Mrs. Goodman's candies or perhaps some honey.

"A man here—" He spoke with pauses. "—is neither bound—by the Napoleonic Code—nor pretensions about 'honor.' He is free to make—only his own choices."

"I don't understand."

"You must think in new ways—if you wish to remain—in Kansas. I have said my last on it. I cannot—speak."

Malcolm snuffed out the cigarette, getting up.

That was settled then, in Malcolm's mind. His plan was to wed Naomi Goodman that very day. Audrey Fontenot must consider herself as having finished second in racing to meet him at the altar.

Besides, he felt he hardly knew Audrey. Comely as she was—a very handsome and talented and seductive woman—she was neither so bright nor considerate and loving as Naomi. He was lucky to have settled on the idea of marrying Naomi.

"I haven't told you all of it," Eugene said as they mounted again, Samuel hugging Ebony's neck in deep sleep.

Malcolm turned inquiringly.

"Audrey has placed her own stamp of honor on this matter," Fontenot said. "She told me before we left Brown—if you refuse to marry her, she means to have you killed."

66

Something had changed in Naomi Goodman's temperament overnight, Malcolm observed.

No doubt she'd been stung by deducing Audrey's purpose. She directed Erskine where to clean up after his arrival from the Grand River. She ministered to his needs, his mouth injuries that seemed to take forever to heal.

But her mood seemed stiff.

When they were alone he touched her arm and looked at her questioningly.

Naomi faced him, her lower lip quivering. "You hurt my feelings, Malcolm."

"I did not," he responded. "Something I did—not knowing when or whether I'd return to Kansas—that's what hurt your feelings."

She looked away to think on that for a minute. Malcolm studied her frown, her appearance of pain, and realized she was reworking in her mind the timing of his commitment. It had come the previous evening, never before. Until then Malcolm had made no pledge. Whatever he'd done up to that moment was done as a man uncommitted.

"What are we going to do?" she said at last, wearily, as though Malcolm must decide the right course for their lives.

"Wed, as planned," he remarked, decisively.

"There's a sadness now, one I can't bear, Malcolm."

"I did *not* violate your honor," he reminded her, "for we had no understandings at that time." He turned back to washing up.

"I realize that now," Naomi acknowledged, "but I feel bad for that poor woman."

Toweling himself, Erskine smirked and shook his head in irony. He'd found Sarah Goodman's hard candies were the key to restoring the use of his injured mouth and throat. He was using them now as one might keep a steam engine lubricated.

"That 'poor woman,' as you call her, was saved from a fate worse than death," he said. "A marriage of monstrous dishonor. Within a few years she'd have lost every spark of her youthful personality, all to pay her father's gambling debt."

"I know all about that. Audrey and I talked half the night, waiting for you and for Samuel and Eugene to return. I know also," Naomi said, "that she has totally different views from mine about right and wrong on many subjects."

"You're damned right she does," Malcolm said, drying his arms and shoulders vigorously. "She thought nothing of leaving me without a penny on that ship. I might have at least been able to bribe my way out of being tossed in the brig. Instead my escape ultimately cost the life of your Uncle Noah. Think about *that.*"

"I have," Naomi said. "Audrey's being here changes a lot. It's given me much to think about."

"I don't understand," he said, putting on a clean shirt he'd bought on credit from the Goodman stock, buttoning the sleeves.

She leaned against the oak stand that held the huge wash basin, then half sat on it. "Malcolm, what will you do after today?"

"What?"

"That's a serious question, Malcolm. What are you trained to do? How will you make a living? My father can't offer you a position in the store, for we're hardly selling enough now to support the family. So he can't pay you. He can only offer you the continuing hospitality of our home. He'd let us live here for a reasonable length of time while you found something to do."

Malcolm shook his head. "I wouldn't want that." He tucked the tail of his shirt into his trousers.

"Oh? Then where would we go after this wedding? Where might we live, with our baby due in less than two months? Malcolm, you're not going to tell me you hadn't thought it all out."

Malcolm was too embarrassed to respond. The fact was, he'd given some but not enough thought to it, certain only that he was possessed of faith in his own resources for survival. He believed that a little application of energy here, a bit of ingenuity there, would help him meet any change in his circumstances.

If they needed a permanent place to live, he would find land, manage a way to come into ownership, dig a well and a privy—even one-handed—then build a cabin, and later a sturdier home. If they needed money, he would earn it at whatever work was available. If they needed protection from an enemy, he would fight and overcome attackers.

That was how Erskine had considered their prospects, but as for details, well—

"Look at me, Malcolm," Naomi said, standing straight and placing her hands on his shoulders so that he couldn't turn away. He hung his head, for he had none of the specific answers he knew she hoped to hear.

"Look at me. I was foolish to have suggested we be married. I still want to marry you, but not till you have a trade. I'll have our child. He'll be called Noah Steven Erskine, as we've agreed. But we won't wed till you come to me and show me you can support us."

"Don't you have confidence I can do that?"

"I have every confidence," Naomi said, her eyes holding his strongly. "But you must arrange it first before we're a family. I won't enter into marriage with you any other way."

She leaned to kiss him lovingly. He was more saddened than buoyed by that, because of her new doubts.

Malcolm decided he'd better go to Lawrence to clear up his status, perhaps become subsidized by Free State forces again.

"I have a job," he said, "or possible assurance of one. Soldier and spy for the Free State."

Naomi's chin was on his shoulder in their embrace, her head back. Malcolm heard her catch her breath, a gasp. "They won't pay you anymore. I checked."

Erskine held her away, unbelieving. "Why not?"

"The Bushwhackers have caused so much trouble, they've finally got Kansas settlers riled to where they'll defend themselves with everything they have. Kansas no longer needs to fund spies and mercenaries. It's developing a completely volunteer defense at last."

"Good. They'll need commanders, trainers."

"They have plenty—qualified and serving without pay."

"None as good as I."

Naomi shook her head. "I won't contradict that, my love. But all are volunteers. To defend the Territory, everything has now become well structured under Jim Lane's leadership."

"Where does that leave me? Supposed to be married today—after we clear up those two jackals in the grove. I was to resume fighting, with your better acceptance of that. Now, no prospects."

"Not—exactly." Naomi embraced him again. "If this is what I think it is, it may be our chance—*your* chance." She backed away. "Come with me."

Malcolm followed Naomi to the second floor, past the Goodman children hurrying to help Sarah prepare the Thanksgiving feast. She led him to a window that looked into the yard at the rear of the house.

"Look there," she said. "I noticed it for the first time at sunup."

Erskine saw, freshly cut into the dirt, a large diagram in the shape a "Y."

Naomi was right to have led him upstairs. At ground level the diagram would hardly have been recognizable as anything significant. From this height, however—

"Where is north from here?" he asked.

"Directly ahead."

"And the stem of the 'Y' is aimed northeast," Malcolm said.

"Meaning—?"

"Black Bob. The 'Y' represents the position of his camp where Wolf and Coffee Creeks meet the Blue. It's a sign he wants me to go to him."

"Just as I thought. Look at me, Malcolm. Listen well. You must," Naomi said, "finish the task here today. Daniel is ready, as you've instructed. He has a plan to capture those Bushwhackers.

"Also, settle matters with Audrey. *I* have a plan for that. Trust me and it will be done. It will take time—a considerable amount of time, I fear. But her honor will no longer be at issue when I've—when *we've* completed arrangements.

"Then," she added, "after you begin the process by talking with her, you'll go see Chief Black Bob. That's the very next thing you'll do, my love."

Malcolm watched her in wonder as she spoke. Her mind was much like his, calculating grand plans and solutions, turning others' lives upside down if necessary, all aimed at making things come out right.

"You think," Erskine said, "the answer for us lies with Black Bob. That's what you meant by 'our chance' when you spoke earlier."

"Yes, I have an intuition about it. See what he wants. I could be wrong, *or* perhaps my hopes for what it may mean are accurate. But I prefer not to discuss details until you've learned why he wants you."

Malcolm glanced out the window again at the sign left by a Shawnee messenger. "I'll leave for Black Bob's camp this evening."

67

Daniel Goodman took charge and described how they would apprehend the Bushwhackers that Jones left in Paola. "Malcolm, you won't appear on the porch as planned."

"You're thinking there's another man the Lykins girl didn't see? A third man on watch?"

"How did you know?" Daniel asked in frank amazement.

"Last night I learned much about this Jones's ways," Erskine said. "I'll agree to your plan—whatever it is. Tell it." He glanced at Audrey Fontenot, who hadn't taken her gaze from Malcolm. Still, she seemed involved somehow in Daniel's plot.

Daniel continued. "It's a lucky circumstance the Fontenots have joined us, for I've needed an attractive young woman to play a role—to literally play-act."

"Merci pour le compliment, monsieur," Audrey said. "But I should protest, you already *have* an attractive young woman available to you here in Naomi, the difference being that she is simply further advanced in her preg—"

"Enough!" Eugene commanded to quiet Audrey. Her bitterness seemed to envelop those who knew her secret. "Just listen and be quiet."

Daniel went on. "Audrey will shortly change her clothes and increase the intensity of her facial makeup. She'll portray a prostitute, inviting Jones's men into her closed carriage—actually the Goodman carriage Samuel and Benjamin are now preparing behind the house. If there's a third man," Daniel said, "he'll reveal himself the instant the two out there climb into the carriage with Audrey."

"He will," Audrey said, fluttering her eyelashes, rocking her hips, "if he's any kind of a *man.*"

Malcolm was not yet comfortable with the plan. "Wait. Aren't you underestimating their attention to duty? These aren't merely unruly Missourians off on a lark. They work for Emmett Jones, one of the smartest and most disciplined adversaries I ever expect to encounter."

"Also one of the most frustrating to work for," Daniel said. "We've done a little research during the night. Zeb Lykins was of great assistance. We've found that Jones keeps his men on a short leash. It's likely the two Bushwhackers out there—and the third, if there is one—haven't been with a woman for weeks, maybe months."

Naomi and Audrey fairly chorused, "Oh, my."

"Jones is some kind of religious zealot when it comes to leading," Daniel continued, "as is John Brown in other ways. Jones keeps his raiders sharp and mean by depriving them of things they enjoy and rewarding them when they least expect it. There've been complaints."

"You have an informant in the Jones camp?" Malcolm was impressed.

"We've traced one," Daniel said with a grin, "that Zeb can reach about third- or fourth-hand. But that's the word that comes out. Good plan, Malcolm?"

Erskine looked at the mantel clock. "It is, but you could run short of time if this is to work. They'll probably withdraw at a prearranged hour. Let me guess you'll have Zeb and his group posted by the square to watch for 'number three.' You—and I suppose Eugene—will be ready to ride hard behind the carriage and overtake it."

"That's the plan. Audrey," Daniel instructed, "get ready. Eugene, give a sign to Zeb out the back way. Also see that my brothers have finished preparing the rig." They left as directed.

Malcolm said, "I congratulate you, Daniel, on arrangements that appear to have every chance of success."

"I'd like to get all this out of the way and those men behind bars," Daniel said with a wry grin, "before the wedding."

"There's to be no wedding today. Naomi prefers we wait, for reasons we've discussed fully. I've been called to Black Bob's camp. I leave this evening."

Daniel smirked and shook his head. "I don't like the marriage delay. I suppose you both know what you're doing. I tell you, though—" Goodman appeared to be looking off into space, then speaking as though he were thinking out loud. "Weddings and romance would be clearer in my mind, if not for two circumstances."

Naomi asked, "What two circumstances?"

"My pining for Jane-Ellen, for one. And my realization that if I knew Audrey much better than I do, I'd probably *not* be pining for Jane-Ellen."

Naomi caught Malcolm's attention and gave him an exaggerated wink.

* * * * *

Daniel's direction of the drama outdoors unfolded as he'd predicted and planned.

Audrey Fontenot, having observed the ways of women of pleasure in New Orleans and Baton Rouge, gave a flawless performance. She was irresistible.

Weary from their overnight watch, Jones's men in the locust grove holstered their guns and accepted Audrey's invitation to accompany her in the carriage. They hitched their horses behind and got in, laughing over anticipated delights.

Meanwhile, Daniel and Eugene Fontenot were mounted and ready.

Zeb Lykins's group grew busy sooner than expected. A rough stranger to the settlement burst from hiding in the high loft of a livery stable on the square. He cursed loudly the associates he'd observed leaving their watch and began running toward the woods for his horse.

Zeb and the others at the square came down on him quickly, tying his hands just as Audrey drove into the square.

Seeing Free Staters ahead and behind, all armed, the Bushwhackers in the carriage surrendered. They, too, were tied and led to jail just off the square.

They would either be tried before a circuit Federal judge for the Territory or taken to Lawrence, where a harsher Free State law might finish them upon conviction. Local officials would decide.

Malcolm led Naomi, who wore a scarf against the increasing chill, for a leisurely stroll around the Paola square. There he congratulated all who'd participated directly in the smooth capture.

As others began to leave their homes to see what activity had just been played out noisily, Malcolm realized he was attracting an audience. Perhaps as many as twenty-five villagers had joined the group. He tested his reacquired voice for speechmaking, not the first time he'd been called on for public speaking and probably not the last.

"Citizens of Lykins County. You all know me, and I feel warm and welcome, thanks to your hospitality. But I can't feel entirely comfortable, nor should you." An uneasy stir was evident in the enlarging crowd.

"We must do all in our power for self-defense, because Emmett Anderson Jones may come seeking his men. These men who've just been captured after their kidnap of Samuel Goodman, who was held hostage for me."

A man interrupted rudely. "What's that to any of us? That's purely a family matter—strictly your affair. And speaking of affair," the man added, looking from side to side for acknowledgement that others might catch his meaning about Malcolm's relationship with Naomi Goodman, "I think—"

Erskine remained calm but stopped the man with, "I care very much what you think, sir. If you speak as a citizen concerned about organizing the safety of Kansans. What you think of me, however—particularly when you border on slander—could cost you your life right here on the Paola square."

"I have the right of free speech, just as you do!" the other man protested.

"You also have the responsibility," Malcolm said, "for all you say, just as I do. And what a man says could have fatal consequences. Do you agree?"

The man quieted himself, but Malcolm pressed. "Sir, do you have children?"

The villager nodded, then said, "Yes, I do."

"Their ages?"

"A girl who'll be twelve years of age, and a boy eight."

"Then the girl is nearly Samuel Goodman's age. Both your children are subject to the same dangers of being taken hostage—for whatever reason enters the devious mind of Emmett Jones and his kind. Wouldn't you say *all* children of Kansas Territory deserve greater safety than that?"

The crowd began to encourage Malcolm. Some shushed the other man for rudeness and agreed that Erskine was making sense—mobilize for self-protection, guard the children and themselves more strongly against Missouri Bushwhackers.

"It's a clear choice—*your* choice," Erskine said, "between exposure to threats of violence by supporters of slavery, or organizing means to counter that threat. When it's clear to ruffians in Missouri that the people here will meet all challenges, that they'll meet violence with equal response, those gangs will *stop* raiding folks this side of the border."

"Can you guarantee they'll stop?" a merchant called out to Erskine.

"Not any more than I could guarantee it will snow tomorrow," Malcolm said. "But the chances of stopping them are *far better* if they know they might *die* for bringing you such trouble. Other settlements are starting to organize for defense. Time that you in Paola quit letting those bullies push you around."

At that a cheer went up in the Paola square. Zeb and Daniel quickly found themselves surrounded by men volunteering for a Paola defense militia. As the village men told what weapons they could contribute, Zeb fumbled for a pencil and paper and enlisted Naomi's help to make a written record.

Observing that his Thanksgiving Day audience had grown to forty or more, Erskine kept their enthusiasm fired with catch phrases—"Statehood without slavery!" and similar cries that brought cheers and backslapping.

When it was done—and after Daniel had invited Audrey to ride with him by a circuitous route back to the Goodman household—Malcolm and Naomi walked homeward arm in arm.

"You're getting your voice back, Malcolm," Naomi observed. "You should think about going into politics. You have a flair."

Malcolm didn't respond but looked straight ahead and registered an incomplete smile.

68

The Thanksgiving feast in the Goodman home was a bittersweet event. There was to be no wedding that day.

Malcolm informed all about his plans to see Black Bob, upon invitation by the Shawnee leader. He appreciated the hospitality and forbearance by the Goodmans. But he must find means of self-support. It was essential.

Naomi appeared proud and supportive of Malcolm's resolution to follow a more stable course, though she said nothing in acknowledgement of his short speech to the family.

Audrey Fontenot, meanwhile, seemed under constraint by her brother Eugene against saying anything more, while a guest of the Goodmans, that might cloud Naomi's hopes.

It was evident to all, however, that Daniel Goodman and Audrey had suddenly taken an interest in each other. Malcolm regarded that as both a blessing and a curse.

As he ate, Erskine considered that Daniel had suffered uncertainties in his relationship with Jane-Ellen O'Brien, a chameleon-like woman. She was now propertied in Cass County. Travel there was increasingly dangerous with acceleration of the Border War. Daniel was now less inclined to pursue that interest.

But Malcolm realized that losing Daniel as a guard against Jane-Ellen's affectionate onslaughts toward him—well, that might free her for further unpredictability.

And *Audrey's* claim on Malcolm wasn't to be taken lightly.

Naomi's claim—one she was wise enough not to press in the threatening style of Audrey—came ahead of all in Erskine's consideration.

A dark side to Daniel's sidetracking Audrey's attentions and interests was Malcolm's belief that his friend deserved better.

Yes, Audrey Fontenot was a skilled woman—an educated companion, athletic and well-formed, much that a man could hope for. Her character, alas, was incomplete. It needed mending. Whether Daniel recognized that or could be the catalyst for accomplishing it was a factor Erskine had no answers for.

Naomi was the only person he knew who might be able to advise, and it was becoming surprisingly evident that she—Naomi—was cultivating her own relationship with Audrey. Perhaps a conversion of the Creole woman to better principles was already under way for Daniel's benefit.

Approximately the same age, both coming on motherhood under the same circumstances—actually by the same man—the two young women otherwise had little in common. Their background cultures differed as night from day.

Malcolm turned to Naomi and glowed in intensified appreciation of her.

"What is it?" she whispered, seeing his look.

"I love you," he said, a little too loudly, sending the younger Goodman children into renewed tittering. He hadn't yet learned to modulate his rediscovered voice, so it had come forth too audibly.

Morris Goodman smiled and used the occasion to ameliorate Malcolm's embarrassment by lifting his glass of wine and rising. "A toast," he declared. "A toast of Thanksgiving."

All who considered themselves adults stood and reached for filled wine glasses. The children remained quietly seated, being content with water and a few of them, in imitation, raising water glasses.

Morris phrased his toast, "To the growing Goodman family. May each of my loved ones find the happiness he or she seeks. For in them, I have found mine."

From the joy that welled up inside him, Malcolm felt tears leap to his eyes. Instead of sipping his wine, he guzzled it to hide his emotion.

Naomi, however, seemed to sense those emotions without looking and made him set down the glass. Still standing, she took his right hand in hers and turned it to kiss the palm.

"And I," she declared in half-whisper, half-announcement, "love you and always will."

Audrey Fontenot, shaking her head, said to Eugene, just loud enough for all to hear if not understand, "I can't compete with that."

When they reseated themselves, Daniel invited Audrey to ride out with him before dark, just for conversation. She accepted with apparent gratitude. "I would like that," she said, obviously humbled by all she'd witnessed.

* * * * *

Later Malcolm readied for the journey to the Blue River valley to see Black Bob. He hadn't much to pack—a few articles of clothing acquired from the Goodman store, weapons given to him or taken from enemies.

On the way to Black Bob he would find the place where he'd buried the special, carefully-wrapped bow and quiver of arrows the Chief had given him. He would carry that gear on Ebony as well.

Erskine wished to ride into the Black Bob camp a full warrior, a role in which the Shawnees had accepted and helped him. He was as much their champion as he was that of the Negro.

Naomi helped him prepare to leave. "Have you spoken with Audrey at all?" she inquired.

Malcolm shook his head. "I approached her when she returned from the square with Daniel. She seemed surprised and—I suppose one could say flighty, fickle, coquettish—still in the role she played earlier today. I wasn't able to get my thoughts out. Besides, she seems now more at one with Daniel."

Naomi nodded with a knowing look. "A woman's trick. She's quite immature. I have a challenge before me, in my dear brother's interest—and ours." Then she placed a hand on her belly symbolically. "We'll wait patiently for you no matter how long you're away," Naomi said.

"I hope to return well before the baby is born," Malcolm said. "I'll go from Black Bob's camp to determine my first steps in the cattle trade I've been considering more and more. I'd like to test the market, which means learning what I can in Kansas City without being apprehended. Possibly moving on to Leavenworth to discuss military contracts for beef with officers at the Fort."

"Those plans will cause you dangerous exposure," Naomi protested.

"I'm good at disguise. I think I can handle that when necessary."

With new resolve he bid his friends and Naomi's family affectionate goodbyes.

In a moment of privacy, Naomi said, "Take care, Malcolm." They kissed passionately.

"I have many reasons to take care," Erskine said. "You and our child are the most important of them."

69

During his ride to Black Bob's, Malcolm recalled Naomi's having described shifts in Free State resistance policy, Kansas's increased reliance on volunteers. From talking with Daniel and others in Paola, he learned reasons this new defense posture by antislavery settlers had evolved in his absence.

Former Governor Shannon, yielding to Washington, had brought the weight of United States forces against Free Staters. Reactions by New England abolitionists intensified over the summer. They stimulated the opening of new trails into Kansas Territory from Nebraska and Iowa. They sent large forces to help General Lane.

Shannon was now gone, forced to resign by reports of his tolerating proslaver atrocities against Free Staters. The new man was Governor John Geary, seemingly more liberal but not yet widely trusted by Lane's people.

Before leaving, Shannon had also become too cozy with the dictatorial Chief Justice of the Territory, S.D. LeCompte, founder of the town bearing his name, Lecompton. The capital was soon to be shifted to Lecompton. The building intended to serve the proslavery lawmakers was, in fact, a multipurpose structure that Sam Jones had ordered built as an investment for rentals.

Geary quickly canceled some of Shannon's excesses, among them establishment of a standing army to crush Free State forces. Geary was also trying to have Chief Justice LeCompte removed from the bench for turning loose a Missouri murder suspect, Charles Hays—so notorious that even a proslavery grand jury had indicted him.

Back-and-forth battles, murders, and acts of vengeance were reaching deeper and deeper into the Territory, with Johnson County serving as the principal corridor.

President Pierce and President-elect Buchanan were compelled to reckon with the fact that people of Northern states were becoming fed up with the violence in Kansas. To Northerners the issue was clear—keep Missourians away from Kansas Territory's balloting places and let the bona fide settlers decide their future.

*****

Malcolm had left Paola too late to make Black Bob's headquarters in the same day. He welcomed the chance to be alone, to think over the reality of needing an income and the unlikelihood of hiring out to Free State leaders again.

Erskine would find a place to camp. Had there been urgency in the sign that summoned him, a turkey feather would have waved from a firmly-planted stick at its center.

Turning northeast he sought the place along Camp Branch where his lodge had been—the hiding place of his ill-fated Jayhawker force.

There, deep in the thick timber, he found the burned ruins. He dismounted. He poked through blackened soil with his boots, finding a belt buckle, a half-melted spoon, and tossing both aside.

After the fire the women of Black Bob's tribe had searched the ruin for bones of his incinerated men and, believing it would have been the wish of their families, buried them in a common grave marked by a rough piece of uninscribed limestone.

Malcolm approached that tombstone and knelt, touching the *chai* at his neck and grateful he still held to life this past year despite several scrapes.

"I wasn't a good leader," he said aloud. "I let my passions get in the way of good sense at times, and you paid with your lives."

Malcolm stared around him in the growing dusk, seeing nothing of particular interest in the greying woods but trying to visualize faces of the martyred men. He said their names aloud—

"Jeremiah Adams....Ralph Lykins....Peter Iverson....Ebenezer Tolle....Ezra Renfro....Calvin Durham....Alfred Willoughby...."

Would Hank O'Brien have carried out his Bushwhacker attack so fiercely against this group if not for the personal feud between him and Erskine? He would never know, and the uncertainty ate Malcolm's insides.

He secured Ebony and unrolled a blanket. He would rest through the night among the spirits of his soldiers.

After he'd settled himself, opened a tin of food, guarded against building a fire in this dry timber—one that might be spotted from the ridge due east—he spread the blanket to fold himself inside. He lay his head on the grave to sleep.

* * * * *

Black Bob's camp had changed since his last visit. A few new babies. Other children grown some. But it disturbed Malcolm to notice whole families had vacated cabins and moved to the Indian Territory. He hated seeing Shawnees yielding to whites' pressure for land.

Chief Black Bob embraced his adopted kinsman. He remarked in the Shawnee tongue about Malcolm's hook. The Chief translated, "Good weapon," and brought a laugh from Malcolm, who confessed that in Arkansas he'd already used it to kill a man.

Tribeswomen were butchering a stag in a clearing and already frying venison. The odor was too inviting to ignore. Black Bob beckoned Malcolm to sit at a table in the sunny but cool outdoors near the main lodge. They would have breakfast.

"Eat well," Black Bob directed, "for we are to ride later—you and I and several of my braves. Something you must see."

Erskine obeyed, hearing the Shawnee leader explain events then unfolding, matters affecting his people.

Evidently negotiators from the United States government as well as from Kansas Territory—from the proslavery forces—were pressing for a new treaty. This one would shorten Indian lands and box the Black Bob Shawnees into a smaller reservation.

"The claim-takers are poised," Black Bob said sadly, then he bit into a rib of cooked venison and stripped it without further comment.

"What can I do to help?" Malcolm asked.

Black Bob chewed for some time. He wiped his lips with a wet cloth a young girl handed him from time to time, as though that were her only mission in life when the Chief dined. He looked around his camp without responding.

Erskine knew better than to repeat the question. Black Bob was neither feeble nor deaf. He liked to think before speaking.

Finally, the Shawnee turned to Erskine and smiled, almost off-handedly responding with the word, "Nothing."

Malcolm started, unsure he'd heard correctly.

Black Bob repeated, "You can do nothing. We can do nothing. They will take all the land, if not by next year then in five years, or perhaps ten years. Where we sit, where we have built homes and planted crops, will be land of the white man."

Erskine asked, "When do you expect the claim-takers to start acting under this new, ah, pre-emption?"

Reference to the hated practice, "pre-emption," was in response to Black Bob's description of how the new treaty would work. The Chief said that as soon as the reservation was shortened by ratified treaty—perhaps even before it became official—white settlers would first claim the opened lands, then start claiming ground that Black Bob's people were unable produce clear title to.

Because Shawnees had been less than formal about much of their ownership—had put all their 33,000 acres of reservation into a common holding—they had made themselves vulnerable.

"It will begin in two months," Black Bob replied. "Make no mistake, we will use the white man's institutions to fight for whatever we can, for as long as we can. But the truth is, Malcolm, this way of life—" He gestured toward the activity around them. "—is over. Ten years more at most, I and my people will be gone from here. You will see....Now eat. Finish. I have something important to show you—something you will enjoy."

Before they rode out, one additional piece of distressing information reached Erskine's ears. That was news that his friend in Monticello, Sam Garrett, had apparently defected to proslavers. The people of the Black Bob tribe who shared that with Malcolm assured him, Sam's action had been taken not from the heart but from a mistaken notion. If he served in the proslavery councils, Garrett apparently believed, he might turn their actions toward a more liberal course.

Malcolm shook his head. *Sam*—who'd gone with him to search for Sylvia, finding her violated and murdered by proslavers. *Sam*—to whom Malcolm had bared his awful grief. The news sent Erskine's mind reeling, making him wonder also that young James Butler Hickok in Monticello might find Garrett's new politics a strain.

Shortly the group gathered to ride out. Black Bob called for an appaloosa mare, among his favorites.

"We are going to visit the land your late wife Sylvia left you," the Chief said. "And you are going to receive it and make legal claim to it, among witnesses." He indicated men of the tribe who would accompany them.

"I have papers for it," Black Bob said. "By accepting, you will remove it from our tribe's documented holdings with our blessing, only because of who you are and what you have meant to us."

70

Malcolm felt excitement in his heart and a tingling sensation over his body. He and three Shawnees followed Black Bob slowly north. One of the Shawnees carried a supply of wooden stakes in slings over his horse.

Erskine was now more acutely aware of his surroundings than at most times. After all, if he was to *own* a portion of this, he should observe what was on or near land soon to be his "home."

They passed through well-timbered areas, peopled sparsely by members of Black Bob's shrinking tribe. All trees but cedars were autumn-stripped. But the Sylvia-trained Malcolm, curiosity whetted by the ride's purpose, recognized walnut trees in profusion. From fallen leaves and trunk features he spotted sycamores, willows, cottonwoods, white locusts, maples, oaks, and elms. And one that had evidently sought sunlight from several directions, branches clearly twisted from its effort. Osage orange.

The plains were also rich in wild blackberry bushes, wild plum, gooseberry—a paradise for raccoons and squirrels.

A cry from one of Black Bob's braves pulled them up. In the distance a white-tailed deer turned and zig-zagged in flight from the approaching party.

The youngest Shawnee pressed for a chase, but the Chief waved off the notion. There was enough meat in camp for many days. Let the deer run and perhaps multiply for another time, he said. Important business lay ahead, he added. Their brother, Malcolm, required a plan for his life.

They heard coyotes yelp, saw woodchucks scamper and possums waddle, heard and avoided a rattler, surprised a family of minks near a stream, and gave wide berth to a slow-moving skunk.

They trotted past a late-nesting killdeer guarding her eggs on the open ground. That reminded Malcolm, spring would bring a return by many more birds than the cardinals and woodpeckers staying through winter. He could look forward to mockingbirds, meadowlarks, bobwhites, robins, doves, swallows, finches, bluebirds, and the tiny English sparrows that enjoyed grooming themselves in pockets of sandy earth.

The Blue Valley—a name already given the region by trappers, though not yet appearing on charts or maps—was certainly a rich place. Malcolm had ridden these lands several times in the past year. He was now more alert to their natural features, proud he was to become linked by ownership.

After they rode to a high point, the Santa Fe Trail lying ahead and visible on the next ridge, Black Bob raised his hand and halted.

The Chief pointed to the ground in front of his horse, then east to a distant rock shelf. From there he drew his finger in the air southward, across a narrow creek. He turned astride the appaloosa to bring his pattern west to a far grove of locust trees, then swept his hand to indicate a return to the place in front of him. Black Bob eyed Malcolm and simply nodded.

"That's more than a quarter section!" Erskine exclaimed. "Easily two hundred acres."

"By right of marriage and inheritance, my brother," Black Bob said, "it is your land. I apologize that it is not so well timbered as other holdings by our tribe. But it is at least adequate in that respect, and it is certainly good for grazing cattle. Do you agree?"

"I agree," Malcolm said, awed by the sight of what was to become his. "And would you agree, neighboring landowners of the tribe might let me lease pasture, if need be?"

"Lease?" Black Bob's eyes grew narrow, his brow wrinkled. Then a wide grin appeared. "We do not lease. We *share.*" The Indian leader dismounted, indicating Malcolm should do the same.

Black Bob crouched and picked up earth from between clumps of prairie grass. He let the wind blow it from his loose grasp. "Man relates to the land only temporarily," he said. "See how it flies in the wind? In the scheme of life and time and earth, that is the strength and worth and duration of our hold on it. All the more reason to use it well."

The Chief stood and began to walk. Malcolm joined in step. The others waited. Black Bob stopped to look around, pointing there to a bounding rabbit—and there in another direction to a singing red-winged blackbird.

"Here is what I hope you will understand, Malcolm. The land, despite papers, despite inheritance, belongs to all. To them as well," he said, indicating the animals. "Just as we share water and air. It is for all—and for all time."

"I can't accept that totally," Malcolm responded in all honesty. "There are times when clear boundaries need to be drawn, clear limits marked, or farmers and ranchers would encroach on one another. That would cause disagreements and conflict."

"The conflict," Black Bob said, "is in the mind." He jabbed his index finger at his head lightly, several times. "Reality is that we are all borrowers and sharers. The land is here for us to use, to care for as long as we can. Meanwhile, we share. Birds, animals—they do not ask permission. They fly over or crawl under fences and come when they like. And we are glad to have them."

A muskrat darted before them, causing Black Bob to look back toward his men and indicate they should observe the animal, where it was headed, where they might wish to do some trapping at another time. They saw and, still mounted, were able to watch it disappear into a draw.

"You may graze your cattle on 'my' land," Black Bob said with a grin playing at his lips and an idle wave to the south, "as I intend to trap on 'yours.'...Come, my brother," the Chief said, clapping a hand on Malcolm's shoulder, "let us stake this claim before a white man rides in and pre-empts us."

Black Bob insisted they go beyond the favorite interpretation of the law, that a stake with a name inscribed on it would suffice for a legal claim. The Chief directed Malcolm to select a home site and stake all corners. Erskine looked at the limits of the land to decide on a place that seemed most likely near a future well.

When pacing of distances and staking were finished, the Chief pressed legality further by insisting on a crude survey, to be recorded carefully from reference points, descriptive features on the land. A brave with a roll of paper sheets in his saddle pocket recorded painstakingly all that Black Bob insisted on.

When all was written—including a temporary will before witnesses—Black Bob arranged a signing ceremony. Each signature would be witnessed by at least two other individuals.

"He is the key," Black Bob said, pointing to a member of the tribe Erskine knew to be named Johnny Parks. "Johnny is three-quarters white, so his signature will be highly respected in any court of law."

Malcolm smiled, realizing that while he himself was also three-quarters white, he was a quarter Negro—legally black—and *that* part weighed negatively in most courts.

"Now the land is mine?" Erskine asked.

"We must deliver records to the Indian agent and officials of Johnson County. I will see to that. Then you may consider the land legally yours. In the meantime, it is yours by claim, and you may take it. You may live on it now. And as best you can, you may keep it, my friend. Considering all that is occurring these dark days, I wish you success in that last part."

Malcolm said, "I won't be returning to camp with you. I want to stay. At least tonight, and very likely longer. My heart is full for what you've done. Thank you. All of you."

Black Bob nodded. "I understand. We understand. And you are welcome."

To Erskine, this was a sacred moment. He was a propertied citizen by law. He wanted to be alone with his thoughts and in conversation with the spirit of Sylvia.

Chief Black Bob and the others mounted and rode off, southward.

Malcolm, standing on the ridge alongside Ebony, watched them disappear into the distant forest along the Blue River.

71

The days blew into a winter of light snowfalls.

With borrowed tools Malcolm began, one-handedly, the building of a lean-to, outfitting the shelter with a crude but serviceable fireplace.

With practice he learned to wield a long axe, sliding the handle within the arc of his hook. Each rise of the tool in preparation for the next chop required a practiced rhythm he mastered by sweaty determination.

Malcolm knew it was vital he learn by trial and error—how to mix good mortar, how to use a timber as a lever to move heavy stones, which trees he should fell and which he should let stand, how to make best use of Ebony for hauling without overburdening the saddle horse.

Before long Malcolm realized there weren't enough hours in the day for all that needed doing, all he wished to get done. He grew impatient with the time necessary for hunting or trapping and skinning and cooking just to keep himself alive. His goal was to build a sturdy home as quickly as could be accomplished for his bride-to-be and their child and to arrange spring delivery of a small herd of cattle.

Complicating that were thoughts of how he might fit into the border fight. He yearned to lead a Jayhawker force again, to chase terrorizing raiders who invaded Kansas Territory at will from Missouri.

By way of the Shawnees he'd sent word to Free State forces that he hoped to renew a Jayhawker role in defense of this land, even if that defense might carry him into Missouri to undermine the attackers at their source.

Malcolm grew impatient also with the need for sitting by the firelight at night—when little or no work could be done—to copy on paper, then revise, lists and timetables for all he must accomplish in a timely manner.

One such chillingly damp night, after the passing of perhaps two weeks and the setting of a stone foundation for his future home, Malcolm heard a voice.

At first the call, or shout, was indistinct. Then it seemed to come from only a few feet away, though he knew that was impossible. Ebony started at the sound, but the steed would have been alerted sooner if the voice's owner was truly near.

Erskine realized that on parts of his land, saucer-shaped as it was here and there, a person could stand in a certain place and speak and have his voice amplified for a great distance. He'd discovered that when Ebony grazed and gave a short neigh at one time, causing him to look up and realize his horse was hundreds of feet away, not beside him.

Now someone else had either discovered that phenomenon or had accidentally happened on it and was using it to keep his distance while communicating. But what was that person saying?

"Ma-a-al-colm," the voice called eerily.

Quickly, Erskine assessed the whereabouts of his entire arsenal. All weapons were handy, he noted with satisfaction. Ebony was close by as well.

"Ma-a-al-colm," the voice repeated in obvious taunting.

This time he recognized the voice of One-Eyed Emmett Anderson Jones.

Malcolm decided not to respond, not to give a clue to his precise position. He threw dirt on the dying campfire.

"Ma-a-al-colm," the taunting voice said again. *"Hey, nigger!"*

Erskine relaxed somewhat—both in realization his position was secure against his being waylaid and on the suspicion Jones was alone.

"You're getting too uppity, Malcolm, thinking you can claim land *white men* are entitled to. And wanting to family-up to *Jews.* Erskine, you've just got to be put out of the way to make room for *real* Americans."

Jones was speaking at a level just above conversational tone, yet he must have been five or six hundred feet to the northeast of Malcolm's position.

"Why don't you answer me, boy? You should really show more respect to your betters."

Malcolm mused on the mystery of why Jones was doing this, how long he intended to keep it up, and whether he could be sneaked up on and killed for the worthless copperhead he was.

As though reading Erskine's thoughts, Jones said in an obvious effort to amuse, "I suppose now you're wondering why I called this meeting."

Erskine chuckled, and Jones must have heard, for the Missourian squeezed off a rifle shot in the dark that pinged off a rock outcropping behind the lean-to.

"*That's* why."

Malcolm felt for his Bowie in the blackness. He began a quick crawl across the ground, sliding in the wet snow toward the origin of the rifle shot.

"You coming for me now? I surely hope so. I'm ready as ever, and I'll do better in the dark than you, what with one eye out—and light and dark being much the same to me."

Malcolm wasn't sure what Jones's capabilities or limitations might be on account of his handicap. All he'd heard was the man was a ruthless and successful gunfighter. By the same token, Erskine knew, Jones couldn't assess whatever skills a handicapped man with a hook might bring into battle.

Jones had witnessed his throwing a Bowie knife, but Malcolm had depended on firelight at the time. In darkness, the snow having nothing to reflect on this overcast night, a knife throw was risky.

If Emmett had selected a spot from which to project his voice, it would also be a spot from which Erskine could hear the sound of Jones's breathing.

Malcolm slithered across the floor of this saucer-shaped portion of his land. He picked up a rhythmic sound, even an occasional impatient sigh from Jones's apparent realization this was going to be tougher than he'd calculated.

Why didn't Jones just pick Malcolm off in daylight? If the Bushwhacker knew his whereabouts, and with timber and rocks for cover, why didn't he just take a well-aimed rifle shot and be done with it?

Suddenly it dawned on Erskine, Jones had a handicap affecting his ability to judge distance. A one-eyed person simply didn't have the depth perception of a person using both eyes.

That *could* be a costly limitation for the Bushwhacker in daylight, but on the other hand—

What in the world?

Jones evidently saw the interruption, too—a torchlight approaching from the Santa Fe Trail. The Missourian uttered an obscenity and scampered for his horse. From the sound, Malcolm knew Emmett Jones had found, mounted, and ridden his horse away in the dark, heading east.

James Butler Hickok was coming down the slope at a trot in the dead of night, carrying a torch to light his way. Beside him, elegantly decked out, was Jane-Ellen O'Brien.

Malcolm stood and shouted to indicate his position in the dark.

The thin layer of snow reflected Hickok's torch and revealed a welcome sight. Malcolm also noticed his heart beating a little faster because of Jane-Ellen's approach, though he had many reasons to despise her.

When they pulled up and held the torchlight so they could see him, Jane-Ellen started to laugh. Hickok shook his head.

"Shoot, Malcolm," Jane-Ellen said, "you're all-over *mud.* What you been doing, crawling on your belly like a snake?"

Erskine told of Jones's visit.

Jane-Ellen responded with, "Oh, *him.* He deserves to be flicked away like a pesky fly, that one. He's bad news. I'll bet seeing Hickok's what made him skedaddle."

Malcolm said, "To what do I owe the unexpected pleasure of this middle-of-the-night visit by—friends?"

Hickock was coming down the slope at a trot in the dead of night. Beside him, Jane Ellen.

Erskine and Hickok shook hands. The young lawman handed Malcolm the torch and dismounted. Then, with Jane-Ellen still in the saddle, he led their horses to where Malcolm indicated shelter.

Erskine rebuilt a campfire and pressed both of them to explain why they'd sought him out in darkness.

"By morning C.C. Catron plans to hit you with eight or ten men," Hickok said. "Jane-Ellen caught up with me in Gum Springs to tell me that. They may send help from there. Word's out elsewhere."

Malcolm shook his head over Catron's still believing in either capturing or killing him or driving him out. He knew he must teach that popinjay a lesson.

Simply because he'd played a role in shaming Catron's brother in Memphis wasn't good cause to plan an attack. Actually, Malcolm knew Catron had other cause to want to snare or destroy him. Not least of them was that Erskine was still a wanted man in Missouri and could be tried and hanged there for slaying so many Bushwhackers.

"I'm here for more reasons," Jane-Ellen declared. "We can talk business. I'm a rancher, and you want to be one. I was north of here when I heard Catron's plan, so I made straight to find Hickok to help you."

She muttered an aside about a shortage of "anyone with balls" for miles around and said Catron had her "so riled, I'll be pulling triggers at him right beside you."

Malcolm didn't know whether to thank her or groan.

"And after the fight's settled," she said, "you and I have serious talking to do about our future."

The implications in Jane-Ellen's tone were clear to Malcolm. She hadn't given up.

Erskine feared no man, but if there was anything he was weak enough to become captive to, it was the wiles of this woman.

72

"Is he aiming to kill me or capture me?" Erskine asked.

Jane-Ellen screwed up her face in the firelight. "C.C.? Makes no difference, because if he drags you over the border, you're a goner."

"She's right," Hickok said. "Once they heard you were back in the area, they decided to finish you any way they could."

"Where does Emmett Jones fit in? Why doesn't he go ahead and make a good try at finishing me, instead of calling out in the night like some—some stupid evil spirit?"

Hickok licked shut the cigarette he'd rolled, then lighted it. "Feeling you out. Biding his time. He'll move one of these days. Likely he'll even stand aside in the morning just to see what Catron accomplishes—or fails to."

Jane-Ellen observed, "Failure by Catron is what I think he's hoping. Jones wants to make himself some kind of hero. Your head would be one of his trophies. He might even get a state job in Missouri from the acclaim, besides the reward. I've heard that's how he operates."

"We don't have a very good defense right now," Malcolm said. "This land's low on timber and has only a few protective places, the house foundation not being one of them. I could suggest one or two deep draws to hole up in, but our defense there could crumble if they decided to come from both ends."

Jane-Ellen removed three pistols from a medium-sized satchel and spread them before her. She'd also brought a rifle Malcolm saw slung on her horse. "*Shoot,* I didn't come here to die, Malcolm." She checked her hand weapons as she spoke, seeing that bullets were in all chambers. "I came to keep you alive long enough to do a little business with you, maybe sell you some cattle, maybe arrange a low-interest loan to you, maybe talk you into more than that."

They heard a voice from the south. "Hallooo-o-o!"

"Who in hell is *that?"* a startled Jane-Ellen said.

"That would be Eugene Fontenot, recently of Baton Rouge and now my very good friend and co-worker in the Underground Railroad."

"The one led all those Negroes up from the Mississippi? About a hundred like? Slaves that belonged to Catron's brother?"

Erskine nodded. "That one."

"Well, 'that one' I just might want to meet."

"He'll probably be with Daniel Goodman, who feels somewhat rejected by you."

"Before they get here, let me tell you. I can't marry a Jewish fellow, you know what I mean? I tried telling Daniel that up and down, in and out, every way I could—except maybe directly. The Catholic's too much bred in me."

"Fontenot's Catholic."

Jane-Ellen sat staring at Erskine in the firelight and gradually broke into a smile. *"Shoot,* Brother Malcolm, if he's handsome and half the man you are, he's got himself a rich wife. 'Sides, I could use the help on the ranch. I don't keep slaves, you know."

"That 'half the man' part," Malcolm cautioned, joining Hickok by getting on his feet, "you'll have to find out for yourself. He's all right in my book....*Over here!"* he called.

Fontenot and Goodman rode in slowly. As soon as they reached the campfire, Malcolm made introductions.

Daniel and Hickok exchanged news. While Fontenot played the role of Southern gentleman toward Jane-Ellen, Daniel hung back. Malcolm was pleased Jane-Ellen and Eugene seemed to hit it off right away. From Goodman's present reserve, Erskine guessed the young man had been pursuing an interest in Audrey Fontenot.

Malcolm asked Hickok, "Who's coming from the north, do you know?"

"Don't know as anybody's actually coming, but they've been alerted. Things've changed somewhat in Monticello, you know, with Sam Garrett cozying up to the folks in Lecompton."

"I'd heard that," Erskine acknowledged. "I think he's misguided, believing he'll sway them."

"I agree," Hickok said. He shrugged. "This political stuff isn't for me, I've about decided. I may give up trying to be a constable and do something else."

"Figured you might get itchy feet."

"I've been offered good work as a teamster on the trail. Wagons, stages. I may take it. Old Santa Fe and other towns between, they're opening up more—new people—and the commercial traffic is getting hot and heavy. Passenger trade, too. Not everyone goes west in a packed wagon, you know, and the railroad's still a long way off."

"If that's what you want to do," Malcolm said, walking with Hickok in the darkness a bit, shaking his head that a youth with such promise as a lawman would consider driving wagons or stagecoaches for a living.

Only the glowing ends of their cigarettes were now visible, but they could see the others near the campfire. Malcolm asked, "You think we've got enough help in this fight?"

Hickok nodded. "Well have to find the best place for aiming advantage, and every shot must count. But I think we'll win the day. It'll come dawn, less than two hours, so I think we should secure the horses, powwow, and find our best position."

* * * * *

"You know how much this dress is worth?" Jane Ellen complained where she lay in the draw, which was still muddy from the last light snow. "*Shoot,* didn't have a chance to change into grubby duds."

"Put it on my bill—with the cows," Erskine said.

Light was breaking in the east—and with it came a group of riders.

Eight horsemen, with Catron's white steed leading, rode toward them from the ridge that carried the original Santa Fe Trail.

At a point where Malcolm knew a marker to be, Catron raised a hand to indicate his group should rein up. Erskine called out, *"Far enough, C.C.! What do you want?"*

"You, Erskine!" Obviously Catron hadn't yet determined Malcolm's precise whereabouts on the property, for he looked over toward where the defenders had tethered horses, then at the stonework foundation, not at the draw where they lay.

A member of Catron's party, however, pulled at his leader's sleeve and pointed. *Now* they'd been spotted, their defensive position measured.

The man who'd done the pointing turned to the others and jerked his thumb first in one direction, then another. Three riders peeled off one way and three the opposite. They would try to take the draw from both ends, as anticipated.

Catron strolled his horse onto Erskine's land.

"You're trespassing, Catron!" Malcolm said.

"I've got a deal to offer you," Catron shouted. "Be a reasonable man and let's talk."

"Say it from there!" Malcolm wondered how long his voice would hold out from yelling across this distance. He was still feeling the effects of his mouth injury.

"We let your lady in Paola keep title to the land no matter what happens to you," the Bushwhacker leader said. "You surrender. Any who's with you goes free."

Before Malcolm could think of an appropriate response, a rifle shot rang out and took Catron in the shoulder. Blood spurted from his light-colored jacket.

Catron grabbed the wound and seemed a bit rocky because of it. The man with C.C. tried to assist him.

Jane-Ellen had fired the shot. Malcolm wasn't ready to condemn her for jumping the gun.

Maybe she planned to force the flank-runners to hurry in blasting instead of sneaking. Their shooting while running would suit the defense better.

Sure enough, they were now firing erratically while advancing on foot. Fontenot quickly picked off two on one end, Jane-Ellen brought down one on the other. Within seconds, half the attacking party was dead or disabled.

Seeing how things stood, the remaining man in one flanking party glanced at the two companions Fontenot had evidently finished. He turned tail and sought his horse.

Shooting was still taking place on the other end, with Goodman and Hickok bringing down the surviving Bushwhacker pair there as they attacked.

When noise from the firing quit echoing, Erskine called to the injured Catron. "C.C., I really couldn't hear you well for all this noise. Now did you say something about *surrendering?"*

Catron didn't respond. Instead he seemed to be directing the rounding up of his dead companions' horses by his two remaining men. Soon they turned and retreated northeast.

"Hey, C.C.! Won't you at least clear your *garbage* off my land?"

Malcolm now stood. He turned to Hickok and said, "I can't even get the fellow to respond when I talk to him. Did you ever see such impolite behavior in your life?"

Hickok seemed annoyed and was grabbing at his cigarette fixings. "Damn it, Malcolm, let me ask you something."

Erskine knew what was coming. He watched Hickok fumble at rolling the tobacco. He tried not to let laughter erupt in his young friend's face.

"Is this *your* land I'm on?" Hickok asked.

"Yes, it is," Malcolm acknowledged.

"Did we just get *attacked* on it?"

"You know it as well as I do," Erskine said, holding his fun in check but now having trouble stifling it.

"Then why in *hell* didn't you fire *one damned shot?"*

Malcolm started giggling. When he could speak, he said with some difficulty, "Just wanted you—to know—how it felt. That time in—Kansas City—"

He could say no more, but Hickok evidently had his memory triggered about the gunfight in which *he* hadn't drawn but let Erskine do all the shooting.

"Next time you come under attack," Hickok said, lighting up, "you can save your own ass. Damned if I'll show up to risk mine."

Malcolm knew that wasn't true. His companionship with this young man was such that each would give his life for the other, if necessary.

That was something new in Malcolm's life.

A code he'd found uniquely in the West. In Kansas.

73

Daniel caught Malcolm alone as the others made ready to leave.

Malcolm was busy noticing that Fontenot was so smitten with Jane-Ellen, it seemed the Creole would have wed her on the spot were a priest available.

Daniel indicated her with a nod. "Watch out for her, Malcolm. She still spells trouble."

Erskine gazed at his brother-in-law-to-be. His eyes narrowed from under the brim of his hat and a wry smile spread. "Daniel, lad, be sure your cautioning is what it should be. A concern for Naomi's interests. Not personal jealousy."

Goodman shook his head. "I'm over Jane-Ellen for good. I have an honest relationship with Audrey. She stayed on in Paola while Eugene looked around for useful work. She's a good help to Naomi, who's having trouble getting around. Meanwhile, Naomi teaches Audrey things she needs to know. After all, life in Kansas has got to be far different than in Louisiana."

Malcolm placed his hand on the young man's shoulder. "Daniel, I think of you as a brother. So tell me, do you truly love Audrey?"

"Naomi asked me the same question. She wanted to know, can I get past knowing both she and Audrey are carrying your children?"

"All right, *can* you?

Daniel looked away, then back and hard into Malcolm's eyes. "If it were any other man, probably not. But this way, and having gotten to know Audrey much better, then I can surely go through with my intention to marry her."

Erskine was surprised the relationship had progressed so far during his absence from Paola. "*Marriage.* Well now—"

"I haven't asked her, but I will. Her Catholic-Creole sense of honor must be tearing her up inside, but she's been kind enough not to set traps, or make demands."

"How do you mean?"

"We've been—intimate. Many times. She might have used our passion and her condition as bases for getting me to propose. She hasn't done that. When I return to Paola, I'll approach her in front of the family. I'll ask for her hand."

Erskine was pleased. "Audrey has shown character under tough circumstances. She'll make you a wonderful wife. And you, Daniel, are as fine a man as I can ever call friend and brother."

Daniel nodded. He seemed pleased but a little embarrassed by all the frank talk.

Erskine turned to wave to the departing Hickok. Goodman began to take his leave as well. He would return to Paola alone.

Eugene would help Malcolm dump the dead left by Catron in a convenient and deep sinkhole Erskine had discovered days earlier. The grave needed only dirt fill after that, and Malcolm had excavated plenty in construction and had been hauling it in a makeshift cart. Fontenot started the grisly work as Jane-Ellen approached.

Malcolm said, "I thank you, Jane-Ellen, for saving my life."

"I don't want thanks right now. I want to know if there's any hope for our ever getting together again."

"Getting—"

"*Shoot,* Malcolm, you're the most exasperating man I've ever known. Having some *poontang.* Making *love.* I know another word and would be glad to shout it."

"Oh, *that.*"

Jane-Ellen turned away suddenly and made a gesture of frustration with one hand, her eyes rolling. She turned back and said, "I'm a widow-woman, thanks to you. I also love you so much I tremble at the sight of you—and sweat at the thought of you."

Malcolm held up his hand, appealing, "Jane-Ellen—"

"Don't try to stop me from saying my piece. We're going to have it out right now."

Malcolm said, "It's never been proved we're *not* brother and sister. There was just my mother's belief before she died, that we're probably not. But she really didn't know. Her baby girl was taken from her when Mama was your daddy's slave, and Sadie Mulligan's baby—"

Jane-Ellen interrupted, saying, "I know all that."

Malcolm removed his hat and beat at his pants leg with it nervously, knocking off grime. "Either my sister died as a child, or—" He looked into her dark eyes. "—or you're my sister."

Jane-Ellen was biting her lip, seething, seeming ready to do violence. "You know the big difference between us? You care about that and I don't. I love you as a *man,* not as a brother. *Shoot,* in my whole life I never expect to meet another man like you. Now you're getting yourself tied up with Naomi Goodman because she's pregnant—"

"That's not— Oh, what's the use?" Erskine moaned, turning away.

"You're torn between wanting to establish yourself as a respectable rancher and wanting to fight like a soldier for Kansas. *I'm* the only one who's ever let you be yourself—who's ever understood you. I'll give you one last chance."

"To do what?" He turned to her, breathing heavily, hoping Eugene wasn't able to hear any of this. "To say what? That we'll be lovers as before? Never. As for differences, Jane-Ellen? Hear *this.* The difference between me and—" He pointed to Ebony. "—that *horse* is that he'll breed with any mare he fancies, while I make my human decision, with my human brain and human heart, to choose *one.* I make a commitment. He doesn't. I choose *Naomi.*"

Jane-Ellen sat on a limestone rock and looked around. "I should have killed you when it was clear you were going to turn me into a widow. Or after you did. Life would have been so much simpler for me with you gone. Of course, I didn't know widowhood would make me rich. I thought I'd be flat busted."

She turned to face him, saying, "You know what I think about, day in and day out? That someday you'll come to me again, quietly. That we'll lie down together. That we'll find what we found before, and more. I live for that dream."

Erskine crouched on a level with her eyes, thinking, studying her. He replayed in his memory the conversation with his mother, about whether Jane-Ellen was his half-sister.

Dahlia's dismissal had been qualified, tentative. *"I have doubts. I can never know for sure,"* she'd said.

That was it. That was all. No proof one way or the other.

Malcolm would try a new approach. "Can we just be business associates, friends, *former* lovers?"

"With nothing to look forward to? I mean, between us?"

"That's right. Nothing but business association and friendship."

"You reckon I ought to marry that one?" She jerked a thumb toward Fontenot.

Erskine smiled. "He's one of the best."

"But he ain't *you*. Don't you understand, damn you? I love *you,* not him."

"And I love you, too, Jane-Ellen. Like a sister."

She sighed, looked down. "I could blow your head off right now for saying that, but I love you too much. It won't go away. It hurts. No matter what man I'm with, you'll always be there, in my mind and heart. That's what you're condemning me to." She looked up again. "I could take it if I knew that even *once in a while –* "

"Forget it, Jane-Ellen."

"You'll change your mind."

"You'll never get me to change my mind."

"I could squeeze you in a business way. Knowing that, you still want me to advance you cattle and capital?"

Erskine looked at her closely, studied the face of the woman he'd known more than a year, the woman with whom he'd had the stormiest relationship of his life—yet the woman he understood least.

"You wouldn't do that. Not if you love me. Just as you couldn't kill me."

"Don't count on that, Malcolm. I'm as unpredictable as you, I guess because I'm probably your sister."

Malcolm threw in, "And you knew all along from first meeting me that you probably were, and in spite of it took me to your bed."

"That's right, I did, didn't I?" she admitted, matter-of-factly.

"That's incest. You knowingly committed incest, Jane-Ellen. That's why I finally ran out on you, realizing what you were doing. Only for that reason."

"Malcolm, you and I still *don't know* it was incest, do we? And we'll *never* know. That's why your running out was a waste of a—good relationship."

She stood, brushed off her dress, picked up the bag containing her weapons. "You ever need a good shot again to save your life—dear 'perhaps' brother, dear 'for sure' love of my life—send for me."

"I thank you for today," Erskine said, standing as well. "And I'll be in touch about trading with you."

"I got me a bank now. Started it with some others in Cass County. I'll send over a representative to meet with you—not here in an open field but in a respectable place. He'll be a neutral. A business type."

"Black Bob's cabin," Malcolm suggested.

"Black Bob's cabin it is," she agreed. "Week from today at noon. You can have anything you want from me. 'Course I'll have to charge you a fair interest."

"Agreed."

"I'll say it again before collecting Eugene to ride with me. You can have anything you want from me."

Malcolm stood staring at Jane-Ellen, head to toe. Physically, temperamentally, there was little about her he didn't know, hadn't discovered. Yet something within her held great mystery for him, eluded his understanding. She continued to intrigue and fascinate him.

There was no doubt of the temptations she represented. No woman had ever offered herself in quite that way to him, but Naomi Goodman had more to give of what he truly wanted.

"You'll do anything I ask?" Malcolm ventured.

"Within reason," she said.

"You were raised Catholic." He nodded toward Eugene. "There's a good man for you. Get to know him. Love him. Settle down with him if you both hit it off. Have lots of children."

While Jane-Ellen stood listening, waiting to hear Malcolm's verdict upon her life, tears rolled down her cheeks. She asked in a broken voice, "That's what you want?"

"For your ultimate happiness—and mine—yes," he said.

She nodded, though hesitantly. "Goodbye, my love." She turned and waved to a waiting Eugene, then quickly brushed the tears from her cheeks and walked toward him and their horses.

Malcolm remained rooted and watched her, studying the way she moved and still aching with lust for her.

74

Malcolm let loose of a sledgehammer wearily. He sat hard on the cold ground of early morning. He dropped his head forward and shoved back his hat.

With peace still so elusive, why had he committed himself to becoming a rancher, a man with family obligations?

Why, when Kansas needed him so badly as a fighter?

Had the lack of a full family in childhood guided his new decisions?

Was it love of Naomi driving him?

Yes, damn it.

Yes!

How would it be for them when time came again for a fight? Naomi was a woman of peace. Strong in her purposes, but without patience for warring and skirmishing. Still, she was a realist, tied to him knowing he had enemies.

She knew, he hoped, what she was getting into.

Malcolm conceded Naomi was better than he deserved. In another environment, like in the East, she would have had her pick of educated men. She'd have wed a brilliant surgeon or university professor—or become such a professional herself. Women were now coming to the fore as equals in intelligence of many men.

Malcolm looked about him, disgusted with himself for planning to place a woman of Naomi's stature plunk-down on the prairie within a short ride of Missouri, expose her to dangers of border life with poor plans for defense and survival.

This was the day he was to meet with Jane-Ellen's banking representative, and he would also see Black Bob at his camp. Almost daily the Chief had sent one or more braves to check Malcolm's progress, inquire about his needs. Always Malcolm had sent back assurances that all was progressing well, no need was going unmet.

Now—and this excited Erskine—he decided on a plan he would discuss with Black Bob.

Malcolm would borrow enough funds from the Missouri banker to finance this new notion, if the Chief thought it made sense.

The enormity of it was so daunting, he was tempted to put it aside as impractical if not impossible. Yet he kept bending his mind to it more and more.

Malcolm stood to gaze about and study how the land fell into hollows, how it rose gently and dipped again toward distant draws. He considered what was underneath, where the limestone lay and how deep. Where the underground streams might be running. He fixed his attention again on the site he'd chosen for their home. He visualized a line running off from a corner, bending here, dipping there, ending perhaps a thousand feet to the south.

Yes, right there. It *could be done.*

Malcolm walked back to the lean-to, where he kept supplies including paper and pencil. He visualized how it would work, how to shore here and secure there.

Given the peculiarities of what lay under this ground, he could do it. Create *a series of tunnels* for safety, for storage, circulating air, water supply. For *escape.*

Erskine rough-sketched the plan, glancing at the sky occasionally to make certain he was allowing enough time for the appointment at Black Bob's. He would take the sketches with him, arrive early to discuss the plan privately with the Chief.

There would be expense—much excavating and hauling of earth, more timber in addition to the supply the home required, venting and piping materials.

Considering everything, he *had* to do it. He had to go to extra lengths.

Underground living quarters in additon to that aboveground. A safe haven.

It could be done in winter below the ground's freeze line—and along that huge, partly surfaced limestone shelf.

Anyone else might think him crazy over such a plan. Black Bob, however, would understand. Malcolm made ready for the ride to the Shawnee camp, almost giddy at the notion of it all.

The Erskine property—home, barn, land—would be the most specially designed of all Underground Railroad stations in Kansas for runaway slaves.

*****

Chief Black Bob listened and studied the sketches. At last he nodded approval in principle. "Do you have a figure in mind for the banker coming here today?"

"I've had to revise it upward."

"How much total?"

"Twenty thousand dollars."

Black Bob shook his head. "They will not lend you that much."

"Why not?"

"Not enough collateral. Your land is not worth that much in the event they might have to repossess. You are figuring a hundred dollars an acre."

Malcolm was annoyed, hearing that. "It isn't worth the original ten thousand I'd planned to ask for either," he said, "so they'll just have to trust my ability to repay them."

Black Bob smiled, then rose from the table and offered Erskine a refill of coffee, which Malolm accepted. When the Chief sat down again, he asked, rhetorically, "A Missouri bank should 'trust' a man named Malcolm Erskine, the outlaw Jayhawker?"

"Business is business, Chief. It will be a good investment for the bank. My hard work—the ranch operations—will assure the interest on the loan and eventual full payment. That should satisfy Jane-Ellen and the others."

"Jane-Ellen," Black Bob said, "perhaps. The others, who can say?"

"Well, how do *you* think I should present this?"

Black Bob was silent half a moment, scratching his chin. "I think you should go ahead and ask for the whole amount. You should also have a figure toward which you can comfortably retreat and still get the job done."

"If I retreat," Erskine protested, "I won't get the job done."

"Yes, you will," the Shawnee leader sassured him.

"How?"

"Your friends will do it."

"What?"

"My braves will help. When they are not planting, caring for the land, they are idle for much of the winter. It will be good work for them."

"But without a full loan, I can't pay them. Also the plan must be kept secret."

"They require no pay, and I guarantee they will keep your secret."

The proposal humbled Erskine. He searched Black Bob's craggy face for the reason behind such generosity. He had done little to deserve the Chief's continuing affection and outpouring of assistance.

"You are wondering why," Black Bob said, busying himself at the table and not looking at Malcolm directly as he spoke. "It is simple. The Shawnee is regarded by most white men as just another savage. But many of our people are Christians, knowing how to give a gift to loved ones at Christmas, and to the Jewish lady, Naomi, at Chanukah."

Malcolm was unbelieving of what he heard as the explanation. "That's *it?*"

Black Bob looked up, eyes twinkling, a coy grin playing on his face. He glanced aside, as though considering whether there was an alternate reason for his offer. He looked back at Malcolm, nodded, and said, "Yes, that is *it.*"

75

"We will be gone from here," Black Bob said, bundling against the cold while sitting on a stack of timbers, "before your son is a man."

Malcolm lowered an axe. Despite the chill, he was sweaty from labor and mopped his brow. He disliked hearing the Chief's dire predictions about the fate of the Shawnees.

Yet he knew Black Bob was right—that the government was revising terms of past treaties repeatedly, letting every advantage go to white settlers at the expense of Indians.

"Before your son is a man," Black Bob repeated, stretching his hands from under his robe to hold the palms over the fire.

"What can I do? I must do something to help," Erskine insisted, crouching near the Chief.

"It is too late. The die was cast long before you arrived in Kansas." Black Bob snorted in ironic laughter. "Long before even *I* arrived in Kansas. No," he said, turning his hands near the fire, speaking without looking at Malcolm, "you must continue in your way and work to free the Negro. When you have accomplished that—and you will—the Indian and *all* people of color will be better for it."

Malcolm thought about that, still crouching. He watched members of Black Bob's tribe draw earth from underground in buckets and spill it into the bed of a wagon partly concealed by a tent. Later they would drive small loads for filling scattered sinkholes. Others worked on the house now taking shape. Still others stood watch on ridges to make certain no one was lingering near to observe this unusual building project.

"My friend and brother," Malcolm said to Black Bob, whose dark mood he seemed at present unable to break. "What you do for me here is monumental. I've communicated this entire plan to Naomi, of course. She has sent word that any of your people dispossessed or stranded, in need of shelter to tide them over, will be welcome to stay with us. All is being made possible by the hard work of your braves and their women. A day will come when history will record their gift."

Black Bob nodded. Malcolm's words had evidently comforted him. "Get back to work. I will go into the tunnel and observe the progress, perhaps do what I can there," the Chief said, rising and starting in that direction. He paused to turn and said, "Surely you have thought of calling this place by a name."

Malcolm stood, drawing up the axe as he did. "Pleasant Valley," he said.

*****

Christmas and New Year's Day of 1857 passed quietly. The ground had frozen to a depth of approximately a foot. Exteriors of the house and barn were done. Work shifted inside. Furniture of Shawnee craftsmen began arriving every few days.

The tunnel was finished. There was no surface evidence of its existence except by intense inspection of the ground, where venting had been installed by means of iron pipes, well-concealed. Underground was a vast area protected by a slightly tilted limestone shelf, and Erskine had insisted upon liberal shoring by sturdy timbers.

The digging carried out almost continuously for weeks by dozens of Shawnees made possible the removal of a couple of thousand cubic yards of earth. Two great rooms were now below ground as well as a tunnel from the house and barn to two distant points for emergency exit or entrance.

No engineer nor architect could have managed better for the special purpose this place would serve, Malcolm believed.

Erskine's well was piped for the home, barn, and tunnel, with hand pumps in place. Naomi would not be required to go outdoors to pump water but could do so in her kitchen.

The privy for the house was near and set in such a way as to prevent contamination of well-water, the slope of the lined ditch underneath heading away from other facilities. A latrine had also been fashioned underground and vented to the surface. Lye was on hand in the tunnel to break down waste. Again, health and safety measures governed its run-off.

The house and barn each contained hatches to the tunnel, hidden by networks of sturdy panels and movable boards.

Malcolm was satisfied. His dream was being translated into reality. Soon, with the help of Shawnees guarding the place in his absence, he would go to Paola and wed Naomi and await the birth of their child.

On a day in January, when he was at work in what was to become the nursery, someone called a greeting from the front doorway. A young Shawnee nicknamed Run-Run asked Malcolm's permission to enter and warm himself by the blazing fireplace. Erskine also invited the young man to share coffee. Run-Run accepted, though he appeared to be in a hurry.

"I have news from Paola," the Indian said.

The youth seemed unable to relax. Malcolm noticed that he strutted with apparent pride, perhaps over being chosen to convey an important piece of information.

"What news?"

Run-Run beamed. "Your lady wishes you to join her quickly. She believes she is only a day away from birthing."

Malcolm prepared immediately to leave, receiving assurances that arrangements had been made to guard the building project and to scout the way for him southward.

The ride to Paola was even and without incident. He kept Ebony at a steady pace that wouldn't tire the animal. By evening he arrived in Paola and went immediately to the Goodman home. Daniel greeted him cheerfully. Audrey Fontenot was by his side and starting to swell in her belly grandly.

"Have someone fetch the Justice of the Peace, please," Malcolm told Daniel. "You'll find me upstairs with Naomi."

"She and the midwife are expecting you. They're using the master bedroom. My mother and the girls are on alert to assist when it's time. And, uh, Malcolm. Would you mind a double wedding?"

Audrey smiled and burst into tears, hearing that. She embraced Daniel.

Erskine studied the Creole woman carefully and became convinced she was changed by Naomi's influence. He was happy this pair had found love.

Malcolm said, "Would I mind? I'd be proud."

76

In the presence of the entire family as well as a few friends from the Paola settlement—all gathered in the Goodmans' large master bedroom—Naomi Goodman became the lawful wife of Malcolm Erskine, and Audrey Fontenot was wedded to Daniel Goodman.

The nervous Justice of the Peace, his small role further diminished by the dominant personalities involved in the wedding rites, sipped wine offered ceremoniously by Morris Goodman.

Malcolm accepted a small glass from his father-in-law as well, raised his hooked arm for attention, and announced to those gathered—

"Before my adopted family, I make this pledge of love to my wife." He turned to his bride. "Naomi, on my honor and on my life, I'll keep you and our child safe and do all in my power to bring joy to you both. I'll be a faithful husband and will work hard and act wisely in order to stand high in your judgment. I'll be attentive to your needs and will seek to serve them as you serve mine by your presence, your intelligence, your character, your beauty, and the gifts of your love."

After drinking about half the wine, he offered the glass to Naomi, who emptied the glass, then wrapped it in a cloth napkin and handed it to Morris.

Then came Daniel's turn—

"My lady is from another culture and a religion I may not understand but most certainly do respect. Audrey, I will honor you in every way and watch you blossom even further into the happy and beautiful woman you were always destined to be. I find every day with you an adventure and a confirmation of my love for you. Let this drinking of the wine symbolize our sharing of the journey we begin this evening."

Daniel and Audrey each drank, and Audrey imitated Naomi's wrapping of the empty glass and gave it to her father-in-law-to-be.

Morris placed the wrapped glasses on the floor and invited the bridegrooms to stamp on them with their boots. Malcolm did not understand until Morris explained to all—

"It is tradition. No other lips may touch such a glass as these young people have just drained in their declarations of love."

All voiced approval and encouragement. Malcolm and Daniel each brought their boots down on the symbolic glasses, which crunched audibly.

To applause and cheers and a cry of *"Mazel tov!"* from Sarah Goodman and her younger children, a fiddler on the stair landing struck up a tune, prompting an exodus from the bedroom for dancing in the Goodman parlor.

Naomi in the large bed put both hands on her belly and gasped. She said to Malcolm and the midwife past the noise, "It's time. Let them have their celebration."

The Shawnee midwife called to Sarah and her daughters to fetch hot water. Clean cloths were already on the bureau. The guests below continued their dancing.

Naomi looked into the anxious face of her husband and said, "That was a beautiful speech, Malcolm. I'll hold you to it, every word. In a few minutes I expect we'll see our child."

"Are you all right?" Malcolm asked, worried over Naomi's apparently troubled breathing and the extent to which she perspired. She was in evident pain of a nature Erskine couldn't understand.

"I'm fine," Naomi said. "The midwife, Blossom, will send you from the room at any moment."

"Now," the heavy Shawnee woman said, pointing to the door, then arranging everything for the delivery.

"Can't I watch?" Malcolm asked.

The round face of Blossom, whose beads and metal jewelry clanked loudly with each step, wore a look of disbelief. "I've never heard of such a thing. *Leave,"* she commanded.

Erskine beat a hasty retreat, meeting Audrey just outside the door as she was carrying more towels.

Their eyes met. Malcolm noticed in them an unspoken message, one that seemed to express gratitude that her life had turned a corner toward happiness because of events they'd shared.

Audrey put her fingers to her lips in a symbolic kiss, then pressed them against Malcolm's lips. A tear broke from the corner of her eye, and she whispered, "Goodbye, lover. Hello, brother-in-law."

"I'm sorry Eugene wasn't here," Erskine said, "but this was all arranged very quickly. Take comfort in the knowledge he's pursuing his own love interest."

Audrey nodded and hurried into the bedroom, leaving Malcolm to ponder the wide range of emotions she must be feeling.

Now, in the upstairs hall, he found himself alone. Most were still partying below. The women in the bedroom were moving about at Blossom's instructions in a way indicating the birth was imminent.

Malcolm sat on a chair next to a hall table, on which there were several books and a lighted oil lamp. He closed his eyes.

"Lord, here I am again," he said. "And again, I don't know if you're there listening and watching every move I make, even directing me. I just don't know. But I need to talk to you—to some power bigger than myself.

"I've made promises, Lord, and to be honest, I don't know whether I can keep them. Tonight I promised to keep Naomi and our child safe. Can I guarantee that? Or am I redeemed if I only try, even at cost of my life, should that become necessary?

"My life's nothing compared with that of my loved ones, except that it must make theirs a happier and safer one. That's what I figure my life is mostly for now. Help me see Naomi through this, and let the baby be a happy and healthy little one.

"That's all I ask."

Malcolm opened his eyes and rose. He paced the hall, every so often going to the door and pressing his ear against it to hear what was happening inside. A couple of times he heard Blossom giving encouragement to Naomi, coaxing her to "push."

He sought smoking materials and realized he'd left them below in his jacket. To substitute he settled for cleaning his fingernails with the sharp point of his hook by the light of the lamp.

At last he heard Naomi cry out in pain, a cry that startled him. Seconds later he heard the faint but distinct sobs of a baby, then suddenly a lusty cry. Malcolm brought his hand to his mouth to contain his joy, else he'd have shouted so loudly he might have alarmed the entire household.

Tears of happiness spilled from his eyes. His heart raced strongly, and he thought he could hear it beat like a drum. He closed his eyes again and held them shut, fearful that if he were to open them, this might all go away, as though a dream.

In a few minutes he heard the door. He opened his eyes. There a slightly bedraggled Audrey appeared, beckoning him, "Come see your son."

Naomi looked weary for the experience but was sitting up, in her arms their baby nursing at her breast.

"I think," Naomi said hoarsely, "you must plan to be a very successful rancher. It's going to cost a great deal to keep this hungry boy fed properly."

Without touching, Malcolm examined him closely, prompting Naomi to say, "Yes, he's all there." Then to his look of worry over her, she gave assurances she was all right, reaching a hand to touch tears on his cheek.

Noah Steven Goodman sucked noisily, at last turning from the nipple and appearing to be curious of what was going on around him, though his eyes were not yet opened very widely.

"He's *red,*" Malcolm observed, sitting on the bed. "Why is he so red?"

"You'd be rubbed red, too, my love, if you'd been locked in a tight place and then forced with a push through a small opening." With a wink and lowering her voice, she added, "You know, that place you seem to enjoy inspecting so closely?"

A giggle erupted from Blossom.

Malcolm leaned to kiss both mother and child.

The baby's hair was not so dark as Malcolm had expected it to be, whenever he did ponder such things. Naomi's Central European background and his own half-Scottish parentage had offset some signs of the baby's Negro heritage, which Malcolm now sought hopefully.

"I want him to know he's part African. I'm proud of that. How will he know?"

Naomi smiled. "Take a good look at his face. It's your face, Malcolm. About as broad a nose as a mixed breed can expect." She chuckled. "Nothing Jewish about *that* nose."

Malcolm said, "I also want him to have signs he's part Jewish. I want him proud of everything he is."

"You needn't worry. That will be taken care of in due course."

"I don't understand."

Blossom approached to pick up Noah and put him in a cradle that had been readied for him. She said to Erskine, "I must return in a few days and do what is necessary for the boy."

Malcolm stood, stunned. "What do you mean? What's wrong with the baby?"

"Nothing, nothing," Blossom assured him. "Ask you wife."

Naomi reached for his hand. He sat again, searching her face for an answer. "You're not to worry, my love. Our baby is to be circumcised. In the absence of a doctor, Blossom has learned how it's done. Many rabbis who are not physicians know how to do it safely."

"But why is that necessary?"

"It's a tradition of my people," Naomi said. "It's also said to be a very hygienic thing to do. I'm really surprised, your mother being Egyptian, that *you're* not—"

Malcolm was embarrassed. He looked about, hoping others hadn't heard. He remembered discussing it with his father once. Morogh Erskine had explained that when Malcolm was born he'd simply not allowed it.

Blossom began to laugh, her stout body shaking like jelly. She came over to where Erskine sat on the bed and poked his shoulder with her elbow. "You be here when I do the baby," she said, hardly able to get the words out for laughing, "and I'll fit *you* into my schedule as well."

Malcolm shrank into himself as he sat, dismayed that his anatomy and, earlier, his lovemaking should have become topics of discussion among the women in the room.

Naomi apparently recognized that and touched him on the arm. "Dearest, you mustn't. Everything is natural and good. We're all family. You must never be embarrassed about such wholesome things."

"Then why couldn't I stay to watch the birth?" he whispered.

"Blossom," she said quietly, in a half-whisper, "was actually nervous about it. She'd examined me earlier today and knew she'd have to turn the baby partly. She didn't want you here for that. Everything's all right now."

Morris and Sarah Goodman entered, pausing to see how their daughter was faring, then went together to the cradle to beam at their first grandson. "Such a happy day," Sarah said.

Speaking to Naomi, Malcolm observed softly, "This is a good home. Many happy things have occurred here. But when will you and Noah be able to leave—to come to *our* home?"

"It's finished?"

"Except for a few inside details, yes."

"I would imagine two weeks." She looked at the midwife for verification, and Blossom nodded.

Erskine said, "Meanwhile, I'll come visit you every few days, perhaps spend a night or two here if there's room."

"Room?" Naomi said. She whispered, "Alongside me there's always room for you, my husband. And I hunger to have you resume your—inspecting."

77

"I know about your Underground Railroad station," the visitor said.

Malcolm's heart skipped a beat. He tried not to show a reaction and continued to puff a pipe in measured rhythm.

When filing papers with authorities for his inherited land late the previous year, Malcolm worked through a Shawnee intermediary Black Bob had recommended. He was this man—a relative of Charles Bluejacket. His name was Johnny Kesibwi. He was a frequent visitor to the Methodist Mission run by Reverend Johnson, where much official activity was centered.

A career Kesibwi appeared to have found ennobling was as go-between in sensitive matters, though most people saw him as little more than a courier. He'd also learned, evidently, that in a life of travel a man could have several homes, several pillows on which to rest his weary head.

How many in Johnny's case was uncertain. Malcolm was aware of a wife and children by Kesibwi on the Wea reservation to the southeast, another wife and children on the Delaware reservation near Leavenworth, and one could only speculate the number of others.

"I know about your station and the tunnel and everything," Kesibwi repeated to Malcolm as they sat in his parlor, a fire blazing in the fireplace.

Malcolm nodded. He knew there might be a price for Johnny's keeping that information confidential. He awaited the Indian's proposition.

Kesibwi cleared his throat, leaned forward, and looked into the fire, saying, "I have a Chippewa woman who has been banished. It is my fault. They accuse her of adultery because I am married."

Malcolm nodded again when Johnny looked up, indicating his visitor should continue.

The Shawnee courier looked again into the fire. "She needs a home, temporarily. She would be no trouble and is a good worker. She could help your Missus. You have a fine barn with living places. I could—" He glanced at Malcolm, who was amused and showed it, then went on, "—visit her there from time to time, if you would permit."

Erskine asked, "Where will you settle her eventually? The Chippewas seem most compatible with the Southern Sac and Fox, but their camp is far from here."

"I have no problem with distance. I have only a problem of choosing a reserve where I have no—current ties."

Malcolm put down his pipe and leaned toward Kesibwi, curious. "How many wives do you have?"

Johnny looked directly at Malcolm, drew himself up in his chair in a prideful pose, and said, "Eight." Then, glancing away and frowning, he looked back and said, "No, *nine,* I think."

Erskine sat back and shook his head. "You should keep better track, or you'll trip over yourself coming and going."

Kesibwi, who still wore traditional wild turkey feathers from his queue, cocked his head to one side briefly, as though indicating he was aware of that and was so far handling it the best he could. It seemed the equivalent of a shrug in acknowledgement and resignation.

"This Chippewa is not yet my squaw. This one," Johnny looked directly into Malcolm's eyes and declared, "is the one I truly love."

Malcolm lifted his eyebrows and nodded, showing no doubt of Kesibwi's sincerity. "What makes her so special?" he asked.

"She is smart, like your Sylvia was. She reads and writes."

"Does she know of your—?"

"Only about the Wea woman."

Malcolm considered what Kesibwi was doing. He was entrusting Malcolm with much personal information that could, if misused, bring trouble down on Johnny's head. In that way he was placing himself deeply in Erskine's debt, perhaps more than was owed for keeping the tunnel a secret.

"She must mean a great deal to you," Erskine observed, picking up his pipe and relighting it, asking between billowing puffs as it caught. "You sure—you wouldn't—like a pipe? More coffee?"

Johnny said, "I don't smoke. Bad for the lungs. No more coffee, thank you....Will you do it?"

Malcolm nodded, saying, "I'll pay her a small wage for helping."

The Shawnee protested. "You needn't do that. She will work for room and board. She will stay in the barn."

"If I don't pay her something," Erskine said, "I would feel like a slaveowner."

Johnny considered that, then agreed. "You are right." He looked at Erskine. "You are a good man. I will do much for you in return for this. Lani-Wawewa, my intended—she is nearly fourteen—will work hard to make your Missus comfortable."

Erskine sighed on that, as though to close it, then did not hesitate to press his new advantage. "There are things I wish to know—about C.C. Catron."

Kesibwi proceeded to bring Malcolm up to the moment with information about Catron's operations. He also changed his mind and accepted the offer of more coffee in order to stay later than planned, for it was snowing outdoors.

Malcolm got up once to look out, glad it was not a driving, dry snow, for he intended the next day to bring Naomi and the baby home.

Erskine learned that Catron had filed township organization papers, renaming Santa Fe Township and giving it the designation Oxford Township, after the community he was laying out near the border close to Little Santa Fe.

Though the village of Oxford was being settled almost entirely by Missourians, Johnny had learned Catron planned to entice wealthy southern slaveowners there as well, mostly Texans. He was offering second and third sons of dynastic plantation families the chance to go into business at this crossroads, where the trail intersected a road north to Dallas and Westport.

"What about Catron's Bushwhacker raids?" Malcolm asked. "I know the snow will interfere, but he's certain to resume."

"Catron is busier selling others on moving to Oxford than he expected to be," Kesibwi said. "Few understand the advantages Catron describes – establishing small shops to make Oxford a commercial center for trail travelers and new settlers."

"How many do you figure he has for his town so far?"

"Perhaps a dozen families, with interest by possibly another half-dozen. It won't be another Westport, but it could become an important community."

"And a proslaver headquarters."

Kesibwi agreed.

"Have any buildings been started?"

"Form poles are being laid out. A few shanties are up. Construction will start with the first good break in the weather," Johnny said.

Erskine considered that quietly a few moments. About four miles east and five miles north of where they sat, shorter as the crow flew, a community was taking root where proslavers would hold sway. It would headquarter the township in which Malcolm now was a citizen and landowner.

If the people of Oxford stuck to their business – to profit from their strategically located community – they might let him alone. Then there was the more likely prospect, that they would use Oxford as a base to start further mischief and bring trouble to Pleasant Valley and places beyond.

All the more reason why Malcolm believed he must reassemble a fighting force.

"Any other abolitionists like me moving in around here, from what you've heard?"

Kesibwi, his rugged, brownish face wrinkling in mirth, sat back and laughed.

"I wasn't asking that to be amusing," Erskine said. "I really want to know."

Johnny shook his head. "As Free Staters go—for this area—you are alone."

"Alone," Erskine repeated.

"Yes, quite alone, *but*—" Kesibwi held up a finger, considering something evidently significant.

"But what?"

Kesibwi bit his lip, apparently uncertain whether to go on with it. Then he blurted, "There is another settlement to begin. Very near. Likely to become very much Free State, if I calculate correctly."

"Where? How far?"

"Northwest of Black Bob's reservation, in a place along the newer Santa Fe Trail out of Westport. A Virginian named John Barton is forming a community. I believe it will receive the same name as we Shawnees have given it."

"Olathe?" Erskine asked. "There's to be a white settlement at Olathe?"

"Yes," Johnny said, "Barton plans to summon me to carry papers filing establishment of the place. So I have been told."

"But a Virginian."

"Not a slaver, if that's what you fear. Barton is a physician, many times visiting Black Bob's camp and serving Shawnees also at the Methodist Mission. He seems to have no other interest in a settlement at Olathe than profit."

"He has good claims there?"

"He has claims bought from the surveyor, Coffman, which immediately makes them questionable, thanks to Coffman's shady reputation. But Barton is pressing a good case by showing interest in establishing Olathe as a county seat, which Johnson County needs."

Erskine considered the information. Compounding the dubious quality of the surveys was the fact Barton would send his papers to the proslaver Lecompton legislature, run by Reverend Johnson. Barton would face a challenge if Free State settlers were too prominent in the picture.

But the pressure was on, Free State advocates pushing in—*pouring* in—through northern boundaries. If Barton was interested purely in profit, unlike Catron who was more political than business-enterprising, he would tell Lecompton he was opening Olathe to everyone, regardless of political persuasion.

Of course, all of that was being done at great cost to the Indians, whose landholdings had been shortened twenty percent by the Johnson-led legislature.

Treaties were being redrawn to cut individual landholdings by Shawnees and other tribes to quarter-section parcels—160 acres. The remainder was being thrown to whites moving in fast behind surveyors. These claim-takers were driving stakes and laying form poles all over Johnson County, sometimes not being careful to avoid legitimate Indian-held land.

"Give Dr. Barton my best wishes at your earliest opportunity," Malcolm told Kesibwi.

"You're willing that he should know you're here?"

"Why not? Everyone else does. And I may as well test his reaction immediately," Erskine said, puffing his pipe thoughtfully, "so I'll know what to expect from that side. I already know what I'm facing from my other new neighbor—Catron."

78

With four armed Shawnees and Daniel Goodman also riding guard, Malcolm drove a mule-drawn wagon containing his family from Paola to their new home in Pleasant Valley.

The journey consumed a full day. Because of a wet snowfall the day prior, there was mud to contend with. By selecting trails not yet worn deeply they were able to avoid the worst of that problem.

A new trail from Paola into the south-central portion of Johnson County enabled Malcolm to see Spring Hill, a place he'd heard was being organized as Free State in general sentiment. They paused to seek out the founder, J.B. Hovey, but failed to find him about.

They avoided the military road to the east—the one joining Fort Scott and Fort Leavenworth—to reduce the danger of encountering riders from Missouri. Furthermore, after such a soggy snowfall the military road would be a quagmire.

From time to time Malcolm glanced at the face of their baby, whom Naomi cradled in her arms. Fortunately, the temperature had risen to the point where they were safe from freezing, yet Naomi still kept Noah as well protected as she could. She seemed to Malcolm in good spirits, excited about the prospect of seeing their home for the first time.

When the party arrived at Black Bob's camp, where they were invited for a meal and where the women admired the infant, the Chief took both Malcolm and Daniel aside.

"Jones wants what he is calling a showdown," Black Bob said.

"One-Eyed Emmett?" Malcolm asked. "He needs a notch in his gun representing someone of my stature, I suppose, to get anywhere politically."

"Not that one," the Chief said. "*Sam* Jones, of Westport. The word is out that he and others are keenly anxious Catron should succeed in establishing Oxford as a proslaver base—for making legal inroads into Kansas Territory."

"Funny you should use the word 'legal'," Erskine said, "when much settling is being done at the expense of your treaties."

"Be that as it may," Black Bob said, "Sam Jones knows you have filed ownership of land perilously close to the Santa Fe Trail. He believes you will use your position to begin raids upon proslavers who wish to settle more deeply into Kansas Territory."

Malcolm thought about the significance of the news. Daniel showed amusement, as though knowing how Malcolm might respond.

At last Erskine said, "They think I've already assembled a fighting force? Possibly they know more than I, because they're indicating that it's time I *did*."

Black Bob shook his head and looked at the ground. "All you need do for now, to give yourself time to gather strength, is let the word go out. Let it be known you have seen to defending your position well and will not be budged, but you have no intention of attacking."

"I will *not* get such a story out," Malcolm protested. "Let them think I'm stronger in force than I am. That way they'll be cautious about even *having* a showdown."

Black Bob shook his head. "You are wrong. That way they will simply send more troops to overcome you, not shrink in caution. By allowing an overestimation of your strength and purpose to linger in their minds, you only increase the determination of the other side."

Daniel Goodman felt it necessary to interrupt. He said, "You're both right. Malcolm, you do need to buy time, but Chief, I agree that showing anything *but* strength and aggressive determination from our side could be fatal. I would just as soon Sam Jones and Catron go on believing we're poised to secure the central and southern part of this county by striking first. To let them believe otherwise would be the beginning of the end."

Black Bob confronted them both, drawing himself erect, crossing his arms, looking from one to the other. He asked, "Then what plan have you in the event *they* strike first?"

Hearing no answer, he added, impatiently, "Well?"

Met by silence again, the Chief said, "The two of you, newly-married, building families, needing to look forward to a peaceful life—you deserve a chance. You must try in some way to make peace for at least the time being. You are in no position to meet a heavy force led by Sam Jones. I will get word to that side in any form you wish. Be cautious what message you send, else you provoke them prematurely—before you are ready to fight."

"I'll never cower to Jones, who is the king of cowards," Erskine said.

"You needn't cower," they heard Naomi say from nearby. She strolled to them. "Excuse me for listening. Oh, don't worry. Blossom and a wet-nurse are caring for Noah. Blossom says a change of diet at times is good, to observe an infant's digestive strength."

"About not needing to cower," Malcolm asked, "what did you mean? You have some idea about a response to Sam Jones?"

"All you need do," Naomi said, "is make a deal. Send word that you will keep your force—fictitious though it may be—from attacking Catron's settlement at Oxford, so long as no proslaver settlers move along the old trail farther west—that you'll be checking to see that they don't violate such a pact. Of course, somehow you've got to be prepared to monitor the trail, in case they test you."

Daniel jumped at that, exclaiming, "*Perfect.* In that way you reinforce what they already believe about your preparedness to fight. But you also give *them* something to hang onto."

Black Bob smiled and nodded. To Malcolm he turned and, softly, he said, "You are a lucky man to have such a wife. Different in ways from Sylvia, but both very wise."

Humbly, Erskine said, "I know." Then, "I'll need messengers. I must contact Abe Milford and others—to see what kind of group I can assemble. We must have a meeting at my place very soon."

The Chief said, "Send word to me when you have selected a date. I believe Kesibwi is out of the area, but we have couriers and can help in that way. And in that way only. You know that we cannot fight alongside you."

"I know that," Malcolm said.

After amenities, handshakings, and the women's exchange of embraces, the traveling party left to move northward, toward the new house in Pleasant Valley.

They approached at dusk, Daniel noticing a light in a window. "Who would that be?"

Erskine peered ahead. He'd forgotten. Johnny Kesibwi's woman must already have arrived, and Shawnees posted around to keep watch had been advised to let her in.

"That must be Lani-Wawewa." To Naomi, "You're to have help from this woman. I didn't know she would arrive so soon or I'd have said something before now. She is, I believe, thirteen or fourteen years old and soon to wed Kesibwi. She's a Chippewa outcast. She reads and writes, I'm told. I've not met her and know nothing else about her."

Naomi, frowning, perhaps over not knowing she was to have a houseguest and helper, asked, "How can you refer to a child as a woman?"

Erskine shrugged. "I call her woman only because Johnny did. Indian girls mature quickly."

Naomi surveyed the house in the dim light of dusk. "It's beautiful. I love you for making us such a house."

Malcolm turned to her as they were pulling up to the front door. "And I love you for what you are about to do—turn it into a home."

Daniel was first to the door and tried it. It was locked. He knocked and turned, asking, "What did you say her name was?"

"I think she's called 'Lani'," Erskine said.

The door opened, revealing in the fireplace glow and lamplights a girl who was fully matured. At the sight of Daniel, who had obviously come in peace, she struck a coquettish pose. Her beauty clearly took Daniel's breath away. Murmurs among the Shawnees who accompanied them indicated they found her to be a surprise.

Naomi turned to Malcolm and, after a few seconds' observation, said, "Have I ever told you how foolish you look with your mouth hanging open?"

Malcolm only vaguely heard what Naomi had said, but he did shut his mouth.

Lani was simply the best-featured young Indian woman he'd ever set eyes on. That was all of it—nothing more—and he hoped Naomi would realize that.

"Make me a promise, quickly," she said.

"Wha— What's that?"

"A promise. I must have it from you *now.*"

Malcolm turned, searching Naomi's face in the soft glow of the lamps shining from inside. "Of course, I will. Promise what?"

"If you ever have her, hide it well. I would rather not know," Naomi said, obviously uncertain whether to smile bravely or to reveal anxieties unashamedly.

"What are you *talking* about?" Erskine said in a hoarse whisper, so others would not be tuned to their delicate conversation. "I and—*that* one?"

Naomi drew herself up with a deep breath. "I know you, Malcolm. Can you honestly say you could *resist* her? *Look* at her."

Malcolm looked at Lani again, who was taking bundles handed her by Daniel from the wagon, setting them inside the door. He turned to his wife and spoke, looking directly into her eyes. "I am yours for life, Naomi. I love only you and want only you."

Naomi smirked. "I find it significant that you didn't answer my question."

Lani prepared bath water for them, then went to her stove-heated room in the barn. Malcolm and Naomi prepared to retire. Noah was asleep in his cradle in the adjacent nursery.

"I do love our home," she said. "I can hardly wait for light to see the ranch, all the grounds, the barn and tunnel—everything." She looked at her husband curiously as he was beckoning her to bed.

"You're very eager tonight," she remarked, "now that lovemaking between us can restart."

That first night with his bride in their home, Malcolm was ardent to an extent surprising even to himself, drawing new sounds of pleasure from Naomi.

Later, when he'd extinguished the lamp and they lay side by side, happy and weary, Naomi said, "It may be a good thing, having that girl around. We shall see."

Sleepily, Malcolm asked, "Who?"

Naomi curled close to him at the beginnings of his snore.

79

"Your idea worked," Malcolm told Naomi, stamping his boots free of snow before entering their parlor.

"What do you mean? What idea?"

Malcolm swung a rifle from his shoulder, set it to one side, then twisted to allow his winter coat simply to slip off—a practice he'd developed since his amputation. He looked down to study the mess he'd made of melting snow.

"Never mind that," she said. "I'll get it later—or Lani will. What idea?"

"On our way here—at Black Bob's camp—you suggested I offer Catron a pledge not to attack his settlement if he and Sam Jones dissuaded proslavers from—"

"Settling farther west," Naomi chimed in, completing the thought. "Now I remember. Of course, it worked. I knew it would." She smirked and crouched to resume measuring an area in front of the hearth, where she'd told Malcolm she would place a hooked rug.

"There are times, woman," he said, "when I want to take you over my knee—for being so smug, thinking you're so all-fired smart."

"Thinking? You *know* I am," she said without looking up, a musical lilt to her voice, as though the conversation amused her. "And that's one of the major reasons you became interested in me and married me."

Erskine sat in one of the chairs near the fireplace. "Come here."

"I'm busy."

"Come sit on my lap."

"Will that chair hold us both?"

"We'll find out, won't we?" With his one hand, but gently, he gave her right arm a pull that wheeled her and allowed her to step and fall into his lap.

Within seconds, husband and wife were becoming deeply affectionate when they heard a startled, "Oh!"

An embarrassed Lani-Wawewa stood in the doorway to the dining area. She had a gurgling Noah in her arms, evidently bringing him to Naomi for his scheduled feeding.

Naomi struggled to get up again. She said, "So much for love in the Erskine parlor." She unbuttoned her blouse and accepted the baby from Lani for nursing. Singing softly to Noah, she moved slowly about the room for the feeding.

"May I stay to watch?" Lani asked.

Malcolm noticed Naomi was still slightly uncomfortable over having Lani around the place. Her face revealed mixed feelings, even at such a simple request as the one the girl had just made. He sat thoughtfully, watching them.

Naomi nodded to Lani. "Yes, you may stay."

The Chippewa girl stepped to the hearth and sat on it, her dark eyes fixed on the baby's blissful nursing.

Malcolm made a sudden and daring decision. He wasn't one who could let tension hang in the air, especially when it discomforted someone he loved as he did Naomi.

"Lani," he said, turning to the girl to ask her a very frank question, one he was convinced she would recoil from in conventional modesty. She faced him, smiling softly and expectantly, apparently ready to serve a minor request such as finding his pipe.

"Lani," he bent toward her slightly to say, "suppose I went to your room in the barn, unbeknownst to Mrs. Erskine, for the purpose of making love to you. You would shun me for being a shameless philanderer, remind me that you are betrothed to Johnny Kesibwi, and perhaps even pack and leave. Am I right?"

The girl's mouth dropped open in evident shock. She turned to Naomi, apparently to see how the mistress of the house was reacting, but Naomi seemed interested only in Noah and shifted the baby to her other breast.

Malcolm, slightly exasperated, felt the need to explain further. "I want my wife to hear what you have to say, so that there's no misunderstanding there could ever be anything between us, Lani. Now, answer my earlier supposition, please. Was I correct?"

Lani wore a puzzled expression as Erskine spoke. She now began slowly to shake her head.

Malcolm was appalled she was taking so long to respond. And he was puzzled to see her starting to shake her head with progressive vigor, instead of nodding agreement. In fact, he felt a touch of panic.

At last she indicated she would reply, and almost simultaneously Naomi burst into giggles. That distracted Lani momentarily, but the girl now answered Malcolm.

"Oh, *no,* sir. I would do *your* bidding gladly. You are my host and have accepted responsibility for my safety and happiness. I would return the favor any time you wished. Come lie down with me whenever you like."

Erskine sat back, stunned.

Naomi was now in such full laughter she could hardly hold Noah and urged between gasps that Lani return the baby to the nursery. Noah seemed satiated and sleepy anyway. The girl got up obediently, took the baby, and left.

Malcolm closed his eyes, baffled. He rested his forehead on his hand. He'd just tried to make his wife feel more secure. Not only had he failed, but he couldn't understand why his failure was so hilarious. He opened his eyes, watching Naomi in her fit of laughter.

Malcolm indicated to her, pointing casually, "Please do something with your blouse. You're leaking."

Somehow that triggered a fresh outburst of laughter from Naomi, who idly grasped at her buttons and obviously had no strength to accomplish such a simple task. Malcolm waited for her to calm herself.

At last Naomi pulled a handkerchief from a pocket, dried her eyes, and looked down to wipe her nipples. Malcolm feared she would squeeze a teat and aim a stream of milk at his face, as she'd done before playfully, but she rebuttoned. Small bursts of giggling continued to distract her.

Lani answered, "Oh, *no,* sir. I would do *your* bidding gladly. Lie down with me whenever you like."

When she could speak, she sat and said, "Oh, Malcolm, Malcolm. You are so *naive,* such a little boy for being a grown man—what?—seven years older than I?"

"I meant to—"

"I know what you meant to do," she said, "and I love you for it. You are truly such a good man, my husband. I sometimes feel I'm the luckiest woman in the world."

"How can you, when I'm such a dunce?" He looked away.

"Malcolm," she said, "look at me. The time I spent in medical school I became as interested in human behavior as I was in physiology. Exciting studies were being started, and I regret I couldn't stay to help continue them. The work led me to read a great deal—cultural anthropology in particular. Oh, Malcolm, it's so *exciting.* I've brought books you're welcome to look through. I can hardly wait till Noah is old enough for me to teach him things. But enough of that—"

"Yes," Malcolm said impatiently, "please explain to me how I just managed to make such a bloody fool of myself."

"I'm coming to that, dearest. What do you know of the Chippewas?"

"The—Chip—" Malcolm was at a loss.

"They're Algonquians, like the Shawnees, but they're from the north. They're actually called Ojibways. The name Chippewa is simply another pronunciation."

"I didn't know they were from the north. How far north?"

"Far enough to have come in contact with Eskimos, whose culture dictates a totally different set of customs in a woman's use of her body than our culture. Do you understand?"

"You're saying Chippewa women, uh—"

"Perhaps not all. But this one has a strong taboo against denying her host—and presumably even a guest, if this were *her* home—anything he wished to do with her, *any* pleasure he wished to take."

Malcolm found that incredible. "All *that* is in those books of yours?"

Naomi started to get up, so Malcolm did as well. He was to make proper arrangements for a dairy cow being delivered that day. After all, Naomi couldn't go on nursing Noah forever.

She said, "Those books—what's in them—can help you understand a great deal." She put her arms around him and held him close, talking past his shoulder. "Malcolm, not everybody thinks as you do, according to your Puritan New England standards, selective though you may be in applying them. Do you remember what I did when we first met?"

"You washed my feet—the feet of a stranger, a traveler and guest in your home. I thought that strange," he said, squeezing her gently at the memory of it.

"It was a cultural holdover for me, going back thousands of years among ancient Hebrews. It was almost instinctive, something quite proper as well as symbolic."

He pondered that, saying, "You're right—about all of it. What you're also telling me is that I should judge neither those around me nor my *enemies* according to principles I would follow. That could be fatal."

"Exactly," she said, "for if you do, they'll have the advantage of you. And if I lost you—" Her hug now became tighter, much tighter.

"You'd survive," he said.

"Not so happily as with you around," Naomi said. "Please live a long life, my husband. I *do* need you. I dislike the war you're fighting, but I also know it's necessary. Which reminds me," she said, pulling away to look at him, "what news do you have?"

"Abe Milford will be here on Saturday. On St. Valentine's day. He's bringing with him fresh recruits. Your brother Daniel is also rounding up young men. And Eugene Fontenot will—"

"*Young* men. How young? Targeting whom for recruitment?"

"We're trying to reach beyond those with wives and families. Even so, the truly young and strong are hard to come by."

Naomi said, "Something doesn't fit. With settlers relying on their sons to plant or work the stock, or to help build homes, I don't understand what 'rounding up' my brother could be doing."

"I've put all of that in their hands."

Naomi made a face and glanced to one side. She folded her arms across her bosom and shuddered, saying, "Not sure what it is, but I have a strange feeling—that you may have given them too much license."

80

Saturday broke as a grey and bitter day. Though there wasn't the feel of imminent snow in the air, the sky was thickly overcast and seemed to convey uncertain threats.

Eugene Fontenot observed to Malcolm, "The morning cuts through a man today. I hope they will all make it here."

Erskine narrowed his eyes to gaze west, looking for a sign of what the ambiguous clouds held. The two were standing outside the barn, which was on a slight rise that gave a good view.

Malcolm said, "I expect these men are Yankees, Eugene. They would know how to bind up against the bitterness, what clothing to bring with them against the worst of winter, how to pace their horses."

"These are things I am learning," Fontenot acknowledged.

"You came to us from Louisiana with thin blood," Malcolm turned with amusement to Eugene to say. "We must thicken it by helping you learn to live with the uncertainties of Kansas weather."

"You have not asked the obvious," Eugene noted, the change of subject between them inevitable.

"All right. How are you getting on with the Widow O'Brien?"

"For some reason, she has warmed up to me as though we have known each other forever."

Erskine nodded to the Creole. "That's good. She is a strong woman and would make a good companion."

"I agree, but I must be careful," Fontenot said. "After all, we Catholics cannot afford to make a mistake about such matters."

Malcolm understood and said, "Both of you should take your time and be quite sure. It will be all the sweeter if you do."

"Ah! I see a riding party turning this way from the trail."

Erskine gazed northwest. There he saw six horsemen aiming for his place. Even at this distance he could tell one of them was

Abe Milford. Now Malcolm turned away, to the northeast, and gave an exaggerated wave.

From afar in that direction a Shawnee guard, astride his horse, returned the wave exactly as given. That indicated all was clear—there were no proslaver scouts to be seen—scouts who may have wanted to report who was going in or coming out of the Erskine place.

Fontenot then tugged at Malcolm's sleeve and pointed south. "There, five more."

Malcolm wheeled and, indeed, there came Daniel Goodman and four others. The timing of the arriving parties couldn't have been more perfect.

From his home came the faint smells of bacon and coffee, and he knew Naomi and Lani were also preparing flapjacks and eggs and biscuits and gravy to feed this small army.

The Erskine dairy cow had proved prolific, so there was plenty of milk and butter. Though he was yet to stock his ranch fully—from which livestock he would later draw his main food supply—he already had provisions stored in the tunnel that included smoked ham and beef.

The eggs turned out to be Lani's contribution, for she was an experienced poultrywoman and had persuaded and helped Malcolm put up pens and a cozy chicken house in the yard.

For her part, Naomi welcomed the opportunity to play hostess to this large party of volunteer Free State warriors.

They would need to be fed, billeted, and warmed. Their clothing would require washing and repairs. She was ready and would rely on the help of Lani—and of Shawnee women who would serve in shifts to staff this new Jayhawker camp.

Later, all the arriving men having taken turns at the barn pump for washing and at the privies as they required, they entered the Erskine home. Fires blazed in both the parlor and dining room fireplaces. A table was spread for fourteen.

"How did you know so quickly how many?" Malcolm asked Naomi as she was hurrying past.

She shrugged and said, matter-of-factly, "I watched the arrivals, told Lani, and she handled the rest. Get them to sit while we prepare to serve."

There were introductions, but nobody expected seriously to remember all names on the first go-round. The important business at hand was to warm their cold insides with good food and hot coffee.

Malcolm sat at the head of the long table, later joined by Naomi at the other end. He surveyed his guests with a mixture of pleasure and mild disappointment.

Most looked green as recruits went, and they were all—with a couple of exceptions—younger than he. In their relative youth they showed only minimal promise of becoming good soldiers.

Abe, sitting at Malcolm's right, leaned to speak confidentially but not to exclude Daniel, who sat opposite. "You know that I can't join you permanently," Milford said.

Fortunately, Malcolm was looking elsewhere when he heard those words. The truth was he *hadn't* known and would have revealed surprise if he'd been looking into Abe's eyes. It was a terrible disappointment. Good old Abe was undoubtedly the best fighter he might have come by.

Erskine turned to Milford and nodded. "Yes, Abe. You're a family man again. While I know I can count on you in emergencies, I can't expect you to put up here like some raw recruit."

Daniel said, "Nor can I stay. But of course, I'll be available on the same basis as Abe, when the going gets rough and you need me."

Malcolm, hiding his now doubled pain, smiled and shifted to pat his brother-in-law's arm. "Don't give it another thought, Danny my lad. You've both done your jobs, bringing me the recruits I've needed. I have no doubt," he said, turning alternately to Abe and Daniel, "I'll be able to train them in no time at all—"

"Stop pretending," Abe said. "If you stop, so will I."

Malcolm looked down at his plate, suddenly no longer hungry. "Give me the worst of it," he said.

Abe shifted in his chair, broke open a biscuit, glopped a bit of butter on it, then dipped it into the gravy and popped it into his mouth. When he was finished chewing and swallowing—all the while Malcolm waiting expectantly—he said, "I practically had to empty the Lawrence jail to bring you this group."

Daniel sipped coffee and, putting down his cup, said, "I went to Fort Scott for the least objectionable deserters. Soldiers whose offenses were so ambiguous, the expense of inquiry, military indictment, and courts martial wasn't warranted. Cases that fell through the cracks in an Army torn by politics right now. All fixed by special discharges."

Erskine leaned forward, stunned. Then, looking from right to left and right again, into the faces of Abe and Daniel while the guests farther down the table chattered animatedly, he asked in a whisper, *"Pardoned criminals? All?"*

Both his comrades nodded.

Abe broke in, saying, "Let me explain something that's happened the past year. To persuade Washington that Free Staters haven't stooped to the same practices as proslavers—the practice of hiring ruffian gangs—General Lane insisted on building a volunteer militia among farmers, ranchers, teamsters, shopkeepers, teachers. He wanted men of substance and decent occupations. Jayhawker bands, on the other hand, are officially frowned on. Lane can't control them. He knows that, and he knows that *you* know *he* knows that. You follow?"

Malcolm nodded, all the while surveying the faces of the men Abe and Daniel had brought.

"Lane also knows he couldn't do without you, without a force right here to stop the likes of C.C. Catron and others hovering inside and outside Santa Fe Township—"

"It's now called Oxford Township," Erskine said by way of correction.

Milford continued. "Lane is prepared to supply you with all the weapons you need and a little money to keep you going as necessary. He sends good wishes and wants you to consider all contact with him entirely unofficial."

"He won't give me any status in this endeavor, will he?" Malcolm asked bitterly.

"Publicly? No. Privately," Milford said, picking up another biscuit, "you're known as his 'favorite outlaw'."

Erskine turned to Abe with a smirk of irony. "He called me that?"

Milford nodded. "There's not a person at this table—excepting Naomi, of course—who hasn't broken some law. Even, uh, what's-his-name—"

"Fontenot."

"Right. *He's* now wanted on a Federal violation in two or three states for running fugitive slaves. At least that's my information," Abe said.

"Are the U.S. marshals working with any bounty hunters in that?"

"I don't think so," Abe said, swirling a biscuit around to soak up the last of the gravy on his plate, then looking up. "Oh my gosh," he said. "Don't tell me he's crossing into Missouri to see Jane-Ellen."

Erskine nodded.

"Fix him up with false identification then," Abe suggested.

Malcolm sighed deeply, looked around, then received a sudden, reassuring smile from Naomi. Upon witnessing her supportiveness, he felt his spirits rise. He needed strength for what lay ahead. He resolved to eat. Before resuming, he asked both Daniel and Abe, "Will you help me memorize their names and give me a rundown on each man? That is, as much as you know?"

With each face at his table, Malcolm was shortly associating a name, soon to be rounded out with information useful to him. Together with Eugene Fontenot and himself, they would constitute his Jayhawker band of Pleasant Valley—

Henry O'Dell, Terence Anderton, Watson Frederick, Chad Brookings, Cyrus Ormsby, Jedediah Blake, Benjamin Ellerby, Andrew Pace, George Morris.

81

Abe and Daniel readied themselves to return to their homes. They stood with Erskine in his parlor for a parting talk.

"Malcolm," Abe said, "before you judge them or direct these men in any way—as your recruits or soldiers or however you want to handle them—you should take time to listen to their stories."

"Stories? What are you talking about?"

"Stories about what it was that set them up crossways with the law," Milford said. "They're really not such a bad lot. Look at Morris, for example. He's quite a polished gentleman, wouldn't you say?"

Malcolm turned to study the New Yorker, George Morris, who was entertaining Naomi with card tricks. "Cards," Malcolm said. "How good is he with a gun?"

Abe raised his eyebrows. "Test him. You may be pleasantly surprised."

Erskine slapped his hand on Milford's back. "My best to Rose."

Abe said, "Let me know if you believe you have a buyer for her land at Camp Branch."

Malcolm shrugged. "Little of it can be farmed."

"It's worth something. If you hear anything, please send word."

"I'll do that," Erskine said. They embraced, Abe then going to Naomi to kiss her on the cheek. He waved to all and wished them luck as a group before shaking hands with Daniel and going out.

"And now, Daniel, I suppose you're going to give me similar advice about the men you've brought."

"Most certainly, Malcolm. They're Army deserters, technically, but good men, as you'll see."

"I'll give them every benefit of doubt. Naturally I'm interested in their character, and naturally I'm interested in their skills. But you must admit, you and Abe gave me a shock at breakfast."

"About our not staying? Or about the origin of your troops?"

"Both."

"I'll take my leave with Naomi now." Daniel went to his sister, who gave him a warm embrace. "I've a gift for Noah," Malcolm heard Daniel tell her. He watched as Daniel pulled from a jacket pocket a small, calico, stuffed horse.

"Wherever did you find such a beautiful thing?" Naomi squealed.

"We've got a supplier out of St. Louis who's sending in crafts made by Amish and Mennonite ladies. This is one of the items."

"Can you get an Amish quilt? I'd go deep into my savings for that."

Daniel agreed to try, then said his goodbyes all around and left.

The newcomers were standing, sitting, leaning in the parlor and adjacent hallways, their modest belongings in small knapsacks slung over their shoulders or at their feet. Erskine summoned Eugene Fontenot to his side.

"Is it warm in the barn?" he asked Eugene.

"Reasonably. Lani lighted a stove in there for us, as well as the one in her quarters and yet another below-ground. And they are all venting well."

"Impress on these men they are not to go near Lani's room, that she is betrothed, and that any man who violates her privacy will have me to deal with."

Eugene nodded. "I'll assign horse stalls and show them their quarters, get them settled. When do you wish to meet with them?"

Erskine looked at a clock at the far end of the parlor. "One hour."

During that time, Malcolm helped Naomi bathe Noah in a tub set on the main table of the kitchen, where the warmth of cooking lingered sweetly. At times like this he tried to drink in every detail of joy they shared. He knew that dangers ahead could cut his life short when he was just beginning to live as a man should.

"You stare at this little boy so intensely," Naomi said, patting Noah gently with a towel, "that you'll rub the skin off him."

Malcolm smiled. "He does give such pleasure, just being here—just being who he is, our son."

Naomi looked up, slightly teary-eyed. She looked deeply into her husband's eyes and said, with a slight crack in her voice while nodding, "Yes, he does."

Shortly after, Malcolm put on his jacket and hat and strolled to the barn. He could have taken an underground route, but until he knew these men better, he hesitated to reveal more of the tunnel network than was so far necessary for them to know.

"Gentlemen, are you all going to be comfortable here and below?"

"Yes, sir," they chorused shyly. George Morris spoke up. "How did you manage the bunks? I mean, how did you get them in?" He referred to sturdy double-decked beds Malcolm had ordered in anticipation of this day.

"The pieces were pre-cut. They were assembled where they stand, by my Shawnee brothers."

"Is this barn the only way out—and out of the rooms below?" asked Cyrus Ormsby.

Malcolm raised a hand in acknowledgement of their concern. No doubt they had heard of the Camp Branch holocaust. Malcolm had been in Lawrence at the time, and news of how the Jayhawker band was destroyed by fire was soon all over town. Shortly after that it was talked about widely throughout the Territory.

"No," Malcolm said, "this isn't the only way out. But I want to discuss other matters first."

"Our records?" That had been Terence Anderton speaking. Clearly he intended his emphasis on "records" as sarcasm, but it was also plain that Malcolm shouldn't take offense.

"Yes," Malcolm said. "Pull up hay bales in an arc around the stove. Mind that you don't get the straw too close. Be seated and, one by one, tell me why you were in jail when Mr. Milford or Mr. Goodman found you."

Anderton spoke up again. "Want to start with me?"

Malcolm nodded, then pulled out his pipe and stuffed and tamped it one-handed. He lighted it from a straw that he had stuck through the stove door. "Yes," he said, "with you. Then let's just go in a circle—or randomly."

Terence Anderton's account was closely involved with the Army's recent up-and-down presence at Fort Scott. After serving as a major military site before and during the Mexican War, the place declined gradually and became a minor frontier outpost. It was officially closed in 1853, but a small force, scarcely enough to be called a garrison, stayed to keep peace among Indian tribes.

The Indians seemed no longer to be warring among themselves or against whites in the region. So guarding and maintaining the military cemetery in the southwest part of the town of Fort Scott became the soldiers' principal occupation. When slaves started running away into Kansas, and when the Missouri-Kansas border turned into a battleground, leaders in Washington were slow to define the Army's role in the new turmoil.

Anderton, youngest of five and uninterested in following his father into riverboat construction, joined the Army in St. Louis in 1855. He was promoted to corporal the following year, when he was twenty-one. Despite the lack of challenge in his assignments, he received commendations for leadership and for his abilities in training others. He seemed destined for another promotion or candidacy for officers' school at Fort Leavenworth. He would have been happy to quit the cemetery outpost.

While papers were being drawn for a transfer to school, Terence was awakened one night and instructed to ready his Cavalry squad for action. Lt. Alan Congleton informed the assembled platoon that abolitionists guiding escaped slaves were moving deep into Kansas Territory after their discovery near the Missouri border, in Linn County north of Fort Scott.

Congleton said the Yankees had a good start and may elude capture for violations of the Fugitive Slave Act. But the platoon would at least try to round up what he called "those po' Nigras out theah in the cold."

They arrived by way of the military road and found six adult slaves, held by a deputy marshal. Anderton and his squad were ordered to take the slaves into a barn, where the Lieutenant would question them. The rest of the platoon was sent as a search party for the abolitionists, an assignment that proved futile.

When Lieutenant Congleton entered the barn, Anderton noticed the officer's attention was caught by a young woman of special beauty. Without looking away from her, Congleton changed his previous order and told Corporal Anderton to take all but this woman to the farmhouse, where a sergeant would carry out the questioning.

Anderton and his men led five slaves from the barn, four men and an older woman. Congleton signaled a soldier who held a lantern to remain. Later, in the farmhouse, as Anderton was observing the sergeant's inquiries uneasily, he decided he disliked the entire arrangement and wanted to know what Congleton was up to.

"I went back to the barn," Terence said. "There I saw in the lamplight our commander raping the woman, like it was his right. I picked up a shovel and hit him on the head with the business end. Unfortunately, I didn't kill him. While I was held for a courts martial, Watson Frederick here—" He indicated a young man sitting next to him. "—helped me out of the hoosegow and we both ran off. We were picked up outside Paola and arrested for desertion."

Malcolm turned to Watson and asked, "Why did you help Anderton?"

Sitting up straight, the young man shrugged and said, "I didn't like what was going on. The woman was scared and crying and begging the Lieutenant not to. And then begging him to leave off before he— Well, you know. Said she didn't want to have a baby. I was the one held the lantern."

82

Watson Frederick's admission of witnessing the crime by his officer raised a question Malcolm had wanted to ask during Terence Anderton's story.

"Instead of an assault on this Lieutenant Congleton, didn't either of you consider turning him in for raping the slavewoman?"

Frederick looked at Anderton blankly. Then Anderton said, "Our word against his wouldn't stand a chance."

Watson added, "Yeah. They'd think we maybe conspired, to get even for some duty we didn't like." The lad looked around the barn at the other men. "Besides, anyone here ever know of a white man arrested for raping a colored woman? Ever?"

None responded.

Malcolm puffed his pipe and glanced at the barn floor, pondering that fact of these men's experience—and his own. He looked again at young Watson, recalling the young man was from Illinois, maybe about eighteen. He said, "Tell us about yourself."

Frederick had been an only child but was now an orphan. While away from the family farm one summer evening—courting a girl over the hill, as a matter of fact—several men carrying torches visited his parents on an angry mission.

Watson's father had left active participation in their church sect. But he'd done so flamboyantly, condemning the presiding minister and elders for hypocrisy. The most fanatical members decided a whipping was in order. They shouted to Elias Frederick to come outside and submit. He refused.

Because summer had been dry, the thatch of a lean-to by the house ignited like tinder when, jokingly, one man poked toward it with a torch. Later he said he meant only to give a sign how they might get the Fredericks out, but not with serious intent.

All in the church elders' party tried dousing the flames by bucket brigade, but there wasn't enough water. Watson's parents had shuttered windows and barred both doors from inside and, with fire raging, were unable to reopen them. They were apparently panicked by the speed with which flames were consuming their home.

The couple died in the fire. The parishioners rode off, carrying shame of what they'd done accidentally.

A Springfield lawyer who'd served in the U.S. House of Representatives heard of Watson's plight. He offered to settle family affairs in a way assuring the boy his rights.

The young man knew one of the lawyer's sons casually and trusted the man.

"I told Mr. Lincoln I wasn't suited to managing the farm, that I'd like to be more seasoned before I tried. He asked what I wanted to do meanwhile. I told him I craved adventure. The girl I was courting didn't seem interested. I'd as soon go off somewhere, I told him. Mr. Lincoln wasn't keen about my drifting, so I suggested the Army. We talked it out, and he helped me get in the Cavalry, like I wanted. Never did charge a fee."

Malcolm leaned forward. "Lincoln," he said. "Same man who served in Congress and opposed the Mexican War?"

"Yes. Abraham Lincoln. A Whig, or maybe now a Republican."

Erskine nodded, then asked, "Does he know about your deserting?"

"I don't think so."

"Write and tell him the story," Malcolm said. "Particularly why you helped Anderton, and all you've seen of the Army's treatment of fugitive slaves."

"Yes, sir. I'll do that, but why—"

"Lincoln and those Republicans need to know the kinds of things you and Anderton have been telling us." Malcolm looked around the barn to add, "I'd like *all* you men to write your families, those close to you. Tell them what you're up to, without writing precisely where you are. I'll see your letters go out properly by way of the Shawnees. You mustn't let those who care about you be sick with worry."

"What if I ain't *got* no one?"

That was Chad Brookings, a fair-haired youth Malcolm remembered was only seventeen and from near Lawrence.

"What do you mean, 'no one'? There's always family, or a friend—"

"What if I don't want anythin' to do with those I useta call family?"

Erskine shrugged and said, "I'm not forcing you to write, son. I'm just suggesting it." Then, "Let's have you go next with your story."

"I'll tell, but I ain't got a crime to be proud of, like these two here." He indicated Anderton and Frederick. "My crime is *actual.* Just plain stealin'. That's how come I was in jail. Stealin'."

Erskine waited and puffed his pipe. When Chad seemed he'd be no more forthcoming with information, Malcolm prompted him. "Why did you steal?"

Brookings shrugged. "I was hungry. I was tired and cold, runnin' around loose, nothin' to do. Not wantin' to go home 'cause I felt I didn't have a proper home to go to."

"Why not proper?"

"My folks split up."

Malcolm became contemplative. "That's it? You're finished with your family because your parents split up?"

"Sure. Wouldn't *you* feel that way?"

Erskine shook his head. "No. What caused them to break up?"

"My older sister was married and gone. One day along comes this sweet-talkin' Southerner askin' for a little bread or somethin'. He'd been on the road a long time, and Maw was alone in the house. Paw was in town. I was doin' chores."

Chad picked up a straw and stuck it in the corner of his mouth, as he'd seen others do in the group. Erskine figured the boy thought it made him look more mature.

"Anyways," Brookings continued, "the fella turns out to be one of them Law and Order agents roamin' the Territory, lookin' for who's harborin' fugitive slaves, lookin' for people like you—" He indicated Malcolm. "I came in the house and overheard his sweet-talkin' my Maw, who's an uncommonly pretty woman, *I* always thought. Next thing, I look in and they's *kissin'* to beat the band. After *that,* in comes *Paw* the other side of the house and *sees it all.*" Chad seemed close to tears.

"'Scuse me a second. Somethin' stuck in my throat." He threw down the straw. "Paw don't say nothin'. He goes to their bedroom and drags out a suitcase and points to it. And Maw, who's been wed to Paw twenny years, stands there a-wonderin' what to do next. The Southerner speaks up and says, 'I believe he's givin' you up without a fight and orderin' you to *leave.* Never mind him, honey. *I'll* take care of you,' is what he says. Then they both ride off on his horse." The youth made a loud sniffing sound and shook his head.

"Paw wasn't the same after that. Me either. I hung around with a gang in Lawrence and we stole things, caused lots of trouble, slept in alleys. Anyways, I got caught. That's the whole story."

Erskine puffed his pipe and pondered through a period of quiet.

At last he said, "Chad, all of us are as weak at times as we are strong at other times. You'll one day forgive both your parents."

Brookings bent his head and appeared to be fighting the impulse to weep. George Morris started to reach a hand to comfort the youth, then he withdrew it, perhaps not to worsen Chad's embarrassment.

Erskine signalled to Eugene Fontenot to come near. "Take Chad below and get him settled." He then crooked his finger and had Fontenot lean closer so he could whisper. "And see if he knows more about Mrs. Brookings's whereabouts."

Fontenot backed away and looked at Malcolm questioningly. In response, Erskine nodded. He'd decided a goal for this Jayhawker band would be to find the woman and try to reunite Chad's parents.

After Fontenot and Brookings left, the polished New Yorker, George Morris, observed, "It's a sad thing, what this border trouble has done to people, to families."

"Why don't you be next?" Malcolm suggested.

"Me? Of course. No family story, mine. You see, no *family*. Mine's the shortest tale of all, I'd guess."

Erskine grew impatient, knocking the blackened ashes onto the floor, then searching for fresh pipe tobacco in his pouch.

Morris was an actor and showman—a magician of sorts. He stood to speak, moving about as he did. A true orphan, having been reared in a Catholic orphanage in New York City, he'd managed to lighten the burden for other boys and girls by arranging entertaining performances, enlisting the aid of nuns in staging them.

As he matured and opportunity arose for him to join a show circuit and tour professionally, Morris packed his trunk and left.

On one recent tour the company played Topeka, where members of the Lecompton Legislature had gathered with their wives for an evening's entertainment.

"I was arrested on the stage for something called 'indecency.' Here in Kansas they make up names of crimes to fit the occasion."

"What exactly did you do?" Malcolm asked.

"Your Reverend Johnson was present in the audience, which proved my downfall. He took offense at something I said in my performance. He has no sense of humor, your Reverend Johnson."

"You can stop referring to him," Malcolm said, "as 'my' Reverend Johnson. He's an enemy of the Free State."

"I'm happy to hear that," Morris said, glancing about the group somewhat animatedly, "for I can't *stand* a man—or woman—with no sense of humor."

"What did you say—on stage, I mean?"

Morris faced Erskine and said, "I merely suggested, for purposes of getting all to laugh, that Mr. Johnson is at heart a *farmer*. The man grinned over that, but then I went on to explain. I said Mr. Johnson maintains his Mission to plow among dusky Indian maidens and slave Negresses, to plant seeds at random for a lighter-colored crop at harvest time."

83

When George Morris had completed his tale, Malcolm's mouth was agape. He remembered what Naomi had said about that habit and recovered quickly to say, "What surprises me is, you got away with your life. No challenge with weapons? For implying the minister romances so-called 'dusky maidens' in his keep?"

Morris replied, "All I know is a Shawnee County deputy came onto the stage and took me in tow. Later I was turned over to Douglas County authorities and placed in the Lawrence jail. I served nearly two months awaiting dispositon of the flimsy charges when your Mr. Milford showed a paper signed by Douglas County officials, a paper releasing me. I'm told that didn't sit well with the Lecompton people. But it was enough to legitimize my freedom."

Erskine noticed that the man—he judged him to be in his late twenties—nearly always paced as he spoke, perhaps a habit of stage presence. Morris also looked alternately among those listening. "The sidearms you wear," Malcolm said, "are new Colts, are they not?"

"I was lucky the touring company was able to keep them for me and see to their safe return to me. Yes. Small caliber. Very light. Would you like to examine them?"

"Show me first what you can do with them."

"Here? In the barn?"

"I assure you," Malcolm said, "no serious damage will result."

George Morris stood before the group, evidently considering for a moment how best to illustrate for Erskine what sort of marksmanship he was capable of providing the Jayhawker band.

Meanwhile, Malcolm was considering Abe Milford's earlier advice—*"Test him. You may be pleasantly surprised."*

Morris at last appeared to have decided, drawing a deck of cards from a waistcoat pocket and fanning them before Cyrus Ormsby, urging, "Pick a card. Any card."

Ormsby complied and drew the six of spades.

Morris held up the card for all to see, then turned to stroll to a distant part of the barn, where he examined one of the sturdy uprights. He found a vertical crack in the beam and slid the edge of the card into it. It remained suspended approximately five feet above the floor, the black symbols visible to the party seated near the stove.

Morris returned to where they were gathered—a distance of perhaps fifty feet. He cocked his head to eyeball the card, then drew one of his revolvers and took aim.

The shot resounded through the barn peculiarly. The size of the structure and its sturdiness produced an acoustical effect bordering on echo. All looked at the card and noticed no apparent change.

George Morris lifted the revolver again and squeezed off another shot. Once more there seemed no effect.

Andrew Pace, whom Malcolm knew to be from Independence, Missouri, and who'd spent more than a year in the Lawrence jail, dug his elbow into Cyrus Ormsby's ribs and snickered.

Again Morris shot, and again, until six bullets were fired.

Completing his evidently unsuccessful demonstration—and now hearing a couple of catcalls and giggles from the group—Morris reholstered his gun. He returned to the beam that held the playing card. He slid it from its place and carried it to Erskine, who smiled upon seeing it close.

"Gentlemen," Malcolm told the group, "we have in our presence the most remarkable marksman with a hand weapon it's ever been my pleasure to encounter."

Leaning forward and flicking open the stove door with his hook, Malcolm held the card in such a way that the fire blazed behind it. Those seated on haybales rose and scurried to see what was so remarkable. Several gasped.

Morris had, with six shots, produced six holes so neatly centered on the spade symbols that none could see them from fifty feet off. Held before the firelight, the six holes were plain to all.

Morris reseated himself, obviously considering his place in the band to be secure.

Malcolm had one more question for the showman.

"Can you ride?"

"I've ridden, but I confess," George said, "there are ways of horsemanship I must learn from you and these, my new companions. I'm truly counting on them."

Erskine nodded, with fresh respect for the New Yorker. Morris knew how to turn a moment of triumph into one of humility, so as not to let those with whom he must work be too much in awe of him. That was a good quality in a member of a fighting force, for others must never assume that any one member can take total care of himself. Each was, in some way, responsible for watching over the next, and so on through the entire group.

Cyrus Ormsby, a man who had one or two years on Malcolm, remarked, "I seen a man shoot *almost* as good as that once—*and* ride like I wouldn't have believed."

That observation sharpened Erskine's attention. "Maybe we ought to recruit him," he suggested.

"Not that one," Ormsby replied, shaking his head with some apparently bitter remembrance. He looked up, gazed at the rafters, and repeated, "No, not that one. A mean one, that lad, and I know for sure his sentiments are with the proslavers—even though he sometimes pretends to be on our side."

Ormsby then looked Malcolm in the eye, squinted, and said, "I'm surprised you ain't already on to who I'm talking about. Man's been moving between Paola and that new place, Spring Hill, pretty regular. Young fella, well-schooled from all appearances. Name of Quantrill—William Quantrill."

Malcolm shook his head. "No, I've never heard of him."

Ormsby asked, "Isn't there a Torrey—or fella with some such name—in Paola? Runs a hotel?"

Erskine nodded. "Yes."

"Well, Torrey's the man brought this Quantrill here from Ohio. Sort of watches over the lad, I guess. Now, I hear, Quantrill's staked himself a claim near Spring Hill."

Erskine decided to remember the name, William Quantrill, and to make further inquiry. "Enough about him. What about you?"

Ormsby shrugged. He dressed like a frontiersman, moreso than did any of the others present. His face was weathered. Malcolm guessed Cyrus Ormsby was a man who'd lived the equivalent of sixty years in the space of thirty.

"Teamster. Grew up right over here—" He pointed generally to the northeast. "—near Little Santa Fe. Back and forth a number of times since the Mexican War over the Santa Fe road. Been a teamster all my growed life."

He shrugged again. "One night I broke the camp rule, got sozzled with one of the folks in a wagon train. I didn't know the man was a slaveowner or I'd never have mixed with him. Unlike most Missourians, I never could hold with a man owning another man. We got into some kind of argument—the rightness or wrongness of slavery. I should've held my tongue. Ain't supposed to get political on the job. But it was *rum* talking. Well, I cut the fellow pretty bad with my knife. A military party turned me over to civil authorities, and I wound up in the Lawrence pokey. The fella survived, so the case wasn't pressed."

Erskine nodded to Ormsby and studied the teamster for possible leadership, considering he seemed the oldest present. Possible, but he wouldn't push that. Ormsby seemed more comfortable participating than leading. Still, Malcolm knew he might need the man's help that way someday.

"Rifleman?" Erskine asked.

"Pretty good shot," Ormsby replied in an appropriately modest tone. "Fair on horseback. Need practice with handguns." He shrugged, as though indicating there was nothing more to say. But there was—

"*And* grateful to you and your friends for my freedom. I'll do you a good job," Cyrus promised.

Malcolm acknowledged that with a look and a slight nod. He turned next to Jedediah Blake, a lad about nineteen. "Haven't I seen you somewhere before?" he asked.

Blake beamed. "I wondered if you'd remember. 'Cause if you didn't, I'd have reminded you. I used to visit John Brown's camp near Osawatomie when you were laid up there. I'm from a farm near there. But a lot's happened since I last saw you."

"Indeed it has," Malcolm agreed.

"I mean, to *both* of us—you leaving the Territory and coming back and getting married and building this place and all. Me joining the Army, then deserting. Well, actually, I never did desert. What it was," Jedediah Blake explained, his face clouding, "I learned my parents and my brother were killed on our farm in a Bushwhacker raid. I guess the Missourians were looking for Brown and his boys, but they'd cleared out long before." He paused to sigh deeply.

"I left Fort Scott without leave when I heard about my family. Everything would've been made right if I hadn't put on civilian clothes to ride out. My superior officer wrote me down as a deserter, not just absent without leave."

"Let me guess," Malcolm said, "that the superior officer of your platoon was a proslaver."

"One of the worst. One of those VMI graduates, you know. The West Point of the South."

Erskine had great respect for products of the Virginia Military Institute. Still, he detested the politicizing of officers that had lately affected the Army. He blamed President Pierce's Secretary of War—Jefferson Davis—for fostering disunity.

It was Davis, a West Pointer as Malcolm recalled, who'd influenced Pierce to sign the Kansas-Nebraska Act into law in 1854. That was the instrument to blame for all present border troubles, precipitating rigged elections ever since.

There was no longer a single reliable policy on which the Army could be depended to base its peacekeeping. Nor could soon-to-be President Buchanan repair that. He was of the same wing of the Democratic Party as Pierce. He'd beaten at the polls the only man Malcolm believed might have brought the nation together again—General Frémont.

John Charles Frémont, first nominee of the new Republican Party, was a man who knew the West, particularly the Missouri-Kansas area, better than anyone in the national limelight. Though a Southerner and married to the daughter of Missouri's former senator, Thomas Hart Benton, Frémont was sympathetic to developing the West in a way Erskine and others like him wanted it to grow—free and with a fair deal for Indians.

Frémont had explored extensively, and— Ah, well. Malcolm broke his reverie about what might have been.

Malcolm nodded acknowledgement to Jedediah Blake, that he was satisfied over the lad's story of being jailed by the Army. Now, once again, he was feeling the tug of politics. He'd felt it in Lawrence, then briefly in Paola, and it was happening again now with thoughts of Frémont and Watson Frederick's earlier mention of Lincoln.

In just over two weeks, however, there would be sworn into office the bachelor Buchanan, so lukewarm to freedom as to be considered an enemy of the Free State.

For now, Erskine knew, his job rested with guns—with the border conflict.

For later he would reserve thoughts of becoming part of the process where decisions were truly made—in politics.

84

Malcolm faced the three remaining men who hadn't yet taken their turn. From their general manner he detected a certain hesitancy about sharing their stories.

Andrew Pace, mid-twenties in appearance, seemed amiable enough and occasionally joshed others. Yet he was a bit too flippant for Erskine's taste. After venturing comments and not always receiving the response he'd evidently hoped for, Pace seemed to retreat into himself.

Malcolm decided Pace would be next to take a turn. He puffed his pipe contemplatively and listened to them all chat, hoping to hear responses by the two young fellows clustered with Pace—Benjamin Ellerby and Henry O'Dell.

They were getting better acquainted. How the men related to one another within the group was an important set of observations for Malcolm to be making. Were they companionable, or was there obvious potential for jealousies and unleashed tempers? Would they make pledges and alliances, or might there be lone-wolf withdrawals?

Pace might have some leadership ability, Malcolm speculated, as did one or two others. It was apparent the Independence man exchanged well with a few but not all.

"Pace," Erskine said at last, bringing everyone to some attention. "Tell us your tale."

Very quickly in Andrew's story it became clear that his legal position remained uncertain, despite his documented release from the Lawrence jail.

Born and raised on a farm near where the city of Independence was later to flourish, Pace had become attuned to frontier adventure by observing three older brothers.

All had left the farm to become drivers on the newly opened trails to Santa Fe and California. No amount of persuasion by his parents could hold young Andrew. At sixteen Pace was making regular runs to supply the military for the Mexican War. Later he drove supply lines for gold-fevered prospectors streaming to California.

The Kansas-Missouri Border War turned opportunity to corruption. Encounters with gun-runners on both sides presented a chance that Pace seized boldly. In violation of ever-shifting Indian treaties, he was caught selling Sharps rifles to Delaware Indians near Leavenworth.

By then all tribes owned firearms, but the appearance of the efficient Sharps on the frontier made for some special treaty-revising, and Andrew stumbled on a technicality.

At that point, Erskine interrupted. "You were released on city and county authority, but you're still uncleared on Federal charges?"

Andrew Pace shrugged. "I guess that's so," he acknowledged.

"Have you done anything to make up for it?" Malcolm asked hopefully, wanting to hear only one answer.

Pace shrugged again. "I gave the Indians back their money, if that's what you mean."

Good enough. If that checked, Malcolm would encourage Chief Black Bob to put in a word with government officials to wipe Pace's offense from the books. If the exchange was equitably settled for the Delawares, it could be done.

"What made you do it in the first place?" Malcolm asked. "Get into gun-dealing with Indians, I mean."

Once again, a shrug from Pace. "I always liked a fast life, is my guess. Like my brothers. That takes money. I did it for the money."

Before his conviction and jailing nearly a year earlier for selling the Sharps to Delawares, Pace had been hanging about saloons in Westport and Kansas City, gambling and womanizing. Handling Pace would require caution, Malcolm realized, but he nodded and said, "Glad to have you with us if you're ready to do the job—virtually without pay and at some risk to your life."

"Anything's better than jail," Pace said. "Looks like I can count on three squares a day and a warm bed and—" He looked about and grinned a bit oddly. "—fair-decent company."

"No women here for you."

Pace nodded. "I know. Remember, I've went without for a year, and it done me no harm, though I think about it."

Erskine nodded. If Pace and the others did their work, he would owe them something more than bed and board, maybe a *soirée.* He would look into that.

"O'Dell?" That was his invitation to the large lad from Wyandotte.

By an almost painful process of questioning and then drawing out answers—as a surgeon might remove a deeply lodged bullet—Erskine was finally able to determine that O'Dell, too, had a somewhat criminal bent, whether or not he could justify such an inclination.

O'Dell was a bootmaker's son and apprentice. By his sheer size, he intimidated a couple of Bushwhacker raiders caught by a well near his home one night. He tied them to a tree, gathered kindling, and was about to burn them alive when their cries summoned help. Except for the fact Sam Jones was a participant in the rescue, O'Dell might never have been charged.

"Why were you about to burn them?" Malcolm asked in a voice under control, so as not to reveal how shocked he was that an eighteen-year-old might do such a thing.

"To teach them a lesson."

Erskine nodded, in painful realization that Henry O'Dell had limited powers of reasoning and no judgment about how to fit the punishment to the crime.

Still, Malcolm knew, he needed at least one killer in the group besides himself, and O'Dell was it.

Erskine turned to the last in the circle, Ben Ellerby of Kansas City, perhaps nineteen or twenty. "Now to you."

Ellerby sat silent.

Erskine repeated the invitation. "We've heard from all the

others. It's your turn to tell us how you happen to be crossways with the law. It's important to me."

One more moment's worth of hesitation could result in Ellerby's exile at best, execution at worst, considering delicate balances at play in constructing this outlawed fighting force.

"If I tell you what happened, must I tell you why?"

Erskine said, "I'll want to know—if *you* know. Yes."

"I *did* desert the Army. I don't have a good excuse like the others."

Malcolm was a little surprised. "But if you're a true deserter, I'm amazed they were willing to release you to Daniel Goodman."

"They let me go because I wouldn't talk about why. They didn't know what else to do with me. I didn't tell why then, and I won't tell why now. Do whatever you want about that."

Malcolm studied Ellerby thoughtfully. The youth was slender, well-proportioned, and handsome, almost effeminate in his appearance. From such features Malcolm was able to guess the source of the trouble. And he would allow such an unconfirmed guess to serve—for now.

Still, he wanted no similar problem to arise here. That thought fortified his earlier resolution to look into arranging some—well, normal companionship of women without jeopardizing this secret enterprise.

"Ellerby," Malcolm announced, knocking ashes from his pipe. "You'll tell me privately what was involved in your deserting—whenever you're ready."

Ben Ellerby's grin—perhaps the first since his coming to Pleasant Valley—was an eloquent display of gratitude for an understanding leader.

Eugene Fontenot, back from placing their youngest charge, Chad Brookings, in quarters below, now sought direction from Malcolm.

Erskine rose from the hay bale, almost sorry to be bringing a most revealing and somewhat companionable meeting to an end.

"Gentlemen," he said, "we'll become organized in a semimilitary fashion, and here's the arrangement for now. All that you're ordered to do will be on my authority. Cyrus Ormsby, I want you to serve as a quartermaster. Make me a list—"

"I don't read or write."

"—with Jed Blake's help, make me a list of all that's required for arming and equipping the men. Eugene, you'll acquaint Ormsby with what we already have on hand. All of you, remember that my companion, Eugene Fontenot, is second to me in command. I'm appointing George Morris as adjutant, or number three. If you have any problems that can't be solved by supplies, as would be handled by Ormsby, you take those problems to Morris. Is that understood?"

All nodded and rose, preparing to become better acquainted with their new lodgings. Just as they were milling, ready to disperse, Lani-Wawewa entered the main part of the barn.

The men were clearly excited by her reappearance since getting glimpses of her in the house. Erskine knew he must make plain to them how this beautiful woman-child was to be treated. Thinking on that quickly, he knew he must also make clear to *her* what behavior he expected.

"This young woman, Lani, who is quartered here in the barn, is my servant and ward. She is being kept safe here as the betrothed of my friend, Johnny Kesibwi, a Shawnee courier.

"There is to be no—" Erskine was having discomfort with this. "—socializing."

Lani's face revealed apparent understanding of the circumstances, the rules Malcolm was trying to describe with difficulty.

"Let *me,*" she urged.

With alarming deftness she pulled from under her garments a Bowie knife and a dusty talisman—a human scalp that appeared to Malcolm to have been taken by one of Lani's ancestors ages ago.

"This is from last month," she lied to the others, "for socializing when I didn't want him to."

Forgetting any temptation to stand there and stare at the Chippewa maiden's ripe beauty, all the men shuffled quickly toward their assigned quarters. Lani held her "trophy" high and received scarcely another glance.

85

Breaks in the weather made it possible for Erskine to arrange horsemanship and marksmanship training and lessons in defensive tactics. All the while, from wherever they practiced, he took care to keep a watch on activity at the ranch.

Erskine began to rely less on Shawnees for security and more on his own men. The Indians would soon be preparing their fields for planting, and they'd already given much that he could never repay. Those whom Erskine assigned watch duty were to carry pocket telescopes as well as a signal flag for communication by day, flares by night.

The realities of economics began to produce—for any who might be allowed to witness the activity—a picture of fairly normal ranching operations. The arrival of cattle and hogs required establishment of routines, allocation of duties, coaching for some with little experience tending stock.

As a person with an address, Erskine indulged in luxuries such as a subscription to *The Liberator,* William Lloyd Garrison's abolitionist periodical, and *The New York Tribune.* Awareness of national events was vital to Malcolm's boosting political passions in his men.

George Morris was of particular help in promoting a Free State ethic, touching sentiments inside each man and shaping those leanings into a fighting spirit. Undoubtedly grateful to receive trust as third in command, the stage perfomer also established a good rapport with Erskine in interpreting current events.

With Eugene Fontenot, Malcolm had yet another relationship. Eugene seemed to regard his leader now as an older brother, a model to follow no matter where the adventure might lead. Fontenot also brought to the alliance a good business acumen, an example to others of loyalty without servility, and a thoroughness about details.

Cyrus Ormsby proved of great value at the fourth echelon. He quartermastered successfully and, as the oldest in the group, provided benefits of experienced wisdom.

Ormsby contributed unexpectedly in another way, because he seemed most at home with managing stock. He literally ran the developing ranch, ordering others about in ways making them glad to be cowboys when they weren't training as fighters.

Erskine observed how Ormsby worked and decided that, if this were a time of peace, the former teamster would make a perfect ranch overseer. Malcolm mounted Ebony and rode to the bluff where Ormsby was watching over the valley.

"Afternoon, Captain," Cyrus greeted him, past a plug of tobacco in his cheek. He also touched his hat in half-salute. They'd taken to addressing Erskine by that honorary title at times, and he hadn't sought to discourage that.

After small talk, some of which had to do with cattle management, Malcolm said, "I'm upset over events, Cyrus, and want to go into action."

Ormsby nodded and listened.

"You recall discussion in the barn about what the Supreme Court has done, about what that means to everything we're trying to accomplish."

Ormsby turned to one side and spat tobacco juice. "I confess, Captain, I'm not all that smart about the law to know whys and wherefores. But I know it would be a blow to *me* to learn I'm considered without rights as a citizen."

Malcolm was satisfied Cyrus had absorbed the meaning of the Dred Scott decision just handed down by the Court. A Missouri slave, considering himself freed by having lived in non-slave states, was ruled without any rights to sue for his freedom—virtually declared a non-person under the law.

"Unlike John Brown who goes off half-cocked in retaliation," Malcolm said, "I'd like to counter that in another way. In a non-murderous way, if killing can be avoided. I'm thinking the way people exploit Negroes, the way they exploit Indians—hell, the way we've all been exploiting *women*—we can now do a little to offset that."

Cyrus narrowed his eyes to watch the cattle below, then nodded. Without looking at Erskine, he said, "You want to go after Chad's mama and bring her back to Kansas. You want to know if the men are ready for that."

Malcolm turned and, making a fist, gave Cyrus a firm but friendly punch in the upper arm. His quartermaster and ranch boss broke into a tobacco-stained grin.

After a moment, Cyrus suggested, "Let's gather Eugene and George tonight and plan it for tomorrow. It's time. The men want action, even if they never have to draw weapons on this one."

Satisfied, Malcolm returned home, went to a desk where he kept his maps and records, and began to plan the small adventure.

Later, he held Noah and rocked his two-month-old son to sleep in his arms. He gave the baby to the increasingly valuable Lani-Wawewa to place in the cradle. He sought Naomi in the kitchen.

Malcolm drew a chair to the table and accepted a mug of hot coffee. He announced, "We're going to kidnap Mrs. Brookings tomorrow and return her to Lawrence."

"Just like that?" Naomi asked, continuing to knead dough on a counter without interruption.

Malcolm nodded and said, "Just like that."

"I don't believe it will work. She wants to be where she is. Her husband's failure to act—his passiveness in the episode—seems the reason she's separated from him."

"You mean, if he'd done something when he caught her being kissed by that Missouri agent, no splitting up would have taken place?"

"Exactly," Naomi said, glancing only occasionally from her work, which seemed to send a good bit of flour dust into the air around her. "The woman interprets her husband's indifference as a numbing of their original love, maybe a sign it died."

She then stopped suddenly and turned fully to Malcolm. "I have no doubt you'll be successful taking her from the Missourians tomorrow. You've enough force in those men out there to do it. But getting her to stay in Lawrence afterward is something else. That's where you'll need to apply something extra."

After a moment, Erskine nodded. "I think I see what you mean. 'Paw' Brookings, with his 'uncommonly pretty' wife, may now appreciate what he had. But he wouldn't know how to handle getting her back. He could lose her again."

Naomi said, "You need more than a plan to get her out of Missouri. I know you want to do that to taunt the proslavers, to let them know you're organized for anything they might throw your way." She held up a wooden spoon and shook it at her husband, lecturing him. "But that won't be good enough, Malcolm. You can't be doing these kinds of things just for your political or military position. You're dealing with people's emotions—making a Border War issue out of the Brookingses."

Erskine was without ideas how to handle a long-term reconciliation of Mr. and Mrs. Brookings. This was a whole new area. The rescue was clear, and his reasons as Naomi stated them were accurate. But the rest?

Naomi said, "I have a plan to reunite them permanently." She turned back to her bread-baking preparations as she spoke. "You'll then accomplish your goal, and the whole enterprise will work for them as well. But," she added as Malcolm was finishing his coffee, "it involves your having to practically make love to Chad Brookings's 'uncommonly pretty' mother yourself."

Hearing that, Erskine choked in surprise. He sent a spurt of coffee flying messily across the table and began coughing, stamping his boots on the wood floor in an effort to recover.

86

"Just what in blue blazes do you mean, I've got to *romance* the lady? You lost your *mind?"*

Naomi stopped working on the bread dough, bunched a pair of fists, and rested them on her hips. "You're thinking of going into politics? Well then, you may as well learn play-acting."

"Play-acting?"

"Yes, Malcolm. Performing. Pretending. All for the sake of manipulating. How else do you think idiots like James Buchanan get people to vote for them?"

"If that's what it takes, I'm not sure it's worth thinking about anymore."

"It's worth it, Malcolm, if you have new ideas to offer and can muster the power to get them into law, into practice. Let me talk to George Morris about this rescue of Chad's mother. He's had stage experience and would be a perfect teacher."

Malcolm got up and held Naomi close. "You're not worried? I mean—"

"About the romancing part? Malcolm, I know you. Whatever else happens out there in the world, I know your heart is here and that you'll always head for home."

"But what if—"

"What? You mean, what if some filly sashays up to you, tempts you?" Naomi broke away to imitate "sashaying," fluttering her eyelashes and causing Malcolm to double over laughing. "I don't worry about such things, Malcolm. I don't let myself think about them. You were heavily experienced and I was a virgin when we met. But I know now, I'll never lose you to another woman. I may not own you as a man, but I believe I own your heart forever. I'm not worried."

"That's what binds me to you more than anything, Naomi. Your enormous self-confidence, which goes well with your intelligence, your character, and all the ways you deal with me."

"Let's seal that with a kiss through all this flour on me—on us now," she said. "And then send George Morris in."

*****

The next day, while leading his band into Missouri, Erskine rehearsed in his mind the evening's coaching by Morris.

By sighting details he'd learned from Sylvia and the experience of earlier excursions in the area, Erskine believed they'd been spotted. That their coming in was being reported ahead.

Malcolm saw a distant break from brush by a saddled horse with no visible rider. He figured that its rider, swung low to the far side, was choosing his path down an incline to conceal his role as a Bushwhacker watchman on the move.

Malcolm was now certain they would either be confronted for battle or targeted by the enemy for encirclement or ambush.

At Erskine's sign, Fontenot peeled off with five of the men and sought a parallel path to Malcolm's, a hundred or more yards distant. Far enough to ward off any surprise action the Bushwhackers might try. Close enough to maintain signal communication.

But their way continued clear, deep into the southern part of Jackson County on a route far southeast of Little Santa Fe, turning now into Cass County. Malcolm credited their freedom so far to the execution of well-practiced deployment.

Fontenot led the marksman and adjutant, Morris, as well as former Cavalrymen Terence Anderton and Watson Frederick, the trusted if not so militarily experienced Jed Blake, and the somewhat dim-witted but powerful Henry O'Dell.

Erskine kept at his side Cyrus Ormsby, Chad Brookings, Andrew Pace, and Ben Ellerby. He doubted there was a test that the groups in tandem couldn't meet, unless by some quirk the watchman's signal might raise a hundred or more of the enemy.

They rode straight toward where Malcolm's studying of information and charts had indicated Chad's mother was now living—in the relatively thriving Missouri town of Harrisonville, reputed to be a Bushwhacker stronghold.

There, he'd learned by cautious inquiry, Mrs. Brookings—Elaine—lived in apparent satisfaction, by choice and in common law, with Lathan Selby. He was postmaster and operator of a general store. Selby also agented occasionally for Law and Order forces in Kansas Territory under the pretext of commercial activity.

Some time the previous year, Malcolm had also learned, Selby's legal spouse in a childless marriage ran off in a wagon train, bound for California. She was lured by a settler in search of a wife—whether or not a good and faithful one.

From then on the Law and Order agent felt freed of past obligations to search for companionship of his own, wherever that search might take him. By chance he wooed a vulnerable Elaine Brookings and, within minutes, enticed her from Lawrence to return with him to Harrisonville.

Malcolm turned in the saddle toward Chad and shouted over the beat of horses' hooves now at canter, "Are you all right?"

The lad, bent low over his horse's neck, gave a quick lips-together grin and nodded.

Erskine knew Chad would be discomforted by everything he would see and hear, not only at Selby's but en route afterward to Lawrence and at their final destination.

George Morris had insisted Chad *not* be given a clue to what was up—not yet—or the ruse wouldn't work with any members of the Brookings family. Malcolm's actions would be pretended, yes, but the reactions of Elaine, of Chad, and of his father, J.T. Brookings, must be spontaneous and real.

Without the need to draw pistols, the Jayhawkers rode into Harrisonville. By quick observation, Malcolm realized nearly all fighting-age men had left, perhaps only minutes earlier, to join a force elsewhere. Only women, children, and elderly folks appeared to be present.

This play-acting mustn't be allowed to drag on.

When they found the Selby General Store, Erskine dismounted, instructed Morris to accompany him inside, and entered the place. To the pretty woman at the far end of the shop he tipped his hat, inquiring after the whereabouts of Lathan Selby.

"Well, I don't know," the woman replied, approaching. "Strangest thing," she said, "he rode off a few minutes ago as though Satan himself were—"

Elaine Brookings stopped, drawing a hand to her mouth suddenly.

Flaxen-haired and younger-looking than her actual years, especially considering she had grown children who included a married daughter, she was—as Malcolm remembered Chad's saying—"uncommonly pretty."

Now her mouth was open in surprise.

It was evident she knew who stood before her. She recovered enough to say, "You've come for me, haven't you?"

Malcolm nodded and said, "Yes, ma'am, we have. And Chad is outside."

Erskine glanced at George Morris, who gave an almost imperceptible signal. Malcolm added, a bit uncomfortably, "Seeing you, Mrs. Brookings, ma'am, I can understand Mr. Selby's hopes and actions."

Mrs. Brookings, perhaps a dozen years Erskine's senior, flashed purplish-blue eyes toward him and said, "I've seen your face often these past weeks on 'wanted' posters hereabouts, Mr. Erskine. But I never knew till this moment the several ways—"

Erskine's heart leapt to his throat. The woman was *flirting.*

"—how *'wanted'* you might be," she concluded in her unexpected response.

Morris, who seemed satisfied over the progress of the scenario he'd been instructed by Naomi to plot and direct, suggested, "Let's skedaddle, Captain."

Malcolm offered a hand toward Mrs. Brookings, as though to lead her away. "Do you have things to pack? We'll give you a few minutes, but you must hurry."

An apparently adventurous woman who seemed willing to be buffeted about by the conflicting emotions and passions of these stormy times, Elaine Brookings said, "I place myself totally in your keep, Mr. Erskine. If what you're doing," she added as she moved her remarkable figure toward living quarters, "is ever viewed by authorities as abduction, I'll testify that I left with you willingly."

Erskine grinned and said, "I'm not worried about being apprehended—at least not for *that* crime. But I appreciate the offer."

When she entered the apartment, he thought he heard her mumble a response, "First of several."

Morris, relieved by Mrs. Brookings's temporary absence, gave in to convulsions of silent laughter and giggling. Recovering, he slapped Malcolm on the shoulder and said, "Why you old lothario, you. You made her give you the 'come-on' even when she knows her *son's* in your company."

Malcolm, controlling his impressions and emotions behind a stony countenance, turned to Morris and replied, "I feel like one of the maidens of the Biblical temples, performing for a good cause. I just hope Naomi was right—that this play-acting will make it work." He glanced about the store. "Check out of that window to see whether Eugene's got everyone stationed well."

Through the glass pane Morris looked about and reported, "So far, so good, but I think you should go in there and hurry her along."

Elaine Brookings came out in a trot, her small satchel stuffed. "No need for that," she said. "Not after I realized with whom I'll be riding."

Malcolm was now starting to worry about the lady's possibly stampeding affections. On their way out, he caught Morris and pulled his adjutant to where he could whisper in George's ear, "When this is done, you explain this whole thing to Chad. You hear?"

87

When Elaine, Malcolm, and George walked out of Selby's General Store, young Chad Brookings dismounted and greeted his mother affectionately and unashamedly. They held each other tightly, the young man obviously fighting tears of joy.

A special look of satisfaction came to Elaine, giving Malcolm a moment's pause.

Erskine thought he glimpsed the true makeup of this complicated mother, an example of many frontier women. Physically unprepared for brutal challenges, they saw their dependency magnified over what it might have been in a more developed environment. That dependency demanded a type of sharing that few pioneering husbands had the knack for.

A marriage on the frontier, Malcolm believed, ranked with the storied man-woman relationships of Biblical days. The partnerships of those times were so severely tested by rough circumstances that only extra display of affections gave reasonable assurance of good outcomes.

Elaine Brookings wanted love *expressed* toward her, freely and unashamedly, and that was all. And Malcolm knew before the day was over he must draw from the dour and unexpressive J.T. Brookings a persuasively demonstrative love for his spouse.

"Let's ride," he ordered. Elaine was helped onto Ebony, and Malcolm swung up behind her. George and Chad scurried to their horses.

The return trip would be made delicate by the presence of precious cargo. Erskine would depend primarily on Fontenot, Morris, and Ormsby if challengers confronted them.

From the way she leaned back into him, Erskine knew this woman was starved for touching. It was all he could do to keep a normal excitement under control.

When Elaine, Malcolm, and George walked out, young Chad Brookings greeted his mother.

"Mr. Erskine," she asked over her shoulder as the horses were prodded into a canter, "what if Mr. Selby has found a force to come take me from you?"

"He'll very likely die in the attempt. If my reputation has preceded me in a way capturing *your* attention, Mrs. Brookings, then I'm sure Selby knows better than to tangle with me."

"How many men have you killed, Mr. Erskine?"

"Ma'am, I honestly can't say. I've lost count."

"Oh, dear!" she exclaimed, leaning into him with added pressure, as though swooning over his perceived villainy—or heroism, depending who judged.

"And how did you lose your arm?"

"I, uh—begging your pardon—cut it off myself to escape a trap. It was that or lose my life."

"Oh, *dear!*"

He worried she might faint, and that would make their return more difficult. After a moment, however, she seemed to have recovered. Erskine concentrated on their cautious flight from Missouri.

Cutting west in a plan to reenter Kansas Territory farther south than where they left it, Malcolm expected they could slip back without confrontation.

All he'd wished to impress on the Missourians—that he'd reassembled a formidable Jayhawker unit, that he stood in continuing defiance of the Law and Order Party despite varying prices on his head—were messages he believed were clearly conveyed by this small adventure.

However—

Fontenot dropped back and signalled to Malcolm, pointing ahead with a revolver now drawn. Less than half a mile distant, on a ridge running almost north-south, stood a force of perhaps thirty horsemen. Most held rifles across their chests, and some were now beginning to bring them to their shoulders to take aim.

Eugene raised his revolver skyward as a sign for all in the Jayhawker party to rein up. They spread out and stopped, still beyond the range of the proslavers.

Malcolm believed the confrontation may have been set up by someone with warring experience, for the sun would be shining directly into the eyes of *his* forces. By numbers and position, the enemy held an advantage.

He must now reverse that.

"Chad!" he called. The lad swung his horse around and approached. "Take your mother onto your mount and wait near, in that draw." They made the transfer, and Brookings did as he was told.

To Eugene, Malcolm said, "I'm surprised they want it in the open. I'd have thought they'd try an ambush in woods, though we never gave them enough time to set one up."

Fontenot said, "They must have ridden hard to get ahead of us, though—to be waiting like that, as though they knew all along what our route would be."

Malcolm reached into his saddlebag for a leather case and drew out his telescope, then extended it and positioned it against his right eye. "You're right," he told Eugene. "Those horses are frothing and ready to drop. One is panting so badly he can hardly stay up." He closed the telescope and returned it gently to its case, then his bag.

Malcolm gave a nudge to Ebony with his knee. His horse turned to approach the draw where Chad and Elaine waited. "Ma'am," he asked, "beg pardon, but only you among us might know. Was Mr. Selby ever in the military?"

"Why, yes," she called. "In the Mexican War."

"Do you happen to know what branch?"

"I do believe he said—yes, Artillery."

"Thank you, ma'am." Then, to Chad, "Follow us by some ten-fifteen yards when we move out."

Erskine walked Ebony back to his main group, motioning to Ormsby.

"Lampblack all, including Mrs. Brookings." He leaned forward as Cyrus uncapped a jar and smeared the cheekbones under Malcolm's eyes. The quartermaster did his own, then proceeded to decorate the entire band similarly, including their guest.

Now Erskine pointed to the center of the silhouetted line that awaited them.

"A *wedge!*" he shouted to all, starting Ebony forward.

Drawing a pistol, he took his right foot from its stirrup and swung his rear from the saddle, letting his hook encircle the pommel. He sank low to the left side, showing the others he expected them to ride Indian fashion for best concealment and handgun attack against the riflemen ahead.

The Jayhawkers now cantered evenly, then pushed gradually until at hard gallop.

The enemy line ahead held. All there raised rifles to take aim.

Selby had apparently undertaken to lead this mission with none of the experience of horsemanship it required, Malcolm decided. Placing his men where the sun would be in the Kansans' eyes was either Selby's luck or possibly planned, but it would not be enough.

Reliance on vintage rifles—and especially on horses too weary for pursuit—would be Lathan Selby's undoing.

Malcolm glanced back and noticed all were in perfect wedge formation, with Chad and Elaine conventionally astride and bending forward low, trailing as instructed.

He glanced ahead again—less bothered by the sun than he might otherwise have been, owing to the lampblack's absorption of the strong light.

When they were within a hundred yards, he saw about eight or more of the rifles discharging, the puffs being caught in the late winter chill like small jets of steam.

Pellets whizzed around them, most of them striking the ground, and then the sound greeted their ears. Ellerby looked as though he'd been knicked on the leg, but he continued his pace.

There would be no time for Selby's men to take aim for another volley. The Jayhawkers had accelerated to a point where they could now begin to pick off Missourians with their revolvers.

Erskine fired the first shots and brought two down. The line ahead was faltering fast. As he rode through and the others in his band followed while firing, he saw as many as five more of the enemy fall. George Morris's aim was especially deadly.

Several Missourians turned and tried to escape. Two of their horses reared, balking at the pressure to which they'd been put with little rest, very likely no water.

Another four men went down from shots by the Jayhawkers, who'd now cleared the line and were being followed safely by the Brookingses.

Malcolm straightened in his saddle and pointed ahead with his pistol, indicating they should continue west toward Kansas rapid-paced.

Though he'd have preferred to return and stand in battle against the remainder, particularly as he'd hoped to confront Selby personally, Erskine knew Elaine's presence made his band vulnerable.

He considered himself lucky to observe only one wound among his men, and that evidently not a serious one. They continued the hard ride another mile before he ordered them to pull up.

During the horses' rest period—and Ormsby's quick attention to Ben Ellerby's slight wound—Malcolm glanced back occasionally and saw no remaining sign of the enemy. The Missourians had evidently gathered their wounded and dead and gone off.

Dismounting, he called to Mrs. Brookings. "I couldn't tell which one was Mr. Selby."

She looked strangely exciting to him with the lampblack smeared under her purplish eyes. She stood alongside Chad, who was wiping his horse's neck with a cloth.

"He was the second one to go down," she said. "You killed him." Erskine nodded acknowledgement.

"You know," she added, now walking and leading him a slight distance from Chad in continued conversation, "in olden times, a knight doing that would have—won the lady."

Elaine Brookings lifted her chin oddly and asked, looking at Malcolm sideways, "You do *want* the lady you've won, don't you?"

"Yes," Malcolm replied, a dry lump forming in his throat from this necessary performance. "Yes, of course I do."

88

Their return ride into Kansas grew more leisurely. Danger from Missouri partisans and Law and Order zealots was behind them. They crossed the border on the eastern approach to a new settlement of claim-takers—a mixture of farmers, merchants, and professional men organizing a town called Aubry.

By that name choice, Malcolm surmised, these new neighbors south of the shrinking Black Bob reservation might be an interesting lot. Aubry had been "Skimmer of the Plains"—Francis X. Aubry—who'd set records for riding the length of the Santa Fe Trail by establishing stations to change horses frequently.

Malcolm maintained a lively conversation with Elaine Brookings, whom he found to be a well-read woman, and with George Morris.

Eugene Fontenot, leading, turned and halted the group while it was still about a quarter-mile from Aubry. Cyrus Ormsby moved closer to the injured Ben Ellerby and informed the others that the young man's wound was worse than first believed. It had reopened, was bleeding copiously, and there seemed danger of infection.

Malcolm assessed the situation as well as their position.

"Eugene, you lead a group to Pleasant Valley, but go through Black Bob's camp. It can't be over three miles north and then west along the Blue. Let the Chief's people minister to Ben's wound. I'll continue to Lawrence with George, Chad, O'Dell, and Pace. We'll deliver Mrs. Brookings safely."

Ellerby surrendered his horse for Elaine's use and was helped astride Ormsby's. Fontenot's group—Anderton, Frederick, Blake, and Ormsby riding with Ellerby—peeled north for Black Bob's place without delay.

"That poor boy," Elaine said. "He was wounded in my behalf."

"Not entirely," Malcolm said. "It's all in the Free State cause."

George turned abruptly in his saddle at the precise moment Mrs. Brookings erupted in a show of outrage.

"You *beast,*" she shouted, taking Erskine by surprise. "You say *all* in the Free State cause? How *dare* you make me and my life a pawn in this absurd war."

It was clear to Malcolm his words had outrun his caution.

George had apparently recognized the error instantly. Elaine was seething with understandable resentment. Morris dropped back and sought to calm Elaine's hostility, but she wouldn't be put off.

"I'll stop ahead—in that place," she said, indicating the Aubry village, "and ride no farther."

Malcolm shook his head. "I'm honor-bound to return you home. It's a promise I made your son."

Elaine glanced around at Chad, who was listening uncomprehendingly to the exchange and was evidently worried again that his parents would never be reconciled. She then turned to Erskine and asked, "Can we talk? Somewhere indoors, alone?"

Malcolm surveyed the place and noticed a crude sign identifying an inn. He nodded, suggesting they rub the remaining lampblack from their faces.

When the Aubry settlers became aware of the identity of their principal caller, they hovered in ways slightly embarrassing to Erskine.

The Jayhawker group entered a saloon—little more than a long plank atop a few barrels and possibly a dozen bottles of whiskey about. Malcolm asked permission to use what seemed a semi-private area off to one side. There he followed Elaine and they sat, the interior warmth of the place now helping to ease the new chill in their acquaintanceship.

At George's instruction, the barkeep brought them each a whiskey.

Andrew Pace appeared to understand it was his role to keep young Chad and Henry O'Dell occupied and out of the way.

As Elaine sipped and after Erskine gulped, he indicated she should speak first.

"Mr. Erskine—Malcolm—we're both false. You're pretending some infatuation for me. Mr. Morris, whom I know to have been a stage performer, is coaching you. Correct?"

Erskine nodded, holding up his glass as a sign for George to have it refilled—the sooner the better.

"Will you please tell me why?" she asked.

"To give your husband, J.T., a chance to show jealousy that will impress you and Chad. To have me provoke him into a fight, which I plan to lose." Malcolm thought to add, "My wife suggested it, all facts that were known to us being considered."

Elaine smiled and put her fingertips to her forehead, closing her eyes. When she looked up, she said, "That's a lot of trouble for anyone to go to, even in the Free State cause."

"Yes, ma'am," Malcolm agreed, accepting a fresh drink from George, who retreated to the main part of the saloon again. "It is, but my wife's a very intelligent woman and I'll go along with her plan, now urging your cooperation as well."

Mrs. Brookings took a larger sip than before, in fact finishing what was in her glass. She put her hand to her bosom, as though feeling it go down.

"It's all unnecessary," she said. "J.T. isn't an unfeeling clod, as you may have come to believe—obviously from Chad's story about my leaving. He's a very sensitive man. Not so demonstrative as I'd prefer, but—not lacking altogether, if you know what I mean."

Erskine was surprised. "I don't understand. You mean Chad *lied* about the way it was when Selby was in your home?"

Elaine shook her head impatiently. "He didn't lie. He told it only as *he* understood it. He's the youngest of your band. A child, really. There are—subtleties of adult relationships he has no way of understanding yet."

"You're speaking in areas," Malcolm said, "that defy *my* understanding. So will you please explain what we're all doing here? And what may be ahead for us in Lawrence?"

"It's true," she said, "that Lathan Selby romanced and kissed me, as Chad has no doubt told you, and that we were discovered by my husband, J.T." She halted, indicating she would like more whiskey.

"Go on," Erskine encouraged her, summoning George wordlessly.

Elaine waited until her glass had been refilled, then she sat silent half a moment. Suddenly, after taking a generous swig, she blurted—

"It is *not* J.T.'s finding me in Lathan's arms that primarily drove us to separate. It was mostly *Chad's* finding me that way."

Malcolm sat dumb, as though he hadn't heard correctly. Shortly it dawned on him what she was implying. He leaned toward her and searched her eyes. *"Chad?"* he asked, nearly choking on the revelation and the name.

Elaine nodded. "He has for some time confused his relationship with me, ever since my daughter got married and left home. I'm confident he and his sister were, well— You know how it is, in some families isolated on the frontier, so—"

Malcolm broke in. "You needn't go on with that," he said. "Yes, I know how it might be. Or is, I mean. With some." Intended reassurance was turning into personal discomfort on this topic.

"Anyway," she continued, "I'd talked the situation over with J.T., who was at a loss what to do. He simply couldn't bring himself to discuss any of it with Chad, though he said he would. We also talked of my going away for a spell, believing *that* might give my son a feeling of independence. You see, I found my personality changing over the problem. I became flirtatious toward men friends, incurring not only Chad's anger—which I didn't intend—but J.T.'s impatience over the whole matter."

"Then," Malcolm said, "your husband's calm acceptance that day wasn't because he lacked feeling? It was because he was resigned to separating you—somehow—from Chad?"

"That's a fair approximation. And all this flirtatious show by me is habit I acquired when I tried demonstrating, indirectly to

Chad, that adult life is full of complicated man-woman feelings, that it *isn't* for children—"

"And yet," Erskine broke in, "he's no longer a child."

"For pity's sake, Malcolm, since he's in your keep now, find him a woman who will teach him uninhibitedly, free of taboos, and make a man of him, will you? Get his mind off me—his *mother.* And help him stop grieving over the departure of his sister. He's a boy—a young man—who needs to express his love for a *young* woman."

Malcolm interrupted again. "An expression of emotion you say your husband, J.T., has no trouble with."

Elaine searched in a pocket of her dress and pulled out a letter. "I absolutely guarantee," she said, handing it to him, "that there's not a shred of difficulty about that between J.T. and me. This is a letter he wrote in response to one from me. Remember, I oversaw Harrisonville postal deliveries for a time, so there was no way Lathan Selby could keep mail from me. I was there half-captive, but half-willingly in escape from Chad." She paused to glance around and wrinkled her nose at the smell of the place, then went on—

"I didn't know Chad had left home and gotten into trouble until J.T. wrote. My original letter to my husband was assurance that while I stayed with Selby, there was *no* physical contact between me and that man. None since that single, solitary kiss that fateful day. And much to Selby's frustration, I might add. I've been faithful—well, reasonably faithful—to my husband twenty years, Mr. Erskine—Malcolm. My flirtatiousness and running off were a foolish pose, a choice of the moment. I'm the one acting, not you."

Malcolm sat straight, lifted what was left in his glass to gaze at it, then finished it off. She handed him what remained in hers. He accepted it gratefully and finished that, too, giving her letter back and summoning George Morris.

"I don't wish to read it," he said to her simply. "It's an altogether dangerous game you've played, Mrs. Brookings."

To Morris, Erskine directed, "You go back to Pleasant Valley with Chad and Pace. Let O'Dell accompany me to the Brookings farm. Tell Naomi we'll stay there tonight and will be home tomorrow. Meanwhile, help Cyrus see that Ellerby is being given whatever treatment by the Shawnees he might need."

George looked perplexed. "Captain, what do I tell Chad?"

"Tell him his 'Maw' and 'Paw' are getting back together again," Malcolm said. "Tell him there'll be no problem between them again, and he has his mother's and my word on it. And tell Naomi I'll explain tomorrow—that we've been outfoxed by secrets of life even *she* failed to consider."

89

In their approach to Lawrence, Elaine Brookings called out and pointed west to show the direction to her homestead. Malcolm slowed Ebony to drop back beside her and Henry O'Dell.

"From your description of J.T.," Malcolm said, "I'm eager to meet him. He sounds like a very solid man."

"He is that," she said. "And I thank you for returning me here. I could never have done this on my own, given the emotions not only on this side of the border but those inspired by the pathetic Mr. Selby, my—well, what do I call him? Captor?"

"No," Erskine said, laughing softly. "I'd call him an unwitting *captive* of a very handsome woman."

Elaine joined in enjoyment of irony that had done harsh justice to the late Lathan Selby.

They soon arrived at the Brookings farm, where J.T. Brookings loudly *"Whoad"* his mule, let the plow strap fall from his shoulders, and ran to greet Elaine.

J.T. was anything but an insensitive man, Malcolm observed with satisfaction. Taking his wife into his arms—actually pulling her into them as she leaned from Ben Ellerby's horse—the farmer wept through his earth-caked features just as freely as happiness allowed.

Shortly, Elaine said to all, "Let me see what may be in the pantry and the smokehouse to make you all a proper meal. J.T., this is Captain Malcolm Erskine, the famous Jayhawker. And this is one of his men, Henry O'Dell. You know, the bootmaker's boy from up at Wyandotte. Show Henry where to take the horses, please, as well as your mule. It's getting onto sundown and I see you've been working extra hard, so no more today. We have guests."

Malcolm had dismounted and was now shaking hands with a slightly embarrassed J.T. Brookings, who wiped his face with the back of his hand and his sleeve, only worsening his appearance.

"I thank you, Captain," he said. "I truly do thank you. Both of you." O'Dell nodded with a grin, unhitched the mule, and taking all lines led the horses and mule toward the barn.

"How is my son Chad?"

"In the best of health. In the best of spirits. He'll make a good soldier for the Free State—and a good man."

"A man," J.T. repeated. "I still think of him as a boy."

Erskine recalled his conversation in Aubry with Elaine and decided not to volunteer to J.T. that he knew about Chad's problem. After all, this man was at a loss how to handle it, according to Elaine, and it was probably behind them anyway.

That evening, after dinner, they enjoyed the warmth of a late winter's fire and talked of the Free State Party's efforts to extricate the Territory from the rule of the bogus legislature at Lecompton.

"I heard down Lawrence way," J.T. said while lighting a pipe, then offering Malcolm the lighted taper to ignite his, "that Buchanan will appoint a new Territorial governor, name of Robert J. Walker."

"Do you know anything about him? Where he's from?"

"Only that he's fair-minded and from Mississippi."

"Well, then," Malcolm said with an unconcealed sneer, "I'll bet he's a Democrat."

"Oh, yes. Of that you can be certain," J.T. agreed. "Buchanan's not going to give us anyone Senator Douglas wouldn't approve of."

"When does this—this Walker get here, do you suppose?"

"Be at least a month," J.T. said. "You know how slow and messed-up things can be in Washington—politicians blowing like leaves this way and that. One fails at the job here, next one is in no blamed hurry to descend into the hell of Kansas Territory."

Erskine found himself enjoying J.T. Brookings's dry humor. He was impressed also with the closeness between Elaine and J.T.—or was that only possible because of Chad's absence?

After they retired, Malcolm thought he heard conversation from J.T.'s and Elaine's bedroom, then realized their separation had brought a need for catching up. From Elaine's audible giggling and other sounds, rhythmic ones, it was evident the couple was enjoying a happy reunion.

Later he was awakened with a hand pushing against his bare shoulder. It was Elaine, seated on the edge of the bed and visible only in the moonlight streaming through the window.

"I should have heard you coming in," Erskine whispered. "I'm either getting deaf or I'm slipping."

"You're just tired. You've had a long day, doing your good work—in the Free State cause or otherwise."

"If you're here for me to make love to you, Elaine, I won't."

"I know that, Malcolm. I have J.T. and he's all I want. Anyway, after tonight I'll quit using the word 'adequate' in my mind to describe him and his affection, replacing it with 'superior'."

"Congratulations."

"I came in only to thank you."

"My pleasure, ma'am."

Elaine Brookings leaned forward and placed her mouth over Malcolm's, kissing him so passionately he fell back onto his pillow while she clung to him and ran her hands over his body.

When she was finished and sat up, Malcolm was out of breath and fully aroused. He fought with himself against resuming their embrace and carrying the situation to natural fulfillment. He ached for some release.

He said, "If you know I won't make love to you—even though tempted, as you could tell—then why did you do that?"

Elaine glanced toward the window. The moonlight caught her face and glinted off her yellow hair, which now hung across her shoulders loosely. The light revealed delightful features of her upper body through her thin nightdress. "Two reasons," she said. "First, that was a thank-you. Second, I wanted you to be the last man other than J.T. I'll ever kiss like that. Now I'm closing the door on my flirtatious ways."

"Your husband is a lucky fellow. And spent for tonight, I suppose, while I'm now in a miserable state."

"I'm sorry. I wasn't thinking clearly." She rose and turned to leave. "I'll set out biscuits and things for you and the big lad. For my sake, go before we're up."

"The sight of me is that tempting?"

"I want to be there for J.T. when he wakes up, if you know what I mean. So, Captain Jayhawker, thank you and goodbye. Please take good care of my son."

90

The orders Malcolm had given for treating Ben Ellerby proved beneficial in more ways than one.

When Fontenot had led part of the Jayhawker band to Black Bob's camp, they stumbled into an informal reception for Dr. Simeon Bell. He was a physician studying the area and considering establishing a practice among settlers. Bell had been swapping stories with Black Bob's medicine men and women when Eugene's group rode in.

Immediately the doctor ministered to Ben's leg, which proved to have retained a chunk of the rifle ball that had been thought only to have grazed the flesh.

Because a tendon was involved in the injury, the physician prescribed a period of rest. For that a place was assigned in the underground barracks of the Pleasant Valley complex, where Lani-Wawewa divided her time assisting Naomi with baby Noah and nursing Ben.

Young Ellerby's recovery in Lani's care had mixed consequences, for Johnny Kesibwi came to visit and observed the activity of his fiancée. The Shawnee courier was less than enthusiastic about the arrangement.

Malcolm knew Kesibwi to be fickle and a polygamist, so after a short time he wasn't surprised to learn the man was shrugging off his commitment to make Lani his bride.

The news Kesibwi brought Malcolm was of greater interest to the Jayhawker commander than the Indian's domestic affairs. C.C. Catron was determined to drive Erskine from Oxford Township, Johnny reported. He added that he had no idea how the man planned to accomplish that.

Catron was having difficulty attracting proslaver settlers to his Oxford community. Erskine's presence nearby was apparently a hindrance.

All Johnny Kesibwi could be certain about in detail, though, was that Catron had been to the Shawnee Methodist Mission to check papers filed there covering Malcolm's title to the Pleasant Valley property.

Somehow Catron had also come upon a complete list of the men in Erskine's Jayhawker group and had made inquiries about their backgrounds.

"That's it?" Malcolm asked.

Kesibwi nodded.

"Then we have nothing to fear from C.C. Catron."

Johnny shook his head. "I wouldn't be too sure of that. He has—resources. And he'll never forgive his being shot when he came here to suggest you turn yourself in to the authorities."

Malcolm slapped the Shawnee's back in a friendly manner several times, partly to let Johnny know he appreciated the concern, partly to give a sign the conversation was finished and the courier ought to be on his way again.

Later, consulting with Naomi and with George Morris, Malcolm received agreement that they would all work on installing a section of milled wood flooring and hold a barn dance. They would invite friendly settlers from Aubry, Spring Hill, and Olathe—people sympathetic to the Free State cause of abolition That way the young men in the Jayhawker band would have a chance for socializing that it was clear they needed acutely. A few were expressing plans to settle down to trades and start families after the border fighting was done—whenever and *if* ever that might be.

There was an undercurrent of hope that much of the outcome of border conflict would rely on actions of Governor Robert J. Walker. If Walker was truly a fair man, as it was being rumored he was, he would listen to reason and end illegal balloting by Missourians in Territorial elections.

But if Walker couldn't stop the illegal voting and the raids on Kansas settlers, Erskine said without hesitation to others, "*I* will."

The change in political leadership would be the backdrop—and likely the main topic of talk—during the social and dance scheduled in the Erskines' barn on a Saturday night in mid-April.

Rotating watches would provide security, each man serving only an hour so that he could enjoy the social affair.

James Butler Hickok had arranged for musicians from Monticello. He promised Malcolm to be present if his schedule allowed.

Daniel Goodman sent regrets he could not come with Audrey, for she was now entering her seventh month of pregnancy and found travel from Paola uncomfortable, if not impossible.

Eugene Fontenot planned to meet Jane-Ellen O'Brien at the border and accompany her the rest of the way to Pleasant Valley. The price on his head was now too high for him to risk entering Missouri alone.

Abe and Rose Milford sent word they were uncertain about coming from Douglas County but would try.

* * * * *

Hearing a knock at his front door, Malcolm admitted a troubled-looking Cyrus Ormsby. When they seated themselves in the parlor, where Malcolm had been cleaning revolvers, Cyrus found it impossible to stay in that position. He got up to walk about.

"Cyrus, what's making you pace around so?"

Ormsby stopped suddenly. Then he broke into a grin and a loud laugh, a trickle of tobacco juice spilling from the corner of his mouth as he seemed to lose control.

Malcolm said, shaking his head, "Cyrus, you're a mystery to me."

"Sorry, Captain," Ormsby said, calming now. "Matter of fact the wording of your question was a coincidence. It's Pace — Andrew — that I came to talk with you about."

"What about him?"

"You recall what it was he went to jail for."

"Selling rifles to the Delawares illegally. But he paid them back and was cleared of charges on every level."

"Not according to Black Bob."

"What?" Malcolm shot to his feet, throwing an oily rag to the wood floor in quick anger.

Orsmby winced, then continued. "This ain't easy for me to tell it, Captain, but the Chief says the part about paying back is still up in the air. The Federal authorities won't sign off on Pace until the Delawares are satisfied."

"Call him in here," Erskine directed.

After a few minutes, Malcolm having resumed his gun-cleaning chores, Pace arrived with Ormsby . The questioning was rapid and direct, and Erskine saw the hostility rising in Andrew from these new suspicions.

In a moment Pace produced a receipt for the return of money originally paid for the rifles. The paper was signed in the name of the Chief of the Delaware nation on the reserve near Leavenworth.

"Why hasn't this been reported to Federal authorities?" Malcolm asked Pace. "They're now refusing to accept the legitimacy of your pardon."

Pace shrugged, shifting his weight from one foot to the other. "I have no idea," he said, shaking his head. "Honest, I don't."

Lani-Wawewa happened through the parlor, carrying Noah. Erskine stopped her momentarily and asked her to look closely at the receipt signature. A literate Chippewa, she'd lived not far from the Delaware reservation and may have seen tribal documents from there.

Lani looked, then shrugged. "I can't say. It certainly looks authentic, but I can't say for sure that it is."

Malcolm nodded and dismissed her, folding the paper and returning it to Pace, who showed obvious displeasure over being doubted.

"It's right that I should know of this," Erskine said. "Everything will be done to clear you, Andrew, if facts show you're deserving. I promise it."

Pace softened on hearing that, stuck out his hand, and Malcolm took it. Ormsby and Pace left.

*****

Late afternoon on the Saturday of the dance, guests and musicians began to gather. Excitement in Erskine's Jayhawker camp soon increased to hoedown rhythm. Fiddlers and a banjo player from Monticello practiced in front of the barn, causing several persons to rehearse their jigging. Young men from Spring Hill showed off cowboy clog steps they'd picked up during a two-day bull auction in Kansas City.

Settlers from Olathe arrived with ripening daughters in tow, much to the delight of Erskine's soldiers. Lani-Wawewa eyed the competition and went to her room to change into native dress and apply makeup. When she emerged to appreciative gasps, she seemed secure in knowing she would be Ben Ellerby's dance partner for the evening, assuming his leg would hold up. To his apparent delight, she clung to him wherever he moved.

The troops except for Ben took watch turns in threes, one each posted at the east, northwest, and southwest for an hour's duration, then rotating with other trios.

As evening drew near, Hickok arrived and sent a ripple through the group over his size, demeanor, and reputation as General Lane's former bodyguard and Monticello lawman.

Erskine continued to hope he would see Abe and Rose, but he knew better than to expect them with any certainty during these troubled times.

Eugene rode in with Jane-Ellen, who greeted all raucously and with apparent joy, though Malcolm knew what her heart held. And he knew Naomi suspected the truth of the never-ending torch-carrying as well.

No announcement was necessary to start festivities or enjoyment of refreshments in the barn. After sundown the music and general conviviality attracted all spontaneously into the specially constructed dance hall.

The barn interior was generously lighted. Musicians perched on a platform with a caller for square and round dances. Cowboy high-stepping predominated. Girls from the south Johnson County settlements took to the new steps with remarkable spirit and some abandon. A few seemed ready to swoon from attention by the dashing Jayhawker soldiers, who were newly scrubbed and on their best behavior.

There was no ceremonious grand entrance by host and hostess. Malcolm and his lady moved easily among the guests. Naomi carried three-month-old Noah and would alternate his care with Lani so that she could dance with her husband.

After perhaps half an hour, the side door burst open and a loud command cut through the music. *"Reach for the rafters, everyone!"* a voice barked.

Erskine recognized Sam Jones, C.C. Catron, and One-Eyed Emmett Anderson Jones. Several more guns-drawn Bushwhackers filed into the barn, lifting holstered revolvers from the men of Malcolm's Jayhawker band.

Sam Jones spoke just as Fontenot rushed to Malcolm's side in an apparent effort to protect his commander. "Don't make any funny moves, Frenchie. Anyway, we ain't here for you – *this* time."

Sam Jones drew out a rolled sheet of paper and read from it.

"In the name and authority of the government of the United States of America, Samuel Jones as deputized agent at my order, I hereby declare that one Malcolm Erskine of the Commonwealth of Massachusetts is to be placed under arrest for illegal claim-taking in the Territory of Kansas. He is further to be held in custody under Territorial law by said-same deputy agent Jones on a charge of flight to avoid prosecution for murder. I hereby set my sign and seal, Samuel D. LeCompte, Chief Justice, Kansas Territory."

As Jones's and Catron's men stepped forward to effect the arrest, Erskine whispered quickly to Fontenot. "Which way did they ride in?"

Eugene said, "From northwest, I am certain."

"Whose watch?"

"Andrew Pace."

91

In front of his guests, the Bushwhackers tore open Erskine's shirtsleeve and stripped him of his hook. They bound him, hand to knees, before carrying him outside and placing him in a buckboard. They drove him to Oxford. There he awaited dawn, sitting still tied, in the stall of a small horse barn.

When day broke, Catron's men sat Malcolm in another open wagon for a long drive that snaked back and forth across the border. He endured silently the shouted abuse first of Oxford settlers and then of other proslavers, all the way from Little Santa Fe through Dallas and then Westport, clear to the Shawnee Methodist Mission.

There his captors placed him in a jail cell. They asked whether he had any legitimate request before being left alone for only routine feeding and collection of his slop pail.

"Yes, I do," Malcolm said to Sam Jones, deciding upon irony because he couldn't think of any reasoning point that the man would understand. "Change places with me. You're the lawbreaker here, not me. You and that hypocritical superintendent of this place, the holy man, Johnson. My legitimate request is you lock yourselves in here for violation of the United States Constitution. But first hand me my hook and let me out."

Jones stood staring at Erskine, obviously not intending a response to that. The bogus lawman's angry breathing quickened, flaring the hairs of his reddish-brown mustache. He stood flush-faced for some time, measuring his prisoner with flinty eyes that spoke a fierce hatred. Finally, he said, "Nigger, when I get through with you, you'll be chopped in a thousand pieces. You'll be little more than a bad nightmare everyone wants to forget."

With a final gesture, Jones cut Malcolm's bonds to let him walk about the cell. A deputy held the Jayhawker's hook, which he hung where Malcolm could see it on a wall opposite the cell.

They shut the cell door with a loud *clank* and padlocked it.

Erskine looked about. His "bed" consisted of a narrow plank supported by two rocks. Under it was a can he was expected to use for eliminating. Otherwise nothing else occupied the cell—nothing but a rat he noticed, staring at him from a corner.

Cockroaches, too, were everywhere—floor, walls, ceiling. Ignoring the intrusion now, the rat went back to feasting on them noisily.

Malcolm replayed in his mind the night's events—

I thought Naomi might collapse in fright. She stood like a rock, and Lani and Ben got the baby safely to the house.

They never found access to underground barracks and tunnels, for all their probing. Must have figured my "cowhands" sleep in the hayloft.

"I don't believe it for a minute," Malcolm had heard C.C. Catron mutter. "Something more's going on here."

Sam Jones feared Hickok's being there could bring the whole Free State force down on them, so he was eager to get the hell out. They got what they wanted – me.

Erskine had watched barn dance guests released to ride home, each wagon party with a torch—and offers of Law and Order escort, which they declined.

When the Bushwhackers were preparing to take Malcolm away, two Missourians had reentered the barn at a run and whispered excitedly to Sam Jones, who'd then turned to Erskine. "Don't know how you managed it," he'd said, "but I thank you for shortening my payroll by one turncoat."

Fontenot had then leaned to Malcolm to whisper, "I ordered Cyrus to finish Pace with a knife."

Malcolm had given an approving nod.

Erskine had also noticed that while the men and ladies seemed calm, there was an exception—Henry O'Dell. The hulking and dull-witted youth from Wyandotte shifted around more than usual.

From snatches of conversation by his captors during the nighttime and early morning rides to Oxford and then the Mission,

Erskine was able to piece together just how Jones and Catron had concluded he was, supposedly, an illegal claim-taker.

They'd pored through papers here at the Mission regarding the Pleasant Valley claim and inherited property. Their key finding was his marriage to Sylvia. Marriage between a Negro and an Indian could be considered miscegenation—race mixing—against laws anywhere, regardless of common practice.

That placed Sylvia's bequest in jeopardy. Malcolm's deed was contestable.

Erskine listened to the rat scurry about. To weigh whatever else they might try him for, he attempted to replay in his mind every killing he'd ever been involved in. When he thought he'd remembered them all, a snatch of memory opened yet another, and there were still more to count.

No way of knowing accurately, but summing all events, he must have been directly involved in the deaths of more than sixty men—maybe as many as a hundred.

Erskine reached into his pocket and discovered his tobacco and cigarette papers, along with a few matches. Without his hook it would be difficult to carry out a successful rolling. By using the slimy bars of the cell for leverage, he might engineer it.

He also looked about to determine whether matches might be of any use toward escape, but there was nothing to ignite, no useful purpose to be served by doing so. He lit the poorly made cigarette and welcomed the chance to inhale tobacco smoke. The effect was sometimes exhilarating, at other times annoying. For now, it was a luxurious relief he could enjoy for a few moments as he tried to plan escape.

Later, pacing in his cell, his tobacco gone and no clear indication how to free himself from this filthy place, Malcolm felt his control slipping.

From time to time he glanced at his hook, which he missed sorely. Without the use of it as a second hand, he felt naked. His torn sleeve hung uselessly at his left side.

That his cell was to be served so infrequently—only for setting food on a box just outside the bars and occasionally for someone's picking up slop—was a limitation against effective plans.

Moreover, he knew so little about the layout of the Mission that he lacked means for useful planning—about what to do next even if he *could* overcome a guard and force his way out. And he realized he might not be allowed visitors.

Malcolm decided to simply wait for those who loved him and cared about him to make their move.

92

Malcolm heard loud conversation beyond the small area that served as a jail, somewhere in the basement of the Mission's trade school. A lively argument. Though he couldn't hear the words, he figured it was about him.

He'd been in this cell two days, fed only a strange gruel made of corn as well as stale bread and water. He slept curled on the plank, where it was all he could do to keep from falling to the filthy floor.

A Shawnee youth had been picked to serve him—to bring him food and carry off his slop can. Evidently that had been arranged in the belief that if Erskine were to try to take anyone hostage to force escape, he wouldn't do that to an innocent Indian boy.

The argument in the far part of the building resumed. Now Malcolm could hear a woman's voice, and his heart leapt. It was *Naomi.*

Apparently there was disagreement whether she could be admitted as a visitor.

He pressed his face against the cell bars, ignoring the slimy touch, the grime and grease that covered everything.

At last doors began opening and closing. Footsteps approached. An older, broad-faced Shawnee caretaker accompanied Naomi, admitting her to the jail area and then the stinking cell. The man turned and exited the other door, closing it and observing them through a small opening.

Immediately Naomi put a handkerchief to her mouth and nostrils, obviously fighting the urge to throw up over the putrid conditions.

The Indian moved off. Naomi said through the 'kerchief, "Malcolm, I'm going to get you out of this place. I can't bear that you're here, much less what they plan to do with you."

"What have you heard?"

"The bogus legislature has convened a panel which returned fourteen indictments against you for murder, aside from other charges."

"Only fourteen?"

"Listen carefully, Malcolm. I'm on my way to Kansas City. Henry O'Dell and George Morris are with me in a wagon. We plan to purchase disguises, false wigs, beards, face paint—anything that will change the appearance of your men."

Erskine raised his eyebrows over yet another grand plan by Naomi. He recalled parts of her plans backfired.

"As soon as they're prepared," she said, "in another day or two, they'll fan out through selected areas along the border, particularly at Watts Mill. There they'll promote the notion that you should be taken from here and lynched."

"What?"

"You heard correctly, Malcolm. A lynching party will get you out of here."

"That's one hell of a gamble everybody's taking with my *neck,* isn't it?" He touched his throat, as though already feeling a rope.

"It's the only way a large enough force can be assembled to pull you out of here. We expect the authorities here would be happy to save the time and expense of a trial—by having you taken away to be killed."

Naomi paused. Seeming near fainting from the stink, she pressed on regardless.

"Your arraignment on charges is scheduled Monday. Once you're arraigned, they might move you to a stronger jail, possibly even to Missouri. So, be prepared that in a few days, either Friday or Saturday night, you'll see from your cell window—"

The sound of reapproaching footsteps reached them. Naomi's time with Malcolm was ending.

"—you'll see torches and hear shouting and abuse against you. I guarantee, husband, the majority of that force will consist of your friends, and they will overcome the rest."

"Why Watts Mill? You said my men will agitate especially there."

"Remember, many of Sylvia's slayers were from around there, and you destroyed them all. Their kinfolks haven't forgotten."

The door to the jail area opened. The Shawnee caretaker indicated they should say their goodbyes. Malcolm gestured that Naomi should not come near. "I'm too dirty," he said.

She leaned to him anyway, puckering to kiss the cleanest part of his face that she could reach, a bit to the side of his nose. "I love you," she whispered, "and I will to my dying day, and beyond—if there *is* anything beyond."

"And I you," Erskine responded, "the same. Forever."

* * * * *

After she left, Malcolm regretted they hadn't discussed Noah. Yet, if there was any problem involving the baby, she wouldn't have held that back. In the care of Lani and the others at Pleasant Valley, the boy was in good hands.

"This is all for Noah," Malcolm said aloud, "and what I did was right. I'll destroy anyone who'd enslave my son for his Negro blood. His blood is as good as any person's, and no different from the white blood in him."

He raised his voice as loudly as he was able. *"Everyone—black, red, or white—must be treated equally! With dignity! In freedom! You hear me, Johnson!?"*

Malcolm imagined the Mission director could hear him. He saw in his mind's eye Johnson sitting somewhere in an office, perhaps just upstairs from the jail cell, thinking about Erskine's words.

Movement again in another part of the basement. Footsteps. With a bang the heavy-faced Shawnee caretaker unlocked and swung open the jail area door to lean in. He showed agitation.

"Brother Thomas," said the Indian, "says it's *goddam prayer time* upstairs! He said to tell you, *no fucking speeches!"* The Shawnee left, banging the door shut.

Malcolm laughed, delighted at the realization—Johnson had heard.

93

On Saturday evening Malcolm heard a bell toll six o'clock. He raised his face to the small window of his cell.

The Mission complex was strangely quiet. Whoever had sounded the evening bell would possibly be leaving the chapel and strolling toward the mess hall for supper.

But on this evening Malcolm saw the same Shawnee youth who brought him his "meals" leave the main trade school building and walk, head down, straight west—away from the Mission property.

Erskine got the eerie feeling the entire place was being abandoned—that word must have reached Johnson and others of the Mission staff about a mob coming for their only prisoner, to settle accounts outside the law.

It seemed the way was being smoothed for the lynching party's success.

Has Johnson spread the word there'll be no resistance?

Malcolm strained to listen at the window for the approach of any large group of people. He heard only a mockingbird, and farther off a cardinal. He moved from the barred window and sat to think it out.

Erskine considered praying, then rejected the notion with a mumbled comment, "God helps those who help themselves."

Now he wondered whether Johnson had ordered locks opened to reach him more easily and without damage to the Mission trade school.

Malcolm stood and grabbed the board he used for his bed. Straining from the effort of doing this one-handed, using his stump for some leverage, he extended the plank through the bars to press an end against the other door.

It *moved.*

The key to his cell must be hanging somewhere out there—conspicuously, so those coming could get to him quickly.

The only comfort Malcolm drew from this was knowing Naomi had started it all, that his disguised rescuers would be dominating the "lynch" mob.

Still, safest not to wait. Now that the door to the small jail area was unlocked, could there possibly be a way to—?

Malcolm rammed the board into the door, and it swung back with a *whap.* The light was so bad beyond, he could see little, yet—

Something by the door jamb glinted. Could that be the *cell key?*

Erskine needed his hook. Quickly he drew the board back into the cell. He started it out between the bars in another direction.

From having little else to look at for nearly a week and now in the dimming light, he knew precisely where his hook had been hung. He knew how it leaned from the shoulder strap tossed over a nail.

If his memory could translate into precise aim and movement—and disregarding that the board was an awkward instrument—he might draw a splintered end of the plank under the shoulder strap and *lift it* from the nail.

A bit to the left, now up.

There!

As precarious a perch as it now had, his hook hung from the end of the board. He could draw it toward him, provided he was extremely careful.

Slowly, quarter-inch by quarter-inch, he drew the board back into the cell, feeling all the while the suspended weight of the metal and leather of his hook assembly, his good left "arm."

When Malcolm finally had the hook in his hand, he became weepy from relief, feeling whole again.

At that instant he heard a voice calling him from outside the building.

"Hey, *nigger.* I won't wait for the party you and your gang arranged. I'm coming after you *now.*"

Malcolm dropped the board and hook and rushed to the cell window. He saw a form approaching on the same path taken in the other direction by the Indian boy.

One-Eyed Emmett had jumped the gun on the "lynch" mob. Somehow Emmett knew it was actually to be Malcolm's rescue party.

In less than a minute, his enemy would be in the Mission trade school basement, would shoot him in his cell or find the key and—

The key.

Erskine scrambled in the growing darkness for the board and his hook. If he could secure the hook strap among the splinters somehow, he might snare the key at the far doorway.

He had to try.

Quickly now, the hook dangling with more certainty of holding, he pushed the board toward where he'd seen the key's faint glinting. The one-handed stretch was wearing on his strength.

Fishing around, his heart beating wildly and sweat pouring from him, he heard Emmett Jones in the far part of the building. Malcolm tried by sound, by delicate touch, to determine whether he'd caught the large ring holding the key.

Jones's ambling bootsteps grew louder.

Malcolm thought—without being certain—that he *had the key.*

If he were to draw the board back this time and discover he hadn't hooked the key in the murkiness, he'd lose time and become Jones's sure victim.

He had to act on instinct. He *believed* he had the key.

Emmett was now only about sixty feet away by Malcolm's reckoning from sounds outside the jail area.

When Erskine had the board all the way pulled in, he dropped it loudly on purpose—to stop Emmett's stride and cause his enemy to wonder what was taking place in Malcolm's cell.

There, he *had* lifted the key.

He pulled his hook into place on his severed arm. Then as he heard Emmett resume his step, he also heard the cocking of Jones's pistol. Another clicking. Two pistols.

Malcolm reached with the key to unlock his cell.

He swung the cell door open with a loud squeak, which stopped Emmett's approach again.

Now Malcolm was free but weaponless, except for his hook—free in the dark and threatened by the approach of an enemy carrying two loaded pistols.

Only now was Erskine able to hear the tardy "lynch" mob whooping it up in the distance. His rescuers were coming for him a little late, though they hadn't anticipated Emmett's discovery of their ruse, the one-eyed man's craftiness.

Torches sent occasional lights and shadows into the jail through the small cell window.

In a moment, Emmett drew close enough in the darkness so that Malcolm could hear him breathing.

Though Erskine had undergone excruciating effort to free himself one-handed by awkward use of the board, he tried to control his own labored breathing so as not to give away his precise position.

Malcolm stood just inside the jail area but outside his cell. He pinned his right side to the wall for bracing, so he could swing the point of his hook upward quickly.

94

Malcolm was poised to strike. With luck he might tear out Jones's *other* eye.

The mob outside drew closer. Erskine calculated its approach wasn't quick enough to discourage Jones.

But he heard his enemy *un*cock both revolvers and move a piece of furniture, as though positioning one of the crude trade school benches to sit on.

Jones laughed and spoke, "Lordy, Lordy, Lordy. I tell you what, boy, this is one funny situation you and I are in right now."

Malcolm estimated Jones was about ten or twelve feet beyond the opened jail area door. He kept his position between the doorway and his cell.

Jones continued, punctuating his speech with chuckles. "Here's the way it is, Erskine. I'm not the only one beat out your Jayhawkers. That bunch on its way now is *real,* you get me? They're going to string you up, or maybe yank off your other arm. Maybe chop off your legs. You never can tell what a mob'll do."

Malcolm was uncertain why Emmett might concoct such a tale.

Naomi had arranged a foolproof ruse and had told him approximately when to expect—

Oh, shit.

Now, feeling a rush of sweat over his whole body, Malcolm realized Jones *was right.*

Emmett had discovered the plot and showed up early. Other Bushwhackers could have done the same.

"Seems," Jones continued, "your bunch has the *awfulest* timing. No telling *when* they'll get here, or *where* they might all be. Tsk, tsk."

It was exactly as Jones described, Malcolm now knew. He must calculate escape urgently, but Jones blocked his best exit from the Mission building.

"I sure was hoping to collect a reward in Missouri for you dead," Jones said. "But I got sidetracked this afternoon. Met a sweet little old farm gal who went all tingly over this eye patch. Do you know, some of these white women in the Territory are the sweetest, most hospitable of any in the West? Well, *of course* you know, because you've been dipping your darky dinger in half of them yourself. That's the word goes around about you."

Malcolm figured Emmett was undecided—either come in shooting now and spoil everybody's fun and collect the reward, or wait and see what a lynch mob will do, later claim being here first and entitled to the bounty.

"So that's what this so-called Free State's all about, isn't it?" Emmett said. "You're just after free love between the colored and whites, right? I mean, *you're* the prime example of mongrelizing."

Jones paused, then, "Oh, listen to them upstairs after you. They haven't found the stairs down yet. Makes it nice so you and I can talk. Only you don't talk much. It's all finally got you in a sweat, right?"

Malcolm sweated freely, but he also felt a draft because he was becoming soaked from head to boots.

Then he remembered where the draft might be coming from.

A place high on the far side of his cell—stuffed tightly with stones laid atop the foundation of the Mission building. When the wind outside was right, it leaked drafts.

Erskine knew he could reach that area by standing on the box now positioned just outside the cell door—the box on which the Shawnee boy rested the tin plate and water cup whenever he brought Malcolm's gruel.

Could he reach and move the box quietly enough so Jones wouldn't hear and enter?

Malcolm remembered times he'd trained himself to move like a cat, *think* like a cat—use mental along with physical discipline.

Every step he now allowed himself was one in which his entire body took part—every muscle. He was full of a single purpose—to get into position silently and quickly for clearing a way out. Without the box, he could never have reached this high place.

Emmett Jones was still talking, but Malcolm had stopped listening. The noise of the mob running through the main floor above spurred him toward his goal.

There. With his hook he'd jimmied the first rock toward him. He stepped from the box to put the rock down quietly. Then he stepped up to let his hook tear at other stones that were giving way, falling to the outside.

A loud shouting went up. Malcolm realized the lynch mob—a *real* one—had discovered the stairway down.

A mighty push by Erskine sent two huge filler rocks out and away.

A man-sized opening invited him to hoist up and shimmy to ground level outside.

Once wiggled free and standing, Erskine wasted no time surveying what was occurring behind him.

He dug his boots in for the run of his life.

The freshness and humidity of the night air were a welcome relief from the dankness and dirt and stink of his cell.

During his escape run—now easily a quarter-mile from the Mission and figuring he was northbound—Malcolm speculated how Jones would explain this to the mob.

At roughly a half-mile distant, he wondered over the whereabouts of *his* gang.

What the *hell* had gone wrong?

Why had his people never come as Naomi promised?

Though he was singleminded over the sure steps he must take toward escape, he couldn't help but think his family and friends at Pleasant Valley had met some awful fate.

Before long, at about a mile and still running, he recognized his surroundings as the outskirts of Westport. He'd been heading north by northeast and had crossed into Missouri.

This wasn't the safest of places for him. But tonight Westport gave him his best chance for freedom and possible recovery of his bearings to head home.

Erskine knew that the McCoy family, which had laid out Westport, had also set aside a place for freed slaves. He would look for their cabins to seek refuge.

He stopped on a knoll to survey the town, now alive with Saturday night revelry. Erskine picked out what he believed was the place where Westport's colored lived.

He scooted low, in case any riders might head in or out on the newer Santa Fe Trail that led from Westport.

He arrived at the nearest cabin in the colored section and sought a window and light. He saw only darkness and moved on to the next.

After trying three or four places, he realized most adult free Negroes were working in saloons and bawdy houses of the town on Saturday night. Waiting tables or working in kitchens—but surely some must have stayed home to tend children.

At last, a glance through a cabin window revealed the presence of one adult—a young woman—reading by firelight inside. He tapped on the pane and saw her jump, startled.

Malcolm decided not to risk her further anxiety, her shouting an alarm. He took a bolder approach. He went to the door, tried it, opened it, walked in, and announced to the cringing girl, "I'm Malcolm Erskine. Have you heard of me?"

The young woman made a nervous sound, and her teeth began to chatter. It seemed she either couldn't move or was afraid to.

Malcolm felt an obligation to check on any children who might be in her care. He opened doors to two sleeping areas and counted five little ones, all blissfully quiet and asleep.

He found the kitchen and helped himself to a large washtub, which he rolled and set near the stove. He emptied a heated water kettle into the tub and sought a pump to bring in more.

Soon satisfied he had enough water and finding soap, Malcolm checked and saw the young woman still petrified with fright, but quiet. That's what was important—that she was quiet.

He turned back to the kitchen and stripped his foul clothes—all of them—tossing everything but his boots out the rear cabin door and stepping into the tub. He sat as well as he could, then dangled his legs over the side and proceeded to lather himself. He dug his fingers into every fold of skin to cleanse the foulness he carried from his jail cell.

When he finished washing his hair and saw the water was dirtier than what he wanted to be sitting in, he got out and found a torn towel to dry himself.

He next sought and found a blanket, wrapping himself in it just as the girl was coming into the kitchen. She looked him over and said, simply, "Malcolm Erskine."

"Yes. I took the liberty of bathing in here. Please burn my clothes in that trash pile outside, and let's dump this water. Come back in to talk about helping me."

As though reassuring herself of reality, she repeated, "Malcolm Erskine. In *my* home. Yes, I'll do that for you."

"You know I won't harm you. Tell me your name."

"Yes, I know. But you sure scared the living daylights out of me. Name's Esmerelda."

"Pretty name," he said. "Pretty girl."

"Thank you."

"Anything to smoke?"

Esmerelda sought and found a pipe and a tobacco pouch. "Daddy's pipe," she announced, handing it to him. "Or one of them."

"You enjoy Longfellow?" Erskine indicated the book.

She glanced at it. "Yes, it's 'Hiawatha.' Have you read it?"

He nodded, wondering where she might have received an education. Then he realized the McCoys were highly cultured and may have encouraged those in Westport's Negro quarter to break the shackles of illiteracy.

"Let's talk about clothes for me after you've burned my other things."

Esmerelda went about doing what Malcolm had asked. She was longer about it than he expected, but when she returned she had a curious look about her and was fingering something hanging from her neck—a key.

"I'm going to do something I never thought I'd do," she said. "Something dishonest."

Malcolm puffed at the pipe thoughtfully, comfortably cleaned, and warmed by the blanket and fire.

Esmerelda held the key so he could see it. "I work at the haberdashery by day," she said. "I'm a tailor's apprentice. Would you watch the children while I steal you an outfit—and risk prison or worse?"

"You don't have to do that," Malcolm said. "I'll go myself."

"In that?" she said, snickering, indicating the threadbare blanket.

"Then take my boots. Break a small pane near the lock, but do it from the outside. Leave my boots inside. They'll trace the burglary to me. Please don't get caught—for your sake, Esmerelda, and to give me peace of mind."

She rose to leave. Chidingly she said, "First thing you said to me— Have I ever heard of Malcolm Erskine?" She broke into a smile. "Take a candle and go look whose picture is pinned on the wall over my bed."

Then she took his boots and left.

95

Malcolm allowed himself the luxury of dozing on the floor while Esmerelda was gone. The flickering fire, the deep-breathing sounds of children asleep in other parts of the cabin, his cleanest condition in a week—all contributed to his serenity. He soon fell deeply into needed rest.

When he awoke, before dawn, he found Esmerelda lying close. Beyond her, neatly arranged on a chair, were a splendid suit of clothes and accessories to make him appear a man of means on the streets of Westport or Kansas City. But his hook and his famous dark face would prevent his strutting about in a manner suggested by the outfit.

So as not to awaken her, he delayed rising. Yet, he must be off and—

To where?

No plan. And he shouldn't be seen in Westport by day.

Gazing around in the pre-dawn light and the glow of fireplace embers, Erskine realized from slight snores that there was another adult in the cabin than was present when he arrived.

Evidently Esmerelda's father had come home from work, and the girl—Malcolm hoped—had explained what was going on and the need for protecting the Jayhawker.

Nervously, he started to rise.

Esmerelda reached an arm to circle his neck. She pulled him back to the pallet on the floor. She seemed determined to smother him suddenly with affection. Malcolm allowed several rapid kisses before he broke away, gently but firmly.

Erskine sought concealment in the pre-dawn to get dressed, though Esmerelda sat up, peeping shamelessly.

At last, suitably clothed, not yet in waistcoat and jacket, Malcolm strolled to the window. Gazing out, he whispered, "I have a wife."

"I expected you would," Esmerelda said, irony in her voice.

"Let it rest where it is," he said.

"Fine with me," she replied, as though amused.

"What happens next around here?" He turned to find her rising.

Esmerelda shrugged. "I make breakfast. You eat."

"No, I mean I need suggestions how to get away from Westport. I appreciate these clothes, but they don't exactly make me inconspicuous. Have you a horse I can buy—or rent?"

"No."

"Do any of the other Negroes in Westport have one?"

"Not that I know of."

"Any money I can borrow to book a stage ride to Olathe?"

"Not enough—but," she said, biting her lip, seeming to hold a secret of some pleasant prospect, "I may have a way for you with a man bound for Lecompton."

"By private wagon," Erskine said, wary but hopeful.

"Yes. Actually, a stagecoach. It's being handled very quietly," she said. "I mean, this man's passage through Westport. He wants it that way."

"Who is he?"

"I'd sooner not tell. Trust me, you'd be in no danger. You'll find safe passage into Kansas with him—far as you want to go. Daddy and I have started working on it."

"What must I do?"

"You must wait in this cabin three days." She leveled her dark eyes at him, watching for his response as she added, "With me."

Erskine gestured impatiently, realizing that if he objected loudly, he'd wake all in the cabin needlessly.

Esmerelda said, "You put yourself in my care when you came into this cabin. I'm responsible now for your life. You have no plan for getting away, but *I do.*"

Erskine hung his head, defeated. "I must have news of my family," he said.

"I understand," she said. "I'll arrange that, too."

*****

By nightfall Sunday—observing all day the visits of Westport's trusted Negroes to stare, greet him, smile, or bask in his presence—Malcolm hadn't yet received a shred of news from Pleasant Valley.

Peter Bartholomew, Esmerelda's father, had gone to church and returned, smiling politely but not yet speaking to Malcolm. He offered a pipe or food by silent gestures. Esmerelda hadn't yet returned from her new errand.

The Negroes of Westport lived communally, Erskine noticed, caring for one another's children as needed, sharing all they had with no thought of keeping track of who owed whom.

Malcolm figured he was in the midst of a closely knit society of some eighteen separate households. None would reveal his presence or whereabouts. Unspoken understandings among this group of freed Negroes seemed a way of life.

Malcolm overheard some refer to Esmerelda as "radical," not because she was more learned but because of what she read and how she felt about the Border War. Malcolm suspected she maintained a connection with runaways.

Erskine looked through Esmerelda's books. He saw abolitionist tracts grouped with classical works of Thomas Paine. Also current romantic literature and poetry.

At last she returned in late afternoon. She dispatched all neighbors and, with a firm but kind look, sent her father to his room, out of hearing.

When they were alone, Malcolm anticipated the news wouldn't be good. The young woman's demeanor signalled that.

"Your family is safe," Esmerelda said, "but in hiding somewhere. The Indians around there have given assurance your wife and baby and a Chippewa girl are all right."

Erskine knew Naomi had gone into the tunnels, but why?

"A platoon of bluecoats—Army—has occupied your ranch. Not your home, but in tents. They've padlocked your house. Pending settlement of issues surrounding your property claim, the Army is protecting what could fall into public lands."

Malcolm snorted and said, "That's a hoax."

"Of course it is. Everyone knows they were sent there simply to drive off your Jayhawkers. Something about a visit you fellows made to Cass County recently."

"Does anyone know where my men are?"

Esmerelda shook her head. "No. That's all I could learn."

Malcolm gave her a look of gratitude. "That's quite a lot, for something happening many miles from here. Can my wife be told of my escape?"

"I've been assured she will be."

"I owe you," he said.

Esmerelda smiled and stared at him. "Follow me, please." She led him into her bedroom and said, "You're mine for two more days. Your visit is the biggest thing I ever expect will happen in my life, and I—"

"Don't continue."

"Please make love to me. Whatever else comes to my life, Malcolm, your touches would give glory to a poor Negro girl. Someone who appreciates literature, romance, adventure, but sews white men's clothing, day after miserable day."

"No."

"I'm not pretty enough? Don't smell good enough? Too dark-skinned?"

"You're—absolutely beautiful. Stunning. Your mind and your good heart add— And the—gardenia scent of you is—intoxicating. But I can't, really. I won't."

"Yes, you can."

She took his hand and bent to kiss it.

"You will," she said.

With her other hand, she raised her skirt and placed Malcolm's hand in a moist place that suddenly drove him dizzy.

96

"It's time to make ready," Esmerelda whispered to Malcolm. Dawn of his departure day appeared through the curtained window.

He said, "You've been good to—"

With a finger pressed to Erskine's lips, Esmerelda halted what Malcolm realized would be an unnecessary recounting of favors.

"We've traded," she said in a hoarse whisper. "You've taught me and given me more than you know. And now I have a place to send runaways, soon as you send word the soldiers are gone."

"I'll sketch a safe route and have it brought here to you."

"Malcolm, I've fallen in love with everything you are. You're my hero. Whatever else happens in my life won't equal the joy of these few days."

"Esmerelda, I—"

"Get on with your life, my love. Make your way safely from Westport today. Return to your family." She kissed him softly, then smiled. "Get up and let me watch you put on your pretty suit. And you can watch me put on my best to see you off."

*****

Later, Malcolm waited at a window by the front door of the Bartholomew cabin. He peered through the curtain for a stagecoach making a special stop to pick him up.

Assurances of highest authority went into making this ride possible, Esmerelda had said. All he need do, she'd suggested, was think of what he might say, given the chance to address someone who could change events in Kansas Territory.

Erskine imagined his stagecoach host would be an intermediary between Free State and Law and Order forces. A person holding a key to future peace in the Territory. Malcolm decided that supervised and fair elections would be enough to talk about.

At last he saw the stage pull to a stop out front. Esmerelda wrapped her arms around Malcolm and sought his mouth with hers. "Go quickly, love of my life." She pushed him gently out the cabin door.

The stagecoach door opened, revealing one person inside—a well-dressed, middle-aged man who held forward a rolled-up paper.

"Get in, Mr. Erskine," the man urged. "I'm newly appointed Territorial Governor Robert J. Walker, bound for Lecompton. And you'll be very interested to see this document."

Malcolm was speechless.

"Hurry, please," the man urged. He was stocky, balding, plain-looking, seeming to be working hard at trying to be friendly. "My driver must signal a small escort of guards. Before he does, I want you to receive this dismissal of Chief Justice LeCompte's charges. Come along. Get in."

Malcolm entered the stagecoach and sat, opening the paper handed him and reading it quickly. He focused on the words, "Erskine as legal combatant to preserve the chartered purpose of Kansas Territorial establishment." Then, farther down, a reference to Sylvia Parks caught his eye. It said she was of "mixed racial ancestry including Negroid in the Carolinas."

A hand was extended to Malcolm in friendlness, and he grasped it.

"I'm happy to meet you at last, Mr. Erskine," the Governor said.

Malcolm replied, "The last of Kansas governors I met was Wilson Shannon. We didn't hit it off too well."

"Oh, yes," Walker said, sitting back, glancing out as mounted and plainclothed Territorial militiamen rode by to take lead positions. The stage got under way. "You met him during the Wakarusa incident?"

Esmerelda pushed him gently out. The stagecoach door opened, revealing a well-dressed man.

"Yes."

"Between you and me, Shannon was a fool—and weak. That's all I wish to say about any of my predecessors—and more than I should have said."

Malcolm glanced again at the dismissal document. Holding it between them, he asked, "Is this legal? You haven't yet been inaugurated."

"It's legal. Inauguration is mere formality. I carry full power of appointment by President Buchanan. The White House telegraphed accord for this, from an Associate Justice of the United States Supreme Court."

Malcolm beamed and nodded. "Thank you. I don't know what made you decide to do this, or how you managed it so quickly. But, thank you."

Walker became silent a moment. Then, gazing at the scenery they passed, he said, "When Peter Bartholomew was a slave near Natchez, Mississippi, he was in town picking up supplies for the plantation. He looked up and noticed flames in a window of my law office. He shouted an alarm, entered the building ahead of firefighters, and, sad to say, inhaled more smoke than his larynx could bear."

The Governor shook his head and looked again out the stagecoach window. "The poor man never recovered use of his vocal chords. I prevailed on his owner to free Bartholomew, who then moved to Chicago, learned the tailoring trade, and got married despite his disability. Esmerelda's mother died in childbirth. Friends in Westport invited Peter and the girl to relocate here, where they're employed and have become socially integrated in a small community of reasonably protected former slaves."

Walker pulled a handkerchief from inside his jacket, blew his nose, and said, "I'll do anything I can for the Bartholomews. You're a lucky man, Mr. Erskine, to have stumbled on them in your escape. And Esmerelda—" Walker shook his head and made a clicking noise. "—is one of the most persuasive women it's ever been my experience to encounter. Imagine how far she might have gone if she were—uh—"

"White. You were going to say white. Sensitive subject, being I'm not legally white myself. But Governor, with this dismissal of the charges, and your feelings about the Bartholomews, I can overlook a lot. Once more, thank you."

"Right is right, Mr. Erskine—Malcolm. I'm old enough that I can call you Malcolm. I know how you Kansans feel about President Buchanan. But it may be a master stroke, his having put me in this job. Like former Governor Reeder, I'm a Pennsylvanian, born and bred. I went to Natchez as a young man and got elected to the United States Senate representing Mississippi. I'm one of the few Democrats who can walk down the middle on this Kansas issue. And I mean to be fair about it."

Malcolm said, "I don't see a middle, not when it comes to slavery."

Governor Walker turned suddenly to Erskine and frowned. "No middle? Think, Malcolm, how long slavery has been a way of life in the South. More than a couple of centuries. Today's slaveowners inherited a social and economic system that only since the Revolution has also become political."

"And the politics of it brought you to Westport, Missouri, to pit vipers like Sam Jones and Colonel Boone?"

"Yes, I met with some of the so-called Law and Order leaders, knowing I would soon meet as well with those of the Free State Party. I'll listen to everyone. As for what I *do,* I'll do only what's right."

"Right for both sides? That's not possible," Erskine said.

"Right according to *law,*" Walker said. "I warned Boone and the others, these Missouri invasions for voting will have to stop." He reached into a leather satchel beside him and pulled out several sheets covered with handwriting. "Here, I want you to see what I've said in the inaugural address I'll be delivering. I want your point of view."

The Governor's trust in Malcolm—over something so important—humbled him.

Erskine took the papers and began to read the neat handwriting. After only the first few paragraphs he looked up, astonished.

Glancing down again, he read aloud—

"You're saying here, 'It is my duty, in seeing that all constitutional laws are executed, to take care, as far as practicable, that this election of delegates to the convention shall be free from fraud or violence....' That's never been promised before," Malcolm said.

"That's right, and it's long overdue," Walker acknowledged. "And it's more than my pledge. It's a solemn obligation. A duty. I intend to carry it out with the full force and authority of my office."

Malcolm continued to read, half hearing Walker's comments, half probing the written words, fully excited by the Territory's being blessed finally with a leader who had a grasp of fairness.

"Excuse me, Governor Walker, but you— You're saying here that President Buchanan has full knowledge of your views and approves of them and—"

"And," Walker emphasized, nodding, "that no work of a Territorial constitutional convention shall be recommended for adoption by the United States Congress *unless* there's a ratification by vote—"

Erskine, in his excitement, interrupted again and read, "A 'vote of all the actual resident settlers of Kansas' in an election that's 'fairly and justly conducted'."

"Exactly," Walker said, obviously pleased to have his words acknowledged with enthusiasm.

"You'll antagonize the proslavers and the bogus legislature at Lecompton simply by speaking such words," Malcolm observed.

Governor Walker stared out the window of the stage and said, "Probably. Can you imagine the spot I'd be in if I had to back those words with force of arms? I hope to God that day never comes."

97

Malcolm scarcely noticed the rapid passing of time in his stage ride with Governor Walker.

After a quick stop in Shawnee, where he saw a sign still referring to the place as Gum Springs, they would soon be on a relatively straight path for Douglas County along the Kansas River.

The pair talked nearly all the while. They reviewed other papers besides the inaugural address. They discussed Walker's plans for running a well-ordered territory, hopes for its standing properly with what were now thirty-one states in the Union.

Before long they glimpsed Mount Oread in the distance, distinguishing the town of Lawrence.

That prompted discussion of Malcolm's earlier visits there, the death of his mother in the raid the previous year, his New England origins, the painful circumstances by which he'd lost track of Dahlia for two decades.

Erskine obviously won Governor Walker's sympathy by that story, if not total understanding, without trying to do so.

Changing the subject, Walker asked, "Will you still be welcome by the leadership in Lawrence? How do you believe they think of you there today, taking into account your—ah—checkered past?"

"I have supporters there. Some in high places. I maintain relative independence now, because I'm no longer paid by the Free State Party."

"My stop will be brief," Walker said, opening a pocket watch. "Everyone has me on a schedule of ceremonies in Lecompton. Will you be accompanying me all the way? I would like that."

Erskine hadn't considered being routed this far from Pleasant Valley. Walker's written dismissal of charges was an unexpected bonus. He could have asked to be excused at Shawnee and headed home from there.

But there was something symbolic about being well-dressed and free again and in the company of the highest official of Kansas Territory—being, in point of fact, the only companion of the Governor in the chartered stage and now a somewhat mutual confidant with Walker.

"Yes," Malcolm replied after hesitating. "All the way to Lecompton." Malcolm wanted to see the expressions on faces of proslavers serving currently—and unlawfully in the view of many—as lawmakers for Kansas Territory.

"Are you armed?" the Governor asked.

"No. Not if you mean gun or knife. But I'm capable of defending myself with this hook. And, from stubborness, I'd probably live to walk or ride toward any man filling me with lead and kill him first."

Walker nodded grimly, remarking, "I'm glad to hear you're not armed conventionally. Weapons and the carrying of weapons make me uneasy, though I understand the need for them." It was obvious the Governor was in awe of Malcolm's strength and frontier wildness and cunning. "How did you lose your forearm?"

"I cut it off to escape an animal trap during a gun battle. It was that or die."

Governor Walker shook his head, looking away and then peering out as the stage began rumbling down Massachusetts Avenue in Lawrence.

As expected, Charles Robinson and James Lane were among the greeters. Lane was grimmer in his countenance than ever, a sign of how skeptically he now regarded governors. Not even the sight of Erskine in Walker's company elicited a show of surprise from Lane.

The bearded Robinson, on the other hand, beamed both in greeting and in pleasure over seeing who rode with Walker. He indicated to his wife Sara within Malcolm's hearing that it was a good sign for the abolitionists' side.

Erskine scanned the area to observe how the town had been rebuilt after its 1856 sacking. He admired quietly the transplanted New Englanders' relentless determination.

Possibly as many as forty greeters were on hand for the Lawrence stop. Walker pledged to revisit, soon after necessary formalities at Lecompton.

Among those present, Malcolm noticed, was the courier, Johnny Kesibwi, who ventured a wave of recognition that Malcolm acknowledged. Kesibwi finally made his way forward and encouraged Erskine to join him to one side.

"Are you riding on to Lecompton with Walker?" the Shawnee asked.

"Yes, why?"

"Emmett Jones is there. He lit out for there after your escape from the Mission, to meet privately with Reverend Johnson and the bogus leadership. They've been discussing how to be rid of you once and for all."

"Well, well," Malcolm said, chuckling. "Won't they be surprised at the Capitol to see me step off the stage as a free man, all charges dismissed?"

"They may shoot you dead on the spot."

"And risk hitting the new Governor?" Erskine scoffed at the notion. "I doubt that."

"Are you armed?"

"No."

"Here. Take this."

"I won't take anything. I, uh, sort of gave my word to Walker," Malcolm said, handing back the Bowie knife Kesibwi was attempting to pass to him covertly.

"Emmett has decided to make himself a rich man on Missouri bounties offered for you."

"How much now?"

"Thirty-five thousand, and soon perhaps forty."

A low whistle of appreciation escaped Erskine's lips, half in amusement, half in a show of bravado for Kesibwi's benefit. "A man could live happily many years on such a sum."

"Take care," the Indian warned, patting Malcolm's back firmly and in a brotherly manner.

"Aren't you going to inquire about Lani-Wawewa? She's safe, incidentally, though I don't know where my soldiers are at the moment."

"She is no longer of interest to me. And your men are scattered, home to respective kin or friends for visits, till you summon them back to Pleasant Valley."

"Have you heard whether the military is still there?" Malcolm asked.

"The Army is there, yes, but reduced to a few soldiers, unsure of the effect of your new legal position."

"They know the charges have been dismissed? How? I only knew myself a few hours ago."

"The Westport Negress sent word two days ago that it was a certainty. As a result, the officer in charge sought and received new orders from Fort Leavenworth. That is all I know....All right, so how is the Chippewa girl?"

"Lani is very well. A good helper to my Naomi, and good for my son."

"I now give her to your son, for a wife if he wishes. I keep more wives than I can handle, I have finally and sadly concluded."

"He is an *infant.* Lani is almost a young woman."

"Same spread in years," Kesibwi observed with a smile and a knowing wink, "as you and our late sister, Sylvia. Correct?"

"Oh, well, in that case," Malcolm said, completely in jest, "I must accept."

Malcolm shook hands in parting, waved goodbye to others at the Lawrence stop, and rejoined Governor Walker in the stagecoach. The escort riders led them from the town at a quick trot. The drive to Lecompton was conducted at a swifter pace, evidently to make up time.

Conversation was more relaxed as the two men grew better acquainted. Malcolm was convinced by the journey's end that Walker trusted him implicitly. He now sought in his own soul the ability to grant the Governor equal trust, deciding he would give the official all benefit of doubt.

Then, arriving at the main building in Lecompton—the Capitol, a large, two-story wood structure—Erskine noticed an array of somber gentlemen standing before the front door.

There, at the center of the assemblage—a gathering Malcolm found comical because of the relatively formal attire worn almost as a uniform by all legislators—was the Rev. Thomas Johnson, chairman of the group.

At the sight of Erskine stepping from the stagecoach, and doing so practically on the heels of Territorial Governor Walker, Johnson seemed astonished, then outraged. It was all Malcolm could do to keep from laughing.

By glancing about, Erskine was able to pick up a glimpse of One-Eyed Emmett skulking among trees near the building. Now, at the instant Malcolm's presence was beginning to bring a buzz of protests, the two enemies made eye contact.

Even at a distance, Erskine imagined he saw a dollar sign forming in Jones's single eye.

98

Malcolm turned because Governor Walker was trying to get his attention.

"I've never told you the price I expect you to pay for my dismissing the charges," Walker said, conducting Erskine to one side.

"Price?"

"Only by a clear case of self-defense will I ever tolerate your killing again. I prefer you consider my action in your behalf a probation, not a license to renew your fits of vengeance and adventurism."

"Begging your pardon," Malcolm replied, showing annoyance, "but I'd hardly call them 'fits.' After all, my first wife was lynched, and no authority existed in Kansas able to do anything about it—nor any in Missouri willing to."

"I understand all that," Walker said, evidently trying to subdue his own impatience, "but I see your so-called Jayhawker work as solely defensive from this point forward."

Governor Walker then grabbed Erskine's right upper arm and held him firmly, as though to drive home his message. The grip was stronger than Malcolm might have expected. "I'll tolerate no further forays, demonstrations, nor any other activity by your Jayhawkers leading to unprovoked killings by you or your men. Is that understood? Can we be friends, Malcolm, and still allow me the upper hand in this?"

Erskine looked at the ground, a habit from childhood when scolded or when vexed by someone's directing him counter to his will.

"I suppose so," he mumbled. "But with all due respect, Governor, I wish you'd get to know more about what goes on around here before you put such constraints on me. I really do," he added, looking up and fixing his gaze directly into the Governor's eyes.

"Trust me," Walker responded, "so that I can forever trust you."

Malcolm weighed the significance of their so-far confidential relationship, one from which the Jayhawker concluded that courage and sacrifice were probably ahead for Walker.

The Governor would need credible support to enforce fair elections and to keep his pledge of popular ratification for a constitution. While Governor Geary had been a great improvement over his predecessor Shannon, this new man was by far the most promising.

Extending his hand, Erskine said, reluctantly, "You have my word. Self-defense. I hope my family and I are not placed in jeopardy by this promise, Governor."

Walker took Malcolm's hand and said, "You won't be sorry."

Erskine leaned to glance toward Emmett Jones, who was moving about in the background for a better view of events at the entrance to the meeting hall.

With a smirk, Malcolm said, "I'm already sorry....Good luck to you, Governor Walker. I'm with you all the way."

* * * * *

Malcolm—unarmed, committed to behave in a manner he was unused to—decided he needed a horse and, if possible, less pretentious clothing for travel. He wanted to leave Lecompton quickly, to be out of range of whatever murderous intentions Emmett held toward him, to be away from other temptations that might jeopardize his regained liberty.

To plan a successful high-tailing out of there, Erskine was now counting on the uneasy dignity of the Governor's being welcomed by the gathering—by scoundrelly proslaver well-wishers on their best behavior.

He began loping afoot at a fairly good pace. One-Eyed Emmett Jones rose suddenly from behind a bush, halting Malcolm with a drawn revolver and a sneer.

In a mocking tone that included a falsetto range, Jones asked, "Where you off to, jiggerboo? They'll be serving puffy sweets and punch inside, maybe hand you yours at the back door."

Malcolm raised his arms in surrender and looked around. He'd unwittingly placed too much distance between himself and the official crowd to be noticed. If he didn't think fast, he'd be a goner.

"Now, uh, hold on, Jones. After all," Malcolm said—in a tone showing the Missourian undeserved respect as a man of honor, not as the snake Emmett truly was—"You can see I'm not armed."

"Well, well. I did kind of think I might have the advantage of you in that. And I really should finish you off right now and drag your carcass back to Missouri, where I'd be made rich by it."

Jones decided to sit on the ground and maintain the drop on Malcolm. "You know, they'd pay me a handsome sum, even if I arrived at the border with just the merest of your splintered bones, long as I can vouch it was you."

Erskine had no doubt Jones was capable of exactly that.

"I heard this new Governor wiped out charges of illegal claim-taking, flight to avoid whatever and so on. Is that so?"

Malcolm nodded. "It's true."

"Well, thank heaven for God-fearing, law-abiding, upstanding Missourians like *me,*" Jones said, grinning, "to correct the errors of such lily-livered and wrong-thinking officials as him." Jones indicated the Governor with a jerk of the head, then spat.

"Personally," Erskine said, "I thought it was a pretty smart move politically. He's a Democrat, you know. If he's going to get this job done, he needs the support of Republicans like me."

Emmett squinted his single eye at that and actually let down the barrel of his huge pistol. "Now hold on there. What in hell do you mean, 'Republicans like me'?" Emmett shook his head, then reached a hand to push his hat forward in mock and vigorous scratching of his scalp. "You? A Republican?"

The man had missed his calling, the Jayhawker decided. He'd have made a better stage actor—in a comic role, at that—than a gunman.

"A Republican?" Emmett repeated. "You can't be. You're a *Nigra.* Not only that, you're married to a Christ-killer, a Jewess. That makes your baby a Christ-hating darky. One I'll have to get rid of too—"

With that Erskine was on Jones in a flash, whipping his hook at him but missing and losing balance. For his trouble he got the revolver muzzle shoved to his nose as he lay flat on the ground, breathing hard.

"Tell you what, Erskine," Emmett Jones said, also panting from the quick tussle. "Let's go out here in this clearing, you and me, and I'll keep the gun and you can use your hook. We'll get down shirtless and have a fair fight."

From his disadvantaged position, Malcolm squinted at the offer, then said, "Call that a fair fight? All right, piece of shit, you've got a deal."

Jones let Erskine up. Each tossed aside his hat, Malcolm his fancy jacket and vest, then both stripped away shirts and stood for a combat pose in the clearing.

Malcolm had failed to figure what he might accomplish by accepting a challenge that included facing a revolver. But it was the only chance for survival Emmett offered.

By now the pair had begun to draw spectators, though a quick look revealed to Erskine disappointingly that the Governor wasn't among them.

One man was heard to mutter, "Classic confrontation. That's Erskine with the hook, and the one-eyed man's kin to Sheriff Jones."

Malcolm reasoned his best approach was to swing his hook offensively and often, not expecting to come so close as to finish Emmett but at least to yank the revolver away.

Emmett dodged successfully, but soon he grew impatient with Erskine's moves and raised the barrel quickly to squeeze off a shot. The bullet caught Malcolm in the right upper arm but seemed not to have damaged bone or muscle. It hurt plenty, however, and the wound bled freely.

Malcolm was convinced he stood a chance only if he could move quickly enough to knock the revolver away. He kept trying until his hook caught the trigger area and pulled the gun from Emmett's grip.

The effort sent Erskine to his knees, and the revolver now lay equidistant between them.

Worst luck of all, that was the moment Governor Walker joined the others to observe this duel.

Malcolm calculated if he and Emmett went for the gun in the same instant, he had the advantage of Jones and would get it first.

Poor depth perception for Mister One-Eye, Erskine remembered. His enemy would be forced to grope, unsure of his reach on a single move.

But could Malcolm even use the gun once he had it?

Emmett would then be unarmed, and to shoot an unarmed man wasn't the "self-defense" Walker said was a condition of Erskine's probation.

Putting aside what he might do afterwards, Malcolm flexed for the jump to the gun.

He saw Emmett poising himself also for a leap.

99

Malcolm wasted no time moralizing.

He needed that weapon.

Steeling himself from a crouch, ignoring his injury, he cat-leapt toward the gun.

Emmett, too, lunged but missed.

Malcolm had figured his advantage correctly.

Now the two regained footing and circled each other, the Jayhawker armed and aiming this time, the Missourian unarmed and snarling in frustration and anger.

Malcolm glanced again in the direction of Governor Walker and caught a knowing look. With that, he dropped his aim and stood still.

"Jones," he said, sighing—pressing the leather casing of his hook against the bleeding wound in his right arm—"I'm going to let you go. I won't shoot an unarmed man."

"Well, that's mighty sporting of you. Stupid, but sporting," Jones replied. "I'd shoot you whether you carried a weapon or not."

"That's you. This is me. I won't do it. Take your horse and head back to Missouri. I'll keep your revolver and—bullets." Ersk ine picked up Jones's bandolier.

The Jayhawker tucked the barrel into his britches and turned his back on Emmett Jones.

Emmett's sneers and snickering made plain his contempt for Malcolm's show of ethics.

"Think you're better than me? Figure because you're the wrong color, you have to show Christian charity, buy a ticket to heaven? Prove you're not ninety-nine percent monkey?" Jones said. "Let me tell you something, Jew-licker—"

Before Emmett got another word out, Malcolm whirled, pulled the weapon from his belt, circled his hook around back of Emmett's neck, and stuffed the revolver barrel half into the man's mouth.

Jones choked and gasped.

"See?" someone was heard by Malcolm to say. "The colored man's a savage after all."

Malcolm said, "I *am* better than you, Emmett. My hatreds don't come from seeing people's differences. They come from seeing mean-ass sons-of-bitches like you."

Erskine pulled the gun from Emmett's mouth when he began gagging on it. He shoved Jones away and said, "Take your stuff and get out of here."

In the background, he heard Walker's voice commanding the others, "Gentlemen, I don't know what you expected to witness, nor why I'm standing here. We've got a territory to run, so let's get to it." The Governor turned sharply and headed toward the meeting hall, leaving no doubt that he expected all others but the duelists to follow.

Malcolm watched them go, paying careful attention to whether Emmett Jones would toss off more verbal abuse for the witnesses' ears before mounting or riding out. He didn't.

A figure turned back from among those walking toward the frontier Capitol. It was Reverend Johnson.

Gruffly the legislative chairman said, pointing downstream, "There's a Delaware squaw—old midwife, actually—half a mile that way on the river bank. She'll attend to your wound and pull out the bullet."

With a nod, Malcolm thanked the slaveholding minister, retrieved his outfit, and walked in that direction.

*****

Erskine visited the Delaware woman and remained in her care overnight, so she could watch for the possibility of infection. He continued to seek a horse to carry him to Pleasant Valley. Lacking success, he aimed himself on foot in that direction.

The practice of walking—resting at watering holes, sleeping under the stars, using Emmett's revolver to bring down game—seemed to help his thinking on such lofty issues as Kansas's future.

And his own.

For several days he headed toward his Johnson County home. All the while he thought and persuaded himself he was now less adventurer and more rancher, less warrior and more father and husband, less outlaw and more solid citizen.

Believing his best course lay in politics, Malcolm considered how he might fit that calling. *"Poorly,"* he said aloud, calling to the nearly undisturbed prairie, a land as beautiful in soft contours and blossoming and perfumey locust trees and wildlife as any free man might want.

Yet, to reach his goals and keep his family safe, politics seemed increasingly a good course to follow.

Deliberately he skirted Monticello, where he might have borrowed a mount easily. He kept walking toward Pleasant Valley, because he wanted this time to think through all his promises and future plans. He was undeterred by occasional bursts of torrential spring rains. He welcomed the challenge to survive in the wilds with only his cunning and a weapon. He fashioned traps as needed, made fire by friction, ate sparingly, wasted nothing.

This long walk he named his "catharsis"—a word he'd learned from John Brown. He was even finding physical strength from the effort. The churning of his mind, however, was exhausting.

At last, coming close to the old Santa Fe Trail and then ascending its ridge, Malcolm gazed on his home in Pleasant Valley. There, outdoors, perhaps by some instinct sensing his approach, stood Naomi holding their son. And Lani as well.

The sight made clearer his commitment to more peaceful ways. He resolved the question finally in his heart.

The soldiers were gone—no trace of their tents.

Near the barn Malcolm saw a few of Black Bob's men. He realized that all the while in his absence, they'd tended his stock and kept the herd healthy.

Malcolm waved his bandaged arm and brought a response from Naomi. He trotted, then ran down the ridge to her—a man changed by circumstances and promises.

100

"You've needed a vacation," Malcolm told George Morris, first of his Jayhawkers to return to the ranch.

Before dismounting, George looked about the porch and glanced toward the barn and outbuildings. Malcolm knew his trusted adjutant sought a glimpse of Naomi. He understood and accepted that the man was enamored of his wife. He knew also that Morris would never violate the trust Erskine placed in him.

Morris turned to his leader with a smile and handshake. "Captain, next time let's you and I work out a period when I'm to take leave. Let's not allow your arrest or an invasion of Law and Order officials be a reason for it."

"Agreed." They sat on the porch to talk. Naomi came out of the house to greet George. She offered him a snack and coffee, and he accepted the latter.

Lani-Wawewa served them steaming mugs. After she returned inside, Morris observed, "She's blossoming nicely, that one. I reckon Ellerby will be wanting to settle down with her."

"We'll see," Erskine said. He felt like a patriarch, able to observe romance budding among young people in his charge.

"I see the border trouble increasing," George said. "This new man, Walker, must have proposed something inciting Missourians to a near riotous condition. I've only heard and read snatches. Can you shed light on it?"

Malcolm welcomed the chance to discuss politics and give a perspective to current events. He explained to Morris how Walker had promised fair elections, unspoiled by outsiders, and Territory-wide voting for a constitution as a foundation for Kansas statehood.

Morris sipped coffee and watched two Shawnee youths play cowboy with part of the breeding herd. He said, "Mighty tall order. Walker's promises, I mean."

Malcolm nodded, saying, "We'll help him the best we can."

"Well," George said with slaps of dust from the thighs of his trousers, "I'd better settle in and get to work. The others will be riding in and— Well, speak of the devil. Here comes Ormsby over the ridge."

Erskine rose to look and nodded. "It's Cyrus, all right."

Over a period of two days all the men returned—Ormsby taking up duties again as ranch foreman and quartermaster of the fighters, the others falling in as before.

They returned refreshed but curious—asking about their future course of action. They seemed happy to be reunited in what would be at least a defensive cause, a more secure border.

None spoke of Andrew Pace's betrayal.

Every few hours one or two rode up—Ben Ellerby receiving a special greeting from Lani. Then came Chad Brookings and the burly Henry O'Dell, who'd caught up with each other on a trail from the northwest. Eugene Fontenot, whom Malcolm now regarded as a brother, returned from the direction of Cass County, Missouri, a clue the Creole was still courting Jane-Ellen.

A second day of reunion brought Jed Blake from the south, who contributed current news about John Brown. "He's turned full attention to the Underground Railroad," Blake said. "He hasn't laid down his weapons, but he's sure a busy man running slaves through Osawatomie to Lawrence and on to Canada."

"Does he get very many through there?" Malcolm asked.

Blake grinned and scratched his head. "Probably not as many as he'd like, considering what old Brown's capable of doing for them. He's been talking about moving his operations clear into slave territory, maybe organizing a slave rebellion."

Hearing that, Erskine looked around at the others and directed Jed, "Take time to rest. Then at your earliest chance, ride to Black Bob's camp. Ask the Shawnees to get word to Brown that if he wants to be free to move south or southeast, we'll take up the work. We'll have this place serve as a major station in the Underground Railroad."

"Yes, sir, Captain," Blake replied. Though obviously tired from his return ride to the ranch, Jed mounted unhesitatingly to cover the few miles south to the Shawnees' community.

Final returnees to the ranch later on were Watson Frederick and Terence Anderton, the latter with surprising news for Erskine—"I think you're an uncle."

"What?"

Blake was returning from Black Bob's camp at that moment, and he shouted ahead of his whoaing. His message confirmed the news—"Daniel and Audrey have had a baby! A girl! Black Bob told me."

Anderton added information, grinning. "I ran into a wagon outside Paola, and folks said they were looking for the midwife to help Audrey Goodman. Asked me if I'd seen Blossom's carriage on the road."

Hearing the excitement, Naomi came out and inquired.

"Seems Audrey had her baby," Malcolm told her. "Daniel and Audrey have a little girl."

"Isn't it early?" Naomi asked.

Eugene Fontenot, now whooping at news of his sister's delivering his niece, offered members of the band a round of drinks in the barn. There he kept a cache of whiskey he'd brought back from his frequent runs to meet Jane-Ellen.

Erskine sensed Fontenot's hidden purpose was to draw others away from a conversation with Naomi that was inevitable. When they were gone, she asked Malcolm, "You were—with her when?"

"Last fall, it was," he said. "Yes, the baby's early by a few weeks. But I'm sure she and Audrey will get the best of care."

"They will, yes," Naomi agreed, biting her lip, searching Malcolm's face. "Don't you—feel anything?"

Malcolm took his wife in his arms, glancing past her at Lani's carrying Noah out to the yard. "Of course I do," he said. "But I mustn't show it. I should put all such concerns aside, take heart in the knowledge she's now Daniel's daughter, not mine."

Naomi backed away to peer into her husband's eyes. "Just like that?"

Malcolm nodded. "Just like that. It was Daniel's choice, knowing everything and marrying her, and all by Audrey's consent. And you and I have made our choice and are handling our lives—with our son."

Naomi relaxed and resumed hugging her husband, squeezing him hard. "No more, Malcolm. Please don't give your seed to any other woman. I realize you were adrift at the time you met Audrey, but—no more."

Erskine thought about how aggressively Esmerelda Bartholomew had sought his affection. He fairly choked wanting to confess to Naomi how that had gone while he was hiding in Westport. But he decided on silence, not to give her cause for concern.

"We should celebrate the birth of our niece," he said, kissing her gently on the forehead. He circled her waist with his arm and led her toward the barn.

* * * * *

As observed by George Morris, trouble was increasing along the border.

Three clear developments had arisen since Governor Walker delivered his controversial inaugural address—

First, although a Democrat, Walker had won the confidence of the Free State Party and had won its agreement to participate in an election scheduled in October. The election would reestablish a Territorial Legislature, and it was hoped the balloting could be free of Missourians' unlawful voting.

Second, on its own side and acting on its own hopes, the Law and Order Party was clamoring for a constitutional convention in the fall. Proslavers were eager to produce a document and submit it for ratification before any Free State-dominated governing body might be established by the October election.

Third, apparently acting independently, Bushwhacker units consisting of young, fiery zealots were stepping up their raids. Either they hoped to show that no Kansas election could be free of Missouri domination, or they were in it for theft and other lawless mischief-making.

The moment of truth was looming, Malcolm knew, and his role as a border defender would be sorely tested during summer and fall.

*****

Within two days after his group had reassembled, the Jayhawker band was called to confront Bushwhackers striking to the south. The raid was so swift, the invaders were gone from the Territory before Malcolm and his men could help the burned-out farmer.

"Gather clothing that neighbors may be willing to give," Erskine directed Ormsby, "and see that this family is housed properly. We've got to work on a better warning system and faster response."

Leaving Ormsby and O'Dell to carry out the assignment, Erskine and the others returned to Pleasant Valley to begin a series of meetings with Black Bob Shawnee representatives and Free State settlers from Aubry.

The best and swiftest riders were given precise instructions for being on alert and on call by day. At Black Bob's suggestion the night warning would be by flaming arrows, except in periods of extreme drought.

One such night warning enabled Malcolm's Jayhawkers to arrive in time east of Aubry, to intercept and scare off a large group of Missouri raiders. A young invader perished when he turned in frustration and charged his horse recklessly toward George Morris. Two older men went down when they reversed their retreat and wheeled on Fontenot and Blake.

After the skirmish, Malcolm felt frustrated and hamstrung by his pledge to Governor Walker. But a promise was a promise. His men groaned, watching the others get away, so he cautioned them, "Don't bellyache about not giving chase. We're still doing a job for the settlers along fifteen miles of border—when we're not cowboying. Let's bury their dead."

Morris protested. "Captain, there are *three.* A lot of digging by torchlight. Why not drag them over the border, less than a mile?"

Malcolm eyed his adjutant in the torch glow. He said, "I no longer subscribe to that, George. I'm trying to be civilized. That's why."

101

"Your plan puts me in a terrible position," Naomi told her husband while she cleaned cabbages. "I should never have encouraged you about politics. I wasn't thinking."

The kitchen pump was a rare home convenience. Sitting at Naomi's worktable, watching her, Erskine was glad he'd designed the place to minimize her labors.

Malcolm would let her speak without commenting. He knew Naomi was "thinking out loud"—her description for it. At such times everything went best if he remained silent.

"Whatever I say to your plan," she said, "I'll lose." She was being rougher in handling the cabbage heads than they deserved, Malcolm thought. "I won't like your being away like that," she said, her helper Lani backing farther when Naomi's motions became more animated. "But it would still be better than your riding out and shooting people."

Malcolm reached for a cleaned celery stalk among a stack Lani had just set out. With deliberate and teasing noisiness, he snapped off a large bite and chewed loudly.

Naomi glanced at him. "You're not funny."

Clearly she'd been shocked by his either-or proposition—that he would run for office and win, and be absent serving in the Territorial Legislature, or he'd stay and continue daily the hazardous job of policing the border. Though it seemed he was giving her a say, the choices threw her off guard.

Naomi took up a large knife and began slicing the cabbages on a cutting board. Preparing meals for ten hungry men was a daily chore of no small proportion. But the way she was going about it today raised the visible worry of Lani-Wawewa. The Chippewa girl rushed to her side and reached, offering to take the knife before Naomi had an accident.

At first Naomi stiffened. Then she showed understanding and yielded to the girl.

"All right," she said at last to a celery-chewing Malcolm, who restrained his grinning. He knew which way Naomi would go.

"All right," Naomi repeated, wiping her hands on her apron.

"Run for the damned Legislature," she said. "Go off to Lecompton or Topeka or wherever the government is going to light."

Now Malcolm let himself grin fully.

"At least that way I won't have to worry your men will bring you back slung over Ebony." A dry sob escaped her.

With that Erskine knew he'd carried this amusement too far. She was more troubled by this than he'd calculated. The new pressures of the Border War were governing her emotions.

Malcolm rose quickly and hugged her as she wept into his shoulder. He said, "I'm sorry," stroking her hair, her neck. "I didn't mean to make you cry."

"Oh, Malcolm," she said between sobs, "just being *you* is all it takes to make me cry. You know that by now."

Embarrassed by having overlooked Naomi's possibly reacting this way, he sought to shift the topic. "You said I had a flair for politics. Have I lost my charm?"

With that he felt her shake, this time from laughing. "Please don't let anyone make a fool of you," she urged. "Malcolm, I've learned that a politician you're not."

"Not?"

"Definitely *not,* because you're too honest to be discreet, too resolute to be compromised."

Though his wife's words were complimentary, Malcolm was a little put out about her assessment and the way she'd stated it.

For all her emotional release, Naomi apparently recognized in Malcolm a disappointment in her explanation. She added, "It's not politics you have a potential for." She kissed him quickly and held his face in order to gaze deeply into his eyes. "It's greatness."

They embraced. Though the moment contained magic for them, Erskine sought to lighten it. He asked over her shoulder, "Why not sainthood?"

Naomi's groan was simultaneous with Lani's exaggerated response.

The Chippewa girl turned for Malcolm's view and simulated throwing up.

* * * * *

Whether fired by the summer temperature or the heat of political passions, wave after wave of Bushwhackers stepped up assaults against settlers of the region. Erskine's group and other Jayhawker units responded, but the attacks were becoming relentless.

Newly built barns were burned almost before they could be put to use. Wheat crops were torched on windy days or nights. Cattle, horses, and pigs were stolen—or freed and chased from corrals or pens to fend for themselves in the wild.

Farmers failed in their efforts to stand up to the surprise attackers. An alarm system and organized Jayhawker defense helped, up to a point, but Missourians grew bolder with each passing week. Some of the Bushwhacker offense was reprisal, due to other Jayhawker units' crossing into Missouri to retaliate for previous offenses.

Little of it was balanced. Much of it was bloody.

None of it showed promise of ending.

The stakes were higher as moments of frontier and national decision grew nearer. By fall it might all be over, everything decided with respect to Kansas's projected entry into the Union as either a slave state or free state.

Congress was at the end of its patience over the border response to its own Kansas-Nebraska Act of 1854. Few members had expected the violence, the illegal balloting by Missourians, the scope of killings by both sides as the way to determine Kansas's future.

*****

A practical reality driving Erskine was knowledge the Bushwhackers generally lacked experience, except for a few veterans of the Mexican War. He found their attacks foolishly organized, recklessly led, at times carried out wildly – and fatally to many of them.

Calculating back to a spring start-up, Erskine guessed his band had slain thirty-seven attackers – men and, regretfully, a few boys – by midsummer.

On the other hand, his own soldiers hadn't suffered a fatal casualty, only temporarily disabling wounds.

The Free State settlers? Those in the southern part of Johnson County under Malcolm's self-appointed protection had lost four of their numbers. Only the knowledge that Bushwhackers had paid a higher price gave Erskine satisfaction.

Such warfare was beginning to defy reason for Erskine. The increased assaults must be bound to a dedication toward preserving slavery that was so fierce, as he saw it, passion ruled before intelligence.

"It's as though," Erskine commented to the visiting James Butler Hickok on a rare night of peace, "the Missourians are against a wall. I fear this border struggle – however it goes here – is a sign something worse is ahead."

102

Hickok asked, "What do you mean, 'against a wall'? *They're* the attackers. And what could be worse than this mess?"

Erskine suspended a tobacco pouch from his hook, then reached in for pinches to stuff his pipe. "They're fighting like cornered snakes, even though they have all the advantage of manpower and spon—spon—"

"Spontaneity," Naomi offered by crisp enunciation as she passed through the Erskine parlor, carrying Noah.

"Thanks," Malcolm murmured, lighting his pipe.

"I never looked at it that way," Hickok said. "Now that you mention it, they seem to be taking foolish chances, as though desperate. Not very smart as war tactics go."

"They've got deadlines to meet," Malcolm said, pointing the pipestem for emphasis.

"How so?"

"In two months—in early October—there'll be a legislative election. The Free Staters intend to go all out. I'm running to become the Oxford Township area representative."

"I don't see how—"

"No, hear me out. The Law and Order Party has called a constitutional convention for the following month. I believe our side will boycott that little circus. If we carry the election, the Law and Order convention would simply be a lame-duck exercise, a desperate effort to come up with a proslaver document to send to Congress."

Malcolm stopped speaking to resume drawing on his pipe so he wouldn't lose the light. Then he continued as animatedly as before.

"The Missourians and the Law and Order people know we've got antislavery settlers pouring in from Illinois, Ohio, Michigan, Iowa, even Nebraska Territory. As fast as they're coming in and staking claims, they're not only signing up with the Free State Party but some are forming or joining Jayhawker outfits like mine. Well," Malcolm said on second thought, "not quite like mine. Some too damned undisciplined."

Hickok drew out cigarette tobacco and papers, saying, "You mean the other side is doomed to lose in numbers, if it waits too long in pushing for statehood with slavery."

"Exactly," Erskine said. "In a few more months, there's no doubt how an election would go here. My best guess is, the proslavers mean to work fast, stir up confusion, and scare off new settlers, if they're to stand any chance in the October voting."

Hickok pondered that, then asked, "All right, now what about that constitution?"

Malcolm shrugged, releasing huge clouds of smoke as he sat back, feeling smug about his conclusions. "Governor Walker is committed against submitting it to Congress if it's not ratified by bona fide Kansans. If we boycott the drafting and ratification of the proslavers' document, what credibility would it have—with him *or* Congress?"

Hickok leaned forward, puffing on his cigarette, then wincing and scratching his neck in some apparent confusion.

"What's the matter?" Malcolm asked. "Do you see a hole in my reasoning?"

The young man looked up, nodding. "Possibly. Possibly. Mind you, I'm not even old enough to vote. But I believe you're overlooking practical considerations."

"Oh?"

"You said Missourians fight like cornered snakes, even when they're the attackers. You sure it's a time factor? Or are stakes for slavery higher than we think?"

"Sure they're high—to them. Abolition would ruin financially some slaveholding farmers not ten miles from where we sit."

"Then," Hickok said, straightening, "what makes you think they wouldn't find a way to buy Governor Walker?"

Erskine snorted. He shook his head. "Oh, no. Not a chance of that."

"You said yourself, something worse is likely to come of this. I know you mean all-out war—a civil war—North against South. To avoid that, wouldn't Walker think twice about being hard-nosed, maybe let proslavers have their way again?"

"War is what I mean, yes," Erskine said, "but I don't think Walker would sell out to avoid it, or for any other reason. The man took a stand in his inaugural address."

"And from what I hear and read," Hickok said, "Buchanan and much of the Democratic Party have been sorry he went and did that."

"That may be, but it's done. Walker told me he talked to Buchanan beforehand and got his backing on all of it. Now the Governor's on record. I intend to help him keep his word." Erskine then leaned forward to ask, "Hickok, how long can you stay in the area?"

Hickok shrugged. "I've got a week's leave, though I'd like to move about a little. Maybe run up to Westport, do a little gambling. Maybe book another shipment to drive to Santa Fe."

"Just out of curiosity," Malcolm said, "what really appealed to you about becoming a teamster?"

"I wasn't seeing enough of the country." Hickok leaned and placed a hand by his mouth to shield his voice from carrying to other parts of the house. "You know how we learned from that fellow Aubry, to keep fresh horses ready along the trail?"

Malcolm nodded.

Hickok winked and held up four fingers. "Well, I got me two beautiful señoritas, one gorgeous widow squaw, and one blond-pussy, pink-titty Swedish gal—stretched a couple hundred miles apart from here to Santa Fe."

Erskine chuckled, cautioning, "Watch it doesn't do you in."

"Now you're sounding like Crazy Carlotta."

"Who?"

"Crazy Carlotta. You never heard of her? A slave in Cass County. Tells fortunes. Her owner lets her go into saloons there. Only she tells me it's not women who'll be the death of me, but *poker*. Calls me 'Mister Bill' and 'Wild Bill'."

Malcolm laughed. He drew out a pocket watch, raised his eyebrows, and announced, "Time for us to leave."

The pair strode outside, into the sultry, moonless night. They checked by low whistling signals the various lookouts arranged for their newest adventure. All posted Jayhawkers responded.

"We'll ride to just outside the Oxford settlement," Hickok said quietly. "The lumber shipment I left there would be unloaded by now, and the team was to be looked after properly till I come for the rig."

"I'll light the way south for you from there," Malcolm said. "I have stuff for torches packed on Ebony. You just manage that big-ass wagon."

They rode to the Santa Fe Trail, then northeast to a point outside Oxford. "Activity seems normal for this time of night," Malcolm observed. "That means no readiness for the likes of me coming on them. Just the same, I'll stay out of sight."

"Good idea," Hickok said. "No sense letting Catron's Blue Lodgers know *you're* here. I don't even want to think about the fuss that would raise. After I hitch my horse behind and drive the wagon a little south, you catch up with me, say about half a mile out. I can manage to that point in the dark."

All went quietly as planned.

Soon, Erskine lighting the way for Hickok, they had the wagon aiming south at an even clip, then they turned east.

At a rendezvous point in Missouri, Malcolm doused the torch. They planned to ride farther in pitch blackness, slowly.

Before long, a low whistle sounded, then another. Erskine knew the signal and halted. Hickok stopped the wagon.

Considerable movement in the brush indicated their cargo was ready. All were rushed into the wagon to take cover under tarpaulins and other materials Hickok had loaded for that purpose.

"You sure you can find the trail again, going due west from here?" Hickok asked Erskine.

"You think I'd have let the operation go this far if I didn't have a way out?"

"Guess not," Hickok replied, resuming his place in the wagon driver's seat. "Lead the way."

Malcolm had previously scouted a trail that required a minimum of fording streams. The Blue River was unavoidable, however. At one point he and Henry O'Dell had placed, then concealed with heavy brush, enough fallen logs across a narrow portion of the Blue to accommodate a wagon.

Only a rainstorm could threaten the safety of these runaway slaves now, Erskine knew. The slightest rise in the level of the Blue would float his makeshift bridge away.

Though the August night air was sultry and threatened rain—lightning and rumbles in the distance—none was breaking over them. Malcolm was also confident of their position and relit the torch.

Seeing the rickety bridge, Hickok was beside himself, standing in the wagon. "Are you *crazy?* That won't hold! And the wheels'll be caught!"

"Trust me," Erskine said, dismounting and sweeping his hook across debris he'd used to conceal the log bridge.

"That whole thing looks shaky as hell!" Hickok protested.

"I've got it secured and a floor on it. Get that damned wagon moving!"

With a *"Giddap!"* the wagon was in motion again, the horses finding footing on the bridge, then the wheels rolling true to cross the river.

When Malcolm pulled Ebony alongside, Hickok asked, "How in hell did you manage that?"

"Anchored in good old limestone," Malcolm said. "O'Dell and I bound the logs with leather straps, braced them at all corners with heavy rocks. We used clay to form a surface to roll you across and knew it would dry in time."

"You could have told me. I near dirtied inside my britches, getting my team and rig across."

"I've got to leave you some surprises, else it won't be like old times together."

"Just like I've got a surprise for you," Hickok said.

"What?"

"Tell you later."

When they arrived at Pleasant Valley, the unloading of the fugitive slaves moved along smoothly. The Negroes entered the tunnel and rooms below. The men of the Jayhawker band saw to their comfort.

The wagon Hickok used was driven to the south for concealment until its next scheduled use for runaways. The four-horse team was led back for stabling.

"This is going to be a busy week," Malcolm observed when their night's work in the barn was done.

"And a mighty interesting one," Hickok said. "Don't forget about your surprise."

"That's right. What did you mean by that?"

"Down below," Hickok pointed. "We've got Crazy Carlotta. Out there tonight, when I told her about you, she said she was dying to tell your fortune."

103

The morning following the slaves' resting safely in the tunnels, Malcolm wanted to see the woman of some renown, Crazy Carlotta.

Had Hickok mentioned her because he knew she'd be aboard the escape wagon? Did his young friend put greater store in the fortuneteller's predictions than he wished to let on? And did he want Erskine to have benefit of mystic intelligence, in the event it might do some good in the Border War?

Malcolm strolled into the barn and asked George Morris offhandedly about the well-being of their guests.

Morris glanced at the barn lookout of the day, Chad Brookings, and seemed satisfied no danger would arise from opening the trap door. Morris then invited his leader to proceed, to go below.

Erskine descended a ladder into the candle-lit tunnel. He checked that the venting was proper for such air-eating illumination. He raised his hand to a series of pipes to determine that they were unobstructed and circulating air. Satisfied, he made his way to the broadest part of the tunnel, where he stood silently and counted five men, six women, and two toddlers. Most sat on the cots.

One of the runaways, a man about Malcolm's age, stepped forward and extended his hand. "I am Josiah," he said, appearing to Erskine to be a somewhat learned man, despite all rules against slaves' being allowed to become literate.

"I am—" Malcolm started, extending his hand.

"We know," Josiah said, smiling. "We know," he repeated, taking Erskine's hand in both of his firmly, tears brimming in the corners of his eyes in company with his joy. "And we thank you," he added.

"Introduce me," Malcolm urged, indicating the others.

Some of the Negroes evidently found it difficult to contain their emotions over meeting the man known widely as a hero at the level of John Brown.

As was often the case in such a group, two women kissed Erskine's hand, a gesture he wished he could discourage.

At last he saw and met the woman of whom Hickok had spoken, Carlotta Edwards. She seemed more reserved in her gratitude over being freed than the others. Malcolm sensed even a slight resentment by Carlotta that she'd been included in this group brought to freedom.

What struck Malcolm most clearly was that Carlotta, though strange-looking in the way she moved her eyes, appeared no better equipped to foretell anyone's future than the man in the moon. She was middle-aged, wild-looking, rumpled. Erskine chided himself mentally for being tempted by superstition, seeking her out.

Abruptly, Malcolm asked to be excused on the pretense of having other pressing matters to attend to. Before leaving he checked whether they were being furnished food and other conveniences to their satisfaction. Josiah, their apparent leader, assured him they were.

Malcolm left, determined to forget the diversion Hickok had pressed on him.

*****

In the two days that followed, before the group of thirteen slaves could move safely to the next station, Malcolm planned another pickup of fugitives.

But an early evening's emergency call to defense intervened. It came to his Jayhawker group by fast rider from near Olathe. Malcolm discouraged Hickok from joining. "I can't let you expose yourself—" he began.

"To danger?" Hickok interrupted, showing offense. "You think I can't handle myself alongside your night-riders? That I'm only a street fighter?"

"I wasn't thinking about that," Erskine said, finding patience to explain. "I was about to say, I can't let you expose yourself to criticism, not danger. You're not working for Lane anymore. As a teamster, you're supposed to be neutral."

Obviously subdued by that reminder, Hickok said, "I know."

"I've got to go now," the Jayhawker said. "Stay here and guard my family and the group below. That's plenty of challenge to help us." He mounted Ebony and rode out to join his gathering force westward, through the dusk.

At their destination south of the Olathe settlement, they encountered a heavy force of Bushwhackers. The enemy had swooped in to harass an outspoken Free Stater on the man's farmstead. The Missourians were *yip-yip-yipping* and setting fire to the barn and fields, pulling down the water tank, chasing animals from corrals, bashing the chicken coop, breaking window panes in the farmer's home.

Malcolm cursed an evident weakness in the mid-county settlers' signal system, a weakness that had allowed an invasion this far into Johnson County.

The Jayhawkers confronted the enemy, and a fierce gunfight broke out.

The attackers were strong in numbers and reckless. Because they'd set fires and were now trying to ignite the house, the advancing nightfall was lighted as though it was still day. That exposed the Missourians as targets, an advantage Malcolm's men didn't hesitate to use. Bushwhackers who'd done their mischief on foot were shooting recklessly and going down quickly. Malcolm wondered whether they were liquored up.

Chad Brookings was shot in both legs, and his horse was shot from under him.

George Morris caught lead in his shoulder but fought on the best he could.

Terence Anderton received the worst of it—a bullet ripping a gash in his scalp that Erskine, on first glance, thought might be fatal to the lad.

Erskine shouted new orders for the uninjured to divide, so some might guide Brookings and Anderton to safety. Morris insisted on fighting by Malcolm's side, despite injury.

Malcolm then withdrew his force to a creek, where the farmer had retreated behind a bank with his family. The women fell immediately to caring for the injured Jayhawkers and stopping the flow of blood from Terence's scalp.

Malcolm considered the best means for routing the Bushwhackers altogether, for inclining the invaders quickly in eastward retreat. The Missourians had already lost four or five dead or seriously injured, but another dozen young attackers were still on their horses and riding through what remained of the property, shrieking crazily.

Observing from a distance, Malcolm determined which man was their leader—a light-whiskered fellow who looked barely over twenty-one, riding a bay horse and stopping occasionally to watch the others, as though checking and then deciding their next course.

"Get that one! Bring him to me!" Malcolm ordered Fontenot. He pointed also to Ormsby and O'Dell.

With a burst of energy, his chosen trio rode out after the man, overtaking him with no trouble, disarming him and grabbing the reins of his bay almost in one motion. They led the protesting Bushwhacker back to Erskine, then Ormsby and O'Dell raced off to beat at flaming crops with rolled saddle blankets.

When the Missourian set eyes on Malcolm, he evidently realized he was about to be invited to quit Kansas by the quickest means, for he put up his hands.

"I know you. Picture's everywhere. You're the killer darky," he said.

"Then you should know," Malcolm said crisply, clearly, "you have exactly two minutes by this watch to round up your damned bandits and get out." Erskine spat out the words. "If you show any sign of *not* heading into Missouri, I'll signal other Jayhawker groups by flaming arrow to intercept and wipe you out."

The man rode off in an instant, shouting to others to mount and be off. As for helping those in the Missouri group who couldn't ride because of injuries, the Bushwhacker leader said, "Leave 'em! Ain't got time. *Ride!*"

Fontenot told Malcolm they couldn't have carried out the threat, for there were no bows and arrows along. Anyway, the remaining wheat crop might also ignite from flaming them. And he doubted other Jayhawker groups were on alert to receive a signal.

"I know all that," Malcolm said. "There are times a man has to bluff. Tonight was one of them."

After making sheltering arrangements with neighbors for the dispossessed family, the Jayhawkers returned to Pleasant Valley.

At the barn Hickok greeted them with news that, out of concern over Malcolm's frequent risk-taking as occurred tonight, Carlotta insisted on reading his fortune immediately.

Erskine had Naomi, Ormsby, and Lani-Wawewa see to the wounded. He ordered Ben Ellerby to summon Dr. Simeon Bell from Aubry to attend to Anderton's and the others' wounds. Naomi was already cleaning and numbing Chad's and George's injuries with herbal compounds, in preparation for Dr. Bell to extract the bullets.

Then, reluctantly, Malcolm agreed to the session with Carlotta.

They gathered in the barn, a few of the Jayhawker soldiers and Hickok, in the light of candles and oil lamps. There Crazy Carlotta Edwards meditated on Malcolm's future.

While Naomi was medically trained—and was needed to aid Brookings and Morris and to direct the care of Anderton—she might otherwise have witnessed the fortunetelling. But she seemed glad not to be available.

From that Malcolm concluded it might possibly have been at Naomi's urging that this activity was being carried out.

Malcolm had failed to calculate that his wife—an intellectual, a scientist, and trained in the often pragmatic dogma of ancient Hebrews—may nonetheless have carried into their marriage a touch of superstition.

The realization amused him.

104

Malcolm looked on this late-night fortunetelling as an ordeal to endure, or his companions would never let up on the subject. He comforted himself that the wounded were being treated—that Dr. Bell had arrived from Aubry and was at work in the house.

Once in New Bedford Malcolm had dropped in on a gypsy fortuneteller who'd pitched her tent on the edge of town. Actually she'd told no fortunes but was a polished extortionist. After flirting and pretending they were alone in the tent, she'd provoked Malcolm's amorousness. With perfect timing, her husband had entered to feign outrage and demand satisfaction—a payment three times the advertised palm-reading fee.

Erskine had sneered at the pair but reached into his stevedore's work trousers to find the required bills for keeping everything peaceful. After that he'd headed for a waterfront saloon and got stinking drunk.

This present situation, however, was far different and ten years removed from the scene with the gypsy woman. Half-amused, half-annoyed by the prospect of submitting to examination by Crazy Carlotta—for whatever satisfaction it might give Naomi or him to "know" what lay ahead—Malcolm sought to treat it lightly.

Immediately in response to his flippancy, Carlotta's expression grew clouded. By her disapproving frown, she let Malcolm know this was a serious matter. He hadn't expected such a reaction, so he decided to show a more respectful attitude.

Carlotta directed him to extend his hand, palm up. She pored over it intently, occasionally using the end of her shawl to wipe her runny nose.

From time to time she glanced up at his face, her mouth hanging slack and revealing few teeth, her eyes uncertain in their focus. She gazed finally into Malcolm's eyes with the same profes-

Carlotta directed him to extend his hand, palm up. She pored over it intently.

sional scrutiny a physician might use to examine some deep medical mystery hiding there.

After returning to his hand, tracing their lines without comment, glancing to one side at his hook and then snorting—as though resenting a professional challenge in which only half the evidence was available—Carlotta Edwards folded her hands in her lap and shut her eyes.

When she'd continued sitting that way for what Malcolm knew to be a full five minutes, he started to speak. Hickok placed a hand on his shoulder to stop him, but too late.

Erskine's unfinished protest—that possibly Carlotta had fallen asleep in the midst of the palm-reading—resulted in her lifting one eyelid to cast a disapproving fish-eye.

Malcolm decided to let the woman play out her act, assuming this was one, and to await whatever verdict she might give, to be delivered in whatever manner she might choose. He would show utmost patience and at least pretend respect for the ceremony.

At last Carlotta breathed a deep sigh and rose to move about the barn. She made directly for his horse, Ebony, who shied at her approach.

Strangely, she quieted the beast with the gentlest touch to his nose, almost as though, Malcolm thought, an angel had come to claim Ebony for the horse gods.

With several of Malcolm's men watching—Hickok as well—Carlotta turned toward the entrance to the tunnel. Reaching the trap door and receiving an offer of help from Hickok and accepting it, she began to descend to rejoin her fellow fugitive slaves.

Throughout, she never uttered a word.

To a baffled Erskine and a disappointed group of Jayhawkers waiting above, Hickok returned in a few minutes. He made light of the matter and relayed what he claimed Carlotta told him. Malcolm had known the young man a couple of years, however, and could tell the situation was more serious than Hickok was letting on.

Outside, on their way back to the house, Erskine said in a hushed tone, "What was all that cock-and-bull stuff you told me and the men? That I'll live to be an old graybeard and maybe get shot by a jealous husband."

Hickok shook his head and said, frowning, "I had to make something up. I really don't know if I ought to tell you what she said." He added, "But I do know I ought *not* tell Naomi."

Erskine stopped him. They faced each other in the night, hearing a great horned owl hooting from its locust tree perch beyond the house.

"Tell me all of it," Malcolm said.

Hickok looked down, then glanced around in obvious embarrassment. "I wish I'd never started this thing with Crazy Carlotta. I truly wish I'd never mentioned her."

"Did you put her in that group of runaways for a joke on me?"

"Hell, no. She wanted to come out of slavery. She's just ornery and cranky and pretends we messed up a profitable deal for her, doing her fortunetelling in the saloons over there for pay."

"Well, let me have it then. What did she tell you?"

Hickok peered through the darkness and caught Malcolm's gaze in lights from the house and barn. He asked, "You don't believe in this kind of stuff, do you?"

"Of course not. But I sure as hell am curious enough to hear what in tarnation she said."

"Well," Hickok began, removing his hat and rubbing an itch at the back of his head, then replacing the hat. "Well, Malcolm, in truth, she says you're not long for this world. But she once said the same for me, so I wouldn't place too much stock in it."

"How long?" Malcolm asked, feeling cold shivers along his upper arms and at the back of his neck.

"She claims you won't live out the year."

Malcolm took that with a straight face. He felt a sudden weakness in his legs but wouldn't reveal that to Hickok. Instead, he grimaced over the foolishness, then let his mouth break into a grin. Soon he elevated that to full-blown laughter, and Hickok was soon caught up in it.

The two slapped each other on the shoulders at the hilarious claptrap Carlotta's foretelling had yielded.

Then, each with one arm around the other, as though in a drunken walk, they aimed for the house, giggles rising from one and setting off the other alternately along the way.

* * * * *

During the night, Malcolm heard Naomi rise from bed and leave their room at least twice. He couldn't imagine why his wife was so restless—unless she was impatient that he hadn't told her the outcome of his session with Carlotta.

Finally, when she returned, he could tell she'd been crying.

"I made Hickok tell me," she said.

"Tell you what?"

"That Carlotta said if you don't change your ways and put away your weapons once and for all, you may not live to see Noah grow up."

In his heart Malcolm was grateful to Hickok for making up a half-truth for Naomi. He knew his companion couldn't help having spilled some of Crazy Carlotta's forebodings to Naomi, for his wife was relentless when there was anything she demanded to know.

To give her assurance, he said, "Well, now you see how false all this fortunetelling stuff is. Because we already *knew* that. A man puts distance between himself and the risks he's been taking, and he's bound to live a longer life."

"Will you?"

"Will I what?"

"Put away your weapons."

Erskine was impatient now, and sleepy. "Damn it, Naomi, we've been through all that. Isn't it enough I can't hit the enemy where he lives, because of some foolish promise I made Walker? I sure as hell won't lay down my weapons and let the attacking Bushwhackers wipe us *out.*"

"You don't have to shout."

"I wasn't shouting. Anyway, I don't think I woke Noah," he observed.

"Lani has him in her room. She wanted him bunking in with her tonight, and I allowed it."

Hearing that, Malcolm considered how the Chippewa girl was becoming increasingly proprietary toward his son. He didn't know whether to resent it or be glad. He decided not to think further about it now but to go back to sleep.

"Come to bed and forget all this," he urged.

Naomi spread her body across his in the darkness and gave him loving hugs and kisses, as though in fear of losing him.

Past her, Malcolm stared into the blackness of their bedroom and in his mind heard Hickok's words again—

"—you won't live out the year."

He gulped to hold back against voicing a protest.

At last, vividly aware of Naomi's warmth and sudden ardor, he rejected Carlotta's predictions of the future and returned to the bittersweet present.

*****

Next day, Malcolm found himself staring at his son, pondering the infant's future as Noah rolled on the floor of their parlor.

The fortunetelling outcome had returned to his mind that morning to haunt him. He tried not to let on to Naomi that he was genuinely worried.

Suddenly he called Lani to watch Noah and stalked out to seek Hickok. He found his friend leading the four-horse freight wagon team.

Hickok was hitching up to make daylight delivery of their thirteen fugitive slaves, under cover of tarps, to a rendezvous point between Monticello and Lawrence. Then he would return to Pleasant Valley that evening.

"Hickok, what else did that crazy woman tell you?"

"What do you mean? I told you everything."

"What I mean is," Malcolm said—gesturing, looking away, trying to make sense while floundering over what might be nonsense—"did she show signs of knowing what she was talking about?"

Hickok looked at the ground. He scratched his chin. He looked around in several directions, squinting in the morning sun, then directly at Malcolm. "I didn't want to tell you this. She didn't want to say anything in front of the men, for fear they'd lose their spirit for fighting if they knew anything bad was going to happen to their Captain. That's why she said nothing till she got below."

"All right, but what else did she say? She couldn't have said much," Erskine observed, "because you weren't down there that long with her."

Hickok looked Erskine in the eyes and said, "She knows everything there is to know about you, except for some names. She knows about your mother, about Jane-Ellen, about some Egyptian charm—"

"The scarab."

"Yeah, that's what she called it. I'm telling you, Malcolm, this woman's got some kind of—" Hickok obviously didn't know how to finish. He looked around again. Then, "She gives me the goddam willies."

105

Malcolm resolved not to think about Carlotta's predictions, at least not to any lengths of unnecessary brooding.

He awoke one morning early, gazed lovingly in the pre-dawn light at the sleeping and disheveled Naomi, and decided he must put his affairs in order—*in case* anything bad should happen.

He should take steps to reinforce legality of his inheritance, he realized—draw a proper will supplementing the quick paper Chief Black Bob had helped draft. He figured he should meet with a sitting judge or court officer to batten down everything properly. He would ride to Lawrence and spend the necessary time there to get it done.

Malcolm was now concerned whether his closest aides were prepared for leadership in his absence. The good side of it was that Eugene Fontenot was spending less time chasing after Jane-Ellen in Cass County.

"You know," Eugene had said to him recently, "I believe it entirely possible she is still in love with you."

"I don't want to hear about it," had been Erskine's response.

"All right, then maybe you would like to hear this," Fontenot had added. "I would like to assume more responsibility for leading the Jayhawkers, if you will allow it."

Malcolm welcomed that but hadn't jump to it straightaway. "Possibly. Let me think on that," he'd replied.

Now, this morning, seeing Naomi asleep and thinking about that episode with Eugene and all the logic it presented, Malcolm finished dressing and decided to place his capable companion in at least temporary command.

Erskine had no doubt of Fontenot's proficiency with arms, no doubt of Fontenot's understanding and adherence to the purpose of the band, nor did he doubt the Creole's devotion to leadership responsibilities.

There was certainly no doubt of Fontenot's courage. The man could lead and fight with a ferocity and expertness approaching Malcolm's. Still, Erskine was glad for the fact of George Morris's and Cyrus Ormsby's presence in the picture, for the former would lend protection by his superior marksmanship and the latter by his frontier wisdom.

When Naomi stirred and awakened, he told her of his plan to be off to Lawrence but didn't detail his purpose.

"Are you going there to consult with attorneys?" she asked, half-awake.

"Now—why would you conclude that?"

"Because I know you, Malcolm, better than you know yourself. Aren't you aware of that by now?"

"I—" He sputtered, gesturing awkwardly. "I would have had to—"

Naomi nodded, shutting her eyes briefly with an air of peaceful resignation. "I know, my darling," she said. "You're right to do it. Go. Know that I love you and Noah more than anything in the world."

"Of course, there's—" She interrupted him by holding up a hand.

"There's something else you must know, under the circumstances," she said, fully awake now in the increasing light. She seemed both amused and in search of approval for what she was about to say. "I'm going to have another baby—I calculate next March."

Malcolm sat down on the bed, stunned. The news seized him with an overpowering joy. Nothing could have sounded better in this time of life than that their family was increasing.

A lump formed in his throat. He drew Naomi quickly into a tight embrace.

Naomi whispered in his ear, "I know that we are your happiness, as you are ours. Take special care and come back to us quickly—in peace."

Malcolm left, his heart and mind filled with plans to expand the nursery, plans for setting aside more time to be with the soon-to-be-born infant as well as with Noah.

If it were another boy—or a girl— But wait. *March.*

Carlotta's words, delivered through Hickok, returned to haunt him—

"—you won't live out the year."

Erskine stopped in the parlor. He watched through a doorway as Lani-Wawewa dressed Noah for the day.

He clutched the mantel, though he didn't know why—perhaps to prevent a dizzy falling, perhaps to feel the strength of the oak and draw a measure of that sturdiness back into himself.

Carlotta's prediction now consumed him. Though he'd sworn not to dwell on it, the fortunetelling presented itself at every turn.

In his throat he felt a wail that wanted to escape.

Alone, in an earlier time, he might have yielded to that. But now? No.

Malcolm drew himself up, took a deep breath, went to Noah to kiss the child good morning, uttered some brief greeting to Lani, and left the house.

Outside he sought Fontenot but found Ormsby first. "I'll be off to Lawrence as soon as possible."

"What's the problem, Captain?"

"Legal matters. You're to arrange and announce that Fontenot is in complete charge in my absence. He's prepared for it and— Why are you laughing?"

Cyrus had removed his hat and slapped it against his knee, giggling quietly.

"Why, Captain, your Lieutenant has already got the men up and ordered practice rides to start in ten minutes—before breakfast. Says he's got some new ideas about riding Indian-fashion, and we're to try them."

Erskine was pleased. He scratched the back of his neck in wonder, how a romance turning sour—as appeared to be true of Eugene's with Jane-Ellen—could instill in any man an ambition toward action. Fontenot was no exception. But Eugene *was* exceptional in other respects, Malcolm concluded.

While saddling Ebony and observing from afar the gathering of his men by Ormsby, Morris, and by Fontenot, Erskine noted approvingly their acceptance of a shift in leadership.

In the natural pauses of preparing for departure, he was able to observe Fontenot commanding the men ably. What newer riding methods Eugene had in mind for the practice, Malcolm had no time to watch. He must get moving to Lawrence and put everything right—make everything legal and binding.

Minutes later, out of sight of the others, he slowed Ebony and then halted. Perhaps he would open one of his talks with God.

Instead, he gazed up and bit his lip. He nudged Ebony westward, fighting a choking sob remaining within, over Naomi's new pregnancy and especially the baby's due date.

Malcolm rode on and muttered—with slow deliberateness—"Are you truly there, Lord?"

106

Summer's end gave faint but hopeful promise to settlers of Douglas County. Most were new to the region, having arrived only months earlier. Those with whom Malcolm stopped to chat confessed the drought was their biggest disappointment, an unexpected price they paid for pioneering.

They asked whether this was something they should anticipate for the future, perhaps team with others to dig waterways from the Kansas River and its tributaries. Erskine assured them the condition was intermittent, noting also he had less than two years' experience living in Kansas.

"There were good years and bad in Illinois," one farmer said philosophically, shrugging.

"And there'll be good years and bad in Kansas," Malcolm responded, in a somewhat liturgical cadence.

Although the motive for his ride to Lawrence had grown out of something dispiriting, he found contacts with farmers generally cheering. By the time he viewed Mount Oread and the town of Lawrence, he felt almost energized by the mood of hope he found among the settlers he talked with.

A final pause he'd planned was to visit Abe and Rose Milford. When he arrived at their place, a caretaker told him the couple had travelled to Topeka to see a cousin of Abe's. Malcolm left good wishes and, despite his disappointment, was amused by the caretaker's startled reaction to his identity. The man's jaw had dropped open. A freshly rolled and lighted cigarette had fallen to the ground. The poor fellow had been forced to dance awkwardly lest nearby straw should ignite.

Turning Ebony toward Lawrence, Malcolm realized by the sun's position that he'd dallied too long on the trail. It was too late to make appointments there this day with attorneys he'd hoped to see.

In his pack were all papers needed for refining his land title clearly and for describing it in his will.

If any gain could be drawn from contact with Carlotta, he had her to thank for forcing him to formalize a will. He simply couldn't bring himself to accept her conclusions, for that would be like believing in superstition. Voodoo.

Malcolm headed for a small hotel, actually the converted home of a wealthy abolitionist tradesman who'd moved on to help develop a Kansas community farther west, a place named Manhattan.

Although night had closed in, he was able to read a sign indicating the place's small saloon had dinners available and—in an annex at the rear, little more than a large tent—*baths.*

After stabling Ebony and booking a room, Malcolm went to the bar. Perhaps he would find sociable exchange with other Free Staters.

On entering he recognized Yancy Banniker, leader of a Jayhawker band at Wyandotte.

Ordinarily, Malcolm would have greeted his counterpart, a rough fellow in his early forties. But Banniker was known to be a generally cantankerous soul, causing most acquaintances to be guarded in contacts with him.

Erskine took a position at the end of the bar and ordered a large whiskey.

As soon as he received his drink, a chiding tone came from Yancy Banniker, as though Malcolm had slighted the Wyandotte area chieftain by not acknowledging his presence.

Malcolm turned, smiled, and nodded, then tossed off a large shot of whiskey, ordering another.

Banniker said, "I don't think you heard all I just said, Erskine."

The tone continued to be a mildly scolding one. The fact that others with Banniker were now tittering like schoolgirls indicated the Wyandotte Jayhawker leader might be in a mood for argument.

Malcolm attributed the situation to drink. He decided this second shot would be his last for the evening. He tossed it down, savoring the burn in his gullet.

"What I said," Banniker evidently found it compelling to repeat, "was that I heard you're retiring from the fighting game, that you're softening and letting a Louisiana Creole and your little school of boys take over in your place."

Malcolm put down his empty glass. He turned to Yancy, smiled briefly once again, and said, "I hope you're not implying I'm yellow."

Banniker made an exaggerated movement with his lips in saying, "The word I used was 'softening.' If you choose to give it a name like 'yellow,' well—"

From Yancy Banniker's joshing appeal to his entourage, obviously seeking approval for his taunting rhetoric, Erskine drew his first anger in days. He decided to rephrase. "Are you man enough to call me 'yellow,' or are you going to sneer around and imply it?"

Banniker straightened, throwing off the restraining hand of an aide who read incitement quickly in Erskine's words.

Yancy demanded, "You saying I ain't a man? You saying I can only talk things roundabout and devious?"

Banniker had begun breathing deeply, rapidly.

Malcolm studied the situation. He strolled toward Yancy and stopped within the reach of a punch. He noticed Banniker had complied with the inn's rules of checking weapons at the registration counter, as Malcolm had, and he was glad of that.

"Yancy," Erskine replied, "that's exactly what I'm saying. I never thought you had the brain to sum it up so well. What's more, now that I'm standing near you—" Malcolm drew a silver dollar from his britches and threw it on the bar. "—let me buy you a bath."

At that, Banniker swung and caught Malcolm on the left side of the jaw.

Erskine went into action, one-handed so as not to do serious harm with his hook to his Wyandotte counterpart. He began a barrage of hard right jabs, interspersed with an occasional haymaker.

One such punch proved devastating to Yancy, who fell backward. He landed in a heap on the floor.

In semi-consciousness, Banniker mumbled to his aides to remove him from the place, for he felt sick and wanted to throw up.

The incident gave Malcolm no satisfaction. He sought the solitude of his room.

Word had spread he was being urged into caution by everyone from Governor Walker on down, and he was possibly taking a softer course. That could be hazardous to a Jayhawker leader. Bushwhackers from Missouri might believe him vulnerable and take bolder risks than ever when riding into his domain.

Malcolm felt no ease about going to sleep that night. He tossed endlessly until he brought himself to a resolution. For the sake of his honor, risks notwithstanding, he would bolster evidence of his courage as soon as he returned to Pleasant Valley.

107

With unexpected ease and at relatively little expense, Erskine concluded all legal work in Lawrence involving his property and his will in a single day.

The ride home was more rapid and direct, yet marked by repeated wishes that he'd never set eyes on Carlotta Edwards. He was annoyed with Hickok for making more of the fortunetelling than good sense would warrant. He was annoyed with himself for being so on edge over it that he escalated a whiskey-inspired exchange with Yancy Banniker into a barroom brawl.

Now, from the ridge overlooking Pleasant Valley, he surveyed his ranch, his home, and pressed Ebony forward into the valley.

Eugene Fontenot had done well, Erskine learned. In his brief absence the Jayhawkers turned out for three missions and received first fire from the raiding Bushwhackers each time. The worst injury, however, was a wound to the neck of Cyrus Ormsby's horse. Fontenot's insistence on additional training in the Indian style of battle riding had proved effective. The wounded horse was also on the mend, as the removed pellet had proved to be of small caliber.

Malcolm decided not to upset the order of present good leadership—Fontenot's dedicated and effective commanding, skillful backing by George Morris, and the wise and energetic presence of Ormsby.

Instead he would personally revert to the role of spy, Erskine decided, for such an activity would serve present needs as he saw them.

For one, he could no longer be accused of shirking responsibilities in order to follow a cautious course inspired by the Governor's probation, his wife's apprehensions, or the fortunetelling.

For another, he knew the Missourians were in an accelerating condition of desperation. He must learn their immediate aims.

While all were witnessing a heavy influx of Free State-sympathizing settlers, the illegally elected lawmakers at Lecompton were maneuvering more actively than ever to give political advantage to proslavers. The next test was scheduled October 5 and 6, the election in which Malcolm was a candidate.

Only a few weeks remained for Missourians to coordinate efforts with Kansas proslavers who currently dominated the Territory's legislative body.

Erskine was confident of yet another invasion by outsiders for the balloting. But heavy settling the past year by new Free Staters north, south, and west should block Missourians' swinging the vote totals this time.

There was less land available for Missourians' casual claims as means of becoming listed on voter rolls. Practically everywhere along the border, antislavery settlers were taking possession of good pasture or farmland. Nearly everywhere, that is, except Oxford Township, largest township in Johnson County.

The delay in antislavery settlement of Oxford Township was due to two principal factors, Malcolm knew—

The original Santa Fe Trail entered Kansas through the hostile villages of Little Santa Fe on the Missouri side and Oxford, just across the line in Kansas. That unfortunate geography cut two ways—Free State settlers wishing to avoid living close to proslavers, and the latter crowd carrying on all kinds of hectoring to discourage them.

The other inhibiting reason was the remaining presence of the Black Bob Shawnees, who still owned a considerable portion of the land in Oxford Township, despite treaty cutbacks. That curtailed the availability of property that immigrants might otherwise have claimed.

Erskine reasoned the next election fraud of major proportions was likely to occur at the Oxford Township balloting station. The township had only a score of qualified voters and a strategically positioned C.C. Catron.

But Malcolm believed he should verify his deductions, and—in the event they were accurate—he should persuade Governor Walker to be prepared to carry out his promise of a clean election.

Erskine was satisfied over the present safety of his family, over the effectiveness of his Jayhawker force, the efficient conduct of the Underground Railroad on his property, and the end-of-summer care of his livestock. He kissed Naomi and Noah one morning and, telling her only that he expected to be gone a few days, ventured alone toward the border.

Except for some of Black Bob's men, few knew the terrain of the area quite so well as Erskine. He knew border-crossing places that would allow his entrance into Missouri completely undetected.

All dry or running creekbeds and covering foliage were familiar spots to Malcolm from past adventures there as a spy.

From recent questioning of captured Bushwhackers, he knew in which forest clearings Law and Order Party meetings were customarily held—and where gatherings of the violent Blue Lodge wings of that force were likely to take place.

Malcolm headed toward one such location on the line joining Cass and Jackson Counties. He was prepared for several days' waiting if necessary. He hoped to witness an actual election strategy conference. To prevent discovery by telltale campfire smoke, he dieted on wild berries and edible roots and was lucky to discover ripe pears on a tree that hadn't fallen prey to squirrels.

After a long day's vigil, unmistakable ground vibrations of approaching horsemen signalled his erasing all camping signs and moving Ebony to prearranged cover.

A Blue Lodge meeting was about to convene.

Erskine climbed a maple tree lush with leaves of fall orange-red, one suited for observation of the meeting. He counted eighteen men assembling. Most of what they talked about was routine, enumerating for one another the names and conditions of the Lodge's sick and injured, moving into harvest reports and even gossip.

When the Missourians' discussion veered toward the approaching election, Malcolm was particularly attentive. In that discussion he learned that Missourians from as far east as Lexington in

Lafayette County and from as far south as Butler in Bates County were on alert to arrive before October 5 for the voting.

Where? At Oxford.

"We done lined us up purt near two thousand men to ride in," he heard one of the Blue Lodge leaders announce. "Catron better have him plenty o' whiskey."

Discussion among Blue Lodgers narrowed to estimates of how many fraudulent votes Missourians should cast to maintain the majority in Lecompton. Estimates ran between 1,200 and 1,800.

Malcolm knew that was true, for Douglas County would go heavily Free State, almost ten to one. Douglas was expected to tilt the results once and for all to a free Kansas—provided there was no interference or offsetting fraud such as that being discussed here.

After about a half-hour's more mingling by Blue Lodge members, they broke up and rode off in several directions.

Erskine returned to Pleasant Valley, bone-tired.

Naomi confronted him. "You've been across the border, haven't you?"

"I guess anybody can see that," Malcolm said, indicating his condition and unbuckling his gunbelt. "Anyone can smell I've been camped out all day. Why?"

"I thought we agreed you're not to take unnecessary risks, in view of what we've—learned."

Erskine turned and said, "We haven't 'learned' a damned thing. Unless you refer to what a ranting madwoman said about me as 'fact,' which it isn't. Naomi, this nonsense about Carlotta's fortunetelling is putting a strain on both of us. I can't think clearly while it hangs over us."

Watching his wife—seeing how she turned aside, wrung her hands, breathed hard so as to stifle either a response or sobs that lodged in her breast—Malcolm began to understand the special and intense strain he'd placed on her.

Moved deeply, he approached Naomi to hug her, but she stepped quickly out of reach—something she'd never done before.

"No, Malcolm. Not now. I must go sit somewhere and think."

108

"Pleasant Valley
"Oxford Township
"Johnson County, K.T.
"September 15, 1857

"The Hon. Robert J. Walker
"Governor
"Kansas Territory
"Lecompton,
"Douglas County, K.T.

"Sir:

"We have become acquainted on levels of mutual respect, because we apply our separate energies toward a common goal – the building of Kansas. Therefore, I feel no hesitancy about the task that follows.

"Your pledge of May, in which you assured Kansas Territorial citizens of proper elections to establish governance of their future affairs, is now in jeopardy of being thwarted unlawfully. Your critics are abandoning all reason and have devised a plan to defy and overturn your stated assurances.

"I can attest that there exists, in fact and deed, a conspiracy against your wish for allowing Kansas Territorial elections to be managed and determined solely among Kansas citizens.

"I have promised solemnly to engage in no violently offensive behavior respecting my operations of Jayhawker protection to citizens of my area, and I have kept that promise. I have found it necessary, however, to conduct surveillance – never once drawing my weapon to do so.

"The past several days I have visited Missouri at some risk to my person, solely in the wish to confirm what I have suspected may be afoot.

"While I cannot furnish names, for I simply do not yet know the identities of the principals I have seen and heard discussing this plot, I have enclosed a diagram showing the precise place of their conferring and of my

surveillance, in Cass County close by Jackson County, and the approximate time and the date of my witnessing.

"Some eighteen of their number came together under the aegis of Blue Lodge affiliation, to discuss an enterprise completely in contravention of law and decency and your own stated wish.

"There is to be in Oxford Township, no doubt a convenient place owing to planned balloting exactly at its border with Missouri, an outrageous fraud that is wholesale in scope.

"As many as 2,000 citizens of Missouri have been 'lined up,' according to words I heard personally, to meet there October 5 and 6 for the purpose of turning the election from its otherwise expected Free State Party victory to one for the Democratic Party.

"I know, Sir, that you are a Democrat, and I do not intend to insult your basic beliefs, the general fairness of which you have persuaded me to accept. Yet you must know that the purpose of such fraud is to win for the proslavery cause a victory that will forever hurl Kansas Territory into darkness as a slave state.

"Entering the approaching balloting with no foreign factor to be considered, the Free State Party has estimated it will win in the aggregate by several hundred ballots. The Missourians' plan, however, is intended to force an effectively opposite result.

"Let me venture to be more precise. The Free State Party has estimated an approaching victory by a relatively small margin. Its victory at the polls seems, by all counts and estimates, an assured outcome resulting from recent immigration into the Territory and the establishment of legal claims.

"An illegal casting of as many as 2,000 ballots by Missourians – even of fewer, say 1,200 – could have a devastating effect.

"The makeup of the Legislature is such, as you know, that its members are elected by District. If cast in Oxford or anywhere in Johnson County, which is paired in the District with Douglas County, that number of votes, even at 1,200, will affect the outcome for the seats of eight Territorial Representatives.

"A factor of eight in the makeup of the Territorial House could vest unlawful power in the proslavers once again. A tally is enclosed for your review on this point.

"Therefore, Sir, I respectfully request that you assign, in whatever manner the power of your good office may accomplish legitimately, a team of qualified and impartial observers to be present at the Oxford balloting. By their presence and monitoring they could insure fairness and authenticity of the balloting, confirming the credentials of those about to vote as Kansans.

"Nothing less than such a close watch, under the authority of your good name and office, will impress the threatening invaders sufficiently for them to stand down.

"I count eleven residences in the village of Oxford as well as five others, including my own, that represent the total landed electorate of Oxford Township. By my count it is not possible for Oxford Township to contain a greater number than sixteen bona fide voters.

"I cannot urge too strongly your subscription to my suggestion of balloting oversight, a proposal I offer in the spirit of our common interests in the integrity of the first balloting under your tenure as Territorial Governor.

"I have witnessed and heard the perpetrators describe their intentions to draw illegal balloting from such distances in Missouri as the Lafayette County seat, Lexington, to the east, and the Bates County seat, Butler, to the south.

"Allowing the time required for this letter to reach you, there remain scarcely two weeks for your arranging a watch at the Oxford Precinct.

"Please, Governor Walker, protect the integrity of the approaching election through this simple safeguard.

"I am a most humble citizen in faithful service to Kansas,

"Malcolm Erskine"

109

Resentments and distancing by Naomi seemed to be diminishing.

Malcolm believed she was accustoming herself to accepting the inevitable. While sworn against attacking, he continued to take serious risks that required understanding and support. Tension at home could distract him dangerously.

Erskine knew Eugene Fontenot and Cyrus Ormsby had urged Naomi not to get her back up over his activities. At the same time, she won from them agreement to watch his moves closely, to speak up when they believed he was about to do anything foolish.

With no regard for the delicacy of the situation, Lani blurted—in a near-scolding manner—her belief that husband-wife disagreements could spoil Naomi's milk and affect Noah. That observation carried much weight with everyone.

A recovered Chad Brookings, doubling back from maneuvers ordered by Eugene, rode in, raising dust. He announced that a carriage was approaching the complex.

Esmerelda Bartholomew arrived with slightly more pomp than Malcolm might have expected. Her Negro driver was in a uniform that appeared specially tailored. A Negro boy about eight or nine years old, in similar attire but barefooted, sat beside him. The boy scrambled to provide a box for Esmerelda to step on as she alighted. She instructed the driver to pull the carriage to a pump and trough in a shady place beside trees, to wait for her.

"That's a grand outfit you're wearing," Malcolm said.

"Everything's changed these past four months, dearest. I'll explain in due course. But your Naomi is watching from a window, so I'll greet you with a simple handshake and proceed directly to meet her. Play this out with me, Malcolm. There's some importance—disturbing importance—to my visit beyond the social call."

Erskine introduced her to Naomi. He emphasized Esmerelda's and her father Peter's arranging his flight from hostile Westport. Arranging also Governor Walker's dismissal of charges.

With satisfaction, Malcolm watched Naomi take Esmerelda into her arms.

When they entered the house, Esmerelda drew something from her large, beaded purse and handed it to Naomi. "A housewarming gift," she announced.

Naomi's eyes grew wide when she opened the small package. "A *mezuzah,*" she cried. "Where on earth did you get such a thing? Thank you. *Thank* you."

Esmerelda explained that a shop in Westport had opened recently handling imported materials, that this symbolic decoration was of Russian manufacture.

Jewish families, Naomi confirmed for her and Malcolm, traditionally fastened *mezuzahs* containing printed prayers to their doorposts.

Esmerelda made a fuss over Noah. Lani readily gave him over. The baby grew cranky quickly, clearly wanting to return to Lani.

Then Esmerelda asked to see the place where fugitive slaves were quartered. Naomi led her into the barn.

Malcolm approached the carriage driver and mentioned he'd noticed a problem with the horse's bit when they drove up. He offered to find a substitute in the tack room and help install it for the driver, who expressed gratitude. The boy was stretched out on the cushioned seat Esmerelda had occupied, fast asleep.

When Malcolm was about to leave the tack room in the barn, he heard Naomi and Esmerelda deep in conversation. Not wishing to interrupt what seemed a serious exchange, he chose to eavesdrop.

"Now that you've told me what enterprise has brought you wealth, Esmerelda, I'm inspired to candor between us. Is that all right? Your current trade is—" Malcolm heard Naomi clear her throat. "—*sex.* Obviously you've had quick success in a prime market, Westport. Now for a related topic, and I don't plan to judge or condemn. Please confide what happened while my husband stayed with you."

"Understand, Naomi, that I *employ* whores, mostly white girls, but I don't rent my own body. As for what happened, I fell in love with Malcolm. It was like someone hit me with a brick. He's a remarkable man. My hero. I'd had his picture from the New York paper on the wall above my bed for months."

"Did you sleep with him?"

Malcolm winced and took notice of a long pause before Esmerelda answered. "I *threw* myself at him. Yes, we made love for the better part of two of the most glorious days and nights of my life. I'm not ashamed to admit that I was the aggressor."

Another pause. Then Naomi said, "Have you become pregnant? He's already impregnated two women besides me, and they're both now married—one of them to my brother—and the other has miscarried."

"I'm not pregnant. I wish I *were,* by him, to be honest."

"That's the bright feature of this conversation, Esmerelda. Your honesty. Despite my knowing what the two of you did, I find your candor endearing. If it was to happen with anyone—and I expected it would—I'm glad it was you. I hope we'll be friends."

"It's clear the motherless child in Malcolm is generally attracted to resourceful women," Esmerelda said. "Compassionate and brainy ones."

Naomi responded with, "At risk of conceit, I'll say we have that in common. The arrangement you made with Governor Walker was brilliant. Actually, life-saving. Let me hug you again in thanks for helping us—and, I suppose, for loving him."

"Malcolm must be on pins and needles wondering whether I'll reveal any of his secrets from Westport."

"My husband, I think, deserves at times to be on pins and needles. Let him squirm. And speaking of squirming, a bit of secret girl talk here, did he—"

At that instant Ebony whinnied in his stall, no doubt picking up his master's scent. That vexed Erskine, who wondered what more the women were discussing so frankly.

Their voices and laughter receded, indicating they were drifting from the barn. Malcolm scurried to the far exit, returning to the carriage by a roundabout path.

After replacing the horse's bit, he confronted Esmerelda when she returned to the carriage. Naomi was nowhere in sight.

"Did you two have an interesting visit?"

"Your wife is fantastic," Esmerelda said. "We've become friends, in spite of my new business activity."

"You're operating a whorehouse?"

"How did you know? I hadn't yet told you."

Malcolm realized he might be letting the cat out of the bag, relative to his listening in the barn. He covered his error by saying, "It wasn't hard to figure, knowing your organizing abilities, the location, and your sashaying around like *nouveau riche.*"

"Good guess, but I don't think you can guess why else I came here today, beyond paying an overdue call."

"I'm on pins and needles waiting for you to tell me."

Esmerelda cocked her head and looked at Malcolm strangely. She said, "Part of it is, I want to relieve your debt to the O'Brien woman, if you'd like to transfer the loan."

Erskine shrugged, only slightly interested but enough to ask at what interest rate.

"No interest. That way I'll be helping the Underground Railroad. That's also my way of demonstrating my love for you is greater than Mrs. O'Brien's."

"Of which I've never been certain anyway," Malcolm confessed, "as to the truth of it, or the depth of it."

"Well, then. There you are."

"I'll think about it, Esmerelda. Besides beauty and talent, you have a generous spirit. Earlier you spoke of something disturbing. Please tell me."

"Governor Walker will deny the request you made by letter—for balloting oversight in Oxford. And there's even worse news, picked up by one of my girls."

"Go on."

"While Walker won't appoint an election watchman, Reverend Johnson has."

"Who?"

"Sam Jones."

110

"Capitol
"Lecompton
"Douglas County, K.T.
"September 21, 1857

"Malcolm Erskine
"Pleasant Valley
"Oxford Township
"Johnson County, K.T.

"My dear Malcolm:

"It is a distinct pleasure to hear from you, even when you bear down so intensely upon issues that have been worrisome. I believe in all sincerity, however, that you exaggerate the danger.

"I have been given most solemn assurances by Law and Order Party and Democratic Party officials, and indirectly by representatives of the Missouri Blue Lodge, that no treacherous activity as that which you predict is to be feared for any of the Territorial voting places.

"As a matter of fact, Malcolm, in order to be absolutely certain that my response to you would be well-based, I delayed writing for purposes of confirming facts. I inquired anew into the possibility of there being a misunderstanding, on the part of those who had earlier given me assurances against false voting.

"When all was said and done, I learned on the highest authority that no illegal behavior such as you describe for the approaching election is even contemplated seriously by any, save perhaps an extreme, radical element.

"The Rev. Thomas Johnson has pledged, in ways leaving no room for doubt, that neither the Democratic Party in Kansas nor the proslavery Missourians will jeopardize principles of fairness and propriety in the approaching voting.

"Malcolm, I know how you feel about the man, for he is a slave-owner and has used his power in the past to further the spread of slavery into Kansas Territory. But he is also a man of God, and for that we must respect his word. A man so pious in every way would not attempt to deceive me in this matter.

"To demonstrate how fair-minded he can be, when I made further inquiry by reason of your letter of September 15, Reverend Johnson offered to have, and has since arranged, that the Oxford Precinct be monitored by experienced law enforcement authorities, to guard against false balloting, whether by Missourians or anyone else.

"Reverend Johnson has assured me that all reasonable resources for successful and fair monitoring of a bona fide election at Oxford will be placed at the disposal of Samuel J. Jones, who until recently carried the title of Sheriff of Douglas County.

"The extra length to which the good Reverend has gone is so convincing to me of his sincerity, I dare not trump his arrangement by issuing an executive order of my own.

"Now, let me become more personal in my reply.

"Frankly, I am disturbed you have resumed the practice of espionage, considering the danger to yourself personally, the position in which the activity places your family, the lack of ethics inherent in the business of spying, and your pledge to me.

"True, you have held your weapons in check in crossing the border. But to spy is an act of aggression, and it is aggressive behavior that you have promised to renounce.

"I am hereby placing you on stricter probation. You are not to visit Missouri of your own volition, while the atmosphere surrounding your presence there is so charged, that you are the target of a veritable manhunt whenever you enter that state. Moreover, your doing so will likely provoke so-called Bushwhackers into further aggression.

"Now, moving to what you consider to be your findings, I have no doubt that you heard a 'plan' spun out by Missourians, but I tell you there will be no such activity.

"A very special effort was made by Reverend Johnson in the course of my inquiry. The Reverend dispatched a fast messenger to Col. A.G. Boone in Westport, Missouri, who is regarded as a leading citizen of the

Western part of that state and a businessman of impeccable reputation and integrity, to confirm there is in fact no effective conspiracy for unlawful voting, neither at Oxford nor at any of the other precincts along the border.

"The answer was returned this morning, and Colonel Boone's personal assurance is in writing before me.

"Colonel Boone, a relative of Mr. Jones I am told, writes and I quote –

> " 'I swear to Almighty God, who is my solemn guide in all matters of personal and professional conduct, that there is to be no unlawful balloting at Oxford or other locales, by my knowledge, which knowledge ought to be considerable, taking into account my position in Western Missouri.
>
> " 'And if it were known broadly, among traditional parties, that such an unlawful exercise as that which you fear might be, in fact, a feasible plan for the approaching balloting, I am confident Reverend Johnson would condemn the same. As you have no doubt discovered in your conversations with the holy man, there has been nothing of substance for him to condemn.' "

"There you have it, Malcolm. The word of two very well-respected gentlemen, though I dare say you find them 'on the other side' of your cause, so to speak.

"I, for one, believe them.

"If I had the slightest doubt, I would not hesitate to do as you suggest, to have my own representatives such as Secretary of State Fred Stanton present for the voting in Oxford. But it is a bad precedent for me to set, just as spying, in order to overhear wishful thinking by radical Missourians, is a bad precedent.

"If I were you, as a candidate, a citizen, a voter, I would simply cast my ballot as will others in good faith on October 5-6.

"I wish you sincerely the best of luck in your effort as a Free State Party candidate for the Kansas Territorial Legislature.

"I pledge to you, Malcolm, that should anything unseemly and inappropriate occur in Oxford, matching your apprehensions in scope or pur-

pose, I will personally visit that place and will invite you, in the event of that remote possibility, to accompany me.

"Very sincerely,
"Robert J. Walker
"Governor,
"Kansas Territory"

111

When dawn broke Monday, October 5, Malcolm awoke and found to his surprise and dismay that Naomi had already left their bed. In recent days a special affection had stirred them, one which he believed was a sign of lessened fears.

He got up, pulled on trousers, and sought Naomi in the kitchen and the parlor. He found only Lani tending to Noah's needs. She explained that Naomi had gone early to the barn—there to see and talk with the men of the Jayhawker band.

Puzzled, Malcolm dressed fully and soon followed, meeting his wife as she exited the barn.

"What are you doing here?" he asked, half-amused by her strange activity at dawn.

"Buying insurance for you," Naomi replied, without flippancy yet evidently intending the response as dry humor.

Erskine groaned. "Not that subject again."

"Always that subject," she said.

"What have you arranged? I imagine you've got some trick up your sleeve because I intend to vote today. And because I'm the only man of this ranch eligible to vote in this precinct, I'll be going alone."

"That's right," Naomi said, moving past him to return to the house. "You intend to go alone. I haven't disturbed even the perception of that. So you needn't feel you're about to be humiliated in front of the enemy."

Malcolm made a grab for her arm to stop her, but he missed.

Now he could only prance awkwardly behind her as she quick-stepped toward home. He called, "Wait a minute. Hey, *hold on* there. You're the most exasperating—"

At his use of that word, she wheeled about, almost causing them to collide.

"I'm exasperating? Malcolm, you're the world's record-holder in that category. But let's not have a spat. Besides, it's chilly out here. Let's get more fires going inside. The barn seemed warmer than the house this morning."

"I'll get fires going," Malcolm tossed back in a protesting tone as she turned to walk on again. "Just as soon as I—" He had to raise his volume to be heard, for she was making fast tracks while he remained both rooted and frustrated. "—learn what the hell you've been up to."

At that last, she whirled before going in, giving him only a coquettish smile.

"That woman," Malcolm said aloud to himself, gnashing his teeth. He was alone outdoors now, the frost glinting in the half-light of dawn. He was at a loss whether to turn to the barn and force his men to confess the plot Naomi had hatched with them or press the issue with her.

The instant Malcolm decided to reenter the house, he heard the barn door behind him, and he turned. There he saw George Morris at the entrance, obviously embarrassed as though interrupted in some clandestine assignment.

Morris gave himself away thoroughly by waving to Malcolm with uncharacteristically jerky hesitations, then by returning inside the barn immediately.

Now Malcolm knew what was planned.

Whenever George Morris and Naomi got together, they intended a little play-acting. Malcolm had no doubt now—his Jayhawkers would be present for the voting, all disguised in one manner or another. They would conceal extra weapons, guarding against the first sign of trouble as he, Malcolm, arrived to cast his ballot. He was confident that was what Morris and Naomi had worked out.

For such a plan to succeed, though, he must pretend not to know. He must back away from pressing the issue. He must seem not to care any longer about her traipsing out to the barn this early.

Hours later, after a hearty breakfast, Malcolm mounted Ebony to ride the few miles to Oxford. Though he had some notion of what corruption he might witness, his spirits were hopeful.

Perhaps the Missourians would miscalculate and provide too few votes to offset the Free State total from Douglas County. Perhaps at the last moment Governor Walker would have had a change of heart. Possiby Walker *would* send Stanton to Oxford to see to a proper balloting.

Perhaps.

Malcolm approached the newly-developed town of Oxford on the Santa Fe Trail and turned south along the Missouri line toward the polling place.

All positive hopes were dashed. There stood a horde of men, border ruffians all—except for Erskine's disguised guards among them. He had difficulty picking them out from the rest.

A table had been set up under a large white-oak tree as a place of balloting. Close by were scores of carousing Missourians, most of them armed, many raising tin cups filled from a whiskey barrel that stood beside the table.

Preparations had been elaborate, Malcolm noticed. He resolved to observe closely all he could, so as to make a complete report to Governor Walker that the worst fears of election fraud were now being realized.

Several taunts greeted Malcolm, who was still astride Ebony. Though he carried weapons, he didn't dare reach for any, or what should be a peaceable process would turn into a bloodbath. Erskine estimated he and his sharply trained men could probably kill fifty of the other side before starting to fall to enemy guns.

And fall they would, for there were a few hundred Missourians clustered in the vicinity, many of them drunk—a motley collection of drifters interspersed with hard-working farmhands.

Malcolm realized, with or without the offending presence of Sam Jones, an election site wasn't a place where any man dared draw a weapon. Should Congress hear of violence at the scene of voting, deployment of armed troops to safeguard future balloting would be the result.

That, Malcolm realized, Missourians wished to avoid like the plague.

He would ride Ebony quietly to the hitching rail near the balloting table, identify himself formally, and cast his vote for the Free State Party.

As Erskine strolled his horse forward, he saw the smirking Sam Jones spread open his coat, hook thumbs into his vest, and turn his head to one side to spit. Jones commented, "Fellas, this is Kansas, and it seems the law allows all kinds to vote, long as they own land. Let him through, then let him be on his way."

"You doin' your job right and proper, Sam!" a Missourian called to Jones.

In further pretended enforcement of orderliness, Jones removed a hand from its resting place on his paunch and conducted with gestures the movement of noisy and jeering Bushwhackers away from the table.

When that area was completely cleared, Malcolm dismounted and steadied Ebony, then walked to the table. He noticed no effort had been made to insure a secret ballot. Instead, a single roll of paper—stretching perhaps fifty feet—was being used to record signatures and choices of either the Free State group of candidates or the Democratic Party slate.

"Would you like a drink?" an official at the table invited Malcolm, indicating the whiskey barrel.

"Wait!" Sam Jones raised his voice to call. "I'll have to draw the line on that. We don't have no dipper," and he began laughing, "marked *'colored'*."

With that, the gathering burst into a cacophony of raucous laughter.

Malcolm imagined himself unbuttoning his britches and pissing in the barrel. But that could start a riot. Instead he signed the roll and cast his vote.

Three days later he learned Oxford polling officials had verified to Secretary of State Fred Stanton that 1,628 votes had been cast there for the Democratic list—and four for the Free State Party.

112

For more than a week after the election, Malcolm was in a state of deep depression, withdrawing from conversation. He showed only mild interest in the comings and goings of runaway slaves, in details of ranching.

He wondered whether to dispose of the property and move his family to Iowa. But he didn't share such thoughts with Naomi. Not yet. She loved this Kansas, in which the Goodmans of Paola continued to find so much promise.

The prospect of the Erskine family's being affected by harsh laws under an entrenched proslavery government was one Malcolm didn't want them to face. The bogus legislature had in the past declared expression of antislavery sentiments a prisonable offense. And to take part in the freeing or escape of a slave meant death.

Until now enforcement proved difficult for what had been a shaky proslavery government. After the latest election and with statehood looming, however, the proslavers might feel free to go to any lengths to enforce conformity.

What Malcolm feared most was the possible invoking of extremes, as in Southern states. Persons holding the smallest quantities of Negro blood were subject to loss of human rights and enslavement.

That meant danger for Noah and the child yet to be born. Malcolm couldn't live with that.

As though underscoring new confidence, Bushwhackers cut their raids to zero.

Kansas citizens anticipated a stranglehold on government by proslavers and an exodus by Free State advocates rather than out-and-out warfare. That mood gripped Eugene Fontenot and others of the Jayhawker band, Naomi reported to Malcolm sadly, for leaving the Territory seemed preferable in the long run.

They'd all fought and lost. They'd stood up in behalf of Negroes and had fallen victim to an enemy without scruples. Erskine had warned Governor Walker of the approaching fraud and had been rebuffed—because of claims of innocence by scoundrels.

All that remained was Walker's promise—that he would *not* recommend statehood to Congress after an election so tainted as this one. But some Free Staters including Malcolm now doubted the sincerity of Walker's pledge, questioning whether Walker had the courage of his inaugural convictions.

In this lull Malcolm looked up from turning earth in Naomi's garden—preparing it to receive the soaking of winter's snow. Unusual activity at the barn surprised him.

Vaguely aware that Terence Anderton had ridden from his watch quickly to report to Fontenot, Malcolm expected that the youth's purpose involved some minor alarm. He expected to see at least half the Jayhawker force ride out to meet the problem.

Instead, Fontenot and the others hovered near the barn entrance. Alternately, Eugene or Cyrus Ormsby or George Morris turned toward the house, toward Erskine, who nevertheless kept his main attention on the garden.

Still, he was aware of the buzzing, and it occurred to him they were hesitating whether to "bother" him. Malcolm threw down the tilling fork, intending to approach them. Before he took a step, he saw Fontenot hitch up his belt and stride in his direction.

Malcolm waited. When Eugene neared the garden, he said, "Walker is riding in to see you. He stopped to tell Anderton he wants to talk with you. Army escorts are with him, but he gave assurance we have nothing to fear from that."

Erskine looked down, picked up the tilling fork again, and dug in, muttering, "I don't want to see him. *You* talk to him. Use the house for your meeting."

Rather than protest Malcolm's instruction, Fontenot turned and stuck two fingers in his mouth, whistling a loud signal. At that, George Morris came running. Erskine watched them hurry past him to enter his house.

Shortly Naomi, a shawl thrown over her head loosely, stalked out with Eugene and George. She grabbed Malcolm by the lapels of his jacket and gave him an angry shaking, crying out, "The Governor is coming to see you. Malcolm, you will behave *respectfully*. Do you understand?"

Fontenot and Morris had retreated rather than share their embarrassment for Malcolm. But they'd calculated correctly, he knew, that Naomi could force him to do anything she wished at this critical point in their lives.

Pushed and pulled by her, Malcolm made for the house and a washpan. He prepared himself for this unexpected visit by Governor Walker.

*****

"I apologize," Walker said. "I was wrong to trust Reverend Johnson."

"Johnson's a bloody hypocrite," Erskine mumbled at a barely audible level. Naomi was present for the meeting, but she remained silent.

Walker continued his agonizing. "The financial motive, the ability to profit from slavery, runs beyond any wish to be right with God and enter Heaven, evidently."

"Bloody hypocrite," Malcolm repeated.

"For me," Walker said, "to have been taken in by pleas of innocence, in the face of evidence you took risks to gather for me—" The Governor was obviously at a loss to continue discussing how the fraud at Oxford had hurt him personally.

Malcolm raised his head to hold Walker's gaze. He would give logic a try.

"In the context of recent history and pressures for abolition, Governor," he said, "anyone holding another in slavery is capable of far worse than false pleading. For a lie to roll off his tongue holds no challenge, regardless whether he wears ministerial cloth or holds community respect for other deeds."

Embarrassed to be lecturing the older man about realities, Malcolm continued nonetheless. "These days defenders of slavery are capable of treachery, even murder—and crimes of that nature have in fact been arranged by such people. *My* crimes were all retaliatory to consequences of theirs. I've been trying to tell you that for five months."

"I know. I know," Walker acknowledged. He nodded with his lips set firmly, as though having made a decision. He slapped his thighs once loudly. He stood. "Will you accompany Secretary Stanton and me on an inspection? I want to see the scene of these—these informalities I've been hearing about."

Startled, Malcolm rose as well. "Informalities? Governor, it was plain and simple fraud."

"*You* know it was fraud," Walker said, placing his hand on Malcolm's shoulder, "and *I* know it was fraud. But for me to declare officially that it was fraud would require many of the principals to go to prison."

"That's what they deserve."

"I know, but what difference to you," Walker inquired with new intensity, "whether I throw out the Oxford vote for informality or for fraud, as long as I throw it out, *eh?*"

Malcolm stood silent, beginning to understand how intricately political were the considerations that a man such as Robert J. Walker must make in his work. And if the Governor were to do exactly as he'd just indicated, that would make Malcolm a politician as well, a member of the Kansas Territorial House of Representatives.

Erskine relaxed. He returned the gesture of trust, placing his hand on Walker's shoulder and saying, "Politics. Don't you just love it? Where is Stanton?"

"He'll arrive early tomorrow."

"Stay here tonight, and we'll all visit Oxford in the morning. We can billet the soldiers as well."

When Walker agreed, those in the parlor heard a *"Whoop!"*

Cyrus Ormsby had been listening unashamedly and now turned to announce the plan to the other Jayhawkers waiting outside.

113

Malcolm greeted the new day charged mentally and emotionally, hope in his heart. He fairly dashed about the house and grounds. He sought to take command of his men again. Fontenot yielded immediately.

Erskine greeted the men in the barn, instructing them to remain close to the ranch for defense and protection of his family as well as for routine chores. The increasingly prosperous ranch proved more and more demanding, particularly as the grazing grass growth would shortly slow by change of season.

Escaping slaves were not expected anytime soon for routing to other stations.

The five soldiers assigned as escort would accompany the Governor's party to Oxford for the local portion of the investigation. Malcolm's men could stay at Pleasant Valley and carry on regular duties in his temporary absence.

The air was crisp that morning, raising Erskine's spirits.

The Governor and his guards were being well fed inside and attended to by the hospitality and good cooking of Naomi and Lani, with Ormsby adding his talents. The hosting of their guests could not have gone better. Erskine paused to say as much to Fontenot, asking that his good feeling about the men's behavior be passed along to them.

Fontenot listened with a furrowed brow, finally saying, "I am worried about this thing with Walker today."

"Worried? What could go wrong? We've got the Army with us."

"You call a few recruits 'the Army,' Malcolm? What do they know about the devious ways of border ruffians?"

Erskine sought eye contact with his trusted Creole friend.

"Eugene, look at me. I'm telling you, I'll be all right. What better protection than to be with the Territorial Governor? Anyway, I'll be armed and have always defended myself adequately."

Fontenot looked down and shook his head. "This makes me uneasy."

"Stop worrying, *mon ami.* You can't give full attention to commanding in my absence if you worry."

Fontenot acknowledged that and, nodding, broke away to attend to his duties.

Erskine found time to chat with each of his men separately before he and the Governor were to leave. With George Morris he discussed weaponry, with Ormsby stores and new supplies, with others the animals, the ranching, or other topics.

Malcolm also met with Lani about Noah and her readiness to help with the baby due in spring. Curiously, she wished to settle the matter of Johnny Kesibwi's release of her.

"Not today, Lani," Malcolm said, starting away.

"Today, Malcolm," she said in a surprisingly demanding tone. He couldn't recall she'd ever used his first name before.

He sighed and turned to listen. "What is it?"

"Have I been pledged to Noah? Am I your future daughter-in-law? Is it true, what I've heard of that?"

Malcolm threw back his head and laughed. "It was a joke," he said. "Nothing more."

"Of such matters," the Chippewa girl protested, "we don't make jokes." While she spoke, her pubescent and wildly budding beauty radiated.

Malcolm surveyed her, head to toe, convinced she was daily becoming more remarkable in appearance. At last he conceded, "Keep to your studies and newly found values. Noah could *not* do better when he's grown and ready, far as I'm concerned. But he's still an infant. Let him grow through boyhood to manhood, and let it all come naturally. If Naomi also approves," he said firmly, "it's arranged."

"Thank you," Lani said with a quick smile. "You realize, I'm not a virgin."

"What does that matter?"

"And my age. I'll be past thirty when Noah becomes a man."

Malcolm tried to visualize a mature Lani but saw mentally only Sylvia, in a white, fringed-buckskin, beaded dress. "Learn, Lani, then teach Noah well. If it's his wish as well, marry, bear his children, be happy, love him always. That's all I can say."

The girl reached up suddenly to hold the back of his neck and draw Erskine's lips to hers. Then, "Thank you. I'm not sure you realize how much your 'joke' has done for an orphaned Chippewa girl's future." With that she ran off to attend to her duties.

Malcolm savored the moment. He remembered how greatly the accumulated wisdom of a woman exposed to both Indian and other cultures had served him.

Now it was time to see Naomi and Noah and determine whether Walker was ready. Erskine found her crying softly in their bedroom, holding their son. "What is it?"

Naomi seemed unable to explain, saying only, "I suppose I'm—happy for you. You're—getting what we must all have—from this visit by the Governor."

"Yes, but we needn't drown our joy in tears." He held her close, Noah still in her arms. Malcolm had a sense of four beings embracing in close love, including the baby in her belly.

Erskine held his family that way several minutes, feeling the trickle of Naomi's quiet tears on his neck, listening to the sounds of Noah sucking his thumb.

At last, ready to go, he kissed them both. He and Naomi were struck evidently with the same thought, for he said, "Take care," simultaneously with her identically spoken wish.

At that they laughed together, baby Noah picking up on the joy of such sharing and giving a small giggle. Malcolm kissed them again, this time long and lovingly. Then he went out to meet Walker and the gathering group.

* * * * *

The ride to Oxford was a cheerful excursion. The countryside was in full fall bloom of color.

A corporal drove the Governor's closed carriage. The escorts rode two ahead, two behind. Ebony was hitched in back of the carriage.

Inside, the two men chatted about plans for the Free State, laws that Malcolm would introduce once he was sworn in as a member of the House of Representatives, articles they would suggest be incorporated into a new constitution prohibiting slavery.

On occasion Walker reminded Malcolm he'd not yet moved his investigation along to where he could set aside the fraudulent votes.

"No," Malcolm replied, "but you will."

Governor Walker nodded, his thoughts seeming to be at great distance from them, and said, "Such a decision will affect the entire nation."

As they neared the village of Oxford, Malcolm pointed out how few residences were there. Walker became quiet as they turned south toward the balloting site. When they arrived they greeted Secretary of State Stanton, who waited beside his open carriage. He'd driven there from Westport, with a stop at the Shawnee Mission, he said.

The soldiers remained in their saddles near the Governor's carriage, which was still manned by the driver, who ordered them "at ease."

As a precaution, Malcolm released Ebony from the tether. Though free, the stallion remained at the spot, ready for Malcolm's signal.

Stanton indicated he wished to discuss something with Walker privately.

Their chat consumed less than a minute, after which Walker approached Erskine. "Fred tells me the Missourians failed to deliver enough fraudulent votes to this site, so they took the rolls to Colonel Boone's office in Westport and copied names from the Cincinnati city directory."

Malcolm said, "They had to get sixteen hundred voters somewhere, because there aren't that many in all of Johnson County. I suppose a Cincinnati book's as good a source as any."

They walked toward the white-oak tree where Erskine had seen the whiskey barrel and table set up for voters. Malcolm described various features of the gathering he'd noticed on the day he voted.

"And the total from Oxford Township that you estimate to be eligible to vote, in the strictest sense of the law?" Walker asked.

"Sixteen," Malcolm replied.

Suddenly a sharp pain gripped Erskine's chest. When he reacted by raising his hand there, as though to protect what had been pierced by lead, he heard the rifle shot.

In slipping from consciousness, Malcolm calculated a sniper had done this from nearly a quarter mile off.

Erskine fell, moaning that he wished his son, Noah, to know of this moment. He looked up into the face of Governor Walker and saw the official's horror over what was happening. He said hoarsely—

"Let my son—know the glory—of what—happened here today."

Feeling blood gush freely from the area of his heart, Malcolm then found it impossible to draw full breath, soon impossible to draw any breath at all.

His eyes still opened to the scene, still taking in the bright, crisp morning about them, Malcolm was aware he would die.

In thirty years, he thought before fading to darkness, he'd lived ninety.

114

The distraught Walker fell to his knees to determine whether Malcolm was mortally wounded. Stanton rushed over and kneeled as well. The Governor put his hand on Erskine's bloody chest.

Walker summoned the corporal, who'd jumped from the carriage. The other soldiers had ridden off after the sniper.

Walker's voice cracked. "Let's get him to a *doctor!* Did you see who did it?"

"Man with an eyepatch," the corporal said. "Rifle from *that* direction." He pointed across the border, toward woods to the southeast. "I had the squad give chase."

"Here, you and Stanton help me put him in the carriage," Walker directed.

When the corporal examined Malcolm closely, he hesitated.

"Well, *lift,"* Walker shouted "Let's pick him up and put him *in."*

"Sir, he's dead."

Fred Stanton nodded and reached to put his hand on the Governor's arm. "Sir, he's gone." Stanton got to his feet.

"You don't know what you're talking about," Walker declared, looking up at his aide. "He's *not* dead."

"Sorry, sir," the corporal said, still examining Malcolm. "I know that he's dead. There's no breath, no heartbeat. Please, sir," the soldier coaxed, softening to the Governor's grief, helping the older man rise, "I'll get help and we—"

"Yes," Walker said, dazed, stained with Malcolm's blood, his chest heaving a sob. "Yes, let's get him home. It's all we can do now."

At that moment Ebony approached and nickered. The animal nudged Erskine's lifeless body with his nose, sniffed the chest wound, stood inert, and nickered again.

Ebony pawed the ground alongside Erskine, then reached to take a sleeve in his teeth and pulled his master over, face down. The stallion repositioned himself. His rear legs buckled and he dropped to the ground, his saddled back to Malcolm's body.

The startled Governor and the corporal moved out of the horse's way.

Rolling slightly and leveraging with a front hoof, Ebony reached his snout. With his teeth, the stallion grabbed the jacket collar at the back of his dead master's neck. He tugged, let go, rolled, turned his head to tug again. By a series of such moves, Ebony gradually pulled the Jayhawker's body across the saddle.

When the stallion seemed satisfied Erskine's weight was distributed belly down over the saddle, arms and legs dangling, he found his footing slowly and stood.

Ebony shook his head and whinnied loudly—whinnied again—then turned toward the Santa Fe Trail and walked slowly, carrying Malcolm home.

By a series of such moves, Ebony gradually pulled the Jayhawker's body across the saddle.

Epilogue

Note: Names of actual historical figures appear in bold-faced type.

One-Eyed Emmett Anderson Jones, Erskine's assassin, squandered his bounty quickly and left the area. In 1862 he reappeared in Aubry. Henry O'Dell, then a Union cavalryman stationed there, yanked Jones from his horse and strangled him. O'Dell never went to trial.

Chad Brookings was a Union hero in the first Battle of Lexington, Missouri, 1861, and was decorated posthumously. J.T. and Elaine attended rites at the National Cemetery, Fort Scott.

George Morris, rejected as suitor by the Widow Naomi, led a Union charge at Gettysburg and was promoted in the field to the rank of major. He became a financier in New York City. He married an Englishwoman and fathered six children, two of whom chose stage careers.

Ben Ellerby sought but failed to win young Lani-Wawewa's hand in marriage. Despondent, he vanished and was never heard from again. Jed Blake won fame as a battlefield journalist. After the war he wrote a book about John Brown, based on recollections in Osawatomie. He tried but failed to trace Ellerby's whereabouts.

Eugene Fontenot became a teacher of languages in a Montreal parochial academy. An escaped slavewoman from the *Delta Queen* recognized him in a wine shop and stalked him for months until he acknowledged her. They married and raised four children, one named Malcolm, and lived into their eighties.

Cyrus Ormsby joined the 1863 gold rush to Montana Territory and then developed one of that area's most prosperous cattle spreads. He wed a young Sioux and fathered eleven children by her.

Abe Milford fathered two sons by Rose and died of a heart ailment in 1860. From farm earnings and from the sale of property at Camp Branch, Rose sent both sons to Harvard. They partnered in law in Washington, D.C., and drew acclaim as Indian rights advocates.

Jane-Ellen Mulligan O'Brien never remarried. She continued to accumulate wealth and political influence in Missouri. On her deathbed in St. Louis in 1913, she confessed she'd had a child by Eugene Fontenot and arranged adoption by a physician, Dr. Pierre Moreau. For reasons unclear, the priest made notes of the confession and misplaced them inside a book that went into an estate sale. The book's purchaser sold the account to a St. Louis tabloid.

In 2003 Noah and Lani Erskine's great-grandson, Daniel Erskine, private investigator, traced a descendant of Jane-Ellen's son—C. Robert Moreau, of Houston—and requested a DNA test. The match was unmistakable.

Westport's Negroes condemned Esmerelda Bartholomew for operating a whorehouse. She moved, reopened in San Francisco, and also founded an orphanage and school for disabled children. She never married. When she died in the 1906 earthquake, a folded news account of Malcolm Erskine's murder was found in her locket.

The Goodmans of Paola prospered. Daniel and Audrey added four children besides the daughter she delivered in 1857. Several of Daniel's siblings migrated west, going into retail and trades in Arizona and California.

Naomi Goodman Erskine in March, 1858, gave birth to Dahlia Sylvia Erskine. Naomi took charge of the ranch, paid Esmerelda's loan ahead of schedule, and trained Lani in ranch management. She resumed medical studies under **Dr. Simeon Bell** of Aubry and **Dr. Celia Dayton** of Spring Hill and received her certificate to practice medicine in 1864. She persuaded Morogh Erskine to move west to enjoy his grandchildren. He died in 1868 and was buried beside Dahlia Bahari in Lawrence.

Malcolm was buried alongside Sylvia at Naomi's instruction. They were the first to be interred in what became (and continues to operate as) Pleasant Valley Cemetery, south of the Santa Fe Trail. Naomi purchased a plot for herself on Malcolm's other side.

In 1866 a settlement began to develop immediately northeast of Pleasant Valley. Residents named it Stanley in 1871, for **Henry Morton Stanley**, the journalist-explorer believed lost in his African quest for **Dr. David Livingstone**, missionary. Later, unable to accept an invitation to acknowledge the honor, Stanley sent a reporter.

The newsman interviewed Dr. Naomi Erskine, among other locals. She confirmed only the factual material that newspapers had carried about Malcolm. She added thoughts later headlined in a Boston paper—*Kansas Hero's Widow Condemns 'Eye for Eye' Warfare as Endless Cycle.*

The Stanley waterway of Erskine's initial hideout is the stream that appears on U.S. Geological Survey maps as Negro Creek (see coordinates 38.85145 N, 94.65477 W). Stanley old-timers refer to it as "Nigger Creek."

The purpose of Emmett Anderson Jones's fatal ride into Aubry was to visit a cousin—**"Bloody Bill" Anderson**, who became a captain in the Confederate guerilla force of **William Clarke Quantrill**. In 1863 the guerillas raided Lawrence, killed nearly two hundred men and boys, and destroyed most of the buildings.

Samuel J. Jones, leader of the 1856 Lawrence raid in which Dahlia Bahari died, left for New Mexico, stung by criticism of his law enforcement methods and rebuffed in his political ambitions. In 1879 a stroke paralyzed him, and he died soon after.

Following exposure of the "Oxford Fraud," **the Rev. Thomas Johnson** helped pilot lame-duck preparation of the proslavery "Lecompton Constitution." But a Free State antislavery constitution likely to win Kansans' ratification was known by Congress to be forthcoming, so the Lecompton document failed to win broad acceptance. The activist minister died early in 1865 when several men fired shots through his front door. He may have been an intended robbery victim, or the shooting was payback for switching sides to support the Union in the Civil War. One local historian has expressed the belief that **Mrs. Johnson** helped arrange the killing.

Two of **John Brown's sons, John, Jr.,** and **Fred**, became mentally unbalanced from guilt over their roles in the Pottawatomie

Creek massacre. **Old Brown** pursued his plan to free slaves by armed insurrection. He seized a government arsenal at Harpers Ferry, Virginia (later part of West Virginia) in October, 1859, and lost sons **Oliver** and **Watson** in a fight with forces led by **Col. Robert E. Lee**. The fiery radical abolitionist, by then bearded, was hanged for treason and murder.

The abolitionist **Dr. Charles Robinson** was first to govern the new State of Kansas, which was admitted to the Union January 29, 1861. A physician, writer, historian, horticulturist, and educator, he died at his Douglas County home in 1894—sixty years before the continuing bigotry in Kansas was spectacularly exposed in the Topeka school segregation case, *Brown v. Board of Education.*

Gen. James H. Lane distinguished himself in the Civil War and represented Kansas in the United States Senate. In 1866 he promoted **President Andrew Johnson's** concessions to Southern whites, angering Republicans who sought expanded Negro rights. Despondent, he put a revolver barrel in his mouth and pulled the trigger.

Christopher Columbus Catron, founder of Oxford, abandoned his settlement during the Civil War and fled with other slaveowners to Texas. Union forces encamped in winter nearby stripped Oxford's buildings to use as firewood.

Chief Black Bob remained as leader of his communal Shawnees, aiding the Union during the Civil War. Ultimately he decided, in the face of accelerating white settlement in Oxford and Aubry Townships, to join his kinsmen in the Indian Territory, later known as Oklahoma.

James Butler Hickok, nicknamed "Wild Bill" in a Kansas City saloon fracas in 1861, became a Union Army scout. Later he served in law enforcement in the Kansas communities of Riley, Hays, and Abilene. He died at thirty-nine in Deadwood, Dakota Territory—shot in the back while holding a poker hand of aces and eights.

Gov. Robert J. Walker—a few days after his and **Secretary of State Frederick P. Stanton's** inspection of the Oxford voting site—issued a declaration October 19, 1857, invalidating ballots cast in the "Oxford Fraud." The order resulted in the Free State Party's first legislative majority. His action caused a furor in Washington and led to the Governor's submitting his resignation to **President James Buchanan** two months later.

The Democratic Party tore itself into geographical factions, a split that carried into the 1860 election. Against **Stephen Douglas** and **John Breckinridge**, presidential candidates for Northern and Southern Democrats respectively, Republican **Abraham Lincoln** won with forty percent of the vote. Southern states began seceding, and Civil War soon followed.

The balloting site of the "Oxford Fraud"—the place of the nation's turnaround on the slavery issue—remains unmarked in Leawood, Kansas, despite historians' and journalists' endeavors. What is etched in some people's memory about Leawood is a covenant that burdened the city's mid-Twentieth Century development—a prohibition against home purchases by Jews, Negroes, and other minorities.

When a young man, the unsung hero, **Robert J. Walker**, graduated at the top of his University of Pennsylvania class at eighteen. He was admitted to the bar two years later. He then joined his brother in a Natchez law practice and was elected to the United States Senate in 1835 representing Mississippi. A disciple of **Thomas Jefferson**, he freed his slaves in 1838. (The high-living Third President had not done the same because his slaves were mortgaged to banks.) **Walker** served as Secretary of the Treasury 1845-49 under **President James K. Polk** and in the time of war with Mexico.

After leaving the Territorial Governorship of Kansas, **Walker** supported the Union. He traveled to Europe in 1863 and negotiated $300 million in bonds to help finance the Union war effort. He died in 1869.

The Jayhawker

Norm Ledgin

Acknowledgements

The Jayhawker first appeared from 1981 through 1984 as a newspaper serial. My wife Marsha and I published the paper in Stanley, Kansas, now part of Overland Park. *The Blue Valley Gazette* covered news of the sprawling southeast Johnson County region that a large school district serves. We intended it to be a "country" weekly, and it was—until cancer laid me low and the paper went to new owners.

Marsha deserves credit for my having taken those 114 episodes and shaped them into book form. Others had suggested it in the twenty-two years of the story's hibernation. They said it was a good yarn and historically instructive. The Border War scarcely resonates today with people crossing between Kansas and Missouri. There's only vague awareness that this is where "Bleeding Kansas" bled.

The historical outcome—the political defeat of proslavers—inspired me to pound an Underwood for 114 Sunday mornings to spin this tale, bit by bloody, passionate bit.

Herschel Golub of Stilwell, a retired teacher, also suggested I pull the episodes together. For several years running he had me tell his students about Gov. Robert J. Walker's overturning the Oxford Fraud, an act that led to the Civil War. Herschel died this year while riding one of his horses, so now I wish I'd done this sooner.

Thanks go to the staff at the Kansas Historical Museum and Library, Topeka; to my keen-eyed reader, Bethine L. Minnis, who checked my editing of redundancies that newspaper serialization had warranted and my intensifying a few scenes the serial hadn't allowed; to artist Jay Reinhardt, who illustrated each episode years ago and created superb new drawings for this book; and, for various forms of encouragement and help, to my son, Alfred Ledgin, and to authors Dave Lieber, Rose Marie Kinder, Chanda Zimmerman, Mary-Lane Kamberg, Karen Heywood, and Rex Rogers, as well as to the staff at Leawood Barnes & Noble and Kathy Roberts of the Stanley UPS Store.

Background for *The Jayhawker* first jumped at me from the *Atlas Map of Johnson County, Kansas* by E.F. Heisler and D.M. Smith, published with loads of descriptive text in 1874. By pure coincidence I own a flea-market copy of *The History of Slavery and the Slave Trade* compiled by W.O. Blake (1860) and was able to take the measure of Robert J. Walker from its yellowing pages.

Long after I wrote the story emphasizing the pivotal importance of events in Oxford Township, I found support for that focus in two sources. The first was a 1902 work I'd been unaware of, *Reminiscences of Gov. R.J. Walker, With the True Story of the Rescue of Kansas from Slavery*, by Dr. George W. Brown, editor of Lawrence's *Herald of Freedom* and nearly as much a Kansas hero as his relative, John Brown. The second, a 1990 bestseller, was historian Kenneth M. Stampp's take on the Dred Scott case, the Oxford Fraud, and James Buchanan's disastrous presidency in *America in 1857: A Nation on the Brink.*

A 1998 book is noteworthy—*War to the Knife: Bleeding Kansas, 1854-1861*, by Thomas Goodrich. Anyone who doubts warring Bushwhackers and Jayhawkers could have behaved so boorishly as I've described should read Goodrich's historical account.

And that leads to my reminder that *The Jayhawker* is a work of fiction. Yes, I named people who lived in that time, and I cast them in roles close to the truth. But, except for incidents historians have documented, this story spilled out of my head.